Under the Harrow

A NOVEL BY

Mark Dunn

Under the Harrow

A NOVEL BY

Mark Dunn

MACADAM CAGE

MacAdam/Cage
155 Sansome, Suite 550
San Francisco, CA 94104
www.MacAdamCage.com

Library of Congress Cataloging-in-Publication Data

Dunn, Mark, 1956-
Under the harrow : a novel / by Mark Dunn.
p. cm.
ISBN 978-1-59692-369-0
1. Imaginary places—Fiction. 2. Domestic fiction. I. Title.
PS3604.U56U54 2009
813'.6—dc21
2009028907

Printed in the United States of America
10 9 8 7 6 5 4 3 2 1

Book and cover design by Dorothy Carico Smith

Affectionately inscribed to
my sister Laurie Kalet and
my brother Mitch Dunn
and to
the memory of my twin brother
Clay Dunn
who left the Dell too soon

An account, most curious, of Dingley Dell and its deceived denizens before and after the dastardly deception, told by one of the duped who was most willing to indite the whole diabolical affair for the delectation of all delving Outland readers. Presented with some notes and a preface.

by Frederick Trimmers, Esq.

PREFACE

Dear reader:

You will find upon the pages that follow my best efforts to chronicle the final twenty-seven days in the life of the ill-fated Dell of Dingley. I have attempted to tell all that can and all that *should* be told both from the record of my own experiences and from the experiences of others as they have recounted them to me. (I take no liberties in imagining the actions or fabricating the dialogue of those individuals who are no longer with us.)

You will note that I have made no attempt to conform the spelling of certain words used in both Dinglian English and the Dinglian vernacular to American English, nor is it my desire to give the book a contemporising idiomatic scrubbing. It is my wish that the Outland reader should read the book exactly as a Dinglian would, its syntactic construction and linguistical presentation constituting important and defining constituents in the ethos of our now vanished homeland. Any reader of Dickens should find the book easily navigable, as the Dinglian idiom is quite Dickensian in structure.

A good many things that the Outland reader will discover upon the leaves of this book will be familiar to twenty-first century American readers, for the community of man is by natural instinct united the world over by those shared exigencies of our species; all must eat and drink, all must sleep, must work, must play; and by the universality of the human condition: we love, we hate, we mourn, we venerate, we laugh and cry and hope and strive to better our lot. The world I have limned upon the leaves of this book will be comfortably familiar to readers of Mr. Charles Dickens and to those strongly acquainted with the latter years of the nineteenth century, for our Dinglian society was built largely upon that literal, historical, and cultural foundation.

However, there is much contained herein that is unique to our segregated valley, and which I will do my best to explain through the course of the narrative. Readers are encouraged to read the explanatory notes I have put together at the end of some of the early chapters, for they serve as important illuminative supplement to the main text. Each entry has been opportunely drawn from articles prepared for a one-volume Dinglian encyclopædia, its compilation halted in 2002 by judicial injunction for failure to submit it for a proper Parliamentary review. The reader will find certain terms within the text of the narrative printed in bold; these link the reader to those related chapter endnotes, which come from the aborted encyclopædia (not to be confused with the *Encylopædia Britannica*, Ninth Edition, about which more to come).

I have no doubt that I shall write other books. However, I am certain that my future years in exile from my ancestral home will little by little dilute the singularity of my Dinglian voice. Here you will find that voice in its purest state. Ten years hence I could easily be mistaken for one of you. I have reconciled myself to my eventual assimilation even as I rue losing some not insignificant part of the Dinglian who lives within me.

But my loss is no matter for your concern.

Read on of my story, and of the story of my doomed compatriots. You may find it a most bracing yarn.

Frederick Trimmers, Esq.
South Williamsport, Pennsylvania, U.S.A.
December 2004

CHAPTER THE FIRST

Saturday, June 14, 2003

Lt has been said that a slow child is an inconvenience to its parents; a slow and ill-countenanced child, an unhappy burden; and a slow, ill-countenanced, and fractious child a veritable curse. Of these three truisms, it is the last that found most fitting application within my brother's family in the person of Augustus' young son Newman, who, at the tender age of eleven, was more child than my brother and his wife Charlotte could easily bear, though he constituted the sort of curse that one hoped, in time, might be dispelled, to the peace and sanguinity of all concerned.

With this aim in mind, my nephew was sent forth from one end of Dingley Dell to the furthest-most opposite end, to be placed under the caring and attentive tutelage of one Alphonse Chowser, Esq., a pedagogical worker of miracles in the field of captious, unyielding boys. The Chowser School would, in attendance to its mission, provide Newman with every granule of the guidance and education that was heretofore deprived him by his own intemperate nature within his small village school, and all the love and kindhearted affection that was not easily bestowed in the lad's familial circle, given my brother Augustus' want of forbearance, his wife Charlotte's nervous complaint, and the couple's daughter (and Newman's older sister) Alice's aversion to disagreeable visage and mental deficiency in a sibling—an indefencible bias on her side, but one often evinced by wilful young girls of thirteen, who have no patience for much of anything that cannot be slipped with frills and lace over the head or patted roseate upon the cheek.

Early reports from the school offered promising evidence of rapid progress. Newman had shewn an especial interest in those esoteric disciplines which characterised Chowser's unconventional (some say Bohemian) approach to education, and had delighted in posting to me a series of letters written almost entirely in a modified version of the hieroglyphic language of the ancient Egyptians, each of which I was fortunately (and somewhat miraculously) successful in deciphering, though my own youthful interest in early ideogrammatic writing had waned somewhat over the years.

Most importantly, Newman's behaviour improved with remarkable expedition, and his pasty pallor retreated, the glow of healthy youth quickly returning to his countenance. Mr. Chowser noted, as well, that the boy's drooping eyes, which often arrested the attention of those who met him and which instantly unsettled the observer, had achieved a lustre that all but redeemed the entire face. Nor did Newman prank and remonstrate half as often as had been his previous wont, nor make of bedtime a thing of dreaded contention for those charged with directing his nightly repose. It was as if my nephew had become, if not a much smarter boy, at least a more tractable one, with every indication given for the continuance of improvement. And every letter received in each of those seven weeks of Newman's residency at the school gave his father and mother, and even his bachelor uncle—who presently takes up the pen to tell this story—cause for encouragement and no small measure of joy.

Alas, such optimistic feelings did not reside long within our breasts, for it came to our attention at the end of that seventh week of Newman's enrolment—and such a grave report it was that the school's headmaster betook himself to deliver the news not by ticket porter or **heliographic** transmission, but in person—that Newman, my beloved nephew and the beloved son of my older brother, had stolen himself away in the dark of night, leaving behind no trace save a brief, scribbled note, which described his intentions; a note undeniably of his own authorship, given its impaired spellings—this from a boy for whom ancient hieroglyphics held much greater appeal than an accurate actuation of the more practical language of his forebears:

Dear Mr. Chowzer,

I am runnning away from yer shcool and see the world and make my-self a man of it and the deuce take you! But tell my mother and pa that I will return and them bring rishes of gold and perl that will make they eyes pop.

With cordial,

Newman

I was present for the interview that afternoon which brought the par-ticulars of my nephew's flight from Dingley Dell to my brother's doorstep. Within the comfortably-appointed sitting room that was my sister-in-law Charlotte's proud domain, we learnt of Newman's desire to seek his for-tune in that world which lay beyond our safely-compassed valley—such an excursion of foolhardiness as is seldom essayed except by men of more than twice my nephew's years and even then only amongst those in want of foresight and sanity.

There would be no going after him. It was seldom done. Once one left the Dell of Dingley, he was lost. This was the rule, though there was also the infre-quent exception. But we had learnt never to fasten hope too firmly upon that exception, given the disappointment that would most likely derive from it.

"Perhaps he'll come to his senses after he's landed himself in the Out-land," said Charlotte, "and will retrace his steps and make his return. He is a rather prosy child, but even one slower of wit than Newman can see what a dangerous thing it is to leave the Dell, especially after all the years of frightful conjecture that has been made about what lurks abroad." Char-lotte trembled as she spoke these halting words and was readily consoled by her husband with thoughtful pats upon the hand.

Daughter Alice, in contradiction to the prevailing mood, sat with folded arms and a languid, indifferent face, bereft of even a hint of concern for her brother's safety. "Egad! What a waste of a perfectly good Saturday night!" The assessment came in a grumbling underbreath that nonetheless carried volume sufficient for all present within the worry-room to hear.

"Upon my life, girl—hold!"

"I wasn't referring to anyone in particular, Mama, but only to the gen-eral climate of the room."

"Howbeit, what a perfectly disrespectful thing to say with your brother gone and perhaps lost forever."

"Newman's known since he was a toddler," retorted Alice, "that one doesn't venture from the valley without risk and consequence. Therefore

I wager that he hasn't left the Dell at all. Ten to one he's up in some tree near the school right now, hanging from a limb like the mischief-making monkey that he is."

Mr. Chowser shook his head. He brushed his hand worriedly across the short, stiff bristles of his close crop, a mindless activity that often served to relax him, though today it was having no effect. "We've scoured the grounds, young lady. We've searched the branches of every tree that might afford his ascent, and have concluded that your brother cannot be found. I wouldn't have come hither had I any doubt that he indeed sought to do that very thing that his missive purported. I'm at fault here. I put us all under the harrow, I did." A heavy sadness subdued the headmaster's address. He had, in fact, been derelict in not keeping a tighter rein on my brother's son and now he wore that guilty negligence upon his wan face and upon shoulders that slumped and did not rise.

"Moreover," the headmaster pursued, "two of Newman's playfellows related to me the young man's strongly-expressed desire to be gone from Dingley Dell and to discover every *good* thing that lies outside our confines. It is now frighteningly clear, Mr. Trimmers, that your son didn't believe anything that he heard pertaining to the dangers of the **Terra Incognita**. He was having none of it and was—say these boys—nearly giddy with glee in anticipation of all those wondrous things he hoped to achieve once he'd shaken the dust and flue of Dingley Dell from his dress."

It was at this moment that my sister-in-law Charlotte, able no longer to contain her despair, released a torrent of tears, which came with howls and honks and coughings, and there was little that any of us could do to mitigate her grief. It was grief of a species that each of us felt in commiserating union, excepting, apparently, young Alice, who sat complacently nibbling buttered bread and feigning boredom.

One could, therefore, easily acquit Charlotte in that next moment for mowing at her daughter with furious eyes.

"I sh-should strike you!" she sputtered, having finally reclaimed her voice. "Such a demonstration of callousness and contempt for your very own brother—it is beyond belief!"

"Yet I own no contempt for my little brother whatsoever." Alice's rebuttal was delivered calmly, and it wanted conviction.

"No contempt? Even as you sit here seemingly *rejoicing* in our loss!"

"*Rejoicing*? What rubbish!" returned Alice with a mouth filled with mashed loaf. "My composure merely gives evidence to the fact that, if Newman *has* left the valley, which I continue to doubt, he will, with all certainty, return."

"And how can you be so certain of this?" I put to my niece.

"Because no one would dare harm a boy as incorrigible as he. I hazard to say that most of the Outlanders whom Newman will meet in this short-lived adventure of his will make wild dashes for their homes and latch all their shutters with trembling hands."

"And yet," began Mr. Chowser, engaging the voluble flaxen-haired thirteen-year-old as if she were his intellectual equal, "young Newman was not nearly so surly and menacing yesterday as he was on that day which first placed him into my custody, for I am quite certain that I was succeeding in my efforts to mould him into the very opposite of how you persist in characterising him. He was, in fact, improving with every day he lived beneath my roof, mark."

"Or perhaps he had simply got very good at pulling the wool over your eyes. Just as he's been doing it to all of *us* for the last eleven years." Alice applied a toothpick indifferently to the interstices of her bread-mortared teeth before adding her codicil: "My brother is a half-wit when it comes to most things, but not where duplicity is required. Here his wits overcompensate for every other aspect of his intelligence that is dull and insipid."

"You wring my withers, Alice, like a choking vise," returned my sister-in-law with wilting asperity. "Go straight to bed this instant!" Charlotte stared at her daughter with wild, reproving eyes and began to pound a knotted fist into her breast. She turned to her husband and said by way of explaining this sudden thumping of herself, "One look at her and the digestive aggravation returns. I can scarcely endure it!"

Alice rose, and, as she had been exhorted, quitted the room without further comment. However, a moment later, obviously prompted by an impertinent afterthought, my refractory niece returned in full filial ferment: "Hear me, Mama. Newman will be back to revisit torment upon us all, and that will be the joke on the four of you. But no one will be laughing, mind, least of all me: the chief recipient of his customary devilish rampages. And so I shall enjoy what few days remain to my holiday, no matter how you may wish to condemn me for it."

As Alice shut the door to the sitting room with such force as to topple a japanned candlestick set upon the mantel shelf, and then was heard to stamp with delicious malice up to her bedchamber above, I wondered for a moment if there could be truth to anything that my young niece had said with such impudent confidence. Perhaps she knew her brother better than any of us. Subscribing to even a small measure of this possibility offered a commensurate modicum of hope, though I would never give her credit for it.

Perhaps he will be back as early as the morrow, I thought as I returned to my own lodgings later that evening. Even within the depths of despondency, I continued to hold within my heart a tiny, most insistent wish: that a promising turn of events would set everything to rights. How was I to know at that moment that there would be turns of events in surfeit, both good and bad, all intricately reticulated? How was I to know that what had happened to Newman would comprise, when all was said and done, only one slender thread in the tightly stitched garment that represented our collective fate, no single incident dictating the course of all the others, but all working together toward a most apocalyptic outcome?

Except, that is, for the very first. This seminal event, which had nothing to do with young Newman, had been born in its retail a few hours earlier at the home of a friend of my mother's and came in the form of a casual conversational reference to a woman who had the night before taken a terrible fall from her upstairs bedchamber window. It was a nasty plunge upon punishing cobblestones, and no one, not even the most prescient amongst us, could guess at that time how important a role the plummet would play upon the stage of that tragedy—a tragedy that we here shall call *The Last Days of Dingley Dell.*

—NOTES—

HELIOGRAPHY, communication between distant points by means of visual signals obtained by reflecting the rays of the sun from a mirror or combination of mirrors in single transmission or relayed transmission, depending upon the circumstance. Short and long flashes emulative of the alphabetical dots and dashes that comprise the Morse code are obtained by opening and closing the operative shutter. Glass mirrors with a plane surface are used; hence the angle of divergence of the extreme rays in the reflected beam is the same as that subtended by the sun's diameter at the point of about 32 minutes of arc, this small divergence rendering the flash visible from great distances. A chief diurnal means of instant communication between Milltown and satellite villages within Dingley Dell, largely employed exigently, although less climacteric uses have also been recorded.

TERRA INCOGNITA, the Latin term for "unknown land," is the name coined by earlier Dinglians for all land beyond the border of Dingley Dell. The term is a bit of a misnomer when one considers that a great deal is known about the "T.I." through Outland writings and through cartographic plates in the possession of the Academic and Lending Library of Dingley Dell. The term is more appropriately applied when speaking of that which is *not* known about the Outland, and more specifically about that portion of the Outland that closely circumscribes the Dell.

A jocular fingerpost once stood upon the summit of the Northern Ridge, directing one to the TERRA INCOGNITA. The sign was later replaced by the even more whimsical THERE BE DRAGONS. Both signs were later removed by trade authorities with a proscription against any further signage in this location.

CHAPTER THE SECOND

Saturday, June 14, 2003

So began what was to become the longest month of my life, given all that eventually took place therein, as events began to transpire with accelerating rapidity over the course of those tumbling weeks. Like a stone dislodged from its shelf upon a craggy hill, one incident gave way to another and then another, the single stone gathering speed in its descent and dislodging in succession a great many other stones along the way, until that first stone, which had been unmoored quite unwittingly at the outset of those remaining crowded weeks in the life of **the lost Dell of Dingley**, begat the avalanche that would bury an entire valley and the unique society which once prospered there.

❧

Now Newman Trimmers had not been the first child to venture from the narrow confines of Dingley Dell. There had been others, none of these young men and women, to anyone's knowledge, having ever returned. My friend Vincent Muntle, who was the sheriff of Dingley Dell, had lost his older brother in a similar manner, and it was upon this date in June of 2003 that he chose to formally remember his older sibling, June 14 being the twenty-fifth anniversary of the boy's departure.

Indeed, the date was a sad anniversary for us both, for it was exactly fifteen years earlier that my mother had died, victim of an overdose of chloral hydrate, prescribed for insomnia. Mama's death was one of the reasons that I had joined forces with those who advocated for the creation of an overseeing Dingley Dell Medical Review Board, and the reason that I volunteered each year thereafter to help prepare that board's annual accounting and general report. You see, the doctor who administered the deadly dose to my mother, Jacob Podsnap, had been responsible for a rash of other serious errors of judgement pursuant to his succumbing to a degenerative case of delirious dementia. Removing the deadly Dr. Podsnap from his murderous offices was a slow process and vigorously contested by his proponents in spite of the anecdotal evidence of his unfitness for that profession—evidence that, had it been properly documented, might have ended his blundering reign of terror some months sooner. I vowed that there should never be another Jacob Podsnap. It was a vow that, now in looking back, I was an arrant fool for having made. As you will soon see.

I had met my friend Muntle on the morning of my nephew's departure, several hours before I was summoned to my brother's house to receive the disturbing news. The bluff and burly lawman was on his way to visit the stone and concrete "bench of perpetual memory" dedicated to his lost brother George. It had been installed by his parents beneath the shady, tranquil boughs of a large oak tree upon the grounds of Heavenly Rest Municipal Cemetery. The brother's name was inscribed on a wooden plate, the bench being one of many such benches in the cemetery, each commemorating one who had left the Dell never to return. There were no other markers for the **Departed** other than these austere places of rest and reflection. As one stood upon a hillock in the middle of the park, one noticed, interspersed amongst the gravestones, a goodly number of these reposing spots—a somewhat unsettling reminder in the aggregate of just how many Dinglians had quitted their protected home in both body and spirit, and were destined never to be properly interred amongst the Dingley dead.

I had often betaken myself to this quiet retreat and wandered amongst its welcoming benches and solemn gravestones. Many of those whose names were etched there were familiar to me. Others I knew from the stories that were told of them or which still to that day were occasionally extracted from memory to elicit a smile or a sigh of commiseration over a glass of warm mulled wine.

Near my mother and father's shared stone was a specific bench that had fascinated me since childhood—one emplaced to remember a gentleman by the name of Roger Rugg. Mr. Rugg had left the Dell long before I was born, but he had scarcely been forgotten (at least not by me). For upon the stone one found not merely the name of this early member of the Departed, but, in relief, the uncanny likenesses of a number of winding, coiling snakes.

What a curiosity!

Both for the very fact of the snakes *and* for their inarguably innocuous depiction. I had wondered in my ever-pondering youth what there was about the man that could have motivated his grieving family to put the images of friendly, happily twining snakes upon his memorial bench. One day I decided to find out once and all the genesis of the ophidian imagery. I went to that man whom I understood in my earliest years to hold the key to every mystery in the universe: my father. I asked him what he knew of Mr. Rugg and what could possibily be the reason for the singular etchings upon his bench.

"Is it not obvious?" returned the parental sage, raising his eyes to peer at me from above the wall of his newspaper, which, though tissue-thin, customarily kept all young intrusive boys at bay.

"That he was like a snake himself?"

"No, my boy. Have another go at it."

"That he *liked* snakes?"

"Ah yes—now there you have it. Rugg was, in fact, quite fervid in his affinity for the slithering creatures. One assumes that his departure from the Dell had less to do with a desire to see the Outland in general than to study the divers species of snakes that lived there in particular. Now does that quench your curiosity, my boy?"

I nodded.

"Then go along and leave your papa to his newspaper. You may tell your mother that the *Crier* says there is to be a lecture at the Burghers' Hall on Tuesday night on the subject of metempsychosis." My father tilted his glasses to give a better look at the printed text before him. He chuckled. "Oh, this is good. This chap says that he cares little what sort of creature receives his soul when his death puts it upon the path of transmigration. He wishes only that it should not find purchase in another human. For 'man is the only creature that prospers by injustice.' How rich. And oh, how very true." And then the wall rose, and my father disappeared behind it, our interview decisively concluded.

I was, at the moment of my chance meeting with Muntle, headed with purposeful steps in the opposite direction from that which would gain Muntle the cemetery. It was obligation that called me; I had been invited, just as I had been entreated every June since my mother's untimely passing, to attend the annual gathering of the "Euphemia Trimmers Memorial Society." An invitation had always remained open for attendance by my older brother Augustus and his wife Charlotte, as well, but Gus could hardly ever bring himself to go. And Charlotte, too, had decided after last year's sleep-inducing assembly to foreswear the visit for every year thereafter as an imposition upon her purportedly crowded social calendar.

"They are dear old souls, every last one of them," my brother would say, "but I cannot abide their tongues. There is such cackling abrasion there, Freddie, and I dare say that I get enough friction in my very own home—what with a mischief-making son and an unruly, disrespectful daughter and a wife who constantly stirs the pot without even thinking of it—to put myself in the way of additional distress by my own volition. This year I'm going fishing. Be so kind, brother, as to extend my apologies—just as you have extended them for all those other years of my non-attendance—and I'll continue to remain in your fraternal debt."

Augustus had made this pronouncement the day before, and I had no doubt that he was at this very moment happily ensconced within his favourite fishing spot on the **Thames**, whiling and whistling away this beautiful sunny Saturday (which was exactly where he was, in fact, until summoned back to his house by Chowser's troubling visit). The bank of the Thames was just where *I* should have been had I chosen not to maintain that relatively undefined, self-punishing sort of allegiance to my mother's memory. It was an allegiance that put me without variance into the company of that group of women who had long been my mother's friends—women who wished each year to commemorate Mama's passing by sitting stiffly within a stifling parlour, lifting teacups to cherry lips and nibbling bits of cake without relish.

"So what is it that *you* do in that cemetery, Muntle?" I casually enquired of my longtime friend (for we had never spoken of our mutual interest in the place). "Sit upon the memorial bench and revisit warm memories of your long-lost brother?"

"Aye. And I cannot help wondering (for I do it each and every year) what he should be doing of a particular moment were he still alive, which I rather strongly suspect that he is not. Of course, I will own to other more peripatetic thoughts, which on occasion divert me from the primary purpose of the visit. For example: something from the natural world inevitably catches my eye—a robin tugging at a worm, for example, or the intriguing shapings of the clouds as they collect themselves overhead. Last year, who should stroll by but the cook at the Chowser School, and we had ourselves a delightful chat."

"Of what did you speak?"

"That was a full year ago, Trimmers. How am I possibly to remember details of a conversation that took place so many months removed?"

Muntle thought for a moment.

And then Muntle said, "Cheese. I believe that we talked of skim milk cheese. Whether there should be much nutritional value to it."

I grinned. "It all sounds quite riveting."

"And you are a turd, Trimmers—a warm, fragrant turd."

"Just what did you *expect* me to say? Skim milk cheese. Upon my life and arse, sir!"

"There was much more that was discussed besides cheese, I'll be bound. And here is another thing that has just come to me, and I cannot think why it was not the first thing to be recollected: she—the Chowser cook—her name is Maggy Finching, by the bye—she knew the lines from John Clare as well as did I:

> 'I am! Yet what I am who cares or knows?
> Sleep as I in childhood sweetly slept,
> Full of high thoughts, unborn.
> So let me lie, the grass below,
> Above the vaulted sky.'"

"Yes, I'm familiar with those lines as well. They're from the **Companion,** are they not?"

Muntle nodded, and blotted a nascent tear from the corner of his eye with his forefinger. "I think of my brother in that last line, the two of us as boys lying on our backs upon the dewy grass. He is *below* the sod now, I suppose, perchance in some Outland cemetery."

"Why do you not let yourself believe instead that he lives amongst the Beyonders and thrives in that way which motivated him to leave our valley in the first place?"

"Because the Departed, Trimmers—the ones who stay away too long— they never return. Why do they not return?"

"Perhaps circumstances don't permit it."

"Shall we give those circumstances their rightful name, Trimmers? I have a better idea. Let us change the topic. This one is much too gruesome for such a bright and beautiful morning as this. In fact, I will no longer detain you, my good friend. You must go and take your tea with the bickering biddies."

"That was rather an unkind characterisation."

"Say it isn't true."

I shook my head and smiled. "It is only for an hour. Almost anything can be endured for a single hour."

"'Tis true. 'Tis largely true."

—NOTES—

THE LOST DELL OF DINGLEY, occasional appellation for Dingley Dell, both evocative and indicative of the fact that its location upon the planet has never been firmly established, and life within the Dell perpetually shrouded in impenetrable mystery. Efforts have been made to discover its location short of making an exceedingly perilous extra-valley investigation; its latitude was long ago calculated through measuring the sun's angle at noon, and it has been, therefore, established that Dingley Dell lies at roughly 41°13' North parallel. However, in absence of a reference meridian, longitude cannot be estimated by any means other than blind supposition.

A close conning of the leaves of *McCormick's Atlas of the World* (copyright 1872) and topographical descriptions of known places that lie upon the determined circle of latitude has, over the years, divided delving Dinglians into competing camps of "position suppositioners," none of whom, for latitudinal reasons, have argued for any point in Great Britain. Nor have there ever been proponents of any of the arid and rugged provinces of Turkey, Spain, and Portugal, nor any point in the western United States—excepting California—(largely too dry elsewhere), nor the Midwestern United States (largely too flat), nor the several Asian "Stans" (too dry and/or too altitudinous).

Over time the following disparate groups have emerged: those who advocate for Campania, Italy, those who believe Dingley Dell to be somewhere installed upon the northern end of Honshu Island in Japan, a smattering of promoters of the Northern provinces of the Kingdom of Corea, a slightly larger number of supporters of one of the several fertile valleys of Eastern China, a sizeable contingent of defenders of the Trinity River Valley in Northern California, U.S.A., and an even larger collection of adherents of "somewhere upon the Allegheny Plateau," which stretches from northeastern Ohio through north-central Pennsylvania. This last, most populated camp bases its belief upon the existence of the availing coal and iron deposits found within the environs of the Dell—a prominent geographical feature characteristic of that selfsame plateau—and the presence of fauna indigenous to northern North America, most noticeably the rattlesnake, the mockingbird, and the common Blue Jay of Canada and the eastern states of the U.S., and, conversely, the conspicuous absence of the European Jay (though this fact may be ascribed to its extinction).

THE DEPARTED AND THE RETURNED, the former term refers to those who leave Dingley Dell and do not return. This number comprises some 250 individuals of every age and walk of life. The latter term refers to those, numbering thirty-five, who did return, each within two weeks of his departure. It has therefore been extrapolated from this data that one's chance of returning from the Terra Incognita diminishes in direct proportion to the number of days spent there, repatriation being all but infeasible when visitation exceeds a fortnight.

It should be noted that those who do return to Dingley Dell are quite incapable of conveying anything that is useful to know about the Terra Incognita, delivering, instead, curiously frantic, feverish, and opiate-like ravings of a fantastical world that challenges belief. Authorities have had no choice but to sequester these men and women in the west wing of Bethlehem Hospital upon Highbury Fields, or "Bedlam" in informal denomination, named for that English lunatic asylum of macabre Anglo fame and legend, lest the returnee infect those round him with the illness of the brain with which he has been diagnosed.

THE RIVER THAMES, primary waterway flowing through Dingley Dell. The river enters the valley through the Tewkesbury Cut in the Northern Ridge, passes in both concerted and meandrous fashion through the entire length of the valley, and finds its subterranean egress through a decades-old re-diversion channel appropriated from retired mining tunnels within the Southern Coal Ridge, the natural outlet—the Belgrave Cut—having been dammed up and its waters so successfully redirected for industrial application that a residual oxbow lake once situated at its foot has been long exsiccated.

Much has been written of the river and its importance to Dingley Dell. What follows is an appropriately descriptive passage from Miss Clara Trotwood's *A Geographical and Lyrical History of Dingley Dell*:

> But who should not believe Dingley Dell to be the most beautiful vale in all the world (if one were to stand with the scarred and scabbed Southern Coal Ridge to one's back), with its fields of rye and oats and corn and mangold set in eye-pleasing checkerboard upon the agricultural northland, and plump rolling downs emeralding the valley's southern reach. And here is the lace that trims

the beautiful green garment: a river of both breadth and majesty, which has flowed the length of the valley since time out of mind; that river which sculpted the valley itself and which is therefore both its mother and primordial primogenitor. This is the river, which we named, in our earliest years and with anglophiliac jest: the Thames.

Attend ye the hurried race of this great storied waterway, powering all of the mills of Milltown and irrigating the paddies of the Wang-Wang Rice Farm, a mainstay for those almond-eyed Dinglians whose ancestors had been brought to the valley, without doubt, from the wet rice field-blanketed continent of Asia. (Indeed, there are other foods that would surely be found by the curious Outlander to be equally exotic: for certainly no English dale produces New World maize in such abundance nor could so many citrus varieties be grown as those which thrive within our teeming hot house orangeries. Nor could any other dale boast orchards of the sort of fruit and nut trees one generally finds only in the more whimsically eclectic British botanical parks.) Into Dingley Dell the Thames sallies forth with wild, thrashing abandon through the deep ravine that it has carved from the less adamantine rock of the Northern Ridge, notching that great, solid mass with alluvial impropriety before slowing by degrees to wander lazily past field and farm, nourishing the piscatorial from its crystal, aerated waters: sustaining all with foot and hoof and wing within the valley with the life-sustaining liquid it gives to surrounding wells and puddles and oxbow ponds; and then flowing ever onward through predominating Milltown and the satellite villages of Tavistock and Hungerford and Folkstone and Fingerpost, town and hamlet alike, drawing power from its replenished speed; then coming to rest in placid leisure within Lake Collier before slipping quietly belowground to flow through the retired mining tunnels and porous recesses of the Southern Coal Ridge where it bids formal adieu to this happy valley.

Without the Thames, there would be no Dingley Dell. O ye Gods of Fluvia! Suffer this life-sustaining river to flow forever through the valley that takes sustenance from it, quenching the thirsty tongue of every creature that calls our valley its home.

THE COMPANION, formally known as THE POETRY-LOVER'S COM-
PANION, a compendium of poetry compiled from illustrative stanzas
of verse found within the *Encyclopædia Britannica, Ninth Edition (1875-
1889)*, or *"Ensyke"* in common parlance. The source of all Outlander poetry not to be found adventitiously within the novels of Charles Dickens,
The Companion was long taught in Dinglian high schools, although since
the 1960s it has largely been supplanted by indigenous verse.

CHAPTER THE THIRD

Saturday, June 14, 2003

I had the fidgets. I could not have kept my feet still for any amount of gold or treasure. I had skipped breakfast and taken hardly anything for my supper the night before, and at some point would have to provender myself with something above the microscopic tea cakes and wafer-sized biscuits that sat upon a plate and were offered to my morning companions and me by the drowsy young woman who kept falling asleep at every opportunity only to be elbowed to wakefulness by her mother with a stentorian, "Revive yourself, Betty, and make the round! Our guests must have another cake! REVIVE, DEAR GIRL! You're quite the walking dead this morning."

There was a reply, which came in the form of a groggy mumble to which the close proximity of my eaves dropping ears gave me full access: the mother—Mrs. Malvina Potterson—had, you see, played desultory ditties upon her **harmonica** through half the previous night as a remedy for sleeplessness that largely benefited the afflicted instrumentalist herself and not—unfortunately—the by-standing (or, rather, by-*lying*) listener. This, of course, left one of the two women at a bit of a deficit and dozing off and fumbling forks and plates, and there was an obvious irony at work here in that the one doing the admonishing was also the very one responsible for that which was being admonished. (At least this was my cursory evaluation of the situation.)

The hour had got itself off to a good start; the profusely brocaded Mrs.

Potterson and her slow-moving (and some say slow-witted) daughter Betty had together greeted me upon the flagstone walk that led to the Potterson cottage's front door, Malvina with open arms and Betty with arms pinned flatly to her sides in the manner of a tin soldier. The embrace of my exuberant hostess gave way to double kisses to the cheek and to the emotional declaration, "Oh, Frederick, we'd begun to think that you weren't going to come, but bless my eyes, here you are, here you are!" Then, directed to her rigid daughter: "Betty, dear, if you will not make our guest welcome with a kiss upon his cheek, then kiss the air at least, or blow him something which approximates a labial greeting."

Betty kissed the air and looked mortified as she did it.

Malvina Potterson continued to bubble and babble as she led me inside and into the fat armchair that her husband had occupied up to the very moment of his death and then a few inconvenient hours thereafter. Betty followed along, her head bobbing, one hand brushing aside a nettlesome fly that had entered the domicile expressly to torment all of her facial projections as it sought a potential landing place, and in the end achieved a small measure of victory in the annals of insectival annoyance by prompting the beleaguered young woman to swat herself hard upon the nose.

Now inside the dwelling to commence my hour-long captivity, I set myself to the task of maintaining a smile of that same duration and a look of rapturous engagement, which said that everything that was spoken within this circle was more interesting than anything I'd ever heard in all of my thirty-four years of conversational audit in surely the most chattering dell in all the world.

While trying futilely to contain my fidgets.

In keeping with the annual ritual, there promised to be talk of my mother's many offices of kindness and talk of some of her more comical traits and habits such as slapping the knuckles of the butcher with a ruler after he had placed a chop on the scale so that he would not be tempted to add an ounce or two with the press of his thumb upon the tray. Or rather I *thought* that this should be the theme and purpose of the morning's visit. But 2003 would prove to be the year in which I'd be most grievously mistaken, as you will shortly witness.

Here are the names of the six women who convened themselves for the purpose of deferential attendance to the memory of my mother, Euphemia Trimmers, upon this, the fifteenth anniversary of her demise: Mrs.

Malvina Potterson (the hostess, as I have noted, in company with that filial child-woman appendage named Betty), Mrs. Sophronia Venus, Mrs. Lavinia Blight, Miss Georgianna Milvey, Miss Antonia Bocker, and Mrs. Rose Fagin. I had known each of these women for all the years of my life. As to their colourful names, they had kept to the long-standing custom in Dingley Dell of choosing Christian names for themselves from the lengthy list of character names given to the world by the imaginative author Charles Dickens—a list of such bountiful eccentricity and peculiarity as to allow the forming of a bond of close denominational similarity, one with another, though Rose did not go along with the queer scheme, preferring instead when it came time for her to pick a name and register it with the **Bureau of Appellations** to call herself simply Rose, for she had sought since she was a toddler to give herself the name of her favourite flower—beautiful in colour and pleasing in fragrance.

It was Rose who sat next to me and winked conspiratorially every now and then when something was said that was frivolous and perfectly ridiculous. And it was Rose who warned me away from the biscuit that had the curl of dog hair upon it (for the Potterson terrier had just been groomed somewhere nearby, and the animal's fur had attached itself to everything about the room). Rose was a stately woman with a firm, raised chin and dark brown eyes that sat deeply within the recesses of her sockets and gave one the impression of sternness and sobriety though no friend of my mother's was warmer and more genial. She agonised through each of these yearly reunions to remember my mother who was her dearest friend, yet scarcely saw her companions upon other occasions except when they paid the occasional visit to her family jewellry shop to touch every little bauble that shimmered and attracted the eye only to return each to its velveteen cushion, and plead poverty and walk out of the shop having spent not even a cent for the privilege of the fondling.

"And where is your brother Augustus on this fine-weathered Saturday morning?" sought one of the two ample-figured constituents of this gaggle, Mrs. Venus—her plumpness so evenly distributed upon her large bones that sitting within an elbow chair (let us say, for example, the one she presently occupied) was a nearly unendurable discomfort to her, and for which reason she was apt to pop up (as best as one of her portly size could "pop") to examine close hand, as an example, the lustrous components of her companions' mourning weeds (for each woman was required to attend the tea wearing funereal black) or to leaf through a cookery book that had been left upon a side table, perhaps in a deliberate attempt by the hostess to disprove the oft-repeated rumour that Mrs. Potterson fed herself and her daughter exclusively on bake-house veal pie and boiled potatoes.

As I thought best how to answer Mrs. Venus's enquiry in such a way as to preserve the good name of my truant brother, Mrs. Lavinia Blight offered up a question of her own for anyone who would entertain it—a question quite remote from the prescribed topic of the morning, my mother. Mrs. Blight, who was an even larger creature, in point of fact, than Mrs. Venus— possessed of an abundance of adipose much differently distributed, her hips being of relatively normal size, whilst her legs and arms were elephan- tine—drew attention away from her visually-arresting appendages to her plump-lipped mouth from which issued a deeply sonorous, almost manly voice. (Indeed, the legs themselves sat like two great tree trunks upon the floor, for my mother's husky-throated friend chose highly hemmed gowns that gave more leg than was customarily available for viewing.)

Mrs. Blight's question was this: had anyone heard anything of the con- dition of the Milltown woman named Mrs. Janet Pyegrave who had taken a tumble from her upper bedchamber window the previous night and had since lain insentient in the Milltown Respectable Hospital where she was not expected to recover?

Mrs. Fagin owned that the poor woman was "still alive as of two hours ago, though she remains unconscious. I know this, in part, because my daughter Susan came home this morning from her nurse's night watch to say that her patient was still to be counted amongst the living, but only provisionally so. Had Susan not spoken of the pitiful creature at all, I would have known this for a different reason: her husband dropt by the shop this morning to bring in some of his wife's jewellry for appraisal."

This revelation prompted a mutual gasp on the part of Mrs. Potterson and Mrs. Venus. Mrs. Venus turned from browsing the leaves of the cookery book to proclaim that she had never in all of her days heard of such a vul- turous act as this, that the wife was not yet dead and here was the husband seeking gain for himself from her anticipated passing. "And to think that he is an **M.P.P**! It is an absolute outrage!"

Mrs. Potterson nodded. "I had no idea that the Pyegraves were in such want of money. Why, he's the most prosperous draper and upholsterer in the Dell. Every squab upon which you sit was stuffed and sewn in his shop."

Mrs. Fagin shook her head. "No, he most certainly was *not* in want of money. What he was in want of was a trade: his wife's jewellry, no doubt of Outland making, for some of the finest pieces my husband and I sell, all of which are crafted here within the Dell by our best local artisans." Mrs. Fagin then dropt her voice and owned that it wasn't her intent to kindle a scandal by retailing the details of the husband's visit. "I merely found it queer that a man who should be sitting puffy-eyed at his wife's imminent deathbed—" Mrs. Fagin stopped herself and shook her head despondently. "Let us forget it. I'm sorry that I ever brought it up."

The florid Mrs. Fagin next turned to me and asked through her regretful gaze if I should be so good as to please change the topic. I made a clumsy attempt at obliging the dear woman by noting how motley and redolent was Mrs. Potterson's cutting garden this year. The observation was roundly ignored by all present except for the garden's owner, who nodded a gracious thank-you, and her dull daughter Betty, who negatived the statement with a shake of the head and the terse pronouncement, "Still there are toads."

"What is more disturbing, my dears," pursued Mrs. Venus, returning to her vise-like elbow chair, "is that Dr. Fibbetson—from what I hear—has done little to help the poor woman aside from setting a leg bone and administering—in a most bored and languid fashion—smelling salts without success. It is as if he does not even *wish* that she should be revived and restored."

"From whom have you heard this?" asked Mrs. Potterson, whilst leaning forward in her chair nearly to the point of tipping herself over. Malvina Potterson was a thin woman whose spindle limbs looked brittle enough to break at this acute angle, and at this moment most resembled a winter-stripped tree bent forward in a heavy gust.

"It was told me by a friend whose daughter is also a patient at the hospital," answered Mrs. Venus, bending slightly forward herself to meet Mrs. Potterson's eye.

"I think, Frederick," said Mrs. Potterson, righting herself and turning to me with a most earnest gaze, "that you should go to see the poor, dying soul, and if things are as they have been described, file a letter of complaint with the Medical Review Board. I think that Sir Dabber and the rest of the Board would be quite interested to know that Dr. Fibbetson is deliberately shirking his Hippocratic duties by this woman. Think of how terrible it should be for any of us to fall from an upstairs window and then be ignored except that smelling salts be passed beneath the nose in the feeblest attempt at restoration. Go, Mr. Trimmers, and for Heaven's sake, learn if the intelligence be true."

I nodded. It was most curious. *I* was most curious to know why the woman had not been better treated—she, the wife of a member of the Petit-Parliament, a *Bashaw*! It made little sense, and sleuthhound that I was, I could not have allowed such a mystery to pass without a thorough probe. "I'll do it, of course," I said, and then added, "in exchange for something of sustenance larger than this Lilliputian biscuit."

I had tried with great difficulty to stanch my displeasure over how meagre were the victuals at this tea, but the battle was lost. I was starving. The clock gave still fifty more minutes for me to suffer through a nearly barren teaboard before I could take my leave without seeming too hasty to be gone, and as much as it shamed me to permit such an impudent suggestion to slip from my mouth, it was a mouth now fully enslaved to my empty maw of a stomach.

"Yes, yes," said Malvina Potterson with a flutter. "I *have* cut the cakes and sweetbreads far too small. There is another plate in the kitchen with comestibles of much greater size. Betty, go and fetch the second plate. Can you not see that Mr. Trimmers is famished?"

Betty rose from the old, broken-spindled Windsor chair, which had been her most recent dozing spot, and quitted the room. She returned shortly thereafter with another tray, and making me feel sufficiently guilty for having ever made such a rude proposition, she looked over the tray's contents and proclaimed it "the most filling collection of edibles ever put upon one tray, a suitable meal for a bear, in fact."

"Betty, do set the tray down in front of Mr. Trimmers and keep yourself quiet." Mrs. Potterson dabbed her handkerchief at her wet forehead—a forehead dripping, no doubt, both from the heat that had risen within the congested room and from the pressure of hosting a conclave of veritable malcontents (with Frederick Trimmers as their most vocal spokesman).

I apologised for my untoward remark and for my sullen behaviour as I pulled a three-cornered raspberry tart from its stack. I explained that I had been up for the greater part of two nights completing a rather longish article for the **Dingley Delver** on efforts by a coterie of concerned citizens to get the Petit-Paliament to outlaw the use of arsenic in the manufacture of artificial flowers—something that should have been done a good many years ago when lead content was reduced in our pewter casting and mercury removed from the fabrication of looking glasses and children's pull-toys. I was forgiven by each of my mother's friends except for the redoubtable Miss Antonia Bocker, who said without a mote of self-censorship that such insolent behaviour was inexcusable under every circumstance, and that I should know better, and that a gentleman should be more like a lady and eat only what is put before him and then only sparingly, for proper etiquette and decorum requires it. Miss Bocker said this with an arch smile that undermined the full sincerity of the sentiment (for Miss Antonia Bocker, did, in fact, like me quite a bit and rarely stood upon prescribed ceremony and decorum herself). Having now seised the floor, this most candid of all of my mother's friends took the liberty of airing an opinion that seemed upon its face quite unsuitable for such a light and convivial assembly as this—a rough and unvarnished opinion for which my companions and I were woefully unprepared.

Miss Bocker, it should first be noted, was slightly older than her companions, and her visage gave more wrinkles than every other woman of her years, for she had spent her life in arduous, hard-scrabble toil to raise herself up from her beggarly workhouse beginnings. She had succeeded remarkably well in building a solid business career for herself without the availing assistance of a single member of the opposite sex, save the banker who extended to her a generous loan when (this is the story told to me by my equally candid landlady Mrs. Lumbey) she discovered that selfsame man in the midst of a secret romantic liaison with his dairyman neighbour's milkmaid.

It was an ornamental stationery business that Miss Bocker first purchased, and it flourished so well that the enterprising woman was able to expand it to address everyday stationery needs as well and to acquire several other businesses in comfortable succession, such as a tobacconist shop and a wax chandlery and a millinery and dressmaking establishment, which put my landlady's dress shop well nigh out of business and earned that lady's consistent enmity. Miss Bocker had even run for a seat in the Petit-Parliament, and would have won and become the first woman in the history of Dingley Dell to do so had she not confessed upon the hustings a staunch belief in social Darwinism, which carried with it a denial of the beneficence (or even, indeed, the existence) of God. For this egregious public trespass Antonia Bocker lost the votes of every appalled Christian in her district. Still she was successful in nearly everything else she did, this fact giving her license to be forthcoming with the most obstinate opinions about all that there was to venture an opinion on (in polite company), including the minor matter of how one should behave at tea, and then the much more important matter of the tumbled Mrs. Pyegrave.

"I have a long-standing association with Richard Pyegrave. He has up-holstered furniture in all of my shops, and I will tell you this, sisters, and you as well, Trimmers: that if I had been married to a man who shewed so little concern for me in my final extremities as to spend time bartering my jew-ellry at a shop—let alone in one of our more middling establishments…"

Miss Bocker paused here to allow time for Rose Fagin of Fagin Fine Jewellry and Plate to take and demonstrate offence at having had her own family business so economically denigrated, but to Rose's credit, she merely waved her hand, unperturbed, thus giving Antonia Bocker leave to continue. "I should, if I were Janet Pyegrave," Miss Bocker went on, "rouse myself from my inconvenient coma, rise straightaway from my bed and, re-gardless of my dress, drag my bedraggled body down to the Inn-of-Justice to file a bill of divorcement. I would not put it past that brute—and yes he is a brute, sisters: a base, hairy-knuckled ape—I've seen the way he orders his workmen about with animal-like grunts and snorts—would not have put it past that brute to have decanted her from that height himself in a fit of domestic rage."

"Antonia!" cried Mrs. Potterson, her cheeks suddenly ruddling them-selves in shock over the accusation.

"I stand by it," replied Miss Bocker, folding her arms resolutely and making her assertion a literal one by rising from her chair.

"Still—oh my dear *Antonia.* You cannot go saying such things. In-sulting Frederick because he is hungry was nothing compared to making this hideous charge against Richard Pyegrave—an upstanding member of our community. A pillar. It is too much, Antonia."

"Yet I have no intention of taking it back. Is it your desire, then, that I should go?"

"What I *wish* for you to do, my dear, is *behave.*"

"Stuff and nonsense! Shall I go or shall I stay? Do I have leave to speak or no?"

Antonia was answered by a flurry of placatory pats and susurrant pal-liations on the part of every woman in the parlour with the exception of the exasperated hostess. Even the child-woman Betty Potterson, who had been wakened suddenly from her most recent nap by the sound of heightened voices, pointed with the others to the vacated chair, signalling that Miss Bocker should sit herself down in it, and then indulged in a private smile as if it had all been pure rapture to take the side of one who opposed her mother.

Miss Bocker stood for the moment in seething silence, unplacated and unpalliated, angered not so much, as was my guess, by the difference of opinion between herself and Mrs. Potterson over how one should comport oneself at a commemorative tea, than by the cold verity of there being a man about whom she had every right to vent her animosity—a man who, whilst reputed to be a fine and worthy member of the Petit-Parliament, and arguably the most accomplished upholsterer and draper in Dingley Dell, was also in her considered opinion a felonious "hairy-knuckled ape."

"I have had my fill," Antonia resumed in a low and choleric tone, "of the men of this Godforsaken vale who rule with one fist poised to punch an opposing face or clout an adversarial gut (such as the combative situation demands), and the other fist closed round chinking bags of coin, because from each orangutan fist devolves one form or the other of this duality of power which has tyrannised the Dell from its earliest beginnings. If guns had not been withdrawn long ago from these environs, I have no doubt that half of the hot headed men in Dingley Dell—that larger number comprising nearly every man *in* the Dell—for nearly all of them—do not deny it, Trimmers—tend to lose their highly combustible tempers over the most insignificant of matters—it is the male beast in them, and the reason for our resembling, at times, the proverbial caged rats all quartered together and gnawing and chewing upon each other's tails—"

"Oh have pity upon our poor ears!" interposed Mrs. Venus in a flutter of spirits.

Antonia Bocker did not leave off, but merely took a pause to fetch her breath and to cast about for a closing consequent to her dangling antecedent. "Then we should all be dead, ladies and gentleman. We should all be riddled with holes like eye-cheese, and Dingley Dell should come to its end." And with this, Antonia Bocker sat down.

"For the love of our Lord and Savior, Antonia!" exclaimed Malvina Potterson in another exasperated appeal to dignified discourse. Addressing her most outspoken guest, she continued: "Your disquisition is wildly inappropriate for a tea party and almost certainly a tea party that seeks only to do honour to the memory of our dear departed friend Euphemia. We will entertain no further outburst from you whatsoever."

Again Miss Bocker rose to her feet and again did she ask her hostess if she should take her leave. "For I will most assuredly go if you desire it. Although I came to speak in quiet, respectful tones of memorial sentiment for that dear woman who bore our friend Frederick, yet I've heard nothing since my arrival but a description in the most mind-numbing terms of what we have worn this past year and what we have put into a pudding and who said what to whom behind the back of whomever else—you see, Trimmers, this was the lay of the land before your own arrival, this mind-less female chitter-chatter that makes me want to reject everything I've just eaten by way of the very same portal through which it was originally admitted."

"Oh Antonia, must you!" This from Mrs. Lavinia Blight, who stomped her tree-trunk legs upon the floor and unsettled both the teacups and the harmonica goblets set upon the escritoire, and for a brief moment made one to think that the musical glasses were about to give a tune. "And if we are to continue along this line another moment, I shall begin to pull out all of my hair!"

Mrs. Potterson nodded to Mrs. Blight in support of the second woman's support of Mrs. Potterson's side.

There was one woman in the group who had yet to say a word, as was her wont. In fact, Miss Georgianna Milvey generally spoke little at all—not here nor, really, anyplace else—and could be largely counted upon to nod her head politely and to smile approvingly at everything that was uttered which wasn't *too* divisive, even if what had just been uttered controverted that which had *previously* been uttered. But now the woman was set to do that very thing which never would have been expected of her. This woman, who wore a squeezed bonnet fastened so tightly about her head that one was hard-pressed to recall what colour was her hair (or even if she had any), actually spoke an *opinion*. The opinion came with such conviction as to put the habitually opinionated Miss Bocker totally off her guard. "Antonia, my dear, let us not merely stop ourselves outside the door to Malvina's home. If there is so much that you find disagreeable with the men of Dingley Dell— and let us agree that without the *men* of Dingley Dell, there should *be* no Dingley Dell, for like it or no, it is they who have borne the heavier burden

in the raising up of this valley to its present state of relatively civilised existence—why simply do you not leave—the Dell, that is? Why don't you
just quit this beastly valley altogether, my dearest?" The normally sedate
and taciturn Miss Milvey smiled. It was a cutting smile, and one that took
a rather good measure of itself.

"*Leave*?" The look of surprise upon the face of the recipient of this
harsh interrogatory gave one to wonder if she had ever been asked such a
pointed question in all of her life.

"I do not wish to offend, Antonia," the beaming Miss Milvey continued, giving all teeth and no small view of gums, "but the plash of brandy
with which I've supplemented my tea when no one was looking in my direction (and it is quite often that eyes are averted from mine for there really
isn't much vivacity in my gaze to engage one, now is there?), well, my dear,
it has made me bold, and so I will make further bold to put to you the following with regard to my previous enquiry: Do you never find yourself ill-
equipped to live in such a parochial place as Dingley Dell—a place in which
mindless gossip stands for serious discourse as a rule and those of us who
are not barely getting by are too busy raising themselves upon pedestals of
importance and privilege to concern themselves with anything of *true* and
lasting worth? Can we not simply agree, my dear Antonia, that we live in a
state of veritable constipation of one sort or another, and perhaps someone
such as yourself who values her own opinion above all others, who forges
her own career over every other office and occupation, is the odd quacking
duck in all of this, and that all of us should join hands in that solemn stipu-
lation and put an embargo on the topic from this day forward?"

Antonia Bocker stared at the woman who had been her friend for years
(though the two had never been close) and who, it could be said from her
expression, did not presently know just *what* to think—stared at her with a
gaping mouth. Then quickly this puzzled, assertive woman recovered herself and composed herself and responded thusly: "My good Lord, Georgianna, what a tongue you have acquired for yourself! And what a beautiful
brain you have been hiding under a bushel! I commend you for making a
solid contribution to our collective discourse beyond 'Hand me a biscuit,
if you please, and if it isn't too much trouble, I shall sit here quietly and
nip it like a mouse in a corner.' In answer to your charges, I shall say this:
that I have done quite well for myself here in the Dell, as you can see, but I
still maintain the right to decry everything about this stifling, costive place

that wants improvement and correction and *airing*. I believe that every woman here has the right—nay, my dear madam, the *duty*—to speak her mind whensoever and wheresoever she pleases, without any conversational embargo whatsoever."

"But Antonia," pursued Georgianna Milvey after a blatant, fortifying swallow of brandy directly from her previously secreted flask, "you contend, as my ears perceive it, that there is nothing about the Dell that does not want improvement and correction, and I must beg to differ. I, for one, am quite pleased to live a life of simplicity and quietude upon the small stipend left to me by my father's passing, and though I have no children or grandchildren to brighten my final days, I anticipate that those days should be incandesced quite sufficiently by the amiable ministrations of a goodly circle of friends and neighbours. And I have my fresh garden greens in the summer, and my peonies and my gillyflowers, and my hydrangeas, which will never be pink owing to too much iron in our soil, but it hardly discommodes me. I am really quite content. I know others who are equally content. Life outside the Dell, however different it should be from life *inside* the Dell, cannot be any better than what we have here. Now where is there reason for anyone to want more than what we already have? May we not laugh and shake our heads at the ridiculousness of those who wish to sit within the Petit-Parliament and play at demigodliness and—"

"You will kindly stop right there!" commanded the offended Miss Bocker.

"No, I will stop you both," interposed Mrs. Potterson.

"Not before I am given leave to respond to this specious claim of Georgianna's that every woman—nay, every woman *and* man in Dingley Dell should be content to live with a simpleton's form of contentment."

"Is that how you think we all live?" asked Mrs. Venus, with no stomping of the legs this time. "In a valley of fools? Though there be things here, as Georgianna says, things that make us happy? That give us peace and comfort? You wish for something more, Antonia, because you strive for something more within yourself. I, however, am content. The rest of us are content—relatively speaking. I know nothing of what lives beyond the ridges and the woods, nor do I wish to. Do not call this blissful ignorance; I will not allow it. Where does the universe end, my darling woman? When did time begin and when will it end? Life is full of unanswered questions. I shall not spend the short span of my few remaining years asking such questions only to receive the answer that such is not for any of us at this time to know. You are different. No doubt, Frederick here will take your side as well."

All eyes were now upon me. "I cannot deny," I faultered, "that my mind runs more to learning all that it is possible to know, all that—" I stopped, finding no way at that moment to make my own case which would not raise hackles.

Antonia Bocker finished for me: "All that circumstances permit you to know, even though there be a great deal rudely withheld from our ken. Trimmers and I abhor the status quo when it shrouds and conceals, do we not, sir?"

I didn't answer. I had already displayed enough ill behaviour for one morning.

"Of course he agrees," resumed Antonia, answering her own question. "I dare say that even Malvina will admit that there are times in which one simply *cannot* sit idly by like the fool in his proverbial paradise and is compelled to go and probe and poke, and teaze out what there is to know about a thing. Why else did she advocate for Trimmers' going to the hospital this very morning to find out more about Mrs. Pyegrave's abominable treatment? It is because she knows what every one of us *should* know— even *you*, Sophronia, and that is this: that ignorance *isn't* bliss at all. And whether each of you admits this fact to yourself or no, we must all grow weary at times from squinting too tightly in the darkness.

"Now let us have our requisite tea-lubricated chin-chin about Trimmers' poor dead mother before the morning has fled. It is the pretext for why we are here and why we have donned black on such a warm morning. And then, Trimmers, you and I will go to Milltown Respectable and ask a few questions. It is never wrong to ask questions, my dears. It is a most healthful and enlightening occupation."

Rose Fagin smiled. Perhaps there was good reason that she had not objected when her jewellry shop had been disparaged. Because, I would imagine, Rose Fagin rather liked and respected Antonia Bocker and nearly everything for which the woman stood.

I recall that my mother had admired her, too.

—NOTES—

HARMONICA, also musical glasses, a musical instrument consisting of a variable number of glass goblets, each tuned to a different pitch as determined by the amount of water poured therein, and played by running moistened fingers along the rim of each, singly or in concert.

BUREAU OF APPELLATIONS, office by which Christian names are acquired and surnames legally changed. Upon attaining the age of twelve, children of the Dell may, if their "nursery name" is not of Dickensian origin, select a name for themselves from amongst the Dickens Dramatis Personae. Surnames may be changed, as well, provided the applicant gives good reason and a formal filing be made with the Bureau. The latter name change occurs less frequently than the former, and generally takes place when originally-acquired family names fail to rid themselves of villainous or otherwise disagreeable connotations, although there are certainly exceptional examples in which names of clearly disreputable and unpalatable Dickensian provenance such as Sikes, Fagin, Pecksniff, Gamp, and Quilp have succeeded to a level of respectability that negates their obumbrate literary origins.

THE PETIT-PARLIAMENT, the chief lawmaking body of Dingley Dell. Composed of nineteen non-salaried M.P.P.'s (members of the Petit-Parliament), the body resembles only in a most general sense that system of government suggested by its name. Its members are elected by district, except in those districts in which tax revenues do not meet the qualifying threshold (as determined by the Petit-Parliament in its previous session). Here delegates to the Petit-Parliament are appointed by the Cabinet.

Eight M.P.P.'s are elected by their peers to serve in the government cabinet, which functions to execute all of the laws passed by the Petit-Parliament-in-plenary. Each minister oversees and administers one or more discrete departments of the government. The position of *Prime* Minister is largely ceremonial and is held for only one year by each of the ministers in rotation.

The Petit-Parliament is unicameral, although it bears passing resemblance in certain aspects to both the British Upper House of Lords and the British Lower House of Commons. Membership seldom passes outside a small and select group of Dingley *haute-familias*, comprised of those families who, according to 1999-2000 Prime Minister William Boldwig, have "throughout history made the greatest and most lasting contributions to the Dell in both word and deed and through generous family patronage."

FOR a more detailed examination of the workings of the Dingley Dell Petit-Parliament, please consult *A House Undivided: A Century of Legislative Progress in the Dell of Dingley* by Julius Gulpidge (Milltown Crier Press, 1990). FOR the arrested efforts to bring pure democratic representation to the "low district" citizens of Dingley Dell, please read *One Man, One Vote: A Dream Elusive* by Daniel Cuttle (Dingley Delver Publications, 1994).

THE MILLTOWN CRIER and THE DINGLEY DELVER, the former a daily publication, established in 1921, distributed to a large valley-wide readership and containing a record of Parliamentary proceedings. Though the *Crier* exists as more than a simple house organ for that institution, it is nonetheless published under its auspices and is generally conservative in its editorial voice.

Its weekly competitor, *The Dingley Delver,* published intermittently since 1977, is financed through subscription, advertisements, and contributions alone, and maintains a much smaller, though far more impassioned, readership. The *Delver* has defended its publication, without success, against a number of repressive and censorial actions taken by the Petit-Parliament, freedom of the press being in no way guaranteed in the Dell of Dingley.

Chapter the Fourth

Saturday, June 14, 2003

T here were a great many things that Miss Antonia Bocker was eager to tell me on that walk to Milltown Respectable Hospital—things that she had perhaps been keeping under her bonnet (had she, in fact, worn a bonnet) for quite some time. Each parcel of intelligence was something that I should have liked to have known as one of the chief contributors to the investigative *Dingley Delver*, although there wasn't a syllable that didn't fly in the face of prevailing opinion and general consensus—such consensus deemed by my friend Antonia "hogwash" and "reeking rubbish." I had never known a woman so willing to take the majority view of things and turn it so thoroughly upon its head. Did she do this for that simple frisson of mischief that would delight, or did she believe all that she said to its very marrow, and it was simply a foregone matter of principle and integrity for her to uphold and defend her minority views?

It was upon this walk that Miss Antonio Bocker took a popgun to the **Suppositive Postulations**—of all things!—and waxed upon the possibility of a revisionist view of the **early history of Dingley Dell**, this after I had finally laid to rest the pen that had indited for two long Irish tea-abetted nights my well-researched if somewhat prosaic essay upon the early years of the Dell for the **Dinglian Day** edition of the *Delver*.

I had not known before this morning this revelatory bit of Antonia's own early life story: that she had in her youth befriended an old man, a fellow inmate of Dingley Dell Workhouse #3, who had made the study of the history of our fair valley quite the obsessive avocation. "He bequeathed to me all of his notes," she said, "or rather all of those notes and writings that I could quickly gather together as the workhouse superintendent proceeded to dispose of every personal effect in the wake of his death, to ready the paper-strewn warren for its next occupant." With a casual air, Antonia added, "Perhaps I'll shew them you, Trimmers. Unless, of course, it's too late to use any of it for your article. If such be the case, then perhaps I'll never let you see *any* of it, for you will have shewn me how little you value your mother's wise friend Antonia as a trusted resource for your commemorative project."

I smiled. I would not be bested: "In the first place, Miss Bocker—"

"Dispense with the 'Miss Bocker,' for the love of Christ, Trimmers. I was Antonia to your mother and let me be Antonia to you as well."

"As you wish it—*Antonia.* The first point which I wished to make before interruption was that I had no idea that you should be a resource for my article on the early history of the Dell. You are a woman of commerce—one who by nature must look forward in her thinking and not backward as would, let us say, a retrospective historian."

"Conceded. And you would never have known of my friendship with Mr. Traddles, unless I had told you. Those are days seldom visited in my memories. Terrible times, Trimmers. Wouldn't wish my early circumstances upon a vicious dog."

"And how is it you're sure of the credibility of what Traddles wrote? Given the grievous austerity of his circumstances, how could you even be certain of his sanity?"

Antonia laughed. "I should think that he probably *wasn't* sane. But there was something about his methods—the way he had of talking to the old ones, taking one hoary account and putting it next to another. There was machinery of some sort working in that strange head of his, even if the brain be somewhat out of kilter. I'll shew you the notes he left me someday. But I suspect that you'll use none of it. His history is quite at odds with the standard, established version. Radically so."

Antonia Bocker became for that ensuing moment altogether lost in her thoughts—thoughts, I had no doubt, pertaining to her friendship with perhaps the only person who had uplifted her during her early-life travails. She smiled to herself. "He saved my life, the old **obsessitor** did, there's no doubt about *that.*"

Alas, we had hardly reached the hospital when I was collared by a **ticket porter**, dispatched by my brother, who had first knocked upon the door of Mrs. Potterson's cottage and then received word that I was to be found upon the High Road to Milltown Respectable Hospital (easily distinguishable from Milltown Indigent Hospital, to which a woman of Mrs. Pyegrave's station would never have been relegated). The gentleman was breathless in his report, having run nearly the entire way from Mrs. Potterson's, but told me enough about my nephew's disappearance that I was given ready leave by Antonia to go immediately to my brother's home in Fingerpost and offer whatever succour I was able.

"I'll stay here and make enquiries about Janet Pyegrave," said Antonia with a look of determination and resolve (marked by pursed lips) overlaid by lineaments of concern for my nephew Newman (largely evinced by the furrowed brow).

"And will report back to you on the morrow," she called to me as we parted. I nodded and waved, and then turned my hand to hail a hackney coach and with minimal negociation arrived upon a fair price to hasten me to the outlying village of Fingerpost.

In less than fifteen minutes I was seated upon my brother and sister-in-law's sofa and listening to the disturbing details of my nephew's disappearance, those details pushing aside, at least for the nonce, all thoughts of the unfortunate and dying Mrs. Pyegrave.

—NOTES—

THE SUPPOSITIVE POSTULATIONS, three passionately held views on why Dingley Dell has been quarantined from the rest of the world. All attempts to reconcile these positions or to bring one theory to ascendance above the others have been for naught. The sole source of outside information which should have proven most efficacious in determining which of the three postulations to be the correct one has been the historic contact afforded Dinglian brokers of trade and their Outlander counterparts through the fortnightly transactions that take place at the Summit of Exchange upon the Northern Ridge. Over the many decades, which span the long epoch of Summit trade, Dinglian brokers have reported absolute, near monastic silence from the Outlanders except when intercourse requires communication of a strictly transactional and commercial nature. Ned Crupp addresses this curious consistency in his 1990 memoir *The Honest Broker: Sixty-five Years upon the Summit*:

> "These men wore cloaks and cowls, and everything about them was shrouded in mystery. They confined their speech without exception to the business of our business dealings with them. Dingley Dell bartered her crops and the articles of jewellry and furniture she made (and which she fashioned and turned extraordinarily well) for those goods that she could not grow or build herself, and all was bliss, except when it wasn't, which was every moment in which we were given to wonder about our whereabouts and if we were destined to spend the remainder of eternity here in this rusticated valley without any useful and current knowledge of the world that lay beyond our border. And this is why, dear reader, not being able to help myself, I asked them upon the eve of my retirement that question which has become the most posited within the Dell: "Which of the three Suppositive Postulations is the correct one?" To which they responded (as I always suspected that they would) with a negatory shake of the head and a concerted return to the business at hand. For this is how rigorously they had been trained, that there should be no departure whatsoever from the automatonic response, no matter how much I wished it to be so."

The Suppositive Postulations are as follows:

1.) That life abroad is a life not to be desired, and the Outlander tradesmen are forbidden to speak of the tribulations of their battered world lest they do injury to our tender ears and delicate hearts. And its corollary: that the last physiologically and psychologically pure and unadulterated strain of humanity remains the denizens of Dingley Dell. Their existence is preserved as living reminder of the anteapocalyptic era in the continuum of the human survival on the planet.

2.) That the plague which overspread the globe in the year 1890, yet spared the Dell in its geographically-segregated isolation, continued to ravage the world over the course of the succeeding years, and although it was eventually vanquished, suffered only a few hardy souls to survive and fructify. Subsistence resources in the Terra Incognita being scarce, it has traditionally been thought best for Dinglians to remain segregated, and for commercial interchange to be closely regulated for the husbanding benefit of both transacting parties.

3.) That a good many Outlanders did live to prosper beyond the bounds of Dingley Dell, but the valley's citizens, in much the same way as farmers who have not been vaccinated against the pox, would submit themselves to certain death should they venture abroad without previous exposure to the earlier pandemic. It is premised that this is the reason that so many who ventured from the Dell did not return, and that those who did come back did so in a grievous lunatic state, bearing evidence of some deleterious agent to which Dinglians are susceptible—an agent which implants a savage and vicious affliction upon the brain.

It is the last of the three postulations which claims the greatest number of advocates, and which explains the decision by most of the denizens of Dingley Dell to remain safely within its confines until such time as, perhaps, a vaccine could be devised that would permit them a disease-free reunion with their human cousins in the Terra Incognita. Venturing precipitously without preventive inoculation, so goes the thinking, would be tantamount to playing cards with fate, their collective hand lacking in trumps.

EARLY HISTORY OF DINGLEY DELL.

An Historical Millennial Essay by Daniel Gamp, Esq.

There are a great many things in the early years of this third millennium of our Christian age that we do not know in addition to the overarching enigma of our geographical location. But there is much that we *do*: the product of over 110 years of meticulous documentation of life within the Dell. We know, for example, that an orphanage was established in the year of our Lord 1882 in the village of Hungerford, into which parentless children from points throughout the world were placed, to be nutured and raised in the spirit of Christian beneficence. It was there in the Magnanimity House Orphanage that each youthful inmate of a certain educable age was taught a practical trade, and it was there on the morning of April 2, 1890, that this society of children—the first generation of Dingley Dell— woke to make a most astounding discovery—a discovery that would dramatically alter their lives and the lives of their descendents from that critical moment forward.

All the adults had disappeared.

Every man and woman, most of whom had served as teachers of skilled trades to the young orphans, had vanished without a trace into the dark night, leaving behind a short note that would have to suffice for explanation:

> To the Children of Dingley Dell:
>
> With terrible fear and wretched sadness we have learnt that a great plague has fallen upon the world. Its blanket of death has overspread every known place on this vast orb with the solitary exception of our isolated valley. It is with equal fear and sadness that we must tell you of that which we have learnt in addition: one of your own teachers has been taken by the pandemic, and has, moreover, exposed each of the other adult members of the community to this most horrible disease.
>
> We have therefore concluded as a group that there is nothing else that can be done but that we should remove ourselves permanently from your society, and pray that the infection has not had

time to spread to you as well.

So we hereby bid you adieu and leave you to your own good devices. We trust that we have trained the older amongst you well, and that you will thrive and grow and make of Dingley Dell everything that it has been our hope to attend and commend.

Do not venture from this cordoned valley or death will most assuredly take you. Remain here and God grant that you may abide in health and prosperity.

With undying affection,

Your teachers

(the names of each appearing in alphabetical order with the occasional appended personal note of encouragement and fond regard)

And so it came to pass that on the second day of April in the year of our Lord 1890, two-hundred, seven-and-fifty children ranging in age from three-years-and-three-months to fifteen-years-and-five-months found themselves left to their own devices. Though their juvenile apprenticeships gave them the skills necessary to build a community based upon the twin foundations of resilience and self-reliance, and though they would take good care of themselves in this valley that had yet to be given the name Dingley Dell, it would still be no easy thing for these young waifs to live without loving adult companionship, and there was the shedding of copious tears born of that painful abandonment (mixed with the tears of relief that the plague did not derange—in the end—the health of even a single child within the Dell). Although none of the Dinglian orphans had ever known the purest form of love—that which exists between parent and child—yet the tender care offered to them by their teachers had been sufficiently sustaining, and would be sorely missed and mourned.

The abandonment, as necessary as it appeared to have been, was made ever the more difficult to bear by the fact that every child, save one, had been left illiterate, the need for the children to learn to read having been superceded by the far more important vocational imperative. Were it not for a certain sewing teacher by the name of Miss Ruby Johnson and her ardent, most-favoured pupil, one Miss Henrietta Weatherfield, the young denizens of Dingley Dell would have been left severely wanting in the means by which they might further an education that did not employ, for example, the loom, the gimlet, the anvil, the bread-pan, or the awl.

The subversive Miss Johnson, as things turned out, had taken it upon herself to secretly violate the rule prohibiting the teaching of any of the orphaned children to read—a hard rule that was meant to be strictly enforced without exception. Every night for a good many months Miss Johnson, through whisper and tiptoe, had invited a most zealously compliant Henrietta to her private bedchambers to take up the Bible, or the elementary grammar, or a worn and ragged copy of *The Eclectic First Reader for Young Children, with Pictures.*

Over time, Henrietta had learnt to read quite well—an irony in that initial season, since, with the sudden exodus of all of the adults, there was nothing left behind for her *to* read, the teachers having hastily stuffed all of their books and journals and every scrap of personal correspondence into bulging carpetbags and capacious portmanteaus.

Except…(And it is a most amazing "except" to be sure!)…for a small library, perhaps overlooked, perhaps deliberately hidden, which was discovered in late summer of that same year by two exploratory little boys. The books were found half-buried in the dirt floor of an infrequently visited fruit cellar—a singular hoard of volumes that had not been hurriedly and irrecoverably carpetbagged! A collection of books, which at that point and ever thereafter, comprehended the entire bibliographic corpus, the full sum and substance of reading matter emanating in the Outland:

— A complete twenty-five-volume set of the ninth edition of the *Encyclopædia Britannica* (1878-1889).

— *The Holy Bible*, King James Version.

— A dictionary (unfortunately missing its cover, frontispiece, title page, and the leaves which comprised those terms from "Aa" to "Ash").

— *McCormick's Atlas of the World,* copyright 1872.

and a set of

— *The Complete Novels of Charles Dickens from* The Pickwick Papers *to the unfinished* The Mystery of Edwin Drood.

There was one other book purported to be found amongst the volumes of the fruit cellar cache, which disappeared very soon after the discovery, only to be discovered the next year accidentally shredded in a cornfield between the teeth of a harrow. The book was titled *Around the World in Eighty Days,* and it had been written by a Frenchman by the name of Jules Verne.

But for the youthful "First Generationers" of Dingley Dell, the "Fruit Cellar Library" constituted an education that would prove to be quite broad in scope and which sufficed to define this receptive league of children and their multiple generations of descendents as English-speaking and English-reading expatriates of some greater Britannic realm. With those soil-begrimed volumes as tool and guide, and young Henrietta Weatherford as first in a long procession of teachers who would add English language proficiency and scholastic erudition to the proud list of our skills and talents, we succeeded over the course of the next century in making our microscopic world slightly less insular, while keeping our collective identity unmistakably...*Dinglian.*

Here is who we were in those early days and the many weeks, months, and years that followed: proud citizens of a state with an affinity for things English (and largely Victorian, for we had no other frame of reference), yet possessed of a conversely noble independence in those acquired attributes that distinguish and commend a people in isolation—people who must proceed upon intuitive inclination in those areas of acculturated human interaction in which Mr. Dickens and the otherwise accommodating authors of the *Encyclopædia Britannica* do *not* apprise. We were a people set adrift by unfortunate, even tragic, circumstances, yet blest by a set of implements-of-the-mind (either accidentally or purposefully left to us), which, in combination with the directives of our own hearts and our own God-given analytical, probing natures, allowed us to navigate our future, even though the course that lay ahead be mirky and disadvantageously adumbrated.

To these books we superadded volumes of our own, created from our very own pens, as we sought to enlarge and aggregate that initial Fruit Cellar Library with the works of writers of our own society (such as the one you are now reading). We did this not only to consolidate our many voices into one, but because, in more practical terms, the tradesmen who came each fortnight to deliver the outside goods that we required brought us no new volumes to read and extol. Each request garnered the same response in the very same words: "We have no books to bring you because there *are* no books." The reply was always delivered with a shrug and in an invariant tone that hinted little at deliberately concealed meaning, and over time our brokers learnt to stop asking. How curious, we privately mused, that this world beyond our vale should be possessed of no new books, or perhaps of no books at all! We were given to imagine book burnings—great conflagrations that reduced every volume to ash. Perhaps, we thought, the leaves of their heritage books were required to heat their homes—sick-houses in which legions of Beyonders lay alternately febrile and shivering with some deadly ague, related, we surmised, to the plague that had originally estranged us.

The tradesmen brought us no new books, or anything else, for that matter, that one could deem "new." It seemed that everything which was essential and provident for human use in the year 1890 was replicated year after year after year upon their rumbling wooden hand-trucks and wobbling barrows. Nothing appeared that hadn't been seen before. Nothing appeared that wasn't historically familiar. How sad, we thought, that industrial progress had become so thoroughly arrested outside our border, when within the Dell, we continued to devise and invent and experiment in the name of societal improvement and technological advancement (that is, when we weren't keeping too comfortably to the old and familiar ways ourselves).

It was not empty boast to say that the candles our chandlers fashioned and sold in the year 2000 burned almost twice as long as did those in use in 1890!

Enterprise, thy name was and always will be: Dingley Dell!

DINGLIAN DAY, August 14, a day set aside to acknowledge that day in 1890 upon which the works of Charles Dickens, the *Encyclopædia Britannica, Ninth Edition, the Holy Bible,* a dictionary and atlas were placed by fate into the hands of all Dinglians to their perpetual betterment. A day of celebration and patriotic pride, marked by public readings of selections from the novels of Dickens, the *Holy Bible,* and poetry from *The Companion.*

OBSESSITOR, name given to a man or woman whose behaviour is characterised by monomania, a number of the most famous Dinglians being so diagnosed, with extreme cases requiring isolation, and less severe cases arguing only for tolerance and, when possible, exploitation of the prodigious knowledge acquired to the benefit of the commonweal.

TICKET PORTER. Following the dissolution of the Dingley Dell Post-Office as a direct result of the Post-Office Scandal of 1957, portage throughout the Dell was taken up by independent Ticket Porters—for voice messages, letters and small packages—and by the Punctual Parcel Delivery Company—for the delivery of larger packages—each service in short order proving a most acceptable and efficient replacement for the discredited post-office (and each proving far less prone to abuse of the mails through neglect and after-hour strumpet parties). Ticket porters are generally fleet-footed men and older boys who use horses only for priority deliveries, although the porters who serve the PPDC always employ a heavily laden van, which, during Advent season, is driven by a man who looks very much like Dickens' Father Christmas.

CHAPTER THE FIFTH

Sunday, June 15, 2003

All thoughts of the unfortunate Mrs. Pyegrave having been supplanted by those of Newman and his fretful father and fearful mother (as well as by those of his neither fretful nor fearful older sister Alice whose callous lack of concern for her brother I found to be rather remarkable), I was surprised to discover Antonia waiting for me outside the **All Souls Church in the Dell**, where I had been dispatched by my sister-in-law Charlotte to solicit a prayer from every morning worshipper on behalf of her missing son. Because I generally spent my Saturday nights in either lengthy scholastic lucubration or equally lengthy frivolous inebriation, both activities typically leaving me abed until nearly noon most Sunday mornings, I seldom found myself communing within these walls, though a friendship since boyhood with the church's pastor, Vicar Upwitch, sent me to this beautiful edifice perhaps once a week to gather up my ecclesiastical chum and subject him to a lively session of beer-lubricated theological jousting at our favourite public-house (I the inveterate infidel, he the habited keeper of the faith).

"Trimmers! I must speak with you!" Antonia's hand was upon my sleeve. Her expression gave urgency and some alarm.

"What is it? What's the matter?"

"Not here. Let us go into the garden." Antonia's anxious and furtive manner had drawn the attention of almost every congregant lolling and chatting upon the church lawn prior to the call to worship. There were awkward smiles for those with whom I was fairly well acquainted and polite nods for all the others as Antonia drew her hand through my arm and piloted me, without my having any say in the matter, to the small contemplative garden, which was presently cast in shadow by the church's campanile towering next to it.

"Here, let us sit," said Antonia, finally letting go of my arm and patting the wooden bench to which I'd been led under only minor duress. As Antonia smoothed and settled her skirts upon the slatted seat, she asked if there had been any word of my nephew Newman.

"None," I answered, lowering myself to sit beside her.

"I can only hope that the boy will come to his senses before it's too late. I am not a woman who prays, but I will keep your family close to my heart in the hours to come."

"Thank you. So am I to assume that you have some news about Mrs. Pyegrave?"

"I have news and I have a request. The woman is all but dead; that much is clear. She may have expired already. I am certain now that there was some manner of foul play connected with the incident. Where is Muntle, your constabulary friend?"

"At the moment? Perhaps in Regents Park or anyplace else where he can sport about in the sun on his only day off. What is it you would have him do?"

"There's someone who has a story I should like him to hear: Mrs. Pyegrave's personal maid. Her name is Tattycoram."

"From Dickens' *Little Dorrit.*"

"Yes, I believe you're correct there. It's an odd name for an odd girl from an odd family—one of the mining families that reside in the hamlet of Blackheath. That is where all the domestic help is coming from these days—the young women and their hacking, wheezing older brothers with black lungs and all-but-empty prospects. That is her history. Here now is her *present* story: Tattycoram was with Mrs. Pyegrave yesterday when I went to see the woman at the hospital. The girl has grown quite devoted to her mistress and was weeping all the while that I was there, for Dr. Fibbetson had already come in and pronounced her insentient employeress dead, only to correct himself when Tattycoram solicited a second listen for the weak pulse.

"After I had got the distraught creature calmed down to such point as I could understand her through her sniffles, she consented to answer my query about her whereabouts on the night in question. She said that she had been standing just outside the room from which the tumble occurred. And did she, I asked her, overhear anything that took place within the room in those moments that preceded the tragedy? She nodded most solemnly. 'And have you any reason *not* to tell me what you heard?' I put to her. Now she shook her head. In a most desponding voice she replied that there was nothing to be gained from withholding, for the master of the house had just sacked her. He had arranged for a return to her family in Blackheath to-morrow afternoon, which, of course, means *this* afternoon. Given what she had heard, I asked her if she thought there could have been some reason for the fall, other than pure accident. 'Upon my very life, I do!' she had cried, before quickly clapping her hand over her mouth as if she had not intended to make so resounding a vocal declaration.

"'But you are most uncomfortable telling me *here*,' said I. 'I clearly see, dear girl, the fear that halts your speech. Would you have an objection, then, to speaking of it somewhere else? Someplace where you will neither be seen nor heard by those not of our own choosing?'

"'I have no such objection,' the girl replied in a suddenly calm and collected voice, as if the opportunity to disclose all that she knew to those who would not do harm to her by it was that very thing she most desired. Now I have suggested to Tatty that she should meet you and me and, of course, Sheriff Muntle, at two o'clock this afternoon. There are unlet rooms above my stationery shop that should serve. And you'll bring Muntle with you?"

"I shall make every effort to get him there."

"Excellent."

And with that, my investigative friend Antonia Bocker rose to her feet and brushed her hands together to put an abrupt cap upon our exchange. "That is all for now, Trimmers. Go inside and solicit prayers for your nephew. I personally find prayers to be a waste of time, but then I am a lost, heathen soul, so you would be advised to follow your own conscience in the matter."

Antonia gave my hand a powerful shake, the hardy grip more befitting that of a man than a woman. Then she turned and strode briskly away. I respected my friend Antonia even as I found myself a bit intimidated by her. I had never before known such a woman as she. To be sure, I was acquainted with several women who very much knew their own minds and would never be deterred from doing what they felt to be right and just. My landlady Mrs. Lumbey was just such a woman. But there was a softness to the demeanour of my landlady that was quite missing from the appearance and comportment of Antonia Bocker, her short, wiry iron-grey hair appropriately suggestive of the steel will that strengthened her mettle.

Antonia hadn't time for tender feelings. There was too much work to be done to allow for any trait that might hinder her from her duties. Perhaps it had not always been so; perhaps in time she would soften in her mien, but for the present, my friend Antonia Bocker was cuirassed in the heavy mail of serious purpose, and it was neither my place nor my intention to seek fault there.

❦

I found Muntle playing **quoits** with three of his young deputies upon the green of Regents Park in the West End of Milltown. The park was one of Muntle's favourite leisure spots and an especially desirable one on Sunday mornings when the more pious Milltowners attended services, and left the skittle, quoits and croquet grounds enticingly empty. "I think that I should like to pitch a tent and live out the rest of my days in this verdant setting," said Muntle in a comically confiding whisper, "would that the weather remained clement. The cemetery is quiet and serene, but there are ghosts there and not a single hob with which to make a ringer."

I led Muntle away from his playfellows so that I might speak to him without our being overheard. One of the deputies, a redheaded fellow, ridiculously over-freckled, eyed us with interest as we strolled away.

"Is *he* the one?" I asked in a low voice, whilst making a slight nod with my head in the direction of the juvenilely mop-topped young man.

"Aye. Boldwig. Billy Boldwig. It wasn't even a month ago that he was thrust upon me. I didn't hold out great hopes for him, but I had no idea that he would shew not even an ounce of promise whatsoever. He is by turns disruptive and indolent, and he all but slept through his truncheon training, in spite of the fact that his mates have nicknamed him 'Billy Club' for the obvious reason. I fear he's going to be a problem and there's really not much that I can do about it."

"Because it was an M.P.P., his own father, William Boldwig of the

General Agency Office, who insinuated him upon you."

Muntle nodded, stopping beneath a large oak tree that gave adequate shade and an accommodating degree of privacy. "You would think that having a father with the power to put you into whatever situation you desired, 'deputy sheriff' should appear nowhere upon a list of prospective occupations. Whilst respectable, the job offers little or no cachet of which *I'm* aware."

"Perhaps Billy hopes eventually to steal your job away from you, Muntle. I would keep a careful eye on him were I you."

I smiled, but Muntle did not. It suddenly became obvious to me that this wasn't the first time that the thought had entered his head.

"Now to my reason for this impromptu visit, Muntle: your presence is requested in rooms above Bocker's Fine and General Stationers at two o'clock this afternoon."

"For what purpose?"

"An interview. Will you be finished with your game of quoits by then?"

"Who is to be interviewed and for what reason? It's my day off, you know."

"Her Christian name is Tattycoram. I don't know her surname. She's one of that small flood of char-girls and bottle washers from Blackheath that are making life so much more pleasant and convenient for our mon-eyed Bashaw class. She has information that should shine a brand new light upon what happened to her mistress, the unfortunate Mrs. Pyegrave."

"By the bye, the poor woman finally succumbed to her injuries this morning. I just received the report of her demise not twenty minutes ago."

"And is there to be an investigation into its cause?"

"We have the cause of death: fall from a great height."

I frowned. "You know what I mean. Was it an accident or was it not an accident?"

Muntle sighed, then turned in such a way as to put his back to his new redheaded deputy who seemed to be edging closer to where we stood, his large floppy ears apparently straining to hear everything that was being exchanged between us.

"Lord Mayor Feenix has nudged me off."

"But why?"

"He contends that there is nothing to be found out, and that any degree of delving should constitute a great waste of my time. There is not even to be an inquest. Pyegrave said that his wife had been drinking, stumbling about, and knocking things over. He put her to bed and thought that she would stay put until morning. It is his assertion that she *didn't* stay put, Trimmers, but rose in the night, tripped over a hassock and went flying out of the open window."

"Do you not find that story to be a bit far fetched?"

Muntle half-shrugged. "A bit…and perhaps a little bit more."

"Tattycoram would think, I warrant, that this account was *beyond* far fetched. As it so happens, she heard the whole thing, listening most attentively outside the door to Mrs. Pyegrave's bedchamber."

"That's what she wishes to do? Offer an earwitness account of what took place in that room?"

I nodded. "Is it required that you seek the Lord Mayor's permission to speak to her?"

"Of course not. It may be a fact that I'm nudged and leaned upon with far more muscle these days than I have been in the past, but I do maintain *some* small vestige of independence in my office, Trimmers. At least for the time being."

This last statement was made in a most circumspect undervoice, for the new redheaded deputy had fully completed his incursion and was now standing only a couple of feet away, signalling Muntle's attention with an "ahem" and a raised, soliciting forefinger.

"Yes? What is it, Deputy?"

"Speaking on behalf of the other players, I was wondering how much longer you wished to delay the game. The tavern is open now and there has been some discussion as to whether or no we should take custody of the tap before the pew-sitters make their thirsty onslaught."

"I've no objection if you want to go along, Boldwig. You needn't have even asked me."

"I interrupt, as well, to enquire with regard to the matter being discussed betwixt the two of you—if there be some small office or service I may render to be of assistance." Boldwig pursed his lips and squinted his eyes in a buffoonish show of earnest sincerity.

"I have no idea what you mean, Boldwig. This is a private conference that has nothing to do with my duties as sheriff."

Billy Boldwig took a couple of self-abasing steps in retreat. "Begging your pardon then. I had it in my head that you were discussing poor Mrs.

Pyegrave's death upon her hospital bed this morning—that Mr. Trimmers here was gathering information to put it into the *Crier*."

I answered for myself: "I don't write for the *Crier*, Boldwig." It was time now for a little blatant prevarication: "And there *was* mention of Mrs. Pyegrave's tragic demise between us, but only briefly and in passing."

"Because…" pursued Boldwig, "I know that Lord Mayor Feenix would prefer that the family be allowed to grieve and bury their dear loved one without prying trespass by the papers or any other sort of meddling for that matter. I know this family quite well, sir, and feel tacitly empowered by the connexion to speak on their behalf."

Muntle brought his eyes to bear on Boldwig without speaking. I knew the hard and penetrating look, having seen it upon my friend's face on previous occasions: the kettle nearly ready to blow its lid but kept in place by a most strongly-applied hand. After taking a breath to rein in his temper, he replied, "First of all, Deputy Boldwig, what is said between Lord Mayor Feenix in his capacity as Minister of Justice and me, in my capacity as Sheriff of Dingley Dell, should be of concern to my deputies if and only if I choose to *make* it their concern—and this goes treble for he who is the most recent addition to my constabulary. Secondly, you have no business knowing *how* the Lord Mayor feels about the Pyegraves, unless you have been obtrusive and prying yourself. Have you been obtrusive and prying, Deputy Boldwig?"

Boldwig gave immediate offence (or at least he coloured in such a way as to lead one to this conclusion). "I most certainly have *not*, Sheriff. My father, as you must know, is close friend to the Lord Mayor and they are both close friends to Pyegrave. Whatever intelligence has come to me I have absorbed merely through inevitable proximity to those amicable attachments. Begging your pardon again, sir, I shall be on my way."

With that, the obtrusive and prying Mr. Billy Boldwig turned to go to that place where he could draw himself a pint, although his withdrawal from our society was by no means tidily executed, for it was accompanied by a series of studious glances over the shoulder, each of which seemed evidential of further opinion and speculation about what his employer might do that a Feenix or a Boldwig or most certainly a Pyegrave should not approve.

"I would fire that officious red-topped turd in an instant, Trimmers, but I should have every member of the Petit-Parliament gathered on my doorstep at my Inn-of-Justice lodgings within the hour demanding his reinstatement. What a low and contemptible cabal holds dominion over this tight little valley! There you have it, Freddie. I am now on record as despising each and every one of these overreaching, obstructionist oligarchs."

"*And* their offspring, my alliterative friend," I added with a smirk.

"Oho to that," agreed Muntle. "Now what is the time again that I am to listen to this tattered woman?"

—NOTES—

THE ALL SOULS CHURCH OF THE DELL, despite its pastorally provincial name, is the largest and tallest structure to be found in the valley, its seven-storey campanile towering over every other building in Milltown.

It had been the life aim of Bishop Richard Tollimglower to see a cathedral of historically massive proportions constructed within the Dell. When the Petit-Parliament refused to allocate the funds necessary for its erection, a more modest church building was proposed but with a compensatory concession: it should have a bell tower of rather impressive size and height such as to dwarf every structure, both natural and man-crafted, within the whole of Dingley Dell. "If I cannot have flying buttresses and imposing gargoyles for my seat of ecclesiastical authority," said the bishop, philosophically, "give me at the very least a lofty campanile with a carillon of bells that will be heard in every nook and cranny of our dale to remind its listeners that God watches in ceaseless attendance from his own Heavenly watchtower above."

So it was done, and it was the Bishop himself who oversaw the construction of Dingley Dell's most ambitious architectural venture and who applauded it and who said it was good and then promptly dropt dead in his raiments within hours of its completion, and was subsequently offered nothing like the funereal pomp and ceremony that had been his testamentary wish.

Tollimglower's successor, the low-church Puritan Vicar Tupman, banished pomp and ceremony not only from the obsequies and exequies attendant upon his predecessor's passage but from every other aspect and office of the All Souls Church. "God loves and watches over us all, this is true, but He does so whether we exalt him with frippery and architectural excess or no. I therefore ring in with our mellifluous and only slightly clanging carillon of bells the 'Era of Simplicity,' and should my flock give objection, I shall be inclined to turn us all into Methodists and have done with it." These words were spoken by the vicar upon the first day of his ascension to that office, which should have been denominated High Bishop, but was reduced by way of ecclesiastical simplification to Humble Vicar, and to the above pulpital peroration was added the injunction that at some point the campanile, which offended Tupman's eye as an unintended tribute to the iniquitous Tower of Babel, should surely come down, brick by brick and stone by stone.

Dinglians, however, would hear of no such a thing, and so the bell tower stood for the next five decades, and the denizens of the Dell became ever the more attached to the tintinnabulation that gave from it, and he who was willing to pay half a florin could climb its ninety-eight steps to look down upon Milltown and to take in the equally commanding prospect of the surrounding valley. So were the coffers of the church filled even on those Sunday mornings in which congregants were feeling more niggardly than usual.

QUOITS, a popular traditional lawn game played by Dinglian boys and men, and more increasingly by members of the softer sex. It involves the throwing of a metal ring over a prescribed distance with the purpose of landing it over a pin (called a hob) set in the centre of a box-like frame filled with clay. A successful throw, called a "ringer," gives a player two points, with twenty-one points being necessary to win the game. Quoits is especially popular amongst public servants as a midday diversion—notably sheriff's deputies, firemen, and government clerks. There is a tournament, which takes place in Milltown each autumn, and which has been most recently won (in impressive annual succession) by a team comprised of Water Rate Collectors, called informally the "Jolly Soakers." The game is played in the United States of the Outland using horseshoes and is called, appropriately, "horseshoes."

CHAPTER THE SIXTH

Sunday, June 15, 2003

Tattycoram was a girl of eighteen with bright blue eyes, a radiant smile, and a complexion darkened, no doubt, by years of having lived within that haze of coal dust and carbonated grime that permanently besooted all who claimed the village of Blackheath for their home. I expected a shy and overly propitiatory young woman and got quite the opposite. Tattycoram was voluble and animated and eager to tell her story in her thick coal-town dialect.

Muntle was last to climb the stairs to Antonia's unlet rooms and was offered a cup of chicory **coffee** before he'd even had the chance to sit down. Antonia Bocker possessed a fondness for chicory that far surpassed her affinity for tea or chocolate or even the unadulterated version of that non-chicorous half of chicory coffee, which was drunk in its pure form only by the wealthiest citizens of the Dell, given its preciousness. "I drink chicory," she explained, "because it was all that there was for me to drink back in the days in which my circumstances were so severely diminished. I grew to tolerate and finally to crave the taste, and because it has less caffeine than does its richer beverageal cousin, it allows me to sleep a bit better. But if you would prefer tea instead, I'll ask Harriet to put a pot on. It is no trouble."

The three of us declined the alternative and endured the chicory, which has little smell but isn't entirely insipid.

The room was spare. There was not much more therein but a few old deal chairs and a moulting sofa upon which to sit and a Pembroke table carved and turned not by the best of Dinglian furniture-makers but perhaps by one of their journeymen progeny. "I will have you know that I don't usually put out my rooms to let in such a sparse state. My last lodger, you see, purchased a few pieces from me upon taking his leave. But enough empty talk. Tattycoram, my dear girl, you must tell us exactly what you heard whilst standing outside the door to your mistress' apartments. It is most important for us to know."

"It was not wot I heerd, aye, but den wot I didna hear."

"What do you mean, dear girl?"

"Dey was feetin' wit da words—hollerin' one t'nother. Den, in da meedle of all of da fussin' and da feetin', I heerd da glass, it break loud on my ears and I heerd her cryin' out of da winder as she fall. For meself, I backed away from da door so's da master Mr. Peegrove, woo-na see me when he coom out."

"And *did* he see you?" asked Muntle writing upon his pad.

"No, he di-na. But here be da ting dat I want you to know bout-tit: his good wife, she fall out da winder, but he di-na leave da room. He in dere all quiet-like and do not go down to find out just how she be. It was like dis, Mr. Sherf—it was like he wos waitin' for her to be dead on da street afore he go. Now a minute or two, dey pass, and dere is a lot of clatter and commotion on dere street below, and so finally he coom out da door and go down da passage and down to da street and I go into da room and I meself look out da broken winder to see him down below a'weepin' and a'wailin' like he know'd noten bout da deed till dat very moment."

I pushed forward in my seat. "As if he were putting on a show through his reaction to it."

"Yessir, yessir. Dat was as it happened."

Antonia, who was taking notes of her own, looked up from her tablet, chewed the end of her pencil in brief thought, and then said, "Tattycoram, my dear girl. You must now try to remember everything that was said in that room prior to Mrs. Pyegrave's unfortunate defenestration. What can you recall of the exchange?"

Tattycoram nodded and took a sip of the chicory, then looked about the room. "Is dere be a sweetmeat or two for me to eat as I be recollectin'?"

"I have a cupboard full of sweetmeats in the shop below, my dear. Harriet, go down and fetch Tattycoram a few liquorice drops."

Tattycoram smiled her approval and began to search her brain with the help of her roving, contemplative eyes. "Dey was feetin', as I done said."

"What were they fighting about, Tattycoram? Do you remember?"

Tattycoram coloured a bit but quickly recovered. "I will tell it, but it be a ting I woo-na in polite compnee normally say."

"We understand," said Muntle. "We will not judge the messenger regardless of how unseemly the message."

Receiving this preemptive acquittal of her character, Tattycoram proceeded: "Da master was a' blazin' over da mistress. He done found out a ting 'bout her—a not very good ting."

"What did he find out?" asked Antonia, licking the end of her pencil in eager anticipation of the intelligence.

"Dat she had been wit another."

"With another—?"

"Not her husband. Dat she was wit another in da flesh-to-flesh."

"Flagrante delicto!" exclaimed Muntle.

"Not necessarily," cautioned Antonia. "How did he find out, Tattycoram? Certainly he didn't walk in on Mrs. Pyegrave in the very midst of the assignation."

Tattycoram shook her head. "And it warn't a man besides. He ain't no more den a boy of eighteen like meself. It be da stableboy Jemmy wot works at da Regents Park. It was head groom who done toll to Mr. Peegrove wot he seen Peegrove's wife a' doin' wit da stableboy in the back of dat dere stable. He tolled it to Peegrove for coin, I 'spect. And Peegrove he go to his wife in da bed and ask her if it be true and she say it were true, every word of it, but he ain't to do a ting bout it, or else'n she'll go and tell everybody 'bout—and here I cain't but hear da words too clearly."

"What did they *sound* like?" I prodded. "The words that you couldn't quite hear?"

"I change me mind. I could *hear* dem, govna. I just can-na remember all da parts a dem."

"This makes no sense," said Antonia in an underbreath. Harriet entered with a tray of sweetmeats, from which each of us plucked up a lozenge except for Muntle who swiped a handful and stuffed them into his waistcoat pocket. (This act confirmed Muntle's love of liquorice, about which hitherto I could only conjecture.)

Tattycoram popped the sweetmeat into her mouth and began to suck it, employing both of her dusky cheeks. "I will tell you wot it sounded like to me ears."

"You do that, dear," said Antonia, raising her voice slightly to be heard above the sound of sucking and slurping (for even Harriet had taken a black lozenge into her mouth to enjoy).

"She say—Mrs. Peegrove—dat she will go and tell everybody 'bout da Tya-dya-dya projette."

"The 'Tya-dya-dya –?"

"*Projette.*"

"You must mean pro*ject.* Oh what a most curious name!"

"It weren't probly dat zactly. But it sounded some-ten *like* dat."

"Yes, I understand, my dear. And was there anything else?"

"She say how she a' goin' to tell everybodys 'bout da fett. She a' goin' to ruin the fett for one and all."

"The *fett?* Like, do you mean fête, as in some sort of festival?"

"I don't know the word, begpardon."

"And how did Mr. Pyegrave respond to this threat by his wife?"

"He yell to her dat she will na do it. He kill her first."

"Did he really say that, girl?" asked Muntle, looking up from his note-taking. "It sounds terribly tidy."

Tattycoram nodded. "It be tidy I s'pose, but it be true, Mr. Sherf."

I struck in, "How much time would you suppose passed from statement of the threat to the point at which we can all now assume Pyegrave pitched his wife through the window?"

"Meebe a minute or two or tree. Dem two went back and forth for a short spell. 'Are you really goin' to go and tell all dem tings?' And she say yes, she's a'lookin' aforward to doin' it. And he ask her again meebee two more times and da answer da same each at every askin', and den he musta gone right to her at dat instant 'cause dere den be a sound like he be liftin' her from da bed, all da covers a rustlin' and da sound of da bedstead thumpin' and bumpin' and dere's a mufflin' sound coomin' too like meebee he got his hand over her moof."

"Her what?" asked Muntle, leaning in.

"Her moof," said Tattycoram, and then she touched her own "moof" by way of demonstration. "And den not a few seconds later I hear da glass a' crackin' and den da sound of her a' screamin' as she go down. It be a horrible sound and I had a mind to go in and find out if it was wot I feared it to be, but den I tink the better of it. I tink dis madman could toss me out dat winder too, so I pull meself back into a corner of da passage and I wait for him to go out. And dat's all dat I heerd and all dat I know."

"You've been quite helpful, Tattycoram," said Muntle, rising to place a genial hand upon her shoulder. "If I require anything further from you, where may I find you?"

"I go back to Blackheath soon as I leave dis place."

Muntle nodded. "Safe travels, child. You've been a great help to us."

As Antonia walked Tattycoram to the door and then down the steps and through the shop to the lane, Muntle and I fell into contemplative silence. Eventually, I sighed and shook my head. "It *does* seem awfully tidy as earwitness testimony goes, doesn't it, Muntle?"

"Cut and dried and bound and sheathed," returned my friend. "But sometimes things *are* exactly what they seem. We have no reason not to believe the girl. Mrs. Pyegrave had taken up with a nice, young, no doubt good-looking horseboy as paramour, and Pyegrave found out. But rather than agree to his demand that she terminate her relationship with the young man, she turns it all back at her husband with a threat of her own, and he is compelled to deliver the consequences right on the spot."

"The Tya-dya-dya Project. Here, though, things get mirky."

"Aye. I've never heard of anything with a name even remotely similar. Have you?"

I shook my head. "Whatever it is, it cannot be widely known…"

"Yet still of sufficient import," interrupted Muntle, "to send Janet Pyegrave to her death for merely threatening to divulge it. That and this 'fête'— whatever that refers to. It really is quite an intriguing business, Trimmers."

"And obviously worth pursuing."

"Yet such pursuit would prove tricky."

"How so?" asked Antonia, having returned to the room to join the conversation *in medias res.*

Muntle folded his arms and chewed upon his nether lip for a moment. "It is, frankly, the servant-girl's word against Pyegrave's. And set one against the other, credibility is generally more heavily weighted on the side of an M.P.P."

Antonia snorted and then began to shake her head. "So are you saying, Muntle, that there is no way for Pyegrave to be brought to justice?" Now Antonia placed her hands on either side of her head as if to still it, although the picture was more of a woman in the throes of torturous exasperation. "For I now have little doubt about the man's culpability in his wife's death. Yet because, at present, everything rests upon the testimony of this one poor miner's daughter, Pyegrave appears set to walk free for the remainder of his days! Do I apprehend the situation correctly?"

"I cannot see means to any other outcome," said Muntle in an apologetic tone.

"Even when you consider…" Antonia's eyes brightened. "…the possibility that there may have been someone who lived in that street who, unlike Tattycoram, actually *saw* it—someone watching in the night as Pyegrave approached the window and tossed his wife out of it as if she were the unwanted contents of a brimming slop pail!"

"If that be so, Miss Bocker, the person has yet to come forward. No, my dear lady, I suspect that everyone was sound asleep in their beds at that late hour."

"Not if the couple's argument carried itself loudly into the street. Perhaps someone was drawn to their window by the noisy contretemps but is presently too reticent to recount voluntarily what they witnessed. Perhaps you need only cast about, then do a bit of tugging here and there to retrieve all sorts of pertinent witness testimony."

"I must tell you, Miss Bocker," began Muntle, clouding Antonia's hopeful countenance with his furrow and frown, "that I may very well be prohibited from pursuing this investigation."

"Stuff and nonsense! You are sheriff of Dingley Dell! It's within your purview to inspect and enquire as you see fit. A woman is dead, my dear sir, and there now exists a decided difference of opinion as to how she got to be that way."

"Sooth to tell, Miss Bocker, I do not maintain the unbridled independence in my offices that you assume. I answer to the Minister of Justice— the honourable Lord Mayor Feenix—who answers, in turn, to the Cabinet at large."

Antonia reacted quickly to Muntle's admission by punching her fist indelicately into a bolster—a bolster, no doubt, sewn by one of Pyegrave's own upholsterers. (Life in the tightly-circumscribed Dell of Dingley was filled with many such little ironies, some funny and flavourful, others bitter and biting.) "A woman lies stiffening upon a mortician's table, murdered by her husband who will never be brought to justice because a collier's daughter is never to be believed. It boggles the brain, gentlemen."

"Indeed," said Muntle. "But don't despair entirely, Miss Bocker. I will endeavour to pursue the investigation as expeditiously as I am able, to see how much I can learn before the Ministry of Justice orders me to close the case."

Antonia shook her head. "That will not do, for they will, no doubt, shut you down from waft of your very first interview. I suggest another course. Set the formal investigation aside. For all intents and purposes you've heard nothing from this char-girl, and I doubt that once she's back in Blackheath there will be much about her story that will venture out, for residing in Blackheath is commensurate with residing upon the distant Malay Peninsula for all that most Dinglians care about that isolated flock. You have only Pyegrave's word that it was an accident that took the life of his wife, and that is how it shall stand, whilst I take a few liberties of my own to ask questions of the neighbours. Would you raise an objection, sir, were I to conduct a few instatutory probings of my own?"

"I suppose not, provided you exercise only the utmost discretion in how you conduct your questionings."

Antonia nodded as I added that "someone should also have a word with the stableboy Jemmy. I should like to know if there is truth to the predicating action: his involvement with Mrs. Pyegrave."

"Your landlady, Mrs. Lumbey, rides at Regents Park, does she not?" asked Antonia.

"Ever and anon," I replied. "She can't afford to make it a weekly outing."

"But you'll go with her on her next visit to put yourself in close proximity with the boy," said Antonia, becoming quite invigourated by the prospect of our extrajudicial investigation. "By the bye, I take it that neither of you gentlemen has heard of anything called the 'Tya-dya-dya Project?'"

Muntle and I shook our heads as one.

Antonia continued: "Given the fact that very little goes on in this valley that is not passed from one to another like a contagious head cold, those few secrets that *are* being kept close must be large secrets indeed, and this one in particular of such significant import that a man should take such an extreme action upon the mere threat of disclosure."

I nodded. It was indeed a Dinglian paradox: that everyone knew everything about everyone else except for those select things known only to a select few. Perhaps the 'Tya-dya-dya Project' was pet name for some nefarious business matter in which Pyegrave, by reputation not one of the

most scrupulous businessmen in the Dell, had engaged to his detriment—
a difficult situation made all the more problematical for him should its
particulars be broadcast by a retaliatory spouse.

For the time being, the thing would remain a befuddling mystery in
both fact and in the very pronunciation of its odd name. But all was destined to come eventually to light, this first stone of revelation having begun
its ineluctable and catalytic journey down that mountainside of earlier
mention.

—NOTES—

COFFEE, a beverage rarely imbibed in its pure, unadulterated state due to
its high cost and scarcity. When drunk by all but the wealthiest class within
the Dell, it is most often prepared through infusion at one of two coffee-
houses in Milltown that employ an infusing apparatus of local invention.
In its pure form it is a drink of luxury for the members of Dingley Dell's
most exclusive club, the Cavendish Coffee-Room.

The beverage is commonly adulterated by one of the following addi-
tives: the ground roots of the dandelion (informally denominated "Wishie,"
nickname for the mature dandelion clock); carrot ("Orange Brew"); pars-
nip ("Sativa," after its species name *Pastinaca sativa*); beet ("Red-cup");
acorns ("Squirrel Juice"); and beans ("Toots").

Chapter the Seventh

Saturday, June 21, 2003

A week had come and gone and there was no sign of Newman. Alice's prediction that if her brother *was* outside the Dell he would make a speedy return had not come to pass.

The worst was contemplated and the worst was ventured in grave whispered voices, but still my brother and sister-in-law had not yet given up wishing and praying for their son's safe restoration to the bosom of his family. Indeed, there was a small ember of hope that burnt within my heart as well, for I had fabricated a plan: in two days the Outland brokers would make their fortnightly visit to the Summit of Exchange, and I was determined to have a word with them to find out what, if anything, they knew of Newman's visit. I knew that even though my nephew could be nowhere now *but* the Outland, there still existed the sliver of a chance that he did not have to go the way of all the other Departed. My meeting on Monday morning would give me opportunity to bellow a little more oxygen into that hope-filled ember. Hundred to one the tradesmen would decline to answer my questions, but I could not let this day go by, no matter how potentially unavailing, without the earnest essay.

The tradesmen were a strange and mysterious breed, saying and indicating little as a rule beyond those things that served to grease the wheels of our mutual commerce: wheels that had spun with well-oiled ease for above a century, and which through all those years of uninterrupted mercantile

intercourse, had afforded a good many Dinglians lives of relative comfort, and for a smaller, more privileged few among us, lives of inordinate
amenity. This is not to say that the privileged did not have their own in-
terpersonal conflicts to resolve or the occasional accident (consider Mrs.
Pyegrave) or debilitating illness from which to recover (though hardly ever
did illness in the Dell rise to the level of outright epidemic or plague, and
we knew that we were quite blest in this respect).

Nor were we ever so unfortunate as to have been visited by any other
form of pestilential pollution. Nor was it required that we should withstand the incursion of marauding Outlanders, nor even the intrusion of a
single rogue Beyonder who through individual initiative might seek to per-
petrate some act of vandalistic destruction or highway robbery upon us.
Nor did any other such harmful purposed calamity threaten our collective
well-being, owing, we believed, to the trust that had been built between the
tradesmen and ourselves—a trust which had been induratively cemented
long, long ago. We came over time to believe that the Outland brokers were
in some large way responsible for our protection, were men of probity and
honour, were men dedicated to the continuation of our unique way of life.
It is for this reason that our own brokers who contracted with these men
trucked with the utmost caution and respect.

It is also for this reason that I made it known to my brother late on
the Saturday night preceding their impending visit that this newly-hatched
scheme of *his* for returning his son to loving parental embrace—a plot that
required the unwilling participation of said tradesmen—was dangerous in
all of its aspects and stupid upon an unprecedented scale.

"Not in one million years, Augustus. And for a myriad of reasons, let
alone the fact that Muntle would never allow it. *Nobody* would agree to it,
for that matter, given the grave risk it poses to us all."

My brother slammed his ceramic mug down upon the table, the
hot liquid spattering the cloth, and pinned me with a glare. "For what
reason would we even tell him, Freddie? For what reason would we tell
anybody?"

"Even without confiding your ridiculous plan to a single soul, brother,
how could you ever believe that such a scheme wouldn't get out? Kidnapping a tradesman, holding him hostage. You don't think that after the other
tradesmen make it known to our own brokers that one of their number
has been gagged and sedated and rudely dragged from the Summit, that

our deed shouldn't within a matter of minutes find its way to the ken of everyone in the Dell? Have you mislaid the very last remnant of your declining sanity and good sense?"

"Still, I believe the plan to have *some* merit."

I looked at my brother as if he had suddenly grown horns. "What merit? Tell me."

"The opportunity to extract information from the kidnapped tradesman—not only intelligence about Newman, but about *everybody* who has ever ventured into the Terra Incognita. It is my hope that should our captive be the sort of divulger who will be happy to cooperate with us in lieu of having his fingers bent back in a manner in which fingers do not generally go, we should find out a most amazing catalogue of things about those who have left us, and especially about those who have failed to return."

Charlotte entered the room, pressing a moist cloth to her head. Fixing me with her pain-squeezed gaze, she asked what had got the two of us so noisy and overwrought.

"This stratagem of your husband's to kidnap one of the tradesmen and force him to tell us what has happened to Newman."

Calmly, because she was weary, but also because she was just beginning to succumb to the effects of the medicinal draught she'd taken, Charlotte asked if it was really necessary to *kidnap* the man to ask him such a thing.

I answered for my brother with a violent shake of the head. "Which is why I plan to go to the Summit of Exchange at the early hour of daybreak on Monday and do that very thing without complicating the matter with the sort of applied duress your husband puts forward as would a raving fool."

"You compare me to a raving fool, simply because I wish to *act*?" rejoined my brother.

I shook my head in silent rebuttal. Augustus' irrational argument had tired me. The whole business was enervating and depressing, and I slumped more heavily into the lap of my chair. Although hope still had reason to abide with us on this night, yet I could not allow my brother to attire it in ways that did not serve. After a silent interval I resumed, "Consider *this*, Augustus: what if after the fingers have been successfully bent backwards the kidnapped tradesman still refuses to tell us what we demand to know? What then? Do we put him on the rack? Do we pour hot oil down upon his head? Think sensibly here, brother. How quickly would any such torturous act drive all of the other tradesmen permanently from our society? Is it your wish for every man, woman and child in this valley to die a slow and inconvenient death in want of those things the tradesmen bring us that are crucial for our survival?"

"No, it is not my wish," my brother mumbled.

"Yet you sit here willing to violate that historic trust with an act of such foolhardy impetuosity as to rate amongst the most dangerous feats of irresponsibility conceivable. This is why highly trained, level-headed and seasoned brokers do our bidding—why they and they alone are responsible for the interaction of trade which sustains us."

"Frederick is right, dear," said Charlotte to her gloomy-faced husband. "It is madness. Don't think of kidnapping an Outlander even another moment. I'm going up to bed." With this, my sister-in-law took her yawning leave.

I thought that Charlotte's summary ruling had put a finish to the debate. Perhaps it had. Perhaps what was subsequently delivered by my irascible brother constituted merely some form of grumbling afterthought: "I don't purchase your theory, Freddie."

"What theory is that?"

"The one that states with unequivocal certainty that we would flounder and die in the absence of outside trade. As *I* see it, nearly everything we take from the Beyonders could be relinquished without insurmountable difficulty. We could easily do without the bananas, the India rubber, the calico and…"

"And tea?" I interrupted. "I see, dear Gus, that you gulp yours down as if it were some life-sustaining elixir."

"Yes, even my tea. And every other indulgence that makes our lives more agreeable and convenient."

I was set to counter that not all of our imports could be categorised as superfluities, but my brother gave me no opening, continuing in the same vein, scarcely taking breath. "Why, every milk cow could drop dead to-morrow morning and we would still make our lardy butterine, which tastes exactly the same as the dairy version. No more cotton? We shall wear more wool! No paper? We shall turn our leather into paper-thin vellum, our sheepskin into parchment! We have come a very long way toward total self-sustenance, brother. Apparently you haven't taken notice."

I pushed my own cup of tea away, some of it sloshing over the rim.

"Why not, then, kidnap the whole lot of the tradesmen, and exact every atom of the information you require?"

"Don't mock me."

"I am not mocking you, Gus. I'm attempting, however unavailingly, to demonstrate the ridiculousness of your position. And you should be grateful that Alice isn't here to see her father in such a puerile state, so as to give further cause for her rebellion."

"She's rarely around, so the point is moot. This night is the third in a row that she has spent with her friend Cecilia Pupker. The two have become inseparable."

A moment of silence ensued. I took breath and pursued in a now somewhat less vexed tone: "Gus. I cannot stress more strongly how grave the consequences should be if you attempt anything that endangers our trading arrangements with the Outlanders, setting aside the fact that you'd be thrown into a gaol cell and never let out again. Perhaps you've forgotten, by the bye, that it's against the law for an unlicensed Dinglian to be found anywhere within the vicinity of the Summit of Exchange on fortnightly Mondays."

"Then how did *you* receive special dispensation to go and talk to them about Newman?"

"Muntle."

"And just how were you able to persuade our 'shire reeve' to permit this circumvention of the law?"

"Don't you recall that the man's own brother left the valley when he was a boy and never returned? If anyone were able to compassionate your loss, it should be he."

Augustus nodded. "It was so long ago that I *had* forgotten. The ones who leave us—we mourn them and then over time the memory of them fades."

"Muntle's memory of his brother hasn't faded. The same way that— well, I shan't say it. The upshot is that Muntle understands what you and Charlotte are feeling. But he still won't permit either of us to tread upon our sacred privilege of contact with these Beyonders and would, no doubt, be seised by apoplexy should he learn what you are *presently* scheming to do."

Gus sighed and lowered his eyes. "I confess that I did not believe you'd purchase even a small portion of the plan. It was born within a father's desperate heart and there it will die."

I placed a comforting hand upon Augustus' shoulder. "I know that desperation and despair will make a man think and say things that aren't his wont. And I know as well that sane and sensible men will check themselves."

Here I told the truth. A part of me *did* know that Augustus would never have carried out such a dangerous plot—no matter how tormented his state of mind. Augustus wasn't one to weep, and he remained true to form here, although I would easily have acquitted a deluge of tears from my older brother if he had been at that moment so disposed. These were terribly rough waters that Augustus and Charlotte now found themselves attempting to pilot, and there was no passage in their journey that would not rock and buffet the soul. Charlotte, for the time being, lay deep in slumber upstairs (for I could now hear her stertorous snoring). I guessed that it was probably laudanum she had taken for her nerves, and that it was now doing its quick business. (I didn't remind my brother that a cessation of contact with the tradesmen carried with it—over time—depletion of all of our medicinal stores, for well nigh all of our drugs came from outside the Dell, including laudanum and every other opiate derivative which had served as effective anodyne to suffering Dinglians for decades.)

The room grew quiet, the Dutch clock, insensitive to all that had previously been bawled and exclaimed and remonstrated, ticking away in automatonic fashion without care or investment. Breaking this interlude of relative silence, Augustus turned to me and said, "Have I permission, Freddie, to come with you on Monday?"

"Muntle presumes that it is only I who will be climbing the ridge for the purpose of colloquy with the tradesmen."

"But would he raise objection to my joining you?"

"Perhaps *I* would raise objection. You're still liable to do something in your present discomposed state that would not be wise." I did not believe this for a second, but it was important to keep Augustus in league with the narrow purpose of my anticipated meeting.

Augustus shook his head with more force than was his habit. "I promise to let you ask the questions. I will recede. But being allowed to come with you will leastways give me the feeling that I am doing *something* that may ultimately bring my boy home."

I agreed to let my brother Augustus enlist in this dubitable cause, and accompany me to the crest of the ridge, the place where Beyonders came fortnightly to give us things.

Would that someone could give us information on Newman. Would that we could learn what had become of him.

CHAPTER THE EIGHTH

Saturday, June 21, 2003

What I did not know was this: my nephew Newman was indeed in the Outland—quite alive and quite well. Turn the hour hand of the clock back to eight o'clock that same morning and one gifted with accurate divination would find him in a queer bedroom in a queer Outland house, sitting a bit uneasily upon a queer and unfamiliar bed.

It was a simply constructed bed bereft of all of the detail work that distinguished even the plainest of Dingley bedsteads. Newman noticed that there were no finials atop the head and foot posts; indeed, there were no posts at all. Nor did he—the grandson, on his mother's side, of a top-sawyer artisan of the Folkstone Furniture Works—behold a palmette upon the headboard, or a rinceau carving gracing the footboard. The bed's oddly patterned counterpane assaulted the eye with swirls of brash colour that suggested nothing in the design but formless paint puddles. Every other piece of furniture in the room was strangely-shaped, yet dull and simple in makeup: a dull writing table (and upon it the most curious metallic box with a glass window and an even curiouser board of buttons imprinted with numbers and letters and various forms of punctuation), a dull chair with nothing to commend it in the way of ornamentation upon its legs—not even the simplest suggestion of acanthus leaf or scroll or cockleshell—a low chest-of-drawers without an apron, and a dull wooden nightstand without a cloth. There was no cheval glass to be found anywhere within the room, nor a clotheshorse, nor even a chiffonier or press in which to put clothing. (There was a small closet, and Newman surmised that clothes went there which didn't go into the chest-of-drawers, but it was all a very peculiar and haphazard, and still rather dull, sort of way to put a bedroom together.)

Newman's rambling eyes could not help but settle (as they had been settling since he was inducted into the room the previous evening) upon the walls. These were plastered with colourful photographic broadsheets of young ladies so scantily-clad that even the most Bohemian Dinglian soul should blush, and frizzy-haired, bushy-faced young men holding oddly-shaped stringed musical instruments somewhat akin to guitars.

Newman had slept soundly (being quite comfortably cushioned and pillowed) throughout the night, and woke early to dress himself and to study his surroundings with a welter of curiosity, but with, nonetheless, the decided, early-attained opinion that those things in the Terra Incognita that were not prurient or starkly-hued were still inordinately plain and really quite drab.

He had come to the house hungry and bedraggled, wet and somewhat cold; for even though it be June, the night had a sharp, frosty bite to it. He had thought the house a farmstead, and would have been quite satisfied to billet himself within its barn where he might curl up within a warm bed of hay. At break of day Newman would have taken a squirt of two from a cow teat and then perhaps filched himself an egg from the chicken coop. Then he would be on his way. Oliver Twist had made his way to London in just such a manner. Or was it David Copperfield? (Newman often confused the two boys, for he was not a terribly retentive reader.) But Newman Trimmers had no such opportunity to play the tramping vagabond here, for the house was *not* a farmstead and his hosts, at all events, would *not* have permitted him to sleep in a barn and steal milk from a cow teat.

It had been a full week since Newman's gleeful embarkation upon his grand tour of the Terra Incognita. He had providently (and greedily) filled his large leathern knapsack with pilfered food from the Chowser larder, and had sufficiently sustained himself from those stores for nearly the entire length of his time abroad. There had been no opportunities for Newman to hunt or fish for his supper since the boy had spent most of this interval held up in an empty house, which he chanced upon in the wood. The house had apparently been long vacated (there was no food in its pantry save a few stray crumbs upon a shelf) and was visited by no one during his occupancy save a woman whom Newman glimpsed through the peeping crack between the door and its jamb as he secreted himself in a closet to avoid detection.

The woman wore red spectacles and pantaloons and stilted shoes, and her hair was short and starched. She spoke quickly to herself whilst holding a little box to her ear, and if Newman had not been looking at her, he would have wagered that there had been another person wholly present to receive the words, so conversational was her tone. Here is one of the things that the woman said into her box: "If I actually *can* get twice what this tumbledown is really worth, Century 21 oughta award me 'Realtor of the Year.'"

Most fascinating to Newman was the fact that the woman arrived and departed in a chariot only marginally similar to the horseless steam fire engine which served the West End of Milltown, being largely a self-propelled box on wheels (and where the steam came out of *this* Outland vehicle Newman had no earthly idea). It was clearly a horseless conveyance, and every now and then there appeared others like it racing up and down the gravelly road outside the house, making loud and impertinent rumblings and roarings that frightened and excited the boy at the very same time.

It wasn't until all of his travelling victuals had been eaten and Newman had grown tired of sleeping upon the house's thinly carpeted floors and had grown unhappy with himself for hiding so long here and suspending his engagement with the world-at-large (which included a possible ride in one of the speeding conveyances) that the hungry, frightened, and now exceedingly bored eleven-year-old Dinglian boy threw his knapsack upon his back and his nomad's bindle stick over his shoulder and ventured out and away from his craven's refuge.

In so doing, Newman Trimmers was promptly assaulted by heavy rain and pea-sized hail that doused and pelted him and finally so slickened his tread that in no time at all he had slid directly down a muddy embankment and into a flooded stream. Young Newman would have been swept completely away (as was his knapsack) and been drowned by the strong, tugging current were it not for the rescuing offices of a fast-thinking man by the curious name of Dean Ryersbach and his twelve-year-old son, who was possessed of the equally-curious name of Chad. The two succeeded in dragging the boy up and out of the swollen creek and onto its bank. They waited for him to take breath and rest himself, and then transported his shivering bones by foot to their home, perhaps a quarter mile away.

It was in this room—*Chad's* bedchamber—that Newman spent his very first night beneath an Outland roof in the company of tangible, flesh-and-blood Outlanders. And now with a knock at the door, he was suddenly being invoked to partake of his first breakfast in their company as well.

"Are you drest?" enquired a maternal voice coming from the other side of the door.

"Yes. Do come in," replied Newman, who could be quite polite given the proper circumstance.

"I have breakfast on the table," said the woman, whose head poked into the room from behind the half-opened door. "Do you feel up to joining us?"

Newman nodded. It was a tentative nod, as if he were wondering for the moment if "having breakfast" carried the same meaning outside the Dell as within.

"Let me see how you look in Chad's clothes. Well, they're a little big on you, but your own clothes were so filthy, I'm going to have to put them through another cycle. And they're really very silly looking—like you ran away from a little stage play. Did you run away from a little stage play, Newman?"

Newman shook his head. He had never heard his clothes called silly before, especially by a woman who looked altogether ridiculous in her own Outland morning attire.

At table, all eyes considered the strange boy who had just the previous day been nearly drowned in a rushing brook, and had come into the Ryersbach family manse begrimed with mud, and tired and hungry, and saucer-eyed and largely uncommunicative, though now he was more willing to speak for himself. You see, Newman was feeling quite relieved to have passed the night unmolested, with his skin retaining its present healthy red hue in contradiction to the oft-told tale of the more mischievous inmates of the Chowser school that Beyonders took especial delight in draining the blood of Dinglian children and quaffing the sanguine liquid in a spiced punch.

"Did you rest well?" asked the mother, whose name, when it wasn't "Mrs. Ryersbach," was "Evelyn."

"Yes, very well, thank you," answered Newman in his most courteous tone.

The young girl—perhaps seven-years-of-age—who sat at the right hand of her mother and whose name when it wasn't "Cindy" was "Pumpkin," chirped: "Chad says he and Daddy found you in a ditch. Do you live in a ditch? Do you have fish gills?"

Newman shook his hand and withheld his opinion of the question.

"You retard," said the girl's brother, insultingly. "Only Aqua-boy has gills."

"*He* could be Aqua-boy," said the little girl with a look of hopefulness that would make one think that this was her greatest wish in the world.

"He isn't Aqua-boy," shot back Chad.

"Shut up! The both of you," said the father, chewing toast.

Newman could not help himself; he gave the father a strongly quizzical look. Dinglian parents seldom addressed their children in such sharp and rude tones. Even workhouse fathers generally shewed good manners unless there was gin present.

"Well, whoever you are, Newman, we're happy to have you," said the mother. "Take some eggs." She pointed to the bowl of whipped eggs on the table. Newman nodded, picked up the bowl, and began to spoon the whipped eggs onto his plate.

"It looks like rain again to-day," said Mr. Ryersbach, glancing out the window. "Chad, turn on the radio. I want the forecast."

Newman suspended his spooning and watched as Chad rose from the table and went to a shelf where there sat a dark box with little buttons and knobs upon it, and a thin, metallic staff rising from the top. The boy did something to the box that Newman could not quite see, and suddenly a voice could be heard—a tiny, reedy voice, which seemed to be coming straight from inside the box.

Newman started at the sound, dropping the bowl of eggs upon the table and sending some of its clumpy contents into his lap, some onto the table and some onto the floor. The bowl struck a jar of honey which sat upon the circular dumb waiter in the centre of the table, popping open the lid and dispatching a sluice of slow-moving, viscous bee jelly toward his place at the table.

"Jesus Christ!" cried Mr. Ryersbach.

"Oh God," blurted Mrs. Ryersbach.

"Spaz," joined in Chad Ryersbach smirkingly.

Mrs. Ryersbach bolted up from her chair to clean up the mess as a man said from inside the box, "… are mourning the loss of their native son, Army Private First Class Timothy Baxter, who was born in Danville and spent most of his life in Milton. Baxter received fatal gunshot wounds while on guard duty at a propane distribution centre in Baghdad. He was assigned to the 82nd Airborne Division, Fort Bragg, North Carolina."

"The radio *is* a little too loud, Chad. Turn it down. Dean, it's going to rain again to-day. Look up in the sky. That's a rain sky. Newman, would you like me to make you some more eggs?"

Newman shook his head as the tiny voice proceeding from the box got even tinier and almost indiscernible.

"You're a strange child," noted Evelyn Ryersbach as she deposited the bowl and the eggs she was able to rake into it, into the sink.

"Creepy weird," Chad added.

"Shut up, Chad," said Mr. Ryersbach whilst glancing at the front page of his newspaper, which Newman noticed was called the *Williamsport Sun Gazette.*

"*Now*," said Mrs. Ryersbach as she pulled her chair up to Newman's, "why don't you tell Mr. Ryersbach and me who your family is, so we can give them a call and let them know you're all right?"

"My family lives in Dingley Dell. It's much too far to call to them. They wouldn't hear you."

"Har, har, har," said Chad in mock hilarity.

"On the telephone, Newman," clarified Mrs. Ryersbach patiently.

"We don't have any of those," said Newman.

"You don't? Hmm." The father took a sip from his steaming mug. "And this Dingley Dell: where is it? Is it a made-up place?"

"Made-up place?"

"A pretend place," explained the mother, attempting to be helpful. "Mr. Ryersbach would like to know, honey, if it's a place you've made up in your head."

Newman shook the head in question and replied, "It doesn't live in my fancy. It lives beyond the mountains."

"Which mountains? *Those* mountains?" Mr. Ryersbach was pointing out the window in the direction from which Newman had come.

Newman hadn't time to answer. "You live with the aliens?" barked Chad.

Newman squinted, as he usually did when something made little sense to him.

"The *aliens*," elaborated Chad. "In the *facility*."

"I don't know what you mean," said Newman, who was fast losing patience with this rude and overly inquisitive family. Then suddenly something redemptive caught his eye. "What's *that*?" he asked, pointing to a glass pitcher of orange liquid that Mrs. Ryersbach was now setting upon the table.

"It's orange juice, of course," said the mother. "Would you like a glass?"

Newman nodded enthusiastically.

"Don't tell me you haven't had orange juice before."

"Only a couple of times. It's very expensive. It comes from the orangery and one drinks it only on very special occasions. I had a glass on my eleventh birthday. Can I have more? Can you bumper it?"

"Bumper it?" asked Evelyn, the mother, as she poured.

"Yes. Fill it to the brim."

"You talk funny," said little Cindy as the mother obliged her guest.

Newman shrugged.

"So are you one of the aliens or not?" pursued the brash son. "Are you from the planet Zargassian 64?"

"I don't know…" Gulp. "…what you…" Another gulp. "…mean." Newman couldn't help smiling; the drink was like ambrosia—or at least it was what he imagined heavenly ambrosia should taste like.

"Stop picking on Newman, Chad," scolded the father. "He's our guest."

"I think he wet my bed."

"He didn't wet your bed. And even if he did, we can wash the mattress pad. So shut up." Turning to Newman, "Son: I am obligated to find out if you've run away from home and where you live. You don't live on the other side of those mountains. That's a private valley leased to a defence contractor. So please tell us where you *do* live, so we can be in touch with your family."

"I don't want you to be in touch with my family. I've *left* my family."

"So that's it, is it?" said the father, glancing knowingly at the mother. "I *thought* you might be a runaway. Where'd you run away from, son? Williamsport? Lock Haven? Milton? Lewisburg?"

Newman shook his head. "Dingley Dell."

"Again with the Dingley Dell," said the father with growing impatience. "Now where in the hell is Dingley Dell? Geographically speaking."

"Dean," said the mother, waving her hand at her husband in a quieting fashion.

"I told you," said Newman with some vexation of his own. "It's beyond the mountains. That's where I come from."

After a long, drawn-out respiration, Dean Ryersbach set down his cup of coffee, placed both hands upon the edge of the table, and leant forward to make his point. "Son. Nobody lives in the valley beyond those mountains. It's totally cordoned off. Some kind of government-sponsored installation is there. Word is, they test top secret weapon systems. Been doing it since World War II. Now. You know that I'm required by law to call the police and report you. So why won't you be truthful with me?"

Newman shook his head. By this action he was signaling that he *didn't* happen to know that his host was obligated by law to report him to the police. But one might also deduce that he was shaking his head to be dissembling and uncooperative, for the look that accompanied the action was dour and sullen.

Mr. Ryersbach resumed: "But I *won't* report you if you'll just let Mrs. Ryersbach and me help you. Is there another family member we can contact? If you've been abused, there are people out there whose job it is to help kids like you."

Newman didn't understand half of what the father of this family was saying. For example, why did he refer to Newman as a baby goat? Newman took another swallow of his ambrosial beverage and wiped his mouth with his napkin. Then, finding himself at a loss over what to say in response, he shrugged.

"Does your father beat you, Newman?" asked the mother in a gently solicitous tone.

Newman nodded. "I mean, he *used* to when I was younger." (This was something about which Newman could say a thing or two, for Augustus Trimmers was never the sort of father to spare the rod.)

"How often would he beat you?" pursued the mother with a troubled look.

"Whenever I would misbehave. Once, sometimes twice a week, out would come the hickory stick."

Mrs. Ryersbach tutted.

Mr. Ryersbach said, "And you're sure that there aren't any other family members you could stay with?" Appalled by the rather slipshod grammatical construction of Mr. Ryersbach's question (though Newman had formerly nursed a contempt for all rules of discourse), Newman Trimmers was happy that Mr. Chowser wasn't nearby to overhear, or even the teacher in his village school, Miss Clickett, who once fell into a paroxysm of tears when one of Newman's desk-mates committed the egregious double error of misusing a reflexive pronoun in the same sentence in which a gerund was left unpossessing.

Newman shook his head. "All of my family lives in Dingley Dell. Everybody I *know* lives in Dingley Dell. I am going to make my way in the world and become very rich and bring them wonderful things." Newman, having now drained his glass of orange juice, held out the empty tumbler for a refill.

"Wonderful things. Like orange juice," said Mrs. Ryersbach with a gentle, almost knowing smile.

"Dingley Dell. Dingley Dell. Now where have I heard the name before?" pondered Mr. Ryersbach aloud.

"It's the nickname they give to the state crazy house, Dad," offered the son. "We talked about it in my social studies class. A long time ago there were all these crazy people there who said that's where they came from."

"And there's no one there who's like that now?" asked Mrs. Ryersbach with a look of concern.

Chad shook his head. "They're all dead. My teacher Mr. Guinter says the only man who talks about Dingley Dell these days is like 150 years old and spends all his time with the snakes and the lizards at the Reptilarium."

Mrs. Ryersbach snorted indignantly. "Mr. Guinter should spend more time teaching and less time telling you kids where to find all the crazies and weirdos of Lycoming County. That isn't why your father and I pay property taxes every year."

"I'm just telling you what he said."

"Finish your breakfast," said the mother, "and go deflate the Aerobed. Somebody's liable to trip over it, all spread out in the middle of the TV room like that."

Newman took the first half of the injunction for himself and ate all that his belly could hold and then feeling actually quite crapulous as a result, he excused himself and went to lie down upon Chad's more permanent bed—the one that didn't have to be "deflated" (whatever that meant), but not before taking a swipe at the honey puddle to have something dessert-like to lick from his hands in the privacy of his guest apartment.

Once safely installed therein, Newman sat for a moment on the side of the bed and licked at his fingers like a hungry bear cub and felt quite the feral beast in the middle of this strange and marvellous place of horseless carriages that sped along like trackless locomotives, boxes that spoke and gave weather predictions, and unfettered access to all of the orange juice that one felt like drinking. Having tongued off most of the delicious honey (for honey was one of Newman's favourite sweets), the boy lay back upon the bed, intent on pondering his future, but was asleep within a couple of minutes.

He woke to the sound of Chad standing next to him, chewing something cud-like that he never swallowed, a mischievous smile screwing up his face. "You're in for it now," he said, referencing with a jerk of the head the soft, low voices wafting into the room through the open door.

"There's a police officer out there," Chad elaborated, "and some lady from child protective services, and they're gonna haul your ass right out of here and you can go and baby-piss on somebody else's mattress pad for a change."

"I didn't urinate in your bed, Chags."

"Cha*d*. My name's *Chad*, Pisspants. And you sure as fuck did. You peed in my bed like a baby without his Pampers. And I know what else you are. You're like that crazy lizard man—the one who says he's from Dingley Doodie Dell."

"I didn't urinate in your bed. I was still wet from having fallen into that stream." Newman, having finally made his point, rose from the bed. "Where's my bindle?"

"Your what?"

"My bindle of clothes. I would like to change into my own clothes. Would you be so kind as to—"

"Stop talking like a fucking fruitcake!" enjoined Chad Ryersbach, clipping Newman hard upon the shoulder and knocking him backwards upon his heels.

Newman recovered his balance. "I don't know what you're talking about. I don't talk like a fruitcake. A fruitcake cannot talk. A fruitcake is a comestible."

"A what?"

"A comestible. And please refrain from pushing me again or I shall have to answer this assault upon my dignity by punching you forcefully in the mouth."

Newman rubbed the sore spot on his shoulder whilst Chad Ryersbach took a step back, as if to better gauge the strength of Newman's threat.

Chad was tall for his young age—at least six inches taller than his unwanted houseguest. "You're gonna do *what*?"

"I have two pugilist medals. I will shew them to you if you will kindly produce my bindle."

"Nutjob!" crowed Chad. There was another bold step forward on the part of the irate Master Chad, and then another stiff-armed push to Newman's already throbbing right shoulder. Newman, his patience now worn to a nub, took a deep breath, and then retaliated against the second assault upon his dignity by punching the rude thief of his bindle directly in the mouth. To make certain that the boy didn't give pursuit, Newman shoved him to the floor.

And then he fled…

…Out of the bedroom, down the corridor, and then with brazen audacity right into the Ryersbach front parlour with his sights set upon the front door. Here he was greeted by four startled faces belonging to Dean Ryersbach, his wife Evelyn, a uniformed and beetle-browed police officer, and a pinch-faced woman holding a leatherish satchel. The two men reached out for Newman as he raced past but caught only air. It was the pinch-faced woman who succeeded in securing Newman's arm and, in fact, sending him stumblingly to the floor. In her attempt to snare the decamping Dinglian boy, the woman dropt her satchel. It flew open and a large number of papers fluttered out. Newman attempted to wrest himself from her grasp and after a bit of a tussle, which quickly set him against not only the woman but the two men as well (as Evelyn Ryersbach stood fretfully by, wringing her hands and crying, "Don't hurt him! Don't hurt him!"), he was able at last to roll himself away in the manner in which Mr. Chowser had instructed his pupils should they ever find themselves engulfed in flames and must put out the fire through their own initiative. Freed now from all the hands that grasped and clawed to take hold of him, Newman leapt to his feet and renewed his flight. Out the door he ran, too fast for his pursuers to catch him, and into the dark woods that environed the country house.

Alas, the boy didn't have his bindle and was by unfortunate circumstances required to wear the oversized clothes of the rude and belligerent Beyonder lad named Chad. But he did possess one thing that he'd had the foresight to keep upon his person: a watch—a beautiful gold Geneva watch that he had taken from Mr. Chowser's nightstand drawer so that he would have something to sell in the Terra Incognita when funds became necessary. Yes, it was stealing; but Newman had every intention of eventually paying Mr. Chowser treble-fold what the watch was worth.

As the boy attempted to reach down into his right trowser pocket to confirm that what he felt bouncing round in there was, in fact, the precious watch, he discovered that there was something papery attached to his honey-sticky hand. It was a paper that had affixed itself to his palm as he had rolled about the floor of the Ryersbach parlour. He hadn't time to stop and look at the paper except to see what it said at the top—three words that made little sense to him: "The Tiadaghton Project." Newman peeled the paper from his hand but did not discard it, stuffing it instead down into the other pocket to be read and considered more carefully when it was safe to do so.

Without thinking, Newman Trimmers found himself running in the direction of Dingley Dell. Newman Trimmers was running home.

CHAPTER THE NINTH

Monday, June 23, 2003

Here is Dingley Dell as it appeared to me on that early summer morning in 2003 when my brother and I made our way on foot to the Northern Ridge that separated this portion of our homeland from the Outland: a large valley with rolling green hills and a motley patchwork of agricultural colour, bounded on the north by a steep rocky incline and on the south by a ridge much different from the other: black and scored, half carved away to extract the coal that had for over a century warmed our homes and cooked our food and besooted our walls and chimneys and the faces of our industrious colliers. In the southeast was the iron pit from which we drew that which made our little world so hard and black and solid and venerable.

The air was clear and bright this morning, and one could see stretching far eastward and westward two distinct forests of some expanse, which sloped upwards as well, but with gentler acclivity than the Northern and Southern ridges. As rite of passage, each of us in his youth had climbed wantonly through those leafy opposing portions of our perimeter, but not much was there to be gleaned by them, save the fact that it was quite easy to get oneself lost therein (once one passed the open vestigial stump-land—evidential of years of harvest by previous generations of Dinglian timbermen—and the currently cultivable timber sward).

The eastern and western woods carried additional risk as well; both displayed a propensity for growing thick and dark with only a short venturing trespass into their beshadowed breasts. And if one pushed far enough into the heart of that sylvan darkness, one reached a tall fence, topped with coiled barbed wire and resembling in construction that same fence which trailed upon the Summit—a fence that paradoxically intimidated the onlooking Dinglian through its impounding insinuation and at the same time contributed to a feeling of protection from unknown forces without.

Having no other dell with which to compare our beloved Dingley (our ninth—and apparently the final—edition of the *Encyclopædia Britannica* offering illustrations of flamingos, and coal cutting machines and Vatican marble sculpture, but not a single, solitary view of an exemplary rusticated valley), we were forever at a loss to know just how our vale might appear to an outsider, the tradesmen, for their own part, taking care not to offer commentary on anything supplementary to their transactions—not even to note the clemency or inclemency of the day's weather!

In silence my brother and I marched past gardens in full blow, serenaded by the happy chirrup of birds that knew nothing of fractured hearts and human loss. In that early season of our journey through dim daybreak, it was easy to forget that Augustus and I were anywhere but the most felicitous place on earth, for quickly does one enter that part of the valley where the hand of man is in slim evidence save for an old, dilapidated cow house, the surviving architectural remnant of a long abandoned farm, where in better light one might read vestiges of the paint-peeling advertisement on its side: "Limbkins Lard—Delectably pure—never goes rancid."

With the cresting of the morning sun over the treetops of the eastern wood, I snuffed out the lantern that had kindled our early steps, inhaled the fresh air of dewy dawn into my lungs and sighed. Here was paradise qualified.

As Gus and I gained that place at which the ridge began its steep ascent, where the foot-and-barrow trail came down to meet the terminus of the Ridge Spur off the Riparian Road, we heard behind us the sound of hoof and wooden wheel upon damp, clodded earth. A gig was approaching, instantly recognisable by its fringed covering and the dappled bay mare that pulled it as belonging to my friend Sheriff Vincent Muntle.

Muntle was as breathless as if he had run all the way, and upon reaching us gave a light tug upon the reins and alighted without taking even a moment to collect himself or to pat down his wind-frowzed hair, standing out from both sides of his head like fuzzy, pronged blinders. If my friend had worn a hat, it had flown off at some point along the way, and he had not halted himself to retrieve it.

"I caught you! Capital!" said he, with a smile less of greeting than of relief.

"Are you coming along?" sought Augustus of our unanticipated companion.

"I'm climbing the ridge to be sure, but alas for you, Augustus, I'll be doing so alone."

"Alone?"

Muntle nodded and turned to me. "This is why I've come so quickly. To tell you that it's no longer possible for you to meet with the tradesmen."

As Augustus stared in puzzlement at the sheriff of Dingley Dell, I solicited an explanation. "What's happened, Muntle? Why has permission for my ascent been rescinded?"

"Because it was foolish of me to have granted you leave for the tête-à-tête in the first place. I hadn't the authority to do so and should have known better." The large man who stood before us, drest differently than when I'd last seen him—with a more formal equipage in the manner of official lawman: all frogs and buttons and soldier-like drab—heaved a heavy sigh, the dreaded thing having now been said and his duty of interception and interdiction duly performed. He took out a pocket-comb, and began to apply it to his retreating bear-grease-pomaded hair, as if to make himself look more presentable to the Beyonders, kemptness and hygiene apparently being key to any successful interchange with an Outlander.

"Do you expect Gus and me to believe what you've just told us?" I asked. "Whatever your reservations about our meeting with the tradesman weren't newly born this morning. Why in truth have you changed your mind?" My expression of bewilderment at that moment must surely have replicated the confused look of my brother.

"My answer is my answer, and that's all there is to it. Now whither could my hat have gone?" Muntle peered down the long, dusty road from which he had just come, as if the hat might suddenly make itself known and then fly obligingly back onto its owner's head. There passed a rigid silence, broken only by a cleared throat or two, and the sound of the sole of my shoe tapping an impatient tattoo upon a stone. Augustus and I would not simply accept this insufficient answer and have done with it.

In that reign of hard silence, the sheriff's will to withhold was whittled down and finally broken in two. It was with a small guilty voice that he finally confessed the fact that there was indeed more to the thing than he had indicated. "It's Pawkins, the Minister of Trade, who won't have it, if you must know. He got wind of your plan—I know not how—and invoked the rule respecting contact with Outlanders. Under no circumstances is that rule to be suspended for those without the requisite license."

"But you're unlicensed yourself, Muntle," I protested.

"Unlicensed to trade, yes, but not to perform my offices as keeper of the peace, wherever those offices may send me. And in that capacity I am suffered to go, should my investigation into the disappearance of the boy require it, and it does."

Augustus' mood had suddenly turned dark and ireful: "I cannot accept it, Muntle! I simply cannot!" My brother's sudden change in disposition was quite understandable. He and I were being deliberately thwarted in our mission to reunite ourselves with Gus's lost son. It was pure Dinglian Draconianism that stood in the way, unless there be something far more insidious afoot.

Muntle lowered his eyes. His compunctious stance told me that, of course, he agreed with my brother and me: the law that confined all contact with the Beyonders to a small group of privileged brokers and their accommodating porters made sense upon every occasion save those in which it made no sense at all, this particular instance being a very good example of the latter. Yet… "Gentlemen, my hands are tied. It is my charge to execute the laws of the Dell exactly as they are written and passed by the Petit-Parliament."

"Petty indeed!" pronounced Augustus. "We'll see that damned law changed, and I'll climb that damned ridge any damned fortnight of my own damned choosing. Who are the brokers to dictate through their cohorts in the Petit-Parliament what the rest of us should and should not do?"

In a quiet voice I interposed, "You know the reasons, Gus—for keeping intercourse with the Outlanders under strict regulation."

"I seek only to ask the men if they've seen my boy," Augustus pursued. "Perhaps they caught sight of him shivering behind a rock in the cold morning mist. Perhaps he fell from some height and was glimpsed crawling broken-limbed upon the ground in need of medical attention. If so, did anybody descend to help? How will I know if there be answers to these questions if I'm not given leave to ask them?"

"You will know," replied the sheriff, "because I'll ask *for* you. Put down on this paper every question you wish answered and I'll do the best that I'm able."

Augustus did not take the paper. Instead, he sat himself down upon the hard ground. He drew his knees to his chest and rested his head upon the knobs. After a moment he looked up to say, "I would like to believe that the Outlander's heart is as large as our own, and yet our circumambient neighbours have demonstrated nothing about themselves beyond a ravenous interest in our apricots, our bedsteads, and our tortoise-shell bracelets. What is it about the Terra Incognita that makes its people so incurious otherwise?"

The sheriff spoke in a soft, subdued tone that betokened his concern: "Some day, perhaps, we will know the answer to that question. For the nonce, it certainly gives the feeling that we have been abandoned by God or fate or whatever is that metaphysical force that superintends this world. And yet wasn't it abandonment itself that brought our forebears to this valley in our earliest days? Was not every child of that founding, foundling generation cast off either by the death of a mother or father or by some form of parental dereliction? A parent's deliberate aberrant wish to push a child away—curiously, the very opposite of *your* desire, Gus, to see your own child restored to your love and care! These are queer things, gentlemen: the ways of the Outlander, as unfathomable to me as any other perplexing mystery of our vast universe, each of which we accept for now simply because we can do nothing else.

"Now, I will climb that ridge and I will ask all the questions that you provide me pertaining to the boy. Perhaps I'll learn something. Or I won't. But for every angry thought that rages within your head against the brokers and against the M.P.P.'s who have put these men into their current position of exclusive authority, let it be mitigated by the knowledge that you have a friend and advocate in *me*."

Sheriff Muntle reached down to shake the hand of my brother, who in taking the proffered paw of my bear-like friend used the clasp to pull himself to his feet. Brushing himself off in the seat, Augustus asked the lawman, "Do you ever wonder what became of your brother?"

"Every day," replied the sheriff gazing off into the distance. "Though in my heart I know that he must be dead. It could be very different, though, with your son. Perhaps there is something different that happens to every man and woman and child who ventures beyond this ridge. I have always wished to know, and I confess to you gentlemen that there was a time in my youth when I considered doing the same thing as your Newman has done. It is devilish difficult to keep emboldened, adventuresome young men such as your son and my younger self confined within this valley—to say to a bright-eyed, inquisitive young lad: 'Here is everything that you may know and now you must not pursue another thing.' It's the reason, I warrant, that 250 of our beloved kinsmen and women have left us. It's the reason that we weep for that fraction who have returned with gruel for brains—those who dare to go and learn of the world beyond the ridges, only to be so cruelly punished for taking up the quest. The sadness of it all is sometimes difficult to bear. Well, I've said enough, haven't I?"

Muntle took out his handkerchief and placed it to his eyes. In Dingley Dell in the year of our blessed Lord 2003, the shedding of tears was not a demerit in the measure of a man, but merely an unqualified aspect of his character.

"So give me your questions, gentlemen," said the sheriff through a sniffle, "and let us find out what we're able."

For a long interval my brother and I walked along, exchanging not a word with one another until we reached the village of Fingerpost. Augustus and Charlotte had always lived here, in first one rented cottage and then another. Gus had tried his best to put food on his family's table, whilst scheming and dreaming of ways to earn a better income through his own creative (and sometimes not so creative) initiative. Alas, not a single one of Augustus' schemes and dreams had ever come to lucrative gain, and in the meanwhile my brother had been forced to make ends meet by working in a succession of disparate occupations. He had been a plasterer, a furniture maker, a dustman, a waiter, an old-clothes man, a ticket porter, a venison packer, and a wheelwright's sawyer. He had earned wages as a fruitier's assistant, a ginger-beer man, a coal-deliveryman, a shoe vamper, a church warden, an office clerk, a sexton, and a fire agency policy copier. His latest job was keeping inventory in a dried fish warehouse; it was a vocation he did not at all relish, and he had already started casting about for some new line of work.

Once inside the village of Fingerpost and nearing his house, Augustus was compelled to stop and speak, and what he had to say sent a chill throughout me.

"I have made a decision, dear brother. I must go and look for my son."

I stared at Gus in disbelief. I could scarcely find breath to say, "But you must know that there is the strong likelihood that such a venture would be tantamount to committing suicide."

"Then are you saying that it is more than likely that your nephew Newman is himself dead?"

I shook my head. "I'm saying that your going abroad in your current state—frantic, wild-eyed, and reckless—will not achieve the objective you seek and may expose you to great harm."

Augustus allowed the weight of my hard words to sit heavy upon his brow for a moment. Then he returned in an angry tone: "You don't know *what* is out there. It's all conjecture on your part. What if Newman is alive? What if he's trapped somewhere and waiting for his father to come rescue him?"

"And what if he is someplace where you shall *never* find him? You're my only brother, Gus. How could you even think of doing such a thing?"

"Because Newman is my only *son*. You cannot hope to know in your bachelorhood, Freddie, how it feels to lose a child."

"I am not insensible to your pain, Gus, but I cannot allow you to do this."

"And just how do you intend to stop me?"

"By any means possible."

"We shall see about that."

I took a deep breath. "Have you not stopt to think of what this would do to Charlotte? To your daughter Alice?"

"Alice no longer wishes to be a member of this family. And Charlotte no longer loves me."

Both statements took me aback—especially the latter. "How can you be sure of such a thing?"

"I've seen it in her look, Freddie. I've felt it in her touch. Ours has been a hollow marriage for some time now—long before Newman went away. I know that he's an unruly, devilish, pranking boy, but I love him with all of my heart, and without him there should be little left for me but a slow march to the silent grave with only my brother for occasional diverting fraternity. So I am prepared to take the risk at whatever the cost. I owe it to both Newman and to myself."

I looked into my brother Gus's eyes and saw the terrible pain of his predicament. And yet I could not, under any circumstances, ratify his decision. "I forbid it."

"Forbid it? Just what will you do, Freddie: have your friend Muntle place me under arrest?"

"If I must."

"You're serious."

"Deadly serious, brother."

Not another word was said. Gus had had his say and I had made my remonstration, and it remained to be seen if what I said would do any good.

CHAPTER THE TENTH

Monday, June 23, 2003

Newman Trimmers staid his hand as it reached out to pull upon the loose bark of the old tree that stood before him. He had for a brief moment sought to know if through actual ingestion he might learn if some part of it was edible. Newman was hungrier than he'd ever been in his life, but concluded as the hand came to rest again within his lap that perhaps he could go another few hours without being reduced to gnawing upon trees and chewing up leaves and twigs.

My nephew had hidden himself in the forested hills that overlooked the country home of Dean and Evelyn Ryersbach since his escape on Saturday. He had begun his journey home with a strong sense about the direction he must go to reach Dingley Dell, but the woods had tricked him, had turned him round, and had left him disoriented in very little time at all. Here there was nothing for a boy to eat without tools of procurement. There were mushrooms, but Newman durst not taste them, for he knew that some mushrooms found in the wild weren't toothsome at all, but poisonous toadstools that tricked the eye. He had come upon the mountain stream that had earlier tried to drown him and had seen a fish swimming therein and had grabbed for it without success and had soaked himself anew, and now he was wet and cold. The sun could not find him here in the wooded darkness. Nor would food walk itself up to him and leap into his lap and ask to be eaten. A deer had approached, and Newman and the creature had considered one another for a long interim before it parted. Newman supposed that the animal had walked up to find out who he was and to learn why he sat shivering and wet and cold and hungry beneath a tree. Who was this creature who did not behave as two-legged creatures usually did—tramping noisily about except for that time of year when they softened their tread to be furtive and cunning and then, paradoxically, to murder the quiet with noisy blasts from their smoking sticks?

It was clear that the time had now come for Newman Trimmers to come down from the wooded hills and find a settlement of some sort that would provide a morsel or two of food to keep starvation at bay. Perhaps he might discover something palatable in the town dustbins, or best of all meet a kindly baker who would take pity on a hungry, ragged boy and tender him a mouldy bun. The thought of the chance to put something into his empty stomach made Newman bold, and so he rose from his pallet of moss and leaves and made his way out of his secluded retreat.

In less than an hour my nephew was standing upon the side of a gravelled road, and wondering where it would take him. Would it lead to someplace where he might nourish himself? Where he could sleep soundly between linen sheets and restore himself for the purpose of essaying once again his long and wending journey home? The answers to these questions would come in time.

For now he must go down the gravelled road. And this he did. By and by, he came to a junction. Upon the shoulder of a smoothly paved thoroughfare stood a directing sign affixed to a metallic post. It said, "Jersey Shore 6 miles." Thought Newman, Am I near the strand of a sea, or is there some great lake close by? (For what else could be the literal meaning of a place called Jersey Shore, except that it should be a littoral one?)

Within the half-hour, Newman had grown slightly less alarmed by the Outland conveyances that raced past him—vehicles of all shapes and sizes. Some were built like waggons and chaise-carts with room for ample storage in the open rear; others resembled Dinglian vans and Pantechnicons with room for storage within. Then there were those that carried only passengers (and perhaps a little something in their boots); and every now and then there came along a great myriad-wheeled monster machine with room enough inside to hold the entire contents of a railroad boxcar. These belched a most acrid-smelling smoke and sometimes blared their horns like the trumpetings of great elephants (or what Newman thought that great elephants should sound like, having never heard one). The loudness of the blasts compelled him in every instance to cover his delicate ears and hasten from the shoulder. Yet he never put himself at such distance from the road that he couldn't feel the whoosh of the warm air being displaced by the prows of the massive man-made beasts.

A driver of one of the smaller vehicles had stopped alongside him to ask if he would like a "lift." Though Newman knew the word to indicate in Dingley Dell a hoisting device, he assumed that this was the Outlander's word for "ride." The cordial old gentleman in the rusting conveyance had asked if Newman should like to be taken somewhere.

Yet, after his rude treatment by the Ryersbachs, Newman trusted no one—not even courteous old men who seemed upon first glance to be well-meaning.

"Thank you for your most kind offer, sir, but I should like to walk," answered Newman.

"I'm going to Lock Haven," said the man, as if he had not quite heard Newman's declination.

"I do not mind long morning rambles. In point of fact, I am rather fond of them. Good day, sir." Newman nodded to indicate that the parley was over and resumed his steps.

The old man sat and thought for a moment and then shrugged and said, "Suit yourself," and steamed away.

After the gentleman had gone, Newman halted himself and took a few deep, calming breaths. He had pictured the man grabbing at him as had the men in the Ryersbach parlour—trying their best to hold and detain him, for what purpose Newman knew not, and possessed of hard looks that did not put his concerns to rest by any measure. Newman vowed in the midst of his narrow escape never to be trusting again, always to be vigilant, and never again to place himself into the custody of anyone who might wish to do him harm.

The boy renewed his steps but soon stumbled over a jutting rock and well nigh fell. He was tired and his feet were dragging themselves shuf-flingly upon the ground, and the hardship of his present situation was not in the least mitigated by the wearing of trowsers much too long for his short legs—trowsers that continued to unfold their makeshift cuffs, only to be trod upon and tripped over to break his stride and nearly break his neck.

I must have some new clothes, thought Newman. These clothes of

Chad's, which were given me, are much too big. I look like a harlequin clown.

Newman stopped himself every now and then to place his hand upon his stomach as if this action would somehow ameliorate his pangs of hunger. He was tired and weak and wanted now to sit upon a log and rest himself, but he feared that in doing so he might never rise up again. So onward he trudged along the side of the road, regretting now for the first time his decision to leave Dingley Dell.

This was a strange new feeling that had taken hold of Newman, and arriving in the thick of his travails, it fascinated him. He thought of what had made him depart Dingley Dell in the first place: he had been different from the other boys at the two schools he had attended. There were those who had said that he wasn't very bright, that he was "walking trouble" and would never improve. He had always looked to the ridges and wondered if there were those who lived beyond them who were more like he was: the imp who had grown into a bit of a hellcat, and who was destined to mature into a fully-fledged delinquent and then finally find himself, at the unfortunate close of his life, a permanently-installed inmate of the Dingley Gaol. Perhaps, he thought, there was some truth to the statement made by the greengrocer from whom he had once purloined a plum, that he had a "criminal nature in embryo." For had he not stolen Mr. Chowser's greatest treasure, his grandfather's watch? Had Newman not stuffed his knapsack with as much food as he was able to pilfer from the Chowser pantry? *Embryo*? Come, come now. The miscreant was already hatched!

Yet Newman Trimmers didn't *feel* like a miscreant. He felt like a boy—a lost boy who wanted only one thing: to return to his mother and father and, yes, even to his sister. Though she nettled him, Alice was still a part of that family that he so sorely missed after all the lonely days he'd spent in this strange and threatening foreign land.

As Newman was walking along deliberating upon his present situation, he noticed out of the corner of his eye a very red vehicle, open-topped like a Dinglian barouche, approaching him at great speed. It rode very low to the ground and as it sped past, it put a buzz into his ears. The vehicle gave him something else as well—a present of sorts: a bulging paper bag, tossed out by one of its boisterous passengers. The discarded bag landed not so very far from Newman's feet. It had writing on it. It said "Burger King. Home of the Whopper." Newman bent down and retrieved the bag. He opened it to discover a container inside, which caused his heart to leap. It had half a sandwich in it! The bread was in the shape of a flat round bun and the meat encased within had been flattened quite successfully into a patty. There was a layer of thin cheese melted upon the meat, and there were greens and slices of tomato stuffed inside as well. Newman smelt the sandwich and agreed with his nose that it should be quite edible. Also within the bag was a closed cardboard tumbler with dark liquid spilling from it and moistening the sides of the bag so that it nearly dropt away from his grasp in its sodden weakness. Newman devoured the strange meat sandwich, which tasted good to him, though it was quite salty. He devoured, as well, the savoury fried food sticks he also found inside; these tasted like potatoes, but only a little. Newman drank some of the dark liquid that swam amongst melting rimes of ice, and liked the sweetness that met his tongue.

Having fortified himself with the contents of the paper bag of food, my nephew improved his steps and marched more vigourously toward the place called Jersey Shore, which was gained by late afternoon.

It was not a shore, as it turned out, but a town—a town with a most misleading name.

Along the high street Newman strolled, marveling at the strange architecture and the colourful placards hanging all about and all the people who were drest in similitude to members of the Ryersbach family and to all the people he had seen in the fast-moving horseless conveyances, each clad dully and simply in colours that Newman had never seen worn in his native Dingley Dell, for there were no such dyes available there.

The first thing that I must do, thought Newman to himself, is to find a pawn shop so that I can put money into my pocket, which will afford me a full meal and a change of clothes and perhaps a bed for the night. Newman knew not whether there was such a shop in the Outland—a place where one could go to take money in exchange for leaving a thing of value behind. He looked for the three balls that he knew to be the pawnbroker's symbol in the Dell and found none. However, what he did find was a jewellry shop, and inside, a proprietor who very much liked the make of the watch Newman presented.

"Nice. Quite nice!" remarked the man who said that his name was Phillips. The jeweller was an elderly man who was, in spite of his age, quite spry and light in the step. He took up the watch, and affixing the watchmaker's glass to his eye to give the treasure a close inspection, popped the watch open to peer at its intricate workings. "Gold hunting watch. Engine turned. Jewelled in four holes. Escape movement. Horizontal lever. Did you know that you can set it to give a little tinkle every fifteen minutes?"

"Yes, I knew that," answered Newman (but really he did not). "It is my choice not to set it in such a way."

"I haven't seen a pocketwatch like this in years. It's rare to find this kind of craftsmanship anymore."

"Except in Switzerland," said Newman, attempting to shew himself duly informed about his valuable possession.

The old man nodded. He had a thick mane of white hair and now combed one hand through it. "That's right. You know your classic Genevas. My son collected bugs at your age. I collected stamps. You collect pocketwatches and I do take my hat off to you." (Though the man was not, in fact, wearing a hat.) "How old are you?"

"I'm eleven years of age."

"So young to take up such a serious hobby."

Newman nodded, acknowledging the compliment.

"Now why do you want to depart with *this* watch, I wonder?"

The man removed his eyeglass to take a better look at the boy who had entered his shop to do business with him.

Newman could not think of what to say other than to take a little bit of the truth and use it to his advantage: "I should like to use the money to buy myself some new clothes."

The man named Phillips looked Newman over. "Yes, those pants don't really fit you, do they? Wait here. I need to go on-line to get a valuation. It shouldn't take more than a minute or two. I want to be fair."

Newman smiled. He was happy that he had come to a jeweller who would be fair. According to his father, most jewellers in Dingley Dell were *not* fair as the general rule, save the Fagins. Perhaps this man was a Beyonder version of Herbert Fagin.

It would come later to me what happened when the jeweller named Phillips went back into his private office. I would learn later exactly what was done and said there: that the old man picked up the instrument, which was called a telephone, and punched its buttons to put himself in touch with another person to be found elsewhere in the town of Jersey Shore, a woman by the name of Ruth Wolf.

Here is what the jeweller said to Ruth Wolf through the telephone instrument and in a voice made very quiet so that the boy standing outside in the showroom shouldn't hear: "Hello, Ruth. This is Phillips. The kid's here—the one they've been looking for. I'm almost positive. No, I didn't ask questions to confirm it; I'm going with my gut. He's wearing some other kid's clothes—they're almost falling off of him, and he's got a Geneva hunting watch he's obviously been carrying around with him since he left. What do you want me to do? Uh huh. No, I don't want to lose him, but I don't want him to get too suspicious. I'm going to give him some money and then ask if he's hungry. He looks like he could eat. I'll suggest that he get himself something at Penny's. You okay with that? I'll call you back on your cell if he decides to pass up the diner and head off somewhere else. Otherwise, get yourself over to Penny's as fast as you can. Where are you? Well, hurry the hell up. I don't want Caldwell or any of his men to get to him before *you* do."

Phillips emerged from his office, with money in hand for Newman.

"You've got quite a prize there, son. You're sure you want to give it up?"

Newman nodded.

"Well, I think it's worth at least a hundred and fifty dollars."

Phillips told the currency upon the counter and then picked it up and placed it into Newman's hands.

Newman stared at the paper money, wondering if the jeweller was giving him too little, but knowing that anything he said along these lines might betray the fact that he was not a citizen of the Outland. For all Newman knew one-hundred-and-fifty dollars could be worth nothing more than one-hundred-and-fifty mil in **Dingley Dell currency**—barely enough money to buy a loaf of bread. Newman needed a frame of reference. His eyes sought and then found some jewellry on display within the glass case next to him. There was a ring for sale priced at "$550" and a necklace for "$750." Newman calculated that "$" must be the sign for "dollar," and that the dollar must be on some par with the Dinglian pound. If such were the case, then he was not getting enough money for his watch and would have to bargain with the old man.

Newman coughed and cleared him throat and then as he had once seen his mother's intermittently depleted brother Leicester do in the presence of a pawnbroker in Milltown's East End, rolled his eyes and cocked his head and said, "Do you take me for a fool, governor? This watch is worth treble that amount and you and I both know it. Now, if you do not give me something in the vicinity of its market value, I shall have to take my business elsewhere."

Phillips stared at the Dinglian boy, knowing now for certain that he was a Dinglian boy, but not wishing to give this important fact away. He chuckled. "You drive a hard bargain," he said.

Newman grinned. This was exactly the reply that his maternal uncle had received upon saying the very same thing when there was a silver snuffbox at issue. Some things, Newman conjectured at that very moment, are no different outside the Dell as within. When it comes to buying and selling and trading, each man seeks to get the better of his trading partner. Perhaps it was simply a part of universal human nature.

Phillips the jeweller told out another three hundred dollars (and still considered that he had got the better deal, for he could resell the watch for several thousand dollars to one of the antique watch collectors with whom he did business).

As he had mentioned to the woman named Ruth Wolf with whom he had just spoken through the conduit of the telephone apparatus, Phillips asked if Newman was hungry, and Newman owned that he was. So Phillips directed the boy to Penny's "Diner" where he could get himself a good chicken sandwich. The suggestion sounded quite appetising to Newman, whose stomach continued to growl even after eating the throwaway meat sandwich and the fried potato sticks.

The transaction now completed, Newman pocketed his gain and left the shop feeling flush and hopeful. He didn't notice the jeweller lingering at the door to make certain that Newman didn't pass by the place where some woman named Penny invited people to dine with her for a price.

To the jeweller's satisfaction, Newman stepped inside the restaurant that had been recommended to him. He took a seat at one of the tables and read through the menu and then asked for a chicken sandwich, as the jeweller had suggested he should, and a lemonade, which sounded as if it should taste as good as had the orange juice he'd imbibed two mornings ago, and then something called "onion rings," because he was curious to know what such things could be. Because he was so excited about his first restaurant meal in the Outland, Newman did not even mind the odd look that the waitress gave him. Perhaps she thought him strange because of the dirty, baggy clothes he was wearing, or the fact that he sat up so straight in his chair (all Dinglian children having been taught to avoid a drooping posture for it was exemplary of rough manners).

The chop-house (for it most resembled one of the chop-houses of Milltown's East End, except that there was more glass and more light, and the tables were shiny and metallic and there were bright colours all about) was fairly empty at this late afternoon hour and for this reason it was quiet save the faint sound of a little music playing. The music came from some-place Newman could not determine, and it sounded a bit cacophonous to his Dinglian ears. He wondered if there was a sound box somewhere about, like the sound box that had produced the voice in the Ryersbach dine-in kitchen.

Newman adjudged his sandwich to be most tasty and he enjoyed the deep-fried loops called onion rings, which were crispy and flavour-able, though quite salty (as he was discovering all Outlander food to be). The lemonade was sweet, yet also sour, just as he had predicted. All in all, Newman quickly concluded that this first Outland meal procured solely through his own efforts was really quite good, and that he would not mind having another one just like it as he made his way back to Dingley Dell.

Ruth Wolf entered the restaurant quite breathless, though she tried not to give the picture of one who had trotted nearly all the way from where she had spoken to the jeweller Phillips. The young woman, who looked to be in her mid-twenties, greeted the waitress as if the two were old friends and seated herself at the table next to Newman's.

Newman glanced up at her as she sat down and thought that he had seen her somewhere before. The puzzled look on Newman's face gave Miss Wolf all the information that she required. She rose from her chair and moved to sit across the table from Newman.

"You think that you know me, don't you?" she asked, pulling a strand of her long red hair away from her grey-emerald eyes.

"I'm not sure if I know you or not," said Newman, whose hand was cupped round the glass of lemonade but was now staid from lifting the beverage to his lips.

"But I look familiar to you."

Newman nodded. "I know not why."

"I'll tell you why. May I sit here? May I speak with you?"

Newman shrugged.

"I'll tell you where you've seen me and then you should feel better. I am Miss Wolf. I work at Bethlehem Hospital upon Highbury Fields in

Dingley Dell."

"Bedlam. You're a nurse at Bedlam."

"Yes."

"I remember now. You came to speak to my fellow classmates and me at Miss Clickett's school."

"That's right. I came to talk about the work that I do on behalf of the unfortunate inmates of Bedlam."

Newman took a sip of his lemonade and swallowed. He set down the glass and looked at Miss Wolf, studying her young face, the face of a Dinglian, who, now drest in Outland clothing, could be thought just as easily to be an Outlander. "What are you doing here?" he now asked. "Have you escaped from Dingley Dell as well?"

Miss Wolf was just about to answer when the serving girl suddenly made her appearance to ask what Miss Wolf would have. "Just a cup of coffee," answered the nurse.

After the girl had walked away, Miss Wolf resumed, "No, Newman. I haven't escaped."

"You remember my name."

"Of course I should remember the name of a boy as bright as you. Newman, there is much that you don't know and there isn't time right now to tell it all. But I'll say *this*: I come and go from the Dell as I please. I am, in fact, the only Dinglian who enjoys that privilege. There are things that I do at the hospital—important things having to do with the care of the inmates there. And then there are things that I do out *here*."

"Were you born in Dingley Dell?"

"No, I wasn't."

"I don't understand. You came from the Outland?"

"Yes. I'll be happy to tell you my story someday and how things came to be, but—" Miss Wolf glanced nervously over her shoulder. "But as I say, we haven't time right now. There are people here—and I don't wish to alarm you, Newman, but you must know the truth—there are people whose job it is to find boys like you, to seek out anyone who has escaped from the Dell, for that matter, and to remove them so that they won't speak of your homeland. So that these other people whom you see all around you should never know the truth about it. Now these bad people have been informed of your escape and they are out here looking for you. As luck would have it, I happened to find you first."

"Why is that a lucky thing?"

"Because it is *my* job, or rather the job that I have chosen for myself among all the others that have been assigned to me—to keep those bad people from finding you. Because if you fall into the hands of *those* people, well, I won't sugarcoat it, Newman: they'll kill you. That's their job: to silence you in the best way they know."

A jolt of panic suddenly struck at Newman's breast. He started to rise from his chair as if he would bolt. Miss Wolf caught him by the arm. "Please. Listen to me, Newman. If you run, if you try to hide, it's only a matter of time before they'll find you. But if you'll only trust me, I can keep them from you. I can take you home. Will you trust me, Newman?"

Newman didn't answer. He knew not *how* to answer this strange red-headed woman who gave him a soft, warm smile, whilst telling him with great urgency the danger that he was in. What he had been told made him feel light in the head. He wanted to believe her. He wanted to trust her. Yet had he not decided that he should trust no one, believe no one? Had not Mr. Ryersbach brought in a policeman and a woman with grasping hands to take him away? Was it *their* intention to kill him? Even the jeweller had tried to cheat him. And Chad Ryersbach had assaulted him. No, Newman thought. He would take his chances with his own fleet feet and with his own strong fists, which had won him two pugilist medals. He was, after all—should he succeed in finding his bearings—only a three-day journey by foot from his home. That is how far he estimated that he had come over the last eight days. He could make it home under his own industry. He had money now and he would buy food along the way when he felt it was safe to do so.

Perhaps, thought Newman, there wasn't anyone at all looking for him—especially someone who might wish to kill him. Perhaps this was a fabrication put forth by Miss Wolf to take him into her own custody so that she could rob him or take him to a work farm to pull up radishes all day, this being another Outland hazard speculated by Newman's schoolmates.

And had it not also been said of Miss Wolf that she was the nurse who puts the inmates into their strait-waistcoats, who plies them with so much laudanum as to make them insensible or babbling? Had not the children in Miss Clickett's school whispered amongst themselves after Miss Wolf had gone that she was a punishing witch without a broomstick but with a great syringe which she straddled and flew all about and used to stab all the little children of the Dell who refused to eat their boiled beef and pease pudding? It all came back to him now. In spite of the warm smile and the soft and sympathetic grey-emerald eyes, there were things about this woman—this fast-talking woman with one foot in the Outland and one in the Dell—that unsettled my nephew, that left him fearfully uneasy and uncertain.

"Begging your pardon: I wish to pay for my food now," Newman called to the serving girl even before she had brought Miss Wolf her cup of coffee.

"I'll get your cheque. What's your hurry?" the girl cheekily replied from across the empty restaurant.

"You're being smart," said Miss Wolf to Newman, nodding quickly. Then to the girl: "Forget the coffee. We have to go. I'll pay for his lunch, though. How much was it?"

"I have money to pay, myself," protested Newman.

"But I insist," said Miss Wolf.

"Very well then, and thank you," said Newman as he rose suddenly from his chair and bowed to the redheaded nurse.

As Ruth Wolf dipped her eyes to look into her leather pocketbook, Newman made his escape. With no less speed and purpose than he had employed to free himself from the Ryersbach house, he made a mad dash to the glazed front door of the diner, threw it open, and disappeared.

By the time the nurse had reached the sidewalk, her temporary ward was too far ahead for her to pursue him, running as fast as his swift legs could take him up the high street of Jersey Shore. She shook her head in frustrated despondence. The jeweller, Phillips, having seen the boy fly past, stepped out onto the sidewalk himself. He and Miss Wolf caught sight of one another and now exchanged looks of hard disappointment that had mixed within them some appreciable measure of fear.

—NOTES—

MONETARY SYSTEM. Serious and early attention was given by the Dingley Dell Petit-Parliament to the development of a serviceable monetary system. An attempt was made in the first three decades of the twentieth century to replicate the Victorian system of farthings and pence and shillings and sovereigns. But it was a needlessly complicated and confusing business, and forever in want of modification and improvement. Consequently, a decimal system of coinage was devised and was put into effect in the year 1929, based upon a proposal posited by the *Encyclopædia Britannica* (Vol. 7, SEE: "Decimal Coinage: a substitute for the "Quarto-Duodecimo-Vicesimal System"). This new system has worked with great efficiency and to this day is so simple in its arrangement that even young children have had little difficulty learning it. Dinglian tots are nonetheless encouraged to recite the following rhyme to remember the denominations:

> Ten mil make a cent,
> And if that ain't spent,
> Add another nine
> To see a florin shine.
> And if nine more florin can be found,
> Pat your back. You've made a pound!

Barter being the chief mechanism of trade with the Outland, the exchange of commodities between parties within the Dell absent a mutual circulating medium, continues, as well, to receive measurable application.

CHAPTER THE ELEVENTH

Tuesday, June 24, 2003

Nothing was learnt from Muntle's trip to the Summit of Exchange. One of the tradesmen had thought at first that he had seen a boy off in the distance standing isolate in a field, but it was merely a scarecrow drest in old, ragged and fluttering clothes, animated by the wind.

This was all that was said.

Muntle had come to deliver his discouraging report to my lodgings above Mrs. Lumbey's Ladies' Fine Dress Shop late the previous night and we had reluctantly taken the news to Gus and Charlotte. Each had received it none too well and Charlotte had slipped from the room, nursing another headache, to complete her packing, for she was to spend a few days with a consoling childhood friend in Hungerford. Charlotte had sought Alice's companionship there as well (hoping for some form of reconciliation between mother and the daughter who now, in all likelihood, constituted Charlotte's only surviving offspring). Alas, my sister-in-law had received in exchange for her maternal overture to the sulky and stony-faced thirteen-year-old a harsh rebuff, delivered in the girl's wonted insolent fashion: "Sit for several days betwixt you and your damask-nosed crony Miss Snigsworth? Watch the two of you tossing off your gallipots of grog as if it were some ancient nepenthe? Pardon me if I decline the invitation this week or any other week, Mama, but I would rather have sharp iron nails driven into my skull."

It was then and there that Alice had decided to spend days commen-surate with her mother's sojourn as guest of her dearest friend Cecilia Pupker. It was a far preferable course of action than being left alone with a "whimpering willow of a father who could hardly be tolerated for a day, let alone a week."

The hour was late when I finally returned to my rooms to retire for the night.

I slept until nearly nine o'clock next morning and then drest and dragged myself down the stairs for a late breakfast of tea and toast and jam in Mrs. Lumbey's dining parlour, and then peeped into the showroom of my landlady's shop where her young apple-faced assistant Miss Casby was modeling a dress that Mrs. Lumbey had just made: a lemon-coloured flannel lackaday frock with a generous number of pockets.

"What do you think, Frederick? It's a house frock for the woman who wishes to remain in retirement for the day. And then when night is come, the whole outfit reverses to become a flannel sleeping gown."

"Yes, I see. The flannel on the outside then becomes a flannel lining for the inside."

"It does indeed!" exclaimed Mrs. Lumbey proudly. "I have created it for the economical young woman of the house who would like to reduce her time at the washboard."

"It's really quite ingenious, Estella."

"And economical," repeated Mrs. Lumbey, stepping back to give herself the full view of the double-purposed dress.

"But does the flannel not make the dress a little too warm?" I asked of the slightly uncomfortable-looking young woman who was wearing it.

"A little warm, yes," replied the oppressively shy Miss Casby with a blush (for it was a rarity that she should be directly addressed by her em-ployeress's arguably good-looking male boarder).

"I should put it directly in the window," said Mrs. Lumbey, darting a glance at the large display window that overlooked the street, "but I would not wish your friend Miss Bocker to see it and make some ungenerous comment about it."

"And what sort of comment would that be?"

"That I continue to run a slop shop and here is my newest sartorial abomination. I should not care in the least what she thinks, but I don't wish to have customers driven away before I'm even able to shew them how a dress magically becomes a sleeping gown."

I sighed. "I don't think that my friend Miss Bocker is as disparaging of your shop and of your skills as dressmaker as you make her out to be. You do her a disservice by characterising her in such a fashion."

Estella Lumbey made no reply. Instead, she turned to her assistant and said, "Run along now, Amy, and change out of the reversible dress. I should like to see you in that new gown of your own making. You told me yesterday that it is nearly finished."

"Yes, ma'am," said Amy Casby, dropping a complaisant curtsey and betraying with a wide grin her eagerness to show off her latest accomplishment.

After Miss Casby had removed herself from the room, tugging a bit upon the heavy flannel that hotly swaddled her neck and arms, Mrs. Lumbey said, "I will have the last laugh, mark me, Frederick. For once word is out that for a reasonable price my customers will be able to purchase a frock that astounds and amazes, there will be a run upon the shop. You will see. Someday I will put that coarse and offensive woman out of business—or at least out of the dressmaking and millinery line. She can sell all of the candles and stationery and cigars she pleases. I'll wager she smokes the nasty things herself, like some boorish wash-house laundress."

I could not help smiling at my friend's sudden agitation over something that lived only in her own fancy.

"Smokes the cigars or the candles?" I chuckled.

"You're making sport of me, aren't you?"

"Estella, I really wish that you and Antonia would make a better effort to get along. I'm fond of the both of you in equal measure, and it troubles me that you're so frequently at odds."

"Need I remind you, Frederick, who it was who started the two of us down this adversarial path? Who it was who opened a dress emporium when a small and humble shop in the very same neighbourhood was serving quite sufficiently the needs of its female residents? She advances herself by breaking every rule of deference and common courtesy in the marketplace, and frankly, I cannot see at all how your society with her serves to your benefit."

"Nor do some people understand why I allow *you* to continue to be my landlady when you're forever caviling and carping and rattling pots and pans early of a morning when I'm trying to sleep." I tried my best to say this without the smile that contradicted the hard sentiment, but could not.

"If you wish to go and live under some other roof, be gone and good riddance, you troublesome ingrate!" Here my landlady could not withhold her own smile. "But mind: no one will feed you better or keep you in fresher linens or listen to your philosophies at two o'clock in the morning. You would be lost without me, Frederick, and I dare you to try it."

I enveloped my friend and landlady in an affectionate embrace, for her knitted brow seemed to require some manner of genial appeasement. She hugged me in return and patted me and then chided me for sleeping so late.

"Last night's late hours were spent in the company of my brother and Sheriff Muntle," I remonstrated.

"I thought you were at the play."

"I gave my ticket away. I didn't feel up to watching the protracted death of little Nell in *The Old Curiosity Shop*. A comedy would have served me better."

"At all events, I thought that you'd taken one of the young women who write articles for the *Delver* with you. You once told me how fond you are of each of them."

I nodded. "I enjoy their company, Estella—most certainly I do—but it is not my season for finding a young woman to whom I should make love. My heart simply isn't in it these days."

"I understand," said Mrs. Lumbey in a soft, almost reverential tone. It was Estella Lumbey's daughter Fanny to whom I had been most devoted, and we had even spoken of marrying once I could better support the two of us with my writing, but fate had dealt us both a terrible hand (and her most cruelly) by ending her young life through an infection of the bronchia that could not be surmounted. Although Fanny's death had occurred a good eighteen months earlier, painful memory of her remained. It was a fact that strangely bound me to my landlady, since she would in all likelihood have been my mother-in-law had her daughter survived.

Here—and I was quite skilled at reading the buried purpose beneath my landlady and cherished friend's questions and opinions—she was saying that perhaps it was time for me to find a young woman who, although she should never take the place of her beloved Fanny, would at least fill part of that void that Fanny's death had so deeply carved into my being. I understood that. Yet still I was not ready.

I could not help comparing every girl I met to Fanny and each fell short of that lofty standard. When one dies who is greatly loved, the loss tends to inflate the feelings of the one who is left behind; it adds a glistening to memories already amply aglow, and lionises the character of the beloved to the point of blind irrationality. Such was the position into which Fanny's demise had put me. And such was the hurdle placed between me and every other girl who wished to win my heart.

There was a little cough in the doorway, which communicated with Mrs. Lumbey's sewing room and her living quarters behind it, and we both looked up to see the gawky, dough-cheeked Amy Casby wearing a dress of her own proud design: a white muslin frock trimmed in beaver, with tartan stockings and a bottle green bonnet from which hung fringe intermingled with tiny cloth butterflies.

It was quite a hideous display outside of a comical costume shop but Mrs. Lumbey applauded the look (as did I) and had Miss Casby to turn round so that we might view the paisley bow that graced the back of the clown's garment.

"A very good start, my dear!" Mrs. Lumbey complimented her apprentice. "I would not have put all of those elements together, but it is a most intriguing mix, is it not, Frederick?"

"Most intriguing," I said to be kind.

"Now go back, my sweet, and remove the busy bow and all the beaver, and give yourself some less—how should I put this?—*Scottish* stockings."

"And what about the butterflies?"

"Oh you must certainly keep the butterflies, my pet. They make the entire outfit sing."

After Amy Casby left the room (happy but a little confused by the logic behind Mrs. Lumbey's suggestions), I asked my landlady the question that I had sought to put to her when first I had come downstairs: "Have you plans this week to go riding in Regents Park?"

"I should like to, but what if there rises a sudden, overwhelming demand for more of my reversibles? I'll have no time for anything but stitching, morning, noon, and night. No rest *or* recreation for the weary. No. As much as Mister Jip might pony-pine for my company, which always brings to him a welcome abundance of apples and sugar cubes for his equine delectation, it is best that I postpone our inter-species tryst for yet another week."

"No riding this week? You're certain?"

Mrs. Lumbey nodded. "Yes, Frederick, I am most certain. Nor *should* I be going nearly as often as I do now. It is an extravagance that I can scarcely afford. So, I'm afraid that you are out of luck."

"What do you mean, 'out of luck'?"

Mrs. Lumbey simpered in a deliberately mischievous manner, and absently brushed a bit of lint from the gown that hung upon a rack beside her. Then she said rather matter-of-factly, "Because I shan't be able to go to give you the necessary pretext by which you should have your chat with that boy-groom Jemmy."

"And how—?" I dropt my voice, lest I should be heard out in the street, the front door to the shop having been left open to be more welcoming to potential customers (though it was mostly flies and gnats that accepted the invitation to enter the establishment at this early hour). "How did you know that I wished to speak to Jemmy?"

Mrs. Lumbey laughed. "I am a shopkeeper, Frederick. Women come hither to do business with me—women who know things and are more than willing to tell me what they know. For example, I know that the boy-groom—the striking young lad with the name Jemmy—was doing a bit more for the late Mrs. Pyegrave than simply walking that beautiful mare out of her stall and saddling her up and giving her every consideration which—ahem—a creature such as that requires. There are questions that you wish to ask him, perhaps to the benefit of something you are writing. The true purpose eludes me, but in time, I suppose, you will either tell me or you will not, and at all events I will eventually hear every detail of it from one of my gossiping customers."

"I am not at liberty at present to give you an explanation, Estella."

"I understand. But if I were given to supposition, I should say that Mrs. Pyegrave's death was in some way related to a husband's rage over discovering that his wife was frequenting the park with something more in mind than simply bestowing apples and sugar cubes upon a favourite horse. There was something sweet that she was giving one of the two-legged creatures who resided in those stables as well: a young man who was just himself learning how to ride."

Mrs. Lumbey left me speechless. Her facility for innuendo and double entendre reminded me of the lustful little book that circulated amongst my playfellows when I was much younger and when manly stirrings had driven my mates and me to engage far less in field games and childish pranks and rambles, and far more in thoughts ineffable, and then in the end interminably effable: *A Young Man's Fancy OR Tit for (Mr.) Tat* by Francis Micawber. Micawber extolled the art of the salacious double meaning and even knocked the virtuous Mr. Dickens from his pedestal of respectability by quoting the following scandalous line from Dickens' otherwise respectable *Martin Chuzzlewit*:

> "She touched his organ, and from that bright epoch,
> even it, the old companion of his happiest hours,
> incapable as he had thought of elevation, began a
> new and deified existence."

(A line that was purposefully omitted from the expurgated edition of that popular novel, though one had only to ask Mr. Graham, the chief librarian of the **Academic and Lending Library of Dingley Dell**, for a copy of the original edition or, for that matter, Mr. Micawber's *A Young Man's Fancy*, or any of the other scandalous writings by the **Dinglian Diddlers**, to be offered the volumes in their circumspect whitey-brown paper-wrappers with a solemn nod that was more in keeping with Graham's refined nature than would be a wink or a nudge.)

"We'll go to the stables to-night," said Mrs. Lumbey, relenting, "after Jemmy has finished his work for the day. Have your word with Jemmy and I'll have my customary appraising look at the gorgeous young man myself whilst partaking of my free visit with that other most adorable creature in my relatively empty life, Mister Jip. But you'll have to go to the greengrocer's and get me some apples, Frederick. I've got the sugar cubes but Mister Jip will neigh most crossly at me if he doesn't get his pippins to boot."

❦

Late that afternoon I did indeed have my interview with Jemmy, a fair-haired and fair-faced young man of eighteen. Sitting alongside him upon his flockbed in the rough-and-tumble hayloft lodgings that had been assigned to him, I came quickly to the point, not knowing just when the head groomsman might return from his afternoon visit to the ale-house in the company of his equally thirsty colleagues in the equestrian currying and equipage trade, and put a summary finish to our colloquy. "Jemmy, there's a question or two that I must ask you, not for publication, mind, nor should you concern yourself that my queries will in any other way bring you under uncomfortable scrutiny."

Jemmy nodded.

"You'll consent to my questions, then?"

Jemmy nodded again. "But I'll tell you right up front that I don't know nothin' about what happened to poor Mrs. Pyegrave. We was friends and friends was all there was to it, I swear upon my mother's grave."

"If your mother *had* a grave, Jemmy. I know for a fact that she isn't dead. Nor would it be my guess that she's already purchased her final resting plot, now has she?"

"No, sir. I was pulling one on you. My mum told me never to lie outright, but she said that a man can stretch the truth now and again like India rubber if there's a good reason for it and it don't do no harm to nobody."

"What's the good reason for wanting to lie to me about Mrs. Pyegrave, Jemmy?"

"What do you think, Mr. Trimmers? I ain't a child no more. And I ain't rich. And if there be ladies what come hither with a few coin to give me and if there ain't no harm to be done, I'll do a thing or two for them for a few florin, I will. I got to eat, Mr. Trimmers, and they pay poorly for what I do here as a stableboy and I got no other prospects right now that I can see in the offning. I do things for the ladies what have money and everybody walks away with a smile on they faces, even the horses, 'cuz I'm a little kinder to 'em and brush 'em a little more gentle-like knowin' I got money for my mama and enough left over to buy a pint or two for meself of a Saturday night."

"So you were never in love with Mrs. Pyegrave. There was never any sort of romance budding betwixt the two of you."

"I don't mean to sound like an odious, um, ogre or nothin', gov'ner, but I ain't ever been in love with any of 'em. Love got nothin' to do with what I do with these women. They know it, I'm right *sure* they know it."

"*All* of them, Jemmy? Did Mrs. Pyegrave know it?"

Jemmy got himself up from the cot and took a sprig of hay and chewed upon it for a moment. "Come to think of it, maybe she didn't."

"Perhaps she actually thought that you had true and sincere feelings for her."

Jemmy nodded. "Could rightly be."

"And of course you never thought to disabuse her of this notion."

"No, sir. I suppose I didn't." Then earnestly: "But how *could* I, Mr. Trimmers, even if I wanted to, 'cuz she paid me the most of all them ladies. And it warn't even like I was *being* paid, come to think of it, which made it all the more better. It was like we was friends, it was. And she saw where I lived and the rags I got to wear for clothes, and then I tell her about how sick my mama is, and it breaks her heart it does, and she decides what she's going to do is she's going to give me some money to help me out, be my *patroness*, is what she calls it. And it's a *lot* of money, Mr. T. And maybe in getting that much money, maybe I did put on a little bit. No, I put on a lot; I'll admit it. Turned my gratitude into something she thought was a lot stronger than what it really was."

I nodded and considered in silence what Jemmy had just said. Then I asked, "Did she ever happen to mention something called the 'Tya-dya-dya Project'?"

"The what?"

"The Tya-dya-dya Project, or anything that might have sounded like that."

"No, I don't believe she ever did. We didn't talk about much that didn't have to do with me or the horses or the stables or them fellows what I work with or my supposed-to-be-sick mama. She liked hearing me talk about myself. She said there was nothing much about her hoity-toity life—them were her words—that a person would care to hear about. And so no, I don't believe she ever mentioned whatever it was you just said."

"But you would tell me if she had?"

Jemmy nodded. "What's the reason I shouldn't want to tell you? What is it anyways?"

"I don't know, Jemmy. I don't know anything about it. I thought you might know."

Jemmy shrugged.

"Thank you for sitting down with me."

I stood to shake Jemmy's hand. "Mrs. Pyegrave was a nice lady," he said. "She might have been a Patricia, but she was still the best lady what ever came to ride here."

"A Patricia? I don't understand. Her Christian name was Janet."

Jemmy shook his head. "Patricia's what the grooms and hostlers all call the lady patricians."

"Patricias. Yes, I see. And was Mrs. Pyegrave, the Patricia, nicer to you than even my friend Mrs. Lumbey has been?" We could both at that moment see Estella through the window standing by her Mister Jip and singing softly into the quadruped's ear.

Jemmy nodded and then delivered in a confidential whisper, "Mrs. Lumbey ain't one to ask from a stableboy more than is normally required. And she don't even tip all that good. But I grant you she's a decent woman. I'm sorry her daughter got so sick and died. And your nevvie, Mr. Trimmers. I was sorry to hear about him, too."

In Dingley Dell, as I may have mentioned, it was hard to keep things from being known by all—unless it was a very big thing, something that put all the little pieces of intelligence to shame—something so large as to shape the very future of the Dell.

But Jemmy the stableboy, it now appeared, hadn't been let in on the secret.

—NOTES—

THE ACADEMIC AND LENDING LIBRARY OF DINGLEY DELL, est. 1922. Dingley Dell's only public library holds over 2,400 indigenous volumes in both published and manuscript formats. Its Special Collections Room maintains the "Outland Fruit Cellar Library" containing all of the Outland volumes discovered in August 1890, with the exception of the *Encyclopædia Britannica, Ninth Edition*, whose highly acidic textual pages have disintegrated over the years.

All volumes of the *Encyclopædia* or *"Ensyke"* have been transcribed and bound into booklets that comprise each of its thousands of subjects, although several booklets were noted missing in an inventory undertaken in 1953, the loss constituting a great setback to Dinglian scholarship, as no multiple safety copies had been transcribed at the time. Relevant lost booklets pertain to the following subjects: EDWARD BULWER LYTTON, SEA SERPENTS, LEGERDEMAIN, JENGHIZ KHAN, INFINITESIMAL CALCULUS, HYPOCHONDRIASIS, and BÉZIQUE (the card game, not the exotic dancer by that name). The booklet on the subject MERMAIDS AND MERMEN, lost for thirty-five years, was discovered in the cupboard of a recently-deceased Tavistocker in 1977, its reappearance gaining a great deal of attention for the Library and inspiring, a year later, the first of Milltown's popular "Mermaid Balls."

The walls of the Library have for many years been graced by the work of local artists, colour plates of illustrations and maps preserved from the *Ensyke*, and the *Anastasia Jarndyce Collection of World Painting*, which includes reproductions of *Ensyke* reproductions of works such as Botticelli's *The Birth of Venus*, Lippi's *The Annunciation*, Velasquez's *Portrait of Philip IV of Spain*, and Reynolds' *Portrait of Dr. Johnson*.

THE DINGLEY DIDDLERS, a group of whimsically ribald writers floruit 1940-1955 who wrote and distributed mildly salacious and occasionally grotesquely obscene verses and character portraits, often deliberately denigrative of members of the Petit-Parliament and other holders of high office in the Dell. Illustrative of their efforts, the following two limericks:

> There once was a sawbones named Podsnap
> Who enjoyed putting damsels on his broad lap.

He paid nary a price
Except for the lice
And a most obstinate case of the clap.

A gentle lady of breeding
Sat in her garden a'weeding,
When up from behind a shrubbery
Rose two naked lovers most loverly,
The lady no longer singular in her breeding.

CHAPTER THE TWELFTH

Tuesday, June 24, 2003

Newman had returned to the wooded hills to spend the night. He was becoming a little used to sleeping lightly upon a bed of moss and keeping himself alert to anyone who might wish to disturb his slumber. There was now an even greater reason not to let down his guard: according to Miss Wolf, there were people in the Outland who wanted to kill him. This thought invaded his dreams and strengthened his resolve to return to Dingley Dell as soon as he was able.

It was hunger that now brought Newman down from the hills at the break of day. Before the town of Jersey Shore had even risen, the boy had succeeded in finding for himself sufficient victuals within a rubbish container behind a large food market. Newman was careful to take into his delicate Dinglian digestive tract only nuts and biscuits and other comestibles that were not prone to rapid spoilage. Already, he was feeling sour in the stomach and not at all himself, and he didn't wish to make things worse by ingesting contaminated edibles that would leave him inconveniently crampish and runny.

After Newman had taken his fill from the large rubbish container (my nephew having never before seen so great a stock of discarded food), he turned his steps in the general direction of Dingley Dell with the sun as his morning guide. Newman vowed to shorten his three-day journey by a full day—that is, if the weather remained clement and if his Dinglian shoes continued to hold themselves securely upon his feet and if he was not stopped along the way by any of those who wished to do him harm, and if—finally—he could navigate his way through the woods, where the sun did not shine, and trust the moss that generally grew on the northern side of the trees to act as his bryophitic compass. (This was a navigational rule of thumb that Newman had learnt in school and then promptly forgotten only to recall it again when he saw a large roadside advertising board promoting patronage at the Home Run Travel Agency through use of the catch phrase "A rolling stone gathers no moss.")

No more than two blocks from the large food market where he had procured his breakfast stood a schoolhouse. It was like no other schoolhouse he had ever seen, for it had a very flat roof and a great many windows that connected themselves one to another in long rows. Although there was a sign in the front that said "Jersey Shore Area Elementary School," he would have correctly guessed the building's purpose from the number of children who played upon its front lawn. There was also a large yellow horseless carriage parked in front. It had the words "School Bus" imprinted on its side. Judging from the word "bus" and from the number of seats inside, Newman supposed that this must be some sort of Outland omnibus especially designed to transport children to the school and then to transport them home again.

Yet, curiously, there were no children *alighting* from the vehicle at this early hour. Instead, they were climbing up and into the omnibus, some of the smaller ones being handed up by attentive men and women who very well could be their mothers and fathers. Newman could not keep his curiosity in check and approached a boy who seemed to be the same age as he. The boy was sitting upon the kerb of the street and eating something from a small colourful bag.

"Good morning," said Newman to the boy.

"Hi," said the boy, squinting up at Newman through the thick lens of his heavy spectacles.

"Where is everyone going?"

"The Reptilarium."

The destination's name sounded familiar to Newman's ear, but he could not at that moment remember how it had come to his kin.

"Are you going, too?" asked Newman.

"Uh huh," said the spectacled boy, nodding.

"What is the Reptilarium?"

The boy, who had a studious look and reminded Newman a little of Dinglian boys who read too much and always knew the answer to every question (not the sort of boys that Newman ever counted amongst his close friends), sniffed a little and rubbed his wet nose upon his sleeve and seemed happy to inform Newman of everything there was to know about the Reptilarium: "You've never been there? It's great. My dad takes me maybe twice a year. The official name is 'Clive and Clare's Reptilarium,' although everybody just calls it the Reptilarium. I don't know who Clive and Clare are—maybe some famous herpetologists or something. Anyway, 'Reptilarium' isn't exactly the right name for it, if you ask me, because it's got more than just reptiles. It's got some amphibians, too. Do you know what amphibians are?"

"Frogs?"

"Yeah. And salamanders and newts. I'm Gregory," said the boy. "I don't know you."

"I don't attend this school," said Newman.

"Neither do I. My church is borrowing the school's bus. Are you homeless?" Gregory looked Newman up and down, taking special notice of his oversized, soiled clothes.

"No. I have a home."

"In school we learned all about homeless kids. We went to a shelter and gave them peanut butter and jelly sandwiches. I thought you were homeless because of the way you're drest. Are you a meth addict? We learned about them, too."

Newman didn't know what a meth addict was, but he was certain that he wasn't one, so he shook his head. Out of the corner of his eye he descried a man looking at him. The man appeared to be one of the fathers of the children who were boarding the bus. It was a penetrating look as if the man were studying Newman in some purposeful way.

Newman sat down next to Gregory, who continued to take particoloured pellets from his bag and pop them into his mouth. He offered the bag to Newman who took a few of the pellets and put them into his own mouth. They tasted sweet and a little like chocolate.

"Do you go to school with all these children?" asked Newman, munching.

"Some of them. But school's out for the summer. I have seventy days of freedom left. I count them down every day. That makes them more precious."

Newman nodded, thinking to himself that this fragile, bookish boy would not last a day at the rough and rowdy Chowser School.

"Where are you from?" asked Gregory.

"Not from here," Newman answered. He had learnt his lesson about telling people that he was from Dingley Dell. It seemed to him now that the only people who knew about Dingley Dell were those with whom he did not wish to associate. Of course, it was at this moment that Newman thought of someone else—another person who lived amongst the Outlanders—who would know quite a bit about Newman's home. Hadn't Chad Ryersbach mentioned a "150-year-old-man" who communed with the lizards and the snakes at the Reptilarium? Perhaps he was a lunatic who had appropriated the name Dingley Dell for his own manufactured life story because he liked the sound of it. But there was another possibility as well: that the elderly man could very well be one of those who left the Dell in its earlier days and never returned—a man who was still very much alive, in spite of what Nurse Ruth had said happened to people who left the valley.

Newman wanted to meet him. He wanted to find out if he was really from Dingley Dell. He wanted to see someone from his home—someone who had once lived the way that he had lived, had once enjoyed all the things that Newman enjoyed and which he now missed deeply. Perhaps the 150-year-old man from Dingley Dell would know a better way for Newman to get home—a way that did not require Newman to retrace his steps through the woodsy, mossy darkness.

"May I come with you?" Newman impulsively asked the boy named Gregory.

"If you have seven dollars. That's what it costs to get in."

Newman knew that he had more money in his pocket than seven dollars. He nodded and smiled as his new friend gave him a few more of the sweet chocolaty pellets.

***

The omnibus was filled, for the most part, by children Newman's age and perhaps a little younger and a little older. But there were a few adults who had put themselves inside the vehicle as well, including the man who had looked so hard at Newman and who now darted a look in his direction every so often as if he were keeping a permanent fix on him. Each look unsettled Newman, but he pretended to pay them no mind. Some of the children gave him strange looks of their own as he climbed into the omnibus and followed Gregory to a double-seat near the back. But their looks were fleeting in the midst of all the roystering merriment. A woman stood next to the driver of the omnibus counting silently to herself whilst moving her finger up and down. Then she turned and said something to the man in the driving chair. He said something to her in response. She nodded.

"Quiet! Quiet!" commanded the woman, waving her stiff, flat hands up and down. The chattering, chirping voices drew down in volume and then silenced themselves altogether. "Children: we have three extras. You new children, please raise your hands."

A boy and girl sitting a couple of rows behind Newman put their hands into the air. Newman did not.

"Raise your hand, Newman," prompted Gregory. "You're new. They have to put your name down."

Newman tentatively put his hand into the air and held it there.

"I need your signed permission forms," said the woman. "New children: please get out your signed permission forms from your parents."

The boy and girl in the back of the bus obediently held up slips of paper.

"I don't have a permission form," said Newman to his new friend Gregory. "What am I to do?"

"Take my extra one," said Gregory. "My mom already turned one in for me and didn't tell my dad. He wrote one out for me just in case she forgot."

Gregory put the required piece of paper into Newman's hand so stealthily that not a soul detected the transaction. "My parents are divorced," offered Gregory matter-of-factly as the woman moved down the aisle to collect the permission forms. "It generally sucks except when sometimes I get things done for me *twice*. I especially like birthdays. Last birthday…"

Newman handed the slip to the woman who gave it a cursory, unstudied glance and continued on her way to the back of the bus.

"…for example," the voluble Gregory went on, "I got both a microscope *and* a telescope. I asked for one or the other and I got *both*! How cool is *that*?"

Newman smiled and nodded as the omnibus began to move. His heart began to race as he felt the vehicle vibrate beneath him. He could not believe that he was travelling along the road in such a miraculous manner, with not a horse in sight to offer propulsion. His skin tingled and he felt a frisson of joy shoot through him. It was hard for him to concentrate on Gregory's chittering, but he owed a debt to the boy for keeping him on the omnibus when surely he would have been forced to alight and stand and watch the large boxy yellow carriage roll away without him.

"Which would *you* have asked for, Newman? A microscope or a tele-scope?"

Newman thought this over for a moment. "They're each quite precious and scientifically helpful in their own way."

"But would you rather study the stars or the microbes? I think mi-crobes for me. In my science class my teacher Mr. Isbell let me prepare all of the slides. I got extra credit."

"The stars," said Newman. "I should like to look at the stars."

Newman thought about the stars and about the night sky. He smiled to himself. It was the very same sky here as that which cowled Dingley Dell. No two places could be as different upon the ground (for why else was the land abroad called the "Terra Incognita"?); yet the sky and the stars and even the clouds that passed from one valley to the next were identical. For a brief moment Newman Trimmers felt slightly less estranged from all the newness that surrounded him. Had he not made a friend—an inquisi-tive boy just like himself? Was the boy not helping him to get to Clive and Clare's Reptilarium?

Newman came to a rather profound conclusion about Dingley Dell and the Outland: that people are the same regardless of where they live. There are some who are bad and there are some who are good, and it served him well to find the good ones who would give him succour and avoid the bad ones who would hurt him. It was really no different here than it was in Dingley Dell.

This was something that Newman's father was soon to learn as well.

CHAPTER THE THIRTEENTH

Tuesday, June 24, 2003

My brother Gus stood upon the crest of the Northern Ridge, at a spot within sight of the Summit of Exchange. Having never before ventured up to this lofty aerie, Newman's father didn't know quite what he should expect to see there. In his fancy, Augustus Trimmers had imagined the place to be a bit more elaborately appointed. He imagined significant architectural detail upon its constituent buildings of trade, and perhaps a flag or two planted in a brace of mutual national comity: the Dingley jack with its stars and broad squiggle (representative respectively of the stellar firmament and the River Thames), and whatever was flown in this portion of the Outland, be it Corea or Italy of the U.S. of A. But in truth there wasn't much to the Summit at all: merely two small warehouse sheds set upon a pavement, and then lodged within a stand of stunted, wind-gnarled trees, a hundred or so yards away, an old and weathered wooden gazebo-pavilion sheltering a few wooden tables and attendant chairs. (Perhaps, thought Augustus, this is where the brokers sit to negotiate terms of barter and trade with the Outland tradesmen.)

Situate upon the pavement in a disordered row was a battery of empty barrows and handcarts. Augustus recognised the one- and two-wheeled vehicles from the times he had seen them coming down from the ridge, carrying all the smaller products of the Outland that were required by Dinglians, and even a few that weren't (designated for that select group of his kinsmen who could afford a taste of luxury in their lives). Augustus remembered that when he was a little boy there had been mules that made the trip, but they had all died during a tetanus outbreak and had never been replaced.

There really was no mystery to the place, and it gave Augustus to wonder if there should be less mystery in the land that lay beyond it. What if the lives of the Beyonders, he mused, turned out to be just as dull and un-intriguing as these dilapidated barrows and these tired and sagging build-ings implied?

Gus posed the question to himself as he laid his knapsack inside the bed of one of the empty barrows, its ironwork rusting away in flakes, its paint curling up in slow, prolonged detachment from its sideboards.

He took a moment to conduct an inventory, to make certain that nothing which should be necessary for his survival in these first days in the Outland had been overlooked.

"Good, good, good," he said to himself, and then appended, "now where the devil is that key?"

The key to which Augustus Trimmers referred had a very important purpose: it unlocked the wicket gate that was set into the tall, wire fence that trailed along the ridge and here separated the Dell from the Terra In-cognita—a fence which, though to his knowledge had never been fully sur-veyed, was presumed to encompass all of the Dell. As a rule, only Dinglian brokers possessed copies of the key, but Gus had been told by his friend Pumblechook, a locksmith, that he owned several copies himself and had once betaken himself and two of his ale-drinking chums upon a daring picnic and drinking party in the near Outland for the sheer thrill of it. What's more, Gus knew exactly where Pumblechook kept those duplicates, and was successful in pinching one of them the day before, when the easily-distracted locksmith had his back turned. Egress from Dingley Dell would, therefore, be an easy accomplishment for my brother.

The same could not be said for his son Newman, who surely hadn't the same convenient means for breaching the cordoning, sharply barbed fence. This particular worry had affixed itself to larger, more general concerns for Newman's safety in the Outland. How did he do it, without incurring serious, lacerating injury to himself?

Finding the key, and settling his mind that his hurried packing had not put him to too great a disadvantage, Gus Trimmers unlocked the wicket and commenced his trip down the other side of the ridge.

From the lofty vantage point that accompanied his first steps abroad, Gus could see a house or two, which looked from this distance not much different from the houses of the Dell. A thick canopy of trees obscured all but these two dwellings. Gus wondered what, if anything, nested or stirred below. Was there a world of life and industry here beneath all of these trees, or was there little if any form of civilisation at this point so close to his own valley home? Must one push much farther, even beyond the next mountainous ridge, to gain the true, reflective face of the heretofore most recondite Terra Incognita? Or was there nothing for hundreds of miles round save a sequence of sparsely populated ridges and valleys?

The trip down the Outlander's side of the ridge took not so long as Gus had guessed that it would, for there was a well-worn and partially-paved path to guide him in his descent (the better to roll a wheel barrow up in the opposite direction)—a path that looked not so very different from the trail that took the barrows and the hand-carts down and into Dingley Dell, laden with merchandise. "I am not yet impressed by what I see," said Gus to himself as he shifted his gaze from his feet to the surrounding landscape, forever on the lookout for some sign of Newman, some clew as to his son's whereabouts—or more disquieting, his final fate.

The children tumbled out of the omnibus in a great squealing and bouncing horde and raced one another to the receiving and main exhibits building of Clive and Clare's Reptilarium. Newman hopped down from the vehicle and glanced up at the large placard that overlooked the park. It said "Reptilarium" in large curving letters and bore the image of a menacing, fang-bearing cobra. "I can't believe you've never been here before!" shouted Gregory, straining to be heard over the din of excited voices. The two boys took their place in the queue that was fast forming in front of the door. One by one each of the children entered the building, as the meticulous woman from the omnibus counted them off, and as the driver and the other man stood by.

The second man seemed to be studying Newman more closely now, his expression staid and unrevealing. Newman didn't understand why the man was scrutinising him in such a sharp way, and then suddenly he understood it perfectly: the man was most certainly in league with the others—the ones who sought him—and, if he was to believe Miss Wolf, the ones who sought him for a purpose that Newman could scarcely permit himself to believe.

He shuddered.

"This is Mizz Edson," said the woman from the omnibus, introducing her young charges to the woman standing next to her inside the building. "She'll be our guide for the morning."

But few of the children were looking at Mizz Edson. Instead, most of the eyes in the room were roving about, taking in the colourful pictures of reptilian creatures that hung upon the dark, carpeted walls, and peeping squeamishly into the glass cages placed throughout the room, each occupied by a different cold-blooded creature.

"Can we pet the animals?" asked a little girl wearing a lattice of miniature metalwork upon her teeth.

"There'll be *some* you can pet," answered Mizz Edson, who wore the same uniform as all of the other Reptilarium employees: grey trowsers and a single-pocketed forest-green blouse. "But not all of them. I'll let you know which ones are friendly and which ones aren't."

There were thirty-two other children in the room besides Newman. He had counted them, too. He wished that there had been even more children who had crowded themselves inside that omnibus, so that he could now more easily hide himself amongst them. The cold look of the Outland man frightened him, and he wished to put himself as far away from him as possible. Whilst Newman was trying his best to avoid the man's gaze, the Outlander took a step in Newman's direction, and whether it was intended as a minatory advance or no, my nephew countered it by pushing his way as unobtrusively as possible through the group of fidgeting, chittering children to a spot nearest the counter where money was paid and guests given tiny cheques that permitted entry into this strange little zoo.

The move left Gregory standing alone. His happy expression disappeared. For a moment Newman felt sorry for Gregory, who now looked quite forlorn. And yet, thought Newman, I cannot find the old, old man of Dingley Dell if this Outlander boy is to be tagging along at my side. I must choose a place to slip away and I must keep long enough to myself so that the hard-looking man will not know where I've gone.

However, Gregory would not be so easily dismissed: "Hey!" he called.

"Come back over *here*! I want to shew you the monkey pen I got at the Bronx Zoo!"

"Anon!" Newman called back, though he couldn't be certain that he'd been heard over the echoing babble of the other children. In the next instant, Newman felt the presence of someone standing next to him. He raised his eyes to behold the face of another of the employees of Clive and Clare's Reptilarium: a young woman with blond hair and a pretty smile.

Thinking quickly, Newman said to the woman, "My stomach hurts. I must go to the privy. Pray, could you direct me to the nearest privy?"

The woman, who seemed for a moment slightly confounded by Newman's Dinglian manner of address (including his previous use of the Dinglian "anon!" for "just a moment!"), collected herself and replied, "The restrooms are around that corner and down the hall. Hurry, though. The tour's about to start."

Newman thanked the young woman with a cordial nod and followed her directions. Although seeking directions to the privy was merely the expedient by which Newman could absent himself from this room, there seemed no good reason for why his search for the old Dinglian man should not begin in this very place of hasty resort, and though he was a boy, he nonetheless pushed open the swinging door upon which had been stenciled the word MEN.

The room for MEN was brightly lit and there were fixtures inside not that dissimilar to those he had seen and used in the house where he had lived alone for a week and in the Ryersbach house as well. But there were also ceramic bowls mounted low upon one wall, which were unfamiliar to him, and a rounded ceramic box upon the wall with a circular mesh upon it.

"Halloa, halloa! Is there an old man in here?" Newman asked the room. The empty room gave back its silent reply.

Newman let out a young boy's singsong groan of disappointment. He went to one of the mirrors that had been set into the wall above what appeared to be rectangular hand-laving washbowls. He studied his reflection in the bright electrical lighting. He did not look well: his face was pale and pasty beneath a thin crust of dirt. His hair was stringy and matted. There was a swelling and a redness to his eyes that made him look as if he had long been crying.

"You look as if you've climbed out of a cave," said Newman to the reflected image of himself in the modern looking glass. "I don't know why someone doesn't take you and put you away with all the jungle animals out there, for you're not fit in your present state to live in this world." Newman, who had known despondency at other moments since he had embarked upon this adventure, now found himself sliding into the deepest trough of despair he had yet to experience. "You're doomed," he said to the reflection of himself. "They'll find you and kill you, just as the nurse had said they would. You should have gone with her. She had a kind face. She wasn't a witch at all."

At just that moment the door swung silently open and a young man entered the lavatory. He wore the employee uniform of Clive and Clare's Reptilarium, with that name and his own name, Roy, stitched upon the shirt pocket. He greeted Newman with a humming smile and went to stand before one of the other mirrors where he picked at his teeth a little with a fingernail.

Suddenly, he turned to Newman and said, "Look at what *I* have." He put his hand under the spigot of water, turned the knob with his other hand and drenched the first hand with water. Then he inserted the dripping hand into his pocket and extracted a small animal using his finger and thumb. It was an amphibious creature of some sort, which wriggled its short legs and darted its head back and forth in the bright light.

"It's a newt," said the man named Roy. "Can you guess his name?"

"If I had a newt," replied Newman, "I should name him Newton."

"Bingo! Great minds think alike," said the man, pocketing his wet pet. "Are you with the school group out there? You'd better hurry up or they'll leave you behind."

"Thank you. I will," said Newman, advancing in small hesitant steps to the door.

"But—" Newman drew a deep breath, for what followed was a bold gambit on his part and it required momentary steeling. "But may I ask you, Mr.—um—Roy, if there is an old man here in this animal place—a very old man who comes from a place called Dingley Dell?"

"Dingley Dell?"

"Yes."

The young man considered the query for a moment. "Hmm. There's nobody by that description on the *payroll* here, but one of our volunteers— hey you *know*…" Roy scratched his head. "I think he's here to-day—Mr. Rugg. He's a snake handler. Mr. Peller lets him come in and help with the snakes, but only the non-venomous ones. He's old, you see, and one slip of a shaky hand—well, there's a big, fat lawsuit."

"He handles snakes?"

"That's right. And he's also a weirdo. A real, you know, *kook*."

"A kook?"

"Uh oh. He's not your grandfather or anything, is he?"

Newman shook his head. "Why do you call him a weirdo and a kook?"

"Well, most snake handlers are religious nutcases. Goes with the territory. Something in the Bible having to do with 'taking up snakes.' But maybe it isn't a religious thing with him at all. Maybe he just likes to play with snakes. Weird, okay? But, like, who am I to talk? I carry a pet newt around in my pocket. But no, Rugg's been a part of the family around here for, like, *years*. Everybody's used to him, and of course Mr. Peller—that's *Clive* to you—he really likes him. How do *you* know the old man?"

"I don't. But I want to meet him. I want to hear him talk about Dingley Dell."

The man nodded and half-smiled. "Right. Dingley Dell. He *does* talk about that place every now and then, come to think of it. It's a made-up place, you know. It's all—you know—" The man named Roy now spun his index finger in little circles round his ear in a gesture that Newman assumed had something to do with having queer fancies.

Seconds later the door opened. Into the bright lavatory room stepped the man from the omnibus who had looked at Newman in such a disconcerting way.

"There you are," said the man to Newman in a very casual tone. The relaxed way in which the words were delivered could easily serve to make one—in this case, Roy—think that he was on familiar terms with Newman. "Everyone's been waiting on you, Newman," the man continued in his artificially cheerful manner, "but I told them to go on ahead, so that you and I could talk." The man turned to the young employee of Clive and Clare's Reptilarium. Now he frowned. "Newman did a bad thing, didn't you, Newman? Newman has forfeited his chance to see the giant turtles."

"They're called *tortoises*," corrected Roy, bristling a bit at the mis-denomination. "*Aldabra* tortoises from the Aldabra Atoll in the Seychelles. What bad thing did Newman do?"

"He can tell you," said the man. "Tell him, Newman. Tell Roy here what you did to lose your field trip privileges to-day."

Newman was too frightened to speak. He was too frightened even to shrug his shoulders. *He knows my name*, thought Newman. *The man knows who I am.*

The man turned back to Roy. "Newman did something that he thought no one saw him do. But *I* did. I always keep my eye on troublemakers like this one."

"What was it?" asked Roy, who now seemed curious to know what manner of delinquent child had entered Clive and Clare's Reptilarium with mischief on his mind.

"He stole a lizard paperweight from the admissions counter. Do you want to give back the lizard paperweight, Newman, or will I have to take it from you?"

Newman recoiled from the man. He could scarcely produce the words: "I didn't steal a paperweight. I did no such thing."

"I saw it with my own eyes, Mr. Trimmers."

Trimmers! Christian name _and_ *surname!*

"I saw you take it from the admissions counter when no one was looking. Now hand it over before Roy here tells Clive and the two of them haul you off to juvenile court."

Newman swallowed hard. He took a step backwards. He bumped his head against the ceramic box. Suddenly, hot air began to blow from the box. He jumped. "I don't have what you say I do," he said. "I don't know what you're talking about. Look in my pockets."

As the man approached Newman in acceptance of his offer of inspection, Newman noticed something clutched in his hand. It glistened slightly. The man reached out with his hand in such a way that the other man—the employee of Clive and Clare's Reptilarium—could not see the secret object. The man put his large hand deep into Newman's front trowser pocket and then pulled the hand back out again and uncurled his fingers. There it was: the paperweight which had glistened slightly on its way into the pocket, and now sat glistening and shimmering quite brightly upon the man's open palm. It was a beautiful paperweight with a tiny baby lizard preserved in its thick glass. The man gave it to Roy who put it into a pocket on his person—one of the pockets that did not have a live newt nestled inside.

Newman didn't speak. He knew that he would not be believed. The Reptilarium employee named Roy looked crestfallen, for it seemed that he had started to take a liking to the bedraggled, searching boy. The feeling was gone now. He turned away and resumed picking at his teeth.

The man from the omnibus clamped his hand upon Newman's arm with such painful tightness that Newman could not withhold a little moan from deep within his throat. Then he led Newman through the swinging door of the lavatory for MEN and out into the corridor that led to the large exhibit room where the children had gathered to be taken upon their tour of the Reptilarium.

"Where are you taking me?" asked my nephew.

"Shut up," said the man, without looking at Newman.

As the two turned the corner Newman could see that the large exhibits room was now empty of children; the tour had already begun and all of the children who had come with him had now been led outside to the park area where the crocodiles and mammoth tortoises lived beneath the open sky.

Newman wished that he hadn't gone into the MEN's lavatory. He wished that he had only put his head in and, seeing that the old man wasn't there, had continued his search through all the other rooms and corners of this strange place. And yet the man named Roy had told him something very important, which he would not have otherwise known: he had confirmed that the Dinglian snake-handler named Mr. Rugg was there that day—that there lived the possibility of success at the end of Newman's search. Now, if only Newman could find some way to wrest himself away from his captor before he could be removed to a place where no one would see him or hear from him again—a place where the mendacious, stony-faced man was certain to do something to him that would make him quite silent and quite dead.

The two moved through the great room where scaly creatures slithered and slinked and flicked their tongues behind glass. They moved in the direction of the admissions counter on their way to the door, which gave on the paved area where all the vehicles were parked. The man had been correct on one point: the paperweight had come from this counter. There were, in fact, quite a few of these paperweights for sale next to the metallic cashier's box.

Newman walked nighest the counter. He walked so close, in fact, that he was able to reach out and pick up one of the paperweights—that he could in truth do that very thing of which he had only moments ago been falsely accused.

The glass paperweight that Newman's hand had conscripted felt heavy and cold in his grip. He closed his fingers round the smoothness of it, taking firm hold of the rounded top. With calculated deliberation Newman raised his arm backwards, as if the half-orb were affixed to some taut catapultic spring. Just as the man was turning to discern the reason for the sudden movement in his side vision, Newman deployed his weapon. The glass pa-perweight struck the side of the man's head with such force as to knock him backwards, his vise upon Newman's arm loosening and falling away. The man emitted a great cry of pain as his face crimsoned, as his legs twisted and buckled beneath him, as his arms flailed uselessly in the air…and as Newman wheeled quickly round and fled back into the hissing, clammy bowels of Clive and Clare's Reptilarium, where a very old Dinglian man draped himself with snakes so that none should know that every word he said about his homeland was the cold and inarguable truth.

CHAPTER THE FOURTEENTH

Tuesday, June 24, 2003

Behind the counter the young woman whose office it was to take the money from visitors and put it into a drawer in the metallic box stood with a full and gaping mouth as she watched the boy-assailant tear away. She watched something else as well, something that she would no doubt remember for the remainder of her days: the stumbling, bloody-cheeked man falling backwards into a special glass cage set upon the floor—an enclosure with a sign upon it that read: "Star Reptile of the Week: the venomous Black mamba." She watched as the weight of the man's body shattered the protective glass. She watched as he collapsed upon the jagged shards, upon the snapping branches, upon the coils and coils of long grey snake—a suddenly very angry snake, which did not scruple to avenge this imposition upon its temporary home by springing at the man and delivering bite after bite after bite to his throat and face, as the man writhed and shrieked (for Black mambas are known not only for the potency of their venom but also for the insatiable repetition of their strikes), and finally, the woman behind the counter watched as the "Star Reptile of the Week" slithered quickly and indignantly away.

Someone else was also watching: Newman. Hearing the sound of the shattering glass he had stopt for a moment to make note of what he had done. By his own hand he had unleashed a deadly snake. At that terrible moment, my nephew felt both pride and fear, though fear was by far the most commanding emotion.

There was a third person watching as well: a different woman. She was at the same time drawing the mouthpiece of the telephone apparatus to her lips to make an urgent plea for help. She and the first woman had climbed upon the cushions of nearby chairs to remove themselves from possible engagement with one of the deadliest snakes in the world. She was entreating her colleagues to procure the antivenom from its refrigerated box in the infirmary, and to lock down and sequester all the Reptilarium visitors until the free-ranging snake could be captured. Then she spoke to someone else through the apparatus: the woman who was both Dinglian and Outlander at the very same time—Ruth Wolf.

Ruth listened intently to the little voice that spoke into her ear through the tiny portable telephone box, pressing it with one hand as the other turned the wheel that directed her horseless carriage. Sitting next to her was Phillips, the old jeweller, who wore a look of some distress but did not speak, lest his companion miss a single syllable of the crucial intelligence she was being tendered.

"Twenty minutes at the most," said Ruth, and then she closed the tiny telephone upon itself and placed it into a recessed tray, which had been moulded between the two front seats of the carriage.

"Angela's spotted the boy?" asked the old jeweller, his troubled brow overlying a scrutinising gaze. "Is he all right?"

"He's at the Reptilarium. My guess is that he went there looking for Rugg."

"Who the hell told him about Rugg?"

"I have no earthly— Look, Newman struck Caldwell. Caldwell was trying to take him away. Newman hit him in the head and got himself free. Of course, Newman Trimmers isn't the only creature at large at the Reptilarium right now."

Ruth Wolf pressed her foot upon the board that made the carriage go faster—a great deal faster.

Gus hesitated, even though there was a bit of carpeting under his feet that said, "Welcome." Yet it would be the first time that he had ever spoken to an Outlander and he wasn't certain how he should appear to him or her, or even what he would say. There had been a moment perhaps an hour earlier when Gus had come very close to speaking to a *different* Outlander— one who in great likelihood would have been quite unfriendly to him. The uniformed man was tipped back in a chair and sleeping within a little guardhouse near the gate that admitted and released one from the fenced compound through which Gus had descended the Northern Ridge. There was no lock on the gate and it was easy for Gus to open it and close it quietly behind him, with the man in the guardhouse snoring away undisturbed.

Gus pulled the framed miniature of his son from his knapsack, and even though it had been painted a full two years earlier, it remained a serviceable and most flatteringly remarkable likeness of the boy. Now he held the miniature in one hand and left the other hand free to curl itself into a fist for the purpose of rapping upon this Beyonder's door.

The house was one of the two buildings that he had seen in the distance from the top of the ridge: a farmhouse. Once he had reached its grounds he could see, as well, the barn, which stood behind it, and the five or six cows that chewed the grass in a small adjoining paddock. Except for the unfamiliar construction of the house (there was a great amount of bright orange brick that gave the dwelling somewhat of a citrus look) and the strange slope of the roof of the barn, this could very well be a Dinglian farmstead, and it was for this reason that he had fixed his courage to approach it first to enquire about his son.

Gus, though set to knock, did not have to, for at that very moment, the inner door creaked open, and there before him stood a woman in perhaps her late sixties. She glared at Gus through the outer door, which was largely constructed of wire mesh. She brandished a small cast-iron skillet—an obviously improvised weapon of defence.

"What do you want?" sought the woman in a harsh and suspicious tone. "Why are you standing at my door? Are you putting literature in my door?"

"I beg your pardon?"

"Are you leaving me a tract?"

"No, kind woman. I have come only to ask you a question."

"I accepted Jesus as my personal saviour when I was fourteen. There.

I've answered your question. Go spread the good news somewhere else."

"Who is it, Mama? Who are you talking to?" Gus couldn't see the second speaker, whose voice sounded more youthful, for the suspicious older woman fully blocked his view into the house.

"Nobody. Go back to your book!" barked the brusque woman over her shoulder.

Now Gus could hear a series of thumps as the other person within the house moved haltingly to the door. From over the older woman's shoulder, a young woman wearing curling-framed spectacles, her hair pinned severely to the top of her head, shewed Gus a friendlier look than did her elderly companion. "Hello," she said. "Mama, let the man in. He wants to sell us something and we'll listen."

"We'll do nothing of the kind!" snapped the older woman, adjusting her grip upon the skillet. "We don't know what he wants."

"Well, then *ask* him, Mama."

The young woman's eager look became ever the more anticipatory. She began to bob a little up and down as if she were stretching herself upon tiptoes and then down again by turns.

"So what *do* you want?" asked the old woman of Gus, without retiring her sullen, probing visage.

Augustus removed his cap in deference to the two women standing before him. "Begging your pardon, kind woman, I am looking for my son. He has gone missing for over ten days and we are fearful that something terrible has happened to him."

Augustus held the miniature likeness out for the women to see.

"That's *him*?" asked the old woman, peering through the wire mesh.

"Yes, madam," said Gus. "He's gained two years since this likeness was put down."

"I don't usually see too many boys around here," said the older woman, softening a little in her address. "You're probably looking in the wrong place."

The younger woman now whispered something into the ear of the older woman. The older woman replied in a full voice: "Absolutely not, Annette! Those Milanos have to last until I can get back to Wegman's."

"He can have mine," the young woman replied in an urgent undervoice. "Let's have him in for tea and Milanos, Mama, please."

The older woman shook her head. "I'm not in the mood for company to-day, Annette, and you are perfectly free to leave this house and see whoever you want. You aren't a prisoner here. There are plenty of people who have overcome their agoraphobia when they finally decide to set their minds to it. And they have gone on to live rich and productive lives."

The younger woman began to sniff, her eyes to tear up.

The older woman sighed. "What's your name?" she asked Gus.

"Augustus Trimmers."

"Where's your car? I don't see it."

"Car?"

"Did you come on foot?"

"Yes."

"How long have you been looking for your boy?"

"Since early this morning."

"Your son's been lost for ten days and you've just now started your search? What kind of father are you? Where do you live?"

Gus turned and pointed. "On the other side of that ridge."

The woman rolled her eyes. "Another one of *those*. Annette, he's all yours. Another mooncalf you can put into your bizarro-land scrapbook." The woman stepped aside to allow her daughter to open the door. Gus could see now with a full view that the young woman wore harnessing metalwork upon each leg. Perhaps, he thought, the metalwork helps her to walk better.

"Meet my nutty daughter Annette. You'll have a delightful time together. I'll be in the barn."

Annette held open the door with the wire-mesh so that the older woman could leave and Gus could enter. Annette was most welcoming. The bit of rubber carpeting upon her porch, which confirmed the sentiment, must certainly have been placed there by her very own hand.

※

Newman ran as he had never run before. He had made a critical decision during the moment succeeding his assault: that he should abandon his search for the Dinglian snake handler who would not, at all events, have been able to save him from the consequences of his attack upon the malefic Outlander. It made Newman sad to think that he had come so close to meeting the old Dinglian only to see his plan so thoroughly scotched by life-threatening circumstances. But the sadness was quickly displaced by the terrible fear that the danger had engendered within him.

Flinging open the rear door, Newman was met by the warmth and light of the strong summer sun. A pebbled path lay before him—a path immediately secured by his swift tread—a path which propelled him past pens of sunning giant tortoises and sunning, langourous crocodiles and sunning, sluggish snakes of all lengths and sizes. Newman had seen a rattle-snake or two in his short lifetime, but that was the extent of his personal encounters with dangerous animals of reptilia class. He ached to stop and view them, as would any boy of his age (for there has always been a curious affinity between boys and reptiles), but there wasn't time for him to do anything now but run—run as if his life depended upon it (which he was certain now that it did).

There were children upon the path—the same children who had ridden the omnibus with him. Some were laughing and gamboling about; others had stopt to gawk at the penned creatures. There were others not from the omnibus—both children and adults—who stood pointing and observing and remarking, each oblivious to what had just happened inside the building that had first disgorged them. They will soon know, thought Newman, and the chaos and confusion that should ensue will help my cause. Newman wished that he could unlatch the wickets to the crocodile pens to unleash further pell-mell to better his chance for escape, but he knew not exactly how such a thing was done. Instead, he began to do that one thing that he was fully capable of doing to achieve similar results: he began to cry with the full force of his hardy, youthful lungs: "Snake! Murderous escaped snake on the loose!"

At first there was no reaction at all from the adults and the children round Newman, who only looked up with placid and indifferent glances at the silly child. Then, as the meaning of Newman's words began to take hold, and as the manufactured sincerity in Newman's dramatised cries began to touch that fearful place in every human brain, there came just the sort of concerted reaction that Newman sought. Someone took him seriously. Then someone else and then another and then another until complete panic took hold—mindless, terror-imbued panic. Some people stopped dead in their tracks. Others began to scurry all about without reason. Fathers lifted their little ones into their clamouring arms. Mothers stepped up upon benches, yanking their young children along with them. How easily the Outlanders frighten! thought Newman.

Then things turned quite ugly. There were scrambles and scuffles and veritable collisions as those who wished to go one way met up with those who wished to use the very same path to go the opposite way. A little girl was knocked down, her hand crushed beneath a rubber sole. A woman held her baby high above her head as if a murderous escaped snake might take an especial liking to any infant that wasn't higher than a tree.

A little boy was flung into a fence, his eyeglasses flying off his face from the force of the impact. Newman noted in passing that the boy's look was familiar to him. He was, in fact, the amiable and erudite Outlander Gregory. Newman reversed his steps and went to pull his scientific chum to his feet. "Don't worry, Gregory. The fugitive snake is safe within that building there," he said, pointing. Gregory squinted. Without his spectacles he could only kick his legs and flap his arms to keep away all the amassing poisonous snakes that he could not see. "This is merely a diversionary tactic that I have been forced by unfortunate circumstances to employ." He spotted Gregory's eyeglasses nesting in a tuft of grass, picked them up and put them into one of Gregory's fluttering hands. "I have to go now, Gregory. Thank you for being so helpful to me and thank you for the tasty chocolate beads."

Still speechless, Gregory returned his glasses to the bridge of his nose and watched with now corrected vision as Newman sprinted away.

What could easily have been dismissed as a young boy's mischievous prank was instead taken for a legitimate admonition, and suddenly circumstances required Newman to say not another word to effect the sort of disorder and mayhem that he required. Hysterical, illogical panic now held sway over that morning's contingent of visitors to Clive and Clare's Reptilarium, one overwrought imagination feeding the next, the resultant turmoil escalating exponentially. A misinterpretation of a broken serpentine-shaped branch beneath a tree propelled a frightened man's flailing elbow into the ribcage of a screaming woman, and obligated a fleeing girl to abandon the woman she had been pushing in a wheeled chair, now toppled upon its side, the girl herself soon tripping over the large stumble-stone of a man who had been inadvertently knocked to the ground by an even larger man with ramrodding shoulders.

Newman stopped for a moment to admire his handiwork and then to feel quite guilty over it, and then was on his way again. A moment or so later he reached another building, this one much smaller than the one he had left. There was a sign on the door that read: "INFIRMARY. EMPLOYEES ONLY. NO ADMITTANCE." He ignored the written enjoiner, threw open the door, and ducked inside.

The front room was filled with cabinets and cages and tables upon which sat various pieces of medical equipment and surgical instruments, the look of the room being quite in keeping with its designation as infirmary for cold-blooded captive creatures. There was a young man standing behind a table, fumbling nervously with a hypodermic needle and a tiny glass ampule.

"What are you doing in here?" he cried with only the briefest glance up from his task. "Get out of here!"

"But there's a deadly snake on the loose out there!" Newman replied in the same terrified voice he had used outside.

"How the hell did it—they told me it was contained inside the North Building." The man now looked at Newman with fearful, goggling eyes. "You're telling me you saw it in the open—you mean on the grounds?"

Newman nodded.

"Jesus!" The man set the ampule down and flicked his finger against the hypodermic. "Look, you better stay here," he said as he dashed out the door.

Newman knew that he could not remain in this place. He knew that even if he were able for the nonce to lock himself inside, someone would eventually come for him and they would find some way to get him. He decided to look for a different door from the one he'd just entered—to go out that other door and then continue his search for some rear egress from the park itself. Surely there was some other way for the park's employees to come and go that did not require one to pass so close to the main exhibits building, or the "North Building," as the man had just denominated it. But Newman had to act fast. There were people who knew what he looked like, people who even should they not be aligned with the man who had tried to kidnap him, would want to take him away and punish him for what he had done to this generally tranquil reptile park.

Newman went through the door that communicated with a back room. There were even more cages in this room—much larger cages—and within them were other snakes and other lizards and other prehistoric animals that he had read about in the *Ensyke*—some of those scholarly descriptions accompanied by illustrations, but most leaving it only to Newman's boyish imagination what such fantastical creatures should look like.

Just such a creature now arrested his eye and halted his step. It was a most curious fellow given to running upon his hind legs back and forth within his long, narrow enclosure, his yellow-contoured mouth open and wide, the folds of his orange neck expanded into a sort of a ruff.

"Frill-necked Lizard," said someone within the room. "*Chlamydoraurus kingii.*"

Newman started. He spun round and found, seated in a shadowy corner of the large room, a little man hunched forward in a chair—a very old man intently observing him through sunken eyes.

"From Australia," the cadaverous man went on. "He's quite popular 'Down Under.' They even put his picture on one of their coins a few years back. Are you hiding from the Black mamba?"

Newman nodded but with only the slightest semblance of conviction.

"Wise choice. They are most deadly. Now, if you wish to take it into your head that I am hiding from the mamba myself, why, you are welcome to the presumption. For I have been ordered to stay fixed to this very spot."

"Why?"

"Why what?"

"Why have you been asked to stay fixed to that spot?"

"Clive—the junior Clive and not the senior Clive who is presently chopping his way through the Amazon jungle—fears that I will go and tangle myself up with that fugitive elapid. They think I'm daft sometimes, these Pellers. Now I ask you, young man: if I were so precipitant as to go draping myself with poisonous fugitive elapids, would I have survived even half of my ninety-four years? Dear me. Now you are but a boy. Do you know what the word 'precipitant' means?"

"It means rash."

"Capital! Who is your teacher, young man?"

"Mr. Chowser."

"I knew a teacher many years ago with the name of Tobias Chowser."

"I have seen his portrait upon the wall of the Chowser School. It was not long ago that I was under the tutelage of his grandson Mr. Alphonse Chowser."

"God bless my weary soul, boy! Are you the one they're looking for—the evasive lad from Dingley Dell?"

Newman nodded and drew closer to the old man. "Unless there is some other. Are you Mr. Rugg?"

"I am in fact."

Newman smiled.

"And how is it that you've come *here*, my boy? Have you truly been so lucky as to have eluded capture thus far?"

Newman nodded again. "I came hither to meet *you*. But I fear that it won't be long before I am taken. The man who fell upon the deadly snake did so because I smote him in the head with a paperweight."

The elderly Mr. Rugg could not help grinning. There were wrinkles upon his face that disappeared altogether and new ones that were formed in the upsweep of his amused lips.

"Caldwell, no doubt. I hear that he and his men have been looking for you."

"People tell you things?"

"I have ears. I have played the doddering fool for quite some time now but I am a very perceptive listener. Now boy, I do not wish to alarm you but there has not been for a great many years even a single immigrant from Dingley Dell—besides myself, of course—who has survived outside our beloved valley for more than a few days. You see, they have got very good—these Tiadaghton people—very good at tracking you all down and disposing of you in the most clean and efficient manner possible. But what you have accomplished, my boy—most exceptional! A capital thing! Yet you're right in assuming that it only increases the likelihood of your capture now. They are a cold-hearted bunch, the Enforcers. Why, the *Chlamydoraurus kingii* over there has warmer blood running through its veins than do the members of that league of determined assassins."

Newman sat himself down upon an empty folding chair situated next to the old man. "Why haven't *you* returned?" he asked his frail companion. "You are only a short journey away."

The old man took his horny and knotted hand and laid it gently upon Newman's head. "There is too much here in the Outland that appeals to me, that enchains my intellectual interest. It has quite spoilt me, I am ashamed to admit. I have the best of both worlds, you know—living amongst the Beyonders but comforted in the knowledge that my homeland lies nestled so very close by. I think that I should like to go home to die when my time is come. Which might come soon. But not this moment."

"There is someone who keeps one foot here and the other in Dingley Dell. Do you know her? She's a nurse."

"Ruth Wolf. Ah, yes. There is a secret society she has formed—the 'Rescuers' they are informally called—she and a few others. They return to Dingley Dell those who have escaped before any harm can be done to them by the likes of Caldwell and his band of gorilla Enforcers. It is quite the meritorious cause they have taken up, and I commend their efforts, but they have, to my knowledge, succeeded only six or seven times since their mission began."

"But alas, Mr. Rugg, all who have returned to Dingley Dell have been taken with that disease which puts them away in Bedlam. I believe that it is called the 'Terror Tremens.'"

"What disease is this? I know of no such disease. Do you see me shrinking with unremitted terror?"

Newman shook his head.

"It must be a means by which to secure their silence. Pray, do not let them diagnose you as such when *you* return home!"

"I shan't let them!" said a very determined Newman Trimmers with a violent shake of the head.

"If I were you, my boy, I would go with Nurse Wolf. I would let her take me home. You will die if you remain on the outside, especially after what you did to the venomous Mr. Caldwell. Now I know that the lovely Rescuer Miss Carpenter who sits behind the cash register in the north building of this place—I know that she is secretly aligned with the rescuing Miss Wolf. And I have no doubt that she has already telephoned Miss Wolf to tell her of your newly discovered whereabouts and what it is that you have done—such a brave young lad you are!—and I suspect that Miss Wolf is already making her way to the Reptilarium. The question is what to do with you between-whiles. I take it that I have convinced you to rendezvous with this woman?"

"Yes. I wish most earnestly to go home and be reunited with my family."

"Smart lad. Now let me think. Soon there will be a number of men—both representatives of the local constabulary and those thugs who do the dirty business of the Tiadaghton Project—who will be combing every inch of this place looking for you. The trick will be to put you in touch with Miss Wolf and *only* Miss Wolf."

As the man sat and thought and gently stroked the white stubble upon his infrequently shorn chin, Newman took a breath to ask, "What is the Tiadaghton Project?"

"It is the very reason for there *being* a Dingley Dell. I haven't time to tell it all to you and there is much that I do not know or scarcely care to know. But I *do* know that they have evolved into a ruthless, diabolical bunch and you are right to go with Miss Wolf to escape their murderous clutches. I will say this much, as well: they are in control of all that goes on in the Dell of Dingley. Tiadaghton is the name of the manipulating machine that pulls the marionette's strings. Now, where to put you, where to put you? Ah!"

Mr. Rugg's eyes grew large within their sockets and his face broke into a wide grin, which attenuated his thin white lips. "Bubbles is feeling much better now and is due to be returned to her permanent habitat by to-morrow. But for to-day, she should be a most suitable companion for you."

"Bubbles?"

"The most docile Boa constrictor you will ever meet. And one of the world's largest: over fourteen feet in length. She's in that very cage over there." Mr. Rugg pointed to a large cage across the room. "Bubbles likes to curl herself in the front and would block any view of you were you to place yourself in the back of her temporary domicile."

"You mean that I am to climb into her cage?"

"Aye."

Newman said nothing else. He knew not at that moment just how it should feel to be sharing so small a space with so very large a snake, no matter how docile she should be.

"It is the perfect place to put you, Newman. And I will go and tell Miss Wolf where you are so that she can come and get you when the coast is clear."

Newman thought about this and then said in a small and reedy voice— not at all the sort of voice befitting a bluff and manly explorer of the Out-land: "What if I were to remain a bit longer here in the Terra Incognita?"

"But did I not hear you to say that you wished to go home to your family?"

"Yes, but what if for a little while longer I were to stay on the Outside, and could do so by taking myself far from this place to some other place where there are not people who are looking for me so that they should kill me?"

"My, but are you not the conflicted little man! Not unlike my own ad-venturous younger self. My boy, I regret to inform you that there are agents of the T-Project throughout the world. You cannot escape their reach no matter how hard you try. I warrant that you will spend your final days skirting shadows and jumping at noises that are made behind you until that last one, which will auger the end of you. It is no way to live. I should know, for I lived in the very same way until such time as it was decided that I was merely a raving fool who could do no one harm. Besides, they were much more lenient with escaped Dinglians in those early days. At worst, they placed us into the state mental institution where I myself have been interned more than once. There is an additional advantage to my case, in that most of these Beyonders think that I do not come from Dingley Dell at all, but have merely created that history for myself from the bits I have heard about it over the years, to give myself a colourful 'character.' You are young and have many, many good years ahead of you, and I would not wish to see you forfeit them in such a foolhardy way. Therefore, do as I advise: go with Miss Wolf when the time comes. But first, let us get you into Bubbles' cage. We have chatted far too long and I am growing concerned that we won't be alone for much longer. Bubbles will like you, and she will be especially fond of you if you come bearing a dead rabbit or two to reward her rejuvenated appetite."

The old man reached out his bony hand to solicit assistance from Newman in rising from his chair at just the moment that both heard the front door to the building being opened. "Sit there for now!" Mr. Rugg whispered with low-toned urgency, whilst signalling Newman to duck beneath a nearby table. "We haven't time yet to—"

Mr. Rugg broke off his dictate as Newman secreted himself beneath the table. The very next moment young Clive Peller appeared in the doorway that joined the two rooms.

"David cornered the mamba in Evans' office. But not before being bitten on the ankle. Where's the kid who was here earlier? He lied about the snake leaving the north building."

Young Clive disappeared into the other room but did not suspend his enquiry and commentary. Along with his voice came the sound of rattling and clinking as Clive prepared another hypodermic of antivenom solution. "I also think he's the one responsible for all this. They said it was some dirty kid in trailer park clothes."

Mr. Rugg walked to the doorway to speak face-to-face with the son of the Reptilarium's owners. "The child was here, Mr. Peller, but he fled only a moment ago."

"Probably for the best. They're gonna arrest his little delinquent ass. The police are already on their way."

"He was a quite frightened—a most frightened little man."

"Now he's going to be a most *incarcerated* little man. Dad's gonna be pissed to the rafters. There are like twenty people out there with all kinds of scrapes and bruises and potential lawsuits dancing like sugarplums in their litigious heads. I can see my inheritance evaporating before my eyes. I could wring the kid's Goddamned neck myself right now."

A moment later young Clive was gone. In the succeeding silence Mr. Rugg returned to Newman, who sat upon the floor with his knees pulled up to his chest, his trembling hands gripping both legs.

"Upsy daisy," said the old man.

"Can I not stay right here?"

"I would not recommend it, Newman. Let us put Bubbles to work to protect you. You're not one of those occasional little boys who is afraid of snakes and snails and puppy-dog tails, now are you?"

Newman shook his head.

"So make haste, lad. We haven't much time."

Bubbles was sluggish. It took a bit of pulling and coaxing to get her to relinquish her preferred spot at the front of the cage long enough for Newman to squeeze and crawl past her. But once the two dead rabbits were produced, her nostrils flared and her tongue flicked, and Newman was well on his way to making himself a new friend. He had to admit that Bubbles was a most beautiful and colourful creature, possessed of ruddy brown skin overlaid with a series of large tan-coloured saddles. Closer to the tail the saddles became progressively lighter before breaking into half rings of cream, these contrasting most sharply with the stark redness at the tip.

"Don't give the dead bunnies to her until you're safely situated behind her. Then she'll know for certain the reason you've come to visit and will be most appreciative."

"And how will she shew her appreciation?" asked Newman, struggling through his fear to bring his question to full voice.

Mr. Rugg smiled. "But is it not obvious? She won't eat you!"

It took scarcely a moment for the old man to rescind his bit of levity, but the damage had been done and Newman's face had blanched.

"Now I know for certain that you're a Dinglian," said Newman as Mr. Rugg closed the door to the cage. "For no Beyonder at such a moment would have jollied me so."

"I jollied you, Newman, to keep your spirits up. Now you sit tight and make no noise that a snake wouldn't make, and enjoy your visit with Miss Bubbles. I'll go off to find Miss Wolf and we will both pray that she'll be able to safely deliver you from this land that does not love the Dinglian."

Chapter the Fifteenth

Gus sat upon the couch next to the plain-looking young woman named Annette and was for a brief period quite happy. The oblong biscuits, which had mint-flavoured chocolate cream sandwiched inside, proved to be a most tasty delicacy, much appreciated by Gus's unsophisticated palate. But this pleasure paled in comparison to that produced by the liquid delight that accompanied it: coffee—pure and unadulterated. And cups and cups of it! Enough, in fact, to make a Dinglian swoon.

"You like it? It's 'Breakfast Blend.' Not too robust. I don't like my coffee *too* bold." Annette kept her head in an inquisitive tilt to one side, waiting patiently for some response from her coffee-gulping and biscuit-bolting matutinal guest.

"I do. I like it very much."

"Glad to hear it. There are people who come here—my mother will back me up on this—who wear strange clothing, just like you're wearing, and are always in a big hurry to be going Heaven-knows-where, until—that is—they get a whiff of the coffee brewing in my Mr. Coffee coffee maker and then suddenly it's like they've just won the lottery! And we'll sit here for an hour or two and drink our coffee in this most perfect and blissful silence until, you know, something finally motivates them to go, but I always think to myself: what a special little moment *that* was!"

Annette dropt her voice to a confidential whisper: "I know you're all aliens, by the way. I'm totally convinced. Nobody else sits on a sofa and drinks coffee like a thirsty man in the desert and scarfs down all my cookies like you've never had a cookie in your life. And, well, it scared me at first. (Go ahead, take the last Milano. Mama can always get more at Wegman's.) It scared me to think that here I was bringing Martians or whatever into my mother's house, and I wondered for a while if it was really a smart thing to be doing, but look: none of you has ever hurt Mama or me and you've never probed us with instruments or anything. In fact, you seem to be quite harmless, you know, just happy to be out of whatever that observational facility is where they've been keeping you—just content to sit here on this sofa and drink coffee and eat Pepperidge Farm products with little ol' me. So I just think, okay, it's nice to have somebody here who isn't my mother, since my disability—my psychological disability, not the fact that I wear corrective braces on my legs—keeps me from leaving the house and ever meeting anyone interesting. I mean it's really, you know, *nice.* Was that T-M-I?"

"T-M-I?"

"Yeah, 'too much information.' Just shut me up if I go on too long. Anyway, after you go—I mean *they* go—I mean, you're all from the same planet, right?—well, in she comes—*her*—my mother—smelling like cow manure—as usual—and standing there in judgement and saying, 'Well, congratulations, Missy, you made a new friend. Another weird friend who will leave and never come back. And what have you accomplished, my lonely crippled daughter? What have you accomplished?' Now Mr. Trimmers, let me ask you this: will you come back and see me again and prove my mother wrong this time?"

Gus nodded. "Once I find my boy, I'll be happy to come for a visit on our trip home."

Gus took a sip of his coffee. He licked his lips and put another spoonful of sugar into the cup to make the taste of the hot beverage even more to his liking.

"You don't mean that, though. It's always the same—really. You come and you drink my coffee and eat up my Mint Milanos and my Orange Milanos and my Genevas and my Tahitis and my Apple Caramel Veronas and my Pirouette French Vanilla Wafers, and after you've had your fill, it's wam-bam thank you, ma'am, and I have to listen to Mama tell me that it had to have been something that *I* did in the end to drive every single one of you away. But I know in my heart that it *wasn't* what I did. I am nothing but the perfect hostess each and every time."

Gus nodded in a way that indicated commiseration. "Perhaps it's simply that the people who come to see you are in rather a hurry to be about their business."

"You're right. I know. I know it isn't me." Annette paused. She said nothing for a moment and then raised herself up from the couch and clomped away with her heavily harnessed legs. "I'll be right back," she said, disappearing into the rear of the house. "I have something I want to get. Enjoy your coffee."

Gus thought about leaving. It would be a good time to do so. But his heart went out to the young woman whose feeble legs were entrapped in metal braces—a woman who resembled so many of the lonely Dinglians who had touched his heart with their empty lives and their inability to achieve comfortable and effective social intercourse. "I'll stay a bit longer, for when am I to have coffee again?" said Gus to himself. "And I'm most curious to learn a thing or two of how the Beyonders live. For example: what is that box with the glass window that sits across from me? What is done with it? I shall ask as soon as she returns."

Gus's hostess did return a minute or so later, with something held mischievously behind her back. Gus didn't ask the question he'd intended. Instead, he sought to know what the strange young woman was hiding.

"You'll find out," she said with a roguish grin. "Now close your eyes."

"I'd rather not."

Annette pouted, her bottom lip protruding and producing a look that intensified the homeliness of her features. "You are hurting my feelings, Mr. Gus Trimmers," she said.

"I'm sorry." Gus rose from his seat. "But I really must be on my way." He tried to sound as casual as he could under the suddenly odd and now somewhat discomfiting circumstances.

"But so soon? You haven't even staid an hour. Most of you aliens stay at least an hour."

"I must find my boy."

"Your boy will keep—wherever he is. He's probably holed up somewhere playing video games. Apparently there aren't video games where you people come from." Annette pulled her hand out from behind her back and dropt a pair of manacles down upon one of the two lamp tables, which flanked the couch. Gus stared at them for a moment without speaking. When he raised his eyes to look again upon his hostess he saw something else—something that she drew from one of the pockets of her frowsy frock. It was a small pistol. The pistol was pointing at Gus.

"What are you going to do?" Gus asked, exerting all of his will to keep himself from stammering.

"Shoot you between the eyeballs if you don't let me handcuff you to this couch."

Gus's gaze darted to the couch. It had flat wooden arms, their finish stained and abraded from general scuffing and perhaps the setting down of thousands of cups of coffee thereupon.

"Sit down. I'm going to shew my Mama that I am fully capable of having a long-term friend."

Gus didn't move. "Would it not stand to reason that when your mother sees me manacled to this sofa, she will not think me under some form of duress?"

"We will tell her it's a game we're playing."

"I'm certain that she'll not perceive it as such."

Annette scratched an itch upon her cheek with the bore of the gun. "You're right. Of course you're right. Then here is what we'll do." Annette opened the drawer contained within the lamp table and deposited the rejected handcuffs therein. Closing the drawer she said, "I will keep this gun in my pocket. And you will return to this couch. And you'll pretend to be that very friend my mother assumes I'm incapable of having—one who stays for longer than an hour and who laughs at my jokes and compliments my hair—which is frequently washed and permanently fragrant though no one ever notices. And we'll do this until she goes to bed and then you'll be free to go."

"And if I do not wish to go along with this ruse, which does not benefit me in the least—?"

"First of all, I'll make you all the coffee you can drink. I'm out of Mint Milanos but we have a couple packages of soft-baked Milk Chocolate Macadamia cookies I've never even tried before—so that'll be a treat for the both us—and look: we'll watch H and H TV."

"What is 'H and H TV'?"

"Home and Hearth Television. And we have a brand new TV to watch it on. My mother just bought it to replace the one she threw the vase at last

Christmas. She'd gotten into one of her 'moods,' and before I knew it, there she was yelling at the TV, 'I don't want Beyoncé at Christmas time! I want Perry Como! What have you bastard TV people done with Perry Como?' Then she picked up the vase and chucked it at the screen. Anyway, this'll be great. It'll get your mind off your lost boy for a little while."

Gus didn't smile, though Annette's obvious hope was that he would subscribe just as enthusiastically to the plan as did she. In a calm and measured voice he said, "What if I were to leave this house at this very moment—squarely against your wishes?"

"Well, then I'd have to shoot you. I wouldn't kill you, because that isn't my style. But I would put a bullet or two into your legs, so you wouldn't get very far, so you might as well park your green alien butt on this couch. On second thought, come into the kitchen with me while I get the Chocolate Macadamia cookies. I'm not letting you out of my sight. And remember: when my mother comes in from her chores to make us lunch, you have to act like we've been friends for years and that you *like* me. Can you do that for me, Mr. Trimmers? If it means you get to keep your legs bullet-free?"

Gus swallowed with difficulty. He tried to say "yes," but the word did not come. He nodded instead and prepared himself for several hours of Outland imprisonment.

❧

At the same time that Gus was following his captor into the kitchen, Gus's son Newman sat in the corner of a very dark cage that was not as large as he would have liked it to be, for two very good reasons: the first was that he could not sit up straight, for even in a seated position, he was too tall for the height of the cage. So he was forced to slouch and curve his back into a position that was a little awkward and which would over time become quite taxing to his neck and spine. The second reason that he wished the cage to be larger was this: Bubbles was curled much closer to him than he would have preferred. In fact, her tail twitched and furled and had a habit of flopping itself directly into Newman's lap. The rabbits had been accepted, then eponymously constricted, then swallowed whole. Now Newman watched as they were being protractedly ingested, the great snake having been restored to her wonted ravenous appetite. Up to now, Bubbles had paid little attention to Newman.

However, the snake was now beginning to grow a little curious about her fellow tenant. Although it had been Newman who had served her dinner, yet she eyed him with a raised head, as if he were someone with whom she had suddenly become unfamiliar. And Newman was called upon by circumstance to do everything in his power to keep from crying out in the sort of abject fear that none but the bravest of souls would involuntarily suffer. She does not plan to eat me or even to bite me, Mr. Rugg has assured me, Newman thought to himself. But she is most menacing in every aspect. Newman took a deep breath, which brought into his lungs the stench of the soiled cage. He coughed. And yet what is the alternative? Death most assuredly at the hands of the Enforcers! Newman's own right hand now fell upon a small pile of bone and fur which constituted the regurgitated indigestibles from one of Bubbles' former meals. He wiped the hand upon his trowsers and reached out and petted the head of his reptilian companion and tried to make the best of things, though his heart was not in it.

Minutes later Newman could hear that people had entered the building. It was much too soon to assume that Mr. Rugg had succeeded in his efforts to put him together with the rescuing Miss Wolf. There was a little grunting and some low talking and then the conversation became louder as men entered the room in which Newman had been protectively installed.

"The empty cage at the bottom," said one of the men. "Careful now, Micks. That mamba's in a pretty lousy mood."

"I swear to Christ, Evans, I thought Animal Control was gonna chop her head off right then and there. Grey Lady, you don't know how close you came to extermination."

"We may still have to euthanize her. She isn't the cuddly cutie that Bubbles is, but can you blame her—I mean just minding her own business when some humanoid asshole drops right down on top of her? Hello, Bubbles, you beauty. Getting better I hear."

Newman receded as best as he was able into the darkness of the cage and held himself very still and very quiet. He fought the urge to cough again, the suppression making the urge grow ever more importunate, while a man stood before the cage and talked pretty-polly nonsense to Newman's coiled co-boarder. Newman tucked his head behind his knees to make himself as small as possible, and prayed that he would not be seen.

Nor heard—the latter proving a far more difficult thing to effect. No longer able to contain his cough, Newman emitted a double hack into the fabric of his trowsers. Though muffled, the sound nonetheless reached the ears of at least one of the two men standing hard by.

"Well, Bubbles isn't *totally* well, Evans. I just heard her cough."

"You idiot. Snakes don't cough."

"How do *you* know? You're not an ophiologist. You're a batrachianist."

"Come on—the police still have a few more questions."

"I tell you—Miss Bubbles coughed."

"Yeah, *right.*"

The voices died away, the outer door opened and closed, and Newman Trimmers allowed himself to cough and cough, now without consequence. Bubbles considered her noisy cage-mate for a moment and then settled herself down for a postprandial snooze.

In the north building, Mr. Rugg was now speaking to the woman named Angela Carpenter who sat behind the admission counter. All around the old man were employees of Clive and Clare's Reptilarium clearing away the scattered remnants of the Black mamba's previous home, other employees escorting frightened families to the front door, medical men patching up victims of the earlier mêlée, and several uniformed police officers asking questions and writing down the answers on little pads.

"I am looking for Miss Wolf," said Mr. Rugg to Angela, who seemed distracted and not very attentive to her enquirer.

"Miss Wolf: have you seen her?" he reframed his request.

"She isn't here," said Angela, looking about. "Somebody said there's another snake on the loose. Is it true?"

Mr. Rugg shook his head. "Calm yourself, dear girl. There was only the one snake and it has been apprehended. The crisis is past."

Angela sat herself down and waved a floppy book in front of her reddened face to calm and ventilate herself. "I'm quitting this damned job. It gives me nightmares. And now they're only gonna get worse. I wish I was still selling beauty products."

"Would you know, Miss Davenport, if Miss Wolf is on her way?"

"How would *I* know?"

"You're friends with her, are you not?"

"Well…yes, but I don't—"

Angela was interrupted by a policeman who set a cracked paperweight down upon the glass counter that separated her from Mr. Rugg. "Is this what the kid used to assault the victim?"

"That's it, I think," said Angela.

"And where is he right now—the assailant?"

"I have no idea," Angela replied. "He could be anywhere by now. Who knows?"

The policeman—a young blond-haired man with a full moustache— turned now to Mr. Rugg. "Did you see it happen? Did you see the kid hit Mr. Caldwell?"

The old man shook his head. "I was in the infirmary." Mr. Rugg thought it best to simply leave it at that, although he could not have said anything else if he had desired to, for at just that moment Ruth Wolf entered the building through the front door, accompanied by her colleague Mr. Phillips. Mr. Rugg knew them both: Miss Wolf, the nurse; and Mr. Phillips, the jeweller. Years ago Rugg had sold some ancient Dinglian jewelry to Phillips and had done so without raising even the slightest suspicion. Perhaps it was luck or perhaps it was simple inattention, but there was also the good chance that it was an intentional accommodation of his secret on the part of the jeweller.

Miss Wolf and Miss Davenport interchanged looks that were insufficiently expository given the presence of the policeman and the elderly oddity named Rugg, and for a moment no one knew just what to do since there were things that needed to be said and couldn't. Finally, the officer was called away and Rugg quickly interposed in a pregnant undertone, "Miss Wolf, it is good that you are here. For I am suffering another bout of sciatica for which I should like to seek your medical opinion."

"I'm not a doctor, Mr. Rugg. You should see a doctor."

"But I am certain that once you addressed the issue—you and no one else—you would clap your hands together and say, 'Ah, what we have here is a brand *new man*! Yes, yes, a brand *new man*!"

Ruth Wolf looked at Mr. Rugg with an abstract expression that lasted no longer than a second or two, when Rugg's double meaning became completely lucid. "A *new man*, you say?"

"Oh, yes. But you must see to it alone."

"But Mr. Phillips is my most able and trustworthy assistant. May I not bring him along with me?"

"Does he subscribe wholly to your methods?"

"I do. I most certainly do," struck in Mr. Phillips, having quickly got the gist of the contrivance himself.

"Then let us go to the infirmary," said Mr. Rugg, "which is the best place for the examination."

Miss Wolf turned to her friend Angela. "Miss Davenport: Mr. Rugg and Mr. Phillips and I will be in the infirmary. But it isn't necessary for you to tell anyone."

The young woman behind the counter nodded. Then she whispered, "God bless you and good luck."

The three were quickly off and away—as briskly as could a threesome go with two of its number of advanced years. As they passed the two medical men who were tending to the half-delirious Mr. Caldwell upon the floor, the patient lifted his head and caught a glimpse of them and gave a startled look that would give one to think that he perceived another Black mamba making its serpentine way to put fresh fangs into his flesh. "Easy, easy," said the medical man, as he and his companion began to lift Caldwell onto a litter.

"We've really got to hurry!" urged Mr. Phillips. "As soon as Caldwell gets his wits back, he'll be in touch with the other goons."

As the three made their way through the rear door and out onto the walkway of the outdoor park, Ruth Wolf said, "Phillips—let Rugg and me go on to the infirmary. You go out the back gate and then bring the car around to the employee parking lot. Have it waiting for us there. And hurry, Phillips. There must be a dozen cops already out here looking for him."

Mr. Phillips nodded and hastened away, huffing and puffing down a diverging path.

Once inside the infirmary, Mr. Rugg led Miss Wolf to the room where Bubbles and Newman Trimmers sat in close grudging companionship. Mr. Rugg unlatched the cage door. One could barely discern, in the darkness, an eleven-year-old boy smiling broadly with relief, a large Boa constrictor now twined indifferently about his shoulders and under one arm.

As Newman was stepping from the cage, the three heard a loud rapping on the now locked front door to the infirmary. "Go! Hurry!" Mr. Rugg enjoined his two fellow conspirators as each glanced fearfully in the direction of the sound. "Dear boy, I will pray most fervently for your safe return."

"Come with us, Rugg," said Miss Wolf, taking Newman by the hand.

Mr. Rugg shook his head. "It isn't my time yet to return. But I'll be back someday, you may depend on it. Be off with you now."

"Thank you," said Newman glancing over his shoulder at the hunched little man. "I'm glad that I came to see you."

"And I was glad to see *you*, my boy. It's been years since I've had the good fortune to see one of my kinsmen. God go with you." Mr. Rugg removed his eyeglasses to put a rumpled handkerchief to his moistened eyes.

There came now another series of knocks upon the door, and then the rattling sound of a key turning in the lock. Mr. Rugg hurriedly re-affixed his spectacles and led Miss Wolf and Newman into yet a third room, where the old man opened a second door—this one leading to the outside. Carefully he peeped out to make sure that it was safe for the woman and boy to proceed. Seeing no one about, he waved the two off and away. He watched as they darted behind a stand of trees and then past a collection of picnicking tables and then disappeared altogether behind a nondescript out-building.

Mr. Rugg returned to the middle room to discover three policemen in the company of young Clive Peller, the trio of law officers standing frozen in their tracks in the presence of one of the world's largest Boa constrictors, free from her cage and moving heavily across the floor to greet them. "Mr. Rugg, you senile old fool!" bawled Junior Clive. "You've let Bubbles out of her cage. Holster your guns, officers. She won't hurt you." Clive Peller waved the three policemen over to help him lift the gentle reptilian giant back into her temporary cell. Two of the young men took a hesitant step forward, whilst the third stood quivering in a puddle of his own making.

Chapter the Sixteenth

Gus sat next to the crippled woman named Annette. The gun was now in the house-frock pocket that was closest to him, so that every now and then as she resituated herself upon the couch he could feel the hardness of the weapon against his leg.

I can bolt from this house, and more than likely she will not have sufficient time to get to the door or the window and take a good shot at me, Gus thought, but there is also the chance that a bullet from her gun will make adequate purchase with my body and I will be winged or felled or worse. I must therefore resign myself to my temporary fate and pray that this insane young Beyonder woman will keep her word and release me when her mother retires. It is not such a terrible thing to be endured, for I am learning much about the Outland through observing the moving pictures in this magic box. Does it not serve me as a true, illuminative window to this world about which I am so woefully unfamiliar?

It was now noontime and Gus and Annette were viewing a little play through the window in the box—the last in a series of plays that kept repeating the same story with different characters. The name of each of the little half-hour plays was invariably "Home Hunters," and each new play gave a couple who, assisted by another man or woman—usually older and more nattily drest than the couple—visited a series of three prospective lodgings through which they would stroll and offer commentary. In strong Beyonder vernacular speech they would say what was good and what was bad about the rooms through which they glided. If there was a yard in the back, they would note how conducive it should be for the rompings of their children or their pet dogs. At the end of each play the couple would come to a mutual decision about what house they should like to buy. Then in the epilogue, which followed a set of interjected appeals for the purchase of various enigmatic household and food items, one would see the couple happily ensconced in their new home—the house having been freshly furnished and the kitchen counters having been newly covered with granite rock.

"It's rather monotonous, isn't it—this series of plays that come out of your magic television box?" asked Gus, the first words he had spoken since telling a tall man entering a room with a low ceiling to mind his head.

"It's a 'Home Hunters' marathon. If you're tired of it, we can watch something else." Annette sneezed. She took out a little paper tissue from a cardboard box and blew her nose. "My mother gave me her cold. This sucks. I hate being sick. So you don't have TV in this Dingley Dell place you come from?" Gus shook his head.

"Then what do you do for entertainment? Do people get together for laser sabre fights? Do you sit around and play holographic space chess or something? I'm trying to imagine what floats an alien's boat."

"I don't come from a pretermundane place, Miss DeLove. I come from just over that ridge. Dingley Dell. It is the valley just behind those mountains. Dinglians don't come from Mars."

"Then why do you look the way you do? Why do you ask me what every other word I say means? Is this a crazy place—this Dingley Dell? Is it full of crazy people?"

"I'm afraid, Miss DeLove, that I can't tell you anything about my home that you would understand, for the same reason that I am slowly coming to only a very limited understanding of the world *you* live in."

Annette DeLove laughed ruefully and sneezed again and then shook her head. "It doesn't take long for a person to understand *my* world. This is it. These four walls you see around you. I don't leave this house. Just like you people don't leave your valley—at least as a rule. We're alike in that one big way."

"It takes courage for us to leave our home. None of us really knows what to expect out here."

"I guess you didn't expect an agoraphobic cripple with a head cold waving her gun at you and forcing you to watch a 'Home Hunters' marathon, did you?"

"I cannot say that I did."

"Would you like another macadamia nut cookie?"

Gus shook his head. He glanced at the television window. A significant exchange between a young house-hunting woman and a young house-hunting man was transpiring as follows:

YOUNG WOMAN: I hate that colour. What is it—magenta?

YOUNG MAN: We can always paint over it.

YOUNG WOMAN: I like the crown moulding, though.

YOUNG MAN: The crown moulding is nice.

YOUNG WOMAN: I think it's fuchsia. That colour. It gags me.

The older woman who is escorting the couple through the house now interposes.

OLDER WOMAN: Would you like to see the bonus room?

Gus had become so engaged in the house-hunting adventures of this particular couple, each of whom had a pleasant voice and spoke in a softer and less nasally accent than did the woman sitting next to him (better to assist him in devising an unobtrusive accent for himself that would make it easier for him to fit in), that he didn't hear the older woman—*Mama* or Mrs. DeLove—enter the room from the back of the house.

"I don't have time to make lunch," she said, slightly winded. "Gloria just called me on my cell. Aunt Lucille's taken a turn for the worse. I have to go to Harrisburg, if I want to see her before—" Mrs. DeLove couldn't bring herself to finish her sentence. "I'm going to pack my overnight bag, because I probably won't be back until to-morrow. I'll get Bill Corley from down the road to drive over and tend to the—Annette, are you even listening to me?"

Annette's own eyes had not left off staring into the windowed television box. Even as Gus was able to pull his own gaze away and look upon his older hostess, Annette's eyes remained deliberately fixed on the glass.

"What is *wrong* with you, Annette? Your Great Aunt Lucille is dying and you won't even give me a minute's worth of your attention?"

"I heard every word you said, Mama," replied Annette sourly. "You've been in the barn for over two hours. Have you not noticed that Mr.

Trimmers is still here?"

Mrs. DeLove sucked in a great amount of air and then blew it all out. "What of it?"

"You give me no credit, *no credit at all, Mama.* I'm not a pariah. There are some people like Mr. Trimmers who come here and actually stay and have a good time with me."

"I have no time for this nonsense. I have to pack."

Mrs. DeLove betook herself to her own chambers and could be heard for the next twenty minutes rustling and clattering about and talking to herself in angry tones. She emerged at just the moment that a new couple in a brand new play were talking about how important it was to have a large kitchen for the purpose of entertaining. Gus wondered how Outlanders entertained themselves in a kitchen. Did they juggle saucepans and baking dishes?

"I'm going now, Annette. You'll be all right while I'm gone?"

"You've left me by myself before."

"Will Mr. Trimmers be leaving soon?"

"I don't know. He might be staying for dinner."

"The last two of those Marie Callender Salisbury steak dinners are in the freezer." Mrs. DeLove walked over and touched her daughter on the head in an understatement of affection. Then she walked out the front door with a valise-like bag in hand. A few moments later there came the sound of the woman's horseless carriage chugging away.

Gus started. "What is that sound?"

"It's the car. You know cars. You've seen cars on TV. What do you Digglians use to get around?"

"Dinglians. Not Digglians. We walk, for the most part. There are horses and hansoms for those who can afford them. The very rich have their own phaetons and cabriolets. I cannot stay for dinner. I must commence my search for my son."

Annette's expression hardened. She rubbed a tissue against her rubicund nose. "I thought we'd agree that you weren't leaving until to-night."

"But you had said that I could leave when your mother retired for the evening. And now she has left altogether to be with her aunt. This nullifies the original agreement."

"Look, buddy, I'm not letting you run off and leave me here alone. You have to stay until Mama comes back."

"That would be impossible. I must look for my boy."

"Your boy is *dead*, you alien moron! They don't let people like you wander around after you've left that valley. They pick you up. I've seen it. I've seen them picking up Digglians right here on this very road. *I'm* the only thing keeping *you* alive right now, so I'm actually doing you a favour by holding you here."

Gus had been so caught up in Mrs. DeLove's departure and the chance that he too might at last be permitted to leave, and was so distracted by an advertisement coming forth from inside the magic television box for something called Depend undergarments (which were reputedly successful at absorbing a copious amount of blue water), that he was not aware of Annette's furtive retrieving of the steel manacles and her deftly snapping one of the cuffs round her left wrist with a click. Then there was a second click. Of this one, Gus was quite aware.

He stared down at the handcuffs that now banded him to this most assuredly disturbed young woman. A wave of hopeless despair engulfed him. "*Why?* Why have you done this to me?"

"You won't believe me, but I'll tell you anyway. It's because I like you." Annette DeLove shrugged and grinned like a bashful schoolgirl. "And because I'll bet you that after a while you'll come to see that I'm not such a bad person either and that we can actually have a pretty nice time together."

Terror suddenly struck at Gus's heart. "But I've already spent time with you—more time than I ever intended. I don't believe that my boy is dead. It's merely something you're saying to keep me here. I know little of your world, Miss DeLove, but I have a very strong sense that you're not being truthful with me. I beseech you to let me go."

Annette shook her head. "Let's find out what this couple plans to do with that hideous popcorn ceiling. Then you can come and help me make lunch. Do you like pimento cheese?"

Phillips was driving Ruth Wolf's horseless carriage. Ruth Wolf sat next to him. Seated behind the two was Newman. Ruth turned her head to address Newman over her shoulder.

"It won't be long now before we reach the place where we can start our climb up to the top of the ridge. I have a key that unlocks all the wickets.

Did you have any idea that I could get you home so fast?"

Newman shook his head. It was difficult to fix his eyes on the nurse; there was too much flying by his window to draw his interest.

Now Phillips spoke: "Newman. How did you get past the fence?"

"The fence?"

"Which surrounds the Dell. How did you get over it, son? We've both been wondering."

"Oh. One of my mates at school said that—what's *that*?"

"What?"

"The tall—"

"It's a cellular telephone tower. So people can speak to one another on the telephone without the need for a land-line."

"Oh. One of my mates said that if you follow the fence long enough you will come to one of the places where someone has made a cut in it. It took me a while but I did find just such a place. It was not a very big opening, but I was still able to squeeze through it."

"Tiadaghton Security falling down on the job," commented Phillips following a few comical tuts of the tongue.

"What is *that*, Newman?" asked Ruth, pointing to a piece of paper held in Newman's hand.

"I wanted you to have it to see what you could make of it. It came from the woman who tried to take me from the Ryersbach house." Newman handed the honey-sticky paper to Ruth. "I can't make much of it myself."

Ruth Wolf read the paper. Here is what it said:

THE TIADAGHTON PROJECT
175 Fifth Avenue • New York, NY 10010

Classified communication

From: Brooks Moseley
To: Blake Sorich-Ward
Subject: Congratulations!
Date: May 15, 2003

Dodged another bullet. I must commend your staff on behalf of the Flatiron Group for all the hard work they put into getting the renewal on the Double Pine River Watershed Protection Order to keep the waters of that endangered river pure and potable for one more year. We sweat this out every winter and every spring your people come through with flying colors. We didn't think you Harrisburg folks were going to pull it out this year especially with Langheart steeling itself (pun intended) to ram through its purchase in a matter of weeks. Why the reprieve—so goes the argument—for a few protected pickerel and white-tailed deer when the river's only going to be permanently polluted in two or three years anyway? (If the Double Pine folks only knew who else was drinking out of that ill-fated river—and here's a hint: they aren't little green men with antennas!)

But for their remaining two months (can we really be that close to D-Day?), the residents of that valley (I'm thinking now of the two-footed human variety) will have crystal clean, drinkable water thanks to your efforts and the continued kindness of the state's Department of Environment Protection. You should all be proud. Be sure to send regional director Yancy a big bouquet of something floral and ferny! I will reimburse.

cc: South Williamsport office; Milton office Attn: Greg Cobb, Jerri Brentano, Luis Medina

Ruth stared at the piece of paper in her now quivering hand, her face suddenly overshadowed by dark concern. She looked at Phillips whose expression carried the same gravity as her own. "Pull over," she said to her colleague.

Phillips slowed the vehicle and brought it to a stop upon the shoulder of the highway. He disengaged the engine with a turn of the inserted key.

"Newman, it is important for Mr. Phillips and me to consult with one another in private. Please trust that we continue to have your best interests at heart, but this is not a conversation that we're at liberty to have in your presence."

"If it is about Dingley Dell, then I have a right to hear it. Dingley Dell is my home."

"Dingley Dell has become my home, as well, Newman. I care deeply about what happens to her."

"What did the paper say? What do they mean about the water?"

Now Phillips interposed. "The memo concerns provisions by which your River Thames remains free of pollution. Sit here, son. Mizz Wolf and I will speak for a moment and then we'll be on our way again."

The two rescuers opened their respective doors and alighted from the vehicle. Newman folded his arms, knowing that he had no choice in the matter. Something was to be discussed that he was certain concerned him greatly, concerned everyone who lived in the Dell. But it wasn't for him to know about. He wondered now if he should ever have given the sticky piece of paper to Miss Wolf. Yet, did not Miss Wolf and Mr. Phillips save him from imminent capture at the Reptilarium? And were they not taking great pains to return him safely to Dingley Dell? Surely they were sincere in stating that they had his best interests at heart. By extension, they must certainly have the best interests of all Dinglians at heart as well. Newman Trimmers had learnt not to trust anyone. Now he must learn how to trust again, this moment posing a particularly pressing challenge.

The two Beyonders took several steps away from the carriage, so that their voices could not be overheard.

Miss Wolf put her hand upon Phillips' arm. "Farber lied to me. She told me they wouldn't even begin to discuss a possible termination date for the Project until late next year, and even that was 'worst case scenario.' What's going on, Phillips?"

"It looks like the financing package for Langheart came in earlier than expected. And they probably aren't willing to sit on the money for the next several years while everyone dithers over what to do about Dingley Dell."

"So you think that this woman is telling the truth about what's going to happen next month?"

"Would *she* have a reason to lie? I'd put more stock in an earlier time frame than a more protracted one. You know that Tiadaghton can move pretty quickly when it needs to."

"But three weeks, Phillips! How do you evacuate 11,000 people in three weeks? And where do you put them all? The Project's land holdings in the South Pacific couldn't accommodate even half of them."

"Maybe they aren't planning on relocating them, Ruth."

Ruth didn't respond. She stared at Phillips, her expression frozen in disbelief.

"They kill escapees, Ruth. They've been doing it for thirty years. What makes you think they aren't at this moment putting some plan into place to exterminate all the rest of the Dinglians in their beds? I wouldn't think that such a thing should be all that difficult to pull off. We're both assuming that the memo refers to helping the Dinglians avoid potential health issues—the kind that arise when people drink from an adulterated water source. All right, now I'm going to ask you to consider an alternative interpretation of that memo. What if they're keeping that water pure and unpolluted to lull the Dinglians into thinking that all is well in the wells of the Dell? Until such point as the Project decides to release whatever deleterious agent into the river will work the quickest?"

"And those lucky enough *not* to drink the poisoned water—?"

"They'll be taken out in some other way—their fewer numbers now being far less problematic."

"It's monstrous."

Phillips nodded. "The final solution. Genocide on a smaller scale than the historical norm, but genocide all the same."

"Jesus, Phillips." Ruth Wolf's body suddenly went limp. She clutched the arm of her friend. He wrapt his other arm round her waist to steady her. Her next words came with difficulty: "And the bodies, Phillips. What happens to all the bodies? Langheart wouldn't be too pleased to know that it was building its vaunted, state-of-the-art steel mill upon a killing field."

"They'll no doubt be buried somewhere. You can't burn that many bodies without making a stink you could smell all the way to Scranton. But the Tiadaghton has been quite efficient in almost everything else they've sought to do, so covering up their dirty work probably shouldn't pose too great a challenge. It amazes me that Dingley Dell has survived for as long as it has with such an engine of evil behind it. In spite of high level governmental complicity, you'd think that somebody by now would have—I don't know, Ruth. Maybe it's time for us at least to *talk* about—"

"It can't be *me*, Phillips. Not given the situation I'm in right now."

"Yet you've been a fairly important cog in their machine. Your voice could prick up a few ears."

Ruth shook her head. "I'm not ready to prick up a few ears, Phillips. I just want to keep doing my job—keep wobbling along for as long as they'll let me. They have my number, *our* number, you know they do, but they don't pull me out. So I'm not going to pull myself out. There are too many things I haven't checked off my 'to do' list yet." Ruth shook her head pensively. "By the way, I'm not so big a cog as you think I am. I wasn't

informed about how and when Dingley Dell will meet its end. This decision was made entirely without me. In fact, Phillips, I believe that I am fast
becoming an obsolescent aspect to this entire operation. Who cares how
scrupulously I keep the Returnees drugged and muzzled, when my job becomes defunct in three short weeks?"

Ruth took a deep breath. "I therefore have no reason not to do what I
had intended all along: return Newman to his family and give him some
time with them before Towlinson and that quack Fibbetson come to collect
him and haul him off to Bedlam."

Phillips shook his head. "No can do."

"He has a right to see his family. It's what I promised him."

"You promised him that you would take him back to Dingley Dell.
You never mentioned putting him right into the arms of his mother and
father, Ruth."

"You're playing with words."

"You can't let him see his family, Ruthie. You can't let him see anyone
but the intake clerk at Bedlam. No one but that small complicitous cadre at
the Hospital can know that he's come back."

"What if we get Newman to promise that he won't talk about anything
he's seen out here?"

Phillips arched an eyebrow. "You think that boy could keep his trap
shut for two minutes? Anyway, Towlinson, Feenix and the others—sooner
or later they're going to know that he's back. And eventually they're going
to find out that it was you what 'brung 'im.' You saw the look on Caldwell's
face at the Reptilarium. He knows it wasn't mere coincidence that you and
I shewed up there the same morning as Newman. He knows that Newman
is your new charity project. Well, it strongly mitigates your culpability in
Newman's return if *you* are the one to deposit him in Bedlam. It'll even
earn you a few brownie points. You opposed the Project by not letting
Caldwell put a bullet in Newman's head but you helped the Project in a
way, by placing him with the other Limbo Returnees."

Ruth nodded.

"Look, honey: you want to get permanently out of Dingley Dell yourself, right?"

Another nod.

"And I take it you still plan to rescue your hospital friend—the one
you went and fell foolishly in love with. You're still planning to take your

beloved Bevan with you."

Ruth nodded once more.

"Then don't muck it up by letting Newman talk. He breathes even a few words about what he's been through out here, there'll be an armed militia of pissed and peeved, pitchfork-wielding Dinglians perched on the Summit as of to-morrow morning. You know that the natives have started getting restless, honey. The Bashaws are getting careless and people have started asking questions. Throwing a loner Returnee like Walter Skewton into Bedlam is one thing but a boy like Newman…"

"But maybe they *need* to get restless, Phillips. Maybe that gives them a fighting chance. They won't be sitting ducks for whatever the Project plans to do with them."

"Right. And then whatever genocidal plans the Project has in store will go into effect immediately—as of right then and there, Ruthie. You and Bevan die along with all the rest of them. I never had you pegged for a martyr, honey."

"Martyrdom might be preferable to spending the rest of my life knowing that I saved my own ass at the expense of everyone else in the valley. I know you feel the same way or you wouldn't have spent the last two years of *your* life helping me save some of these runaways. The Dinglians didn't ask for this life. And they sure as hell don't deserve the death that you think is being devised for them."

"Then I suggest you find a small and circumspect group within the Dell, unconnected with the Petit-Parliament or any of the other Bashaws. Go to them. Explain what's happening. Explain the consequences if they move too swiftly. But also explain to them the consequences should they choose not to act at all."

"There *is* a group that I know of—they meet every other week. It's ostensibly a poetry society, but I don't think it's poetry they're discussing with one another, given the make-up of their membership. I don't know the exact purpose of their meetings—maybe they're researching the true history of the Dell, rather than the official bogus version. Maybe they're planning some class uprising against the excesses of the Petit-Parliament. But I'm pretty sure they'd be the bunch most willing to listen to me—to take seriously what I could tell them."

"And in the meanwhile, you'll send Newman to Bedlam to buy yourself some time?"

Ruth Wolf cast a worried glance back at my nephew.

"It breaks my heart, too, Ruth. To have survived as he has in this forbidden place, and then to be put away in Bedlam for all his pluck. But you can't lose sight of the bigger picture."

Newman wasn't looking at Ruth Wolf and Phillips anymore. His gaze had been captured by a pencil-trail of manufactured cloud high up in the sky. Newman had always wondered what they were, these strange clouds, and now he knew. Phillips had told him. Phillips had told him a great deal about terrestrial man and his ability now to reach up and touch the sky.

Newman Trimmers had always wanted to touch the sky. It is not so strange a wish for a valley-bound boy to have.

Darkness had settled in, and it was difficult at first to find the head of the trail that would take the three up the eastern wooded ridge. In time, though, it was located, and Phillips and Ruth Wolf shined their hand torches upon the ground to light the way. The trail branched off in two directions: one spur went west through the thickest part of the woods and terminated at a wicket. Here one entered the Dell without fanfare and sometimes even a bit covertly through the eastern perimeter. The other spur meandered northward to join the higher Northern Ridge where it ended at the Summit of Exchange. Ruth and Phillips had considered taking the first spur, for it was certainly the far less-traveled of the two, but there was an important reason that they could not—a reason to be conveyed shortly.

In addition to the fence that girdled the whole of the Dell of Dingley, there was another equally oppressive fence that separated those who managed the Project from the casually curious or deliberately prying Outlander. It was through this enclosure that Gus had come down from the Summit upon his own journey into the Outland, little knowing how lucky he was not to be detected by any of the Tiadaghton personnel who worked in that compound, generally a hornet's nest of activity, except for those quiescent mornings in which even a guardhouse could become a dormitory.

But Gus's son Newman hadn't taken either route on his trip out of Dingley Dell. Instead, he had broken through the encircling Dinglian fence in a place far distant from the Tiadaghton Compound. The path that Ruth Wolf and Mr. Phillips and Newman now took was unfamiliar to Newman, though the look of the thick, crowding trees nonetheless comforted him, the smells and the soft muted sounds of the nocturnal forest reminding him that he was drawing close to home.

These woods were once closely and heavily patrolled, but it was simpler and cheaper now to track down a Dinglian *after* he had fully left the vicinity of the valley and to deal with him upon that terrain. For once in the Outland, Dinglians were, as the reader has no doubt observed, quite conspicuous in their appearance and address. It wasn't easy for one of Newman's countrymen to hide who he was from an Outlander—especially from an Outlander whose job it was to make him disappear forever.

Even though the woods were supposedly empty now of threats, Newman did not let down his guard, and continued to worry that men like Caldwell might still be in pursuit of him—that even in this late hour of his rescue there were those who sought him to do terrible harm to him for having brazenly walked amongst them. Newman would not feel completely safe until the three had reached the Summit and he could see his welcoming homeland spread out below.

The climb was slow and quite taxing in places where the ascent was difficult for an old man such as Phillips, or even for a boy and young woman with insufficient illumination to guide their way. On more than one occasion, Phillips, who had been leading the other two to keep the pace of his companions in line with his aged gait, stopt and remarked that he had lost the path altogether, and some time was spent in reclaiming it. On another occasion the climb had so tired and winded the septuagenarian that Ruth Wolf was compelled to ask if it would not be better for him to end his escort and suffer Newman and her to make their way up to the Summit without his companionship.

Phillips shook his head. "I'm not leaving until I see the two of you standing safe and sound on the top of that damned Northern Ridge," Phillips had vowed in a wheezing underbreath that was, nonetheless, easily heard by Newman's keen ears.

"But I'm also worried about your losing the trail on your way back down from the Summit," responded Ruth Wolf gently.

"So I lose the trail—what of it, Ruth? I'll park myself on a rock and wait until morning when it's light."

The climbers pushed onward and upward and held to the path through the woods and toward the Summit, which they eventually gained later that night. The Summit of Exchange was untenanted. Phillips had privately feared that he might find one of Caldwell's Enforcers waiting there, or any of the Tiadaghton men, for that matter, who would put a last-minute finish to Newman. But no one was there. Ruth Wolf had won her battle for Newman's life. She had convinced the Project's decision-makers that it wasn't worth anyone's time to kill Newman now. This was how it generally worked—the cat and mouse game with the Project.

Newman released a little satisfied sigh to find himself so close to home. He looked out over the twinkling valley. It was still too early for all but the youngest Dinglians to be abed there. What were his parents doing? he wondered. Was his father reading the newspaper or working an acrostic? Was his mother darning a stocking or playing patience with her cards? Were they thinking of him, wondering what *he* was doing in that same moment?

Newman also peered into the darkness close by, looked round him at this spot he had never visited before. There was the faint outline of the gazebo, and there were the warehouses, and over there, the large iron wicket through which the Beyonder tradesmen came fortnightly with their Beyonder foods and dry goods—meagre offerings when compared with all the things he had seen for himself in the Outland. Newman was eager to tell his mother and father of the discrepancy that existed between what was given to Dinglians upon the Summit and what they could easily obtain for themselves if they lived in the Outland: boxes that talked and played music, other boxes that allowed one to speak to a person over a great distance, onion rings and salty meat sandwiches and horseless carriages that moved like lightning, and all the orange juice one could drink. There was a great deal more that young Newman could scarcely wait to tell his parents and to tell anyone else who would hear him. For he had returned without any sign of the Terror Tremens having taken hold of him and surely would not be consigned within the imprisoning walls of Bedlam.

It only stood to reason.

"Be quick, Ruth," Newman now heard Phillips say behind his back, and the boy assumed, most naturally, that the old jeweller was referring to the process of returning Newman to his family.

There followed in that next instant the sound of Ruth's medical satchel being snapped open and then a rustle and a clink and a click. Newman turned to see a medical syringe clutched in the nurse's hand.

"What is that?" asked the boy.

"An injection you must have before you enter the Dell."

Phillips rolled up Newman's sleeve. Nurse Wolf dabbed at Newman's arm with a wet cotton ball and then inserted the needle. Within only a few seconds Newman began to feel sleepy. "Is it the shot that's making me drowsy?"

"Yes, it is," replied Miss Wolf.

"Must I be drowsy?"

"No, Newman. You must be fully asleep."

A moment later the strong sedative took effect on Newman's brain. Phillips caught the boy as his legs splayed out from under him and his head dropt back.

"There is a good boy," said Ruth Wolf sadly. "There is a very good boy."

Ruth and her fellow Rescuer beheld my unconscious nephew for a moment in mutual silence. Then they lifted him up and put him into a barrow. "Are you sure that I can't help you get him down the ridge?" asked Phillips.

Ruth Wolf shook her head. "I'll be fine." She took out her little box telephone and pressed several of its tiny numbered buttons. "I just paged Towlinson. He'll be waiting for me with the van when I get to the bottom."

Ruth Wolf looked at the crumpled body folding in upon itself to fit into the tight barrow. "I feel like shit, Phillips."

"Double that for me, Ruthie."

"Call me by my real name. It's been ages since I've heard anybody say it."

"Megan," said Phillips, taking his friend and fellow renegade into a warm and close embrace. "Little Megan Hester. I can remember all the way back to when you were just a baby."

"I feel just as helpless right now."

"I know, sweetie. I know."

Another moment passed. "I should go," said Ruth Wolf, finally pulling herself away and sucking in an emotional sniffle. "Watch your step on *your* way down, Phillips."

The jeweller nodded. "Be safe, Wolf," he said. "As terrible a thing as it is to place a boy into that Victorian madhouse, it's still better than what might have happened to him on the outside."

"Yes, I know. And I'll make sure to keep an eye on him."

"He goes right to the cock-loft?"

Ruth shook her head. "To the basement first. There's a holding room there. That's where we'll keep him for the first couple of days—until we can figure out which of the bensodizepines are going to work best on him. Then we'll put him with the other Limbo Returnees. Only a few staffers at the hospital even know about the room. And it's really not such a bad place. There's quite a collegiality among the inmates, since almost all of them are members of a pretty prestigious club."

"Those who have been to the Outland and beheld its wonders," said Phillips with a nod.

"Beheld them all to themselves. Goodbye, old man."

"Goodbye, Meg."

The two parted. Phillips stood and watched for a moment as Ruth Wolf turned her covered wheelbarrow southward and began down the Brokers' Trail that led to the valley floor. Then he turned to begin his own caliginous descent down the forest path that pointed to the Outland and to all of its wondrous wonders.

Chapter the Seventeenth

Tuesday, June 24, 2003

My only marginally informative visit to Regents Park Stables had diverted me for a short time from indulging in worry and concern over what my brother Gus had said to me in his despairing hour. But now Gus and the frightful earnestness that characterised his need to launch himself from Dingley Dell in search of his son weighed heavily and importunately upon my thoughts. I rose next morning determined to engage my brother at his place of employment, where he kept watch over how many fishes came into the dried fish warehouse and how many fishes went out. I wished to make certain that Gus had taken this latest perilous scheme of his and tossed it decisively into the dustbin of impractical stratagems—a dustbin, I might add, overfilled with like deposits from a most injudicious mind.

Gus's superintendent Mr. Mell reported to me upon my arrival that he had just received word by ticket porter that my brother had decided to accompany his wife Charlotte on her restorative visit to her friend Miss Snigsworth and would therefore be stopping in Hungerford for the next several days. Gus's present whereabouts were confirmed by the letter I found addressed to me, secured beneath the iron knocker upon the front door to Gus and Charlotte's cottage in Fingerpost. Appended in postscript was a request, attributed to Charlotte, that I be so kind as to water the roses and geraniums and scarlet beans, and a notation as to where in the outhouse I would find the watering-pot (for Alice could not be trusted to interrupt her Pupkerian holiday to do it, nor would they choose to enlist the widow Chillip who lived next door and once mortally drowned Charlotte's American aloe in a full tub of water as if it were watercress). The prosy nature of the missive gave me hope that my brother and sister-in-law were attempting as best they could to return themselves to some semblance of normal life, clouded to be sure by the loss of their son, but needful of disallowing grief to reign despotically over the remainder of their years together.

I returned to my lodgings and made every effort to turn my concerted attention to those articles I'd promised the *Dingley Delver* that were behindhand. But my mind was not wholly suited to the task and I soon found myself upon a long and musing ramble about the Dell, sorting my thoughts, revisiting conversations with my brother and with Muntle who ached even to this day for the companionship of his own brother. My steps took me by and by to the Wang-Wang Rice Farm teahouse, which had become my favourite place of private contemplative refuge. As I approached the structure, which had been modeled in the shape of a pagoda, I could not help thinking of my nephew and how late I had sat up with him on cherished Saturday nights playing dominos and backgammon and his own version of miniature battledore using kitchen spatulas, and how at other times we had corresponded like bearded, angle-limbed Egyptians using the ancient language of hieroglyphics, or had stuffed our gullets with apricots from the Scadger clan's fruit grove and then hid sticky and snickering behind a hedge when the men of that rustic family returned from their weekly hunt with freshly-slain venison for the spit, oblivious to our mischief.

As a very young boy Newman had once built a pagoda of nursery blocks. It was rather good, as I recall.

Upon entering that oriental outpost, I was unprepared for the intriguing sight that greeted me. There, huddled in a dark corner of that jessamine-scented tearoom, were the librarian Uriah Graham and the Vicar Upwitch. The room's only two occupants (excepting myself) were poring over something spread out upon their table, Upwitch's hand rhythmically patting the head of his companion with noticeable affection.

Seeing me across the room, the pastor exclaimed, "Saint George and the Dragon!" and quickly withdrew his hand as if from coals upon a hot stove. "As I live and breathe—it's Frederick Trimmers come all the way to Nanking!"

I put out my hand, which was heartily wrung by each of the two men as Upwitch signalled that I should draw up a chair and sit myself down for a visit.

"My dear Mr. Trimmers," said Graham in his soft and genial manner, "for what possible reason have you come such a distance to grace us with your presence to-day?"

"My visit here isn't exceptional, Graham," I answered good-naturedly. "I come to this oriental hideaway now and again for the peace and quiet it affords me." I cleared my throat. "As apparently so do two other men with whom I'm acquainted."

The two men in question exchanged a pregnant glance before Upwitch turned his gaze to me in reply: "Dingley Dell, as you know, Trimmers, offers few quiet corners, with everyone always out and about and into everyone else's business. Consequently, Graham and I tend to seek out those few retiring spots for the, um, solitude. By the bye, look at the map that my multi-talented friend has nearly completed, which we have been inspecting at our undisturbed leisure. It gives the entire valley with every road and tree and nearly every stone put down."

Graham coloured and adjusted his horn spectacles (though they were sitting quite comfortably as they were) and offered the simple retort, "My friend exaggerates."

Graham had not the thick blond mane and chiseled statuary good looks of his friend Upwitch, who was known to elicit a swoon or two from the female members of his congregation when sweltering circumstances required a loosening of the surplice and sometimes its removal from the body altogether. Graham was of a softer, more feminine variety of man, perfectly suited to his studious profession of librarian and academic author, but nonetheless sun-browned and solid-limbed from his love of exploratory perambulations to every green nook and stony cranny of the Dell, equipped with sturdy boots and a dependable walnut hiking stick.

I turned the map to view it in its proper orientation and was quite taken with the work that Graham had done. "Masterful is the only word for it," said I.

The librarian accepted the compliment with a proud grin. "I do not fancy any of the standard maps, you see. Do you know, for example, that none of the current maps give Belgrave Dam in its proper scale? Slipshod work, sir, and inexcusable."

"Our former mapmakers seemed to have cared little about the south-ernmost portion of our valley," I elaborated. "Perhaps because the un-sightly mine is there, and Blackheath, the unsightly collier's town, and the iron pit."

"Equally unsightly," said Upwitch.

I nodded. "It is none of it pretty, but certainly undeserving of carto-graphic neglect."

"Hear, hear!" said Upwitch. The table grew silent. Upwitch composed himself. "We continue to pray for your nephew, Trimmers." Lacing the fin-gers of both of his hands together in a prayerful attitude upon the tabletop, the vicar continued: "Such a tragedy it is to lose a loved one to the Terra Incognita. There is a high fence circumscribing this valley but still it does not stop a person who is determined to leave us."

"There are also breaches in the fence that help one to that end," added Graham. "I had thought to mark them upon my map, but then reconsidered, not wishing to tempt other boys to do the same as your nephew has done."

Graham took a sip of tea just as the proprietor of the teahouse, Mrs. Wang-Wang herself, came to ask if I would have my customary cup of apple-tea.

"Yes, of course, Mrs. Wang-Wang, but bring biscuits as well. These gentlemen seem to be in a self-denying mood to-day and I'll not have it. Tea, in my opinion, is best imbibed with a sweet viand, wouldn't you say?"

"Yee," said Mrs. Wang-Wang, "yee" being the way that the members of the eccentric Wang-Wang clan stated the affirmative.

"What brings you here, Trimmers, in the middle of an afternoon?" asked Graham, as Mrs. Wang-Wang toddled away.

"Or *rather*," I laughed, "'why aren't you back in your garret above that dress shop, Trimmers, writing about all things Dinglian?' I should ask the same of *you*, Graham."

Upwitch answered for his friend: "We've been discussing, amongst other things, an article that I have been deputed by Graham to write for his *Dinglian History for Young Readers*."

"Ah, Graham," said I, "you have returned to the *History*. I thought that you had abandoned it."

"It needs to be written now more than ever," said Graham. "And Up-witch is just the man to put down the chapter on the All Souls Church. Nothing so lengthy a treatment as to comprehend the entire structure, but merely a few enlightening paragraphs on the history of the bell tower itself, for this is what would most fascinate a young reader."

"It really *is* the only thing about that disproportional building that anyone—forgive my candour—much cares to know," I opined.

"No offence taken, Trimmers. It's rather an architectural anomaly, now isn't it?" laughed the vicar.

"Upwitch was telling me of the campaniles of old," struck in Graham. "Places of refuge and asylum for religious and political dissidents."

"I recall a little school paper that my brother Gus wrote upon that very topic. Ever thereafter when he found himself at the insalubrious end of my father's disciplining ferule, he would vow to go to that very place for safe harbourage from the man's patriarchal wrath."

"And did he ever have cause as a young lad to make good upon that vow?" asked Graham.

"Not that I'm aware. Besides, here in Dingley Dell, there is no law on the books that gives a cleric leave to take a fugitive into his custody in the manner of the medievals."

With a smile from my weekly philosophical sparring partner Upwitch: "Nor is there a law upon the books, Trimmers, which expressly *forbids* it."

I lounged back in my chair and threw my arm over the top rail in a show of relaxed engagement. "My dear most reverend Upwitch, should I come now, so late in our friendship, to regard you as insurgent, a, hum, *provocateur*?"

"However do you mean?" asked Upwitch, plucking a gooseberry jam biscuit from the generous platter of pastries and sweet-breads proffered by Mrs. Wang-Wang—snatching it, in fact, before the good woman had even the chance to set the platter down upon the table (placement there being tempo-rarily delayed as Graham quickly sought to retrieve the spread-out map so that our hostess wouldn't think it a tablecloth of cartographic design).

"I'll tell you my meaning, Upwitch," I returned. "That there are those in this valley who have stood in historic opposition to the powers that be, but cannot act to overthrow the government for want of sufficient am-munition."

Upwitch nodded. "Now by ammunition do you mean the *literal* arming of ourselves with—what have we at our disposal here?—sticks and stones and a few sharp-ended implements from the Iron Age, or do you mean by the term 'ammunition,' sir, the lack of a seasoned and reasoned rationale for toppling the state in a sort of bloodless coup?"

I thought for a moment, stroking my chin in a way that I had taken from my often-cerebrating father. "To be sure, Upwitch, there are a significant number of reasons for changing the administrative guard however we may wish to make the change. Permit me to give you two such reasons."

"By all means, give us two!" replied Graham with uncharacteristic animation. (Was there something potent within his tea? I wondered, given this leave-taking of the librarian's customarily composed and coolly self-possessed demeanour.)

"The refusal of Mr. Pawkins of the Trade Ministry earlier this week to allow my brother and me to surmount the Summit to ask questions of the tradesmen that would give us some idea of the fate of my nephew Newman. I understand the reason for the law, as I apprehend the reasons behind *most* of the laws that the Petit-Parliament passes, but there is never an allowance for extenuating circumstance or any other form of exception. Here would have been a very good occasion for invoking both."

"Oh, but sir," said Graham, taking up this thread, "there are exceptions abounding. Throughout our history. Yet it is only the governing class that receives consistent exemption. It is an entirely lopsided system. I've studied it for years. Do you not agree, Slingo?"

Slingo—also known as Vicar Upwitch—nodded. Then Slingo coloured.

"Is that your new name, Upwitch?" I asked, whilst enduring the throes of subduing a hardy chuckle.

"It is not the name I selected for myself at the Bureau of Appellations, but rather a pet term that Uriah has selected *for* me."

I composed myself and resumed, "There are other matters as well with respect to personal liberties that go wanting. The restrictions, for example, put upon visitors to Bedlam. You would think the place as it presently exists under the heavy-handed rule of Dr. Towlinson to be more a prison than an asylum for the insane and mentally-infirmed. Is it written in the laws of the Petit-Parliament that all who pass through its admitting gate should be so inhumanely demeaned?"

The two men shook their heads as Graham tutted.

Confided Upwitch, continuing that same train: "A great many of my parishioners have come to me seeking my intercession with respect to this very matter. They seek so very little from Towlinson, really: only that they should have a few minutes more to visit with their loved ones who have been incarcerated in that dismal place. Heretofore my efforts have been to no avail and the visits remain painfully brief. As for the Returnees, it is even worse, for they are permitted no contact with their families whatsoever!"

"They say it is the mental affliction," said Graham in a skeptical tone.

"And I call that swine-milk!" howled Upwitch, slamming the flat of his hand upon the tabletop. "No, it's absolute roguery, that's what it is. I cannot put my finger on it, Uriah, but I know I'm right. And it makes it quite difficult for me to stand behind my pulpit and speak the word of our most compassionate Lord and Saviour, and to expound upon the Golden Rule and everything else pertaining to the lifting up of the least amongst us, whilst those bloody Bashaws who sit before me with every advantage— to such an extent as is allowable by our constrained circumstances—think only of how to self-aggrandise and expand their base of power and privi- lege—sit before me in their gated pews and nod and sing and pray and put a coin or two into the collection basket in parsimonious hypocrisy, and frankly, I'm losing all patience for it."

"My word, Slingo!" exclaimed Graham in mock distress. "You've be- come quite the clerical Communist!"

"I tire of it—that is all that I'm saying," said Upwitch. "Trimmers would grow weary to see it, too, if he ever cast his shadow over the threshold of my church. But I know his heart on the matter. I've read what he's written in the *Dingley Delver*."

"I dare say," I replied, "that Bishop Tollimglower is presently rolling over in his grave, to hear so much disrespect being directed toward our Patrician class. He was one of them, you know."

"I am sometimes given to wonder about his true allegiance," said Up- witch, looking off into the distance as if Tollimglower were standing some- where out there himself, and commanding his thoughts from a distance.

"What do you mean?" I asked.

"He was pomp and quite a bit of privilege, but there was something else within him—I have read his diaries preserved within the rectory— something desirous of seeing through the opaqueness of our existence in the Dell. I believe, and you may take your shots at my theory if you wish, but I believe a part of him sought the construction of our towering cam- panile not simply for its grand architectural swagger, but in an attempt—a symbolistic attempt—*to know God*."

"Know God?"

"Through the ability to stand upon the tower's pinnacle and take into one's view that land which lies spread out far beyond our valley—to know if God smiled upon that land as well. Or is the Terra Incognita, instead, some Godless realm set against us? 'We're here for a very short interval in the span of eternal time, and occupants of a very tiny place'—this is what he wrote into his diary, for it never came out in any of his homilies—'a tiny place that must be made proud, that must be made good, that must be guided by the hand of God…and it is not. Yea, it is my studied opinion that it most decidedly is *not*.'"

"And was there anything else in his writings," I asked, "to further expand the point?"

Upwitch shook his head with sadness.

"Something is wrong here," he whispered. "Something is very wrong. I cannot put my finger directly upon it, but I know, as did the man who held my office many years before, that it is real and that it grows, and I know as well that there is a close connexion between that which beshadows our valley and those Dinglians who pass our laws and run our factories and manage our emporiums and distribute the goods that come down from the Summit—an association with those who smile and strut and never give evidence that all is *not* charmed and all is *not* wholly fine and beautiful in the Dell, as if there is some great feint, some grand counterfeit being worked to their benefit. Perhaps you're right, Uriah, that it is the clerical Communist in me. But I stand by my feelings and will defend their legitimacy to the end."

I sat for a moment nodding, not speaking. But there was something that needed to be said, and so I said it: "Mrs. Pyegrave didn't find Dingley Dell to be charmed and beautiful. She was exceptional in that respect."

Upwitch nodded.

Graham said, "It is the consensus of my friends on the staff of the *Encyclopædia of Dingley Dell* that the woman was murdered by her husband. This is why her entry must read, 'expired at a too-early age of undetermined but suspicious causes.'"

I nearly smiled. "Who now is the traitorous agitator?"

"Aye, sir," returned my fellow scribe. "There is indeed power in words. Most of the lasting change that has been forged in the history of this world from what I have read in the voluminous *Ensyke* came not from a wielding of the swift and bloody sword of battle but from the shaping scalpel of ideas, and what are ideas, Trimmers, without the words to deliver them? I live for words. We shall, all of us, live and die by our words and the words of others. At least if there be truth to the dribblings of those learned compilers of the *Ensyke* and our most prolific Mr. Dickens! For they have given us the lens that equip the spyglass with which we view the world, a glass that has been ground and fashioned by the very words that *they* have written."

We remained at the Wang-Wang Teahouse until long after the sun had fled the sky, and then the three of us strode back to Milltown together. It became quite dark along the way but there was enough moonlight filtering through the clouds for each of us to see his feet and to see the stones of the road that wended before us, and for me to see with near certainty two hands folded together as hearts will sometimes do.

CHAPTER THE EIGHTEENTH

Friday, June 27, 2003

Mrs. DeLove had found it necessary to spend two additional nights at the side of her aunt at a hospital in Harrisburg, Pennsylvania, as the old woman teetered between life and death, and ultimately chose to invest herself for a little while longer in the former. Her niece returned to her home in Lycoming County and discovered a most curious thing: Mr. Trimmers was still there. She learnt this not immediately upon her return, but it was not long thereafter that her daughter came to her with a most strange look planted upon her face—a look that could not be quickly translated into words.

"I haven't slept, Annette," said Mrs. DeLove, dropping her luggage heavily upon the floor of her bedchamber. "I'm very tired and I don't have patience for game playing. What's wrong? Tell me what's the matter."

"You remember the man who was here when you left?"

"Mr. T-something. Trimmers. Yes, I remember him, Annette. What happened? What do you need to tell me? Did he hurt you? I knew after I started for Harrisburg that I shouldn't have left you here all alone with him, but I wasn't thinking too clearly at the time. I was so worried about your Aunt Lucille."

"I'll tell you, Mama, if you'll let me get a word in."

Annette sat down on her mother's bed and folded her hands. The odd look on her face now transformed itself into an amalgamated display of guilt and contrition and the ever-present disquiet.

With a sudden seizure of maternal alarm: "Did he…*rape* you?"

"For God's sakes, Mama, *no*! He didn't do *anything* to me. It was what I did to *him*."

Now Mrs. DeLove found need to sit herself down so that she might be better prepared to receive whatever horrible thing her daughter was about to confess. "Tell me, Annette. What did you do to that poor man?"

"I kept him here. Against his will. I handcuffed him to me."

"You did *what*?"

"I handcuffed the two of us together."

"Sweet Jesus, Annette!"

"I used a pair of Daddy's old police handcuffs."

"It's time to put you away, Annette. I mean it this time. You're certifiable."

"I knew the minute I did it that I shouldn't have. But by then—" Annette suspended her confession and took her head into her tremulous hands.

"By then *what*? Say it, Annette."

"By then it was too late. By then I realised that I'd taken the wrong key from the drawer in Daddy's workroom. I knew just from feeling it in my pocket that it wasn't going to fit the handcuffs. I knew that Mr. Trimmers and I would have to go looking for the right key."

"And how long did *that* take?"

"A day and a half."

"Sweet Jesus!"

"The more we looked, the more scared I got that Daddy'd lost the key or had thrown it out or something. I was afraid I'd have to call a locksmith. And then people would know that Mr. Trimmers was here. It was awful, Mama, and you weren't here to help me."

"But you found the key. That's the important thing. Where was it?"

"What?"

"The key, Annette? Where was the goddamned key?"

"Lying on the floor behind Daddy's workbench. But by then—"

"By then what? Speak to me, Annette. Where is Mr. Trimmers right now?"

"In the extra bedroom. He's sick."

"What do you mean sick?"

"I mean that I think he caught my cold."

Mrs. DeLove shrugged. "So we'll give him zinc lozenges and Tylenol and he'll be up and around in no time."

Annette shook her head. "He's *really* sick, Mama."

"How can he be really sick? It wasn't even that bad of a cold. You told me so yourself."

"It must not be the same with the Digglians."

"The Digglians?"

"The ones who live in the fenced-off valley. I don't think they've been exposed to the same viruses or whatever that we have. I think that's why it hit him so hard."

Annette took her mother to the door of the extra bedroom. She opened it slowly and quietly so as not to disturb her slumbering, febrile guest. Her mother put her head in. Glumly she said, "Yes, I see," and gently closed the door. "What have you done, Annette?"

"I wasn't thinking. Should we call a doctor?"

"And let it be known that one of *them* is in our house? Do you think that doctors are any better at keeping that kind of thing to themselves than locksmiths? Provided we can even find a doctor who makes house calls, how long do you think it would be before someone came for him—one of the others—the ones who go after these cursed people? You remember the man they killed? Right in front of this house. *He* was a Digglian, too. Was it only coincidence that this was when your agoraphobia took hold?

"No, ma'am, I will not have that kind of thing tugging the hell at my conscience, Annette. We're going to have to deal with him ourselves. And if you ever let another one of these Digglian weirdos into this house, I'm going to drown you in the bathtub."

Annette nodded, looking even more contrite and more self-depre-cating than before. "I like him, Mama."

"What?"

"I said that I like him."

"Are you in love with him?"

"I don't know what love is, Mama. I just know that I like him. I feel sorry for him. Especially after what I did to him."

"You're one piece of work, Netty."

"I know, Mama. I know."

CHAPTER THE NINETEENTH

Saturday, June 28, 2003

ntonia Bocker stood in the doorway to her stationer's shop and smiled. It was nearing noon and the doors would soon be closed, not to open again until Monday morning, and here were so many customers clamouring for the attention of her lone Saturday clerk, Miss Hexam, that Antonia could scarcely believe her eyes. Miss Abbey Hexam—a serious young woman with plain and simple features that vanished from memory once out of sight—was pulled this way and that by the determined men and women bunched about the counter, each apparently desirous of making Miss Antonia Bocker the most successful ornamental and practical stationer in the history of the Dell.

Abbey Hexam looked up from writing in her sales book to see her employeress silhouetted in the open doorway, and gave a smile. Antonia had never been one to put her salesclerks in a difficult way when it was quite easy for her to step in and don the mantle of salesclerk herself to alleviate a customer crush-and-rush. And so Miss Antonia Bocker let the door close behind her and marched with a singularity of purpose up to the crowded counter and thereupon became clerical partner to her young employee, much to Miss Hexam's situationally-restrained delight.

"What *is* this?" Antonia marveled to her clerk in an underbreath. "You would think that there was a sudden shortage of ink blotters and sealing wax in the Dell."

"*And* clasped morocco diaries. I've sold three just this morning."

"That all of our lives should be so interesting as to be documented between pebbled leather! Good morning, Mr. Meagles, I hope that you have not been kept waiting long."

"Not long at all," said the short balding man standing, slightly stooped, before Antonia. Mr. Meagles smiled, his mouth drooping on one side from a bout of apoplexy from which he had largely recovered save the facial wilt. Job Meagles was bailiff and clerk to the honourable Judge Price Fitz-Marshall, chief justice and administrative magistrate of Dingley Dell, and though quite devoted to his employer, was generally undeserving of the frequently levelled sobriquet "Mr. Toad."

"And how is Judge Fitz-Marshall?" asked Antonia, whilst withdrawing a sales book from a shelf below the counter.

"Never better. I have my shopping list here somewhere. Ah, yes." Meagles extracted a slip of paper from his coat pocket and presented it to Antonia.

Antonia conned the paper, then looked up. "But Mr. Meagles, this is the list of what was needed last month. Do you not have a different list for to-day?"

"Oh, dear me," said the absent-minded bailiff, patting all of his pockets. "I do. Of course I do." Mr. Meagles eventually produced a second list that contained only one item: red tape—for tying up paper bundles.

"How extraordinary," said Mr. Meagles, scratching his head.

"*Most* extraordinary," said Antonia. "I've never known the judge to require so little from my stores. Has there been a recent contraction in his caseload?"

Mr. Meagles shook his head. "We're actually quite busy. And it is not in the judge's nature to be improvident about keeping stationery supplies on hand. But then look about you, Miss Bocker. With all the customers here to-day, I see not a single one who is affiliated with either the Petit-Parliament or the Inn-of-Justice."

"I would not have taken notice if you hadn't pointed it out, Mr. Meagles. Business continues to thrive for all of us positioned several rungs down the ladder of power and prestige in the Dell, but it has come to a standstill for those at the top. It is very curious, my good man. Quite a puzzlement. But let us not become obsessitors about it. And since you are come to buy a spool of red binding tape, at least, may I impose upon you to know if the judge has made his ruling on the death of Mrs. Pyegrave? I understood that there was to be no inquest, but what was the exact ruling of the judge?"

"It was published just this morning. The death of that poor woman was adjudged to be an accident—a terrible accident that might have been avoided had she not been drinking heavily and in a most self-abasing state."

"But that would make a case for suicide, would it not, Mr. Meagles?"

The diminutive man gave a slight nod, worked his slanted mouth a little as if he would answer, then looked about with some nervous concern upon his brow and withheld his reply.

Antonia took the arm of the judge's bailiff and escorted him back into her private office. "We will not be heard here, Mr. Meagles," she said with quiet assurance as she bolted the door. "Pray tell me, as you feel inclined, why Judge Fitz-Marshall, given evidence that poor Mrs. Pyegrave was in such a dismal state of mind as to take her own life, did not rule thusly."

Meagles put his lips near to Antonia's ear and said in a sunken, confiding voice: "To spare the family from public humiliation, for suicide, as you know, Miss Bocker, carries a stigma with it. To think that a couple so blest as the Pyegraves could have its distaff half of the union so unbearably unhappy whilst the husband continued in his affable, hail-fellow-well-met fashion was too much for Pyegrave and his brothers to put out for public consumption, and so the fall was ruled an accident, and the cause severe intoxication."

Antonia nodded and tossed a nugget of coal, which served upon her work desk as paperweight, back and forth between her hands. This empty occupation gave her time to think of what next to say, though she later confessed to me that the thought which proved the most impertinent within her mind at that moment was that Janet Pyegrave could not have been the depressed sort of person that Pyegrave had described, for she had given her heart to a young stableboy who most certainly put a youthful glow upon her cheeks and a spring to her step. (It only stood to reason!)

"And Mr. Pyegrave and his brothers find no measure of disgrace in the fact that the depression was either induced or attended by drunkenness? Is not inebriety also stigmatic?"

"Somewhat, I'll grant you, Miss Bocker. But 'attended' would be closer to the correct characterisation, for a good many who drink do so to find respite from depressive thoughts. It is a natural and readily available anodyne, is it not?"

Miss Bocker nodded, thinking, as she later confessed to me, that the judge's ruling was a pile of horse excrement. Not that her casual questionings of the Pyegraves' neighbours had given her anything with which to refute either the judicial finding or Pyegrave's account of that tragic evening! And Miss Bocker had nearly given off speaking to those others who lived on Park Lane save a quiet and retiring woman of Antonia's light acquaintance who occupied the house just next door to the Pyegrave's townhouse. The woman, who was nearing her dotage, rarely left her home, except to take her little dog each week to have a different-coloured bow fixed to his head.

The private interview concluded, Miss Bocker bid the bailiff good day at the shop door, returned to the counter, and turned her attention next to she who was standing closest to her in the buzzing queue: Maggy Finching, a robust, if slightly flushed, large-figured woman in her middle years who served as cook for the Chowser School. Miss Finching wore a peach-coloured velvet bonnet that instantly captured the eye.

"Good morning to you, Miss Finching, and what brings you so far afield of that quaint boys' school in the distant heather?"

"Mr. Chowser has given me two days leave to attend to some personal business. I must have a new hat and—"

"Yes, I can see the new hat. It is quite captivating."

"Do you not think so? The Milltown milliner is a marvel. What is his name? Ah, Mr. Glamour! Mr. Glamour the milliner is a rare marvel."

Antonia nodded and smiled and touched the nap of Miss Finching's new bonnet—a riot of colourful ribbons and artificial flowers—and found pleasure in its softness.

"And a new lace tucker since my present one has unraveled and withered itself before the hot stove. And, of course, a brand new frock." This statement came accompanied by a titter. "Oh, dear me. 'Frock' is much too *slender* a word for a woman of my capacious girth. Let us simply call it a 'dress.' A 'dress for a woman of a certain overwhelming size.'"

"My dear Miss Finching, there is no profit in speaking of yourself in such self-depreciating terms."

"You're right. Nor was that even an accurate depiction of myself. The Finching women have always had large bones. I'm the first in my line who didn't spend her life milking and calving. I'm proud of my position as cook for all of those hungry boys. And Mr. Chowser has been a most generous employer. And my size, besides, is no detriment to my duties, and upon occasion, I dare say it can even be an asset, especially when there is a side of meat to be conveyed from the butcher's waggon to the kitchen and no hobbledeboy nearby to impress into my temporary employ."

Throughout the preceding proclamation Maggy Finching had directed her gaze not at Antonia Bocker but out the front window and toward the busy street that passed the stationer's shop. Antonia could not help noticing. "Miss Finching, is there someone you're expecting to see out there?"

"Oh, no. Not particularly."

"Then let us do business together. How may I be of service to you?"

"Yes, yes. I have letter paper with the name of the school in the heading, you see, and Mr. Chowser wishes—because there is a little bit of school business that I must transact on my trip as well—wishes a crimpled edge along the sides as one finds in the finest handmade paper. Can you crimple the edges for a not unreasonable sum?"

"I believe that I can."

"Happy day! I will leave it here then and—" Suddenly, something caught Maggy Finching's eye. It produced a little gasp in the viewer, and from this point forward hustled and compacted all of her remaining words to Antonia, so that they ran together in one long unbroken torrent: "ExcellentnowpleasetakethesesheetsandsendthembyPPDSifyouwillImustgoIreallymustTataMissBockerandgoodday!"

With that, Miss Finching hurriedly tied the strings of her new peach bonnet and waved herself out the door in a quick waddle.

Once in the street, Miss Finching said "oh dear" to herself perhaps three times and looked ahead, peering beneath the shade of her flattened palm, and then groaned a little to think that the object of her search, just a moment ago caught within her sights, had now eluded her. But then in a trice she re-discovered that which she had sought—*he*—not so far ahead that she could not catch it—*him*—for it was a man. A man whom she knew.

"Hurry up, you fool!" she mumbled to herself in a most distressful tone. "You cannot let him get away!"

For Miss Finching's quarry was indeed "getting away," having stopt for only the briefest of moments to peer through the window of the miniature painter's equally diminutive gallery, there to squint at the tiny paintings set upon dolls' easels, and there to curse his ineffectual eyesight for missing the smaller details, and then to move quickly along.

"Perhaps he'll glance back and see me," she said quite aloud to herself, "but no, I shan't have *that,* for my plan is to stroll up to him casually and as if unawares."

Whilst Miss Finching continued to ponder her predicament as the object of her interest put greater and greater distance between himself and his unknown pursuer, there was a private family drama taking place in the jewellry shop on the other side of the street at very nearly the same time (for this be the memory of all parties who imparted to me what was happening as the minute hand of the clock crept to that spot in which all hands pointed upward). Mrs. Rose Fagin had shut the door and latched it and turned to her daughter Susan who sat upon a skirted stool beside the flat, glass-covered display cabinet, which showed an eye-catching array of coral bracelets and polished jet necklaces and gem rings that sparkled in the gentle gaslight. The third player in the drama, Herbert Fagin, stood next to his daughter with his delicate fingers (much the better for jewellry handling and watch repair) resting upon his daughter's heaving shoulders.

Susan Fagin had been crying even before she arrived at her parents' shop, but now the bung had been fully removed and the tears fell quite gushingly.

"Have a blow," said Mrs. Fagin, offering her daughter a handkerchief. Susan took the handkerchief and blew her nose loudly with it and dabbed at her moist eyes (but not in that order) and sat down quietly, without telling a word of what had brought her to such a sorrowful state.

"Take all the time you need, my love," said Rose, seating herself at the side of her only child.

Susan nodded and blew her nose again and prepared herself to tell what the matter was.

Outside the jewellry shop the man urgently sought by Maggy Finching stopt again to take a toothpick to his teeth (having eaten a late breakfast at his habitual chop-house and finding some portion of it still residing within his mouth.) Being offered now the opportunity she desired to come upon him as if by chance, Miss Finching executed that very feint, right there in the street with nearly half of Milltown hurrying hither and thither to conduct their commerce before the close of this business half-day.

"Sheriff Muntle!" she declared with a manufactured look of surprise, "How pleasant it is to see you here!"

Taking her hand warmly in his own, Muntle smiled and said, "The pleasure is entirely mine, Miss Finching. And quite the good fortune, for is it not the case, my dear woman, that you seldom take yourself this far from the school?"

"Yes, yes, relatively speaking of course, as one must speak of *all* things within the Dell. You see, I am on my annual shopping excursion." Miss Finching touched the brim of her bonnet by way of illustration.

"Aye. Fetching," said Muntle with a nod. "I recall that it was during your last year's sojourn that we enjoyed that pleasant little interlude at the Municipal Cemetery. You with all your parcels and bandboxes piled about you—"

"And you with—well, yourself."

"Right you are, old girl, and we had that most delightful little chat about—now what was it we discussed, Miss Finching?"

"Cheese, Mr. Muntle, and how much we both adored it."

Muntle smiled and nodded. "I recall it as if it were only yesterday. And have you time for another interlude, Miss Finching? Could you make time to sit with a dear old friend and sip something warm or perhaps cool—whichever suits your fancy on this day that wants neither to be too hot nor too cold?"

"I am charmed by the very possibility of it," said Miss Finching, having obviously been asked that very thing that had been her heart's objective all along.

The two repaired to the Chuffey Bakery, which had chairs and tables inside where those who could not wait to devour their loaves and pastries at home were given leave to wash them down right there upon the premises with milk or tea or chicory.

"I make better buns within my own kitchen," confided Miss Finching proudly, "and will make some for you on your next visit to the school."

"But let us not tell Chuffey, for he is a worrisome man who would lose three nights' sleep over it were he ever to find out. How is the headmaster Chowser? I've not had sheriff's business up that way in quite some time."

"He still mourns the loss of the Trimmers boy."

"As do I. I am a second bachelor uncle, in a way, to the lad."

"Have you never married, Mr. Muntle?" asked Miss Finching, as she poured tea from the pot that had been put before them.

"I regret to say that I have not, Miss Finching. And yourself?"

Maggy Finching shook her head. "But I am compensated by serving as mother, of a sort, to quite a brood of boys at the school."

"They are quite the handful, I should think."

Maggy Finching flinched. Then she apologised much more than was necessary, for there had just been an accident; Maggy, not being able to take her eyes from Muntle's warm and friendly visage, had consequently over-poured the cup and soaked the table and there now ensued a scramble to sop it all up before Mr. Chuffey should find out, and one hand inadvertently overspread another and was not removed, and Maggy Finching was most happy to see the first part of her plan to win Muntle's heart go quite swimmingly. Quite puddled and swimmingly indeed.

CHAPTER THE TWENTIETH

Saturday, June 28, 2003

Susan Fagin had dried her tears and then burst into a new round of sobbing and then blotted her eyes once more and blew her nose clean and was now prepared to speak...

...With, that is, another ounce or two more of paternal prodding:

"Is it something to do with the girls with whom you live at the Nurses' Dormitory?" asked the father. "Have they taken to teazing you again about the size of your feet? It cannot be helped that we have large feet in this family. And there is no shame or scandal in it. In fact, it makes the cobbler quite happy to charge an extra florin for the additional leather required for the insoles."

"It isn't about my feet, Papa," replied Susan Fagin, still attired in her nurse's uniform with its obligatory little mob cap—a medical costume which often invited people to ask Miss Fagin far from her places of employment to give close inspection to a whitlow infection upon the finger, or to put her hand upon a forehead to divine a fever.

"Has something dreadful befallen you, my child?" asked Mrs. Fagin, who now betrayed her wonted placid demeanour with moderate maternal hysteria. "Tell me that there is no disease of the womb. We are prone to diseases of the womb on my side of the family—even those who have not borne children."

"It cannot be her womb," expostulated Mr. Fagin. "It must certainly be her bear-sized feet."

"Enough!" erupted Susan. "You're both being most alarmingly ridiculous. It is neither my womb nor my feet. It is not *anything* that has happened to *me* for that matter, except that I have been made the undeserving recipient of a rather disturbing bit of intelligence, which I know not how to interpret."

"Well, perhaps you should start, dear," said the mother in a much calmer tone, "by fully unbosoming yourself to your father and me. That is what mothers and fathers are for. It is our most worthwhile purpose in life: to offer love and succour and parental advice to our only child."

"And only *then* to sell broaches and pendants, and collect rents on our several rental properties, if you wish to know the proper order of things, my darling girl," said the father who had begun to knead his daughter's shoulders in the way that most relaxed her.

"Do you remember my telling you both of the unfortunate Mrs. Pyegrave who was brought into the Respectable Hospital? How abominably she had been treated by that most disreputable charlatan physician Dr. Fibbetson who then left her there upon her bed to expire the very next day?"

"Of course we do, my love, and we can scarcely abide the thought of what was done to her any better than can you." This from Mrs. Rose Fagin who had begun to thread her daughter's fingers through her own so that Susan should be ever the more relaxed and quieted and further reminded of her parents' love and their interminable interest in her well being.

"Well, there is a little more to the story; it pertains to that critical moment in the poor woman's final terrestrial hours that was witnessed by me and me alone."

"Whatever do you mean, daughter?" asked the father, his massaging hands suddenly stilled by surprise.

"Everyone who visited Mrs. Pyegrave—everyone who came to her room as life slowly ebbed away from her—even the housemaid who wept such tears upon her mistress's pillowcase that I was compelled to change it lest the patient catch cold from the dampness—saw an insensible woman, dead to all who came and went. Everyone, that is, save *me*."

Mrs. Rose Fagin's eyes goggled and her mouth formed a rosebud with her lips.

"Whatever do you mean, my daughter?" asked the father, putting his palm upon the shiny glass display case and smudging it—a thing that was *never* done in this shop but which mattered not the least in the midst of this most riveting revelation.

"I mean that there were a few minutes—not many—in which the patient returned to her senses and was awake, though a bit groggy, but awake enough to speak to me, and to be coherent in our impromptu exchange. And to tell me something she felt should be told to *someone* prior to her demise."

"She confided something to *you*?" asked Mrs. Rose Fagin. "How queer! A nurse whom she hardly knew!"

Susan nodded. "For there was no one else around, and she knew not how long it should be before unconsciousness should steal her away again."

"And have you the desire to tell us, darling? To tell us what she said?"

"I must tell *someone*, Mama, for it frightens me so dreadfully. I have little slept or eaten in all the days and nights that have passed since I was conscripted as that woman's solitary auditor."

"Oh dear child! For so long you have carried about this terrible burden!" This from the mother.

Then from the father to be helpful: "We have broiled fowl and mushrooms left over from last night's supper. I will take you upstairs to it, and there is a cold meat pie, and your mother would be happy to make you anchovy toast."

"Hush now, Herbert. She can fall to, as soon as she has said what she came hither to say. Proceed, my darling daughter. What do you wish us to know?"

Susan nodded and rose to her feet and took a step or two and turned back to face her most enrapt parents. "There is a society of men and women," she began, "here in the Dell. Men and women of a certain high station—owners of our largest firms, members of the Petit-Parliament and their wives and a few of their children—those who have reached their majority—they form a special, secret society which deals with the Beyonders in ways that far exceed the prescribed intercourse between our brokers and their tradesmen counterparts at the Summit of Exchange."

"In what excessive ways would those be?" asked Mr. Fagin. "Did Mrs. Pyegrave say?"

"Ways that give them advantage and profit over all the rest of us."

"I don't understand," said Rose Fagin, gathering the plaits of her work blouse into her fist in unconscious agitation.

"Each has sworn a vow never to divulge the workings of the society upon penalty of—" Here Susan Fagin stopt and swallowed before finishing her sentence: "Upon penalty of death."

The three Fagins sat for a moment in hard silence, the operative word "death" commanding the room.

"The woman was obviously delirious," said Mr. Fagin with a casual shrugging of the shoulders that seemed deliberately effected to put his wife and daughter at ease. "Out of her head. Those beleaguered, fevered dreams failing to recede even in her brief wakeful moments. Do you not see it? Though awake, the woman clearly remained in the thrall of her nonsensical nightmares."

"Then, Herbert, you do *not* believe there to be such a society as the one described to Susan by Mrs. Pyegrave."

"Do *you*, my dear?"

"I am more inclined to believe it than not."

"How so?"

"Ponder *this*, husband: is it really such a far-fetched thing—a secret society—when one considers that to which present circumstances subjects us in a slightly less cabalistic and fantastical fashion? Has there ever been a collier or ploughman to serve in the Petit-Parliament or even a barber or schoolteacher? With the exception of my friend Antonia, can you name a single person in the history of the Dell who rose up from attenuated beginnings to build several thriving businesses?"

Rose Fagin turned back to meet the worried gaze of her daughter. "What else? Tell your father and me everything that was imparted to you by this dying woman."

"There was a little more. She loved a stableboy who worked at Regents Park but the husband would not have it. She defied him. She threatened to tell everything she knew about the secret society if he didn't leave her to the boy who gave her far more happiness than Pyegrave himself ever did—a society which stood in service to something called 'The Tia-daction Project.' *This* is why he pitched her from the window. And she was prepared to tell it all to me so long as she remained conscious and relatively lucid. But this is all that was said for she quickly lapsed back into the sleep that delivered her a few hours later to her death."

"Still—" remonstrated the father, his receptive expression conversely giving no hint that he *didn't* believe every syllable his daughter had just uttered. "Still—they could merely have been the narcotic ravings of a woman possessed of anything but a clear head."

"Yet consider the specificity of it, my darling Herbert," reasoned Rose. "Janet Pyegrave didn't paint it with a broad brush. Delirious ravings are rarely so cogently pointed and particularised, now are they?"

Susan Fagin knitted her fingers in worry until her mother pulled the hands apart and patted them to calm and soothe her. "So that is all?" asked the mother, having regained her own composure.

The daughter nodded and said, "And you must not tell another soul."

"And we shan't," said the father. "We will keep it here only amongst the three of us."

"We cannot tell the sheriff?" asked Mrs. Fagin of her husband.

"No one," interposed Susan with a quavering voice. "If there be truth to it, and if anyone finds out—anyone who could do me harm, we'll regret that even a single syllable ever left this room."

Mrs. Rose Fagin nodded. It was hard to keep such a thing to oneself, but for the sake of her daughter's safety and peace of mind, it could not be disclosed further. Privately Mrs. Fagin cursed the late Mrs. Pyegrave for revealing the existence of this secret society in the first place. What manner of society punishes a disobedient member by so drastically abbreviating her life? It frightened Mrs. Fagin to think that constituent members of such a dangerous and evil fraternity might reside so near—as near, in fact, as the General Agency Office next door, whose owner and master agent, one William Boldwig (father of the previously-introduced Billy Boldwig, neophyte deputy sheriff of Dingley Dell) was in close league with Richard Pyegrave. In fact, wasn't Mr. Pyegrave on the most intimate terms with *every* scion of wealth and high station in Dingley Dell, both those Bashaws who owned large houses in Milltown and those who had fine family estates throughout the Dinglian countryside? (As well as the most highly-advantaged who boasted one of each?)

Mrs. Fagin entreated her daughter and husband to drop the subject, and the three fell to the leavings of broiled fowl and mushrooms and a meat pie, and Susan was given three slices of anchovy toast, their savoury goodness making her smile and pout at the same time (from the salt), and this dirty business that had long plagued her was to be put forever behind them, for it would do no good to speak of something so vague—to address so cloudy a charge, and so shadowy an accusation.

Susan had said all that she knew.

Or had she?

In truth, as it would later be revealed to me along with all the other details of this story, which came to my ken at various points in the offing, Susan, in fact, *hadn't* told her parents everything there was to tell about Mrs. Pyegrave's deathbed disclosure. There was one thing more—something that she chose to wait and share with her friend Hannah Pupker, oldest daughter of Montague Pupker, one of the richest Bashaws in Dingley Dell and owner of a great deal of real property, including both buildings and unimproved land, and, most notably, owner and chief proprietor of the Pupker Emporium, the largest dry goods and sundries establishment in the valley. Susan wanted Hannah, her best friend, to know what Janet Pyegrave *knew* about a certain room: a hidden room beneath the cellar of the Emporium—a *sub*-cellar, if you will, and how it would prove the truth behind Mrs. Pyegrave's dying disclosure.

Tangible proof. A whole room full of it.

CHAPTER THE TWENTY-FIRST

Saturday, June 28, 2003

The sun was setting and I could find no candles. I knew not where my brother and his wife stored them within their house. At any other time I would chuckle over the fact that the village of Fingerpost was most decidedly *not* the West End of Milltown, which had put in a great number of gas lines, so that I was able, on occasion, to sit up late into the night by the generous light of gas-burning desk lamp (until such time as Mrs. Lumbey came to apply her knuckles to my door and demand that I put out the light and spare her another exorbitant monthly payment to the gas-rate collector).

I had finished with my watering of all of Charlotte's many flowers and plants, and had taken a meal from my sister-in-law's larder of foods that had not yet moulded or spoilt, and now I was prepared to relax a bit and draw a book from that part of my father's small library that had been oddly bequeathed to my older brother, the infrequent reader, if I could only discover the whereabouts of the candles. It would be in keeping with Charlotte's provident nature to have taken them all with her to her friend Miss Snigsworth's house in Hungerford, for "Economy" could verily have been Charlotte's middle name. You would take that name as well, if you had been married to my perpetually insolvent brother.

But then I found them…in a drawer in a little table in the drawing room. I huzzahed not once but twice, for my evening was now set. I could settle back and enjoy the quiet of this sleepy, tranquil village, and the quiet of my brother's dark and empty house, which was a rare and welcome contrast to the bustle and hustle of Milltown, a veritable city (in Dinglian terms) that did not close its shutters until well past ten o'clock post meridiem. And even in the depths of night there one might still find oneself awakened by the hourly peal of the clock atop Burghers' Hall or the mangled harmonising of late-night revelers stumbling home from the town's various public houses. There was also the barking and mewing soliloquies and colloquies and veritable choruses of every furred and four-footed creature turned out upon these warm summer nights, each animal quite adept at dodging both boot and bolster chucked from the window of a slumber-deprived bedchamber.

I lifted the candle to light the bookshelf and peruse its Dinglian volumes, some of which I hadn't visited since childhood: *Oliver Twist, the Man*; *Acrostics for Every Name and Occasion*; *Jiniwin's Jest Book*; and one of my personal favourites, which had inspired me, in part, to become a writer, *The Curious Bogleman and other Tales of Dinglian Horror*. Yet I left all of these volumes untouched upon the shelf, and took down, instead, my mother's sketch pad. I hadn't seen it for several years and thought for a time that Gus had lost it in his family's latest removal or that Charlotte had accidentally put it out with the rubbish.

I settled into my brother's easy chair (which had formerly belonged to my father) and opened the pad that was more book than pad, in actuality, its thick leaves carefully stitched and bound together with a proud artisan's hand. My youth lived upon these pages. And Gus's as well. My mother was a gifted artist and the likenesses she created most striking. They rejuvenated long put-by memories of a relatively happy youth, though my father did not make the season altogether perfect given his frequent bursts of anger and frustration at a world much too small to contain him. But where Papa dropt a shadow, Mama shone a light, and there was sufficient equilibration betwixt the two to buoy my childhood to an adequate level of normalcy.

However, I wasn't long in the chair before I heard something outside the house not at all representative of the customary nocturnal quietude of this village. It was a woman's raised voice: serious, admonishing and a little frantic. I rose quickly from the chair and went to the window.

There before me was the proprietor of that voice—a young woman, standing in the middle of the dusty twilight-shaded lane, facing a shaggy dog of some size, the creature growling and bearing its gums in an overtly intimidating manner.

"Now you stay right there! Right where you are, buster!" said the woman.

From the window, I called, "Oho! Pepper! Pepper! Withdraw this instant, boy!"

The shaggy Pepper turned his head, and recognising a familiar face in the window, left off growling and gum-bearing, and began to wag his thick tail. I stepped out onto the porch and was instantly greeted by the great creature with happy paws upon my chest and a wet tongue upon my chin.

"He really is quite friendly. You needn't have worried," I called to the frightened young woman in the lane.

"If that's the case," she rejoined, "then you and I have different definitions for the word 'friendly.' Another half-minute and I would have been his dinner."

"That's nonsense," said the Widow Chillip, standing upon her own front porch next door. "Come, Pepper! Supper!"

"I walk down this road every night, madam," said the young woman, "and your Pepper has always let me pass. But to-night he has decided to become quite territorial."

"Mayhap, Pepper didn't recognise you in the gloaming," said the Widow Chillip. She slapped her side to bring her dog to heel. "As Mr. Trimmers has already said, he's quite the friendly dog—that is, unless he's provoked."

The young woman, whose hair, even in the dying atoms of daylight, appeared quite red, placed both hands upon her hips in a rather disputatious posture. "I didn't provoke your dog, madam. I was merely walking down the road, minding my own business."

"Mayhap it is your medical bag. You're the nurse at Bedlam, are you not? Do you always carry it with you? Mayhap it frightened Pepper. Sometimes the veterinarian Mr. Smallweed comes with just such a bag as that, and he inevitably produces something with which to poke and perturb poor Pepper. That is my theory. Goodnight to you both and I apologise to you in earnest, Miss Bedlam Nurse, for whatever inconvenience Pepper has caused you." With this, the Widow Chillip spun theatrically upon her heel and led her shaggy, scraggly, small horse of a dog into her cottage.

The Bedlam nurse and I could not contain ourselves and smiled in concert over the comical display. I stepped down from the porch and the nurse came toward me so that we should meet in the middle of my brother and sister-in-law's brick walk, bordered by colourful flowers of the season that stood a little straighter from the tall drink of water I had just delivered to them.

"I am Ruth Wolf," the woman said, extending her hand to shake, "and Mrs. Chillip is correct—I work as a nurse at Bethlehem Hospital."

"Frederick Trimmers. This is my brother's house. He and his wife have gone to spend a few days in Hungerford."

"Yes, I've been to Hungerford. It's slightly smaller than Fingerpost, isn't it?"

"Not much more than a few cottages and a communal well, really. Are you in a hurry to get yourself home? I could make us tea."

"I'm actually in no great hurry to get home per se. Only to get off my feet. If there is something upon which I may sit in your brother's house, I should enjoy a little company that isn't bedridden or medical by profession. Although, if you are the Frederick Trimmers whose name receives mention now and then at all of the hospitals where I work—for I am on call at the Lung Hospital and the Milltown Respectable Hospital as well—"

"But not the Indigents' Hospital?"

"Not officially, although I do make visitations there on my own twice or thrice a week. I was just going to say that your name is not unfamiliar to me. I believe that you are instrumental in preparing the Medical Review Board's report each year."

"'Instrumental' may be overstating my duties," I said, holding the door open for Miss Wolf to enter. "I am but a lowly scribe. At all events, your name is quite known to me as well."

My brother and sister-in-law's sitting room was dark now, the single candle beside my reading chair doing little to illuminate the rest of the room, and so I took a moment to go about and light and place a candle here and there to give more light.

"Has your brother not an oil lamp of some sort?"

"He has the lamp. Just not the oil. You might have noticed that the price of oil has risen a bit in the last several months, and he and Charlotte can no longer afford it. Well, I shouldn't speak of my brother behind his back. He and my sister-in-law do what they can to get by. Who is to say that I wouldn't be in similar straits if I had two additional mouths to feed? Well, one extra mouth in truth, at least for right now."

Miss Wolf sat down upon an ottoman, carefully placing her bag upon the floor next to her. Her expression became both grave and sympathetic.

"Yes, your nephew still resides in the Outland, does he not?"

"I'd not use the term 'reside.' We don't actually know just what has become of him."

"You're close to him?"

"Oh yes. Quite. I cannot say the same for my niece, but they are both very different creatures. Some find Newman hopelessly incorrigible, but I see worth to his character where others may not. He plays the role of the simpleton, but I know he is not. Let me shew you something."

I rummaged in my pockets to find a letter written by Newman several weeks earlier, sent to me from the Chowser School. I don't know why I continued to carry it with me, or perhaps, then again, I *do* know why: to keep the spirit of my nephew close at hand, as the chance of ever seeing him again waned.

Miss Wolf took the envelope and unfolded it. "Oh, isn't this intriguing? He has written his letter to you in—what is this? If I am not mistaken, it's like Egyptian hieroglyphics. Now are these symbols you have made up betwixt yourselves?"

"On the contrary. They are true and historical hieroglyphics that Chowser has taken from the *Ensyke* and taught to his boys."

"I am sorry that I never met your nephew Newman. He sounds quite fascinating." The statement was made to me in a steady and even tone, and the composed features of Miss Wolf's face did the job as well of not betraying to me the truth that lived behind the falsehood of the declaration.

"You have never?"

Miss Wolf shook her head. "Not that I can remember. I cannot even think of what he looks like, though I live only a few houses down the lane. He has in all likelihood been inside this house or off and away each time I have passed."

"He looks very much like his father. And a little like me. May I put the kettle on for tea?"

"Please," said Miss Wolf, stretching her limbs upon the ottoman, and looking all about the room with interest. "This is where you grew up— right here in this house?" she called to me in the next room.

"No," I called back. "That house is no longer standing. This is a house that Gus and Charlotte lease from my friends, the Fagins."

"I see. Can I not help you, Mr. Trimmers?"

"Not at all. Make yourself comfortable."

Ruth Wolf did make herself comfortable, and when I returned to the drawing room after lighting the stove we both fell into a rather desultory conversation about her work at the various Dinglian hospitals. Especial mention was made of Bedlam, where Miss Wolf informed me she spent the greatest amount of her time tending to the sundry patients and especially to the victims of the "Terror Tremens," that disease exclusive to those who return from the Outland.

We spoke as well of Miss Wolf's own childhood. As the story went, she had been an invalid for most of her life, finally overcoming a multiplicity of childhood ailments and infirmities and then dedicating the remainder of her life to the healing of others.

"I've always found it rather odd," I mused aloud, once I'd set the tea tray down between us, and my popping up and down had subsided, "that your parents never made mention of your existence all the time that they were alive. And then there was the carriage accident—please stop me if this is difficult to speak of."

"No, no. I am not so troubled by the recall of those events as I once was, for time has been a balm."

"Yet it has only been two years."

"I mourn my father and mother, Mr. Trimmers, but I do not allow memory of them to keep me from tending without distraction to my important work. You mentioned the fact that my existence was kept hidden until their deaths—now that is not quite true. There were quite a few who visited me when I was bedridden. I was simply never in sufficient health to be permitted to leave the house." Miss Wolf smiled archly. "You know a bit more about me than most. Are you planning to write of me some day— perhaps for that dissident newspaper that publishes your work?"

I laughed over Miss Wolf's perspicacity. "You don't think yourself worthy of a profile in the *Dingley Delver*?"

"Yet I am merely a nurse."

"'Merely a nurse.' Come now, Miss Wolf. I have heard it said of you that you are the very best nurse in Dingley Dell. And after only two years' training!"

Miss Wolf shifted a bit upon the ottoman. "Perhaps my reputation merely reflects my determination to rise from my bed like Lazarus and make something of the life that I saw spanning ahead of me. I will admit to working quite long hours. Even now, I rarely take a day off."

"But perhaps you should. Is there harm in giving oneself the occasional holiday? Is there harm in doing what we're doing now, for that matter: sitting at tea and speaking only of inconsequential matters?"

"Is that how you would characterise our conversation? I was thinking that it felt quite the opposite."

"Quite the opposite?"

"Like an interview of some sort."

I took a moment to consider the directness of Miss Wolf's assessment. "Have I been playing the part of inquisitor? If so, I humbly beg your pardon, madam."

"I didn't say that it was necessarily untoward of you to interrogate me. I'm merely curious as to your motives."

"My motives? Hmm. Well, I did come to your rescue, Miss Wolf, and as hero of this little play, perhaps I give myself license to eschew propriety to *some* extent, considering the circumstances."

"That is a rather silly line of reasoning. Chivalry obviates propriety? I've never heard that said before." Miss Wolf's smile had a mischievous quality that was quite appealing. It brightened her whole face and illuminated her amply lashed green eyes.

"What I *meant* was that the circumstances that introduced us were of such an exigent uncommon nature that to reintroduce formality and decorum after the fact, as it were, seemed, at least to *me*, unnecessarily inelastic."

"So you gave yourself liberty to regard me at the outset as an old friend—an old friend about whom you might wish to learn more than you already know—is that it? I must say that it's a rather interesting approach to endearment—as such approaches go."

"Endearment, my good woman? You think that my primary motive has been to endear myself to you?'

"You do have a charm about you."

"As do you."

"Resolved then, um: that we are both charming."

"And I regret, Miss Wolf, that our paths have not so intimately crossed before now. I should have liked, when you were an invalid child, to have brought you soup or something."

"And I should have been most grateful to have had it, and would have slurped it up with relish."

"My dear Miss Wolf, what is happening here?" My face and neck had suddenly caught fire. I wondered if it was the same with my companion.

"We are—" Now there came a breathlessness to my lady's voice that was all the more intriguing and tantalising. "We are each of us making a new friend, I suppose."

"I'm happy that you accepted my invitation to join me for tea," I said, taking Miss Wolf's soft, freckled right hand into my less soft and far less freckled left hand (for I had moved my chair close by the ottoman, thus putting us face-to-face, or hand-to-hand, as it were.)

"And I am most happy that the invitation was extended," replied Miss Wolf in her breathy way.

I now took up the other hand.

"This is rather precipitant," said she, looking down at both hands being held in a rather bold and, yes, somewhat untoward way, given that neither of us was wearing ice skates nor were we doing figures upon a dance floor—the only two circumstances which came instantly to mind that did not require an admixture of affection to bring delight to the encounter.

"More precipitant than *this*?" I asked, and then gently pressed my lips to her cheek.

"Perhaps not," said Miss Wolf, closing her eyes in something that I would like to interpret as private rapture, although it could merely have been a simple, circumstantial frisson of momentary pleasure.

"You are a bachelor, with no wife," said Miss Wolf.

I nodded, probing the green depths of her eyes with my own somewhat dull brown ones.

"And you have no lover, no paramour, no woman to whom you have already pledged your heart?"

"Madam Inquisitor, I have none. I had a love—my last—her name was Fanny Lumbey."

Miss Wolf nodded soberly. "Yes, yes. A sad case. I read of it in my training."

"She was the last woman whom I—"

She nodded. I suspended.

"And whom could I myself have loved from that invalid's bed? Those who came and went—the men, that is, who ministered to me—were there to heal, not to win my heart."

A moment of silence passed and I kissed Nurse Ruth Wolf again, this time upon the lips. When our lips parted, she sighed. Then she cleared her throat, and then she took the heels of her hands and pushed me gently away from her. "Yet I cannot."

"Why?"

"Because I have lied to you. There *is* someone else, and I would never, *could* never forget him in a raw moment of passion with a man whom I hardly—It is all quite foolish."

My spirit was broken. I felt at that moment thoroughly trod upon. "This is foolish?"

"No, no, not foolish. No, no, not at all. Only untenable. You understand? You do, don't you? Think if Fanny had lived. You would be married by now and the three of us would be sitting here together, respecting all decorum with napkins spread upon the knees and properly clinking our teacups and saucers with our spoons. Is this not true?"

I nodded. I certainly would not have kissed Miss Ruth Wolf with Fanny sitting here—nay, with Fanny anywhere else but beneath the hard earth.

"So let us suspend this encounter before it begets regrets."

I nodded once more. "Although I will forever repine what was nearly ours."

"Is that true? Why, Mr. Trimmers, you are a veritable romantic." Miss Wolf rose from the ottoman and took my hand and gave it a proper shake.

At that moment, something came suddenly to mind. I crossed to my brother's easy chair where I had left the sketchpad. I picked it up and began to leaf quickly through it. "I have a—yes, here it is."

I shewed a particular sketch to Miss Wolf. It was of my brother Gus at Newman's age. "I find the resemblance here to be rather remarkable."

"Yes, I see what you mean."

"But you haven't met Newman."

Miss Wolf cleared her throat. "I mean the resemblance of your brother as a boy to the way he now looks as a man."

I studied the sketch, unaware of how deftly Miss Wolf had just concealed her misstep. "Yes, there is still quite a bit of the boy-Gus remaining in his adult features."

"Thank you for the tea, Mr. Trimmers. And I thank you as well for saving me from the jaws of the Widow Chillip's canine sentry. This has been a most interesting—"

"May I—" I interrupted. "Begging your pardon, Miss Wolf, but may

I play the role of inquisitor just once more for the purpose of asking a parting question?"

"If it isn't of too prying a nature."

"The one to whom you have pledged your heart—is his name known only to you, Miss Wolf, or may I have knowledge of it as well?"

My auditor responded with a slightly reproving wag of the finger. "You should know his name so that—what?—you should challenge him to a duel or a joust or some other such medieval thing? No, Mr. Trimmers, I'll not indulge you by divulging it. At least not now. There are circumstances which militate against our union—his and mine—so any public declaration of our affection would not be wise."

"I see. I understand. Good night, Miss Wolf. Don't forget your medical bag." I picked up the bag and handed it to the nurse, who had in those brief moments of our time together seised my heart and held it close to hers and then returned it to me, slightly rumpled.

She thanked me and departed.

A slightly rumpled heart was better than that which had preceded it—a broken and mourning heart. I felt revived and in the end did not repent the encounter at all. It was all I could do to keep myself from stepping next door and shaking Pepper's paw in gratitude for having made it all possible.

CHAPTER THE TWENTY-SECOND

Sunday, June 29, 2003

I rose early in the morning to work on the Medical Review Board's yearly report. I had been at the task for scarcely above a quarter hour when I heard two gentle taps upon my door—taps that were quite familiar to my ear. More than likely my landlady Mrs. Lumbey had heard me stepping about her creaking floors and had thoughtfully risen to bring me tea.

But there was no tea tray left outside my door. Instead, there was the good woman herself, her generally bright and pleasant countenance transfigured by perturbation and worry.

"What is it?" I asked, ushering her into my sitting room. "What's the matter?"

I bade the good woman sit down and she did so without hesitation. I took a chair and drew it next to hers.

"It concerns Miss Pupker. She came to me last night in a most wretched state."

"You refer to the older of the two Pupker sisters: Hannah?"

Mrs. Lumbey nodded. "The older and more *agreeable* one. That state being, of course, the rule, I do fear that her wonted affability has been exceptionally tested by events of late. She was in such a frightful way last night, Trimmers. She could not be still, even as I took her hand and patted it most assiduously to calm her."

Mrs. Lumbey required a moment to compose herself, fanning her hand a little before her face. I waited patiently for her to resume. I did not wish to hurry her with the sort of impatient entreaties that generally characterised my parleys with my older brother Augustus—even before the loss of his son—or my good friend Muntle.

"The cause was this, Frederick: Hannah, the poor girl—she came to me last night, enlisting me as her confidante. We have become quite close, as you know, since the death of her friend Fanny. Hannah, you see, had overheard something quite terrible which she needed to unbosom."

"And does the matter keep itself only between the two of you or are you at liberty to relate to me its particulars?"

Mrs. Lumbey nodded solemnly. "I see no reason that you shouldn't know of it. 'Twas an exchange between her mother and father she secretly audited. They had no idea that she was standing just outside the parlour room door imbibing every syllable interchanged between them. You see, Trimmers, the two had put their daughter to bed with a warm cordial to make her sleep. After they had quitted the room, she spat the soporific liquid into a vase, not a drop of it having been swallowed, and so she was quite wakeful to overhear what was said."

"And why was it so important for her to hear what her parents were saying in her absence?"

"Only the week before she had been discovered by her father in a place that she should not have been. He was quite upset, I should say—most terribly agitated against her, more so than she would have thought him to be, given the obvious innocence in the trespass."

"Where was she found, Mrs. Lumbey, that Pupker should be so violently put out with her?"

"She hasn't said, and I cannot get it out of her. Perchance she'll tell *you*, Trimmers. She's always been quite fond of you."

"Fond of me. How do you mean?"

My question elicited the smallest suggestion of a grin upon her full lips. "You have always been kind to her, ever since she was a young girl. I recall the way that both of those girls—Hannah and my dear departed Fanny—nipped at your heels like playful puppies. Unlike the other older boys, you always stopt to offer a kind word about the dress of their dollies or to pay compliments to their curly locks. (I appreciated the compliments as well, Frederick, having spent long sessions applying the curl papers to Fanny's naturally straight tresses.) Your kind attendance was all quite affecting to see. Even though your friendship with Fanny bloomed into love, your amity with Hannah did not recede. She wonders, in fact, why you come so seldom these days to her father's sundry shop to visit."

"In a word, Mrs. Lumbey: Pupker."

Mrs. Lumbey nodded. "Hellhound of the first order. I cannot even bring myself to look upon him."

"Nor I to feign any manner of civility with *her*, alas."

Mrs. Lumbey did not suspend her agreeable nod. "He connives to gull every customer who sets foot in his shop into paying far more than his merchandise is worth. He is a merchant of the lowest order, Frederick, and a discredit to all of us who make our living in this otherwise respectable profession. It astounds me that the brokers continue to deal with him at all, let alone bestow upon him the choicest of imports."

Mrs. Lumbey was right to ventilate her hostile feelings toward Montague Pupker, and I was fain to second her opinion. There was a history of animus between Pupker and half the citizens of the Dell, which couldn't be ignored.

"So it should come as no surprise to *me*, Frederick, that the man is a disreputable father as well. Indeed, both of Hannah's parents give love to their two daughters most sparingly, but Hannah is by far the more maltreated and maligned of the two."

"What is it that they seek to do to her?"

"It is unspeakable."

"Pray speak it nonetheless."

"Petition Judge Fitz-Marshall for an order of lunacy to put Hannah into Bedlam."

"Into the asylum?"

"Alongside all the lunatic and deranged of Dingley Dell. It beggars belief. There's nothing wrong with Hannah, save the sort of reticence and self-abashment that one finds within the temperament of many of our more sheltered young women."

It was difficult for me to hear what my ears were recording. "For what reason would they seek to do such a thing, Mrs. Lumbey?"

"I cannot give you the full reason, Frederick, for I know not yet where it was that Hannah went that set her father so terribly against her. But I can tell you *this*: that Mr. and Mrs. Pupker intend over the next several days to concoct situations in which Hannah cannot help but appear to even the

most casual observer to be compromised in mental facility and discomposed in the worst possible ways. And they have already begun the process."

"How do you mean?"

"They make frightful noises at night when she is abed—the sort of
noises that a ghost would make, and they touch her with feathers—at least
it feels this way to her—as she sleeps so that she awakes to feel the touch
of a ghostly hand upon her skin. And she cries out in fear, as would be the
inclination of *anyone* who found herself waking to the skeletal touch of a
bony wraith. The parents are there when she wakes to say that she has been
screaming thusly for a long season. She surmises that Cecilia, her sister, is
in on the business as well, for upon wakeful occasions she will deny the
spectral noises that Hannah hears even as they pervade the darkened bedchamber with penetrating clarity."

"And you're certain, Mrs. Lumbey—don't misread me here—that
there is not the slightest chance that Hannah could indeed be teetering
upon the brink of insanity and that the overheard conference between her
mother and father could not have at least *some* foundation of legitimacy?"

Mrs. Lumbey shook her head whilst giving the kind of stern look that
comes when I fail to tidy up my apartments after several days of bachelor
negligence. "I've never been surer of anything in my life," was my friend
and landlady's ardent rejoinder. "If I were not, I shouldn't have asked the
poor dear girl to stop with me last night."

"You mean to say that Hannah is presently within this house?"

Mrs. Lumbey nodded.

"And do Mr. and Mrs. Pupker know this?"

Again, Mrs. Lumbey nodded. "You were at your brother's house last
night when Hannah came, with her mother and father and sister in close
and angry pursuance. Your niece Alice was tagging along as well. Is she
stopping with the Pupkers whilst Augustus and Charlotte take the country
air in Hungerford?"

I nodded. "But don't ask me to explain her affiliation with that family."

"Then I shan't. At all events, I sat with Hannah in my bed chamber
and held her hand and listened to *her* side of things as Mr. and Mrs. Pupker
and their daughter Cecilia sat and paced by turns in my front parlour, the
odious father bellowing that the girl must be turned over to him without
further delay. I emerged to say that I didn't agree, and with some resolve
I instructed Montague Pupker that he and his wife and their younger

daughter and, of course, Alice (since she wasn't come to see her uncle) should leave my premises immediately, for I had decided that Hannah would remain with me for the time being and that the matter, as far as *I* was concerned, had been fully settled."

"A most commendable act, Mrs. Lumbey," I said, shaking my landlady's hand. "And what was Pupker's reaction to this brave stand on your part?"

"At first he would have none of it, and there was stomping and bluster and protest in repletion, but he must then have come to realise that although Hannah lived beneath his own roof, one could make the case that she had reached her majority and could therefore make up her own mind about where she should spend the night."

"Even if the mother and father believed her mental capacity to be impaired by lunacy?"

"That case has yet to be made. Remember that the conversation which Hannah overheard last night was about that which was being plotted and schemed, but had yet to come to full fruition."

"Meaning that perhaps you rescued Hannah before her parents could engineer evidence sufficient to prove *non compos mentis*."

With a self-assured nod of the head, Mrs. Lumbey returned, "I hope and pray, though, that there was little truth to their vow to return to-day with the sheriff and fetch her home by whatever means could be secured."

I took a breath and then a moment to compose myself. "I should like to see her when she rises."

Mrs. Lumbey nodded. After an interval of silence, during which each of us allowed the facts of this troublesome matter to cure within our thoughts, she turned to me and said, "Trimmers, pray tell me if I did the right thing."

"To be sure, you did. But it's now up to the two of us together to discover what was done or seen by poor Hannah that has placed her within such desperate straits. I'll speak with her, if she's calm and will permit the interview."

❧

I was relieved to see that Muntle came alone. There was not a single Pupker hiding behind tree or lamppost to spring upon Mrs. Lumbey's shop and adjoining lodgings to reclaim their fugitive daughter. This happy fact would afford me the chance to argue for Hannah being given leave to re-main with Mrs. Lumbey without cross-questioning by the Pupkers. Be-sides, as I may have mentioned before, I didn't like Pupker and chose to avoid intercourse with him at every opportunity.

Unfortunately, Muntle came too early to allow time for me to see Hannah prior to his arrival, so there was not much more that I could convey to my friend on Hannah's side, given my reluctance, without de-tailed corroboration from the young woman, to mention the parental scheme to drive their daughter insane—or, rather, to create the appearance of lunacy within her—nor did I feel that I should mention that there was a place visited by Hannah that had set her father upon this present course, not knowing what that place was nor how important a role its disclosure would play to her cause.

So I made her case as her advocate based upon the singular fact that Hannah was a grown woman, and as such had the right to withdraw from her family for whatever reason should be her choosing, which did not in consequence put her into the women's ward of one of the Milltown work-houses, nor into a dirty gutter in a state of impoverished self-negation, as would sometimes come to a woman in Dingley Dell without family, for-tune or position.

"Consider her to be, at least for the nonce, the ward of my landlady," I said to Muntle as I poured from the pot of tea that Mrs. Lumbey had thoughtfully sent up for our refreshment.

"Though she is beyond the age of compulsory guardianship?"

"Then consider her independent."

"I must see what the law says."

"I know what the law says, Muntle. It says that Hannah Pupker has every right, should it be her desire, to stop with Mrs. Lumbey. You're only here, I warrant, because that repugnant blackguard has put screws to you to haul her home, with or without legal justification."

"Trimmers, your accusation that the man has overriding influence over me is odiously unfounded. I answer only to the law."

"I'm not assailing your reputation as sheriff, Muntle. I'm only saying—"

The sheriff raised his hand to put an end to this train. "Here is the truth of the matter, Trimmers, and I draw you generously into my confidence as friend to tell you the following by way of background: the Petit-Parliament has just this forenoon passed legislation which authorises the removal of all of the residents of the vagrant Scadger camp so that their mean shelters can be razed and more apricot trees planted in their place."

"And where are all the displaced Scadgers to go?"

"Housing has been secured for them in Milltown. The Petit-Parliament maintains that this barefoot, dishevelled clan has remained dissociated from the rest of the valley population for far too long, and though they live at the farthest most eastern reach of our Dell, it is time to bring their gipsy-like subsistence beneath the apricot trees to an end."

"Because they are polluting the fruit."

Muntle shook his head. "Their children are badly fed and poorly drest, Trimmers. Adult or child, it makes no difference—one's full dietary requirements cannot be met by apricots and ground nuts alone, nor do apricots and ground nuts provide the necessary materials for the making of shoes or any of the other indispensables of daily life."

"You sound as if you're in agreement with the Petit-Parliament."

"On this issue, I am *quite* in agreement. It is far better in my opinion for the Scadgers to live close-at-hand and be educated and uplifted than to have my deputies and me galloping far and wide to put scattered clamps upon their scuttling, mischief-making indigence."

"You raised this topic to tell me something about Pupker, but I cannot, as yet, make the connexion, Muntle."

"The connexion, Trimmers, is this: Pupker owns several buildings in the East End Mews that he is willing to let to the Scadgers at a quite reasonable rate. This is a very good thing, since the cost will naturally have to be paid out of community coffers, the whole lot of those impoverished gipsy-like knife-sharpeners and basket-weavers having not two florins to rub together."

I shook my head and well nigh snorted. "Yet I've never known Pupker to be philanthropic without deriving some concurrent benefit. What's the catch?"

The sheriff sighed. "That the Petit-Parliament and, more specifically, its cabinet ministers, give more faith and credit to *this* particular act of public largesse on the part of Pupker than to any of his former deeds of civic benevolence."

I laughed. "To my knowledge there have been *no* former deeds of civic benevolence from that execrable purveyor! And I take issue with your present characterisation of 'largesse' at all events."

"Howbeit, Pupker will heretofore have a greater voice amongst those who claim the attention of the M.P.P.'s. It is the way of things, Trimmers. One hand greases the other, and whilst a few benefit in surplus, others such as the soon-to-be-homeless Scadger clan may profit along the narrower margins. It is the reason, if I may be honest, for the Minister of Trade having raised objections to your climbing to the Summit of Exchange to discuss the whereabouts of your nephew with the Outlander-tradesmen."

"Because Pupker first objected?"

Muntle nodded without lifting his head. It was an admission that he would have preferred not to make.

"Pupker hasn't anything better to do with his time than to devise ways to check and obstruct *me*? Has thwarting the intentions of Frederick Trimmers become, as of late, the man's favourite avocation?"

"I don't know, nor do I have the time to puzzle it out. I will only say that Montague Pupker has never been one of your great admirers—let us both stipulate to it—nor will your advocacy of his refractory daughter do anything but add more fuel to the fire of his dislike for you, especially should you choose to pursue this matter with the girl beyond this day. Perhaps I *will* hazard a guess here: it is your feelings for Hannah that abrade him."

"But I *have* no feelings for Hannah Pupker beyond simple friendship," I protested.

"He doesn't see it that way."

"I cannot account for his misinterpretation of my friendship with his daughter, nor do I wish to waste time anatomising it."

"Well, I shan't be the one to tell him he is wrong on this account, Trimmers. Perhaps in your heart of hearts you do feel something beyond a platonic attachment for the young woman. I have myself in recent days wrestled with similar feelings that will not make themselves so clear."

"What do you mean, Muntle?"

Muntle coloured.

"Out with it, man."

With bashful reluctance: "The Chowser cook—you recall my telling you of the afternoon that she and I spent in the cemetery last year?"

"Discussing cheese."

"Amongst other things, turd. I chanced upon her again just yesterday. We spent another delightful afternoon together. I am inclined to visit the school soon on official business."

I interposed with a laugh, "Such business as yet to be concocted."

Muntle nodded animatedly. "I must find out if this small stirring within me for this dear woman may lead to something far more serious. Now, my dear Trimmers, who is to say whether or no your heart carries you along the same path with Miss Pupker."

How ludicrous that Muntle should presume my thoughts to stray to Hannah Pupker, when ever since last night I could not stop myself from thinking ever and anon about the Bedlam nurse Ruth Wolf, and how appealing her features had appeared to me in the softly diffused candlelight of my brother and sister-in-law's drawing room, and how we had been most intimate, and how close we had come to melding ourselves in that most intimate mode of coupling that God and human evolution have devised!

"At all events, Trimmers, whether there is truth or no to what some have always said about you and Hannah Pupker, nothing can be allowed to muddy the proceedings, especially with regard to the Scadger matter, nor will I simply stand by and watch you ruffle the feathers of the Petit-Parliament's strongest ally and, at present, its greatest benefactor through your affinity—however it should be defined—for Montague Pupker's daughter, nor for reason of your overwhelming distaste for Montague Pupker himself. Moreover, Pupker will not believe that, given his felicitous standing with Parliament—he being a virtual member of that body himself—there should be nothing that I can do as sheriff of Dingley Dell and servant to that august assembly to restore Hannah to her family. Pray suffer me, therefore, Trimmers, to fulfill my obligations and return her to her parents and let us all put an end to this whole prickly affair."

I shook my head and crossed my arms upon my chest. "I will not, Muntle. I will not fold my hand as a matter of the strongest principle. I'm not so easily compromised that I should see a young woman placed into a madhouse so that no one's 'feathers be ruffled.'"

"Madhouse?"

"What?"

"You said 'placed into a madhouse.'"

"Did I?" I closed my eyes and repined. I had put my foot in it.

Muntle stared hard at me. "My hearing is not as good as it once was, Trimmers, but I am fairly certain that I just this moment heard you to say that the girl might be placed into a madhouse. And as there is only one 'madhouse' in Dingley Dell, I am certain that your specific meaning was

Bedlam. Now, out with the rest of it, if you know what's good for you."

"Alas, Muntle, I've told you too much already."

I took a silent turn across the room, Muntle watching me, waiting to hear what next I would say. Finally I resumed: "And regardless of what I have unfortunately blurted, there's no fair reason that Hannah Pupker should be forced to return to a family that so thoroughly maltreats her."

"I hadn't heard that the young woman has been made miserable within that household. Would you care to tell me what you know?"

"Things have been spoken to me in confidence, Muntle. I haven't leave at present to retail them, nor do I know the half of what there is to know of Hannah Pupker's plight. At such time as I become better informed and once permission has been granted, I shall be more than eager to disclose every detail."

Muntle stepped back and regarded me with a half-smile and a thoughtful rub of the chin. He shaved only every third day or so and there was often a bristly aspect to the face that gave him the look of one too invested in the duty of his offices to attend too closely to personal hygiene. "Although this places me in an awkward position with regard to the Pupkers, I've known you too long, Trimmers, not to trust you when you say that my trust in you is paramount to your purpose. I thereby grant you— albeit with a decided measure of disinclination—the time you require to learn everything that it may behove me to know to put a cap on this matter before it draws in the Petit-Parliament, which employs me, by the bye, and which would hold me accountable for an unsatisfactory resolution to this matter."

"And what will you say to Pupker betweenwhiles to put him off?"

"The only thing I *can* say: that the poor girl has taken ill, and cannot be moved, and cannot see anyone, and this will have to suffice for the near term. But mark me, Freddie, I can hold off the family for only so long. It's up to you to put an end to this thing in such a way as to mollify everyone concerned."

"I'll do what I can," I said, instantly regretting the heavy charge that had been invested in me. "Perhaps when I speak to Hannah, I'll have a much clearer picture of where things stand."

Sheriff Muntle departed without his hat. However, within moments he returned to snatch it up and plop it roughly upon his large head. There was a business-like formality to his mien, yet a smile escaped in spite of himself:

the smile of a friend—a friend who knew the way of things, but who also knew that there was right and there was wrong, and there was nothing more right in the world than the cause of those who championed, at some risk to themselves, the former over the latter.

CHAPTER THE TWENTY-THIRD

Sunday, June 29, 2003

Hannah was sleepy. Her eyes considered me through creases. Yet I could still see that they were shot with blood from the young woman's having lain awake for a good many hours the night before, and having shed tears all the while, and there having been insufficient hours intervening for a natural reversal of the ocular rubrication.

"I'm here to help you," I said in a low and tender voice. Her nod—a slight tip of the head—indicated that in her heart she knew this. Now the next matter to be settled was this: how forthcoming would Hannah be in disclosing those events that had led us to this unfortunate juncture?

We sat in Mrs. Lumbey's kitchen across the table from one another. My landlady paced close by. Her constant motion was distracting, and I bade her sit down. "Or is it your wish, Hannah," I asked of my table companion, "that Mrs. Lumbey should quit us altogether and that you and I should speak in private?"

Hannah shook her head. "No, no. My rescuing angel may hear what it is that I will say. I've thought about it through much of the night and it's been a terrible burden for me to keep these things inside, so I'll tell it the both of you, but pray you may not breathe it to another soul!"

We—the rescuing angel and myself—nodded as one. Yet I knew that Muntle would want to know as well. I decided not to pursue the matter here, but to wait until such future time as I could make a convincing case for adding the sheriff's name to the list of Hannah's selective confidantes.

Hannah Pupker was a sylph and softly winsome young woman, resident of that twilight land between "pretty" and "beautiful." Even in taking a sip of tea from the cup that had been placed before her, she executed a fluidity of movement that brought to mind a lithe dancer, comely in face and comely in motion. Hannah returned the cup to the table but kept her palms pressed against it, as if her hands required the heat to keep themselves warm. Although this early summer morning was just as temperate as any other, yet Hannah Pupker seemed to be feeling a great chill upon the air. She shivered, then she sipped again, and then she said, "My father keeps a cellar deep below his shop. It is not the cellar storeroom which my sister and I frequently visit, nay, which a good many have seen when they have followed us down to find the particularly elusive item that often turns up there. But it is a second storeroom hollowed out beneath this one—a sub-cellar, which in all of my years I had never before discovered."

"How curious!" remarked Mrs. Lumbey. She sat deeply absorbed, her right hand poised with a bite of cake, not permitting it—as yet—to reach her partially gaping, receptive mouth.

"And how did you come to learn of the other cellar's existence?" I asked.

"Susan Fagin told me."

Neither Mrs. Lumbey nor I could withhold the startled looks that overspread our faces at that moment.

"How is it that Susan Fagin knows about this secret sub-cellar?" asked Mrs. Lumbey, the hand still holding the uneaten cake in mid-air.

"It was told her by Mrs. Pyegrave. Told to Susan and Susan alone."

"And how did Susan come to be privy to such intelligence?" I asked.

"The woman told her things before she died. Other things as well, which she did not reveal. But Susan felt that I should know about the sub-cellar and what was in it, since it lay beneath my own father's emporium."

We sat quietly for a moment, the three of us, digesting what had been said.

After a brief interval of silence, Hannah resumed: "One reaches the burrow by descending a musty set of stairs. These stairs are hidden behind the cupboard that contains the older porcelain cups and saucers—those that have lost favour with our customers. I never knew until last week that the cupboard isn't like any other, for it doesn't always hold fast to its spot along a wall in the upper cellar. You see, it has the capacity to *turn*, and the wall itself to turn out with it. One must only pull at a certain cup upon a certain side peg—this is what Susan told me—and something of a mechanical nature then causes the cupboard to pivot upon its hidden internal axis, revealing those stairs that lead down to the room below."

"One pulls at a cup upon a peg!" I exclaimed in unchecked amazement. The mechanical has always fascinated me. I begged forgiveness for the interruption and bade Hannah continue.

Before she could do so, Mrs. Lumbey asked how it came to be that Hannah should find herself alone and undisturbed in the cellar-storeroom, conveniently situated to pull at the cup and put the cupboard into motion.

"Quite simply this: Mrs. Gallanbile sought a salt spoon. Her playful new puppy had run off with her present one, and no doubt buried it somewhere in the commons. I wondered aloud if there might be a spoon in Mrs. Gallanbile's preferred pattern downstairs in the old relegation-cupboard. I went down alone to the storeroom and the cup that puts things immediately into motion caught my eye. It was hanging incorrectly, just as Susan had said that it would be; rather than depending upon its side in the manner of its companions, its rim kissed the cupboard itself most inordinately."

Mrs. Lumbey nodded and continued: "I myself hate to see such things out of sorts. One must have order and decorum within one's home *and* one's shop if one is to have any hope of lifelong sanity."

Hannah nodded with polite indulgence and resumed: "I pulled upon the cup as I had been instructed to do and in that same moment, the peg upon which it depended extended itself toward me, and the cupboard became unfastened from whatever was inside, which had held it securely in place, and it swung dramatically upon its axis, as I have said—so dramatically, in fact, that I couldn't help jumping back in a most surprised state to marvel at this most curious phenomenon, made ever the more astounding by the sudden revelation of the descending staircase formerly hidden behind it."

"Susan hadn't mentioned the staircase?" I asked.

"Of course she had. I was simply unprepared for it—unprepared to behold with my own eyes the existence of this room that I'd never before seen nor heard mentioned by either my parents or my sister."

At this, Mrs. Lumbey popped the bite of cake into her mouth, but did not chew. As one suspends one's breath in excited anticipation, my landlady postponed mastication for a full minute at least, before beginning to work her jaw in a most abstracted manner.

"Now the stairs were quite dark. I lighted a candle and proceeded to discover what mystery lay beneath my feet. I knew that my younger sister Cecilia would, in due time, come to fetch me; Mrs. Gallanbile was waiting, and Papa doesn't like to keep customers waiting (though he has done every other regrettable thing to a customer that can be imagined). Yet I also knew that I wouldn't have another opportunity to find out what was in the sub-cellar for quite some time. Mama and Papa were each abroad this particular afternoon, but they were expected back shortly and would remain in residence for the balance of the day and perchance all of the morrow, as well.

"So I took the candle to light my way and crept down the wooden stairs, and I could tell after only my first two or three steps that the room was by no means empty. I could make out the outlines in silhouette of a good many things, none of which I was able to conclusively identify save a number of cardboard boxes. As I continued my descent, the things that had been stacked and lined up and ordered about the room did not betray their mysterious nature. Each unboxed item remained most unfamiliar to me. Some appeared to be made of metal of some sort, and others of metal and glass. Still others had apparently been fabricated from some light ceramic that I was certain I had never before seen. It was as if this were the laboratory of a scientific madman—but not just any everyday, garden-variety madman. Here was the potential domain of a crazed man of science like none other, for nobody I knew in our valley—sane or otherwise—could have crafted those things that sat amongst all the boxes of varying sizes. Where, I asked myself, were the madman's smoking flasks and bubbling beakers and the galvanometers to gauge the conduction of electrical currents hither and thither?"

"Forgive me for interrupting, dear," said Mrs. Lumbey with an expression of perplexity that replicated my own puzzled look, "but could you not identify even a single thing within the room? Was *everything* contained in that sub-cellar of unfamiliar shape and design?"

Hannah nodded. "I touched an object and then another, and they were quite cold to my fingertips—hard and cold. Some had long ropes, fashioned, it would seem, of India rubber, which snaked and coiled from the inside. One of the snakes communicated with a plate upon a wall. It was the strangest assortment of things I had ever seen in my life. I knew that my father must have acquired these things from the Outlanders, but none had ever been put into the showroom upstairs nor had they even made their way to the storeroom directly above my head.

"It was at this most unfortunate moment that the outline of my sister materialised at the top of the stairs, her arms akimbo, one foot tapping an impatient tattoo. 'Shame on you, Hannah Pupker!' she scolded. 'Loitering down here whilst Mrs. Gallanbile remains above, upbraiding me in that shrill voice of hers over your lengthy absence!'

"It took me a moment to compose myself, Cecilia's sudden appearance having severely unsettled me. Then I asked my sister quite pointedly if she knew of the room.

"'Yes, I know of the room,' she replied with an indignant toss of the head, 'but *you* have no business being here. It is of no concern to either of us.'

"'But what *are* these things?' I pursued. 'This thing here, for example.' I touched the top of a hard narrow box with buttons and slots upon the side. 'What is it? Or this? Or this?' I placed my hand first upon a box with a glass window too opaque to view what was inside and then upon a machine of some sort with numbered buttons. 'This thing has writing upon it. It says "Cuisinart Espresso Maker." What is Cuisinart espresso and why would a person wish to make it?'

"'Egad, Hannah! Do I care? Ask me if I care.'

"My sister's tone was harsh and reproachful, and yet I persisted: 'Did each of these things come from the Outland?'

"'I have no doubt that they did,' she said. Then Cecilia added: 'But none of it should concern you in the least, Miss Nosy-body, and if you don't remove yourself from this room at this very instant and procure that ancient spoon Mrs. Gallanbile has requested, I shall be compelled to drag you up both flights of stairs by your hair.'

"I stared at my fifteen-year-old sister to glean if she had lost her juvenile mind. Here stood I in a room never before revealed to me by my father, amongst a strange assortment of sealed boxes and metal and ceramicoid objects that made no sense at all, and which gave every reason for further investigation, and the only thought that lived within Cecilia's dimly-lighted brain was that I should come up to attend a restive customer who after examining the spoon in question would, no doubt, as was her custom, decline either to purchase it or even to have it set aside for future consideration!

"'I refuse to join you upstairs, Cecilia, until you tell me the purpose of this room and what all these things are for.'

"'And *I* have told *you* that I don't *know* what they're for. Nor do I give a straw. Perhaps they're small presses and little miniature wardrobes and divers mechanical wind-up toys that are made by the Beyonders, which our father sought at one time to sell in Dingley Dell but then decided *not* to. They are most ugly, at all events, and I don't wish to look at them another second, and you are a fool, Hannah Pupker, if you remain here in some ridiculous attempt to figure them out. I'll make this bargain with you: if you come up the stairs with me before the passage of another minute and forget that you have been down here, I won't tell Papa of your trespass.'

"'But I should like to ask him a great deal about this room when he returns.'

"'I would not do that were I you. He gave me stern warning never to come down here. You have interloped and will not be better treated.'

"'Now how on earth could I have interloped, Cecilia, when I was never issued like-injunction?'

"The question was never answered, for at that very moment a shadow made itself manifest next to my sister. The adumbration bore the outline of my father and its presence, ominous and forbidding, frightened me to my very soul. Papa didn't speak. He came down the stairs in a sweep of fury, and taking me roughly by the wrist, wrested me up and out of the room. With an angry shove, he restored the cupboard to its previous situation against the wall, the opening to the stairs now closed tight. Loose cups flew off their pegs from the force of his free hand, sailed across the room, and shattered into hundreds of shards upon impact with the hard slate floor.

"The suddenness and precipitance of this action terrified me, and I let out a startled half-scream, which was immediately aborted by the clap of Papa's hand over my mouth. For one horrible second I felt as if he were bent not only upon silencing my voice, but also upon preventing my taking in all future breath. But I quickly checked myself; it was surely the scream—my thoughtless, reactive scream—that had propelled the brutal assault of his large hand upon my mouth. He will pull away, thought I, and then apologise for taking such a drastic and violent action.

"And he *did* pull away. Scarcely a moment later." Hannah lowered her eyes. "He did not, however, offer an apology."

With mention of the stifling hand, Mrs. Lumbey had let out a startled peep of her own. I held myself in check but could not stop shaking my head in disbelief. With the succeeding revelation, Hannah's female auditor heaved a long, commiserating sigh. Obviously, the right thing to do had not been done, but when had Montague Pupker ever done that which was generally expected of every good burgher *or* father?

"'You're never to go down there again,' said he. 'And you will forget everything you've seen there.' I couldn't withhold the question that crouched so brazenly upon my tongue; I asked my father without reservation what they were—all those things that I could scarcely identify—a veritable storeroom of inexplicable merchandise. 'They are nothing that you should know about,' was his gruff reply. 'Nothing at all. Expunge what you've seen from your mind. Go upstairs now and wait on Mrs. Gallanbile. The old crone has reached the state of impatient nuisance. Go along! Take yourself away from here!'

"And that was the last that was said of the room by anyone. Even Cecilia, who at first would not answer any of my subsequent private enquiries, took later to responding with a convenient, albeit mendacious 'I have no idea what you're talking about. There's no such room. You're daft.'"

"Upon my very soul!" exclaimed Mrs. Lumbey.

"I've heretofore kept my promise to my father, and in addition, I plan never again to raise this futile matter with my sister who foils and frustrates no matter what one asks of her. I've kept my side of the bargain. Yet now Papa knows that *I* know and he cannot stop himself from looking at me in either a suspicious or apprehensive manner. It is quite discomfiting. I'm now convinced that it is his aim to have me declared insane either to silence me or to create doubt about the veracity of any account I should in future make as to what I saw in that nether room. Such an account can come only from the mouth of a madwoman, he will say, and people will heed him, as they always do, and I shall be in a hard spot, no matter how one looks at it."

With this, Hannah Pupker sank back into her chair and exhaled deeply, as if she could not possibly have relaxed herself until every bit of her story was related in confessional fashion.

"And now you have told *us*," I said in as comforting a tone to Hannah as I could offer. I noted that her hand was trembling, her brow beaded with the perspiration of worry. "And whilst it was quite commendable that you should unburden yourself, it nonetheless keeps unanswered the important question of what exactly is in that lower cellar. Also why should revelation of the room's contents inject such fear into the heart of your father?"

"And my mother as well. She also treats me differently. Both of them regard me now as if I'm a stranger in their midst."

"Can you even guess at what those things were, which you saw within the room?" I asked.

Hannah shook her head slowly and reflectively. "I have pondered it at length. They resemble nothing with which I'm familiar. I must confide something to you both. I am mortified to say it, but I *will* say it: I wonder if those boxes have come to us from some distant world."

"Surely you can't mean that!" declared Mrs. Lumbey. "Some other world?"

"Yes. I cannot help thinking this. I cannot help thinking that the room is filled with merchandise received not from earthly Outlanders, but from Outland purveyors of a most *un*-earthly origin. This is my only explanation."

"You shouldn't apologise for making such a conjecture," I said. I had hoped that my voice carried with it the soothing tone that characterised the earliest moments of our exchange, and yet, my blood was up and my curiosity whetted and there was much that I was now champing at the bit to discover for myself. "The sheriff and I must go down there ourselves, and as soon as possible," I resolved aloud. "What *we* find there cannot help but exonerate you, Hannah. Your father will be forced to explain everything."

Suddenly, Hannah's face became blanched of all colour. "But you mustn't!" she cried out in fear. "You simply *cannot!*"

"But otherwise, dear girl, you will be made the fool or worse." It was Mrs. Lumbey's turn now to bring young Hannah Pupker to the point of reason. "Without proof of what you've seen, your parents will deny everything that you say." Mrs. Lumbey had seated herself next to her guest. She twined her own plump fingers through Hannah's slender digits to settle and calm her, but the gesture seemed to do little good. Hannah shifted her delicate frame uneasily in her chair and finally uprose, whilst retrieving her hand so that it could be employed in such agitated, fitful wringing as to tug upon all but the most hardened heart.

"But I *don't* plan to say another word. I don't intend to breathe even a single syllable to another soul. We must, all of us, put this into the tomb of silence and walk quickly away. I cannot even conceive of the consequences, should we pursue it!"

"Yet last week you didn't quail," I countered. "Your curiosity transported you boldly down the stairs of that nether cellar and into the darkness without hesitation. You made your cursory inspection without thought or care as to potential consequences."

"This is true. But now my mettle has weakened. I shrink most terribly when I think of what my family wishes to do to me because of my trespass."

"But that is the point, my dear," said Mrs. Lumbey. "That they now seek to have you placed in Bedlam whether you speak or do not speak. It matters not *what* you do, for you are become a danger to them by your very liberty. And by the bye, your mother and father and sister can no longer be regarded by you as family. They consider you to be a stranger and so you must consider them as likewise alien to your blood and to your heart. Do not shrink, my darling child. Suffer Frederick to take this matter to the sheriff and give that good man leave to place it into the hands of the law."

"The Sheriff will not think me insane?"

"He's known you all your life, Hannah," I replied.

A moment passed, and then another. Finally, Hannah signaled her consent with a nod.

"The lid is off the kettle and the heat below is coming to full flame," Mrs. Lumbey continued by way of summary, "and things will reach a boil, whether one wishes them to or no."

"I *have* opened a veritable Pandora's box, haven't I?" rejoined Hannah with a quivering lip. "And nobody can undo what has been done here."

"However, I wouldn't put it in *those* terms," said I. "It was never *your* parcel, but something your *father* has secreted that is at issue. Forgive me for speaking ill of the man whose blood you carry in your own veins, Hannah, but I don't like the sound and substance of anything you've told us this morning. It must be investigated. Have I your permission to go directly to the sheriff with that which I now know?"

"Directly?" The word gave her long pause. Hannah was torn and tormented by her predicament. There was no safe path—each possible avenue being strewn with nettles and pocked with holes to sprain and trip and perhaps cripple the farer along the way. But one takes a journey through a series of single steps. And this first step put the foot upon solid ground. "Very well," said she in a soft, even strain. "I suppose you must."

Mrs. Lumbey and I greeted Hannah's decision with a reception of nods and compassionating smiles.

"You are much too lovely a girl to have to reside with lunatics," appended Mrs. Lumbey on her way to the stove to reheat the kettle. "And we simply cannot have *that!*"

CHAPTER THE TWENTY-FOURTH

Monday, June 30, 2003

Muntle scratched his head. He coughed. He composed his features and then he said, "It is all quite unbelievable."

The two of us were strolling along Rudge Street in Milltown, my having joined him on afternoon rounds. It was generally the duty of the deputy or, in exceptional circumstances, the tipstaff (or vice-sheriff) to watch the streets for things amiss, but on this particular Monday post-noon hardly a deputy was eligible for patrol, nearly all of the young lawmen having gone to the cricket field. The game, which had been initiated at Regents Park the previous afternoon between the Sheriff's League and the Barbers' Brigade (an historic rival), remained tied when suspended on account of darkness and had this following day been resumed to determine which team would face the Hustling Hostlers in the tournament's final match on the following Sunday. The sheriff himself was eager to complete his rounds and be off to extend befitting motivational encomiums to his bowler and his fielders, but he also knew that there was plenty of time for him to demonstrate his support, this particular bout conceivably lasting another five or six hours.

"Do you mean, Muntle, 'unbelievable' in the sense of 'preposterous!' or is your meaning something more along the lines of 'I stand here amazed but won't deny what you've told me'?"

"The latter of course. Have I any reason to doubt what you've just said?"

"None whatsoever. So you'll come with me, then, to see it for yourself?"

Muntle thought over the proposition but didn't speak.

I pursued: "It won't take you much out of your way, and you'll view with your own eyes what Hannah Pupker's eyes have beheld, much to her detriment."

Sheriff Muntle, having stopt at the corner of Rudge and Dorrit, cleared his throat to make his response, as, at that instant, a young boy whose name I recalled as either Tom or Toby approached us with broom in hand to sweep the equine and bovine ordure off the cobbled lane in anticipation of our desire to cross without soiling our boots.

"We will not cross here," said Muntle to the child, "but are only suspending our perambulation for a brief interval. Nonetheless, here are three mil to thank you for your interest in our well being." Muntle dropt the tiny coins into the young boy's small, outstretched hand. Tom (or Toby) pocketed his gain with a smile and then tipped his frayed cap before turning to accost the couple (the glazier and his wife, the miniature painter) who casually strolled a few paces behind us.

The youthful crossing sweeper was amongst the poorest of the valley, nearly as indigent a child as any within the barefoot Scadger clan. Mind, no child starved in Dingley Dell who could open his mouth to take thin, eleemosynary gruel into his empty maw (and publicly-bestowed brimstone and treacle for the constitution was given, as well, by the charity ladies—or charity "ladlers" as they were more humorously denominated), but a good many of our younger Dinglians (and quite a few of the older ones as well) had little to their name beyond the bread that they received at the workhouse and the various dispensaries of beneficence, or those crusts earned by the sweat of their own brows or the exhausting enterprise of an eking parent.

Dingley Dell, in spite of every good effort to turn it to utopia, endured a system of class and caste, which closely paralleled that with which we had become quite familiar through the works of Mr. D. and the authors of the *Ensyke*. The system was put into place quite early in the long epoch of our existence, born of the greed and sharp wits of a group of First Generationers who saw fit to seise the larger farms and estates subsequent to their adult evacuation and then to hold them within their families in virtual perpetuity, not unlike the unapologetic aim and purpose of the landed gentry of Queen Victoria's realm. It was vexing to everybody whose ancestors had not the expeditious wherewithal to do the same, but each of those generations that came thereafter settled, at all events, into an attitude of acquiescence (of a sort) to their fated lot, such resignation amongst the "have lesses" discouraging the fomenting of revolt or any concerted movement toward republicanism, so long as one was permitted to pursue the vocation of one's calling, or, in the case of the poor, under-skilled and dimwitted, to receive their roll with butter (or lardy butterine) and the occasional tumbler of mitigating ale.

I, like Muntle, carried mils about in my pocket to bestow upon the poor with daily munificence. There was not much that a mil could buy, but ten would give a cent, and ten cents a florin, and before one knew it, a man (or boy) might find a pound's worth of the small-valued coins within his pocket, and a pound would buy a great deal in our small mercantile world in which there was not much to buy of *great* worth, but a great store of available goods of significantly lesser value.

"What are you getting at, Trimmers? That we should go at this very moment and pray access to this sub-cellar that Hannah Pupker limns? And upon what grounds would I compromise my legal offices to do this? For even if we find such items as those matching the young woman's vague description, where has a crime been committed?"

"There is no crime, I suppose," I returned. "At least none upon the surface of the act. But doesn't it strike you as strange that there exists within the Dell such a room, withheld from view, possessed of contents that can scarcely be understood? Haven't you even an ounce of curiosity about the whole business?"

"I suspect as was one of your own proffered suppositions, Trimmers, that they are articles of furniture fabricated outside the valley, which do not please the eye, and which for this reason Pupker withholds from public display. I find more logic to this hypothesis than the one that presumes some other-worldly, astronomic origin."

We strolled along the walk toward the promenade that gave a lovely prospect of the indolently meandering Thames. I could tell that Muntle was dangling upon the proverbial horns of that dilemma which argued for Pupker's privacy, yet gave equal weight to civic curiosity. Here was an officer of the Dell whose sworn responsibility to provide for the safety and well-being of the general population militated against the right to suspicious concealment and secretiveness on the part of any single member of that same population. Pupker was a man with an excellent standing before the Petit-Parliament, but such a position of patronage and favour didn't give him leave to operate his business under deliberate clandestine coverture. Or did it?

"Consider as well the treatment of the daughter by each of the other three members of that family," I added. "Although she was never well-favoured, they now regard her as if she is a veritable pariah amongst them."

Muntle did, in fact, consider this unfortunate truth in thoughtful silence as we gained the promenade and began to amble upon its weathered wooden planks. There were small skiffs upon the river, and even a punt or two in the middle where the channel had been only shallowly dredged. Along the opposite, reedier eastern bank trooped a tagrag and bobtail bunch from the Scadger clan—one of the six Scadger brothers—leading his brood to the Pupker Mews.

Muntle stopped to register the scene. "Would that they *all* went so willingly to their new home," he mused aloud. "That appears to be Harry—the second oldest of that family. He's always been the most sensible of the tribe. He knows a good thing when he sees it."

As the family drew nearer that point which offered our best vantage, I saw that Muntle had identified the brother correctly; there was Harry and there was his wife Matilda, each drest in cast-off and multiply-mended clothing, the husband in an old worn and faded blue camlet coat that did not befit the warm season, dragging a large gunnysack, which, no doubt, contained most of his family's paltry possessions. Matilda wore what certainly represented her "finest": a tawdry squeezed bonnet and shawl over a castoff pinafore and smock, both threadbare and depending nearly in tassels. Behind the parents trailed their five children of various ages and sizes, the oldest, perhaps thirteen, a girl of well-nigh-skeletal frame and a near bewigged death-head sitting upon hunched, brachiate shoulders. The girl, whose name I could not recall, had a scrofulous-like cough, which completed the pitiable scene.

I had met this girl and each of her brothers and sisters, as well as the mother, when I had sat down several months earlier in the jerry-cobbled, apricot-tree-shaded wooden structure that had formerly served as a poor excuse for a domicile. I had sought and received upon that visit an interview with the father for the purpose of placing an appeal in the *Dingley Delver* on his behalf and on behalf of the other members of his familial clan who lived in similar impoverished circumstances nearby. That winter had been especially severe, but the Scadger brothers were too proud to ask anything of their valley neighbours beyond the small income they derived from their tinkering, and the women from the sale of their plaited baskets (baskets which Pupker and his ilk bought for mils and turned to great profit through trade with the Outlanders for goods of significantly greater value). I did not ask for charity from my *Delver* readers, but instead encouraged an increase in the patronage of Scadger vendibles during these hard times, so that the youngest and most vulnerable of the clan wouldn't starve or freeze to death.

Although Harry Scadger had acknowledged my kindness with a pledge to eternal friendship, his brothers did not. Moreover, they permitted their pride instead to feed resentment and suspicion of my motives—motives that nonetheless resulted in a sharp increase in business, and the opportunity to purchase blankets and quartern loafs and hard sausage, and to see every adult and child in their band—even the several consumptives (for Harry's oldest girl was not alone in being stricken by this affliction)—brought safely through the fell season.

Harry was different from his brothers in many ways, and it touched me to see that he didn't plan to resist the inevitability of eviction from the apricot grove. Muntle and I followed the family with our gaze until they had rounded a corner and disappeared from view. Others on our side of the river were observing them as well, with expressions that ranged from the mildly curious to the clearly indignant. There were a good many Milltowners who lived on the western side of the Thames who, I predicted, would not countenance a Scadger invasion. Yet the Mews, being quartered in the town's poorer East End, district gave some protection, for there was little cause for the Scadgers to cross the river and "pollute" the finer neighbourhoods of Milltown with their impecunious presence, except under the most exceptional circumstances.

For my part, I regarded the finer neighbourhoods of my town with an opposite species of disdain. That in a land so narrowly circumscribed, so small and potentially insignificant when set against the rest of the immense world, one should exhibit the same snobbery and contempt for the less fortunate who hobbled and begged amongst us as was evinced in the works of Mr. D., the same derision and loathing of the lower classes that appeared to make a mockery of the mission of our Lord Jesus Christ— this was a conundrum which irked and nettled me upon a daily basis. I gained no satisfaction from society with any of those lofty and high-toned

Milltown Bashaws who rolled perambulators under fringed parasols, who twirled their silver-tipped canes, who rode in private cabriolets and fine chariots-and-four, who wore silk turbans and bonnet-caps trimmed with little damask roses and high-crowned hats upon their swelled heads, who turned up their noses or avoided looking upon all those who did not, *could* not do or have these things on account of limited means. It utterly bewildered me, and though I kept my feelings largely to myself, at times those feelings must have shewed themselves upon my face in the burning cheek or the lip-chewing mow. Perhaps it was just such a grimace which at that moment drew my friend Muntle's eye and turned his own lips opposite-wise into a cryptic grin.

After holding the look for a long moment, he said simply, "You care far too much for your own good."

"What do you mean by that?" I rejoined.

"You're a sensipath. *I'm* a sensipath. It will be our undoing, you know. 'Sympathise—do not sensipathise.' This is what my mother once said to me in my boyhood. I was standing before her, one hand cupping a crippled, dying baby bird that had fallen from its nest. With my free hand I wiped away tears that I could not bring under controul. And my mother said, 'You may feel sorry for the little bird, son. But you must do so only to such extent that you do not become one *with* the bird. For if you *become* the bird, you cripple yourself, as well.' These were hard words to hear, Trimmers, but I think sometimes that you and I would be better off if we heeded them a little more often."

"I hadn't thought of things in that way."

"Our collective mortal existence is congested with pain and inequities of circumstance. It is our natural calling as sensipaths to attempt to change and make better those things that are conducive to change. But those things that cannot be improved, we must not permit to destroy us. Although having just imparted those kernels of wisdom, I must say that I've spent most of my life trying not to let my sensipathic nature get the better of me, and I have not always achieved success. I wish you greater luck, but in the mean time I feel compelled to remind you that what you feel is largely the product of a different set of chemicals in the brain than, let us say, that fœtid stew that swirls inside the craniums of the Montague Pupkers of our world."

I smiled and shook a finger at my friend Muntle. "It's all brain chemicals, then, that make me want to help the Scadgers? Where is the human heart in all of this?"

"Oh it's there, my friend. There are directive chemicals in that organ as well. It's *all* chemical, you see. Humans are nothing but a slosh of chemicals orbiting an adamantine core of survival intuition. But recognise that it's an inconvenient trait for a Dinglian to own, this investing oneself too deeply in the well-being of others."

Muntle didn't look at me as he gave voice to his opinion. He stared off into the distance—over the rooftops and church spires of the West End, out toward the Northern Ridge, topped, like a frothy dessert, by a fluffy creampuff of billowing clouds.

"And do you have some reason other than the most general for why it is an inconvenience to concern myself too fully with the concerns of others?"

"Besides the fact that it is debilitating, consider also that the day will come when none of it will make a difference. The day will come, sooner or later—it's only a matter of time, dear chum—when all that we cultivate here for good or bad, in poverty or in luxury, will be gone."

"And we shall all be dust," I hurriedly added. "I'm quite aware of the mortality of man."

Muntle shook his head. He turned to face me, pinning my gaze with the sharpness of his own look. "I don't mean finality in the eschatological sense, Trimmers," said he, "but in the much more immediate, specific sense of the future of the very soil upon which we presently stand—the Mother Valley—Dingley Dell."

Muntle paused, his words apparently halted by a thought. It was, as I would soon come to realise, a most important thought, for there was a profound decision to be made; I could see the thing being contested through the windows of his eyes and in the now serious turn of his lip and the contemplative corrugation of his brow. Would he convey it or withhold?

The contest finished, the decision made, my friend Muntle, sheriff of Dingley Dell, leaned toward me and in a grave whisper disclosed the following: "This thing, you see, cannot last."

"This *thing*?"

"This construction, this fabrication—all that you see round you, Freddie. Dingley Dell."

"My brother has made a similar claim in his more pessimistic moments."

Muntle shook his head. "There is only incidental similarity, for Augustus doesn't know half of what *I* know."

I didn't respond. It wasn't clear to me at that moment Muntle's meaning. I gave him leave through a silent nod to continue.

"Hear me, Trimmers. This place. Our valley. It's a patently false construction. There are things about Dingley Dell that do not follow reason."

I affected to laugh. "And since when has the sheriff of Dingley Dell taken up philosophy as a secondary vocation?"

Muntle ignored my flippant question and pursued in his raspy whisper: "These *things,* Trimmers, are being catalogued, are being anatomised, are being placed like tiles into a great mosaic, one by one, incrementally arranged. It is the big picture we are after, my friend."

"The big picture?"

"Of who we are, *what* we are. Why we are here. For what purpose. To what end. And yes, finally: *how* it is all destined to end."

"Muntle," I said, in a deep tone, which surprised even me by the degree of its sobriety, "are you become mad?"

Ignoring the query, Muntle replied quickly and earnestly, "There are three others with whom I meet on a fairly regular basis. I would not call us a society per se; we're quite an informal little gathering, but it is here in private conclave that we paste together, piece by piece, the bigger picture."

"What do you mean by 'bigger picture,' Muntle?"

Muntle and I gained a bench, which overlooked the river and, more specifically, the bridge that crossed it—Westminster by name (after that famed London crossing). It was here upon the bench that one could see the beshadowed comings and goings of the poorest of the Dell—those without homes who refused to resign themselves to a life of rigourous and punishing regimentation at the workhouse. Here two, perhaps three dozen Dinglian vagrants—the "People-Under-the-Bridge" or, more unkindly, the "Trolls"—eked out a bare subsistence—more deprived and elemental than even that of the lowliest of the working poor of the East End of Milltown— scavenging from dustbins, dropping improvised lines and lures into this mud-coloured bend in the river. It was a hard and brutal life and one that shook my sensipath tendencies to their core.

Yet it was here, where one could see these miserable destitutes huddle and scuttle in the shadows, that Muntle wished to sit to deliver the second half of this most curious revelation about how he often chose to occupy his free time.

"We are universal skeptics, Trimmers. It is in our nature and it is our calling. My three friends and I don't believe anything that has been told to us about this place. We question *everything*—from the details of our orphaned beginnings to the reason that you were not permitted to meet with the tradesmen at the Summit last week. We believe that everything has a false—a 'veneer' reason, if you will, and then a true reason beneath it, and we have made it our mission to learn all the true reasons and to patch them together into some unified theory as to why Dingley Dell is…well, *Dingley Dell.*"

Muntle took a breath. We both watched in silence as a little boy standing upon the pebbles that overspread the eastern bank of the river threw sticks into its languorous current. The boy was drest in tatters, his face besmudged with grime. He smiled to see his little sticks go far, but betwixt the smiles there lay permanent lineaments of melancholy, for this was a boy with no hopefulness in his young heart, who could see nothing ahead for himself but a most bleak future.

"I want you to come next week, Trimmers. I want you to be a part of our little enquiring group. I've known you long enough to think that we could benefit from your own inquisitive mind."

"Even if I *don't* happen to think that there be something more to Dingley Dell than that which we see before us and that which we have always been told?"

"Are you being deliberately contentious? Can you possibly take everything you see about you at face value?"

"I don't know. There are some nights that I lie awake in bed for hours asking myself those very questions. Other times I don't care. I turn my concern to those things in our society that are broken and must be repaired in the here and the now."

"But perhaps the imperfections you perceive in the here and now are intricately connected, hand-in-glove with all of the bigger, shrouded questions. I've heard you and Gus say it before—in fact, just the other day—questioning, for example, why the Petit-Parliament maintains such unassailable power within this valley. I've heard you ask time and time again why membership in that hegemonic body is limited only to those with great wealth and property. For we have no king, Trimmers, who was enthroned 'by the hand of God.' We are a government of men. Why should that government be a plutocracy rather than a democracy? Why is it the

Parliament and not some more egalitarian governmental body that gets to decide where the goods that we take from the Terra Incognita should go—that decides who will be allowed to bid for them and who will not? Why, for example, does the greengrocer Jinkins receive nothing from the Outland that he may sell from his bins and shelves, but the fruitier Mortimer Riderhood, who owns the largest and best-stocked of those establishments, is given an exclusive contract to sell every banana and currant and fig and pine-apple that makes its way up the far side of the ridge? Why, for example, does your friend Pupker receive the best of the foreign herbs and spices and his competitors must settle themselves with the middlings? Why are Summit transactions conducted in such secrecy that I was held at a distance of several hundred yards from the trading pavilion the other morning and was forced to ask my questions about your nephew in closely monitored interviews beneath a tree?"

"And has your group come up with answers to any of these questions beyond a simple assumption of avariciousness on the part of members of our ruling class?"

"We do not come up with answers, Trimmers. We merely formulate conjectures—strong conjectures based upon the evidence we have gathered."

"And have you a conjecture, Muntle, for why Summit trade is kept so secretive and closely regulated beyond the fact that—as I have oft been told—one must tread easily with the Beyonder tradesmen lest they take easy offence and abandon their habitual transactions with us?"

"Yes. I will put it simply: it is a canard."

"A canard. How do you know?"

"Come to our next meeting and ask every question you'd like. We shouldn't be discussing such things out in the open like this."

"Permit me to ask, though: is there a name for your little group that isn't quite a society?"

"We don't consider ourselves a society when in company with one another, but there is a counterfeit name that we put forth should anyone ask why we meet. We call ourselves the Fortnightly Poetry League. You see, the conceit is that we gather together to read poetry to one another."

I smiled. "And does a poem every now and then surreptitiously slip itself into your intercourse?"

"Only when one hears a passerby through the cottage window and we are required at that moment to reinforce the illusion of our purpose. But by design, no. We have far more important things to do in the course of our short time together."

"Permit me one last enquiry, Muntle: may I know the names of the other three individuals who make up your little hugger-mugger gathering?"

"In time, Trimmers. But not now. Come to the meeting. You'll be surprised to discover who attends, for as it so happens, you know each of them quite well."

Muntle looked about and gave himself some time to think and then said, "The end is coming, my good friend. There are things that we know— things that you'll soon know, and things that ultimately we *all* shall know. This is why we cannot, *must not* look beneath Pupker's shop. Because what Hannah Pupker saw there *shouldn't* be seen by anybody else, lest it give Pupker and others who command the Dell reasons to think that there are those such as the members of the Fortnightly Poetry League who have become curious, who have become restive to know the 'whys' and the 'why nots.' For think on this, Trimmers: questioning the way of things is an exceedingly dangerous business, not to be engaged without the raising of eyebrows, or the raising of hackles, or the engendering, in the possible extreme, of the worst sort of enmity against us.

"So pray suffer me go to Pupker and make arrangements with him to visit his lower cellar at some designated point in future, for by now, he surely knows that his daughter has disclosed to you the details of her visit there, and that you have more than likely informed me as well. I shall schedule the inspection for, let us say, next Monday, and he will agree to it without hesitation, for that will afford him ample time to remove everything that is there, and the appearance of blissful ignorance on my part will preside, blissful ignorance, my dear friend, being key to the preservation and longevity of those of us who must continue to gather information methodically and incrementally, and in secret, protected communion."

I should be grateful, I thought, to be taken so thoroughly into Muntle's confidence. Yet with knowledge came solemn responsibility. I had known since I was a small boy that there was something quite odd about a protected valley which lay near the 41st northern parallel, in which a small collection of people lived in a sort of self-imposed quarantine in much the same way as did their forebears of five generations past. There was something quite strange about all that we had been taught about our valley home—that each element of our existence, which should feel right and

comfortable and familiar, resembled nothing that was limned and conjectured about the world at large upon the leaves of the instructional volumes
of the *Ensyke*. "But that is the *world* and *we* are Dingley Dell, and mark me,
there is a great difference," my teachers would conclude. And it was this oft-
articulated refrain which echoed throughout my school days and which
still reverberates against the hollow walls of my majority. It was as if we
had always been living in a dream world from which one day we should all
awaken; yet in waking, our sensate world would prove to be no less dream-
like and fantastical as that of our insensate state.

Chapter the Twenty-fifth

Tuesday, July 1, 2003

arly this morning I returned to Fingerpost, ostensibly to check on my sister-in-law's plants, but I knew the true reason for my trip: that I should perhaps be so fortunate as to meet up with Ruth Wolf in the lane, for I had thought about her more than perhaps I probably should have over the course of the previous two days. Whilst my thoughts did not rise to the level of obsession, I was at intervals quite occupied with meditations upon the woman. I would not be so bold as to go by her house and linger there in hopes that she should come out (for I figured that if she worked late hours of an evening she would not work early hours as well, and would be somewhere within the house or thereabouts). Yet something happened on my visit to Gus and Charlotte's cottage that put thought of Ruth Wolf and all of her prepossession and redheaded pulchritude completely out of mind.

As I approached the house, I noticed a ticket porter whom I knew by the name of Samson (a stick-boned individual not at all representative of his brawny Biblical moniker) pacing back and forth in front of the little picket fence that separated the front garden from the lane. He perked up when he saw me, and hailed me with his hand, though I had no intention of avoiding him. "Mr. Trimmers!" he called.

"Yes? What is it, Samson?"

"I've been waiting for your brother. I've knocked and knocked and he doesn't come to the door, and I thought that perchance he was out for his morning constitutional."

I shook my head. "Gus isn't a 'constitutional' sort of fellow, Samson. More to the point, he isn't in Fingerpost. He's stopping in Hungerford with Mrs. Trimmers."

Samson looked perplexed. He held out the envelope in his hand. "But how can Mr. Trimmers be in Hungerford with *Mrs.* Trimmers when this missive is from her *to* him?"

I took the envelope and looked at its inscription: 'From Mrs. Charlotte Trimmers, Hungerford, to my dear husband Augustus Trimmers, Fingerpost.' "It's most curious, Samson, for my brother told me that he would be joining his wife thither just hours after her own departure for that village. May I have it?"

"If you will find him and deliver it him, I have no objection. But I cannot allow you simply to drop the envelope into this rose bush."

"No, Samson, I assure you that I will not."

"Because it's marked 'Personal Delivery,' which means that it must be put directly into the hand of the recipient."

"Yes, yes, Samson. I understand what the phrase 'Personal Delivery' means. May I have it?"

Samson relinquished the missive and I gave him five cents—a more than generous gratuity for his trouble.

I waited until the porter had left to unfold the envelope and read the personal correspondence therein between wife and husband—something I would never do without very good reason. My very good reason was confirmed by the contents of Charlotte's note to my brother.

> My dear Gus:
>
> Nearly a week has passed and you have sent no word to me of how you are getting on in my absence. Do you not miss me even a little? Camilla has been quite a dear and has worked so very hard to improve my spirits, but your absence makes the task so much the harder for her. I do miss *you,* my dear, and though we quarrel and though I spend my days in bed or in tears (or both) I do not think, as we prepare ourselves to live the rest of our lives without our blessed Newman, that I am strong enough to live without you as well. Please come to Hungerford and see me. It is a pleasant place and Camilla is a good cook—much better than I am. You

and I will repair what is broken between us and we will weather this together, as loving husband and loving wife. You will see.

With all my heart,

Charlotte

My brother had done a clever thing, you see. He had led everyone, including his own younger brother Frederick, to believe that he was in Hungerford with Charlotte and her childhood friend Camilla Snigsworth. At the same time he had led Charlotte and Camilla to believe that he was abiding in Fingerpost. But there was no sign that he had ever set foot in his own house the whole week that had passed since Charlotte's departure. Perhaps he was hiding himself away in Tavistock or Folkstone (though he was not well enough acquainted with anyone in those villages to sponge a visit there), or had joined miners in Blackheath or the Scadger apricot pickers for that matter, but I did not believe it. My gut told me exactly where he was, and the reality of it sickened and frightened me. Gus had gone into the Outland to seek his son. He had more than likely commenced the trip only a few hours after I had tried to talk him out of such a suicidal mission. As always, my brother had followed the dictates of his heart over the wisdom of his head and had turned a deaf ear to every good reason offered against that which he had stubbornly set his mind to do. I hated him at that moment for his foolhardy, headlong impetuosity. I hated him for effectively removing himself from my life, from the life of his wife who was clinging to this broken marriage by her fingertips. But hatred for one you love never lasts. Shortly thereafter my animosity toward my brother—a brother I feared I would never see again—was replaced by a deep, crippling sadness. I sat down upon a bench in my brother and sister-in-law's front garden, the missive crumpled in my hand, and I bowed my head and wept.

All of that day was spent in a great quandary over what to do about Gus. I was inclined one moment to go after him, and the next to see dangerous folly in such course of action. Mrs. Lumbey and Hannah Pupker and even Mrs. Lumbey's customarily unmeddlesome dressmaking assistant Miss Casby forbade my venturing out of the valley using the very same reasoning that I had used to argue against my brother's leave-taking. It was the same case that Gus, no doubt, had made to his young son through his customary offices of parental inculcation, which had not been heeded.

Therefore, the question was whether I should follow in the steps of my nephew and brother, or put an end to the lethal family pattern once and all.

"If you go, Frederick, you will break my heart," said Mrs. Lumbey. "I have lost my only daughter and as I have come to regard you as something of a son, I will die of devastation to see a second child depart from me forever."

An unsimilar but equally strongly worded proscription was delivered by my friend Antonia Bocker. It would have been seconded by Muntle, had he not been off to the Chowser School to inspect a sudden and most disturbing theft of cabbage sprouts from the Chowser greenhouse, the criminal act having been brought to his attention in an earnest letter from Maggy Finching who felt that a thorough investigation by the sheriff of Dingley Dell (and that officer alone) was in order and the sooner the better.

That afternoon I received the report from Antonia of her visit with a woman by the name of Mrs. Gargery who lived in Park Lane in an old, ivy-choked brick residence next to the Pyegrave house. There was a stark contrast of appearance betwixt the two abutting houses; the Pyegrave dwelling, proud and spruce and stone-stolid, seemed almost offended by its close proximity to the aged and mouldering structure that Mrs. Gargery occupied, one of the top story windows of the former being of the eyebrow variety, which made for a comical picture of supercilious judgement upon its neighbour. The Gargery house would have been pulled down long ago had its equally-superannuated owner and occupant not remained stubbornly extant, defying the published actuarial averages by a number of years.

Antonia stood knocking intermittently—knocking and waiting, knocking and waiting—for she knew that Mrs. Gargery had a servant, she knew that Mrs. Gargery must be at home (for the woman hardly ventured out more than once a week), and she knew, further, that Mrs. Gargery could scarcely be called unsociable from this bit of daily behaviour which characterised her: as was her habit, the old woman opened her front door each morning and put herself into a decaying rush-bottomed chair that had been permanently emplanted upon her porch. There she would sit, holding her pug-dog in her lap and making his little paws to wave and salute at passersby when not sharing with her snub-nosed pet a rasher of bacon, the canine nibbling from one end and the ancient hominian nibbling from the opposite end and the two coming together into something resembling a kiss, which was either droll or revolting depending upon one's opinion of pugs.

Antonia could see the front window curtain drawn slightly back as if there were someone peeping out. "Only persistence will win this day," she said to herself, determined not to suspend her knocking. In time the door opened and my friend found herself bidding good morning not to the lady of the house, but to the lady's intermittent companion, Miss Georgianna Milvey, late of the Euphemia Trimmers Memorial Society.

"Good God, Georgianna, has something happened to Mrs. Gargery?"

"Not at all."

"Then why would no one come to the door? Was that you hiding behind the dimity, wishing that I should go away?"

Georgianna nodded, with nary an ounce of compunction in her address. "I wanted very *much* for you to go away, Antonia, and that is why I instructed Sarah the housemaid to withhold as well. Mrs. Gargery cannot abide even a small dose of your fiddle-faddle in her present state."

Georgianna stood in the doorway as if she were an impeding sentry, her arms folded athwart her breast.

"Fiddle-faddle! Good Christ, Georgianna! I've come only to put a few delicately-delivered questions to your hostess about the injury and subsequent death of her next-door-neighbour, Mrs. Pyegrave."

"And I say on behalf of my hostess that she does not wish to speak of that night. She is doing her very best to erase the events of that dreadful evening from every corner of her memory. It will not serve for you to bring it up."

"I see." Antonia took a deep breath to steady her nerves, for Miss Milvey, like most of the other members of the Euphemia Trimmers Memorial Society, had a way of setting her teeth on edge. "May I at least step in to bid my friend good morning?"

Georgianna considered the request with wandering ruminative eyes, gave a reluctant nod, and stepped aside to permit entry.

Mrs. Gargery was to be found in her sitting room lounging upon a chaise longue, wearing a tiara and eating a boiled egg. The old woman was partial to breakfast and preferred no meal that did not resemble it, though her partiality to such an unvarying repast should seem monotonous to some. Since she had lived to be quite old and had all the while remained relatively hale, the issue of whether such a limited diet should be in some way injurious to her health had been settled in favour of her odd dietary preference many years before.

"Good morning, Mrs. Gargery," greeted Antonia. "You are looking quite blooming this morning."

"I feel very well indeed, Miss Bocker. I do not sleep as soundly as I should like—I suppose this is one of the customary drawbacks of advanced age—but otherwise I am rather enjoying my twilight years. I believe that you know my good friend Miss Milvey."

Antonia nodded. "Yes. Georgianna and I are well acquainted."

"And what brings you to Park Lane of a morning?" asked Mrs. Gargery, languidly stretching herself upon her chaise as if she were an elderly Cleopatra luxuriously awaiting her grapes.

Antonia interchanged a look with Georgianna. The admonitory expression of the latter said everything to Antonia that needed to be said without words. Antonia acquiesced: "You were on my way, my dear, and I thought I should stop to see how you are. I have been meaning to do it for some time. You do not venture out to the shops as a rule, so we must come to *you* for the pleasance of your society."

Antonia now settled herself into a chair and Georgianna did the same with a bit of a groan.

"Who am I? I am no one," replied Mrs. Gargery. "Nothing more than an old woman in an old house with an old dog that farts." Bethinking herself of her dog, she looked upon the creature lying drowsily at her feet and smiled. "Oh, but you have lost your little bow, Mr. Toddles. We must go out and get you another." Turning to her two guests: "You must not look upon him when he is so woefully underdrest. It mortifies him."

The mortified creature began to snore most nasally.

"Shall I ring for tea?" asked the old woman. "I am so sorry that Miss Milvey made you stand for so long rapping upon the door. She told me that you were that young deputy sheriff Boldwig. And that he was come to ask another round of questions. And I simply cannot endure another session of his impertinence. He is a most rude young man."

Antonia glared at her fellow Euphemia Trimmers Memorial Society compeer. "She told you that I was Deputy Boldwig? My dear Georgianna, perhaps to-day is the day that you should finally have yourself fitted for spectacles!"

Georgianna turned away, one hand surreptitiously searching about her person for her secreted flask of gin—the elixir that made life for her slightly more bearable.

"And as for Deputy Boldwig," Antonia continued, "I was not aware that there was an official investigation into the death of Mrs. Pyegrave. I was given to believe, as I think we all were, that the cause of death had already been determined and the book closed."

"Perhaps Sheriff Muntle pursues it nonetheless," said Mrs. Gargery. "And in a decidedly *un*-official manner."

Antonia was poised to say, "I think not." Or even: "I *know* not. For our good sheriff could not take such independent action without incurring the displeasure of the Petit-Parliament, and so I must conclude that this is either a rogue investigation by a rather roguish novice deputy, or the young man has been so directed by an agent unaffiliated with the offices of his shrieval employer."

But Antonia said none of these things. In fact, she could not give voice to so much as a single musing from those thoughts of intrigue that now accosted her. What she said instead was put in the form of a query: "If you do not mind my asking it, Mrs. Gargery, what sort of enquiry has the young man been making?"

Here, Georgianna struck in with a stentorian "But she *does* mind! She minds it very much. I mind it, too. Must we fill our lives with questions, Antonia—always questions! I have done with it. And I know that Mrs. Gargery has had her fill as well. Now we were sitting here, Mrs. Gargery and myself, having ourselves a quiet, a most lovely little chat about hyacinths and forget-me-nots and…"

Mrs. Gargery completed the statement with "jessamine and peonies. And there was also brief mention of hollyhocks."

Georgianna affected to smile. "Yes, there was. You said how much you adored them and how easy they are to grow when the soil is properly composed. And I added that one must also be patient, for hollyhocks are biannuals and do nothing the first year but sit small and unblooming within the bed and one is tempted to rip them up for their impertinence and thrash them against the houseside." Georgianna checked herself. "At least this is what I hear that *some* gardeners will do."

Georgianna now averted her eyes to Antonia and formed her look into a reproving glower. "A perfectly civilised and perfectly quiet and delightful exchange—that is what we had before you arrived, Antonia. And

Mrs. Gargery was calm then, whilst she is decidedly *not* calm now. And you are to blame. You and the deputy and everyone else who wishes that a poor dead woman should not be permitted to rest in peace but must be conversationally exhumed upon a daily basis so that her death should be anatomised for some sort of ghoulish pleasure."

Antonia rose from her chair. "Georgianna, it is difficult to engage you when you drink."

Georgianna Milvey seemed not to know just how to marshal a defence, for the flask was in her hand and her lips were moist.

Antonia continued: "Now a young man who purports to be asking questions on behalf of the sheriff's office has come here. He may have no right to do so. However, I believe that *I* have the right, on behalf of the deceased, to find out—if only to put my own restless thoughts upon the matter to bed—what it was that was seen by you on that fateful night, Mrs. Gargery, and what it was that you have told the stupid boy who struts about as if he were sheriff himself."

Mrs. Gargery made her reply to Antonia's exclamatory explanation of herself not in words but in the singular gesture of placing the back of one hand to her brow, as if she would faint.

"Sarah!" called Georgianna. "Sarah! Quickly! Your mistress is crapping out!"

"I most certainly am *not* crapping out!" declared Mrs. Gargery in a sharp, corrective tone. "I have a headache." To her personal maid, who had just stepped into the room from her station just outside the door: "Sarah. Get me a headache powder if you will. I am being assaulted by loud voices. Miss Milvey's voice grows especially noisy and shrill when she takes to the flask."

Georgianna shrunk into her chair, mortified to the point of instantaneous muteness.

"Here is what I told the young man," said Mrs. Gargery, turning her gaze to Antonia as the comely maid Sarah withdrew from the room. "I said that I heard a scream. It did not wake me for I was already awake and reading. I do not sleep well at night—perhaps I have already said this—and was reading a book. I believe that it was *Oliver Twist: The Man.* He grows up to become a cheese-monger, you know. But that is neither here nor there. I was reading my book and I heard a scream which coincided with the sound of breaking glass. And I went immediately to my window..." and then gesturing toward the window of reference, "... this window right here, in fact, for I often spend the night here in this room and upon this very couch, not wishing to climb the many steep stairs to my bedchamber. And there she was—lying not so far from my very own house, her limbs moving a little to tell me that she was not dead—but oh such a horrible, ghastly sight! Poor Mrs. Pyegrave, all bent and broken and so severely lacerated by all the broken glass. And such a pool of blood there was, expanding from beneath every corner of her!

"For a brief moment I knew not just what I should do. Surely, thought I, there will be others who will come—others who heard the breaking glass and her terrible plummeting scream and will hasten to her aid."

"Such as your maid Sarah?" asked Antonia.

"Oh goodness, no. The girl sleeps with plugs in her ears, because the attic squirrels keep her awake otherwise. It was only I standing at that window, and yet something within me nonetheless propelled me to the door, even without my bedrobe wrapt round me. I took up Mr. Toddles (for he was trembling just as much as was I, and I felt that we should comfort one another) and the two of us went out into the street to render what assistance to the woman we were able. And for a short time it was only Mr. Toddles and myself and Mrs. Pyegrave alone in the street. And as I spoke to her to see if she was still conscious, Mr. Toddles jumped from my arms to make his own judgement of the scene by sniffing the poor woman whom he knew from her many passages hither and thither before our house. I was so afraid that the broken glass would cut his little paws that I snatched him back into my arms but not before he had drawn from the victim's hand a folded note card just about this size." Here Mrs. Gargery stretched her forefinger and thumb apart to give an approximation of the card's size. "I pocketed the card from Mr. Toddles' mouth and returned my thoughts to ministering as best I could to the woman, as the street began finally to fill itself with my neighbours all come to either help the victim or to gawk at her, such as their inclination directed."

"And is it true, Mrs. Gargery, that Mr. Pyegrave was amongst the last to come down to the street?"

"Yes. Quite true. I found it most curious. I continue to find everything about that tragic accident to be curious to this day. Miss Milvey will not suffer me to speak of it, but I am happy to confess to you, Miss Bocker, that not a lot of it makes much sense to me."

"And this you told to Deputy Boldwig as well? How odd you found it that Pyegrave took his time in coming down?"

Mrs. Gargery shook her head. "Nor did I think it should be his business to know about the card. In fine, I told the deputy nothing more than
the fact of what I heard from my couch and then the fact of my wandering
out and then being joined by others. I elaborated for *your* benefit, Miss
Bocker, because of how much of a burden it has been to carry the particulars of that strange and tragic night upon my solitary shoulders."

"Yet he continues to return to ask questions."

Mrs. Gargery nodded. "Twice again and is ruder still with each new visit."

"What sort of questions does he ask?"

"The same. Always the same. But there is one in particular that seems
the most pressing. And I have come to the conclusion that this is the one
that largely necessitates each of his insolent visits."

Sarah had returned with Mrs. Gargery's headache power in a paper
upon a pewter salver, and a glass of water, and Mrs. Gargery permitted the
interruption so that she could medicate herself. "Thank you, Sarah," she
said. "Go up to your room now if you will. There is a private matter which
I wish to discuss with Miss Bocker."

Dropping a curtsey: "Yes, ma'am."

As Sarah was repairing obediently to her room, Mrs. Gargery whispered
to her guest (the one who was not slipping into a gin-induced slumber in
her chair) that Sarah was the best servant in the Dell. The reason for her
most dutiful servitude was this: Sarah had been shewn Mrs. Gargery's last
will and testament, and now knew for certain that which she had always
been told: that she was the old woman's sole heiress. "I did this," explained
Mrs. Gargery in a brief digressive admission to Antonia, "because I sought
to guarantee faithful and loving subservience in my declining years. And it
has worked, has it not? See how she hops to?"

"You were saying—about the one question—?"

"Come now, Miss Bocker, can you not guess? It is about the card that
Mr. Toddles took from the poor woman's bloody hand. Someone has, no
doubt, been looking for it."

"Someone? Whom do you mean?"

"I cannot say. But I have read the card and its contents are intriguing—
the words that are engraved thereon, and those as well that someone has
pencilled upon the back."

"And have you shared those words with anyone else?"

"Oh bless my life and soul, Miss Bocker—I could not possibly do such a thing."

"Would you tell *me*, Mrs. Gargery?"

The old woman raised a wary eyebrow.

"And just why should I bring you into my confidence, Miss Bocker? There cannot be two more dissimilar women in all the Dell. Why, I have much more in common with Miss Milvey who knows only of flowers, and spends her days in quiet, unobtrusive inebriety, than I do you."

"Have we not always been friends after a fashion?"

"Have we? I once caught you sniggering at me when you passed my door."

"Sniggering? No. Smiling? Perhaps. Good God, my darling woman! You were feeding a rasher of bacon to a dog and taking such transporting delight in it!"

"Which makes me some sort of daft and doddering old fool. Is this not your *true* assessment of me?"

"It most certainly is not!" protested Antonia, sitting herself down upon the end of the chaise. Mrs. Gargery courteously retracted a leg to give her guest more than a mere perching-seat. "My dear Mrs. Gargery, believe me. It is not in my nature to deceive anyone. I have achieved success in business through honesty and plain dealing. Certainly you know this. Recall how easily went the negociations between your husband and me when I purchased his tobacconist shop—let alone the good price that I gave him. Have you wanted for anything from that sale? Perhaps we have not become the best of friends over the years, but I have always held you, and will continue, my dear, to *hold* you in only the highest regard. It is no more odd to me that you should sit in your doorway of a morning and feed bacon strips to your dog than it should be that I—and now I shall make a rather large confession to win your confidence—that I should find in my heart the capacity to love a woman with far greater fervour and passion than ever I should love a man."

"My word, Miss Bocker! Is this the reason that you never married?"

Antonia nodded.

"And was there ever a woman to whom you surrendered your heart as most women surrender theirs to men?"

Antonia nodded. "But the transaction was only one-sided and never made privy to the other party. I loved only from afar, Mrs. Gargery. For good or bad, there it is."

"Myself as well."

Antonia drew back in surprise. "*You?*"

Mrs. Gargery nodded with a schoolgirl's pert bite upon the nether lip.

"But what of your husband?"

"He was a dear. But I didn't love him. Not from the true depths of my heart. Our marriage was a fine friendship—a partnership, if you will, but nothing more. I confess, though, that I too have only loved—*truly loved*—from a distance. Though even in my dotage, may I say that the beauty of my fair cherry-lipped Sarah does not much tire the eyes—not even old ones like mine with a haze upon them? Good Lord, how emancipating it feels to say such a thing to another after all these many years of silence upon the subject. Now, dear sister of the heart, let me shew you the card and you will tell me what you think it all means."

CHAPTER THE TWENTY-SIXTH

Tuesday, July 1, 2003

It was late afternoon when Antonia and I entered the Wang-Wang tearoom. In contrast to my previous visits, the establishment was far from empty. There were several other couples present with whom I was either fairly well acquainted or knew in passing (for so many faces in the Dell were familiar to me, given that only 11,000 souls lived therein), most of the patrons huddling and cuddling in the shadows: Mr. Creakle, the unhappily married bottle-maker, keeping amorous company with Mrs. Babley, the equally unhappy wife of Babley, the coach painter; Mr. Chestle, the dance master, with Mr. Glamour, the milliner; and there in the darkest corner of all sat Jemmy, the handsome stableboy, twining his fingers through the hair of Mrs. Packlemerton, the chinless wife of the distiller. Seeing me, Jemmy retreated even further into the shadows. In fact, all who were present at this time seemed either a bit disturbed by Antonia's and my sudden arrival, or greeted us with pregnant looks and conspiratorial nods.

"If this is where you come to be alone, Trimmers, I would premise that there are more isolate places than this so obvious trysting spot."

"Do you judge these people, Antonia?" I retorted in a lightly adversarial tone.

"Absolutely not. When it comes to morality, I'm a neutralist. I judge only my feet. Which hurt." Quickly checking her querulous demeanour:

"I'm sorry, Trimmers. I know that you're worried about your brother and I am being insensibly petulant. Forgive me."

I nodded. Mrs. Wang-Wang came to take our orders. Once given, Antonia resumed, "And I cannot quarrel with your reason for bringing us here. Estella Lumbey and I have been like oil and water for so long that I don't even recall a time when we were ever friends. The last thing I should wish to do is make you uncomfortable by insinuating myself into her presence, knowing what could come of that. Moreover, my own apartments are being painted, so this place is the perfect alternative. Quite discreet. Discretion, in fact, appears to be its hallmark."

This last statement was made, I have no doubt, to elicit a smile from me, but I could not bring myself to it. It was difficult for me even to concentrate on what Antonia was saying, so plagued with worry was I over Gus's decision a week ago, apparently fully executed, to go off and look for his son. The fact that he had yet to return augured a tragic outcome, and deeply hampered my ability to think of anything else. It was all that I could do to look at the card that Antonia now slid across the table for my examination.

"What is this?" I asked, picking it up.

"The engraved invitation I was telling you about. I do not recognise the paper upon which it was printed. Notice, as well, that there is gilding along the edge. We do not gild in Dingley Dell. What little gold comes into this valley, as well you know, quickly finds its way into the mouths of our richest citizens as dental fillings. The invitation was most certainly printed in the Outland."

Here was the invitation:

> *You are most cordially invited to a Fête champêtre*
> *to celebrate a century of trade*
> *upon the Summit of Exchange*
> *2:00 pm, Tuesday, July 15, 2003*

"Now turn over the card and look at the reverse," instructed Antonia.

On the back were several words pencilled by a hasty hand: "portmanteau, bandbox, hatbox." I stared hard at the scrawled inventory. "Do you suppose this was inscribed by Mrs. Pyegrave herself?"

Antonia nodded. "Because I believe that once received, the card never left her possession—that is, not until Mr. Toddles extracted it with his slobbering canines."

"It was as if she wished to take it to the very grave with her," I said.

Now Antonia shook her head. "Or perhaps her true intention was quite the opposite. That if her voice was to be silenced, she would allow the card to speak in her stead, post mortem, as it were."

"And what does the card mean, Antonia, besides the fact that there is to be a celebratory festival on the Summit on the 15th?"

"I will make a guess, Trimmers, but first let me tell you what I have learnt from a wise little owl who sits upon his perch in Judge Fitz-Marshall's chambers."

"Mr. Meagles."

"That very bird." Antonia leant forward to convey a confidence through a whisper: "I shewed him the card, and once he had recovered from the shock of seeing it in my own grossly illegitimate hands, he actually became somewhat receptive to my enquiry. The card does indeed in its professed purpose invite the bearer to a fête to be held upon the Summit of Exchange—an exclusive gathering to which only the ruling elite have been summoned, ostensibly to honour and celebrate the long amity between our brokers and the Outland tradesmen. Now I didn't shew Mr. Meagles the words on the back, not knowing even to this day how much I should trust him, but he did lead me a few steps in the right direction by *hinting* that there could be some other even more important objective than the stated one."

"That objective confirmed by Mrs. Pyegrave's directions to herself of what she could carry with her thither."

Antonia nodded. "Putting down what she had been told by mouth: 'portmanteau, bandbox, hatbox.' When do we use such items, Trimmers?

"In the course of travel," said I, stating the obvious.

"And where would one travel from the Summit that should require the use of *luggage*?"

"Clearly out and away from the Dell and into the Outland."

"Capital deduction!" Antonia tucked the invitation back into her reticule. "But let us say, rather, *permanently* into the Outland. For it is quite clear to me now, Trimmers, that the High and Mighty Bashaws of Dingley Dell are flying the coop. The date of their flight is July 15, and the stalking-horse is the fête. And what are we to do about it? Not a blessed thing, Trimmers. Not a blessed thing."

"And why should we *wish* to do anything about it?"

"For reason of what may come next. Why would they flee a place, unless that place—with all that they presently gain from their ascendance and dominion here—be one in which things are set to take some sort of very different turn?"

"Perhaps trade is about to be terminated."

"Perhaps. Or perhaps something worse is in the offing. I cannot imagine it. I cannot imagine the *reason* for it. There is too much that we don't know, Trimmers. But I surmise that everything we do not know should be regarded as cause for alarm. I wish to invite you to a special meeting—"

"The next gathering of the Fortnightly Poetry League?"

Antonia nodded with a look of amused astonishment. "How have *you* come to know of our private league?"

"Muntle has told me. And he's already extended me an invitation. And I now know the identities of two of its four members. If I am lucky, I will learn all of your names even before the meeting convenes."

"You are actually *quite* lucky," said Antonia, turning to send a nodding greeting to the two most recently arrived of that day's visitors to the Wang-Wang tearoom, Vicar Upwitch and Uriah Graham. "For the gentlemen in question have just entered the room."

I nodded and they nodded, and then they joined Mr. Chestle and Mr. Glamour, who was adjusting his wristbands to shuffle cards whilst his friend Chestle peeped coquettishly from behind an oriental handfan.

———

Vincent Muntle stood looking about the Chowser School grounds and shaking his head. "I cannot find it. Is it invisible?"

"Is *what* invisible?" asked Maggy Finching, who stood next to him, looking not about the grounds but up into the sheriff's searching eyes.

"The greenhouse. From which the cabbage sprouts were allegedly stolen."

Maggy began to giggle. "I must return to the kitchen and begin preparations for the evening meal. We have an extra mouth to feed this night and

I want our special guest to be happily sated by evening's end."

Muntle grinned. "So I am staying the night, am I?"

"And another night or two as well, if I am to have my way," chuckled Maggy with a carefree fillip of the finger to Muntle's nose.

"So there never was a stolen sprout."

"Nor is there even a greenhouse, you silly puss—only a few cabbageless hotbeds. I brought you here under blatantly false pretenses. Are you cross with me?"

"On the contrary. I commend the ingenuity behind all of your subterfuges—even the one that engineered that chance meeting on Drood Lane."

Across a nearby meadow now trudged Alphonse Chowser. The meadow was quite crowded at the moment, having been turned into a rugby football field by a number of the upper form Chowser School boys. There were moans from some, as the headmaster's sudden distracting presence upon their "pitch" led to a muddled, collapsing scrum; but there were cheers, as well, for the boys' beloved leader. "Carry on!" shouted Chowser to the pile of players, who were now all heads and limbs and youthful guffaws.

Reaching Maggy and Muntle, Chowser addressed the latter: "Has our very own Bow Street Runner solved the mystery of the captured cabbages?"

"I have," laughed Muntle. "And the solution is as follows: that there *are* no cabbage sprouts to be restored to their rightful owner, but there *is* a cook who in filing a patently false report has deterred a busy sheriff most egregiously from his appointed rounds."

"Even the busiest of sheriffs is entitled to the occasional holiday, Muntle, and now that you are here, you will not be permitted to return to your wonted offices until you have had a bit of leisure and a happy helping or two of Maggy's batter pudding with saveloy and pickled kidneys."

"And that is only the first course!" exclaimed Maggy with a lick of the lips, for Maggy loved her cooking just as much as did any of its other myriad partakers.

As the three crossed the improvised rugby field, inadvertently dismantling in their passage a fine play with significant advance, and thus engendering a polyphonic chorus of both groans and whoops (distinguished by the degree of allegiance to the player carrying the ball at the time), Chowser threw an arm round Muntle's neck. "If you ever decide to retire your badge and enter the field of pedagogy and boy-herding, I should very much like you to come and work for me. I know that Maggy would, too."

"And what if the opposite occurs?" asked Muntle. "That I should take Maggy away from you to join me in Milltown as my…" Then with a whisper into that man's ear, so that Maggy should not hear, "…*bride*?"

"Well, I should be most unhappy to lose her. But I should nonetheless understand the very good reason why."

Maggy blushed, knowing exactly the gist of that which was said, and how very close her beloved was edging toward a full marriage proposal.

CHAPTER THE TWENTY-SEVENTH

Wednesday, July 2, 2003

I completed my draft of the medical review board's annual report and delivered the pages next morning to the board's chairman, a portly, wheezing, slack-gaited man by the name of Sir Seth Dabber, who quickly dismissed the latter section of my work as superfluous. "I know what the doctors in the Dell have been doing as of late, Mr. Trimmers, and whose work has been meritorious and whose has fallen short of the mark. I've commended the former and petitioned my colleagues on the Board for dismissal of the latter, who number only two, and who should, in my opinion, be removed to some other line in which they will not misdiagnose and make a dangerous nuisance of themselves."

"May I ask if you count Dr. Fibbetson amongst that second group?"

"I do not. I must say, Trimmers, that you make a compelling case of malpractise against him with regard to the Pyegrave case, but it doesn't quite rise to the level of de-certification, as the evidence against him is based upon anecdotal hearsay without sufficient peer corroboration. As to the doctors for whom there *is* sufficient cause for dismissal, there is a problem with that course of action: we, at present, have no replacements at the ready, save the two fledgling lads who passed their exams only last week, both of whom, I warrant, will promptly upon instatement prescribe something or other out of youthful inexperience that will place a burden upon the lung or heart, and incite a claim before the Petit-Parliament for financial compensation on the part of the unfortunate patient's survivors, and as head of the Medical Review Board all will fall upon my head. So you see, sir, what a fix I'm in, and how I should like to chop out the last paragraphs of your report like some ugly boil to be lanced."

Dismissing the analogy (Dabber's medical similes often clanged and thudded as ill-executed attempts to burnish his medical credentials, which were in a word *none*, the man having gained his position on the basis of his standing in the community and his generous charitable support of three village infirmaries), I noted that I was on friendly terms with one of the two medical training graduates. "In fact, I know the young man quite well," I added, "and can state without equivocation that you should put your utmost confidence in him."

"Timberry?"

I nodded. "Mulberry Timberry's father and my father both worked for a time as sawyers in the saw-pit at the Folkstone Mills Furniture Works, before the elder Timberry bought a cow and became a dairyman. I watched the young man grow up from a baby and know him to be a very bright and conscientious physician-in-training. He will be a credit to the profession, I assure you."

"Has the lad finally begun to shave?"

"For a couple of years now, or was that a jest?" (I could never tell when Sir Dabber was having his bit of a laugh, for his expression never changed; the man always seemed to be in the midst of making a very serious effort at catching his breath and then contemplating how he would devise the next breath to come.) "If I may be so bold, Sir Dabber, you do Timberry a great disservice by presuming youthful incompetence."

Dabber opened his snuffbox and took a pinch. The large man displayed a tendency to foppishness that was undeserved. In his youth he had wrestled upon a mat in the manner of the Greeks and had downed the largest buck in the eastern wood as was ever felled by bow and arrow— that record holding itself in perpetuity given the fact that hunting in both woods was now prohibited (though the law was broken now and again, almost exclusively by members of the congenitally-venatic Scadger clan). Over time, Dabber had settled into a semi-indolent life of service on somnolent supervisory boards (in which one was rarely charged with much to do but listen and nod and cast votes with the prevailing majority in the spirit of approbative accord), and membership in music societies and art leagues and the like, his having acceded to his father's sizeable fortune, garnered in the line of coal extraction. It had never been Dabber's wish to run for a seat in the Petit-Parliament, leaving such doings to those "whose eyes do not cross at the very mention of budgetary allocation, taxonomic contingencies, periodic parliamentary review of statutory instruments, commission report abstracts, continuing resolution debates, and rules of order begetting paradoxical *disorder* through self-serving misapplication. The mere thought of such a culture of prolix bombast brings a tight constriction to my delicate throat."

Semi-indolence had not, however, served well the quinquagenarian's constitution. His excessive avoirdupois had taken its toll upon his locomotion. He had also begun to drink more than one in his condition ought, one night stumbling in a drunken stupor upon his housemaid and breaking two of her ribs.

The family mining interest had been sold and his wife had passed away, and the one child, an imbecilic boy, had been placed under the care of Bedlam custodians, and Sir Dabber's days were much too long and languorous and his humour often splenetic and his eyes rheumy from his affinity for both port and porter. I dreaded meeting with him upon each occasion in which my offices as a writer-for-hire were required to put down some medical matter or other that required formal documentation, the aforementioned report being an ongoing example.

I could sit and nod and only privately repine the interview until my much-anticipated withdrawal be effected, or I could defend my friend Mulberry Timberry who did not deserve to be depreciated by the chairman of the Medical Review Board simply on the basis of his youth and present inexperience.

"And what a ridiculous name it is: Mulberry Timberry!" Sir Dabber appended in exclamation, after taking a sneeze from application of the snuff. "Two berries in the same name. Were his parents daft?"

I knew his parents well. They were not in the least bit daft, though their sense of the comical sometimes led them to inject jollity into places in which it wasn't generally to be found. Even to this day, I could be no better cheered upon occasions of despondency than by a visit to that harlequin house. Charles Timberry and his wife Julia were also puppeteers who in itinerant fashion strolled the lanes of Dingley Dell and here and there put on Punch and Judy entertainments for the children—and a good many child-hearted

adults—when they were not pulling upon the udders of their lady Guern-
seys both to fill the pails for their dairy customers and to spray foamy teat-
milk into the faces of one another in mischievous divertissement.

"Daffy, yes, Sir Dabber, but daft, I should say not. Now, if there is
nothing else that you require of me, I must be off."

"As it so happens, Trimmers, there *is* something that I require of you.
Will you stay for tea? I have cake."

I could not help rolling my eyes in annoyance, happy that my back
was turned to the importuning gentleman and that I was nowhere near
the large pier glass that would have afforded him a look at my reflected
disrespect.

"I'll stop for a bit longer then, Sir Dabber, but cannot delay for too long
my other appointments."

Dabber smiled. "Other appointments? Do you not sit hunched over
your little writing desk above Mrs. Lumbey's dress shop all the day long
and scribble away as would some Bedlam obsessitor? Can you not delay a
return to your chicken-scratching for two hours more? Come now."

"Still, there are things I must—" I broke off and heaved a noiseless sigh.
"Well, there is nothing *too* pressing to which I should attend, I suppose."

I was got.

"Excellent! Sit, sit. Arabella! Where is the teaboard? What detains you,
girl?"

The aforementioned Arabella flew into the room at the clarion mention of her name, all the tea things upon the tray rattling and clattering
from her jostling carriage. I could only presume that Arabella, who had
been in service to Sir Dabber for at least the last five years, was paid quite
well for being so brashly ordered about, servants in Dingley Dell who did
not come untrained and unseasoned from Blackheath constituting a precious commodity as labourers who could, in most cases, do a great many
other things for a florin that did not require demeaning obsequiousness
and self-abnegation.

Dabber kept quiet until the tea had been poured and the cake cut and
portioned. Following the young woman's hasty departure, pursuant to a
stern and dismissive look on the part of the master of the house, Sir Dabber
(the Sir being affixed to his surname for no reason but personal whimsy)
looked at me with an earnest aspect and said in a sober and even tone,
"You know of my child—my little Bevan—Good God! He isn't so little

anymore, now is he? He must by now have attained his twentieth year. The boy—I must call him such, for I cannot think him ever a man with a brain that does not cerebrate beyond that of a low monkey upon his very best days—receives a visit by me once a quarter. I take him sweetbreads and other tasty things for his nonetheless rather undiscerning palate and I sit and hold his hand and sometimes I hum to him to draw out a smile. Well, it is time again for a visit—overdue, in fact, but I'm having difficulty finding the resolve to betake myself to that dreary place. I know that I must—it is a father's bounden duty to see his child at least four times a year, even if that child be imbecile and wholly incoherent."

"Are you nevertheless asking that I go in your place, Sir Dabber?"

"Upon my word, I am not! I am merely seeking your company for the duration of the excursion. For I will endure the visit much more comfortably with a companion standing at my side who will draw my son's eye, so that he doesn't stare at me vacantly and sometimes drool and drivel as if I am a leg of roast mutton that will anon be his to gnaw and savour."

"Is there no one else whom you might ask? I have no history with the boy. He will wonder at my presence."

"He'll wonder at nothing of the sort, for his lizard brain doesn't wonder at anything but what he will eat and where he will lay his head to sleep. He's an automaton of a sort, a kind of unhuman thing with which I have been saddled and plagued for all of the last ten years for doing nothing more terrible than siring him and giving him my surname. I would weep over the injustice of it all, had I any tears left to shed."

"Have you—" I faultered, for the question was harsh, "have you, Sir Dabber, no love left for the boy? Has all compassion for the young man and his plight taken its leave?"

Rather than taking offence at the question, Dabber dropt his head and willingly nodded, the shame in the admission reducing the gentleman to silent self-debasement. After a quiet interval, he delivered through a wheeze, "I once loved Bevan, but it was all squandered affection, as if one were cuddling and dandling a stone. I have endured his society, but now it exacts a heavy price from me. I wish sometimes that he should simply die. On occasion…" And here the large, lugubrious man's admission took on a still more confiding tone, "I even *pray* for it."

I did not judge Sir Dabber's motives. Should I have found myself in identical circumstances, could I not have felt the very same? Yet the hospitalised young man was still a human being who deserved a tender hand whether his brain be akin to that of low primate or lizard or stone. Bevan Dabber deserved compassion from his father. But the father deserved clemency from me as well. I would not wish to trade places with him for worlds. Perhaps time *had* hardened him to his son's condition; I would not excuse it, but I couldn't fully deprecate his position. At all events, I would be unable to escape the commission that had been given me (for no temporisation on my part would have been believed) and so I agreed to go with the father and to sit next to him as he in turn sat beside his only child, the young man of twenty who bore his surname and resembled him slightly in the chin and in the eyes. He would hold that young man's cold hand (for cells within Bedlam were drafty, frigid places) and speak to him in those dulcet tones that calm and soothe the breast.

For there was nobody else to do it. Sir Dabber had only one friend, and apparently (to my surprise) it was I.

"When do we go?"

"This afternoon. Visitation, as you know, is permitted only on the first Wednesday and third Sunday of the month. If we miss this opportunity, two-and-a-half weeks must pass, and I'll feel dreadfully guilty for every day that intervenes."

CHAPTER THE TWENTY-EIGHTH

Wednesday, July 2, 2003

It was not my habit to visit Bedlam. It was a stark and forbidding place that was best avoided if there be no compelling reason to betake oneself there. Yet however one felt about it, one could not help noting its rather intriguing architectural design, the Georgian style being quite the anomaly in this valley of mean fairy tale cottages of Tudor crisscrosses and a rather vague attempt at the Romanesque as evinced by some of our larger houses and public buildings (but without the heavy and more ponderous masonry that marked that style). This being said, the mansion house, which had been years ago converted to hospital, offered none of the lightness and eye-pleasing symmetry representative of the Georgian ideal. First, the roof had been lopped off in sugarloaf fashion to give the building a Mansard-like topping that mocked the Georgian elements. And with the construction of an appendage in 1925, which was designated the "West Wing," Bethlehem Hospital upon Highbury Fields was forever thereafter in want of symmetry. Its extravagance of windows gave the building the look of some hard-angled creature with twenty too many eyes, who gazed ominously when he gazed at all, for a good many of his portals had long been shuttered in permanence against the harsh, exposing sun. Nor did the grounds offer respite from the grim austerity of perpetual twilight, the asylum's garden and courtyard being canopied by oppressive boughs that overhung its paths and darkened the prevailing mood as much outside as within that severe and dismal edifice.

My brother and I had a male cousin who had been interned there for many years and whom we had never visited. Indeed, many of Bedlam's residents had lived (if life it be) in that sad but purportedly indispensable facility for just as long as he. The clearly insane, who would do grave injury in close company with other inmates, were confined within separate isolated quarters; yet the number of patients overall, and the scarcity of space available for their segregation from sound-minded society, required a mingling of the imbecilic with the overly nervous and overwrought, those who imagined themselves (with some innocuity) to be famous personages interposed amongst the birdish chatterers and the palsied and the feeble-minded and dodderingly senile.

Young Bevan Dabber was not alone in his affliction. His imbecility, as his father explained it to me on our walk to Bedlam, whilst quite singular in the manifestation of its symptoms, was shared by a number of other inmates of various ages. There was a lack of intellectual apprehension and cerebral engagement in the afflicted, but there were also other traits that marked the disease, as well: a tendency to rock and sway the body, to caw at times as would a crow, and to cover the ears as if they should be muffed, to sit with the fingers straight and held apart one from another, and, when sleeping, to keep the limbs splayed outwardly in rigid fashion, even though the room may be cold and the need to curl and coddle the appendages self-evident. Interestingly, noted Dabber—for he had studied the case files of other patients who resembled in this unique form of imbecility his son Bevan—there was such a consistency and uniformity in the manifestation of the symptoms that a Dinglian doctor several decades earlier was able to give a name to the condition: Rokesmith's rigoritis, taken from the doctor's own name, but not with any measure of pride, for Dr. Rokesmith never succeeded in devising a cure.

Rokesmith's rigoritis was, as I recall from last year's Medical Review report, the third most prevalent of afflictions to visit Dingley Dell, the first and second being, respectively, consumption, whose sufferers were tended either in their homes or as patients within the aptly named "Lung" Hospital, and "Terror Tremens," the most disturbing of all possible names to be affixed to that disease of the mind that targets those who leave the Dell and then return in a thoroughly demented state.

For years, the Petit-Parliament had spoken of making improvements that would reduce this unfortunate quartering within Bedlam that required the co-mixing of the various aberrants. But nothing had been done.

There was a desk in the front hall of Bethlehem Hospital upon Highbury Fields, at which visitors were required to stop and register to gain a few tidbits of time with those loved ones who resided there. Upon our arrival Sir Dabber and I found ourselves at the end of a long and slow-moving queue.

Nearing the point of finally addressing the registrar, we could not help overhearing the following exchange taking place betwixt that selfsame gentleman and the woman who held the spot in the queue directly in front of us. Her name was Jemima Pilkins. She was the wife of Dan Pilkins, a Milltown mason. Mrs. Pilkins was a tall and somewhat brittle-looking woman who reminded me of a willow bending stiffly in the wind. She had been put into a state of great agitation from the moment of gaining the registrar's desk for the purpose of seeking visitors' tickets both for herself and her two daughters, each of whom stood quietly at her side wearing looks of great expectation, due to the following unwavering presentation of recalcitrance on the part of the registrar:

"I'm sorry, Mrs. Pilkins. It just isn't possible. Not possible at all." The registrar, whose name was Howler, though the name did not fit (for the man rarely raised his voice above an audible whisper), was all calmness and equanimity, even as the expression of the woman standing before him turned pinched and sour.

"But you wouldn't let us see my brother last month either. Nor the time before that," replied Mrs. Pilkins, stating a fact that both certainly knew.

"You're correct on both counts, Madam." Howler had not left off shaking his head, perhaps to enforce more fully his disallowance, though the words and the motion of the head would now appear to the casual observer to be incongruously matched.

"Nor even the time before that. And the time before that one. Indeed, Mr. Howler, you have yet to grant permission to my daughters and me for a single visit with my brother Walter, ever since the day of his return from the Terra Incognita a full four months ago!"

This was true. Mrs. Pilkins' brother, Walter Skewton, was the most recent adult Dinglian to venture beyond the valley, and then to return. Mr. and Mrs. Pilkins had welcomed the young man with open, loving arms upon the moment of his late-night appearance on their doorstep. They, like all of those who were present for the joyous homecoming of Jemima Pilkins' younger brother, were bold in refusing to subscribe to the general fear that every Returnee to Dingley Dell (after whatever interval of time abroad) posed such a dire risk to the general population as a potential carrier of that dreaded infectious disease of the brain that he should be thoroughly shunned and certainly never touched!

I was familiar with the incident from having reported on it for the *Dingley Delver*. Dr. Towlinson had been summoned by circumstances to the Pilkins cottage along with Dr. Fibbetson, Sheriff Muntle, and Lord Mayor Feenix (who, in addition to being Minister of Justice, was also Minister of Health) for the express purpose of removing the young man to Bedlam, to be examined and thoroughly evaluated. The transport was swift and uncontested, the situation deemed grave, the disease in the quickly-rendered medical opinion of doctors Towlinson and Fibbetson having spread throughout the young man's brain and into his heart and limbs, thus necessitating his permanent immurement in that hospital, in a form of isolated confinement that disallowed visitation even by close family members.

"Mrs. Pilkins, the order, which placed your brother into quarantine, has yet to be rescinded. Contact with him would be inadvisable even should there be no such order, his having contracted one of the worst cases of Terror Tremens that Dr. Towlinson has ever had the unhappy office to diagnose. Yet you continue to come hither with maddening regularity, possessed of some wild hope that circumstances will miraculously change, despite the fact that there is absolutely no precedent for improvement in your brother. He remains more ill to-day than he was upon the first day of his confinement. The visit is nearly always a waste of your time and mine, and frankly, madam, I don't understand why you continue to put us all through it."

Jemima Pilkins lowered her head and said with quiet determination, "It is my profound hope, Mr. Howler, that Walter *will* one day improve."

"It is naturally our hope that each victim of this unfortunate disease will prove the exception to the general prognosis. But such a thing has yet to occur. Pray go along, so that those standing behind you in the queue may receive their visitor tickets before the day is done."

Yet Mrs. Pilkins was not in an obliging mood. "I spent an hour with him on that first night—the night of his return. My husband, our daughters, several neighbours—all of them as well. I kissed his cheek and he held me in his arms and stroked my head and could not stop speaking of every wonderful thing that he saw in his voyage abroad. He appeared to me clear-headed and quite hale upon that night."

"Then your eyes and ears have deceived you, madam. For whatever wonderful things were spoken of that evening, they could not possibly have been anything but the ravings of a lunatic mind. It's the pattern, Mrs. Pilkins—a pattern with which we've become quite familiar." The registrar's voice gave no animation. The tones produced were dull and laboured and unsympathetic. Mr. Howler, it was quite apparent to even the most casual observer, did not enjoy his offices; when he was not turning away men and women such as Mrs. Pilkins with a dismissive bureaucratic hand, he was putting visitors' tickets into the hands of other men and women who more closely resembled Sir Dabber—those who came to visit their loved ones under the onerous weight of filial or maternal or paternal obligation. There were sick people in Dingley Dell, to be sure, plagued by afflictions of the brain, or given brains at birth that did not function as they should, brains reduced in capacity that would never improve, or which had been knocked insentient from a fall from a horse, for example; or strangulation in the womb; or, in the case of one philandering Dinglian spouse, by the swing of his wife's retaliatory rolling pin. It was all rather trying for every family member to see his kin in such a diminished state, but still there was a duty to be borne.

However, blessed be those who approached the hospital with more than good intention and dutiful step. Blessed be they who imbibed the brew of optimism and hope—a bitter brew sweetened only in its final swallow, when that which was wished for finally came to pass. Mrs. Pilkins longed to be just such a woman in full, and there were others: loved ones of other sufferers of the dreaded Terror Tremens. Such a cruelty it was to family and friend to see a cherished brother, or son, husband or wife, colleague or chum return to the Dell, only to be snatched away nearly upon that instant and imprisoned, as if the disease were some perpetration of felony to be severely punished. It was tenacious hope that brought Jemima Pilkins one Sunday and one Wednesday of each month to this dark and cheerless building along with her teen-year daughters Charity and Mercy, in the belief that this day would be different from all the others, that upon *this* day something of the attributes which she drew for her daughters' very names might imbue and soften the hardened heart of the registrar of visitors, but it was frustration and distemper that staid her departure.

"I mention the hour I spent with my brother four months ago, Mr. Howler," Mrs. Pilkins rejoined, fixing Howler with an icy glare, "to say that we—all of us—spent time in close company with him, and to-day I stand before you bearing no sign at all of having contracted the disease which removes him from us. Nor do my daughters shew evidence of having caught it, nor anyone else who showered my brother Walter with hugs and kisses on that joyful night turned so tragic by his forced removal from us. I am inclined to conclude that the disease isn't communicable at all in his case, and for that reason there should be no reason whatsoever for your persistence in keeping us away from him."

"Then, Mrs. Pilkins, I would advise you to take up the matter with Dr. Towlinson. It is not for me to contravene the rule that Returnees shall have no visitors under any circumstances."

I could not at that moment keep myself from intruding, and I did so by leaning forward and putting my head between the two sloping shoulders of Charity and Mercy. "Begging your pardon, Mr. Howler," I began in a deceptively casual lilt, "I'm curious to know (and it amazes me that I have never put this enquiry to you before) if there ever *was* a Returnee who was permitted a visitation either by family member or friend. Or have they all—without exception—been wholly and permanently quarantined?"

The registrar cleared his throat and then replied, "Certainly there have been exceptions."

"May I know, then, which of the inmates, who once communed with the Outlanders, have been allowed visits with their loved ones?"

"I haven't the names at present. But mind, sir, that it must be established that the illness has receded to such point that it won't spread to others. That is cardinal."

"And how long does it generally take Dr. Towlinson to establish this fact of recession?"

"I don't know." Turning to Sir Dabber: "Would *you* know? You once served on the board of this hospital. What are the criteria?"

"I wasn't aware that there *were* such criteria, Howler. But now that you put it to me, I'd imagine that all devolves to Dr. Towlinson to make that determination, and that it remains a discretionary matter for that gentleman alone."

The matter now having been placed back into the lap of Mr. Howler, official gatekeeper of Bethlehem Hospital upon Highbury Fields, I said, "Then we should like to see Dr. Towlinson. May we have an interview with him directly?"

Crusty irritation now reconfigured the countenance of my companion. "Trimmers, we didn't come hither to intercede on behalf of Mrs. Pilkins' lost cause." With a bow of apology to that good woman: "Not to cast a single aspersion on the *worthiness* of your cause." Then back to me: "We *came*, in point of fact, to see Bevan, and that is all."

"Yet it is an issue that confounds me, Sir Dabber," said I in stubborn pursuit of my newly established mission. "It's also an issue in which I am now partially invested given the recent departures of my nephew Newman and my only brother Augustus."

"I had heard about your nephew but was not aware that your brother was gone as well."

I nodded solemnly and resumed. "Should we all be so fortunate as to witness their return to Dingley Dell, I should like to know if I—and my sister-in-law Charlotte—will ever be permitted to see them subsequent to their sequestration, or must we, as in even the best of cases, wait an interminable number of years for that privilege?"

"The matter is all quite hypothetical at the moment, wouldn't you say, Trimmers?" returned Dabber with an impatient tap of his umbrella's ferule upon the hard floor.

"Nonetheless, Mr. Trimmers' advocacy is much appreciated," said Mrs. Pilkins, with lips that half-smiled, no doubt, for the first time since she set foot that day within the asylum's great front hall.

I dropt my voice for a private conference with Sir Dabber. I reminded him that I was doing him a favour by accompanying him on this trip to see his son Bevan, and it was only right and meet that he should reciprocate my kindness by indulging my promotion of Mrs. Pilkins' four-month-long cause. Had Newman and Gus never left Dingley Dell and the matter remained in the abstract with regard to my own curiosity, I should still at all events wish to find out why it was that none who had left our valley and then returned was ever permitted to see his family, even, in some cases, after many long years of agonising separation. It made no sense—never had. I could not help recalling what Muntle had said to me only two days before: that it was his belief and the belief of the others who gathered with him (for a purpose other than reading poetry) that there was a false reason conveniently put forward for everything that happened in the Dell and then a second true and hidden reason. Was this the case here?

"You cannot see Dr. Towlinson because it's his afternoon off, and he doesn't conduct interviews on his afternoon off. It is unheard of," said Mr. Howler, with finality.

"This is his afternoon off?" asked an elderly farmer, listening with his ear-horn. The farmer's name I recalled as Matthew or Mark (or Luke or John; the mnemonic I used for this gentleman placed the man somewhere within the ranks of that scribing quartet of gospel apostles).

"That's what I just said," snapped Howler with a curved and nearly snarling lip, contemptuously dis-acknowledging the man's hearing infirmity.

I surmised that, given the way that some in the queue closed about to better hear our exchange, there just might be others amongst those present on this day who were either themselves in straits similar to those endured by members of the Pilkins family or were sympathetic to Mrs. Pilkins' struggle through sensipathic solidarity.

My supposition was confirmed by the following observations:

"Sometimes I will speak to a person on *my* afternoon off." This from Mrs. Jellyby, who supervised the laundresses at Dingley Dell Workhouse #3.

"That isn't at all germane to the matter at hand," replied Howler dismissively.

"Where does the good doctor spend his afternoon off? Where is he at this moment?" asked Miss Clickett, Newman's former village schoolteacher, who had come to visit her sister Minnie who was being briefly interned for a climacteric nervous condition.

"How should *I* know?" replied Howler, growing more bilious with each moment. "In his study, I would warrant, but don't hold me to it!"

As a farrier by the name of Stiltstalking was opening his mouth to speak, Howler appended, "But he's left specific instructions that he isn't to be disturbed. That is always the way on Wednesday afternoon. Now if you will all kindly—"

"Not even for a matter of dire importance?" interrupted Chuffey the baker.

"This most certainly doesn't rise to that level, my dear sir, and if we are to have revolt here on behalf of the perpetually-persistent Mrs. Pilkins, then I will be forced to summon orderlies to clear this hall and send each and every one of you back to his home."

Sir Dabber, who had bristled at my involvement as an impediment to his wish to see his son as soon and as quickly as possible, now be-mantled himself with a public garment I'd never before seen him wear: disdained and demeaned man of the people.

Brandishing his rather large enfolded umbrella as if it were some menacing mace or spear, the gentleman, his full cheeks puffed out and deeply coloured, plunged into the following wheezing, rather remarkable declamation: "My dear Mr. Howler, I have sat at intervals upon the supervisory board of this hospital, it being a *public* institution and answerable to the citizens of this valley whose taxes pay for its continuation and upkeep, and I must say that your obdurate behaviour can only be taken as offensive and insulting to every man, woman, and child in this hall. You have no authority here but to follow the rules you've been given as to who may enter and who may not, and you are obliged, nay, institutionally *obligated* to refer anyone who questions or contests your interpretation of those rules, or voices any grievance with regard to said rules, to the author of those selfsame rules, that person being Dr. Towlinson, who, I happen to know, maintains his office on Visitation Wednesdays to be available should there be matters pertaining to visitation that might require his immediate attention. *This*, sir, is just such a matter, and if you do not suffer Mrs. Pilkins and her daughters *and* my friend Mr. Trimmers, *and* myself to proceed to a direct and immediate interview with the good doctor, I shall use every ounce of the clout which I still maintain with the board of directors, each member of whom is a close colleague of mine in medical society, to see that you are promptly discharged from your position as registrar of visitation for this institution without hope of future reinstatement!"

Mr. Howler swallowed, his face having attained a most interesting plastery pallor. He had been trod thoroughly beneath the hooves of that large-framed authority known as Sir Dabber, who had hitherto represented himself as nothing more than a silent, perturbed man in a queue, no more important to eye and ear than a cold and silent sconce upon a wall. "I will take you to the doctor's office this instant, by all means," stammered Howler, who then bounded up from his desk with such a forceful application of bodily intention that the chair was tumbled backwards and the hand, which joined the voice in indicating the young man's newly-found purpose in life, swept itself in sloppy gesticulation across the bundle of visitor tickets, brushing no small number of them onto the floor, this collateral misfortune compelling the flustered and fluttering gatekeeper of Bedlam to deliver the following adjuration to his gaping-mouthed spectators: "Do not touch the tickets. Remain where you are. Let the paper slips lie! I will return shortly."

In his patter across the hall with the five of us skating and skittering on the slick linoleum to keep up, Howler resembled some diminutive animal I could not bring fully to mind. But having raised his voice to a degree which had never before been heard here in this large and echoing chamber, he made me smile to think that the surname Howler on this particular day quite befitted the man, and that perchance it was the exception rather than the rule, in more cases than even this one, that commanded when it was most necessary.

CHAPTER THE TWENTY-NINTH

Wednesday, July 2, 2003

Mr. Howler, finding the door to his employer's study agape and its official occupant absent, bade that we all be seated within that room whilst he went searching for the man who paid his wages. The room was not a large one, having once served as a cozy bedchamber within the mansion home that was the hospital's previous incarnation, but it was spruce and lavishly furnished. A fine mahogany triangular press dominated one corner. Scattered about were a Spanish mahogany desk, several leather-bottomed elbow chairs, and a couch to match the design and wooden filigree of its companion pieces. All were exemplary of the finest furniture construction in the Dell—a top line rarely found outside the home or office of the most patrician of Dingley Dell's Bashaw class. A fireplace, girded in expressive marble, had been set into the handsomely wainscotted wall, that very architectural feature making it obvious that the room had been improved *after* the commencement of Towlinson's reign, for the hearth frame matched in colour and pattern the marble top of a small lamp table also found within the room, as well as a decorative lintel imposed above the door.

The room was, in fact, far better appointed than even those libraries and studies I had visited within the homes of the Dingley Dell's most titanic titans of industry, their league comprehending a half dozen or so gentlemen, who were themselves heirs to our earliest enterprisers in the sectors of coal and iron ore extraction and furniture manufacture and textile production and fruit and vegetable factoring.

Mrs. Pilkins, who was of that class which, whilst not by definition "poor," scrimped and saved and did without to put a goose upon the Christmas table and warm shoes round her daughters' feet, commented upon her exquisite surroundings through a breath-whistle of incredulity and an appeal to Charity and Mercy to be "ever so careful not to touch and soil anything."

Mercy Pilkins, the younger of the two sisters, with eyes opened wider than even her mother's, consented to the injunction with a nod, but appended withal, "Still, Mama, I should like to curl up in that easy chair, and take down a book and never leave!"

Charity, who shared her mother and sister's sentiments, was loathe to take a spot between the two upon the beckoning couch when she could instead stand and run her fingertips along the smooth wooden grain of Towlinson's desktop, those fingers quickly migrating to touch the items which rested thereupon, in clear violation of her mother's enjoinment. All were things that a man would use in his attendance to the needs of the one-hundred-some-odd mentally-defective men and women (and a small smattering of mentally-defective children) who had been placed under his care: an opened foolscap pad with figures pencilled between its blue lines, a closed ledger, an ink well and pen, a ruler, sealing wax, wafers and pounce box with powder within to blot ink (Charity confirming this with a peek beneath the lid), a string box and fire-box and then another item that could not be identified, but which the young woman took into her hand to overturn and poke and squint at.

"For the sake of Heaven, put that down," exhorted the girl's mother. "We weren't brought into this private chamber to dandle the doctor's personal effects."

"But what is it? I should like to know," returned Charity in weak remonstrance. From where I sat, the item didn't resemble anything I'd ever seen before. I myself was curious to discover its purpose. I rose from my chair and held out my hand for the girl to give it up. Having done so, Charity went to sit with her mother and sister, as Sir Dabber joined me at desk-side.

"Can you make it out?" asked Dabber. The item was largely flat with dimensions of roughly five inches by four inches. It was composed of some material that seemed an amalgam of ceramic and metal. It was black. There was a rectangular glass window at the top, which slanted upward, as would a propped-up bed. There were a number of raised button-like squares—I counted twenty-four—some containing the imprint of numbers placed in an oddly reversed sequence: 7,8,9, then below these 4,5,6 and so forth. Here is what was imprinted on the squares upon the top row: MC, MR, M-, M+, then down the right side, the mathematical symbols for dividing, multiplying, subtracting and adding, the button with this last imprint being longer width-wise than its neighbours. Next to it was a button bearing the double bar sign for "equals." At the very top just below the curious window were buttons bearing the imprints "off" and "on." Next to these buttons the letters AARP had been written in unfamiliar script.

Peering over my shoulder Sir Dabber marvelled aloud, "It must be some sort of calculating device, similar to the theoretical calculating machines of Mr. Babbage, but look at it, Trimmers: note how very small it is."

"Perhaps it's a model of something that has yet to be built. A good many of that famed British mathematician's calculating machines lived only upon paper, although there were perhaps smaller non-functional versions that he put together to shew the design. There's only one way to know what it is for certain."

I touched the tiny raised platform with the word "on" inscribed upon it. At that instant a naught followed by a full stop appeared most miraculously within the window. My hand trembled. I set the device down upon the desk and took a backward step. I felt as perhaps did the primeval cave dweller upon first encountering the mystery of fire. Instantly, I berated myself for acting so foolish. I squared my shoulders and reclaimed the device, and after chewing upon my lip for a moment, announced, "We will ask it to perform a calculation. Sir Dabber, what is something arithmetical that we might wish to know?"

Dabber thought for a moment, whilst tapping his fingers on his lips. "There are 107 patients in this hospital. Seventeen are, like Mrs. Pilkins' brother, Returnees from the Terra Incognita. Ask the machine to tell us the number of those within this place who would *not* be so classified."

"Ninety," blurted Charity, wishing to be helpful.

"I should like the *machine* to tell us," admonished Sir Dabber. "Hush now. We must figure how one goes about putting down the figures."

"I should think," said I, "that one must first touch the buttons that comprise numerals of the first term: 107." This I did, the full three-digit-number appearing in that very same miraculous way as did the original naught.

"And now," said Sir Dabber, his voice lifted to higher pitch in excited anticipation, "poke the subtracting button, so that we should order the sequence in the same way that one would put the operation on paper."

I nodded and pushed the button with the horizontal line upon it, which we presumed must stand for subtraction. Within the window, there was no change. The "107" remained undisturbed.

"Don't despair, my friend. Push buttons for the next term, the seventeen." Dabber's breath was hot upon my neck and made the hair there stand on end, but I didn't, nay, *couldn't* ask the esteemed man to remove himself. We were discoverers in tandem, and his participation a welcome adjunct in the spirit of collaboration. I pushed the "one" button, and then the "seven" to give seventeen. The 107 promptly disappeared, its place now taken by the newly pushed seventeen.

"And now the equals sign!" cried Charity, who had sailed to my side, for she could not hold herself upon her seat when there was so much magic afoot only a few paces away.

"Yes, I see the sign and I'll push that button." It was a simple thing to do, but when the correct number, ninety, appeared within the window, my hand once more began to tremble.

"That was a simple operation. Let us try a much more difficult one," suggested Dabber. He took the calculating device from me and pushed buttons to divide 66,666,666 (comprehending all the space that the window allowed for putting numerals thereupon) by 12,345,678. The answer was 5.4000003.

"Is the quotient correct?" asked Charity in an eager, nearly breathless voice.

"If it is not, it must come quite close," I replied. "Sixty-six divided by twelve gives five-decimal-five, but let's put the longer operation upon a page and see for ourselves." I was about to take a piece of foolscap from Dr. Towlinson's desk when I heard voices emanating from the outside corridor. I put the device down upon the spot in which Charity had discovered it and quickly took to my chair. Sir Dabber claimed the chair next to it, whilst Charity returned herself to her mother's couch with equal alacrity. The voices outside the room were strong and carried themselves quite clearly into the office.

"Where are they now?" The first voice sounded gruff and also quite vexed in tone.

"Why, in your study, of course. That's where I asked them to wait." The second voice most certainly belonging to Mr. Howler. It lacked composure and confidence.

"Have you suddenly reverted to the age of two? Since when have I allowed anybody to enter that room in my absence?"

"I'm sorry, sir. I wasn't thinking. Yet the door was open. I assumed that you'd be returning in only a brief moment."

"You assumed incorrectly, my dear Howler. And I should have locked that damned door when I left upon my errand. Yet, nonetheless, due to your negligence of duty I must now contend with—" With a great interruptive sigh of impatience: "Who is seeing to the other visitors? Go along. Quickly now, Howler, or we shall have the entire populace of the Dell prowling our halls and performing acts of scattered mischief."

"Yes, sir."

As we unwelcome guests listened to the corridor voices, we exchanged uneasy looks. Yet it was young Charity's face that gave evidence of the greatest discomfiture. In fact, in the briefest instant that worrisome countenance suddenly contorted itself into a display of true horror, striking commensurate fear within the hearts of all of the rest of us.

"Good God, Charity, what is it?" I put to her from across the room in a poorly elevated stage whisper.

"The machine! The little calculating machine! It's still—!"

The time for explanation having expired, Charity leapt from her seat and flung herself at the desk where she fumbled with all of her fingers to take up the computational device and find upon its face that button which returned it to its former dormant state, the button being in both my estimation and fortunately hers as well, "Off." That button having now been pressed and the permanent occupant of the room having now appeared in the doorway of his premises (his head turned to make certain that his employee was moving with all expedition in the direction of his downstairs post), the girl promptly placed herself at the window and assumed the posture of one lost in her meditations, which her mother now disturbed to abet the conspiracy. "Charity, dear, come away from that window and sit yourself down. Dr. Towlinson has arrived."

With a deliberately effected (and quite convincing) carefree air, Mrs. Pilkins' oldest daughter acceded to her mother's wishes and wordlessly repaired to the couch, sitting herself, it should be noted, upon both of her hands, each in need of having its discernible tremor withheld from the view of Dr. Towlinson, lest they betray to him the pretense behind her otherwise commendable performance.

"Good afternoon, Sir Dabber," said the doctor, who to my knowledge was fast approaching his sixtieth year, though he was a specimen in apparently prime and robust health. Dr. Towlinson wore horn-rimmed spectacles, which he now adjusted upon his nose as if the better to identify each member of that impertinent quintet that had stoutly stormed his office.

"And Mr. Trimmers. And good afternoon to you, my dear Mrs. Pilkins and the Misses Pilkins."

Having clasped hands with each of us (excepting Charity) in the quick and prosy manner of a farmer shaking the last drop of milk from his dairy-cow's teat, the doctor moved to his desk to take his place behind it, doctors, like any member of the more exalted professions, being well aware that placement behind one's desk offers the best advantage for commanding a room with authority. In this respect Towlinson resembled nothing so much as a judge upon his bench or perhaps a butcher before his block, cleaver in hand.

"We beg pardon for the intrusion, Dr. Towlinson," said I, "but it's doubtful that Howler would have allowed us to see you without some application of assertiveness on our part."

"Do you really mean *Howler*?" posed the doctor with a grin, "or *me*? For I left strict orders with my registrar that I would be entertaining no visitors this afternoon."

"Unless there rose a matter of some importance," Mrs. Pilkins corrected our host, "which this visit most certainly concerns."

It was at this moment that Towlinson made a discovery that raised his brows and set his mouth aslant. He noticed the calculating device that had been left upon his desk. It was obvious from the unsettled expression upon his face that it had not been his intent to leave the thing in full view of anybody who might approach his office. Perhaps it lived always and without exception within that very drawer into which he now deposited it and quickly locked it away. Having put the thing out of sight, he scanned each of our faces for some indication that its presence had registered with us. Each visitor made his or her face as blank as could be possible, Mercy even feigning to wipe something from her sister's eyelid, as if to use this bit of business to demonstrate a lack of awareness of anything of an extraordinary nature within the room, including a most miraculous calculating machine that could not have been believed had we not all clearly seen it in its full and glorious function.

Each of us had made a decision upon that very instant not to enquire about the device, for what would it profit our present cause and how easily could it prove to over-complicate our efforts here? Yet I, for one, would not soon forget it, for its existence begged a number of questions I should like to have answered. Here, however, was neither the time nor place to ask them.

Dr. Towlinson seemed to relax, having apparently decided for himself that we had not trespassed upon his desk and in all likelihood had not seen the computator (let alone used it to divide 66,666,666 by 12,345,678 to gain a quotient that placed a "three" seven full spaces behind the decimal, producing the requisite result in less time than it took me to blink even once in utter disbelief!).

"If you refer, Mrs. Pilkins, to the hospital's decision to keep your brother Walter Skewton in a continued state of isolation, there is nothing to be said. The quarantine remains in place and you will not be given leave to violate it."

"Yet it is my belief, Dr. Towlinson, that he has been incorrectly diagnosed, for as I told Mr. Howler downstairs, nobody who sat with Walter on the evening of his return has been taken ill. Not a single one of us!"

"The disease may be in a state of hibernation or incubation, my dear lady, and if it were up to me, I would place each of you into quarantine yourselves given your close proximity to Walter on that night. But it just isn't possible for us to go about putting large groups of people into observation cells at the expense of the general ratepayer. And so we will count our blessings that, so far, nobody within your household seems to have contracted this terrible disease. And let us leave it at that."

"Before we 'leave it at that,'" I interposed, "may I ask if you will permit Mrs. Pilkins to, at the very least, view her brother at a safe distance?" I prided myself on this attempt to bridge the chasm between the two positions. "Perhaps Mr. Skewton may be brought to a window and engaged from some vantage point on the grounds below."

Towlinson dismissed the idea with a resolute shake of the head. "That would be out of the question. The young man is asleep."

"Then wake him."

"I cannot. Mr. Skewton is presently under the influence of one of our strongest soporifics and cannot be roused for love or money."

"Why?" I asked, sliding forward in my chair with impatience.

"Why what?"

"Why has he been so heavily sedated?"

"Because—forgive my bluntness, sir—he is mad. Because he spends most of his waking hours attempting to remove himself from this place with such violence and such calculated expenditure of energy that he can scarcely be subdued. I eschew that dreadful three-letter term, 'mad,' madam—" now having returned his sombre gaze to Mrs. Pilkins, "but in the case of your brother I shall make exception: Walter Skewton is a veritable madman. He will not improve. Nay, he worsens with each week. His is a most grievous case, a fact that I did not wish to convey to you for fear that the disclosure would have a devastating effect upon your sensibilities and upon the sensibilities of your fragile daughters. But since you must have it, the truth is this: that the man whom we hold in strait-waistcoat is no longer the same man you knew as your brother. *That* man, I regret to inform you, is as good as dead."

Mrs. Pilkins did not reply. All of the wind had fled her sails and she sat slumped and withered upon the couch, silent tears streaming down her cheeks, each bookend daughter doing everything with attentive strokes and pats to assuage her misery, their eyes bedewed as well.

It was Sir Dabber who chose next to speak: "Dr. Towlinson, has the hospital board been apprised of the young man's condition?"

"They'll be informed at our next scheduled meeting on Monday evening."

"And what is the present status of the other Returnees?"

"What do you mean, sir?"

"How similar are their respective conditions to that of Mr. Skewton's?"

"Quite a few are nearly as bad. We've tried large doses of every remedy that can be compounded: bromide of potassium, belladonna, chloride of aluminum, ferrous sulfate, quinine, tartar of arsenic, stramonium tobacco. It is all for naught, my good man. The tragedy of it haunts my dreams and disturbs my waking hours. When I at life's end prepare to depart this world, my inability to heal these men and women will constitute my greatest professional regret and disappointment."

"But you say that Mr. Skewton's condition is the worst? There is no one amongst the other Returnees whom you could say displays more acute symptoms than does Mrs. Pilkins' unfortunate brother?"

"There was Mr. Gamfield, but, alas—do not speak of this outside these walls, for his family has yet to be told—he died this morning. In the midst of a fit. He was being conveyed to the bathing room and threw himself against a wall and cracked open—" The doctor lowered his voice now in deference to the tender ears of the females in the room. "Cracked open his skull. There was significant loss of brain matter. The skull must have been weakened in its constituency from the gentleman's having struck his head repeatedly against the wall of his own cell as the most grievous idiots do."

Mrs. Pilkins, having heard every word, gasped and then was seised by a paroxysm of tears that did not abate even as she was being led by her daughters out of the office and down the corridor and away. I reached for her hand to give comfort as she passed but could not secure it. Nor did she see my look of commiseration, nor the look of sadness upon the face of my companion Sir Dabber.

"And there it is," said Dr. Towlinson, as the sound of the footsteps of Mrs. Pilkins and her attending daughters died quickly away. Towlinson clasped his hands together as if in relief over their departure.

"And the inquest—has it been scheduled?" asked Dabber.

"It will be done as soon as possible. We must put all of this behind us. Now if there is nothing else to be discussed, I am very busy and must be on my rounds. It is my primary goal to see each visitation Wednesday proceed as smoothly as possible for my visitors as well as for my patients and those who tend to them. It is all a very carefully-orchestrated business and I am the conductor who holds the wand."

The doctor, who, apparently, thought himself a symphony conductor, rose from his chair and offered his hand. The three of us shook in silence, and in like silence were we escorted from the chambers and out into the passage. Noting our reticence, Towlinson, with one hand gripping the door handle, released a long sigh through his nostrils. "I take it that my brief discourse on the unfortunate state of things wasn't what you came to hear."

"Indeed not," said Sir Dabber, dispiritedly. I merely shook my head in wordless concurrence. Dabber had one thing more to say, which he delivered in a subdued voice: "Things were not so difficult when I served on the board. The Returnees were more tractable then, and their situations less severe."

"The disease has progressed. To a man. One might chart the course of one and apply it to all the others. Here is the thing that most disturbs me and I will tell it you in all honesty: Mr. Gamfield was not the exception. He was actually, in my studied opinion, the vanguard."

Dabber returned: "Meaning that every man and woman who was once in the Outland and has returned to Dingley Dell faces the eventuality of violent death within this place?"

Towlinson nodded with gravity. "And let us be thankful that we are able to contend with them *within* these walls rather than without so that others will not be harmed or leastways collaterally inconvenienced. It is my educated conjecture that the trajectory of each man and woman so afflicted leads to the very same end. Some will take longer to succumb than others, but the course is the same. Now, gentlemen, I really must be about my rounds." Towlinson turned and closed the door behind him. He drew a key from his waistcoat pocket and locked the door, then gave the handle a pull to test the fastness of the lock. Without giving so much as a parting glance in our direction, he strode quckly down the corridor and was gone. Dabber and I were left standing in stunned silence.

"I don't believe him," I finally took breath to say.

'Nor I," said Sir Dabber. "Something is direly amiss. I cannot put my finger on it. Yet I am deeply disturbed by it."

I nodded.

"But alas, there is nothing to be done about it to-day. On Monday I shall go to this month's board meeting. I have leave to attend as emeritus member of that body. You will come with me."

I shook my head, less in disagreement than quandary. "That is a closed meeting, Sir Dabber. Surely, I would not be given leave to attend."

"I will plead for your presence under a petition of special circumstances. I want everything that is said in that room put down on paper, and your shorthand will serve us invaluably. Formerly the board has not kept minutes of its proceedings, but from now on we must have an indisputable record of its business. Come. Let us see my boy before the day has fled."

"May I ask you one question before we proceed?"

"Of course."

"During your full tenure upon the hospital board, what was the reason given for why victims of the Terror Tremens, all of them Returnees from the Outland, were denied visitation by their family and friends?"

"The contagious nature of the affliction, of course."

"There was never another reason put forward—even one that you may have accidentally overheard?"

Dabber shook his head. After a thoughtful pause, he said, "Although I have always found the policy to be rather Draconian in some of its aspects. Consider, for example, the fact that it wasn't only face-to-face contact between patient and non-patient that was disallowed. There was a proscription placed upon all written correspondence as well."

"And do you not recall thinking this queer, even unfair at the time?"

"Somewhat. But I was never one to second-guess decisions made by the board. Generally speaking, I simply deferred to the better judgement of Towlinson and Fibbetson on such matters. Yet now that I stop to consider it fully, I do find it most disturbingly queer, and, yes, patently unfair, and I intend to ask for a more detailed justification at Monday's meeting."

As we headed down the long gallery that led to the cellar stairs, the imbeciles having been temporarily relegated to the cellar chambers whilst their rooms above were being refurbished, I thought of the magical calculating machine and how it added and subtracted and divided and multiplied numbers, and told one exactly what one wished to know of an arithmetical nature. It did not, most obviously *could* not, answer those questions that most often pressed upon the minds of Dinglians: Why, in truth, did this place called Dingley Dell come to be? For what purpose? And to what end? And where were we all to be when every question had finally received its answer? More immediately, what other wonders and horrors remained hidden within the valley, privy only to the Towlinsons and the Pupkers amongst us?

Yet this strange day was far from done. As miraculous as was the calculating device, and as tragic as was the intelligence pertaining to Walter Skewton and the unfortunate Mr. Gamfield (who hadn't even ventured from the valley with adventurous intent, but in coincidental pursuit of his runaway Newfoundland pup), even far greater peculiarities of this day lay only a few steps and a few moments away, and in meeting them, two more pieces of this rather large puzzle, which was being offered to us both intentionally and inadvertently, would be put directly into our hands and heavy would they weigh, though there be some modicum of hope affiliated with them both.

CHAPTER THE THIRTIETH

Wednesday, July 2, 2003

There was no reason to *creep* into the dark cell that held Sir Dabber's son Bevan and three other victims of Rokesmith's rigoritis, but creep we did nonetheless in respectful silence. The attendant who unlocked the door, a roughly-hewn young man from the village of Tavistock whom I knew only as Oscar, informed us prior to shutting us in, "You rap upon this here door, when you got to go. I'll come set you free."

"Must we visit with him *here*?" asked Dabber of the attendant. "Can he not be taken up to the garden? There are benches there beneath the trees."

"And light and air," I added.

Oscar shook his head and rubbed an itch upon his pocked nose. "The 'rigors' don't get the grounds. They stay put where we puts 'em."

The door closed with a loud clang and in that jolting instant we joined the company of Bevan and three other men, each of whom was rocking back and forth upon his own cot, seemingly oblivious to our presence.

"My heart breaks for each one of them," said Sir Dabber, touching the corner of his eye with his oversized pocket-handkerchief. "And to think that there is no cure. It's most difficult to abide."

I touched Dabber upon the arm and pointed to his son. "Go and sit with him. Take his hand. Deep within him he must know that it's you come to visit."

The large man sighed and nodded and moved to sit next to the young man who bore his surname and a bit of his look. "You should sit on his other side," Dabber entreated me. "He may like it that there are two who are come to be with him."

I did not wish to sit next to Bevan. He stank. It had been a while since he had been bathed. There were crumbs clinging to his chin stubble and encrusted morsels lodging within the corners of his mouth. Bevan's long, matted brown hair remained in an upward sweep as if he had been standing in the wind. I imagined the pitiful young man running his hands upward through his locks over and over again as some of the "rigors" were wont to do.

Sir Dabber lowered himself carefully upon the hard cot, and took up his son's bony hand. He held it as he, no doubt, had held it on each of his former visits. A cockroach skittered aross the floor, stopping at Bevan's unshod right foot, and then making bold to traverse it. Bevan did not acknowledge the prickly passage of the verminous creature. The young man's begrimed face gave nothing but a blank stare, a look no different from that which greeted us when first we had stepped into the cell.

One of the other men cawed. It was a single shout, which sounded very much like that of a crow, and then there was silence in the small dark room—a room that smelt of unwashed flesh and unlaundered linens and mouldering food and dank water. I could not tell which of the room's two buckets was used for what, and I had no desire to investigate.

"These conditions are appalling," said Sir Dabber with an atrabilious shake of the head. "I don't care that the lodgings are only temporary until the rooms are finished upstairs. It is medieval. Barbaric! This is a hospital, for Christ's sake! A place for hospitable healing."

I nodded. I was equally repulsed.

"I intend to find out exactly how much longer these men will be made to live here in this veritable dungeon!" proclaimed Dabber, his brow knitted in consternation.

Dabber's raised voice had unsettled one of the other young men who looked up with a frightful expression.

"Contain yourself," I admonished my exercised companion.

Dabber nodded. He turned to behold his son, fresh tears forming in his eyes. "What a life you have led, my child. And how cruelly have I disparaged you. I should never have thought so little of you. You were always a burden, but from this day forward I vow to do better by you. I will be a far kinder and far more loving father to you, mark me, my dear boy."

I turned my own gaze to Bevan Dabber and witnessed thereupon a most amazing thing: the young man had also begun to cry. A tear was trickling at that very moment—one errant tear only—down his left cheek. But in its tiny rivulet upon that dirty face, it brought both Dabber and me to an even greater state of emotional affliction. The tear served as a simple but stark reminder that the young man was still human. And then came something else that made the same point in an even stronger, more dramatic way: *Bevan Dabber spoke!*

"Hear me, Papa. Give me leave to say a thing or two." (Sir Seth Dabber could not have found his voice at that moment even if he had wished to, his son's words having put him into a sudden, nearly apoplectic, stupor!) "I have been healed, Papa. There is a nurse here who has done it. Miss Wolf. You know Miss Wolf, I believe, as the child who lay abed with withering lungs and a crippled heart in Hungerford village—a child whom no one ever saw. No one saw her because she is a fabrication. Miss Wolf is a Beyonder who needed the means by which to pretend that she had always been one of us. Two years ago she came hither and two months ago she began to heal me, and now I am well and the rigoritis is gone."

So now I had come to know some of the truth about the mysterious Miss Wolf, and to receive answers to a few of those puzzling questions I had had about her early life and that sudden and miraculous recovery coincident to her supposititious parents' death. But one question led to another, and then another. Did Mr. and Mrs. Wolf participate in preparations for their "daughter's" integration into the Dell, or did their deaths merely open a convenient portal for Ruth's entry under the guise of being their daughter? (I was later to learn that it was the latter, Ruth being absolved, moreover, of my suspicions that she had been somehow complicit in effecting the exigent death of her "parents.")

I did not betray to the young man that I knew her. Instead, I prepared myself to listen to this most earnest and commendatory invocation of her with feigned ignorance of any knowledge of the subject at hand.

Bevan took a long breath. I seised this opportunity to say that it was extraordinary, nearly beyond belief, to think that he had been healed of a disease that had never before known a cure. But one thing at a time: why was he pretending otherwise?

"For the time being, I must counterfeit myself in the way that you saw me when first you entered this cell. Miss Wolf was brought here for a sinister purpose that she has not disclosed to me—a purpose that plagues her soul. She is working to divest herself of those duties one-by-one. But she also redeems herself by performing good deeds where she can, and in ways that will not disclose her true identity here in Dingley Dell. She has healed me, Papa. She is secretly healing others as well; she has the drugs to do this—drugs procured from the Outland.

"Papa, I love you. And if you love me half as much as I do you, you will keep what I have told you to yourself. I shouldn't be speaking to you. I should be keeping up the pretense of my illness. Yet your tears have compelled me to give balm to your suffering, to tell you in confidentiality that I am well. I am trapped within this place for a short time longer and must continue the counterfeit for the sake of Ruth Wolf, so that no harm will come to her for what she has done to help me and some of the others, but I had to tell you, to lift the heavy burden I have placed upon your heart and which you have carried about for lo, these last ten years."

"I was so very cruelhearted in my thoughts of you until only a few moments ago," said the father, his choked voice aching with remorse.

"Yet you must acquit yourself, Papa. I was become no longer a son to you. I was a cross to be borne—a ragged, splintered, broken thing. Think no more of it, Papa. Now you must promise me—the both of you—that you won't communicate a word of what I've told you to anybody."

Sir Dabber threw his arms about his son and did not release him. The last of the interchange was spoken in voices muffled by the close embrace of the two men—father and son, not only reunited (for many years had passed since Bevan had been a happy, healthy boy) but also newly born in each other's arms.

"Your revelation raises a very large number of questions," I said, keeping my voice to a whisper.

"Very few of which I'm able to answer," said the young man.

"Cannot or *will* not?"

"Cannot. I have told you almost all that I know. There is only one thing more, and it will frighten you, so you must be stout."

Bevan withdrew his head from his father's shoulder. Sir Dabber eponymously dabbed at his wet eyes with his expansive handkerchief.

"Papa, and you who are his friend—"

"The name is Trimmers."

"Yes, I will in time learn all the names of those who presently live in this valley, which I have for so long occupied in imbecility and ignorance and darkness. Here is the thing that must be said; I have no reason not to believe Miss Wolf, and so you must believe her, too: the world moves forward. The world outside of Dingley Dell moves ever onward. It has always moved thusly. It is we who have remained trapped in a time gone by. It is an oppressively complicated business. There are dangers in this new world that must be addressed. Dangers to us. In time, Miss Wolf will tell us how we are to confront them. But all must be done with great care and caution. We are fragile, she says. We are the china and porcelain that sit protected upon a shelf but once withdrawn may break in a thousand different ways. She says that we are beautiful to behold but it is inevitable that some day we shall be pulled down from that shelf, for we have gathered too much dust there, have draped ourselves too much in the cobwebs of our suspended lives."

"But here is a silver lining to it all," said Sir Dabber through a wheeze, for the mould and must within the room were taxing his respiration. "My son has been returned to me! After ten years you and I are again truly united in mind and spirit, father and son. And I cannot help celebrating, even if it be in private fashion, my wonderful good fortune."

Sir Dabber imprinted a kiss upon Bevan's dingy forehead and struggled to rise. The tremendous gravity of what had been told, the shock of seeing his son without the splayed and stiff limbs, nor rocking back and forth, nor cawing like a rook—every aspect of the few preceding moments had weighed so heavily down upon him that he could hardly return himself to his feet. I rose quickly to take his arm when it appeared likely that he might topple over or faint away.

"Rest assured: we won't betray your trust," said I to Bevan, who remained upon the cot. Yet I dissembled. I had to tell Sheriff Muntle, and now all of the members of the delving Poetry League. They had every right and reason to know. These were important pieces for the mosaic they were putting together. But the young man must not be troubled on this account.

So I dissembled.

"You fear for the well-being of this young woman?" asked Sir Dabber of his son.

Bevan nodded. "Frightfully so."

"Is it because you love her?"

Bevan smiled. "She has resurrected me."

Now Bevan paused. "And she is beautiful."

And finally, Bevan blushed.

I had now received the answer to at least one nagging question from that pivotal week: to whom had Ruth Wolf given her heart? And there he sat—a boy, several years younger than herself, fully dependent upon her, literally resurrected by her. Had she healed him because she loved him first, or did she come to love the man he became under her cure? These speculations made me feel guilty, intrusive. I backed away from them. I vowed to release Ruth Wolf from my heart to pursue this path she had wisely or unwisely chosen for herself. Indeed there was love here that no one had a right to judge or define—least of all Frederick Trimmers, for whom love in the abstract remained elusive and capricious.

"When may I come to see you again?" asked Sir Dabber of his son. "On the next visiting Sunday?"

"We must not raise suspicions by too frequent visits, Papa."

"But this deplorable room—you must be removed from it at the earliest possible moment."

"That time will soon come, Papa, for Ruth tells me that there have been other complaints about the conditions down here, and so the renovation is now moving along more quickly upstairs. But it serves me to remain in this dungeon. Down here I am seldomly observed. Here Ruth may come to see me without worry of interlopers or keyhole peepers. With each visit, my darling Ruth feels more and more at ease to tell me things. And there is so much more to tell—a *world* of things."

Sir Dabber nodded. A moment later we stood before the heavy iron door, listening to the clink and click of its latch. As the door creaked open, pushed by the youthful hand of Oscar the attendant ("Turnkey" would be a more appropriate appellation), Bevan Dabber resumed his previous state. His stare became glossy and he began to rock. The hands went up to the ears. He cawed.

"He's telling you goodbye," chuckled Oscar. "That's his crow-like way of saying 'ta'! Somebody should put these boys upon a stage. It would be a true hilarity to see it—at least for those who don't got to clean they's stinking dovecote each and every bloody day."

The statement drew no response from either Sir Dabber or myself. It was safest to leave Oscar's odious opinion unchallenged.

CHAPTER THE THIRTY-FIRST

Wednesday, July 2, 2003

This day of revelations was not done. As Oscar conducted Sir Dabber and me to the beshadowed staircase that would deliver us from this dark dungeon of human abjection and mental affliction, I stopt before the door to one of the cells, which had been left so widely open as to give a full view of its interior. Although the cell was empty, yet it captured the eye nonetheless for what had been put upon its black walls. All four had been chalked with such a riotous display of arithmetical equations that one might take it for the oddest sort of black and white wallpaper. It was as if one of the room's former occupants had sought to use the cell's flat black surfaces as instructional chalkboards (and even so, could not successfully fit upon them all that he wished to convey). I could not take my eyes from the patterns of mathematical chalkings and stood looking into the room through the dim and dusty light that filtered through an ivy-shaded window near the ceiling.

"Ain't it too amazin'!" exclaimed our conductor, the attendant Oscar. "Was just a coupla-three weeks ago we had the obsessitor of all obsessitors in here: Jeremiah Chivery. Down in this hole for all of two day and two night, and lookee what he done wrought!"

I remembered when Chivery had been admitted to the asylum. Though the mental infirmity that so characterized him had taken hold many years earlier, it was only in recent months that the affliction had been marked by a disturbing acceleration in its progression.

"Now I don't know what all them mathematical scratchings adds up to," Oscar continued, happy to play the role of our cellar cicerone, "since it spilt itself out of the most lunaticky brain as ever was squeezed inside a human head. But could be they add up to some earth-shaking theory or such. Could be all them madman's numbers and symbols hold the very key to the whole blooming universe! But they ask me to erase it all away when they take him upstairs from this temporary lodging. And I aim to do it. I do. But just not yet. It's too pretty I think. Look it all over, gentlemen. It'll cost you only half a florin for the privilege. It's quite a picture. I'll wait for you outside."

Sir Dabber and I nodded to young Oscar, appreciative of his only marginally-avaricious generosity in allowing us to inspect (for a small price) the walls that had once enclosed the "obsessitor of all obsessitors": one Jeremiah Chivery. Until his conventional life came to an abrupt end with his transportation to Bedlam, Chivery had been professor of mathematics at the College of Dingley Dell (informally denominated "Oxbridge" and sometimes "Camford" to conflate the names of those two illustrious English institutions of higher learning, neither of which bore any resemblance whatsoever to the CDD).

Professor Chivery was a peculiar gentleman, driven to put down numerical equations that may have had some importance or may only have been the pencilled (and chalked) ravings of a genuine madman through the medium of mathematics (at least these were the competing perceptions at the time). Chivery's colleagues at the college were never able to decipher any of the notebooks he had left behind—had been unsuccessful in making any sense of anything that he put into mathematical formula, outside the equations that the school's curriculum required him to impart to his students. It was concluded by most that this obsessitor was everything that Dr. Towlinson had concluded him to be: a certifiable lunatic who spoke his own language of numbers—numbers that had no bearing upon anything practical and could never be translated, for they lived only within his abstruse thoughts.

Yet standing before this most extraordinary display of numerical graffiti, one could not help being impressed by the sheer beauty of its presentation. There was poetry in chalk upon those walls, and it should be a sad day, I thought, when Oscar would finally have to accede to the wishes of his employer and scrub it all away.

Sir Dabber stood looking at the walls in silence, and thinking, I have no doubt, nothing at all about the unrestrained numerical ravings that had been inscribed upon them, but about his son and the possibility of having him back, hail and hardy and restored to full sanity. It was I who gave the walls full scrutiny and in doing so came to see in one small corner at the bottom of the wall that ran to my right, something that did not resemble a mathematical formula at all—something that was quite different from everything else round it: a sequence of ancient Egyptian hieroglyphics.

"I cannot believe it!" I exclaimed.

"Cannot believe what?" replied Dabber, shaken from his reverie.

"This—in the corner here. There are no numbers here, nor mathematical symbols. The markings are all in hieroglyphics. I recognise these ideograms from my own childhood interest in this most exotic language art."

"And what do you make of it? Can you decipher it?"

"I'll certainly try." I sat myself down upon the dirty stone floor to give the sequence a closer examination.

The first symbol in the progression sent a chill throughout my hunkered frame. I could not help shuddering, and Sir Dabber could not help noticing my astonished state.

"What is it, Trimmers? You look as if a ghost has just passed before you."

"I presume the first ideogram to be some form of salutation. The glyph here is a man with a long beard. It generally means an august person, a person of some rank, a god or demigod, if you will. This ideogram has always been my rather comically self-important way of signing my own hieroglyphic missives to my nephew Newman, who took an interest in the ancient art when a pupil at the Chowser School."

"One might think, therefore, Trimmers, that the hieroglyph is addressed to you. Read on."

I studied the next symbol: a rectangle with an opening at the bottom, which generally stood for "abode" or "a place" as if it were the simplest form of an architect's floor plan. I continued to muse and decipher aloud for Dabber's benefit: "Here is then a reference to a place—it is a specific place, I warrant."

"What place?" asked Dabber, finding himself helplessly drawn into the mystery.

"The next glyph should give us more information. Here we have a representation of stairs, which is exactly what it purports to be: stairs, or the locomotive act of *mounting* stairs. Now I should think that the symbol in connexion with the previous term should refer to someplace with stairs—someplace of more than one storey."

"There are quite a few such places in Milltown," said Dabber.

"But note that the writer has made the stairs taller than the symbol generally allows. He is telling us, I'm certain, that the place to which he refers is a place with quite a number of stairs."

"There are only two such places that come readily to mind, Trimmers. The All Souls campanile—which is nothing but stairs and quite a few of them—and this very hospital. Could it be that the writer is directing us up those very stairs we find beyond that door?"

I nodded effusively. "I wager that he is telling us of his next anticipated address. For note that he is no longer here within this cell." That thought which I had not hitherto allowed myself to think now cast itself most impertinently upon my brain: that this hieroglyphic sequence had, in fact, been chalked by my nephew Newman. For who else could have done it, and what would have been the odds that another author would have addressed his message to *me*?

There was now quite an urgency to Dabber's wheezing voice: "What do the other glyphs mean? There are five more.

"The last is a closing. The writer is identifying himself here."

"What is that?"

"Can you not tell? It is a wing: the symbol for flight. It is how Newman signed his own hieroglyphic letters to me when we would write back and forth. Newman always said that he should be a bird in some other life: a bird of some majesty."

"And you're certain of this?"

"It simply cannot be mere coincidence, Sir Dabber, especially when coupled with the salutation."

"And the other four symbols?"

"A roll of papyrus, indicating writings or books or…oh, let me think… there is another meaning: yes, yes. *Thought*. To *know*. And now, this one is easy: it is the crocodile, which stands for concealment. Then the symbol for a tie—the tie that holds a papyrus roll together. This means, again, writings or books or knowledge of some sort."

"And again the crocodile. It is most impenetrable, Trimmers. I cannot see how you can possibly make heads or tails of it."

I pondered the sequence in silence, going over each of the possible denotations conjunctively. "I don't think, Sir Dabber, that the glyphs for papyrus and roll-tie are merely illustrative of the fact that I am a writer. Newman would not expend himself in merely stating the obvious." Suddenly, in the midst of my composed and sedate interpretation of these symbols, I was struck by the import of their very purpose: that my nephew Newman was attempting to communicate with me. That he had been *here* within this very cell—a place in which he most obviously did not wish to be—and devised, using the only tools at his disposal, a means by which to tell this to me—with only the slightest chance that his effort should be discovered and correctly interpreted by an unintended recipient. It was a gambit that had little chance for the most desirable of outcomes: that his uncle might eventually find his way to this particular cell—but regardless of its rather long odds, it had paid off. For was I not standing here reading his words?

Or were those odds not long ones at all? I would presently find out.

"He is here, Dabber—being concealed within this very building."

"The crocodile, Trimmers. *Concealment*. There you have it."

"Yes, but why the second crocodile?"

"The other—well, what does one do when another one hides, Trimmers?"

"We go to look for them."

Dabber nodded and smiled. "The second crocodile therefore means that very thing. He wishes you to find him. It couldn't be simpler."

"I wish that somewhere in those ideograms there gave an elaboration for *why* he is being secretly held captive here."

I rose from my crouched situation and stepped out into the corridor. I called to the attendant Oscar who was half-dozing in his chair. "You there! Have you any knowledge of the person or persons who occupied this cell after Chivery?"

"I have not."

"Why do you say that with such assurance?"

"Because there are certain folks they bring down here that I'm not permitted to see. That is when they send me up the stairs to work in the scullery or clean out all them piss pans. I prefer it *here* if you want the truth of it, where I can keep my hands dry of suds and piss."

I returned to Dabber and to the hieroglyphic message from my nephew.

"Perhaps we are straining too hard to see that which is most obvious," said Dabber, continuing the thread of our exchange. "Let us therefore use a bit of Chiverian mathematical logic for our own benefit. There were seventeen Returnees, prior to the unfortunate death of Mr. Gamfield, all of whom have allegedly been taken ill by the Terror Tremens. Now we have another Returnee, your nephew Newman, who returns us to the original figure of seventeen. For he was slipped in here unbeknowst to you or his mother or even to poor Oscar out in the corridor. Why?"

"Not because he has been struck ill by the Terror Tremens. For if that be true why should we not have been told that he now resides here?"

"Because there is another reason for his secret incarceration. Let us think of what that could be."

"What else can it be but this, Dabber? That each who is held here should not be given leave to speak of what they know—what they have gleaned from time spent outside the Dell. There are things that they've seen, things that they *know,* which cannot, nay, *must not* be revealed."

"It is all quite crocodilian—the whole business—isn't it?"

I nodded. "And perhaps Newman isn't the only one who has been slipped in here in the dead of night in such a crocodilian fashion. If this be true, Dabber, there should be no reason that Muntle could not enter this hospital on the morrow, writ in hand, and search every room for every Returnee who is being held captive here."

"But who would sign such a writ? Judge Fitz-Marshall? I think not, Trimmers. Based upon what—a suspicion? A collection of Egyptian hieroglyphs? Fitz-Marshall wouldn't do it. Nor should any of the other magistrates, possessed of not a single independent streak amongst the lot of them. No, we cannot do it by prescribed and lawful means, Trimmers. Just as I cannot go to Judge Fitz-Marshall and demand the release of my son on a different form of habeas corpus."

"My nephew is entreating me with chalked fingers to help him, however I can. In want of an ideogram for the imperative, he is *imploring* me to look for him! It is all here. I see it now in his missive to me."

"Let us not be precipitant. Let us take some time to think of a proper course of action both for my son Bevan and for your nephew. And for whomever else is kept against his wishes within this increasingly perilous place and must be freed. There is something terribly malignant in all of this, Trimmers, I am sure of it. We must therefore tread with great caution from this point forward. Lest—if nothing else—the kindnesses shewn by this Beyonder nurse Miss Wolf be discovered and perhaps punished, and Bevan lose his advocate-angel and his healing medicaments."

I nodded, recalling my recent encounter with Miss Wolf and wondering how it could possibly be that an advocate-angel (who shewed a *devilishly* angelic side to me as well) should first start along her ministering path with the hard steps of a destroying monster. Then I knelt down and with my sleeve scrubbed away the Egyptian markings that my nephew had made, so that no one else should find them.

Sir Dabber nodded his agreement with this protective action, wheezed, and gave the slightest shudder. Then Dabber said this: "There is another kindness that Miss Wolf has done for us. I'm certain now that it must have been she."

"Yes? What is it?"

"Miss Wolf has set your mind at ease that your nephew has been safely returned to the Dell."

"How has she done *this*, Dabber?"

"By sending me this note." Sir Dabber drew a crumpled piece of paper from his vest pocket. "It was slipped beneath my front door yesterday. You will see that it was penned anonymously, but who else could have written it but someone who wanted to make certain that you accompanied me to-day?"

I took the note and read it. This is what it said:

> Sir Dabber:
> You must not go alone to see your son to-morrow. As one who knows best Bevan's current state, I entreat you to take a companion with you to lend you a supportive and consolatory hand. Think upon the words of the writer Frederick Trimmers who wrote so eloquently upon the plight of the beleaguered Scadger clan: "Anguish and woe to him that walks alone by choice or by cruel natural design. But comfort and joy to him that would accept the succoring hand from without. Can it be any other way? The woeful one must find courage to invite that hand of aid and comfort, which had previously been eschewed. It is the best course for keeping loneliness and isolation at bay and for improving the spirit."

"*I* wrote that?"

"If you did not, Trimmers, it was attributed to you for a purpose—a purpose for which I was its most receptive recipient. For did I not ask you to accompany me? And was not your candidacy suggested by that missive in its cunning manner?"

I nodded, the mystery of Ruth Wolf growing, even as more about her had been revealed. "The angel seems, in a sense, to be ministering to us all," I said musingly.

Dabber and I summoned Oscar so that we should be escorted from this dreary place—a place that had ironically fed the two of us with the morsels of renewed hope. Sir Dabber and I were now determined to visit this building again when we had a better sense as to what could be done for those we loved who were interned here. In the meantime I would speak with Ruth Wolf and find out all that I could from this woman whose conscientious heart grew with every new mention or thought of her.

CHAPTER THE THIRTY-SECOND

Wednesday, July 2, 2003

Just what *was* Ruth Wolf's original commission? I wondered and pondered. Could it really be true that an Outlander had been working here in Dingley Dell without detection, performing acts of evil in her nurse's habit and then repenting and atoning in an equally important way? My head was spinning as I accompanied Sir Dabber back to his manse.

The housemaid Arabella was gone. She was off buying a summer frock and bonnet and visiting with friends in Pedlar Place (a working class neighbourhood in Milltown)—things she would otherwise have been doing the previous Saturday afternoon had she not been drafted by Fips, the butler, to help him polish all the silverware and plate, which was growing tarnished from neglect. With the death of Lady Dabber, Dabber Hall had begun to lose its polish and lustre, and although it would never be mistaken for Miss Havisham's decomposing Satis House (of *Great Expectations* reference), the mansion had its own repletion of dust and cobwebs, the equally present mould and mildew, no doubt, aggravating Dabber's ongoing respiratory difficulties.

Upon our arrival late that afternoon Fips could not be found. Later he was discovered ensconced in his room upstairs on this, his alternate afternoon off, reading something borrowed, no doubt, from the Academic and Lending Library. More than likely he was perusing the transcribed *Ensyke* article devoted to France, because Fips believed himself to be of French stock.

"We may speak freely and in confidence in my sitting room," said Dabber. "Fips will not descend those stairs unless there be a fire, and even then I should possibly have to haul him bodily from his interminable appointment with the Gauls."

We drew chairs before the fireplace, though there was no fire therein, this being early July. A silence passed between us, as each of us communed with his own thoughts about all that we had witnessed on this most eventful Wednesday afternoon.

"My head is most muddled," said Dabber, finally, taking out his snuffbox. "I have not the faintest sense as to whether this is all some sort of wild dream. Are we upon the brink of something of awesome consequence, my friend, or have I instead partaken of a large dose of opium unawares?"

"I'm no longer certain of anything myself at this moment," was the only thing I could think to say in response.

"Is it really possible," continued Dabber, "that the cavalcade of time has marched itself forward and left us all behind, just as my son has said? What then should be the reason that we have been kept here as antiquities? Is that what we are, Trimmers? Or are we more like curiosities in some scientific zoological park?"

I wanted to reply that perhaps our being kept here for so long in this secluded valley served to our benefit. Perhaps there *was* some grave and deadly pestilence on the outside, the avoidance of which had allowed us to survive, nay, even to thrive after a fashion. Perhaps Bevan could feign his rigoritis for a time, but such a thing as purportedly infested the brains of each of our Returnees—such a thing could not possibly be counterfeited. Or could it? I wanted to say that surely there were terrible, life-threatening illnesses beyond our border and that we had not yet the means to protect ourselves from them. Yet I said none of these things to Sir Dabber, for in the darkest recesses of my heart, I had come to feel that I could no longer trust any of those former theories for why we were here. To-day was the day that I began to view everything through a different prism, one refracting cynicism and grim doubt.

I settled back and tried to relax with my new friend Sir Dabber before his cold, boarded fireplace, attempting, as well, to clear my mind. But the gears and pistons of Dabber's own mind were turning and chugging without respite. "So many questions, so many mysteries to be solved!"

"Conjecturing about such things will only bring us to the point of derangement, Sir Dabber. Let us have some port."

"A capital idea! And you must call me Seth. Together we have peered into the darkness of the great unknown, and such an experience should remove all ceremony from our private society, don't you think?"

I nodded and smiled. Sir Dabber sneezed, then wiped his nose with his handkerchief and rose from his chair. "We must drink ourselves into the cups of temporary oblivion, or—you are right—we should be made mad by evening's end."

Both of us in agreement as to the soundness of this course of action, we proceeded to drink ourselves into a most comfortable state of cloudy half-forgetfulness. The instrument of our necessary transformation into creatures that did not worry about the fate of Dingley Dell was first port, then Madeira, and then champagne, and lastly strong brandy. In the last hour of this lengthy, rather diversified indulgence in the grape, I had even begun to see things in a slightly positive light (A window of opportunity! A ripping challenge!) and did not mind in the least that my new best friend Seth had taken the liberty of reducing my name further in familiarity to *Fred*.

Gus woke and opened his eyes halfway. He looked all about him through thin, crusty slits. He was in a room that was dark and unfamiliar to him. There was an electrified lamp sitting on a table next to him, but it gave very little light. He was lying in a bed, but he didn't know at first what bed it was. But then by little and little, his memory began to uncloud itself. Bits and pieces of the last eight days and nights began to come forward in his re-assembling recollections. Gus had drifted for quite a long season in and out of high fever, his mind swimming in a swamp of thick delirium. Other moments gave more lucidity. Gus touched his hand to his now cool forehead. The fever had broken for the last time, although he felt greatly weakened by the trial of his illness, as if a heavy weight continued to press itself down upon him. But it wasn't long before my brother was fully cognisant of where he was and even of how he had got there.

Gus was conscious, as well, of the fact that he was not alone. Sitting in stiff-backed chairs against the opposite wall of the room, drinking from steaming coffee cups, were the two women who had spent the long week nursing him.

"Awake at last!" said the older of the two, Mrs. DeLove. "Do you feel better?"

"I do, yes," said Gus.

"Your last fever broke a couple of hours ago. We've been giving you an antibiotic. The vet had prescribed it for a spaniel we used to have, but apparently it works on human pneumonia, too."

"We thought you were going to die," said the younger woman, Annette.

"And I didn't know how in the world I was going to get you buried," struck in Mrs. DeLove.

"There was no doctor to attend me?"

"Are you a comedian?" asked the older woman in a rhetorical fashion. "They'd haul you away and do something awful to you. Didn't you tell him, Annette? Didn't you tell him the things we've seen?"

Annette shrugged a little. "I tried to."

"It was a decision we had to make," explained Mrs. DeLove. "Would you like tea? Annette, go and make some tea for Mr. Trimmers."

Annette rose from her chair, her braced legs clicking and clacking. She turned and addressed Gus. "Or would you like some coffee?"

Mrs. DeLove answered quickly on behalf of her patient: "Tea is easier on the stomach. And use the store brand. Mr. Trimmers has already cost us enough money." Annette nodded and hobbled from the room.

"How long have I lain here?" asked Gus of Mrs. DeLove. "All the days and nights seem of one piece in my head."

"*Too* long. Annette and I were to the point of 'recover or die already, Alien.' I'm not kidding you, Mr. Trimmers, you have been one super-sized headache for my daughter and me."

Gus struggled to pull himself up a little upon his pillows to better see the woman who remained partly obscured by the shadows of the room. "Why didn't you just let me die?"

"You think I wanted that on my conscience? You know, they let us live here—the ones who oversee your valley. They let us stay here because they think we're a couple of loony tunes who aren't going to get in their way. But aside from the fact that Annette goes off her rocker every now and then— case in point, this whole ridiculous handcuff episode—well, when it comes right down to it, we're just as sane or insane as they are. I don't know why they keep you there. I don't know where you come from or much of what you're about. I *do* know you have no idea what the real world is like, as if they're keeping you all in the dark on purpose. And I also know *this*: you're a human being and you don't deserve to die from some germ you don't have any immunity to, so that's why Annette and I have been playing Florence Nightingale for the last several days. Because it wasn't your fault your boy ran away. And it wasn't your fault you got sick. And I'll tell you something else, Mr. Trimmers: whatever Annette tried to tell you about the way they go after you people is true. We've seen it right here on my property: one of you funny-drest escapees, shot dead right in the back. We watched it from this very window, and then we spent the rest of the day hiding down in the basement to make them think there'd been no witnesses."

"But they *have* to know, don't they?—that you've been watching them all of these years?"

Mrs. DeLove shook her head. "Couple of loonies, like I say. And lucky for you we loonies decided to save your life in two different ways this week."

"You mean keeping me here. And then nursing me when I was ill."

Mrs. DeLove nodded. She took another sip from her cup.

"Then I thank you doubly."

"You don't have to thank me. You just have to get yourself well and then get yourself back home. There's something going on—a lot more of those unmarked trucks and vans going in and out of the big fenced compound down the road. You should be back home in your valley where it's safe."

Gus nodded. He was quiet for a minute, and then he said, "Do you think my boy Newman is dead?"

Mrs. DeLove sighed and drew her shoulders up into a half-shrug. "If he's still out here, then maybe his chances aren't so good. But I want to believe that he's made it back home by now. And you need to be thinking the same thing. Oh, the little painted picture you brought with you—I put it in a frame and set it on the table so you could look at him. Not the lamp table. The other one."

"Thank you," said Gus, picking up the miniature of his Newman to give it a closer look.

"Nobody takes pictures in Dingley Dell?"

"Takes pictures?"

"Photographs."

Gus shook his head. "The tradesmen never brought us any cameras."

Annette clomped back into the bedroom. "Your tea will be ready in a minute," she said to Gus, moving to seat herself on the side of the bed. "I made you English breakfast tea. Because of how much you like England and Dickens and all that."

"Thank you."

"I wish I could come with you, Mr. Trimmers. I like all that you've told me about Dingley Dell."

"It probably *is* a very nice place," allowed Mrs. DeLove. "But Annette hasn't left this house in fifteen years."

Annette nodded and then cast down her eyes in sad regret. "Someday I *will* though, and I'll climb that ridge over there and I'll come and visit you."

"You won't climb the ridge, Annette, because of your legs. But Netty Girl, if you ever *do* someday find the courage to put your sorry ass outside this house, I will personally hire somebody to carry you piggyback all the way to the top of that mountain and then all the way down again, and baby, I'll be shouting 'hallelujah' all the Goddamned while."

Annette broke into a smile. There was a warm look between mother and daughter at that moment that wanted no words.

Gus now fixed his eyes upon his former captor: "Will you at least step out upon the porch to wave goodbye to me when I get strong enough to make my return trip?"

"I wish I could. I really want to." And then Annette gave a hopeful smile and quitted the room to check on the tea.

❧

I will move temporarily ahead in our story to tell you that Gus, with the help of his two Outland nurses, was put squarely upon the recuperative path, and two nights later under cover of darkness found sufficient strength to make his homebound journey. And a long and exhausting journey it was for a man who had only recently recovered from a near-fatal illness—a trip requiring a steep and steady climb up the spur that his own son had earlier taken to such a prominent height as the Northern Ridge. Yet as hard as it was for Gus, he essayed it with a burning desire to find his son returned home himself and happy and well, pushing back thoughts as best he could that Newman had been tragically lost to the murderous aims of that unknown force that the DeLoves had adumbrated.

Up the ridge Augustus Trimmers betook himself on that dark Friday night with the strength of a man only partially restored to his usual mettle, and with huffings and pantings and a stumble here and there and frequent rests upon the sturdy ash walking stick he had been given by Mother and Daughter DeLove. At last upon finally surmounting the mountaintop, Gus paused to behold the darkened valley of his birth, only faintly sparkling under distant Milltown street lamp, and then Gus turned to give a final parting glance back at the black, unwinking Outland—deep and dark and pricked only by the tiny glow of the DeLove porch light, still electrified long after his parting. Gus wondered if she was still there, still standing upon the porch, having found the courage to step out from behind the imprisoning walls of her mother's house for the first time in fifteen years. Taking the clean night air fully into her lungs. Sending off her new Digglian friend with hopeful, heartening words and a whispered prayer on his behalf and one bag each of Milk Chocolate Milanos and Strawberry Veronas. Proud of what she herself had just accomplished, as monumental an achievement in those mere three or four steps as a walk across the entire Commonwealth of Pennsylvania!

CHAPTER THE THIRTY-THIRD

Thursday, July 3, 2003

My head throbbed. I had taken far too long to rouse myself from the bed in which Dabber's manservant Fips had deposited me (pursuant to a word-slurring appeal by his employer that he *must* be the one to tuck me beneath the coverlet, for I could not execute the task myself whilst in such a severely intoxicated state, and Dabber was in no condition to do it, finding himself in a similar situation of full prostration.) It was post-noon before I could bring myself to rise and dress and force a piece of dry toast and the yolk of an egg upon my topsy-turvy stomach, and then to transport myself with a slack and painful gait out of the front door of Dabber Hall, having been medicated by the master of that lonely household with a salutary dose of salicylic powder that had at least reduced the size of the hammer that assaulted my recovering temples to something well nigh endurable.

I was prepared to betake myself to the offices of my friend Sheriff Muntle to relate the details of the preceding day when I recalled that Muntle would be unavailable for private counsel until eventide, owing to his having removed himself to the Chowser School for the purpose of investigating a matter of the utmost importance: that hothouse thievery of earlier mention. Having absented himself from Milltown for two days, the sheriff consequently found himself deprived not only of my society and all the intelligence I was fairly bursting to convey pertaining to the momentous events of the previous day, but also active participation in other events of that period, including—as I would later learn—a fresh example of rude impatience on the part of Montague Pupker in the form of the most clamant species of door-pounding and door-kicking as had ever been evinced outside a shop, this protracted display of insolent public impropriety sending my landlady Mrs. Lumbey (the imperiled protector of Pupker's even more imperiled daughter Hannah, and owner of said door) into such a tizzy as to engender thoughts within her fervid brain of dropping a heavy mangle or iron safe from an upper storey window down upon Pupker's raging head.

Thinking of Muntle and of Pupker and of the appointment that was to take place between those two gentlemen on Monday with regard to a certain sub-cellar containing a most amazing inventory of mysterious items, I was reminded of something along these same lines that I had seen from Dabber's terrace the night before when my host and I had stepped out to take the night air, my mind fuzzy with drink, my vision hazy. In that late hour, through the fog of inebriation, I descried some three or four blocks away a waggon stopt before Pupker's emporium being loaded from the cellar trap by three dark figures whose features would have been impossible to discern even had I been cold sober. All of the cargo was boxed and crated and would not have drawn interest even had there been passers-by at this desolate hour. "Ah," I said to myself. "I was wondering when the deed would be done, and I see that Pupker doesn't procrastinate."

"When what deed would be done?" enquired Sir Dabber, peering with squeezed eyes into the night without knowing what he was supposed to be looking for.

"It is no great matter," I replied. "At least not for the present. Bumper me, my good sir! Your guest is positively parched!"

I shelved the memory for later review, and was making every effort to direct my halting alcohol-poisoned person toward my own lodgings above Mrs. Lumbey's dress shop (where I hoped to cover my pounding head with a blanket and sink back into the arms of recuperative Morpheus), when I noticed a barefoot man in rags and tatters backing his way out of the apothecary's shop across the street, in response to an angry injunction by that business's proprietor to "Go along and never cast your dirty shadow upon this upstanding establishment again!" The door was then promptly slammed shut in the man's face. During the seconds that succeeded this overwrought rebuff, the penuriously-attired man stood in the manner of one giving close inspection to the wood grain of the door's outer face (for quite close was he in proximity to it when he had been summarily dismissed by its closure), or perhaps the man's eyes were shut tight as he was taking this quiet intervening moment to compose and steady himself. Shortly thereafter the shabby man turned round to behold the street and all potential witnesses therein, and in so doing, revealed himself to be the pauper Harry Scadger, who had only four days earlier quitted his clan's gipsy-like encampment within the apricot grove, and moved himself, his wife Matilda, and their five children to the Pupker Mews, as he had duly been directed to do.

I could not take my eyes from the man who looked many years older than his true two or three and thirty, life for all of the Scadgers, young and old, being steeped in toil and hardship, impairments of fate that aged the body with great acceleration and put frightful creases upon faces that rarely smiled or found any measure of joy or delight in the mortal journey. Raising his eyes to meet mine, Scadger acknowledged me with a nod that did not alter the despondent expression upon that wontedly cheerless countenance.

Having done this, he appeared prepared forthwith to quit this spot, and even took one step away from the door, as I, in turn, made up my own mind about approaching and detaining him. Anticipating my putting to him a question about what had just occurred, he raised a hand to sign that he did not wish to speak of it, leaving me then to stand in his presence and execute a mundane greeting that served neither of our interests beyond empty salutation.

"And it is quite a joy to see you as well," said Scadger quite mechanically (for what was to be found particularly availing about this most mortifying moment?).

"Have you found work in Milltown yet?" I asked.

"Soon I may be hired at the grist mill. I hear, as well, that there is now an opening for inventory-keeper at the dried fish warehouse." Scadger's voice trailed off. He was distracted. I did not pursue the fact that it was my brother's departure from Dingley Dell that had created the vacancy of Harry Scadger's reference. It would have served no good purpose at the moment. At all events, it was quite apparent to me that Harry didn't wish to speak to me about this or any other thing, shifting as he was from one leg to the other in a scarcely-concealed indication of an impatient desire to be on his way. Even in the best of circumstances our society had been a bit strained; though our intercourse had always been cordial, there existed between us that imposing wall of class and economic estrangement—a wall that now towered even higher after what had just taken place.

"I must be off," he finally said. "You must come and visit Matilda and me after she has prepared our new home to receive guests. It should not be long. Already the rooms are tidy and clean. But, alas, we have nothing yet in the way of furniture for a guest to sit down upon!"

Scadger affected to smile. It was a hollow thing, this attempt at good cheer.

I could restrain myself no longer and asked the very question which the poor man most dreaded: "Why on earth did Skettles eject you from his shop? What was the trouble?"

"Begging your pardon, Mr. Trimmers, I do not wish to—"

"Come, come, Scadger," I pursued with little concern for his present state of abashment. "I've assisted you in the past. Perhaps I may be of some service in *this* particular instance."

There succeeded no response. Instead, Harry Scadger lowered his eyes and bowed his head, as if this combined gesture of abasement should be sufficient to end my pursuit and send me on my way. Yet I was resolved to get to the bottom of the matter, no matter how long it took and at whatever cost to the man's feeling of self-worth.

"Come now, Scadger."

"I have no need of taking money from you, Trimmers, should that be your primary goal in detaining me. The Charity League has kindly lent a small sum to Matilda and me with which to situate ourselves and the children in the Mews and to tide us over until I am able to secure gainful employment."

"Forgive my persistence, Scadger, but I must now know ever the more why Skettles would have you dismissed from his shop, if indeed you had money to pay for his apothecarial compounds. Was there something you sought that he was unable to provide? For I am familiar enough with your character to know that you would never have entered his shop bent only on provocation."

Scadger nodded. "I *did* seek something from him. Something for my daughter Florence. To quell her cough. Unfortunately he had nothing to sell me."

"That's rot! Of course there must be elixirs or syrups upon his shelves that will suppress or sooth a cough. Let me have a word with him."

Scadger clasped my arm. "I implore you not to advocate for me in this matter. Your good offices have been helpful to my family in the past, and for these ministrations, I'm most grateful. But there's nothing that can be done here, and your auspices in this instance, however kind and well-intended, will only do harm."

"Did he refuse to serve you?"

"Yes. But—"

"And was it because you live in the East End?"

Scadger nodded. "Because I now live in the East End like a pauper. And because I once lived beneath the apricot trees like an animal of the field."

"And is there no chemist in the East End with whom you may trade?"

"There are no chemists in the East End."

"Then you have no choice but to purchase your physics on *this* side of the river."

"And yet—"

"One man's money should be as good as any other's, Scadger. Now you've told me that he wouldn't sell you a syrup for your daughter. Is this also the reason that he ejected you from his establishment? I want to be clear on this, man. Did you do anything else to warrant this final indignity?"

"My presence within the shop was deemed an offence to two of his other customers—two women of breeding. They commented upon it both in word and gesture." Here Scadger demonstrated "gesture" by pinching his nose. "I made haste to withdraw at that moment, but apparently I did not depart quickly enough to suit Skettles, and so he took it upon himself to have me removed by force of his own hand—and no doubt made the necessary show of it for his preferred customers. I will recover, Trimmers. It is my daughter Florence who sadly may not."

"She has worsened?"

"Aye."

"Then you must admit her to the Lung Hospital. Immediately."

Scadger shook his head. "There's nothing that can be done for her there. It is the place to which consumptives go to die. I would prefer to have my daughter at home when it is her time to leave us."

I nodded. Scadger had spoken truthfully about that place. Rarely did one depart its wards in better condition than when he or she went in. And because it ministered to the most consumed amongst the consumptives of Dingley Dell, it was death that most often and most tragically emptied each of its thirty or so beds in turn.

"Scadger, my good man, at least suffer me to go inside and purchase a syrup for your daughter as your surrogate."

"He will sell to *you*, I have no doubt," said Harry Scadger with uncharacteristic rancor.

Skettles the apothecary allowed the purchase now that the presence of Scadger was no longer polluting his shop, but the merchant charged me twice the going price. William Skettles, like his brother-in-law Montague Pupker, was a man who did not permit compassion to dilute commerce, and often used the vehicle of retail trade to serve more selfish ends—such as, in this case, making a lesson of an East Ender who sought to sully his premises with the effrontery of his mere presence, *and* making an equal lesson of the man who sought to help said East Ender. It was odious in every facet, and I wasn't sure at that moment which of the two hateful brothers-in-law I despised more.

Scadger and I were soon crossing on foot the Westminster Bridge, which connected the West End of Milltown to its bastard brother, the East End. The bridge wasn't frequently traversed by West Enders of a certain elevated rank (most Milltowners of that caste preferring to cross the river, when their travels took them east, via the Waterloo Bridge (north of town) or the Victoria Bridge (south of town). Artisans and tradesmen of the working class used Westminster when necessary to ply their trade within the weazen, dilapidated neighbourhood that now included Scadger's new domicile, and now and then lowly men in Scadger's impoverished league were driven by necessity to venture in the opposite direction to bear the sort of cold reception that had come to Scadger in Skettles' apothecary shop.

The bridge, in this sense, had become a loose link between two very different worlds, and a stark reminder of how distinct one Dinglian was from the next, even as we all had been forced by estrangement from the Beyonders to band together in a form of consolidation that should have been blind to all class and fortune. Here stood we all at one end of that other bridge—the metaphoric one that joined Dingley Dell to the Terra

Incognita, and there on its opposite end stood every Outlander behind a thick, obscurant wall of fog and mystery. Though the irony of it was quite clear to me, it was now become even more illuminative on this particular day and in this particular way, the possibility now existing that the world beyond our valley could very well be everything utopian that we had ever dreamed of *or* everything nightmarish that a Dinglian had reason to fear. All of it promised to be of such transformational import as to make those differences between Scadgers and Pupkers, West Enders and East Enders, the high brow and the low class altogether petty and immaterial, and to-tally inconsequential.

Two women of class and breeding had pinched their noses to feign revulsion (for there was, in truth, no polluting stench emanating from Scadger despite his soiled garb) and a chemist had denied a sick young girl something to ease her destructive cough. Sir Dabber's son Bevan, even having regained his sentience, had sat with three others in a dark and dismal hole beneath a hospital that executed refusals and disallowances as its wont and in the face of every appeal to clemency; pauperish Scadgers were being relegated to filthy mews, which still, I had no doubt, reeked of the equine manure that had marked their former employment, because it served their duplicitous owner's feint to good civic stewardship. Whatever truth there was to there being something outside the valley to put an end to life as we knew it in this final season, Dingley Dell was fairly rotten at its core withal, and, one might argue, partially deserving of its impending demise.

Yet what of those who wept over the inequities, who ministered to the sick, who attempted to uplift the poor? What of those who followed in every way the teachings of our Lord Jesus Christ, whose life was paragon? Were these virtuous exceptions to the rule sadly noted above to receive some form of dispensation, some accommodation, some compensatory kindness?

My head continued to throb as I contemplated such onerous questions, and as Harry Scadger and I reached the eastern end of the bridge (this end left without whitewash as if impoverished East Enders were not even deserving of so much as bright paint and clean varnish upon their own side of a public construction). My meditations received an abrupt check by the sound of my name being called by someone to my rear. The voice belonged to my young friend Mulberry Timberry, who quickly overtook me and seised my right hand with both of his own to better execute a most violent shake.

"Thank you, sir, thank you, thank you, and again I say thank you."

"And for what reason do I find my arm being nearly wrung from its socket, Timberry?"

Scadger had stopped a few steps ahead of me and now turned to behold what was transpiring behind him with a curious cock of the head, a tilt shared with brothers who perhaps learnt to display inquisitiveness by observing in their own puppyhood how curiosity was most often demonstrated by the many mongrels that survived in the apricot grove by means of scraps and vermin of the field and large doses of Scadger affection.

"I've just spoken with Sir Dabber. Oh, I beg your pardon, sir," said Timberry to Scadger. "Your servant, sir: Mulberry Timberry. Although I must admit that I don't know you."

"Scadger, Governor. Harry Scadger." Another hardy double-palmed pump of the hand, this time for Scadger.

"Ah yes, one of the apricot clan. I haven't seen much of your people, but in my own defence, you *have* lived a rather isolated existence on the whole."

"To be sure we have, Mr. Timberry," answered Harry Scadger.

"Please don't call me 'mister.' For as of to-day, my good man, I am in name *and* fact…a doctor of medicine." Turning to me, with a face flushed with excitement and overflowing affability: "You see, Sir Dabber has decided to recommend to the licensing sub-committee of the Medical Board my installation as practitioner-in-full. It is as good as done. And I know, Trimmers, that I have you to thank for your promotion of my lifelong objective. I can think of no other way to shew my gratitude other than to say thank you until I grow blissfully hoarse."

"No. You mustn't do that, Timberry," I replied with a chuckle. It would have been difficult *not* to smile and congratulate and join the young man in his infectious celebration. "We shall drink to you, Timberry, as soon as I am sufficiently recovered from my foray into the vineyards with Sir Dabber last night. But for now, I must accompany my friend Scadger to his new home in the Mews. His daughter Florence is in a bad way and we must take her this medicine."

"I'll join you," the young doctor returned. "The young girl shall be my very first patient, though my shingle has yet to be hung."

Scadger eyed the sprightly young man with some suspicion. "We live in the East End. In the Pupker Mews."

"Yes, I naturally assumed that this was to be our destination."

"And you do not demur?"

Timberry shrugged. "Why should I?"

"There's only one physician who condescends to treat patients in the East End. And if I may be candid, sir, one is better off not to summon him, for his cures are sometimes more injurious to the patient than the complaint itself."

Timberry laughed in a boyish manner that reminded one in an instant how very young he was to be taking up the mantle of physician and healer. "You must put him totally out of mind, Mr. Scadger, for he has been retired. As of to-day that most decrepit old gentleman joins the ranks of the superannuated set. I am to be the one who attends to the poor of the East End from this day forward, and I relish the challenge, I most certainly do! Lead on, my good man. Let me attend to your infirm daughter Florence, full stop, end of discussion." Seeing the bottle of cough syrup in my hand, Timberry took it and examined the label. "This is good. This will help. What we need here in Dingley Dell is a *true* sanatorium for our consumptives; the lung hospital is nothing more than a scrofula warehouse. I cannot believe that I am a doctor now! Trimmers, I am walking upon clouds. Now I must be subdued when I see the girl. I must be subdued and sober and evince maturity."

An interval of quiet succeeded these words as we walked along. I couldn't help thinking of how happy I was for Timberry and how grateful I was that Sir Dabber had changed his opinion of the young man based upon my own good opinion. It was good that Dabber and I were now allies, each warmed by the incandescent rays of mutual respect. It would be good as well to have as many allies as fate would permit in these days to come—days that would put each of us to the test within that crucible that would prove to be unlike any other that the mind can possibly imagine.

CHAPTER THE THIRTY-FOURTH

Thursday, July 3, 2003

If one were to take a torch to the Pupker Mews and reduce all the structures therein to elemental charcoal and ash, and then sweep away the smoking ruins, and leave in its place a stark, besooted vacancy, one would say that this was a far, far better thing one did, than to leave extant that which presently assaulted the gaze and troubled the heart. Stables they once were, and little more than stables they still seemed to be, and how merciless it was to think that two-legged beasts should adapt so readily to a place hardly fit even for quadrupedal habitation!

Yet this is where Harry Scadger and his devoted wife Matilda and their three girls and two boys set up their new home, for they had no choice in the matter. Theirs was a building not much larger than the smallest of cottages in the Dinglian countryside, and where a wall or two of pasteboard had been thrown up, one could pretend the separation of rooms, though one could have just as easily strung curtains or erected tattered, moth-nibbled Japanese screens to achieve the same flimsy effect.

But to Harry and Matilda Scadger, a home was a home. And lodgings in the Pupker Mews were, at all events, more home than the couple and their children had ever known before. For every year that had preceded their present situation, the family had occupied mean and lowly domiciles that were little more than sleeping barracks of castoff plank and scavenged log. Everything that one did in a wakeful state was done out-of-doors and under sun, moon and stars, and even during eventide a drowsy Scadger might lie supine upon an old, frayed hearthrug or a soiled charity-bestowed counterpane, which served as crude floor mattress, and gaze through chinks in the ceiling at the night sky through the sort of rude skylight that required no glazing.

"What you see round you much improves upon our previous circumstances," said Scadger, leading Timberry and me to his newly occupied dwelling. "Mind the rubbish," he cautioned, stepping deftly over a dust pile near the front door. "They have not yet carted away the refuse from this long-vacant by-street. But I am told that it is to be done quite soon."

The loud creak of the door, which did not hang easily upon its rusty hinges, proclaimed better than any bell or butler's declaration our arrival, and in a trice, the three of us found ourselves in the company of four members of Harry Scadger's young brood—two boys and two girls—each of whom either tugged upon the skirts of their father's fustian waistcoat or pulled at his trouser pockets in want of something to eat.

The object of their quest lay within Scadger's waistcoat pocket, and it was from this deep pouch that the man withdrew a paper of assorted nuts and currants "given to me by the kind charity woman who is overseeing our case." This was said to Timberry and me to explain why such a poor man who was not a thief could be in possession of so much tasty treasure. The papa then commenced to passing a few tidbits to each of the children, who, in the manner of little baby birds, opened their beaks (whilst cupping their hands to give an alternate means of receipt). As Scadger was about the business of distributing the treats, his wife Matilda entered from the rear rooms, wiping her hands upon a flannel cleaning cloth.

"Good afternoon, gentlemen," said she, dropping a small curtsey. "I didn't know, my love," this to her husband, "that we were to have guests to-day or I would have done a much better job of brightening up these dreary rooms." Mrs. Scadger used the back of her hand to push a fallen lock of hair from her eyes. Her tresses were wilting in these stifling rooms, and perspiration beaded upon her flushed face.

"This isn't a social call, per se, my love," said the master of the house. "I have brought Dr. Timberry to see Florence."

"A *doctor*? You have brought a *doctor* here?" exclaimed Matilda, craning her neck to look behind us and out the door and into the lane.

"Right here and at your service, madam," said Timberry, waving his hand as if he were hailing a hackney. "You may call me the boy physician, but I won't mind it. Where's the patient?"

"In the back room," said Matilda, her face still registering some measure of confusion. Matilda led Timberry away as the father followed behind. I waited amongst the children who were gobbling their nuts and currants as if these were to be the only morsels they should eat this week.

As Scadger reached the door of communication between the rear rooms and the front parlour (if parlour it be; the room in which I stood was wanting of furniture save a wooden bench, a camp stool and a ricketty table and chair, where, one imagined, the family took turns eating each meal), he turned to beckon me to join him.

"Perhaps I should stop here," said I.

"Nay, nay. You must see her. Florence has heard much about you and about your brother and your father. She wishes to be a writer like you. Have I not told you this?"

I shook my head. I could tell from the casual tone of Scadger's voice and from the collected expression upon his face that he had heard of neither my nephew's nor my brother's departure from the Dell. How such a thing could be was not difficult to surmise: the Scadger orchard was an exclave, isolated like no other place in the Dell, save the coal-town of Blackheath. That which was known within an hour or two by nearly every other Dinglian, via the flash of the heliograph and the fleet-footedness of the ticket porter, sometimes took many additional hours or sometimes several days to reach the ears and ken of our valley outcasts. I would tell Scadger all of the news in time. For now, I did as my friend bade, and followed him—in silence—into the next room.

The oldest of the Scadger's children lay propped upon a couple of pillows on one of a trio of small beds. The room was dark and smelt, as did every other room within the lodgings, of old mouldy hay and iron tools, and gave even a lingering hint of horseflesh. There was also the faint scent of apricot. Having lived amongst the fruit trees and having harvested their issue year after year before moving to the Mews, the Harry Scadgers—each member of this family, including the sick girl who lay before me—exuded the fruity scent as if it came directly from their pores, and its residue of sweetness did not offend.

With the sudden appearance of her father in the company of two men, one of whom she knew from my past visit to her former alfresco lodgings,

Florence's face brightened. Not only had the girl met me before, but had not Scadger spoken of me in my absence in complimentary terms? I took her hand. She smiled and put her other hand to her mouth to shield me from her latest croupy cough.

"Good afternoon, Florence," said I.

"Good afternoon, Mr. Trimmers," replied Florence after the cough had subsided, and with a blush that put some colour into her pale cheeks.

"And this is Dr. Timberry, dear," said Mrs. Scadger to her daughter. "He is come to treat you."

"Thanks in part to this syrup which your father has procured to ease your cough," Timberry added, as he touched the thirteen-year-old girl gently and diagnostically upon the forehead.

How kind and modest Timberry presents himself to his patients, I thought to myself, humbleness being a credit to a physician. One cannot learn such a manner; it proceeds from one's heart, and how that heart considers, as is its wont, the worth and feelings of others. I knew that there was something that I had always liked about this young man. Even as a boy, Mulberry had shewn a level of compassion and mercy that was striking for a child, sheltering all manner of injured animals, both feral and domestic, in his miniature veterinarial infirmary, and nursing a good many of them back to sound health. It was by Mulberry's hand, as well, that the Judy puppet, which squawked when struck by Punch in each of his parents' public puppet presentations, donned forever a fresh sanitary bandage upon the head so as to give one the sense that the battered Judy was forever on the mend.

Florence's upturned eyes beheld her physician with obvious regard. He was a fine-looking man, whose darkly handsome features might appeal to a girl in the early blow of womanhood. After a brief interval, the patient returned her gaze to me. "Oh, Mr. Trimmers, I've read many of the things you've written, and I believe that you should write stories. I'm sure that they would be good ones."

"Stories." I smiled.

Florence nodded and grinned as well. "I should like to write stories myself one day."

"And perhaps you will. Perhaps we both will, although I must say that there is too much of interest all round us that is real and true for me to feel so greatly inclined to fabricate things for the purpose of reader delectation."

Curiously, this statement, which should have passed with little attendance, drew the most amazing interchange of knowing glances amongst daughter, mother and father, each pregnant with some meaning I could not fathom.

I pursued: "And have you, Florence, any stories that you've heard, which you may wish to put down?"

Florence nodded. "And a good many more that I should like to change to my own liking."

"My daughter doesn't like *my* stories the way they are," laughed Scadger. "Nor do her siblings. Perhaps it is a parent's duty to lace his tales with sugar and treacle, but I rarely do it."

Scadger turned to wave away all of the aforementioned siblings who had gathered about the door to see what was to be done with their ailing sister. "Away! Away!" he enjoined them in a stern, paternal voice. To me he said without severity: "Perhaps we should each of us withdraw, and leave the doctor to his patient."

"An excellent idea," said Timberry, rolling up his sleeves. "I should like to give the child a full medical examination, so that we may know exactly where things stand. Mrs. Scadger, if you will serve as my attending nurse, I would be most grateful."

Matilda Scadger nodded and executed a slight bow that gave evidence of her good breeding in spite of the mean circumstances of her workhouse youth.

Scadger and I stepped from the room. There was no door to be shut to give privacy but only a curtain, which was pulled across the portal.

"Come," said my host, signaling with a nod that we should repair outside. "There are a couple of things that I should like to discuss with you."

I nodded and followed Scadger out the front door and into the quiet, rubbish-filled by-lane. "Ours, as you can see, is the only building in the lane presently occupied. But I suspect that my brothers will come to take occupancy here before too long. Why, just this very forenoon, Zephaniah came to tell me that he now sees merit to my reasonings and is giving serious consideration to following the path that I have blazed. It's a good thing, for there isn't much case to be made for remaining behind. But my brothers are stubborn men and will make it most difficult for themselves before things get better."

"And is there no way that I may be of assistance in this matter?" I asked.

Scadger shook his head. "If I may beg leave to speak candidly with you,

Trimmers, my brothers haven't much respect for you."

"You must call me Frederick, if we are to continue to be friends."

Scadger nodded.

"And why do they feel this way about one who has never done a thing to harm them?"

"To be sure, you have done nothing that deserves even an ounce of their enmity. Indeed, not only have you never hurt them, but also I must say, Frederick, that your efforts on behalf of my clan have far exceeded even my own expectations. My brothers are purblind in this and everything else that would redound to their benefit. They do not have the capacity to put their faith in anyone whose surname isn't Scadger."

"But perhaps their feelings about *me*, at least, will change over time."

"Yes, yes. We shall bring them round, even if we must do it one brother at a time. I wish that there were somewhere we could sit. There is much that I have to tell you—much that you should know. The time is come to discuss with you things that I have long postponed disclosing. I hadn't intended on doing it to-day, but you see, fate has turned an inopportune day into a most opportune one."

"You intrigue me, Harry."

We had halted our stroll in the middle of the lane. An old mottled cat, which fended for herself, came close to us to see if we would offer her a scrap. Finding no comestible in hand or upon our person, she crept on, sniffing and pawing through the rubbish that lay strewn about in search of something that would fill her empty stomach. There were rats and mice that thrived within this forgotten lane, and she would soon eat if she would but be patient for the night.

"Let us go round the corner. There's a small pot-shop there. One cannot say much for it, but we may have a pint if you're game."

"Only if you permit me to pay," said I.

"It is not my design to traffic in your generosity, Frederick."

"Still, it's the least that I can do in exchange for whatever intelligence you may wish to share with me."

Scadger and I struck the bargain with a quick handshake. As we were set to make our way to the public house, we both noted Harry's oldest son David creeping toward us with small, stealthy steps.

"Mr. Trimmers and I are going to talk close-by, David," said Scadger to his son, "so go and tell your mother that we plan to remove ourselves for a bit. And when the doctor is done, please be so good as to ask him to join us at the Ox and Crow."

"Yes, Papa."

"Now run along, son, and do as I say."

"Yes, Papa." Curiously, the boy resembled to a striking degree my brother Gus at that same young age, and I could not think of him without feeling a deep pang of sorrow. As was usually the case since discovering Newman's Egyptian markings in the Bedlam cellar, I settled and soothed myself (as best as I was able) by thinking that if Newman had returned to the Dell, even against his own wishes and by means that kept him under lock and key, perhaps his father had also come somehow to be secretly consigned to that lunatic house, and it would only be a matter of time before I could see them both. I admitted to it being a dubious hope, just as one hopes that a drowning man will suddenly bob himself up from the churning sea and take the lifeline just when all appears lost, but this possibility, however slim, had nonetheless become *my* lifeline, and I clung to it for what little peace of mind it gave me.

David took a step back, but didn't retreat in full. There was some hesitation to his withdrawal and the desire to say something else to his father perched upon his parted lips.

"What is it? Out with it, boy," said Scadger.

The lad obligingly tendered the following words, half question and half entreaty: "Are you going to tell Mr. Trimmers about who I found?"

Scadger nodded.

"And you'll tell me what he says—who he thinks she is?"

"Of course I will, David. I would never keep a thing from you. We are the dauntless duo, are we not?"

David smiled and nodded.

"Now be the obedient young helperman and go tell your mother where we have gone and that she isn't to worry."

David nodded, turned and ran back into the house.

"'Who he thinks she is': what does your son mean by this?" I queried.

"I'll tell you presently. Let's not discuss it here. I trust not even these cats and rats to keep overheard confidences to themselves."

CHAPTER THE THIRTY-FIFTH

Thursday, July 3, 2003

The Ox and Crow was, uncontestably, the smallest tavern in Dingley Dell. There were three tables, a bar counter, a stone hearth, and not much else besides. The public room was encompassed by dull walls that had been formerly wainscotted and tastefully ornamented but now stood bare and differently shaded in those places where shelves and sconces had previously been affixed—indications of better days (for this neighbourhood of the East End had not always been one given over to impoverishment and destitution). There were three labouring men sitting at the table nearest the bar, and then another man who slept upon the pillow of his arm at the next table. The third table was empty, and beckoned us by default. Here we took our seats, as the publican, a man I vaguely knew by the name of Peecher, came over to ask us what we would have, though all that there was, was gin and porter and beet sugar rum and some perry ale, which I learnt from the rather forthcoming owner had been accidentally denatured and could not be recommended.

"I'll take a pot of porter," said Scadger.

I asked for gin, the spirit being by no means my favourite, but the only thing I could think of that would be tolerated by my weak West Ender's constitution. Many a man on my side of the Thames, unaccustomed to the insalubrious potations of the East End, had lain writhing upon their cramping beds from having imbibed the sort of befouled labouring man's beverage that conversely passed without complaint through the tempered tracts of those, like Harry Scadger, whose digestive systems had become inured to the effect.

After taking a drink of his dark brown beer and wiping his mouth with his sleeve, Harry looked me squarely in the eye and said by way of brief prologue: "Three, no—almost four weeks ago my son David was playing upon the bank of the Thames where it wends closest to the apricot grove. He wandered up a little farther than was his usual habit and there he dis-covered it—*her*—lying there at river's edge."

"*Her*?"

"The body of a dead woman. She was drest in clothing I had never seen worn by a woman in the Dell. And there was a small, thin, leatherish sort of valise of a very odd make, which lay next to her. All was wet: the corpse, the valise. She had apparently been carried along by the river and then de-posited in this spot. David left the body to come fetch me. Perhaps twenty minutes passed before he returned with me in tow.

"By that time someone else had arrived and was inspecting the body on his own. It was Dr. Chivery from Oxbridge. The professor was so atten-tive to his investigation that he didn't take notice of us at first, but finally he did look up with a slight start and asked what David and I knew about her.

"We could offer nothing more than that which we could all see with our own eyes. Dr. Chivery had already gone through the valise and was now clutching in his trembling, attenuated fingers two soggy pieces of paper that he had obviously removed from the case.

"'And what is it that *you* have found out?' I asked.

"'Nothing good,' the professor answered cryptically. 'And you and the boy will only make matters worse by divulging any of what you see here. It is of paramount importance that we keep knowledge of this dead woman's presence to ourselves. Now we must find a place to bury her—someplace where her grave will never be discovered or disturbed.'

"I suggested to Chivery that it might be better to fetch the sheriff, but he remonstrated vehemently against that course, having convinced himself that there should be additional calamitous consequences should a public report be issued and an inquest held. 'Trust me, I beg you,' he concluded.

"Together David and the Professor and I dragged the woman quite some distance from the river, and using two broken shovels from my brothers' work hutch, we buried her in a secluded spot near the timbermen's sward.

When the deed was done, I asked Chivery if I could see the papers that were now tucked into one of his pockets—the papers that had so disquieted him. He shook his head. 'There is something that I must do,' said he. 'Something that these papers compel me and *only* me to do.'

"As much as I desired to read what frightening words had been put upon those leaves, I agreed not to deter Chivery from his self-appointed mission, not even guessing what that mission might be. You see, Frederick: I *did* have good reason to trust this man. When I was a boy, he had been my teacher. He didn't remember *me*, considering me in this later year just one of many members of a large family clan—nameless to him except that I be a Scadger. But though his fading memory would not recall it, he and I had had a richly productive season together, which I shall limn for you shortly. I mention it here to give reason for why I would extend to the professor every consideration for the course of action he chose for himself to the exclusion of my son and myself, and trusting that the course should be the right and proper one."

"And what day was this, Harry? Try to remember the exact day."

"It was a Wednesday. I should like to say that it was the first Wednesday of last month."

I drew out my pocketbook, which carried a small calendar card within it. "June 4. Two weeks later Chivery was removed to Bedlam. I happen to know a little something about those intervening days. He spent a good many of them neither eating nor sleeping, but writing his equations in a mad fury upon the board in his classroom. Those who observed him said that he was carried away, in a most wild and obsessed state."

"Surely it must have been something upon those papers that put him into such a frenzy," said Harry.

I nodded. "And here is something more: I saw the continuation of those ravings upon the wall of a cell at the asylum when Sir Dabber and I visited that place just yesterday. I wager he's writing still, in whatever new room they have put him. What happened to the valise?"

"We kept it, David and me."

"And what else was in it?"

"Small personal items as a rule. All from the Outland: a very colourful photograph set into a shiny metallic frame: photographic likenesses of a young man and woman wearing the same odd clothing as the dead woman was wearing—spare and indecorous, though the colours be bright. There were these things as well: empty folders and transparent packages of tissue paper, and a most remarkable pen, which writes from ink held inside. I know that there were mechanical pens of this sort in the earliest days of our valley history, but it is rather astonishing to think of how sophisticated *this* pen is by comparison, for it does the job of releasing its ink so efficiently. Oh, and a little ceramic doll now in the possession of my youngest girl, Louisa—it is the figure of a little boy, perhaps eight or ten inches high, standing with a grin. He wears a uniform of some sort, and holds a stick. It is too narrow to be a cricket bat, so David and I have deduced that it must be suggestive of an American baseball bat. Oh yes, and his head sits detached upon a spring and bounces when you touch it."

"I should like to see it."

"I'll shew you each of these things when we return to the mews. These *and* the mechanical objects which also lived within the case—objects for which I could not readily glean a purpose, except for the one that seemed to be some sort of small calculating device."

I nodded my head with great interest. "Yes, yes. I've recently seen such a device as this myself, and have even had the opportunity of making an arithmetical calculation upon it."

Harry Scadger ran his hand through his thinning, blond hair, and leant back a little in his chair. "I should like to know what was on those papers— the ones that put Dr. Chivery into such a state of agitation, and which in the end resulted in his being committed to Bedlam."

"As would I. For the time being, though, there is no getting to him. He is sealed away in much the same manner as are others who have important things to tell, should they only be given leave to speak."

"Others?"

"Yes. Returnees from the Outland, deliberately cordoned off from the rest of us."

"But they are sick."

I shook my head. "I strongly suspect now that the sickness is a fabrication, a pretext for their incarceration. Do you know the dead woman's name? Does it appear on anything in the valise?"

Harry nodded. "Michelena Martin. I'm glad that I told you of her, Frederick. You are the right man to know. But there is something else as well—something having nothing to do with her, that I must discuss with you."

"Yes?" I drew back. I took a pull on the gin drink. It tasted fœtid in my mouth and I could hardly bring myself to swallow the vile liquid. It was the sort of concoction one put upon a wound to heal it faster. I could not believe that it shouldn't burn its way through my tract like lye or acid.

"I had been wanting to speak to you about this other important matter for quite some time, but Matilda wouldn't let me. 'Let sleeping dogs lie,' said she. 'But,' said I, 'Frederick Trimmers isn't a dog, or at least not the sort of dog to bare the gums and make things unpleasant for us. Nor do I think that what I have to convey should do anything but bind us stronger in our society with one another.'"

"Then by all means, you must tell me."

My companion nodded. He took a deep breath, and then in a soft voice he began: "There is a great secret that has been kept from you and your brother. I have known it for some time."

"Yes?"

Suddenly the drink didn't taste so vile. I drank it heartily to quell the feeling of unease rising up within my breast.

I could count perhaps upon the fingers of a single hand the number of times that Harry Scadger and I had sat and spoken thoughtfully and earnestly with one another. Society and circumstances didn't generally permit it. Yet I had always enjoyed my exchanges with this unique man. He was perspicacious and quite bright, and our encounters had always left me with a better sense of things, my understanding having been illuminated by the fresh, articulate perspective of his simplified station.

If one hadn't been told that Harry Scadger was amongst the poorest men in the Dell, one should think him to be nothing short of scholar, teacher, or even erudite member of the Petit-Parliament. Soon I would learn the reasons why.

For in addition to his intuitive intellect and common sense, Harry had been favoured, when just a boy, by the kindness of a mysterious benefactor. "The man had sent word to the apricot grove," Harry revealed, "that my brothers and I would be provided a tutor, whose services would be paid in full by the benefactor. Thus, each of the six sons of Solomon Scadger would be afforded an education, through the learned offices of Dr. Chivery, that elseways would have been denied us by our impoverished and societally estranged circumstances. In spite of the generosity of the offer, my brothers turned it down, preferring to continue as their father had, illiterate and uneducated. I, the second oldest offspring of that family, proved the only exception. For a good many months, I received a singular education from, inarguably, the most brilliant man in Dingley Dell. I received my schooling in the face of the taunts and ridicules of my brothers, my youngest brother save one—Melchisedech (or Mel for short)—even succeeding in dropping, from an overarching limb, a Dinglian grammar upon my head as I took a nap between my studies, and nearly putting me into a state of irreversible insentience.

"Over the years, I'd nurtured this early taste for books that set me apart from my proudly-unread brothers, and this fact drew rancor from them, though Papa remained supportive of my efforts to uplift myself. In point of fact, my father was more than merely supportive, eventually encouraging me to leave the grove and seek my fortune in Milltown. But I refused to go and turn my back on my brothers, who had taken wives and started families and were forever being gulled by every tradesman with whom "Scadger and Sons" (the name facetiously applied to my under-enterprising family by our many betters) did business. Devolved to me was the responsibility of keeping the books, such as they were, on behalf of this collection of knife-sharpeners and basket weavers who seemed to all the valley little more than idiots with industrious fingers. But in staying behind to help my family eke out an existence that kept them all from dropping dead of everything imaginable that could befall a family of pastoral innocents, I put my light under a bushel and pushed all my grand life plans to the back of the hearth shelf. And in Solomon Scadger's last lingering hours before succumbing to a kick in the head by a passing mule when the driver failed to see a sleeping man lying too close to the road, my expiring father nonetheless found voice enough to thank me for overseeing the family business—and this acknowledgement warmed my heart more than anything else that he could have said in those expiring moments—and reminded me that all of my services to the clan had not been for naught. And there was something else that was said to me by my father in those final pre-mortem breaths. Something really quite extraordinary.

"Papa confessed to me that he was, in fact, *not* my papa. At least not by blood. And that my brothers are not my brothers-in-full, but only half-brothers."

I shook my head in disbelief. "And had he always known that he wasn't your true birth father?"

Scadger nodded. "But it was in those last moments before his death that he told *me*—five years ago in August. He revealed to me the name of my true father and the identity of my benefactor, and as one might guess, the two were one in the same." Harry Scadger expired a deep breath and then *in*spired a long, contemplative drink of porter.

"And how was it that your brothers' father could be so certain that you weren't his blood son?"

"Because I was conceived during his separation from my mother. There was a period of time several months before my birth during which my presumed father lived apart from my mother in the workhouse. Those were the days before he and my mother put down their stakes beneath the apricot trees. They had first lived under the Westminster Bridge with all the other vagrants of Milltown. People-Under-the-Bridge—that is what West Enders call them. Solomon Scadger was taken for tramp and beggar, though in truth he was neither—only a man who had fallen upon hard times. And he was removed to the workhouse, at the same time that my mother and my older brother—then but a baby of two—were shewn kindness and taken in by your own father and mother."

"My father—?"

"Yes. Your father *and* my father, for they are both the same."

"I cannot believe it."

"You must believe it, for my mother wasn't one to prevaricate." Harry raised his hand to seek a fresh pot from the publican. "It is for this reason that Matilda cautioned me against telling it to you. That all the good that may come from our being bound together as brothers might be undermined by the hard truth of how I came to be, by the fact that my mother was taken in carnality by your father whilst both were wed to others. I apologise for speaking so candidly here, but there is no other way for me to present the facts to you."

I slid back into my chair, numbed by this news, stilled by what the disclosure said about my father. "How is this possible?"

"Your father was kind to my mother and my older brother Sol, each hungry and penniless and clad in rags. But there was a price to be paid for that kindness. And I am the dividend."

I wished at that hard moment no further company with Harry Scadger, even if his name should, in truth, be Trimmers, and so I stood to go. I had often borne the wrath of my father, as had Augustus. Papa was an angry, bitter, and cynical man who left this Earth (a victim of pipe smoker's labial cancer) still at odds with everything that life had bestowed upon him—a candidate, if there ever was one, for leaving Dingley Dell in some manner *other* than a burial box, had he ever found the courage to make his escape. By the same token, Papa was, by turns, a loving man, a compassionate man, who bore the pain of others even as he railed against the general causes of that suffering which was the lot of most of the denizens of Dingley Dell. He was a tangled, convoluted, enigmatic man, whom Gus and I could never fully unravel. And in the end, I could see Papa taking pity on Harry Scadger's mother in her terrible plight, and then taking her to his bed for the pleasure of her voluptuous body, regardless of how even the thought of such a thing would have shattered my mother.

I loved my father and hated my father but ultimately would not, *could* not with good conscience hold black feelings in my heart against his "dividend," for Harry no more embodied the misdeeds of that man than did Gus or I. My heart softened.

"Sit," said Harry, clasping my wrist with his hand. "Don't go. Find it in your heart to accept me as your brother. Up to now you have helped my family and me out of a general sense of compassion for the most diminished amongst us. Now I ask that we vow to assist one another as brothers of the same blood."

I sat down. For a long while I said nothing. And then suddenly there was very much to say: I told Harry Scadger about our nephew Newman, about how he had left the Dell, and how I now believed that he had returned. I told Harry Scadger about his half-brother Augustus who had gone off looking for Newman and whose whereabouts were now unknown. I didn't forbear telling him everything that had been told to Sir Dabber and me by Dabber's son Bevan. I spoke in more detail of the calculating device found in Dr. Towlinson's office, which matched the description of that which had been found in the dead woman's valise (this fact later confirmed when I was permitted to view the instrument in Harry's custody). I took Harry Scadger into my confidence with few qualms, bolstered by the strong intuitive sense that ours would be an alliance upon which I could strongly depend. For Harry Scadger had no alliances or attachments of his own, save an allegiance to his brothers—an allegiance built more upon a sense of family obligation than upon an intellectual or philosophic commonality. I had Muntle and now Sir Dabber with whom to exchange theories and confidences. Harry had no one.

And so Harry Scadger and his wife Matilda and his son David and each of David's siblings had sat and viewed the contents of the woman's valise and had wondered within the circle of that family what it all had meant, and had wondered what words lived upon those damp papers from the Outland that Dr. Chivery had so hastily squirreled away. They had done this without context and without a clew as to how important these pieces could be to the great mosaic.

After a quiet and contemplative interval, I turned the subject to our detached childhoods, Harry obliging me by describing in broad strokes and a little pin-point the conjoined lives of his half-brothers and himself. He spoke of his deceased stepfather and mother, and I, in turn, told of the father that Harry had never known except through the man's paternal patronage, and of Harry's half-brother Gus, whom Harry had met only in passing. I fought back tears to recall the hard life that Gus had led (a life I could not help fearing in dark, quiet moments had now come to tragic end).

By the close of that long brotherly colloquy, the tavern was become a much duskier and far sleepier place than it had been upon our arrival, even the labouring men who had been in the beginning a bit loud and bois-terous now slumping groggily in their chairs. In the hush of that deadened room, we soon heard the click of the street door handle being turned, and then saw the sharp angle of summer evening sunlight slicing across the hunched backs and shoulders of some of the tavern's inmates. We beheld a young man standing proudly erect within that fog of dust motes suddenly illumined, and I could tell from the shape of his youthful silhouette that it was Dr. Mulberry Timberry. Cupping his eyes to better see into the room's darkness, the doctor made us out, and strode briskly toward us, letting the door behind him close with a muted catch.

"Good evening, gentlemen," said he. "You both look worn and weary. I was told that this was a lively, convivial place."

"Dr. Timberry," I said, rising to my feet to better formalise my intro-duction, "I'd like you to meet…my brother Harry."

"*Half*-brother, to be precise," Scadger corrected me. "The time had come, you see, for me to tell my friend Frederick that he is a bit more to me than friend and that he has, in fact, a blood relation in the apricot line."

Timberry shook his head in amazement. He was eager to hear the story of our linked parentage, but not as eager to address the condition of Harry's oldest daughter; whilst Florence was not amongst the worst consumptive cases he had seen in his studies of the disease at the Lung Hospital, she was, nonetheless, in a very bad way, and if we did not treat the illness quickly and aggressively, she would, by his estimation, succumb within two or three months.

I thought of Ruth Wolf and how she had healed Bevan Dabber with her Outlander drugs. Were there drugs that doctors used for consumptives in the Terra Incognita? Was this disease, often referred to by its scientific term "tuberculosis," as deadly a scourge amongst Outlanders as it was in the Dell? I would not be shy about asking this of Miss Wolf in my very next encounter with the woman. Nor would I forbear asking her about a good many other things now that I knew her true identity to be that of covert expatriate Beyonder.

CHAPTER THE THIRTY-SIXTH

Thursday, July 3, 2003

Unwittingly, I took a page from Muntle's book.

I left the East End and journeyed back across the Westminster Bridge, only to find myself gravitating inexorably to the Heavenly Rest Memorial Cemetery. Passing first beneath the great iron entry arch, I bent my steps toward the gravestones of my mother and my father (who now I knew to be the father of Harry Scadger as well) and to the gravestone of the love of my young life, Fanny Lumbey. Then, my obligatory obeisances having been made, I began to wander about in aimless reflection, finally coming to rest upon the "Bench of Perpetual Memory" dedicated to Muntle's brother George.

I wondered as I sat there how long my own brother must be gone from the Dell before I should consider putting in a bench in honour of *his* memory. I wept in this spot, not only over the potential loss of my brother, and the veritable loss of my mother and father and my dear Fanny, but also over the impending loss of my ancestral home. Because I knew in my soul that the only reason that prosperous, well-settled men such as Pupker and Feenix and Fitz-Marshall should pack their bags and leave Dingley Dell was this: that the valley was soon to change in some dark and perilous way that I could not begin to fathom. It was a fearful thought, but one that also beset me with a sense of great sadness.

I bowed my head and stared abstractedly at the green grass cushioning my feet. It was some time before I raised my head again and I did so because I heard my name being invoked by one who had come upon me. The voice belonged to my friend Sheriff Muntle.

"Ah," he said, "you have found some comfort, communing with the spirit of my lost brother?"

I shrugged. I pulled myself heavily from the bench. "You were away at the Chowser School longer than you said you would be."

"I have asked Maggy to marry me."

"And did she accept?"

"Aye. We are to be wed as soon as circumstances permit. There is, of course, the minor matter of where we shall live. Chowser doesn't wish to lose his valuable cook, and this is no time at all for me to resign my position as sheriff. Let us walk, Trimmers. We must go to Fingerpost. Your sister-in-law needs you. She is newly returned from Hungerford and has just received news of Gus's journey into the Outland. You should have sent word to me, for it came as a shock to me as well."

"There was nothing that you could have done. I didn't wish to cast a cloud upon your visit with Miss Finching."

"Still, I am your friend."

"It seems these days that friendship exists *only* for the purpose of commiseration. Every former purpose for platonic union appears to have been subverted by circumstances that can only be met by impotency and ineffectuality. We cannot go after Gus. There are a great *many* other things that we are unable to do for our friends. Is Charlotte alone?"

Muntle shook his head. "By luck, Miss Bocker chanced upon her on her return from Hungerford and accompanied her the rest of the way to her cottage. Knowing what Charlotte would discover when she arrived home, Antonia held her hand and explained in as dulcet tones as that woman's gruff demeanour generally allows the reason for Gus's absence. Your sister-in-law is taking the news quite badly, Trimmers. It is best that we hurry so you can be with her."

Gus was right. When we arrived at the cottage, Charlotte lay distraught and moaning in her bed, although according to Ruth Wolf, who sat nearby, she was just beginning to yield to the sedative she'd been given. Antonia paced the floor, waiting as well for Charlotte to drift off.

Seeing me, Charlotte struggled with drowsiness to ask me if it were true about Gus, for she still could not bring herself to fully believe it. I could do nothing but agree to that which had already been said, but I added that I still held out hope for his return. Charlotte had scarcely made a feeble nod in response when a hard and fast sleep overtook her, and her two female attendants, Muntle and I were given leave by circumstances to withdraw from the bedchamber.

"She was quite upset when I arrived," said Miss Wolf, snapping her medical bag shut. "But I have put her under the influence of a strong sleep agent. It was good that I was passing by at just the time that I was most needed."

"Given her fragile and nearly demented state," added Antonia, "I know not what Charlotte was capable of doing to herself once she realised the true reason for Gus not being home to greet her return."

I devoted the next hour to informing my companions of everything I had learnt over the last two days, and Antonia in turn discussed with us the invitation that Mrs. Gargery (or rather her pug dog) had taken from the hand of Mrs. Pyegrave as she lay crumpled and bleeding upon the cobblestones of Park Lane. Ruth Wolf had sat and listened as if she too had every need to hear all that was said, taking especial notice when I voiced the name "Michelena Martin." Ruth's presence seemed a natural thing, as if there were no doubt that she should be in this room, that she should be a part of everything discussed here.

But eventually the time came for Ruth to reciprocate. We had questions for *her*—a good many questions. Would she indulge us? That was the top question on the list.

Her answer was a most welcome one; not only would she indulge us, but she had, in fact, been hoping for an opportunity to address us, to put herself before the Fortnightly Poetry League, about which she had heard a thing or two. "I know not what your *true* purpose is, but I should like to bring you into my confidence nonetheless. It is time that some of you who have been marching for so long in the darkness should be given a little light to see where that path has been taking you."

And so Messrs. Graham and Upwitch were summoned, and within the hour an ad hoc meeting of the Fortnightly Poetry League was figuratively gavelled to order with all members present.

Ruth Wolf waited patiently for the librarian and vicar to be fully apprised of all things pertaining to miniature calculating devices and riverside corpses, a miraculous cure for Rokesmith's rigoritis, and a cellar filled and then suddenly made bereft of merchandise from the Terra Incognita.

"There is this as well," said Antonia Bocker, handing Upwitch the card of invitation that had come from Janet Pyegrave.

The vicar responded by asking Antonia, "Just what *is* to be celebrated on July 15? The fact that another crate of expensive champagne has been hauled up to the Summit for the exclusive relishment of the Petit-Parliament?"

"Perhaps I should defer to our Outlander guest to tell it," said Antonia with a nod to Miss Wolf.

Ruth Wolf beheld the faces that stared in rapt attendance within the close room—beheld them as if from some great height, for was it not true that the nurse had situated herself upon quite the lofty precipice in this engagement? For a moment I began to fear that she intended to go back on her word—that gathering us together was merely a ploy by which to receive as much intelligence as we were willing to give *her* and then renege on her promise to be equally forthcoming with *us*.

Muntle was thinking along the very same lines: "There are five people in this room, Miss Wolf, who have put a good deal of the puzzle together, but we cannot finish it without your help. We pose no danger to you, should you withhold the fact of our society and all that we know from those who could do us harm. But mark me, madam, we may do great harm to *you* if you decide to change your mind about cooperating with us. We could tell every man, woman, and child in this valley the details of your clandestine activities here. I wager that you wouldn't be sitting within this room entertaining our suppositions and receiving our facts, if you did not yourself nurse terrible qualms in your own breast about what you have been asked to do in the name of this mysterious 'Project' that manages our lives, exploits us, and preys upon our ignorance. Something is afoot. We know it now and we know that we have been put in the way of some great veiled peril. You are the link between that which threatens us and the means by which we may save ourselves. Do you wish to help us, madam, or do you wish to doom us all—yourself included—to whatever destruction these people are capable of inflicting?"

Ruth Wolf looked to me. Then she took a measure of the other anxious faces within the room. Finally she drew breath to say, "While I wish to help you in whatever way that I can, I cannot bring back your brother, Muntle, nor yours, Trimmers. Nor do I know what has happened to your nephew."

"You know nothing of Newman?" I asked, quite astonished to hear the words, given what I now knew of her rather circuitous efforts to inform me of Newman's present involuntary tenancy in Bedlam.

"I assure you I do not."

"I don't believe you, and you know *why* I do not believe you."

"How on earth could I have knowledge of the boy's whereabouts?"

"Because you work in Bedlam and because I found proof that he is being kept there and because you are the very one who led me to that proof."

"I can't possibly apprehend your meaning, Mr. Trimmers." Ruth Wolf turned away so I could not scrutinise her face for the sincerity I should certainly find lacking there.

I was set to offer the theory put to me by my friend Sir Dabber—delivering it, if circumstances required it, to her very back and shoulders, but was deterred by the staying hand of my friend Muntle. "Leave it to rest for now, Trimmers."

"Yet how can I trust anything else that this woman now says?" I rejoined in an undertone and with a hard look at that person whom I now believed, in spite of her earlier efforts to put a balm upon my mind with regard to my nephew, was now working against the release of that same cruelly sequestered child.

Antonia answered my rhetorical question with a concrete answer: "She will tell us what she wishes us to know, and *we* will have to decide what is true and what is not. For all we know, Trimmers, the woman will prevaricate when necessary to keep us in check—to prevent our storming the walls of Bedlam as if it be our own Bastille. We cannot have that, now can we, Miss Wolf? The five of us, dashing about, forming militias, creating havoc, ruining your plans to get away with Bevan Dabber and make a life for yourself far, far from this doomed place. Am I close to your ultimate purpose here, Miss Wolf—a purpose that would be compromised, perhaps altogether obliterated, should we all go about half-cocked and disturb the peace of this valley in such a way as to cause all your selfish schemes to go awry?"

Miss Wolf turned to face her inquisitor, and in so doing, to face all of the rest of us as well. She did not colour, nor did her expression change from that of stoic impassivity. "It's largely rubbish, of course. Most of what you just said. But I *am* in agreement with the predicate of your premise, Miss Bocker: that panic and havoc and precipitant action would not be wise—would induce retaliation upon a rather grand scale. Now I am happy to tell you what I know of the Tiadaghton Project and to explain what my role has been in it, but only for the purpose of helping us all to keep our heads, to effect a careful and studied analysis of present circumstances with all the tools of cool intellect that have marked your previous fortnightly gatherings. Mr. Graham knows what I mean, do you not, sir—your being a man who has spent a long and fruitful life in dispassionate research—in investigations divested of unproductive emotionality. Is this not the wisest course, sir?"

Mr. Graham blushed at what he perceived to be a compliment (for never before had he been commended for his dispassionate, emotionally-divested investigations).

Miss Wolf continued: "In this matter you must *all* approach your present situation just as I approach my own rueful position—one from which I do eventually hope to extricate myself—without giving license to dangerous, sudden impulse."

"Yet," struck in Mr. Upwitch, "do you or do you not intend to steal away with young Mr. Dabber in the dark of some forthcoming night and be done with all of this—with all of *us*?"

"Do I wish to leave this place and never return? I most certainly do. Is it my wish to go arm-in-arm with the man I love? Yes. One hundred times yes. But it is my fate to remain here for the present. I am powerless to do much more at this unfortunate juncture than that for which I was hired: to maintain through sophisticated chemical therapies the illusion of the disease you call the Terror Tremens."

"So that is what you do," said I.

"Surely you had figured it out by now."

"So you will confirm for us," joined in Muntle, "that there is no such mental affliction."

"That I most certainly will confirm or I should never have been given a job here," replied Miss Wolf matter-of-factly.

"You say 'to do much more than that for which I was hired,'" I interposed, "yet you have healed Bevan. I saw him. I spoke with him. You were not hired to do this."

Miss Wolf nodded again, this time with obvious discomfiture. She lowered her eyes and could very well have been at that moment mistaken for a different sort of woman altogether—one made suddenly ineffable by thought of love. "I have done a little here and there to assuage my conscience, which grows more troubled by the day. I plan, as well, to give drugs to your Dr. Timberry to administer to young Florence Scadger. The medicine will treat her tuberculosis and eventually heal it. Outside this valley the disease is quite manageable with proper treatment and rigourous attendance by the patient to a specific pharmacotherapeutic protocol."

"And who else have you helped?" asked Antonia.

"I have been making secret, unscheduled visits to the patients of the Lung Hospital over the last couple of weeks, administering the same drugs to them that are used on the outside. It is a lengthy series and I pray that it will do some good. I intend shortly hereafter to give all of my Outland medical supplies over to Timberry so that he should continue in my stead. I'm not an ogre or a monster, though I will admit that some of what I do and do not do these days is motivated by fear for my own safety. I cannot help it; my situation is growing precarious.

"Now this has reminded me of the woman whose dead body was dis-covered by young David Scadger last month. I knew this woman, or at least I knew *of* her. The Tiadaghton Project is a massive construct that ably pro-tects itself from any threat, be it large or small, and especially that of the renegade variety. Apparently, Miss Martin had become just such a threat—a cog that was set to fly off the machine and draw dangerous attention to it. The Project has its rules and those rules are adhered to without variance. Everything serves the illusion that Dingley Dell is everything you see round you: a sheltered, pastoral, Victorian entity, a quaint and curious anach-ronism in a modern world. But there is another deception, which must also be maintained: that which is presented to the rest of the world—that this valley is home to a highly restricted government-sponsored installa-tion wherein sophisticated weaponry is manufactured and tested, though there be no small number of those who believe a different story entirely: that visitors from some other world reside here. It's a fiction no one goes to great lengths to disprove since it sends the imagination far afield of the actual truth about this place."

Here looks of astonishment were exchanged amongst Miss Wolf's silent auditors. To think that there are those who believed Dinglians to be ultramundane!

"It has been my job," Miss Wolf continued, "to keep quiet those who return from what you call the Terra Incognita—to keep those who have viewed life in the twenty-first century as it truly is from threatening the health and functionality of the machine. I silence the Returnees by creating the necessary symptoms of the Returnees' disease: I bring about narcolepsy and dementia and disorientation when it is called for. I induce seizures in the most intractable patients."

"Were you responsible for the death of Mr. Gamfield?" I asked coldly. "I understand that he beat his head against a wall until his brains spilt out."

Ruth Wolf lowered herself slowly into a chair. In a hushed, nearly imperceptible voice she said, "That isn't true, nor was it my doing. Gamfield's death came, in fact, at the hand of Dr. Fibbetson, who took it upon himself to supplement the pacifying drugs that I had already given the patient. The man is more than mere bumptious idiot. He is an imbecilic menace. The grisly, fictionalised account of Gamfield's death was put forth to create the necessary fiction that the disease—this spurious disease—has worsened in its manifestation and symptoms. While the families of the patients have become more impatient, the patients themselves have also grown more restive. And it is no easy task to keep men and women under lock and key perpetually sedated, especially those who do not go easily into their restraints or fall most readily into the required stupor. The Tiadaghton Project would prefer that every escapee from Dingley Dell be captured and summarily executed, and a good many have been. *Far* too many..."

My heart leapt into my throat at that moment to hear confirmation of what I had come to fear. Antonia and Muntle were taken aback as well. Slingo took Uriah's hand, or perhaps it was the other way round.

"But there are those, as you know, who *do* make it back. And they must be dealt with. Bedlam is the place where they are quarantined. It is where I do my job. And it robs me of a piece of my soul every day that I am at it. I would gladly walk away—no, *run* in a fast sprint from my duties here if I could. But I would be writing my own death warrant. Just like Michelena Martin did, for I am certain that she too was trying to get herself away as fast as she could."

Muntle ran his hand across his chin in rigourous thought, then flung that hand with a sharply pointing index finger in the direction of the now most forthcoming Miss Wolf. "Tell us why the Tiadaghton Project is coming to its end."

"It appears that Dingley Dell has been purchased by a private industrial concern. A modern steel mill is to be built here, of such size and sophistication as to make your tiny steam-puffing foundry look like a child's play-toy. It seems that we, unknowingly, have entered the end times."

"And you knew absolutely nothing of this?" snapped Antonia.

"Upon my honour, Miss Bocker, there were things that I had been told were coming in the offing, but nothing so immediate as this. It was only quite recently that I learnt about the Fête champêtre. I suspected that it should be the vehicle through which certain privileged residents of this valley—the Bashaws, as you call them—would receive their sanctioned release from this place, but I could not confirm it for myself until this moment, seeing here what Mrs. Pyegrave wrote on the card. Emigration is the Project's way of rewarding its helpmates in Dingley Dell for their many years of service as insider agents."

"Whither will they go?" asked Graham.

"I suspect that what awaits the members of your Petit-Parliament and their kinsmen and families is relocation to some secured and exotic place—perhaps an island in the South Seas, since the Project owns hundreds of acres of holiday property throughout the South Pacific. I would imagine that they'll be spending the remainder of their days in compensatory tropical comfort."

"And what of the rest of us once they go?" asked Antonia. "What are they to *do* with us?"

"I don't know," was all that Miss Wolf would say.

"May *I* guess?" asked Muntle. "Allow me to offer two possible contrasting outcomes, each dependent upon how the following questions be answered: what should happen to the administrators of the Tiadaghton Project once word of what they have perpetrated becomes known? If laws have been broken—both those of man and those of God—will our mysterious overlords be required to answer for them? Is there a price to be paid for what was done to us over all the years, and if so, will they attempt to avoid that cost by covering their tracks by any means? How these questions are answered should determine whether we shall simply be evicted, or whether we should be dealt with by some other more terminal means."

"I believe there to be only *one* possible outcome," said the Reverend

Upwitch grimly. "For did we not hear Miss Wolf say that many who left the Dell were murdered to guarantee their permanent silence? I should think that our own lives are of equal negligible value to these filthy Outland assassins."

"Consider as well the depravities to which the Bedlam inmates are daily subjected," added Mr. Graham. "There is not a glimmer of humanity in such treatment of any of us, not within the Dell or without. Why should it be any different when the book is closed?"

"They will not—nay, *cannot*—permit the true story of Dingley Dell to be freely told," I added. "The administrators of the Tiadaghton Project will have no choice but to still every voice that remains after the Bashaws have fled. There is only one solution, and we all know what it is."

As each of the men in the room pondered the looming possibility of his own demise, the two women in our company repaired briefly to Miss Wolf's home to fetch an ice pail containing a certain canned beverage to be imbibed during the unveiling of the true and unvarnished history of Dingley Dell, courtesy of Miss Ruth Wolf, impromptu annalist of this now-forsaken valley. I was most eager to hear every detail that Ruth chose to offer, and was curious about the taste of the flavourful potable, which the teller had procured from her secret larder for our refreshment. The beverage was of Outlander origin. It was called *Wegman's Cola*.

Chapter the Thirty-seventh

Friday, July 4, 2003

After pouring the beverage from several cans upon mountains of ice within our tumblers we each took an appraising sip.

"I've never tasted anything quite like it," said Upwitch, smacking his lips and holding the clear glass away from him to examine the umber colouring of its contents.

"Quite sweet," said his companion Graham. "A little syrupy, but quite good."

The attention of my scholastic and bibliophilic friend was now drawn to the discarded cans from which the liquid had been decanted. He picked one up and assayed its weight upon his palm. "What is this? It cannot be tin. It's much too light."

"It *isn't* tin," responded Miss Wolf. "It's aluminum. Or alu*min*ium in the parlance of the Brits."

Graham squeezed the can; it gave way, readily crumpling in the centre. "That's quite impossible."

"And why do you say that?"

"Because aluminium is more precious than gold or silver. Bars of it were, in fact, exhibited alongside the French crown jewels at the *Exposition Universelle* of 1855."

"Yes, and Napoleon III reserved a set of aluminum dinner plates for his most favoured guests," rejoined Miss Wolf. "I'm familiar with the illustrious history of this metal. Back in that day, Mr. Graham, it was prohibitively expensive to extract the metal from bauxite ore. But that has changed. Nowadays we turn aluminum into beverage cans and sell it by the roll for kitchen use in even the poorest of homes."

"Remarkable!" Graham examined the crushed can in his hand as if it were some new species of miniature mammalian fauna that he could not wait to take home to dissect and give taxonomic name to.

I picked up a can myself and ran my inquisitive fingers along the contour of this sculpted element of nature, which I'd never before seen (for there was nothing within the Dell made of aluminium to my knowledge—not a single, blessed thing). It was as if I were holding a golden ingot in my palm, or clutching a cluster of shimmering diamonds. Here was the Terra Incognita in metallic form: the precious made commonplace. I was curious to see how else that equation manifested itself in the land beyond the Dell. What else of value had the Outlanders diminished in worth and merit? I knew for one thing that there were those within that large tribe of humanity who placed far less value upon human dignity, upon self-respect and self-determination, upon human life itself. I was ready to hear everything else that Miss Wolf was willing to impart about people who would make aluminium into toss-away cans and humans into mammalian refuse.

And she could see it. In my eager eyes. In the corresponding looks of anticipation upon the faces of each member of the Fortnightly Poetry League. "Sit back. Relax," said Miss Wolf. "I'm about to tell you a story which, in the cant of some of my fellow Beyonders, 'will knock your socks off.'"

"Where to begin now. Where to begin." Miss Wolf paced back and forth with tumbler in hand, the beads of condensation from the ice cubes trickling down the side of the glass. "Once upon a time—oh, let's not start it out like that."

"You may begin with the orphans if you please," said Miss Bocker. "Why were they brought here in that very first year?"

"Is it not your wish to know first just where in the world you are?"

"We reside somewhere in either the state of Ohio or the state of Pennsylvania in the United States of America." This from Muntle who spoke for all of us except the vicar, who still held out hopes of our being in Italy (where glorious campaniles grow up like toadstools—or so he supposed).

"And how have you come to this conclusion? I'm curious."

It was Graham who offered the answer: "Because even a child—sorry, Slingo—can deduct from all the empirical evidence that we reside somewhere about the Allegheny Plateau."

"*I* will offer more specificity than that," struck in Antonia with no small measure of pride. "That we are situated in the county of Lycoming, the largest such geographical division in Pennsylvania. Have I guessed correctly?"

Miss Wolf broke into a smile. "You are precisely right. And how have you come to this accurate conclusion?"

"A friend of mine from my workhouse youth surmised it in notes he made and which I gathered together after his death. I expected to find some truth in what he had taken from the mouths of some of our early forefathers—many of whom were still alive when he was a young man—but it isn't until this very moment that I finally receive confirmation that the first of his several hypotheses is true."

"And how specifically did it come to his ken?"

"From his *kin*, it turns out," returned Antonia, grinning at her homophonic cleverness. "It was his own grandfather who told him. He was one of the original orphans, and as a child had quite audaciously asked of the conductor of the train that brought him to the edge of this valley wither it was that he was going, and the conductor whispered the destination to him when no one was looking. So you see, Miss Wolf: there are a few things about the Outland that some of us have known, which do not happen to come from *The Encyclopædia Britannica.*"

"Ninth Edition," added Mr. Graham helpfully.

"Ninth Edition. Thank you, Mr. Graham."

Miss Wolf considered this fact for a moment and then asked what else Antonia's friend had learnt from the elders.

"This and that. Surely you don't expect me to speak so freely about everything I know, but I *will* say that I shall not hesitate to use what my dear late friend Mr. Traddles has written upon his dirty paper scraps as that gauge by which I shall keep you honest."

Ruth Wolf seemed wounded. "Miss Bocker! I have no reason *not* to speak with you honestly and forthrightly."

Antonia elevated an eyebrow. "We shall see."

And with that, the obscurant mummified shroud, which had swaddled Dingley Dell for well over a century, began layer-by-layer to be peeled carefully away. Those salient facts that had been as unknown to the residents of our fair valley as all the mysteries of the night sky and every infinitesimal secret locked within the most miniscule molecule upon a microscopic slide now found illumination and explication and life and breath and free and unfettered airing within that simply-appointed sitting room, whose attendant lay in ignorant drug-induced slumber upon her bed up-stairs.

Never before had a Dinglian been privileged to hear the deepest secrets of his existence revealed and explained. Perhaps those who left this valley came to understand a few things prior to their demise or their ill-fated return, but never had a Dinglian been placed into such a glorious position of unqualified receptivity. We would take every advantage to learn all that we could and would try our best (and fail) to keep our tongues silent through the unveiling except when a point demanded further elucidation, or commentary was wholly called for. But first…

"The orphans," Antonia reiterated. "Why were they brought here in the very beginning? For what purpose? My friend Mr. Traddles wasn't able to learn it and none of us has ever known it."

"Well, let me tell you first the *original* reason and then we'll take up the second one, which was mandated by altered circumstances."

I could not help myself: I leant forward, wearing, I have no doubt, the look of a young child who must know everything there is to know about a fantastical storybook kingdom. In a sense, Dingley Dell was itself just such a storybook place with a cloud of mystery overhanging it, as magical and mystical as any of the children's stories to which Mr. Dickens had alluded. (Who was Cinderella? we had always wondered. Or Jack the Giant Killer or Sinbad the sailor? For they receive only the briefest mention in the novels of Dickens, and the tales ascribed to them aren't provided upon the leaves of the otherwise most eclectically informative *Ensyke*.)

"Dingley Dell," Miss Wolf began in the steady, starched voice of a professor standing stiff-armed behind his lectern, "which as you know was given that denomination by your ancestors in accordance with their wonted affinity for all things Dickensian (and in this specific case, *Pickwickian*), began life as a rustic valley comprised of a small village or two and a smattering of farms and a goodly amount of acreage, which was uncut and unfurrowed and pristine in nearly every way. And there was abundant wildlife here in those days and a scenic prospect, no matter where one stood, of such primitive beauty as to soothe and nurture the most troubled human breast. No prettier spot on earth could be imagined, prettier it was than even that which our present-day eye beholds, for Dingley Dell was greener then and the sky above it bluer, it would seem, and more vibrant, and the sun much warmer in its radiance. A true Arcadia.

"But a rather odd sort of Arcadia, orographically speaking, for the valley that would come to be known as Dingley Dell lies within what is known as the Allegheny Front—the dividing line between the eastern edge of the Allegheny Plateau escarpment…"

"…and the lower Allegheny Mountains," broke in Mr. Graham, excitedly.

"This strange conjunction of different land forms created something most unusual—a contained valley put down almost as if it were a basin or caldera, with high ridges running north and south, and lower thickly-wooded ridges running east and west. Almost unique as valleys go.

"And it was in this unique, isolated Arcadian state that the valley presented itself to a handful of men from Philadelphia who came hither to camp and fish upon the banks of the river you call the Thames, but which is known elsewhere as the Double Pine. These were men of science, big thinkers, staunch supporters of Mr. Darwin's theories, of which I suspect you know a little something."

That being put in somewhat the form of a question, Mr. Graham nodded in the affirmative.

"And it came to pass that these men, with no small fortunes to their names, decided to buy up all of this valley for the purpose of conducting an experiment on a rather ambitious scale. They wished to learn if Mr. Darwin's theories were correct and if a species of animal—in this case, the one that comes by the scientific designation 'Homo sapiens'—would in an identical environment evolve in much the same way over time as did our primate ancestors. Would the fittest remove the less fit, the stronger supplant the weak, the brightest bring to extinction the dim-lights? But you see, the experiment did not—could *never* resign itself to answering those questions alone, for there were many other theories which these scientific men were hungry to test, other questions for which they sought answers: how, for example, does language and culture develop when there are no precedents upon which to build? How would societal institutions grow with no historical or generational models to emulate? In its purest, most unadulterated form, the experiment would require that its subjects be infants—infants brought to the valley in their most unformed state, and then left there to raise themselves, like Tarzan without his apes—no, no, you wouldn't know Tarzan, would you? Edgar Rice Burroughs didn't foist that vine-swinging gentleman upon the reading public until around 1912. But the unfortunate fact of the matter is that baby humans *aren't* precocial—not at all like cheeping, self-reliant little chicks. They are quite the opposite, their *altricial* nature demanding that they be nursed and nurtured for a time, or else they should die in the crib and the experiment come to naught. It was for this reason that children above the age of three were procured, and that even then all children were afforded—over a period of several years—sufficient training in very rudimentary forms of survival, as well as education in the sort of trades that might readily be found in a rural society of the 1870s. Any advancement beyond those basic skills imparted by specifically selected vocational teachers would be effected by the children and their descendants alone, and that would be the thrust of one aspect of the study. The scientific men were most curious to see how these young innocents and their descendants evolved over the years, how they should build upon what they'd been initially taught, and I must say, to interject a personal note, that in fine, you've acquitted yourselves quite commendably."

I nodded to thank Miss Wolf on behalf of the other four Dinglians in the room, as well as our accomplished brothers and sisters, over 25,000 in number, both the quick and the dead. Then I interposed, "So this then is the reason why nothing that could not be obtained by a citizen of the 1880s was ever brought for barter by your tradesmen."

Miss Wolf nodded whilst taking a sip of her brown drink. "A task which, I might add, became more and more difficult with the years, for so many of the objects that fitted and graced the everyday lives of citizens in the 1880s ceased to be manufactured over time. An entire clandestine industry therefore sprang up with the singular purpose of providing you Dinglians with such items as would have been used a good many decades ago: bear grease for the hair, for example; and macassar oil; outmoded, even currently illicit pharmaceuticals, largely of the opiate family; gas-light fixtures and steam engine fixtures and engine pumps; and oysters—tons and tons of oysters that must be brought at some expense from the Atlantic coast to feed the conceit that the superfluity of these shell creatures which existed in Dickens' day continues still. (It does not, by the bye. They're quite a delicacy nowadays.) What else? Hmm. Steel knitting needles—for you could never make them here the way they were once made in London. All manner of tobacco except for the ready-made cigarette, which didn't hit its stride until after your quarantine began. Obtaining significant quantities of dry snuff has been especially difficult, I understand, because hardly anyone in the Outland takes snuff anymore."

"Then what *do* they take?" sought Muntle, who occasionally turned to the snuffbox when his pipe was unavailable.

"They dip it. They dip a mash of it and apply it to the gums."

"Revolting," commented Antonia Bocker. "Disgusting and revolting."

"What else?" mused Miss Wolf aloud. "Ah, yes. Exotic and now largely extinct perfumes and men's scents."

"Bouquet du Roi?" asked the vicar.

"Gone with the ages."

"Bay rum?" sought Graham the librarian.

"Will always be with us."

Mr. Graham released a sigh of relief that was shared by Muntle and myself.

"You've grown so successfully self-sufficient with your printing presses and your glass-blowing factory and your iron foundry and all your other mills and manufactories that it is only the more esoteric items, as you know, that generally find their way into the tradesmen's waggons."

"Not including," I interrupted, "those modern conveniences—a few of which have accidentally come to our attention—items that we must assume were never meant for common Dinglian consumption."

Miss Wolf nodded as all of our thoughts descended into Pupker's sub-cellar.

"It's quite fascinating," said Antonia, "this attempt to keep us married to the 1880s. Though in a good many cases we proceeded along entirely different lines from that fusty decade. You will note that the corset is rarely worn these days. The shelf bustle, in fact, disappeared back in the 1920s."

"And the wearing of layers and layers of petticoats, I note, has also gone out of fashion," said Miss Wolf. "Much to the delight, I am sure, of every woman in the Dell."

Antonia nodded as Ruth Wolf grinned. "At all events," continued the nurse, "everything went quite according to plan for the organisation, which early on acquired the name 'The Tiadaghton Project.' That plan included first and foremost the eventual prescribed exit of all of the orphans' vocational instructors. Indeed, every adult in the valley."

"Their departure being facilitated by that most deceitful of all deceptions—a worldwide pandemic," said Antonia. "Mr. Traddles figured this out for himself, though few others could make such a leap with certainty."

"It was the only pretext by which the children could be left to their own wits and industry. But things hardly ever go as planned. Miss Johnson and her illicit pupil Miss Henrietta Weatherfield were the first flies to befoul the ointment. How dare that kind lady teach her little sewing pupil how to read when the experiment expressly forbade the acquisition of any written language not of the subjects' own creation? It was at that moment that Tiadaghton was well nigh abandoned, for it was the development of a unique written form of language that the philological members of that original scientific cadre most sought to study and analyse. Things were upended further when that renegade cache of books was inconveniently discovered in the fruit cellar."

"How did they come to be there?" asked Muntle. "Generations of Dinglians have wondered."

Miss Wolf looked to Miss Bocker. "Does your Mr. Traddles have a theory?"

"He has none. It could have been accidental divestment, or the books could have been left behind quite deliberately. Do *you* know, Miss Wolf?"

Ruth Wolf smiled mischievously. "I *do* happen to know. Or at least I know the legend that was passed down to us over the years. But I'll not tell you now."

A collective groan rose up and then receded. We *had* reverted to schoolchildren. It was quite an amazing thing to behold.

"But rather than jettison the experiment and ship all the children off to various and sundry orphanages, and then fall into desponding wistful musing over what might have been, the conductors of this unprecedented sociological and anthropological experiment chose, instead, to adapt themselves to modified circumstances and to entirely recalibrate their objectives. Ultimately they decided to sit back, clipboards still in hand, and observe the effect that *David Copperfield* and *Great Expectations* and the

Encyclopædia Britannica (Ninth Edition) and the Holy Bible (King James Version) might have upon their subjects. Could it be possible for those subjects to inadvertently replicate Victorian/Dickensian England here in Lycoming County, Pennsylvania? With access to the Christian Bible, would they become a Christian society? How much value would they put on education? Would the voluminous *Ensyke* make them intellectually inquisitive? The overarching answer to all of the above, as you all well know, was yes in capital letters."

"What is 'Tiadaghton'?" This from the ever-enquiring Uriah Graham.

"The name of a forest nearby. Shall I freshen your drink?"

Graham shook his head. No doubt the sharp mind within that thoughtful man's head was reeling to the same degree as was my own. It was difficult to hear of the sheer nerve and audacity that characterised the actions of those who in their pre-murderous incarnation had nonetheless criminally uprooted our ancestors from their childhood homelands and deposited them in this orographically anomalous test tube to try out "theories" upon them and upon their every descendent.

I essayed to steady myself and suppress my outrage. I knew that my anger would only grow in intensity as the baneful perpetrations being detailed and expounded upon by the informative Miss Wolf began, themselves, to intensify in perniciousness—as by little and little that picture of abominable, villainous exploitation began to take form and shape. "So they observe us?" I asked, attempting to compose myself.

"I beg your pardon?"

"Observe us, Miss Wolf. Have the administrators of the Tiadaghton Project always been about the business of observing and studying the residents of this valley whose ancestors they intentionally placed here?"

"Yes, in one way or another. What began as a scientific endeavour transformed itself in short order into quite a commercial one. You see, Dingley Dell became, to put it bluntly, big business."

"*Business*?" Antonia, the only merchant in the room, took especial note of the word.

"Yes, Miss Bocker. It was a natural progression, this being America, the most capitalistic country on earth. And remember that Tiadaghton came along in the 1880s during that first golden age of capitalistic excess. It was a time of unprecedented agglomeration of individual wealth, during which an industrial titan could make as much money as he was able to squeeze from the strained sinews of the men who laboured beneath him. This was the period during which Dingley Dell came into its own. You have somewhat the same sort of dynamic at work here in the Dell, albeit in microcosm: the privileged, entitled few lording their privileges and sense of entitlement over all the rest of you. From very early on we sought out your Bashaws for their inside assistance in our undertaking in exchange for generous compensation."

"You're speaking of the ones that Graham and I have come to call the Moles," said Upwitch.

"Yes. It is they who have always helped us to keep things running smoothly, they to whom the Project has always been historically indebted."

"And their compensation—?" asked Upwitch.

"The Moles, as you call them, have been and continue to be rewarded for their assistance with those little baubles of modern civilisation that we felt inclined to bestow upon them—all of which have been kept largely out of the view of the rest of you—the calculators, the radios, the televisions, the phonographs, the laptop computers, the food processors, the espresso makers, the hand-vacs, the Walkmans, the iPods—"

Upwitch shook his head in stupefaction. "Aside from the calculator, I don't know what—"

"I'll explain them all in time, Reverend Upwitch. My point is that the world has progressed apace. Electricity alone powers a good many things that serve to make a Beyonder's life far less toilsome than your own. What was shared with the Moles was always meant to be kept well hidden. Unfortunately, Mr. Pupker, for his part, hasn't been as scrupulous in recent days with the distribution of these twenty-first century lagniappes to his comrades as the administrators would like to see, but that's a subject for some later discussion."

"So you know about the sub-cellar?" I asked.

Miss Wolf nodded. "It served, until Wednesday night, as the subterranean warehouse for all of our little gifts of gratitude to our inside agents."

"How appropriate," observed Muntle with a dark grin, "that the Moles should take their presents from a hole in the ground!"

Following a moment of subdued collective laughter, Miss Wolf painted a vivid picture of how Bashaw cellars throughout the Dell had been secretly used for years as playrooms of Outland design and accouterment.

"But what may be found in these cellars doesn't hold a candle to what you would actually find in the Outland," continued Miss Wolf. "Suffice it to say that it is a highly mechanised, electrified, electronic world that lies beyond this valley—one which your Returnees could hardly put into words—or having described it with a small modicum of success, they could only be thought mad from the utter outrageousness of their reports. Can a Dinglian even begin to wrap his brain round the concept of airplanes that fly faster than the fleetest bird, traversing the entire globe in only a matter of hours?"

"'Airplanes.' You mean 'aerial planes,'" interposed Mr. Graham in polite rectification. "A Dinglian may wrap his brain around it quite easily when he considers that the *Ensyke* predicted that it was only a matter of time before the problem of artificial flight would be solved. It has always been believed that the Beyonders had, as a result of the ravages of that pandemic—the one that we now know was counterfeited—abandoned all attempts to fly by mechanical means. We now see that what the *Ensyke* predicted did indeed come true."

"And yet," struck in Muntle, the inveterate sky-gazer amongst us, "if Outlanders are flying hither and thither in their expeditious contraptions, why have we never seen a single one above our heads?"

A correction from Mr. Graham: "There *was* one, Sheriff Muntle, which was observed in the summer of 1949."

Miss Wolf nodded. "I'll confirm the incursion. A plane accidentally entered the restricted air space over your valley."

"I recall something about the event from my childhood," said the vicar. "My great uncle Thomas was one of those who saw it, though few of the witnesses were believed. He said that it buzzed and hummed and was most decidedly mechanical. I remember thinking how much I should have liked to see it myself. *Still* would, in fact."

"Yet, Reverend Upwitch, you see airplanes in flight every day. Or at least their contrails."

"Contrails, Miss Wolf?" asked Graham.

"Yes. A shortened name for condensation trails. Above 26,000 feet, Mr. Graham, visible trails of condensed water vapour are formed—a by-product of engine exhaust."

"I *have* seen them!" exclaimed Graham. "But I always assumed them to be of some unfamiliar meteorological origin."

"Whilst my sky-gazing nephew Newman," I struck in with a smile, "once surmised that they might very well be laid down by some manner of man-made machine."

Through an open window at the opposite end of the dark room now appeared a bright shaft of reflective moonlight, as that orb became fully unveiled in the sky by retreating clouds. I shifted in my chair to look up at the glowing satellite, to think of aerial-planes flying at incomprehensible speeds in silhouette across its luminous face.

"And we've been *there*, too," declared Miss Wolf, noting my temporary attendance to the moon.

I did not doubt the truth of what Miss Wolf had said, though I knew that she hadn't been honest in every answer she'd given us to-night—most notably pertaining to the whereabouts of my nephew Newman, and perhaps even to the location of Newman's father. She had some reason there to prevaricate, but why would one lie about such a thing as flying to the moon? Was it not simply indicative of the fact that life outside the Dell *had* moved forward, just as Bevan Dabber had said that it did—and at a most extraordinary pace? It deeply wrenched my soul to think upon it—to think of all that Dinglians had missed during the many years of their imposed isolation. I spoke my regretful thoughts aloud in a contemplative under-breath: "All the books never read. All the plays and musical concerts never attended."

"Or the thousands of movies that you missed," added Ruth Wolf.

"*Movies*?" asked Mr. Graham.

"Motion pictures. Magic lantern shows that move and speak and sing and reflect the world upon a wall. Americans became quite good at making movies. But while I sympathise with the utter abjection of all you have missed, I also envy your hundred and twenty-one years of blissful ignorance about everything that has gone wrong in our world during that time."

"It hasn't always been bliss, Miss Wolf," said I. "Life for us, as you must know from having studied our society, has never been as idyllic as one would think."

Miss Wolf nodded. She had been standing at the window, gazing thoughtfully at the moon. Now she withdrew her gaze, turned, and settled herself into an empty chair.

After a brief contemplative interval, I directed us back onto the original thoroughfare of our discussion: "You said that the Project strayed by necessity from its original purpose. That somewhere along the way it became a commercial enterprise of significant size. What did you mean?"

"Exactly that. The Tiadaghton Project expanded and metamorphosed, and in the end became a profit-making enterprise of great scope and breadth. Nearly all of the Robber Barons—the name given to those business potentates who became obscenely wealthy through their industrial and financial rapaciousness—shared a fashionable fascination for this little slice of synthetic Victorian England nestled ironically in their own American backyard. And they poured millions of dollars into its upkeep, guaranteeing Dingley Dell many happy years of solvent patronage.

"It took no time at all for the Robber Barons to fall madly in love with this place and its colourful people. These and the men who came after them drew from their extravagant bank accounts to create from their obsession with Dingley Dell a secret society whose membership was kept deliberately small and select. Through the help of your Moles, mechanisms were put into place for a more detailed accounting and monitoring of the goings-on there—hidden telephones were installed, then wireless telegraphy, remote radio broadcast facilities, then secreted video cameras—or rather—how should I put this?—devices that may capture a moving and speaking image as photography captures a still picture and which transmits that image through the air to some other place. Are you keeping up with me, gentlemen…and Miss Bocker, or have I hopelessly outpaced you?"

"I think, rather, the latter," admitted Muntle. "But proceed."

"Suffice it to observe that there are this day a large number of ways for those who administer this present-day version of the Tiadaghton Project to keep abreast of a great deal of what you and your fellow citizens do and say, both through devices which transmit your activities and your conversations, and the reports they receive from their agents."

"Yet we are safe to speak here?" asked the vicar looking nervously about. "You will confirm that no such devices have been put into this room?"

Miss Wolf nodded. "As a rule—and it is a rule I have never seen violated—monitoring equipment is installed only in public places."

"And does Dingley Dell still continue to be the hobbyhorse of the very wealthy?" asked Antonia.

"Not so much now as formerly. Many have lost interest and quitted the society. There's a tribe of pygmies, recently removed to an isolated compound in southern Utah, that is drawing a bit of attention from many of our rich members—the lives of transplanted hirsute and squat-legged

African dwarfs being much more entertaining to easily-bored billionaires these days than the now rather prosy and parochial lives of bonnet-wearing, pudding-eating neo-Victorians. Which brings us then to the latest phase of the Project, of which I have not been apprised, and about which, as I earlier mentioned, I know only anecdotally what lies ahead. I should like to think that after the M.P.P.'s and their families have been gotten away, that someone will arrive to make a grand announcement, to lay out a detailed timetable for the evacuation of the valley. I should like to think that continued evacuation would be effected with gentle care and respect, that each Dinglian will be given the requisite vaccinations to guard against those illnesses from which you presently have no natural protection. I should like to think that funds would be allocated for your comfortable resettlement, that some of you will find a home with the Amish or one of the other plain-living Anabaptist denominations. There seem a number of outcomes— *positive* outcomes that do not allow for only pain and heartbreak and—"

"And extermination," said Muntle somberly.

"Yes, I know. I regret that I cannot deny that possibility as well."

"Are these men truly such monsters?" asked Miss Bocker.

"It has happened before," replied Miss Wolf in a tone of sobriety matching that of her interlocutor. "And there is even a word for it. Genocide. It came with the wholesale slaughter of six million Jews in the 1930s and 1940s by a German dictator by the name of Adolf Hitler. There is an older word, as well, that was appropriated for this unthinkable act. The word is 'holocaust.'"

It was quite telling—the fact that Miss Wolf could not give a definitive answer to the question of our future. I was convinced now that she had been placed with deliberate intent into the uninformed darkness. She was, in effect, more like us now than like those from whom she came. Perhaps it was because they could no longer trust her.

My heart had softened towards Miss Ruth Wolf. I would not trade places with her for worlds: fully trusted, fully embraced by no one—not we Dinglians nor the Outland masters for whom she worked. She was adrift.

And she was beautiful.

But she would not be mine.

CHAPTER THE THIRTY-EIGHTH

Friday, July 4, 2003 and Saturday, July 5, 2003

L ater that day, Muntle was dismissed from his office as sheriff of Dingley Dell.

It was Lord Mayor Feenix himself who had informed him of the Petit-Parliament's decision. Feenix came to Muntle's apartments in the Inn-of-Justice, accompanied by the man who was to take his place—or rather the *boy*, for Muntle had lost his position to none other than his lowest deputy, Billy Boldwig, whose behaviour, in spite of the rather grave and humiliating circumstances, was marked by callous exuberance for his new position and for his new lodgings—it being required that Muntle vacate his apartments immediately and the boy registering nothing of Muntle's devastated demeanour, except that he moved slowly.

I did not know any of this at the time. My friend Vincent, being a proud man, confessed to me later that he had been reluctant to tell anyone. When one's professional life comes to a sudden, ignominious end, even the most garrulous of men are apt to keep quietly to themselves.

❧

At dawn the next morning I was awakened by a scream. I thought for a moment that it had been emitted by some wraith within my dream—for I always dreamed heaviest in the hour prior to waking, and at that moment was immersed quite deeply in a goblins' croquet game. (Please don't ask me why, for I have never played it.) I sat up in bed and listened. Muffled voices filtered up from Mrs. Lumbey's dress shop showroom below. I quickly donned my robe, threw open the door to the stairwell that led down to the shop, and hurriedly but cautiously descended the dark stairs (for the sun, though rising, had yet to infiltrate every nook and cranny of the passage).

Mrs. Lumbey stood in the centre of the showroom, wearing her dressing gown, her hands outstretched to coax her frightened apprentice Amy Casby, crouched and quivering in a far corner of the room, to come into her enfolding embrace. The girl quickly consented to Mrs. Lumbey's offer of temporary harbourage and stood for the moment weeping and clutching, but giving no explanation for what could possibly have incited such a fearful outburst.

A moment later, Hannah Pupker appeared. There was genuine concern written upon her face as well for the woman with whom she had formed a loose friendship of circumstance. Gathering the plaits of her own gown in a distempered hand, she darted her eyes about the room to descry the cause of Amy's distress (wondering all the while if her provocative presence here were somehow implicated).

"Speak up, dear girl," said Mrs. Lumbey to her assistant, whilst gently smoothing back the young woman's sleep-tangled hair. "Dry your tears and tell us what has frightened you so."

"It frightens me still, Mrs. Lumbey. *He.* That man there, lying behind the dress rack. See his legs jutting out like those of a corpse?"

The three of us, who had yet to notice the legs, now positioned ourselves to do that very thing. But the legs were no longer simply fixed in their spot; now they *moved.* Behind a row of frocks and gowns a man now seemed to be pulling himself up from a prone orientation into a seated one, his identity masked by the wall of vendible wardrobe in front of him. Once drawn up, the legs disappeared altogether.

"I heard a noise," whispered Amy, her voice quavering. "I thought that it was Mrs. Gallanbile's cat come in through the cellar window. But that is no cat!"

"Whoever is hiding there," I sternly commanded the unseen interloper, "kindly make yourself known this instant."

There ensued the sound of someone struggling to raise himself to his feet. It took a moment for the man of mystery to complete the task and a moment longer for him to step aside of the clothing rack and reveal himself to the four of us.

For a second I felt as if my eyes were playing tricks on me—that it was a ghost standing before me—one come back briefly to commune with the living after a season with the dead. For a brief second I could not believe that my own brother Augustus, holding himself weakly and unsteadily against the pole, which supported one end of the clothing rack, his legs all but buckling beneath him, had materialised into flesh and blood before my very eyes.

"As I live and breathe!" exclaimed Mrs. Lumbey.

"It is my brother Augustus," I said to Miss Casby to calm her fluttered spirits. "He will not harm you." I went to Gus, took him by the arm, and led him to a chair.

"Dear, dear man!" said Mrs. Lumbey. "You look as if you've been trampled by a coach-and-eight, and have lived to tell the story."

"Yes, and I feel exactly the same," replied Gus.

"What is required, you poor dear? Food? Drink? You've taken a little rest through the night upon my showroom floor, but that will not do. When you're able to make the climb, Frederick will take you up to his bed."

Gus nodded. In a broken, crusty voice, he said, "I should very much fancy a longer, more cushioned sleep, for Beyonders know nothing of Eiderdown."

As Gus and I shared a look of fraternal affection which for the moment required no appendance of words, Mrs. Lumbey began to issue instructions; Amy was to put a kettle on for tea and her boarder Hannah was to go to the larder and get bread and butter and cold beef and anything else that would provide her famished-looking visitor needed sustenance.

"You've come back," I said to my brother, not knowing what else at that odd moment to say.

"By the very hardest."

"Where have you been all of these days?"

"First held captive by a mentally-infirm woman in the Outland, then kept enchained by near-mortal illness upon a bed."

"But you must have gotten better or you wouldn't be here," I observed.

Gus nodded. "In the end the woman and her mother did what no other Outlander would have done: they nursed me back to near health and facilitated my return to Dingley Dell. But I am still weak, and weaker still after my return trip."

"And was your son Newman anywhere to be found?" asked Mrs. Lumbey after a slight hesitation.

"Alas. I never got to him. I had hardly any time at all to seek him before the woman took me for her prisoner." Gus turned his gaze to me now, wearing an expression upon his pale, gaunt face of the most tangible species of hopelessness: "Then Newman hasn't—isn't—"

I shook my head. I could not tell the truth to my brother at that moment. The fact of the boy's return had to be carefully, thoughtfully conveyed, or there was no telling what Gus would do in the way of trying to rescue him. I didn't want to see my brother put into Bedlam as well. I would give him no reason to reveal himself and be taken into custody.

Gus released a most heavily freighted sigh and dropt his shoulders. "Yes. I knew it. In my heart I did know it."

"And did you see *nothing* of the Outland, Gus?" asked Mrs. Lumbey, attempting in a purposefully blithe voice to rally my brother by way of conversational distraction.

"Nothing in actuality but the inside of the house where I stopt. I did, however, see a great deal of the Outland, pictorially speaking, through the window of a television."

"What is that?" asked Mrs. Lumbey. "A televizy?"

"I'm too tired to explain. Ask me after I've rested."

"How did you get into my shop?"

"Through a half-open area window to the cellar. So I should not be detected."

"And wise it was that you didn't go to your house," I said. "Or did you?"

Gus shook his head. "Credit your older brother with *some* sense, Freddie."

"You can remain here for as long as you like," said Mrs. Lumbey with a smile of conspiratorial accommodation. "It is become a safe house of sorts already, hasn't it, Frederick?"

I nodded.

And then Mrs. Lumbey explained—as quickly as would still serve the topic—the saga of Hannah Pupker, her discourse ending by the time of the appearance of that same young woman, who bore a platter of every food that she could procure from the Lumbey stores.

Scarcely a half-hour later, I helped Gus up-stairs to my rooms and put him into my bed where he quickly drifted off into needful slumber—but not before he took brief leave to ask me sleepily if I would go to his house and tell Charlotte that he was back in Dingley Dell and that he was safe but that he durst not return to his house. So she must come to see him here.

I sat in a chair and watched my brother sleeping soundly for a minute or two as thoughts raced through my head. When should I tell Gus what I knew about Newman? What should I tell him—for that matter—about all that had taken place during his ten-day sojourn in the Terra Incognita? For events were transpiring more quickly now, and with each new revelation our small world seemed more and more at risk of disappearing forever.

But at least Gus had come home. And that was cause for gratitude and quiet celebration.

When I reached my brother's house, I found my friends Antonia Bocker and Dr. Timberry sitting in the front parlour and speaking in al-most cheerful tones.

"Has Charlotte taken a turn for the better?" I asked.

"She has indeed," said Antonia. "And we have Dr. Timberry and that Beyonder marvel of a nurse, Ruth Wolf, to thank for it."

Timberry, blushing, picked up the thread of Antonia's explanation. "Mrs. Trimmers was having a most terrible and fearful night and I did not wish to simply administer laudanum and see her put out for the next twenty or so hours, so I poked about in the traveling dispensary that Miss Wolf left with me, and found something that the accompanying apoth-ecary's book said was good for distress and unease. She demonstrates none of the negative ancillary effects that generally characterise the Opiates pre-scribed for the same complaint. It is called Xanax, by the bye, and it is most amazing in its efficacy."

"I've brought my maid-of-all-work Harriet to give your sister-in-law a much-needed bath, Trimmers," offered Antonia. "And the ablution seems to be a further lift to her spirits."

"And I have something that will lift Charlotte's spirits even more," I said eagerly. "Gus has returned. He is resting himself in my bedchamber above Mrs. Lumbey's shop."

"My dear Trimmers, I am thrilled beyond words!" Antonia shook her head in joyous disbelief. "In this time of so much to mourn and fear, he has done the impossible: your brother has come back to us all in one piece!" With sudden concern: "I take it Gus is still all in one piece?"

I nodded with a grin.

Antonia resumed: "That he should have returned by his own wits and industry is more than a joy, is it not, Dr. Timberry?"

"Indeed."

"Mulberry," said I, "I would like you to examine Gus at your earliest convenience. To make certain that whilst he is quite exhausted and somewhat malnourished, there is nothing else the matter with him."

"I will have a look at Hannah Pupker, as well, for she has undergone quite a trial at the hands of her father."

But Hannah Pupker's trial was hardly over.

Within two hours the young woman had lost her battle to keep herself from immurement within the malignant walls of Bedlam. The good protective offices of Mrs. Lumbey and the good legal offices of Sheriff Muntle had not been enough to prevent it, and by that point-in-time, Muntle's offices were no longer his to employ anyway.

This we discovered upon my return to Mrs. Lumbey's in the company of Mulberry and Antonia and my sister-in-law Charlotte, who had yet to be told that we were taking her to be reunited with her lost husband Gus so as to prevent onlookers from deducing from her rapturous expression the fact of her beloved's return.

What awaited us when we gained my landlady's shop was nothing to be wished for and everything that had been dreaded: the new chief law enforcement officer of Dingley Dell—the absurdly freckled, red-topped Mr. Boldwig—was at the very moment of our arrival in the midst of transporting a combative, yet wholly frightened Hannah Pupker out the front door of Mrs. Lumbey's shop, as several other men stood close by with folded arms and penetrating, satisfied visages. The men were Hannah's own tyrannical father, Montague Pupker; the dictatorial director of Bedlam, Dr. Arthur Towlinson; the malpractising, malodourous Dr. Fibbetson; and Bedlam's empty-headed orderly Oscar, who stood hard by the open door of the van, which had been requisitioned to convey the young woman to her new address.

Trailing Boldwig and his captive out the door was a most distressed

Mrs. Lumbey and her equally discomposed assistant Amy Casby.

"What is this?" I enquired, interposing myself between the sheriff and the van.

"No business of yours," replied Boldwig with a cracking voice that had yet to settle upon a consistent adult pitch.

"Where's Muntle?"

"Cashiered and put on quarter pension on account of his incompetency," offered Pupker. "Now you are blocking the way of our new sheriff, so kindly step aside."

I directed my next question to the new Boy Sheriff: "Where is Muntle at this *moment*?"

"Clearing out his lodgings at the Inn-of-Justice so that I can move myself in. He's being very slow about it, by the bye. Slower than even those apricot eaters Mr. Pupker just had me throw out of his mews."

"Is this true, Pupker?" I asked. "You have evicted Harry Scadger and his family?"

Pupker nodded. "I try to please my brother-in-law when I can."

"Now, Mr. Trimmers," pursued Billy, "if you do not suffer me to do my duty here, I will have no choice but to make your arrest the second official act of my brand new tenure as sheriff of this Dell."

I glanced at Hannah, who seemed at the moment to know not what to do, for she didn't want to go with Boldwig—this much was clear—but did not know how one might successfully contest such a thing.

It was Mrs. Lumbey who spoke next: "I'll ask it again, Pupker: under what charge is your poor daughter being arrested?"

"She *isn't* being arrested, Mrs. Lumbey," replied Dr. Towlinson snappishly. "The sheriff is merely assisting me in transporting her to Bethlehem Hospital."

"By whose order?" asked Antonia, stepping forward, and delivering her question in an equally clipped fashion.

"By *my* request," retorted Montague Pupker.

"And under the signed order of Judge Fitz-Marshall," Dr. Towlinson added. "I have the order here if anyone wishes to examine it. The commitment is perfectly legal. A commission of lunacy was convened last night and the judge ruled that the girl should be consigned with all due expedition to the hospital for treatment."

"Who in attendance at that hearing spoke on behalf of Hannah's own wishes?" I asked.

Dr. Fibbetson, who was given to speaking in a flubbery way as if he were a squirrel carrying winter nuts about in his mouth, replied on behalf of his medical colleague, "The girl has no say in the matter. Do we forestall treating a man with boils until we should fully interview the carbuncles themselves? I think not."

Mrs. Lumbey could not restrain herself: "Dr. Fibbetson, you are a blithering, lip-flapping fool!"

"Bless my heart and eyebrows, I have never in my life been so openly disparaged!"

"There's more of that to come, you chuckle-headed marvel of medical malfeasance!"

"Hold!" enjoined Dr. Timberry. "Dr. Fibbetson, you and our colleague Dr. Towlinson know that there are two sides to a sanity dispute and you have done Miss Pupker here a grievous injustice by not hearing her side or having that side advocated by another party. I recall from my training, and I believe that it was you who taught it to me, Fibbetson, that lunacy is a difficult affliction to diagnose, and for this reason every caution is customarily taken to make certain that the rights of the patient to liberty are not errantly abridged."

"I cannot remember saying any such thing!" protested Fibbetson.

"You can't recall what you had for breakfast this morning, you doddering old fool!" Mrs. Lumbey would not check herself, and continued to vilify the appalled and affronted surgeon standing before her. There was a look of serene admiration upon the face of Antonia, who was rather enjoying the plucky spirit of her inveterate adversary. "It is *you* who should be put away, you lunatic medical incompetent, rather than this poor girl who has done nothing worse than find herself at odds with a dictatorial father. I extend that assessment to you as well, Dr. Towlinson, for Bedlam is become the equivalent of punishing prison for the human mind."

"My dear Mrs. Lumbey, are you quite through?" asked Pupker, his nostrils flaring.

"For the nonce." Mrs. Lumbey folded her arms and jutted her chin in a show of holding her ground.

Through pursed, indignant lips, Pupker continued, "Because I will not permit another black word from you that impugns my character or the character of my friends and associates."

"And what do you intend to do about it? Have *me* thrown into Bedlam as well for mental deficiency?" Mrs. Lumbey's cheeks were puffed out and reddened by the temperature of her anger. "I see nothing here but a father's attempt to punish his daughter for no longer wishing to live beneath his roof." Mrs. Lumbey now addressed herself to all the rest of us: "We all know what a patriarchal despot this man is. If I were his daughter I should have fled the family manse at the age of four." Mrs. Lumbey was scrupulous in avoiding the larger reason for Hannah's present travails—that she had seen things she was not supposed to see and now must be put away to prevent her speaking of them too widely and in a way that would produce difficult consequences for her father and others in his league.

"I'll no longer remain here to be so maliciously slandered," said Pupker to Sheriff Boldwig. "Put my daughter in the van and let us be on our way."

Boldwig nodded and tugged upon the arm of Hannah Pupker. Hannah wrenched her arm away and fell back into the clasping embrace of Mrs. Lumbey. "I implore you, Papa," said Hannah, regarding her father from over the shoulder of her temporary protector, "not to put me into Bedlam. You know in your heart that there is nothing wrong with me. Don't do this cruel thing to me, I pray!"

"It is for your own good, my daughter," said Mr. Pupker in so indifferent a tone that one would think he was reading words from a book. "Your mother and I want to see you made well and this is the only way that your health and future happiness can be secured. Now go with Boldwig and let us end this ridiculous spectacle."

"Step aside, Trimmers," said Dr. Towlinson in concurrence. "And you, too, Dr. Timberry, if you do not wish for me to petition for the revocation of your brand new medical license for conduct unbecoming a physician. Let us end this unnecessary intervention on behalf of this poor young woman. Suffer the sheriff to pass with the girl, or I shall ask him to arrest you."

I didn't budge. Moreover, I took a step to put myself even more obdurately between Boldwig and Hannah Pupker. Timberry did the same, coming to stand to my right, just as Antonia positioned herself upon my left, so that the three of us became a triumvirate of bricks in a single wall of opposition. All the while, Mrs. Lumbey wrapt her arms round Hannah to do her own part in opposing this unjustified removal of her adopted ward.

The silent deadlock lasted for nearly a minute, for neither I nor my friend Dr. Timberry nor my friend Antonia Bocker was willing to step aside—even if our refusal to do so should result in our arrest—so that a conniving, unloving father and his accommodating accomplices, including a newly-sworn sheriff who wasn't more than a mediocrity in every aspect of his former deputyship—all members of that secret fraternity of inside agents who would save themselves at the expense of the rest of us—should not take an innocent young woman and subject her to a most undeserved fate. It was an offence and an outrage that Muntle should be removed from his office (on what I would later learn was the wholly manufactured charge of shrieval misconduct based upon his unauthorised trip to the Chowser School), but what was being done to Hannah Pupker—innocent of innocents—was tragedy in exponential terms.

Hannah finally broke the silence herself with these words addressed to her father: "Papa. You know exactly why you wish to have me put away, and I will not say it here, but you know that it has nothing to do with the question of my sanity. It is a ploy—a ploy that has been born of a scheme concocted by you and Mama to protect yourselves from public disclosure of certain acts you have perpetrated and the prevention of whatever consequences may rise from them. I know now that *you*, Sheriff Boldwig, benefit from this silence as well, or else you would not be so complaisant and obliging with my father. I know that *you*, Dr. Towlinson, are also in some way in collusion with my father or you should not be so ready to do his bidding through your medical offices. Likewise, Judge Fitz-Marshall can only be of that same covert fraternity. I know not what it is nor what it does but I do know that I am now to be sacrificed to it, simply for having gotten too close to whatever secrets it keeps. Sheriff Boldwig: I will not submit to being put into a deep and cooperative sleep, nor will I agree to whatever else should befall me in that house of horrors that Dr. Towlinson superintends. Subsequently, I say to you the following: that you will have to strike me down with a heavy truncheon before I will suffer myself to be trundled off with you."

With that bold declaration, Boldwig turned to Pupker and Pupker turned to Towlinson and all heads nodded almost in synchronicity, and then the new sheriff reached into his satchel and produced something that had never before been seen in all of the 113 years of Dingley Dell: a gun. More specifically, a revolving pistol.

I stared at the evil Outland weapon, half-curious and half-frightened out of countenance to find it here in Dingley Dell after so long an absence.

I turned to look at Pupker. "In all the years of Muntle's tenure as sheriff of this dale, Pupker, he was able to uphold the law through use of his wits and billy club alone, and rarely did he even have much cause for employment of the latter. This whelp of a sheriff has been in the employ of the Petit-Parliament for only a few hours, and lo! he cannot even bring a frightened young woman, half his size, to heed his authority without deploying this implement of modern brutality. Are there others, Pupker? Other guns, other twenty-first century weapons that you have had brought here to maintain the power of your cabal? If you will authorise their use upon your own daughter, is there anyone upon whom you will *not* use these weapons to keep all of us in a state of subservience to your wishes?"

It was clear to me now. At that very moment it was become translucently clear what was happening: the Dell was to be put under strict martial controul to maintain order until July 15, the day that each member of the Petit-Parliament and those who closely orbited that nefarious body would climb to the top of the Summit of Exchange and turn and look for the last time upon the valley that had been their home for all of their years. Dingley Dell was to be kept placid and quiet in its valedictory days by whatever harsh measures would do the trick. Those who were ignorant were to be kept ignorant. But those who were coming to see the way of things would be put under restraint, tossed into gaol cells, strapped into strait-waistcoats, or perhaps even shot squarely between the eyes (the most efficient means of acquiescence yet devised!). With the removal of Sheriff Muntle there was no law left in the land that did not comport with the self-serving objectives of the Petit-Parliament, for laws could be made up exigently as things went along—the needs of that body being narrowly focused upon how best to preserve the peace (at whatever the cost) so that a smooth and tidy departure could be effectuated for the bastard Bashaws of Dingley Dell.

The way of things was made even clearer to me in that next moment when the trembling, clammy Boy Sheriff's finger accidentally pulled the trigger and the gun was fired, the thunderous crack of its discharge echoing off all of the buildings in the vicinity of Mrs. Lumbey's shop, its bullet streaking past my ear and shattering into thousands of little pieces the show-window glass behind me.

I heard Amy Casby cry out (as she dropt herself into a little ball upon the ground), and Charlotte make a similar, more deep-throated cry. I heard uninditable epithets stream from the mouth of the window's owner. I heard Antonia Bocker murmur, "madmen" in a deep underbreath. And I heard most pronounced of all (though the words did not rise in volume any louder than anything else) Hannah Pupker say that she would go, without further objection, to Bethlehem Hospital upon Highbury Fields, to keep us all from bloodshed. "I will not have my friends made dead to keep you from tying me to a bed and sedating me," she said to Dr. Towlinson in capitulation, though her tone was that of bitter imprecation.

Boldwig put the gun away. Pupker allowed himself at last to take in full breath. His startled face and indeed the equally startled countenance of Dr. Towlinson had said that neither man had intended for the gun to be fired. It was merely a prop in the little play—a means to an end. Perhaps it would have worked its business without the shot, but that was now past, and its aim had been achieved nonetheless (although its literal aim could very well have produced the death of one or more of us).

"I cannot afford to have this window replaced," repined Mrs. Lumbey in near tears. "The glazier charges a fortune and I don't have it."

"I will pay for it, dear," whispered Antonia with a hand of commiseration resting upon my landlady's shoulder.

"Thank you, Antonia. You are a treasure."

Had the two women finally ended their long feud? It appeared so.

"I will hold the both of you personally responsible should anything happen to Miss Pupker," I assailed Pupker and Towlinson as Hannah was being led by Boldwig to the van.

Hannah took another couple of steps and then stopt. "I will go to Bedlam but only on the condition that I do not have to ride in that thing which looks to me like the tumbrel which conveyed Sydney Carton to the guillotine in *A Tale of Two Cities*. If you do not agree to my request, then you will have to shoot me."

There followed a hasty conference amongst the three older men and the freckled boy (the Bedlam turnkey Oscar being excluded), during which I exchanged a brave smile with Hannah, who seemed far less fearful now than she had been moments before. Somehow she had a found a measure of courage that I hoped would sustain her through the dark days that lay ahead.

"You have only ten days to endure it, Hannah," I whispered, "and then they will all be gone and we will have you back."

"Stop exchanging confidences with the prisoner!" enjoined the sheriff in his squeaking pubescent voice.

"Is Hannah Pupker now a criminal?" exclaimed Mrs. Lumbey, with blistering stridence.

"Criminal? Of course not!" Boldwig sputtered. "I misspoke. She is a lunatic. Not a prisoner but a detained lunatic. That is all."

"And that is quite enough as it is!" declared the "lunatic's" father. "Such shame has this ungrateful minx brought down upon her family. Very well, Hannah, you may walk to the hospital. Dr. Towlinson and I have agreed that it should do you no harm, though this promenade before our neighbours will be a most mortifying blot upon our fine Pupker name!"

"Yet," returned Hannah in an angry underbreath, "as I have come to regard myself as no longer a member of your family and carrier of the Pupker name, I shall not care a straw. In fact, Mr. Pupker, I own only the most contemptuous feelings toward you for what you seek to do to me. Yes, *Mr. Pupker,* to whom I no longer maintain even the most reedy of family allegiance."

With a nod of the head by Dr. Towlinson, Oscar was bade to take the reins of the chestnut mare that pulled the van and to be on his way. Doctors Towlinson and Fibbetson joined the Bedlam minion upon the box, and without speaking another word the three rolled away, leaving Pupker and Boldwig to walk along either side of the criminal who was purported to be a lunatic but was, in fact, only a frightened young woman who had found a stalwart side to herself for which she was to be most highly commended by the allies she left behind.

CHAPTER THE THIRTY-NINTH

Saturday, July 5, 2003

My brother Gus could not help himself.

He had watched the siege and then the capture of Hannah Pupker—had observed it all from a peeping spot behind the curtain of one of the windows of my up-stairs rooms, and then had crept down the stairs and stood behind a Cheval glass in the dress shop showroom and was there situated so that when Charlotte entered the room after all had grown quiet and Hannah had gone, he could step out and take her by the hands and kiss her upon the lips and dry those tears that would flow so freely to see him returned.

But it did not happen exactly that way. Gus stepped out and Charlotte promptly fainted away. However, it took hardly any time at all to revive her, and her cheeks were quickly thereafter flooded with those anticipated tears, and husband and wife—kept several days asunder by the most trying and frightful circumstances—could not now be wrenched apart for worlds, as their loving embrace was far too strong.

Charlotte urged her husband to come with her to their house, but was quickly dissuaded. It was too dangerous to risk his being seen, and so this was to be his address for the time being and no one must know that he was here (besides those who knew it already and swore not to reveal the fact to another soul.)

"Then I'll come to stop here as well, to be at my husband's side," said

Charlotte. "Frederick, you will have to find another place to sleep, for your older brother and I are now laying claim to your bed."

"And I am happy to give it up to you," said I.

We repaired to Mrs. Lumbey's breakfast parlour, where we gathered about the table: Gus and Charlotte, and Antonia and Timberry, Mrs. Lumbey and her assistant Amy and I. We drank tea and ate sweet seed cake, and cheese and celery, and Gus hungrily fell to a dish of kidneys and the remnant carcass of the roast fowl that had been Mrs. Lumbey's supper the night before, and some anchovy toast drowned in egg sauce, whilst I breakfasted on a basin of mutton broth, and Antonia and Timberry shared a slab of potted ham and then three or four raspberry tarts. Amy nibbled upon a morsel of cheese, as would a finicky mouse, whilst Mrs. Lumbey finished the morning's porridge, and then we all had a peppermint drop and pronounced the meal an unqualified success.

Gus was coaxed by Mrs. Lumbey into telling some of what he had seen and experienced in the Outland. He spoke for a few moments on the topic before I interrupted him. "I'm sorry, Gus, but I cannot hear the end to this story. My mind is too much on Harry Scadger and his family now turned out from their new home. I must go and find them."

"I'll go with you," said Timberry, "to see how young Flora is doing."

"What is this most sudden interest in a Scadger?" asked Gus, without sharpness but nevertheless with a free-and-easy manner that reminded me that I'd yet to tell Gus of his connexion by blood to Harry and his children.

"It is this, Augustus: Harry Scadger, the second oldest of the Scadger brothers, is your half-brother. Our father was also *his* father. I haven't time to tell you the details of how this came to be. You must, for now, simply accept it. We have a half-brother. And we have a half-sister-in-law and several half-nephews and nieces, and all, I fear, are put in some jeopardy now by their expulsion, and I must know if they'll be safe."

"A Scadger—our brother? I find it almost too incredible to believe!" said Gus.

A darkness fell upon Charlotte's face at that moment. I knew with certainty the reason for it: Newman. Gus noted the change in his wife's expression as well, and as Gus would often do, he turned a sad reflection into something that must have a culpable author. As often would be the case with my brother, I became that author.

"But no more incredible," he continued, "than to think that you have now substituted these half nephews and nieces for the one nephew-in-full now apparently banished altogether from your thoughts."

"You cannot believe that, Gus!" I earnestly rejoined.

Antonia rose from the table and beckoned me with a crooked finger to join her in the passage. When we had both assured ourselves that a confidence or two could pass between us without being overheard, she whispered sagely: "Frederick, your brother and sister-in-law are in great need of hope about their lost son. Perhaps you should tell them where you believe Newman to be, to give their minds some small measure of ease. It's the right thing to do, you know that it is."

"And my impulsive brother will take this information and promptly put himself in the way of God-only-knows-what sort of danger through a reckless attempt to effect Newman's rescue. He will—as a result of this fool's errand—find himself likewise enchained within that place, and who knows what will happen to Newman in consequence? Perhaps to prove that Newman hasn't been there all along, he will be made to disappear altogether and for good. It is a risk I dare not take, so I must keep Gus and Charlotte in the dark about it for a while longer, for everyone's good."

"And yet…"

"How you've softened, Antonia."

"I haven't softened. I may not be a sensipath, but I am still fully capable of feeling in my breast what it is like to be put asunder from one greatly loved. I am as human as you are, Trimmers."

"I never said elseways. I simply—"

"I concede that your argument is the stronger. Let us suspend this discussion. There is silence in the breakfast parlour as all are no doubt straining to hear what we're saying."

I forbore telling Gus and Charlotte about where I believed that their son was being kept. Timberry and I excused ourselves and started off for the apricot grove, where I hoped to find my half-brother Harry, reaffiliated by necessity of circumstance with his other half-brothers.

Upon reaching the grove, Timberry and I were received with brusqueness and calculated indifference by Harry Scadger's oldest brother Sol. "Harry ain't been here," he said, poking a whittled twig casually between his dingy teeth. "Didn't know he and the wife and the kidlings was evicted. Could've told him you get nothin' from them high-handed snakes and swindlers that you don't got to give back or you ain't a-goin' to have to pay for in the long run. We'll take him back if he comes to the grove, but I figure he's got too much pride to slink back to the likes of us now."

The brother who had been resting upon a deadfall log now uprose, turned without ceremony, and walked away.

Before Timberry and I began our return trip to Milltown, I wanted a moment to look about. It had been a good while since I had last visited the apricot grove, and I noticed that there was a bit more of the Scadger presence emplaced there. The settlement had become a small hamlet of sorts, composed of old, weather-rotted deal wood shacks appointed with castoff rubbish-pile appurtenances to create some semblance of domesticity. Here was a rustic tinker's table and over there a weaving place for some of the women, with half-completed baskets and straw hats strewn about. Most members of the clan were doubtlessly off at this moment harvesting salad weed, for the Scadgers had become adept at finding nutritious wild greens to put upon a plate that anyone else would extirpate as an inedible garden nuisance.

Our delay in withdrawing from this spot was quickly rewarded by the appearance in the distance of Harry's brother Zephaniah, who waved to us and called my name to detain me as he ran toward us.

After raising a hand for permission to fetch his breath once he had gained us, Zephaniah Scadger finally exhaled: "My brother Sol said you were here. He told me what happened to Harry. You'll find him beneath the Westminster Bridge, I wager, but that ain't the reason I require to speak to you."

"What is it? Oh, Timberry, this is Zephaniah Scadger. Zephaniah, this is Dr. Timberry, the most recent addition to the medical fraternity of Dingley Dell."

"Pleased to make your acquaintance. My brother Sol—he didn't tell you about the deputies comin' by this morning, now did he?"

I shook my head.

"I need your view of things, Mr. Trimmers. Now, you know better than most the way of things, so I ask you this: they says we're to leave the grove by mid-week. Now, they've been a-sayin' this for quite some time now, and we give it no never-mind. But it's a new sheriff now, they say—one what ain't a'goin' to abide our staying here the way the last one—that Muntle— did. Now as them deputies was leavin', one of them says something of a confidential nature that one of my kidlings hears, and she tells it back to me and my brothers. Them two deputies, now they be talkin' one to another about what's goin' to happen when we all get moved into the middle of the Dell—when all of us on the edge gets pushed in with everybody else."

"Zephaniah, I'm sorry, but I don't quite understand what you're trying to tell me."

"They's goin' to light it all on fire, Mr. Trimmers. This place—the Chowser School, Blackheath—everything along the edges of the Dell."

"*Who*, Zephaniah?"

"They's callin' them the 'Enforcers.'"

"The Enforcers?"

"My brothers and me—we don't scare too easy, but we do worry for our families. That's why we's armin' ourselves with the bows and arrows and such-like to protect ourselves, when they come with the torches."

I shook my head in disbelief. Timberry was equally staggered. "I've heard nothing about this," I said helplessly.

"Here's what my brother Mel he says. It's his theory. He says they's gettin' ready to bring an end to Dingley Dell. But first they got to get us all into one place."

Timberry now interposed, "I don't quite understand, Mr. Scadger. Upon what evidence is your brother basing this theory of his?"

"I tell you now but you cannot let on to the new sheriff what you know."

"Why should I—or Mr. Trimmers here—have reason to betray such a confidence?"

"If you're a Scadger, doctor, you learn not to trust nobody. I guess it's come time, though, to put a little faith into *somebody*, and I think that Mr. Trimmers, he done a little good for us, and you being his friend—now I make bold to tell you both: we've seen encampments—in the eastern wood."

"Encampments?" I replied. "What do you mean, Zephaniah?"

"Outlanders with guns. Waiting. We've seen more than one of them camps. We're stealthy in the wood, can move ourselves through it with our eyes closed. But with open eyes—this is what we see. They're gatherin' themselves for some wicked purpose, no doubt about it."

"Inside or outside the fence?"

"Inside. That's cheeky, hum?"

"Quite," I replied. "Zephaniah, you and your clan cannot stay here. If the deputies don't succeed in removing you, the Outlanders are apparently prepared to come in from the woods and route you themselves."

"Sol and Mel and my other brothers—we've made our decision. We're goin' to take a stand."

"But that would be suicide," countered Timberry.

"This orchard is all that we have. This *valley* is all that we have. Why should we move into town only to die in whatever way they've done chosen for all the rest of you? We make our stand here, that's what we do—right here where our Papa put down his stakes many year ago."

I could not argue with Zephaniah's reasoning, though it was blind clan pride that largely motivated it. I gave no response. Nor did Timberry know what to say. However, it wasn't necessary for either of us to reply. What was required of me were answers to a very specific line of questions, put next by Zephaniah Scadger in all earnestness and with no small measure of concern.

"Is Dingley Dell coming to its end, Mr. Trimmers? And for what reason? Have we displeased the powers that rule this valley?"

"What do you know of the powers that rule Dingley Dell?"

"Nothin' that I could say for certain. But I know that they watch us. That they laugh at us. We've done heard them talk about us in the midnight encampments. How we're like little string puppets. How we don't be human. My clan has lived for many years on the edge of Dingley Dell. Here is where a man is closest to the Outlanders. Here is where a man gets the strongest feeling that the path we're on ain't one of our own making. Is Dingley Dell coming to its end, Mr. Trimmers? And why is such a thing to be?"

"I won't dissemble, Zephaniah. I believe now, as do several others with whom I affiliate, that our days are indeed numbered, but the best course is not to keep ourselves divided, but to band together to fight whatever is being planned for us."

Zephaniah shook his head. "It ain't possible. Ain't nobody but yourself would band with a Scadger. We're on our own. Always have been, always will be—right to the bloody end."

As Zephaniah had predicted, we found Harry and Matilda and their five children beneath the Westminster Bridge, settled uneasily amongst the People-Under-the-Bridge. We gathered them up and conducted them to the empty apartments above Antonia's stationery shop. She was waiting for my brother and his family with boiling water for the washtub and clean linens and open arms.

I related to Harry and Antonia what I had learnt from Harry's brother Zephaniah. A dark, foreboding silence supervened—the sort of quiet that only intensified the fear of what was being carefully and diabolically arranged for all of us, Scadger and non-Scadger alike. And what was to become of us in the end.

CHAPTER THE FORTIETH

Monday, July 7, 2003

Ruth Wolf stood beneath the strange tree-like steel tower that the Dinglian metals-sculptor Waldengarver had erected upon the grounds of Bedlam asylum two years earlier. It bore a strong resemblance to four other Dinglian towers whose construction offended the eye of most who viewed them, but would never be removed without plenary Parliamentary approval. Waldengarver had been commissioned by his brother Lord Mayor Feenix to put up all five of the "steel trees"—one of which stood atop the Northern Ridge near the Summit of Exchange and another of which was erected upon an outcropping of the Southern Coal Ridge, where coal-dusty collier boys and girls climbed and begrimed it to adorn its metallic branches with Christmas ornaments and garland of their own impoverished construction, giving at least this one tower amongst the five a look of near-festivity during the happy holiday season.

Ruth Wolf stood beneath the oddly welded Bedlam tower for good reason. This was the best place to engage the secretly-purposed tower to transmit the signal emanating from her portable wireless telephone—to direct it to the ear of her colleague in the underground rescuing league, Phillips the jeweller. The tower did the equally serviceable job of returning Phillips' reciprocating signal back to her, bouncing it from one tower to the next like invisible saltatory voltaic arcs. The magic in the transaction allowed the two to speak as if they were standing within natural earshot of one another.

"Hello," said Ruth Wolf into the tiny rectangular telephone.

"Thank God you called, Ruth. I was starting to get worried." It wasn't a tiny rectangular pencil-case of a telephone into which Phillips was speaking, but the voice-amplifying mouthpiece of a much larger tethered variety of telephonic device. The apparatus sat upon Phillips' desk in the cluttered back office of his jewellry store.

"Things have been crazy," Ruth replied. "They've summoned me to to-night's hospital board meeting. I have every reason to believe that I'm about to get canned. I have to get out of here, Phillips. I went to talk to Chivery up in the attic room just a few minutes ago. He didn't make much sense, but he gave me something. It sent a chill down my spine. It's a memo from Michelena Martin to Patty Kreis. Does the name Martin ring a bell?"

"I know that she works pretty high up in the New York office. Corporate Command, inside Flatiron, right?"

"Co-director of Victorian Research, actually. But she doesn't do that anymore. She resigned in late May. Guess what she's doing now, Phillips?"

"Drinking Mai Tais at some Club Med?"

"Think: dust. Think: biting it."

"I don't get it. Why would they kill her?"

"She'd obviously become a risk to them in her retirement. So she had to be taken out. But here's a nice little fun fact for you, Phillips: they didn't take as much care at all in how they disposed of her body. She and her briefcase, which must have been latch-chained to her wrist, washed right up on the bank of the Thames, deep in the heart of Dingley Dell. That's where one of the Scadger kids and Professor Chivery found her. Chivery got the printed copy of a fairly damning exchange of memos she'd been carrying around with her, and put it right into my hand—how it's all going down. They're going to blow up Tiadaghton Dam, Phillips, and flood the valley."

"Jesus Christ."

"Hey, look, it's time for me to grab Bevan and the two of us get the hell out of here. Otherwise they're going to kill me, Phillips. They're going to fire me and then they're going to kill me to keep me quiet, to keep from mucking up their final act. And who knows where in bloody hell *my* body turns up."

"All right, now. Calm down. Let's think this through."

"First me. Then everybody else in this Godforsaken place. Look, I should go. I can't—someone's going to find me here. I'll call you again when I get to a more secure location—I'm guessing the top of the Southern Coal Ridge, before Bevan and I make our descent. Phillips, I'm rethinking what we talked about the night we brought Newman back here. If my days are numbered then I'm not going out without making a little noise. I've gathered more than enough evidence to make a rock solid case against them, against their whole operation."

"And I've also given this some more thought myself, Ruthie, and I'm not so sure anymore. Spilling the beans on the Tiadaghton Project—that whole shit-load of beans, honey—"

"But if we can get to the right people fast enough—if we can get some protection for ourselves—"

"And just who are the right people? This thing goes all the way up to the White House, Ruthie. The Pentagon's had a place at the Tiadaghton table for the last sixty years. This isn't us with the slingshot facing off with Goliath. It's David and holy frickin' Godzilla. I'm not a young man, Ruthie. I've lived my three score and ten and then some. But I still have no great desire to throw myself upon a live grenade, especially if there's a chance that we don't end up saving a single life at the end of the day. You know how hard it's going to be to get this evidence to somebody who isn't already compromised by the Project."

"Not everybody's in on it, Phillips. Congress has always been kept deliberately in the dark. You get it to the right Congressman—"

"It doesn't matter, Ruthie. You've still got a global conspiracy here over a century in the making—run by some of the richest men in the world and with the tacit approval of nearly every occupant of the White House since Taft. And history records what happened to those who didn't want to play ball. They poisoned Harding, took shots at FDR and Ford to bring them in line, and as for that Boy Scout from Massachusetts—the one man with balls enough to try to put Tiadaghton out of business—well, history tells us exactly what happened to him in gory, Technicolor detail. Look, let's take this thing a step at a time. First, let's work on getting you someplace where nobody will find you. F.Y.I., honey: I've called a meeting of the Rescuers for Monday. I've been wanting to tell you: we're going to disband. Our job is done. Don't come to that meeting. It's too dangerous. Get yourself lost, baby. I mean it."

"Phillips?"

"Yeah?"

"I think they're getting sloppy. Or else they've maybe got a couple of inside subversives who've taken to monkeying around with the machine."

"How do you mean?"

"I mean that the Project never should have allowed a dead body to go floating down the Double Pine like that. I mean that I'm seeing other examples of how they've started to drop the ball. I think the Project is starting to unravel—not in a big way—just little threads being teazed out here and there—people who might have found out that Tiadaghton's about to be shut down, and they've decided to engage in a little light sabotage while they're still able. Or it could just be plain Project burnout: folks who've simply stopt giving a shit about their jobs."

"And are you saying that this kind of climate could be of benefit to us?"

"Maybe in the short run. Openings get created. Opportunities suddenly present themselves. The members of the Fortnightly Poetry League can certainly speak to that. But these chinks could also serve as a wakeup call for Flatiron to go get themselves a much bigger pail of Spackle. Look, I have to go."

"Go. Be safe."

"I'll do my best."

Lord Mayor Feenix was the last to arrive. The mayor of Milltown and Health Minister of Dingley Dell was a man in his middle years who compensated for his diminutive stature through daily stints with the dumbbells, the medicine ball, and the Indian clubs. The result of this rigourous exercise regimen was a thick muscularity that gave the mayor a brutish, bulldog look, marked by a wide, full neck, and limbs that seemed more muttonish than human.

The Bulldog surveyed the faces of those gathered within the wood-paneled room that served as convening place for the Administrative and Advisory Board of Bethlehem Hospital upon Highbury Fields (the informal appellation "Bedlam" never being uttered between these dignified walls). He gave deferent nods both to his equals and to his inferiors as he took his place at the top of the conference table.

"Good evening, gentlemen, and a good evening to you as well, Miss

Wolf," said Feenix in a voice that was two parts croak and one part glottal abrasion. "I understand, madam, that your presence has been requested for a very important purpose that we shall take up shortly. Ah, Sir Dabber, yours is an old and warmly familiar visage. I'm curious to know what brings our senior-most emeritus member to this table after so long an absence. I am, however, even more curious to know why you've brought Mr. Trimmers along with you. Is there a piece for that scandal-mongering *Delver* that its favourite reporter wishes to write, perhaps on the subject of the recondite workings of our mysterious organisation? For if such be the case, I must caution the gentleman against pursuing it. Perhaps he isn't aware that there exists an embargo against the publication of any of the particulars of our confidential proceedings."

"Mr. Trimmers doesn't wish to write about Bethlehem, Lord Mayor," interposed Sir Dabber, whilst patting a handkerchief against his freshly perspiring forehead. "I have engaged him to indite minutes of this meeting for the purpose of retaining a permanent and official—albeit private—record of our proceedings."

"I see," piped Lord Mayor Feenix, nearly grinning. "Now what do we think of that, Dr. Towlinson?"

Dr. Towlinson did not think much of it at all: "We've never had need of a permanent record before. The idea is ludicrous." The doctor's tone was sharp, his manner defensive.

Sir Dabber turned to face the hospital administrator who sat to his right. "Ludicrous, Dr. Towlinson? To do that which the Petit-Parliament has itself been doing for the last one hundred years? If this body purports to have any legitimacy whatsoever, then let a written record document its proceedings."

"Do you think our memories are going, Dabber," retorted Towlinson, "that we should not be able to recall what is discussed at these meetings?"

"It is not simply what is discussed, Towlinson, but what is being planned and schemed and brought to fruition to the detriment of this institution and its inmates. I want the record to clearly shew who is responsible for every decision made here." Dabber sat back in his chair and folded his arms across his ample belly.

"I am without words!" ejaculated Dr. Fibbetson in a sudden, horrified swoon.

"Notify the press," riposted Dabber, "for that is something worthy of publication."

There was a bit of laughter about the room that could not be helped. Even Chairman Feenix smiled at Fibbetson's expense. Sir Dabber continued, "By the bye, Dr. Towlinson, Frederick Trimmers is an excellent stenographer—perhaps the best in the Dell."

"Mr. Trimmers is also an agitator," opined the head of Bedlam, bending his dark gaze full upon me.

"He is no more agitator than you or I," countered my defender with an even more assiduous application of the handkerchief to his wet brow. "Moreover, gentlemen, I was once the chairman of this hospital board and can say that in my lengthy tenure there was much greater attendance given to institutional openness than I see now. The place is now become a castle keep of concealment and huggery-muggery. And as this is a publicly-funded asylum, I, for one, will no longer brook the argument that what takes place here is not the business of every citizen in the Dell."

"A rather stunning indictment, Sir Dabber, if I may say so," pronounced the Lord Mayor, leaning back and locking and then unlocking the muscular fingers of his muscular paws in a thoughtfully amused manner. Several heads within the room nodded in staunch agreement—these heads belonging to the four other men present besides Dr. Towlinson and the medical mal-practitioner Egbert Fibbetson: three M.P.P.'s of inconsequential supernumerary status, and the eminently redoubtable Judge Fitz-Marshall. Those keeping their heads in dissenting abeyance were Sir Dabber, his exigently-enlisted amanuensis Frederick Trimmers, and the intrepid Ruth Wolf, who at this moment was about the business of sedulously avoiding my look, lest anyone in the room read complicity in our familiar glances.

Ruth feigned a casual air that only thinly mantled her true feelings of trepidation. For she knew as well as did I that there must be some dire reason for her summoned presence here, and the longer she was made to wait to hear what it was, the harder it would be to bear the suspense.

"Yet," responded Sir Dabber to the Lord Mayor's flyaway characterisation of his explanation, "there is too much that has taken place in this hospital as of late about which the public has been kept purposefully uninformed. I take up, first, the matter of the egregious relegation of some of our most needful inmates to deplorable quarters within the cellar."

Dr. Towlinson scarcely gave Dabber time to finish his charge before putting forth his defence: "The refurbishing of the upstairs rooms obviously took longer than had been anticipated, but you should be glad to

know that the renovation will soon be complete, and that all of the inmates who have been kept below-stairs in temporary quarters will, in fact,
be removed to more suitable rooms shortly. And surely, Sir Dabber, you
know that you need only have asked, and better transient accommodations
would have been promptly arranged for your son. It was your choice and
your choice alone not to pursue the matter, your having put the boy largely
out of sight and out of mind for yea these ten years past."

Upon this allegation of parental neglect (and the rather flippant and
disrespectful manner in which it was tossed out), Sir Dabber leapt to his
feet with both fists doubled up. "Mendacity!" he thundered.

I who was seated on the other side of him now rose to calm and quell
his erupting anger. Others about the room got quickly to their own feet,
desirous, apparently, of not being fixed to a chair should there be hurlings
of fists and other things made rudely airborne. As Sir Dabber did not, in
fine, do much more than simply repeat the word "mendacity" in a tone that
would put it amongst the most insulting of epithets, it was easy for me to
get him back into his seat and by extension the rest of the Board members
to return to their own berths about the table. Ruth Wolf, for her part, did
not rise but, instead, receded slightly into her chair as if wishing to disappear altogether.

"Take up your pen, Trimmers," said Sir Dabber, " and make note of the
following items for discussion at this month's Star Chamber."

"Oh how he jests!" cawed Dr. Fibbetson.

"Just who is the current chairman of the board of this hospital,
Dabber?" queried a suddenly no longer sunny Lord Mayor Feenix.

The question was left unanswered as Sir Dabber with restored equanimity and sober resolve launched himself into a rather remarkable list of
everything that was the matter with present-day Bedlam, in the sense of
both gross incompetence and deliberate malefaction. "Visiting days and
hours are purposefully truncated to curtail time spent by inmates with
their loved ones. Inmates are subjected to brutal, almost animal-like conditions—yes, both below and above stairs, for I have at last opened my ears
to all the reports of those who do manage to see their friends and family
members, only to discover for themselves the lengths to which this hospital
will go to rob these men and women and children of their dignity."

"Baseless calumny!" interjected Dr. Fibbetson, his mouth, thereafter,
fixed into a permanent expression of outrage.

"I am not finished, Fibbetson. I have yet to mention the trickery and connivance that has latterly taken place between *you*, Judge Fitz-Marshall and the administrator of this hospital under the instigating direction of Montague Pupker—a travesty of justice that sets a dangerous precedent for future misapplication of the law within the Dell. I speak of the young woman, Pupker's oldest daughter Hannah, who is no more mad than any man or woman in this room, with the possible exception of Fibbetson here, who has been known to parade about in the early hours of the morn drest only in his bedroom smalls."

"I am a sleepwalker, you dolt!" exclaimed the offended Dr. Fibbetson.

"And have you been somnambulating through your many bungled surgeries, Fibbetson? You, sir, are the worst doctor with whom I have been professionally acquainted since the reign of the infamous Dr. Popsnap, whom I understand was your revered mentor. And you have the audacity to add your worthless opinion to the chorus of those who will put Miss Pupker into this dismal place for reasons that have absolutely nothing to do with the fitness of her mind. Gentlemen, Miss Pupker has no business being an inmate of this hospital, and I demand that she be released at the close of this meeting." Sir Dabber paused just long enough to give extra freight to the sentence that followed: "Along with my son, whom I wish returned to my own care."

Lord Mayor Feenix exchanged an indecipherable look with Dr. Towlinson. In a sedate and measured tone he said, "Are you finished? Because if your rant has reached its terminus I should like to say that both Miss Pupker and your son Bevan were placed into our custody through a process of proper legal consignment, indicative of nothing but concern for the welfare of the patient."

"That is rot!" snapped Sir Dabber. "And besides, hospital commitments, no matter how they have been effected, are not irreversible. They can be undone by this very board, in fact."

"If you want your son home with you, Dabber, I'll not stop you," said Lord Mayor Feenix. "Anything to reduce the temperature of your growing aversion to this institution. As to your other charges, I will authorise an investigation. You are right that things have not run as smoothly as of late as they once did."

Dr. Towlinson's face now gave a look of some confusion that was brought to rein by a pat of the arm by the current board chairman, the rising and falling of his beefy paws bearing strong resemblance to a bear rapping upon a captured bee hive.

"In defence to our esteemed colleagues, Doctors Towlinson and Fibbetson," said Feenix, "the charges you have made, while possessing some merit, do not address the difficulties presented by this sudden degenerative turn in the conditions of our T.T. patients."

Sir Dabber knew now just as surely as did I the deceit of the spurious Terror Tremens and even some of its underlying purpose, but demonstrated a savvy prudence in not raising the issue under these circumstances, and thereby betraying to the men in the room the degree to which we had informed ourselves about the inner-workings of the Tiadaghton Project.

"And what of Hannah Pupker?" I struck in. "Is she to continue to be made prisoner in this place based solely upon a father's singular fallacious charge of madness?"

"Stay your tongue!" ordered Lord Mayor Feenix. "You have no voice in this meeting, and, moreover, the matter of young Miss Pupker has already been addressed by the court."

"Through self-serving machination," added Dabber, saying that very thing that I should have liked to say, had I a "voice in this meeting."

"I'll hear no more about Hannah Pupker, who blithers and drools in her chambers even as we speak, for I saw her just moments ago in my monthly round of inspection." The Lord Mayor indicated that the topic of Hannah Pupker had come to its end through the sudden application of his paws and eyes to the various papers collected before him.

During this brief interval, I succumbed to the desire to bend my eyes to Ruth Wolf, who responded with a slight and almost imperceptible shake of the head. It was not she, the nurse was thus telling me, who had made Hannah Pupker "blithering and drooling."

A sickness rose up in my stomach, accompanied by a feeling of profound helplessness in the cause of Hannah Pupker.

The Lord Mayor took a deep breath and rearranged his Bulldog bulk in his chair. "So Dabber. Take your son at the close of this meeting. By all means. He shall be one less mouth to feed and one less reeking slop pail to empty. Shall we make this official, gentlemen? Shall we have a vote? Let me see the hands of those who agree that the "Rokesmith Ruin," Dabber's son Bevan, should be released this very evening to the custody of his father."

All the hands of those who had standing in the meeting rose, save one—Towlinson's with some hesitation, and Fibbetson's after seeing the way that the majority would go. The single exception was the lugubrious Judge Fitz-Marshall, who professed a policy of never reversing a lunacy commitment to which he had been judiciary signatory.

"Fitz-Marshall, you are outvoted," said the Lord Mayor. "The boy will be released. Moving on now to that grave matter which brings Miss Wolf before us: Miss Wolf, your attendance at this meeting has been requested for the following reason: that you should tender your resignation as nurse in service to Bethlehem Hospital upon Highbury Fields, such resignation effective upon receipt."

Lord Mayor Feenix pushed a piece of paper and quill to Nurse Ruth Wolf. She stared down at the paper, neither speaking nor moving her hand to affix her signature to it. "Your services to the Lung Hospital will also be terminated. You will surrender your medical bag this evening."

"I don't have it with me," said Ruth Wolf in a small voice.

"Where is it?" asked Towlinson.

"At home."

"No, it is not."

"You've been to my house?"

"It has been searched. The bag was nowhere to be found."

"What difference does it make?" asked Ruth Wolf, putting forth the pretense that the contents of the bag should have no value at all.

"It makes a very great difference," said Towlinson with a pregnant, knowing look. "And I should like its return—to my office—to-morrow morning at the latest."

"I don't understand why I am being dismissed," said Ruth Wolf in a mechanical voice that said she knew quite well a number of underlying, unspoken reasons for her termination. But she was nonetheless curious (as was I) about what should be the *purported* grounds for her departure from the institution, which had employed her for the entire length of her sojourn as counterfeit Dinglian.

"Am I to believe that you actually do not know?" shot back Towlinson, playing the role expected of him. "If I must say it, then I will say it. An investigation into the recent death of the T.T. patient Gamfield has pointed every finger to your singular culpability. Moreover, there was an eyewitness to this murderous act: one of the orderlies who attended you in Mr. Gamfield's final moments. He was present to see you administer the drug that sadly ended Gamfield's life."

Ruth Wolf raised an eyebrow in dubiety. Now that the axe had fallen, she did not appear quite so nervous. The thing was done, her course now set. She could afford to be a mote contentious, a bit wise to the mechanics now being employed to remove her from Bedlam.

She cut her eyes to Fibbetson. He would not engage her with his own.

"The orderly stated that the patient was very much alive when you entered the room, madam," Towlinson went on. "It was you who killed him. Either with specific intention or through gross neglect, it is no matter. You are unfit to continue in the employ of the hospitals of the Dell. Sign the paper. Return your bag on the morrow and let us put an end to the sorry chapter of your tenure here."

"Yes, let us indeed do that," said Ruth Wolf in a sarcastic underbreath. She picked up the quill, dipped it into the ink well that accompanied it, and affixed her signature dutifully to the document before her. Then she rose from her chair. "Sir Dabber. I shall wait for you and Mr. Trimmers in the corridor to assist you in conveying your son to Dabber Hall."

"Hold please, my dear," said Dabber, rising from his own chair. "I myself have no further need to continue with this meeting."

"Now that you've received that chief thing that you sought from us all along," said Dr. Towlinson with a dark chuckle. "I have never said, sir, that you are impenetrable. Take your son away and spend the remainder of your days cleaning up his incontinent shit. That will be your lot, you fat, wheezing old fool."

I watched my friend bunch his fingers once again into fists and wondered if his pugilistic abilities rose to the level of his laureled youthful wrestling proficiency. I would not receive an answer to my musing, for Dabber did not tarry to exchange blows with his detractor, removing himself instead with a quick and contemptuous sweep from the room.

Together Dabber, Miss Wolf and I stepped away from that place where we had won a small triumph, but where one of us had suffered a great defeat, and made our hurried way through the asylum's labyrinthine passages to the cellarage stairs.

Momentarily deterred by Oscar the attendant's unwillingness to admit us to Bevan's cell without proper authorisation, we did not have to wait long before consent came in the form of a verbal directive from Towlinson's assistant Howler, who had been hastily detailed by his employer to this very purpose.

None of us—our number now having grown to four, with young Bevan Dabber in tow—spoke a word until we had safely assembled ourselves within Dabber's cabriolet, and even then there was not much speaking in the first moments of our situation there, given that the lovers Ruth Wolf and Bevan Dabber had a personal need which took precedence: to embrace and to wipe away with great tenderness their mutual tears, and to wonder if the angels of fate had not for once smiled upon a Dinglian in a rare act of good, deserved fortune.

Only when the lovers had released their mutual hold upon one another and acknowledged with gratitude the father who sat happy and beaming to see his son restored to health and restored as well to his freedom, and acknowledged, in addition, the father's friend who had had a hand in seeing this moment come to pass, did the nurse say in a burst of confession and contrition, "Now, Trimmers, let it be said, that I did lead you to your nephew. I wanted you to know that Newman was now in Bedlam, just as I did *not* want you to know that it was I who had put him there. Newman would have been killed in the Outland had I not rescued him. I'll tell you everything else you should want to know about him, for there is nothing left for me to hide. I have been made ignominiously redundant by the Tiadaghton Project. No longer an asset. Now only a liability."

"Does Timberry have your medical bag?"

"Yes, and a store of other drugs which I was able over the last few months to smuggle into the valley, thankfully without detection. He must guard these drugs with his life, for amongst them is enough isoniazid and rifampicin to cure every consumptive in Dingley Dell. That is, if there is to be any Dinglian extant after July 15. For I was able to see Chivery earlier this evening and have taken from him the two memoranda which he drew from the briefcase—rather—what is the Dinglian word?—valise, yes, of the dead woman, Mizz Martin. I knew of the woman, Trimmers, and I know now that I am marked to receive the same punishment as she for my acts of subversion against the Project. That is why Bevan and I must leave this very evening whilst we still have any hope left for escape."

I shook my head dispiritedly. "Gunmen are already gathering in the woods, and, no doubt, upon the Northern Ridge."

"How do you know this?"

"The Scadger brothers have seen them. I must advise against this course you wish to take, Ruth."

Now it was Bevan's turn to speak, to earnestly counter my attempt at dissuasion. "Ruth and I haven't many choices here, Trimmers. All that we can do is take the path that carries the lesser risk."

"If that be your decision, my son, then I choose to go with you." This from Sir Dabber. "And we will not go unarmed."

"Knives against guns, Dabber?" I interposed.

"But also strength in my own two hands."

"And infirmity in your pursy lungs, my good friend. Reconsider."

Sir Dabber shook his head. His look now darkened even as a smile graced his lips. "I have had my son returned to me. I do not intend to lose him again."

Father and son beheld one another in tearful silence for the succeeding moment.

"And my chances of survival here are not so much better than they are out there," said Dabber, handing to me the papers that he had been browsing since they had been given him by Miss Wolf upon our entering the cabriolet.

Here is what was on the papers:

Tiadaghton Project Communications Center
mKreis@tiadaghton.com
Re: Your ShoCKinG NeWS!!!!
Date: May 30, 2003
From: Patty Kreis
To: Michelena Martin

I am floored. Knocked totally on my ass, girl. You haven't even given me enough time to get you a buh-bye card. Print this. Keep my sentiments close at hand, baby, as you go off and make your honest living in the world. (Better late than never, right?) My heart may be black as coal, but I'll still miss you bunches.

I agree with everything you said, except that I can't see any other way out of this. The ant farm has to be exterminated, case closed. I also disagree with you on one other minor point: I'm quite confident that if we've been able to keep a lid on this thing for the last 121 years, there should be no reason why things should have to fall apart NOW. I, for one, will do everything I can to keep that from happening. I'm much too young and beautiful to spend the rest of my life behind bars.

Anyway, Missy, it won't be the same at Flatiron without you.

(Can I treat you to a farewell lunch at Mesa? Please say yes. Don't limit my goodbye to this impersonal electronic hand-wave.)

Original Message.

Tiadaghton Project Communications Center
mMartin@tiadaghton.com
Re: Leaving the Project
Date: May 30, 2003
From: Michelena Martin
To: Patty Kreis

Patty-cakes:

Today is my last day at the Flatiron Building. I have no plans to come back.

I know it'll seem awfully sudden to you, because I don't think I've ever mentioned how unhappy I've been here lately. But in truth, I've been thinking about getting out for some time now, and loping quietly off into the sunset. Yesterday's executive meeting cinched it. The ant farm analogy that Lipson introduced (and which Livingston and DeFeo cleverly embroidered) was an aptly droll one, and I laughed along with everybody else, and maybe it's because I've been at this job for so long that I didn't think at the time about what it all really means.

But now that I've had a few hours to let it sink in—to consider everything that was said (including how truly depraved most of that gallows humor shit was), after digesting all the gruesome details of how this is to be "effected" (how clinically Medina chooses his words)—I'm not only put off by it, Patty-cakes, I'm quite nauseous. We always knew there had to be an end to it—I just never thought I'd be here when that final chapter got written. And I suppose, officially I won't be. Because this little rat is preemptively jumping ship. At least I plan to jump ship once I clean out my desk and my computer files and make that final farewell trip to Pennsylvania on Monday. It's there that I'll make my obligatory "cut me loose" appeal to Yelavich and Brentano. Brentano will understand. I think she's sensed that I've wanted out for a while now. Yelavich, on the other hand, might make things difficult. I do, after all, know where a lot of the bodies are buried. (That statement goes from the figurative column to the literal on a very grand scale in just a few short weeks.)

Fact is, Patty-cakes, I just never acquired in totality that tough leather hide that the rest of you seem to wear with pride. Last time I looked, I still hadn't sprouted cojones beneath these comfortable K-Mart cotton panties. I mean, Campbell had been Special Ops for Christ's sake, and Reyes and Wilson and Weinberg would shove their own mothers down the basement stairs for the right amount of money. But I kept getting hung up on the fact that the subjects of our study are actually—all right, drum roll, wait for it, wait for it—people. (I also have a soft spot for kittens.) And there you have it: Michelena Martin's big dark secret. A lot of lives are about to be snuffed out and I'm not altogether happy about that. Now don't misread me here, Cakes. It could be a very good thing that one of our richest playfellow-subscribers has decided to have a go at old-fashioned brick and mortar enterprise again. That Langheart's actually going to turn that cobweb-covered Victorian amusement park into a vehicle for Rust Belt job growth. Who'd have thunk it? And who wouldn't commend him for it?

But it doesn't quite pass my personal smell test—you know, the smell of dead bodies not really being one of my favorite scents. And here's the other thing, Patty: I'm tired. I'm bored with the Dickensian freak show. And I'm ready to do something else with my life. Michelena Martin has left the building.

BTW, my prediction: Phase Seven isn't going to be the perfectly-executed piece of hydraulic theatre everyone thinks it'll be. Wam, bam, thank you, dam! Because nothing ever goes the way it's planned. And things WILL get out. Just you wait, 'Enry 'Iggins, just you wait! All those horribly messy facts and details of how this modern day Atlantis met its end. Things that historians will be writing about for decades. The carnage will not stay hidden within that drowned valley. Bodies will someday be exhumed from that erstwhile iron pit, both those newly dead and all of those corpses of yore that will have to be dug up and transferred from the cemetery. Just how DOES one kill off 11,000 people and keep the whole thing safely beneath one's hat?

And I will walk away with my twenty-year pin and my desk tchotchkes and wonder how a project with such relatively innocent beginnings became in the end so spectacularly wicked.

The Flatiron is a beautiful building in its own slendiforously funky way. But sometimes just looking at it makes me throw up a little in my mouth.

Love to Nichole and Layne and Valerie G.

PS: If your I.T. boyfriend McSprinkle doesn't nuke all traces of this transmission, I will personally come looking for you and kill you.

CHAPTER THE FORTY-FIRST

Monday, July 7, 2003

Dabber wept. He could not help himself. In less than an hour he would be turning his steps permanently from Dabber Hall, his lifelong home, inherited from his ironmaster father. He would be letting go of a lifelong collection of fine furniture and exquisitely fashioned art objets and everything that his income and his class had bestowed upon him. Sir Dabber could have had much more, had he made friends with other members of the gentry, had he served in the Petit-Parliament, had he not made the choice to live his life of wealth outside the usual margins and thereby unwittingly inoculate himself against the sins of his compeers. In exchange for his independence, Sir Seth Dabber had, most importantly, been kept uninformed of the details of the Great Lie. His novelty as a rich and powerful man who had nary a single rich and powerful friend now served him and served those of us who had used his good offices for our own benefit. But with his departure those days would come to an abrupt end.

For Sir Dabber was now poised to steal away with his newly reconciled son and the woman who stood a very good chance of becoming his daughter-in-law. And such a thing was far too great for the man to absorb in so short a span of time. So Sir Dabber wept. As he and his valet Fips performed the chore of selecting an article or two of clothing that Dabber could stuff into a knapsack, the large man put his handkerchief to his cheeks to wipe away the silent tears he shed without recess over all that he was leaving behind and for every uncertainty that the future now held for him. For his part, Fips' own eyes were anything but dry, nor could Arabella, Dabber's housemaid, withhold a vocalised expression of her own grief. Standing in the doorway to Dabber's bedchamber, she sniffed and snorted and blew her nose and wondered aloud in a bit of a word-wail what was to become of her.

"I've left you with plenty of money, my dear," snuffled Sir Dabber in return. "Upon my soul, dear girl, I've deeded to you and Fips the whole blooming house! No master would ever be so generous as I."

"Begging your pardon, Sir Dabber, that isn't what saddens her," corrected Fips. "It is the simple dismal fact that you are leaving."

"But leave I must. For I shan't be apart from my son, and he has no desire to part with his beloved. It is as simple a story as any you would read in English or in French. Now take this slip of paper, Fips. It's the combination to my safe in the library downstairs. Go and take out all of the silver therein—I have a little store of Outland pieces from my dealings with those who trade with the Beyonders. Silver is of great value in the Outland and will help Bevan and Miss Wolf and me to better make our way to safety there. Keep a coin or two for yourself and for Arabella, to provide for that day in which you may also find yourself abroad. And look sharp, man! We haven't much time."

Downstairs in Dabber's library, Bevan and I paced. Miss Wolf sat upon a sofa and watched the face of the grandfather clock that had been one of Dabber's most prized possessions. (It was one of the finest made in the Dell; its several companions had drawn top trades from the Outland brokers.)

Muntle had come, as well, from his new lodgings in the Fagins' apprentice quarters, having watched Dabber Hall from the shadows, waiting for our return to hear the upshot of the meeting of the Bedlam Board. With one hand my good friend poured himself a glass of stiff brandy-neat. The other hand held within it the exchange of memoranda between the two Tiadaghton Project employees, which he had twice read since his arrival, and upon which he was now seeking detailed exegesis.

Turning to Ruth Wolf, Muntle enquired, "What exactly does this mean?"

"I call your attention, Sheriff, to the words 'hydraulic theatre.'"

"There is another telling phrase in the missive," I struck in. "This 'wam, bam, thank you dam.'"

"A flood," said Ruth Wolf with a nod. "Brought about by dynamiting the nearest dam upriver: the Tiadaghton Dam. This would be my guess."

"Good God," said Muntle.

"It should not be too difficult a thing to collapse the dam by such means, to place hidden charges there. And consider that the force of the water upon the Tewkesbury Cut would be of sufficient strength to rip away large chunks of the porous rock that delineates that narrow opening. The water would have free rein to wreak its havoc upon this valley." It was apparent that Ruth Wolf had studied the topography of our region, just as she had thoroughly informed herself about everything else about our valley home that would serve her in the course of taking up residence with us.

"Then I must assume," I said, "that our own dam to the south—the Belgrave—which prevents the Thames from exiting the Dell in any way other than through its subterranean discharge channel beneath Southern Coal Ridge—I assume that they are expecting that it should hold and thus allow for a rapid collection of floodwater within the valley basin."

"Thereby drowning all of Dingley Dell," said Muntle gloomily.

"But what of those who cling to rooftops and the like?" asked Bevan.

"The force of the water will no doubt collapse all but the sturdiest of our buildings," said I. "And those structures that remain intact will be left fully underwater. As for those lucky few who have somehow purchased a few extra moments of survival upon the floating debris, there will, in all eventuality, be armed Outlanders standing at the ready to come in when the waters recede and pick off each of them one by one. It is no different from their obvious intent to slay all of those who are lucky enough to make their way to the woods or halfway up the ridges as the floodwaters race in. We will be fish-in-a-barrel as the saying goes. Do I have down the last chapter of our story as you would envision it, Miss Wolf?"

Ruth Wolf thought for a moment and nodded. "That would be the cleanest way to effect it. Then once the floodwaters have fully subsided, all of the dead bodies will be deposited into the iron pit, just as Miss Martin had said, and sealed for the end of time. Despite her predictions to the contrary, there stands the distinct possibility of complete and total success in this murderous venture."

"Then we should act without delay," said Muntle, bounding over to Ruth Wolf and myself to take first my hand and then Miss Wolf's in his usual exuberant, demonstrative manner, "to get as many of us out and away from this doomed valley as we are able before the floodwaters are unleashed."

"And how would we succeed in such an undertaking without Feenix and Pupker and all the others getting wind of it, Muntle?" I asked. "Think clearly, man. They already suspect that we've something seditious in the works—that we stand poised upon the brink of outright insurrection. Now how much of a vault of the imagination would it require to re-ascribe our insurrectionary motives to something not communistic at all, but to that which threatens them most of all: our growing realisation of the true nature of Dingley Dell? The Moles cannot be blind to the fact that as events have escalated on their side with the approach of their day of rescue and repatriation with the Outland, some of us should begin—as indeed we have—to become more observant, to become much better at putting together the pieces of that no longer inchoate mosaic."

"Aye," said Muntle, nodding slowly, his exuberance for immediate action having dissipated. "Especially when so many of those pieces of late have been so generously handed us. Trimmers, you make a compelling case for keeping our heads, and keeping our feet planted firmly upon the soil of the Dell. At least for the time being."

"And to that end—the end to be achieved by our collective cerebration—I should enquire as to the specific whereabouts of the most celebrated cerebrater in the valley—Professor Chivery. Where within that Minotaur's maze of rooms-within-rooms in Bedlam, Miss Wolf, would we find this brilliant gentleman?"

"On the top floor. In a secured room in the building's attic. He was put there amongst the Limbo Returnees."

"The Limbo Returnees—now who would they be?" asked Muntle.

"Those who have either come back to the Dell under their own industry or have been conducted here by the offices of my rescuing group. Those like Trimmers' nephew Newman who are assumed to remain still in the Outland."

"And that is where they are keeping Newman?" I asked.

Ruth Wolf nodded. "I enquired about him just this evening. He is well. He is safe. And he has become quite adept at winning backgammon for toothpicks."

I smiled. Muntle did not. "Why do they not simply kill all of them in that attic room if their presence here is unknown to anyone but that small group that attends them in the asylum?"

"Towlinson, to his credit, refuses to stain his hands with the blood of a single Dinglian," said Ruth.

Muntle laughed dryly. "I cannot believe that the ogre has grown such a conscience as that with which you impute him."

"Granted, it is a small conscience. But even Gamfield was never meant to die. Fibbetson accidentally injected him with a second dose of the general soporific."

"A point of fact which you had no recourse to rebut at this evening's meeting," said I.

Ruth nodded. Bevan drew near and took her hand in his.

"In your interview with Chivery, was there anything else that was said?" I asked, suddenly thinking that whatever intelligence had been imparted by Chivery to Miss Wolf would vanish with her, until such time as we were able to meet with the quarantined man to learn it ourselves.

"He said very little except this: that 'his calculations proved that all of it could work. The first stage and the second.' He was most cryptic in this regard, and so I asked him whatever did he mean. 'You'll see,' he said. 'But you must release me to do any good. My calculations cannot be of benefit if they are not to be applied with the utmost speed. Take these papers,' he said, giving me the memoranda between Miss Martin and Miss Kreis. 'Use the papers to win my release. Time is of the essence. Time is of the essence.' I recall all of the words he communicated to me because he began to repeat himself until the appeal became almost nonsensical in its redundant utterance."

Muntle now turned to me with a look of the most profound urgency. "Yet there should be a great deal of sense and order to what he said. Once one knows how the words are to be interpreted. We must go to Bedlam, Trimmers. You and I. We cannot wait until Towlinson and Fibbetson and the others have fled. By then it will perhaps be too late to use the product of Chivery's calculations to our benefit. What could he mean? We will draw it out of him."

"And what if we fail, my friend?" I asked. "And we are put under arrest in the course of the attempt? What good will we do in a gaol cell?"

"And have *you* an opinion one way or another, Miss Wolf?" Muntle asked. "To attempt to effect a rescue earlier rather than later or to wait and employ caution as the overriding watchword?"

Ruth Wolf spoke without hesitation: "I would go in. As soon as you can. To-morrow night, in fact."

"You would do it?" I asked, surprised that Miss Wolf should answer so quickly and with such adamancy.

Ruth Wolf nodded. "Whilst I do not believe that Towlinson or any of his minions would take such rash and murderous action as to vacate that attic room through the wholesale slaughter of its occupants, each day that draws nearer to the day of departure for the Moles makes for the possibility of circumstantial, unwonted actions—actions that put certain men and women—yourselves included—into a most precarious state. I would not wish to think that at some point between now and July 15—well, I shall not say it. What I will say is this: there is a particular person who shares that room with Newman and Chivery and several others, whose name should be of interest to you, Sheriff. His last name is Muntle. You see, Vincent, your brother George is there. He is, in fact, the longest held of the Limbo Returnees."

As we bid our adieus to Ruth Wolf and her lover Bevan Dabber and Bevan's father Sir Seth Dabber, Muntle sat upon the sofa in Dabber's library, shaking his head in disbelief over what he had just been told, and asking over and over again of anyone who would hear him, "Could it be true? Is it really possible that George lives? Or is this a dream from which I will soon awake?"

Outside, I stood back and watched as Ruth was being handed into the cabriolet that would take her two companions and her to Road's End in Black Heath. Suddenly, I was struck by something else that had come up in that most revelatory Thursday night and early Friday morning gathering of the Fortnightly Poetry League. "Miss Wolf," I said, "would you indulge the curiosity of this scribbling and enquiring amateur historian for one last time?"

Ruth put her head out the window and nodded.

"The books that were found by the First-Generation boys in the fruit cellar—the only books that were left here when all the adults fled in that early epoch of Dingley Dell—you said that you would later tell us if they were left there by accident or were placed there on purpose."

"On purpose, if we are to believe the story. The perpetrator's name was Elizabeth Cochran, a young woman from Armstrong County, northeast of Pittsburgh. She is better known by her pen name, for she was a writer like you, Trimmers: Nellie Bly. She had just returned from a seventy-two-day trip around the world—a record-breaking trip—and came hither to live for a while so that she could write about a very special orphanage that she had heard was being been built here—an orphanage that would give a home to children from around the world. During her visit, Miss Bly learnt quite a bit more about the place than she ever expected, and was troubled by what she found out. The Project administrators learnt, in turn, that she intended to write an exposé, something she had gotten quite good at doing, and a serious threat was made against her life. She was quickly escorted from the valley, but not before she was able to secret her travelling library away in a place that she hoped would later be discovered by the children. To protect her identity, she removed all of the identifying bookplates. But if you look in one corner of the frontispiece for *Our Mutual Friend*, you will find her name written there: "Pink." For this was her childhood nickname.

"I hope that you appreciate the irony of it, Trimmers: that Dingley Dell exists to-day, forever reverential to the written word, because a female writer left behind the means to literary expression in that hollowed-out fruit cellar."

Ruth Wolf lowered her voice. "Ask the vicar to pray for us, Trimmers. For Bevan and Sir Dabber and I have agreed amongst ourselves that we are not going into hiding. We have decided to advocate on behalf of the Dell— to find someone in a position of power who will listen to us, who will join hands in helping us to rescue this valley."

"Always the rescuing angel," said I, and then after I had said it, I could not be certain if it was spoken aloud or merely expressed within my head.

Ruth Wolf and her lover Bevan Dabber and his father Sir Seth Dabber climbed the Southern Coal Ridge for two reasons: it presented a much more difficult ascent than the Northern Ridge, and so, it was hoped, would be less carefully guarded by Tiadaghton sentries, and Ruth Wolf hoped, as well, to make good on her efforts to keep her partner Phillips apprised through the course of her exodus from the Dell of Dingley through application of her small portable telephone. The climb would be a difficult one for Sir Dabber, whose lungs were often taxed simply by walking too quickly across a room, but he was nonetheless determined to accompany his son and the young man's devoted fiancée wherever their travels should take them.

Sir Dabber's lifeless body was discovered by two romping collier's children the very next morning, not very far up the ridge. However, it wasn't respiratory difficulties or coronary arrest that had brought an end to the man's life; it was the loss of blood to the brain pursuant to the severing of that gentlemen's right carotid artery. One of his two climbing companions had died similarly; Miss Wolf had also suffered a terminal attack upon the neck—both through a slicing open of that selfsame artery and the jugular vein that coursed next to it. Dabber's other companion, however, did not die through a slit throat at all; there was evidence, instead, of a rather violent struggle, which produced multiple stabbings into Bevan's chest and back. All three bodies had been left where they fell in an obvious attempt to forewarn any other Dinglian with escape on his mind against making such a foolhardy attempt. The bodies were a gruesome find, and the children who first discovered them were put into a greatly unsettled state for the remainder of the day.

There was no sense from any of the members of the mining families who viewed the bodies nor from the sheriff's deputies dispatched to collect them nor even from Dr. Fibbetson who was detailed to serve as coroner over them (such responsibility requiring no more than a simple pronouncement that the three corpses were indeed dead), that two of the three individuals had been most deeply in love, the two having fallen several yards asunder, and having not even been afforded the consolation of dying in one another's arms.

CHAPTER THE FORTY-SECOND

Tuesday, July 8, 2003

The two girls often strolled together of a morning, but most especially upon those recent mornings following ejection from the emporium run by the older girl's father and from the family's finely-appointed apartments above. This particular morning the two had not even been given leave by the father to take a little breakfast, being sent, instead, to Chuffey Bakery for that very purpose. The reason was this: the father sought that neither his daughter nor the friend whom he was coming to regard as a daughter should be present for rather important conferences and preparations related to the large undertaking that loomed in the near offing. The undertaking was, of course, the somewhat elaborate removal of the "Eighty-three Elect" to the Summit of Exchange upon the Ides of July (July being one of the four calendar months whose Ides fall on the 15th), the M.P.P.'s, and all those within their closest orbits to be immediately thereafter spirited off and away from their ill-fated ancestral valley home, and out and abroad into the Outland—a worldwide tract that promised the most wondrous post-Victorian perquisites of privileged life.

It had only been two days since Cecilia Pupker and her best-of-all-possible-friends Miss Alice Trimmers had received a bit of rather important information from Cecilia's father. That illustrious worthy, who had been placed in charge of the Fête champêtre and who was responsible for every detail of its incumbent arrangements, decided only then to tell his daughter the true reason behind the recent flurry of activity engendered by the exclusive celebratory event. With this revelation came the father's injunction to his daughter to gather in due course a few items of clothing and a few items of sentimental attachment, for she was leaving Dingley Dell with only a little luggage and would never be coming back. The disclosure was received at first with quite a measure of filial displeasure on the part of Miss Pupker (and with great observational fascination on the part of Cecilia's best-of-all-possible-friends Alice Trimmers). The younger of the two Pupker daughters was so displeased, in fact, that she made a show of baulking and bridling and stamping her foot in a most unbecoming manner. Remaining in this place in which she had been largely sheltered and pampered and made relatively happy was far preferable, said she, to being cast to the winds like the peripatetic children of Israel.

"And what will you do, Papa," speculated Cecilia in her closing argument, "if I choose not to go with you and Mama? Whatever will you do then?"

"Why, I know exactly what I should do, my obstinate daughter. Your mother and I will simply depart this vale without you. You are free to stay behind. You are free, should you wish it, to keep company with your lunatic sister in Bedlam for that matter. But I must caution you that Dingley Dell in our absence will be a not very hospitable place, and will little resemble the familiar Dingley Dell of this day."

Cecilia Pupker was seated upon a cushioned all-weather settee as her father paced up and down the terrace. Her look was one of clear concern and anxiety (attended by manufactured petulance), such a look being one that rarely visited the girl's face, it generally being carelessly languid, bearing hardly a lineament of worry. "Whatever do you mean, Papa?"

"I'll not say it with your friend Alice present."

Alice patted down the plaits in her skirts to give her hands something to do so that they should not betray too strong an investment of interest in the discussion at hand.

"And what do you mean by that, Papa? For Alice cares not a straw about those whose names have been left off the invitation list. Who are they to her, for she is one of us now," said Cecilia, turning to her friend Alice.

"One of you, yes," said a blushing Alice, who allowed her cheek to be delicately kissed by Cecilia to punctuate the sentiment with demonstrative affection.

Montague Pupker suspended his pacing and stopt before the chair occupied by Alice Trimmers, late of the Trimmers family and greatly glad, as just noted, to be done with them. "Is there truth, Miss Alice Trimmers, to what my daughter has just said? Is it true that you care not a fig what is to happen to your family or to any of those countrymen of yours, for that matter, who are to be left behind after our departure?"

"I care nothing whatsoever," said Alice boldly. "They bore me to tears. My own family drives me so mad that you could put me directly into Bedlam alongside your other daughter, and I should like it better than having to a take another meal with Mama and Papa when even upon their very best behaviour."

"Do you truly mean that, Alice? Do you truly mean that you could actually go off and leave your family here to whatever fate awaits them and feel no compunction whatsoever over the abandonment?"

Alice nodded. Then she shrugged. "They are dead to me, Mr. Pupker, and will always be dead to me. Hand me a shovel, sir, and I shall be first to dig a hole to inhume them."

"Good God, girl, how forcefully do you renounce your very own family! And may I ask why?"

"Because my mother is a flighty, fluttering, pecking little bird that does nothing but chirp and peep when she isn't scowling and sputtering and slapping the cheeks of those who incommode her."

"Your mother strikes you?"

Nodding: "So hard across the face that she sometimes leaves a handprint there. It is most mortifying."

"And your father—"

"A man of no talent and little ambition who had no business siring a family given his unwillingness to offer us anything but perpetual failure in every office and facet of his being. I will not speak ill of my younger brother, though, for he is probably dead. He has successfully severed his bond, just as I did, and I will commend him for that at least, though my flight to the embracing bosom of my friends the Pupkers—"

Here Alice Trimmers gave a beatific smile to shew affection for her newly adopted family.

"—has proven a far more practical route to sanity and sanguinity."

"A solid course, my child," said Pupker, resuming his contemplative pacing. "A most solid course. Now Cecilia, dear daughter, here is what we intend to do, because I know that you have been upon pins and needles over whether Alice will be joining us: we shall have the circumstantially-orphaned Miss Alice Trimmers…" (With a courtly bow to Alice.) "…come with us to the Summit and emigrate with us to the Outland. There is no reason that she shouldn't. So let us set your worrying little mind to rest on this count right this very moment."

Consequently thrilled beyond words, both girls sprang up from their seats to put their loving arms round the neck of their benevolent bene-factor. "And perhaps," continued Pupker as he detached himself with a chuckle from all the clutching, supple young arms, "with Alice's coming, you will find it in your own troubled heart, Cecilia, to join us now with a renewal of spirit and with a full and happy endorsement of our course, and leave off being morose about departing a place that is soon to become nothing more than a fast-fading memory. Shall we not all together, my dear girls, turn over a new leaf—begin this brand new chapter of our lives with an ebullition of glee and optimism for our well-paved future?"

"Of course we shall!" cried both girls in unison. Then there was a si-lence, which was shortly broken by a question from Alice: "So your other daughter, then, is to be left behind?"

Pupker nodded. "What else can be done? Hannah has been legally con-signed to a madhouse. I doubt that I can gain her release as much as I try. Fate has determined that you, Miss Alice Trimmers, should take her place, and one never argues with fate."

"I thank you for taking me along, Mr. Pupker. But what if I should see my father out there? How am I to present myself? Whatever should I do?"

Montague Pupker now turned to fully face my inquisitive niece. He threaded his hand through her long brown tresses, allowing the fingers to linger there for a moment so as to better feel the softness of her youthful locks. "Such a chatterbox of questions you are! But you'll not worry about that one for another moment, fair Alice. Rest assured that your father will come nowhere near us. He'll no longer bring shame upon you. Nor soon will your mother. You have my word on that. Banish them from your thoughts, my child, just as they have, no doubt, banished you from theirs."

There was simplicity to the statement but there was little truth to it. For two mornings later Alice Trimmers had her own jolt of displeasure—and a rather consequential one it was at that—when in the course of that quiet forenoon stroll with her new spirit-sister Cecilia—both girls bending their steps to the Chuffey Bakery to break their fast—the two were halted by a sight of a most disturbing character. Through the upstairs window of Alice's Uncle Frederick's lodgings above Mrs. Lumbey's Ladies' Fine Dress Shop, Alice and Cecilia saw the following: Alice's erstwhile mother, recently installed therein, and Alice's erstwhile father, raised by all appearance from the proverbial dead, crossing the room, their arms locked in connubial affection.

"Away from the window, you two!" I called to my brother and sister-in-law from the other side of the bedchamber in which I had just a moment before disturbed their morning solitude with the presentation of a fully provisioned teaboard. None of us being aware that there were four most critical eyes staring up at us from the street below, I appended rhetorically and a bit mootly, "Do you wish to be detected by a passerby?"

"Not at all. We weren't thinking," said Gus, drawing the curtains and throwing the room into temporary darkness. "But it is become a true bother to keep ourselves from the bright light of morning, brother."

"It beseeches one, morning does—teazes and beseeches," offered Charlotte, looking blissfully upon her husband, the marital ties between the two strongly restored.

"I sometimes feel, brother," continued Gus, "as if I am already interred behind the dark walls of the gaol or within the Bedlam mad hospital."

"Better darkness here than darkness there," said I, settling myself down into a chair to take my own morning cup from the tray.

I had decided that this was to be the morning in which I would inform Newman's parents of their son's present whereabouts, that so much had I said upon the subject of remaining calm and collected and unprecipitant and in the more practical sense of keeping Gus's own whereabouts scrupulously hidden, that he and Charlotte would surely now take the news about Newman and cherish it in their hearts and give leave to Muntle and Timberry and me to do what needed to be done. What was to be done was this: that we should rescue the boy from Bedlam, just as we strove to rescue three other personages of great worth from that institution: Hannah Pupker, George Muntle, and Professor Jeremiah Chivery, there being great practical value in emancipating the last inmate on that list, for Chivery would finally tell us what all of his calculations had been about and whether they should reveal something in the arithmetic of his obsession that would be useful to our efforts to save Dingley Dell from extinction.

It was time, I thought, to tell everything to Gus and Charlotte, to bring them fully into the circle of those most informed about what was happening here. It was time to reveal those facts that had been kept deliberately from the ken of nearly every other citizen of the Dell who was not a member of the Fortnightly Poetry League (or an adjunct of that esteemed body) nor a constituent member of the Eighty-three Elect.

But once again I could not do it. Here was my brother crossing negligently before an open window, totally unmindful of his safety. Who is to say that he would not be equally neglectful in forcing upon us his own reckless participation in our still-formulating rescue mission?

I laugh. I cannot help myself. *Mission*. Muntle and Timberry and I: rescuing swashbucklers! The humour lies in this: that there was never opportunity to give the venture more than minor preparatory thought. Because of what was to happen next—something that would constitute quite a troubling turn of events and propel this story into its final tumultuous chapters!

With astonishing speed and devastating consequence, not only for Gus, but for all of us who resided in Mrs. Lumbey's townhouse, and then for several others who associated with us, Alice and Cecilia's sighting succeeded in dislodging a rather large boulder from its precipice upon that high hill of early metaphorical mention, thus setting the avalanche into full, tumbling motion. Within two short hours a number of us were put into the Dinglian gaol, whilst Gus was conveyed to Bedlam to be placed under lock and key, his name to be indited into the records of that institution as the most recently quarantined victim of T.T., Terror Tremens.

Here is how it all came to pass with blistering velocity:

Alice Trimmers stood beneath the window through which she had espied her mother and father. My niece expressed shock at having found her father returned and hiding and possibly diseased and spreading same to her mother and in only a matter of time to everyone in the contagion-prone valley. "We must tell someone! Oh, Cecilia—we must tell someone this very instant!" pressed Alice, still staring up at the window even after the curtains had been pulled together, the occupants having failed to register their daughter's appalling discovery of them.

What supervened thereafter was a hasty, hurtling return to the Pupker Emporium for the two girls, where they had opportunity to describe what they had seen not only to Montague Pupker, but to Dr. Fibbetson as well (that venerable surgeon having just come to seek permission to carry along with him into the Outland an extra valise containing his precious morphia suppositories). Also there was Sheriff Billy Boldwig who had wished to confer with Pupker over arrangements that would employ his constabulary in the offices of protection for the privileged pilgrims in their procession to the Northern Ridge.

In hardly less than an hour there was a pounding upon the Lumbey door that went unheeded, and then a storming of the dress-making redoubt by the increasingly intrepid Boy Sheriff Billy Boldwig and two of his accompanying deputies, the aforementioned Dr. Fibbetson (who contributed not much to the proceedings beyond rear-guard panegyrics to the success of the venture), and Montague Pupker, who was most eager to find cause in the way of conspiracy to harbour a diseased Returnee that would implicate every one of those who defied him upon the day of his elder daughter's involuntary hospital confinement.

What a perfect turn of events for Pupker and Towlinson and Lord Mayor Feenix! Now there was a legal pretext for putting all of those who darkened the path to that impending day of release directly into the gaol, there to be held without bond (for the seriousness of the charge settled the issue of remanding on the side of the Moles) until such date and time as their incarceration became moot.

In a matter of two hours several individuals of great import to this story were rounded up and put under lock and key within the compound known as the Inn-of-Justice, the place in which courts sat in session, and where prisoners sat (upon hard iron cots), and where the newly promoted Billy Boldwig sat in his newly-gained lodgings, and pridefully polished his very own gun (when he was not abroad upon his shrieval rounds).

I was taken along with my sister-in-law Charlotte, my landlady Mrs. Lumbey, and her assistant Miss Casby, from the premises of Mrs. Lumbey's Ladies' Fine Dress Shop and from those rooms situated behind and above it. The arrest employed use of the threatening end of Sheriff Boldwig's shiny new firearm and a growing measure of self-assurance on the part of the newly-minted lawman. The arrest included as well an ancillary report for all ears, just relayed from the remote coal-town of Blackheath, concerning the deaths of Sir Dabber, Nurse Ruth Wolf, and young Bevan Dabber.

Hearing the report, I was at first too staggered to speak. Likewise, Mrs. Lumbey could not bring herself to say a word. Charlotte and Amy Casby wept. It was my brother Gus, very soon to be relegated to a dismal cell at Bedlam, who found voice to ask of no one in particular, "Who could have done such a thing?"

"Drunken colliers, no doubt," volunteered Fibbetson. "I've seen far worse from that low and murderous bunch of black-skinned reprobates."

In a low voice, Montague Pupker broke into sudden soliloquy, perhaps not realising that he was employing his tongue to the audit of all the ears round him: "And fine riddance to you, Miss Wolf. And to your every mis-placed attempt to heal those who did not deserve your secret ministrations and for your every act of treachery." Then recalling himself, he addressed us all in full: "I'll mourn Dabber—a good man in his quixotic way. I'll not mourn the death of the self-styled Miss Nightingale. As for the young man, I haven't an opinion one way or another. Those Rokesmith Ruins are a rather inconsequential bunch, wouldn't you say? Now, now, Deputy, you're being far too rough in attaching the handcuffs to Miss Casby's wrists. Please remove them, sir, and allow me to shew you how it is more gently done." This Pupker proceeded to do with equal parts care and equal parts palpable, pawing lechery.

Having newly secured the restraints to that whimpering innocent, and having taken as much delight as he was able to take from such a proceeding in a public place, Pupker drew breath to address me with a self-satisfied look: "Sheriff Boldwig has neglected to give the second obvious charge that now arises to put you even deeper into the Dinglian gaol, Mr. Trimmers: We have evidence that you assisted Miss Wolf and Sir Dabber and his son in their ill-fated escape. This constitutes a criminal act, sir."

"Indeed, it does not!" I protested.

"As of yesterday morning it is most assuredly become one," responded Dr. Fibbetson. "For the Petit-Parliament met and voted it into the Book of Criminal Statutes. From that point forward, Trimmers, anyone who at-tempts to leave this valley or assists in the escape of another will be charged with a felony."

"Upon what grounds?" Mrs. Lumbey demanded to know, her wonted dander finally taking voice.

Pupker laughed. "There is no requirement that the Petit-Parliament must give grounds for *any* law it passes, my dear woman. Though if grounds you must have, let me say that we no longer wish to bring disease into the valley through those who escape and then do us the injurious disservice of returning." Here Mr. Pupker looked hard at my brother, who should be diseased to such an extent that he would be put into summary confinement, but was, instead, most casually and negligently handled by Boldwig and one of his deputies, such as to give a ready lie to all that had just been said.

After Gus was put into Bedlam, and Mrs. Lumbey and Amy Casby and my sister-in-law Charlotte and I were placed into cells within the Dinglian Gaol (the cruelty of this most recent sundering of Gus and Charlotte making the scene one that would be most wrenchingly difficult to describe), the extended roundup of co-conspirators and suspected accomplices continued in earnest. Muntle was found at the Fagin jewellry shop. Because my friend regarded the capture (in addition to his other objections in concert with my own) as representative of a vanquished opportunity to finally see his brother George after a twenty-five year separation, he did not go easily. Muntle resisted every moment of the apprehension and did so with such energy and industry as to draw a sympathetic and combative Herbert Fagin into the cause, his obstructive enlistment resulting in his arrestment as well, much to the horror of his onlooking wife and daughter.

Antonia Bocker was taken without struggle from her stationer's shop and it was all that she could do to secure continued liberty for her clerk Miss Abbey Hexam, for the hastily-drawn warrant named this young woman as well for having committed no greater crime then being in close proximity to Antonia by reason of her daily employment in the fine and everyday stationery line. Equally troubling was the arrestment of Dr. Timberry's parents for protesting the seizure of their son, who was visiting his mother and father at the time. There succeeded quite a row when Charles Timberry began to take swings at Sheriff Billy with a cricket bat in the manner of his anarchic Punch puppet, and Mrs. Julia Timberry, in a futile attempt to aid and abet her handcuffed son, began to scream at the top of her lungs in the most animated fashion of a battered Judy puppet.

Only two men from our motley bunch of renegades escaped capture: Messrs. Upwitch and Graham, for neither man would open the door to the All Souls Church under a declaration of "right of asylum" no matter how hard the freckled fist of the law beat upon it. Each man knew that the attempted arrests were politically-motivated, that the Tiadaghton Project represented dictatorial despotism at its most extreme, and that each member of the small confederation of those who opposed the Project (that fraternity including Messrs. Upwitch and Graham amongst its core membership) were eligible for religious sanctuary under longstanding common law. (They knew, as well, that each of the doors to the All Souls Church in the Dell were made of solid lignum vitae, the hardest wood in the world, and that any attempt to batter them down was doomed to failure.)

This sudden thwarting turn placed the young sheriff and his deputies in an awkward spot. Lord Mayor Feenix was called in to help facilitate the irksome removal.

"Vicar Upwitch, it is the Lord Mayor of Milltown rapping now. Please open the door and admit me so that we may speak."

Came a sonorous pastoral voice from behind the door (both Upwitch and Graham standing defiantly on the other side of that secured portal, Upwitch with proud, raised chin and Graham wringing his hands in fret and worry): "Speak of what, sir?"

"The warrant that Sheriff Boldwig holds in his hand. It is a warrant for your arrest and the arrest of your friend and fellow conspirator, Mr. Graham, and it must be executed."

"If you are come to assist in this ridiculous legal charade, Lord Mayor, we'll not admit you. Mr. Graham and I are exercising our right of asylum."

"There is no such right within the Dell of Dingley, Reverend Upwitch."

"Not every right possessed by the citizens of this valley devolves from the pen of the Petit-Parliament, sir. Some rights are bestowed by our Creator. They are intrinsic to our species, sacrosanct and inviolable, especially in the face of the sort of rampant tyranny that now infects this Dell. Will you deny, Lord Mayor, that several of our friends have been arrested to await an indictment of conspiracy to commit criminal acts that are without any merit whatsoever?"

"Of course I'll deny it. I'll deny it in full voice, young man." Then in an undervoice to the sheriff, came a mumble and then a whining murmured defence made by its recipient, something easily gleaned by the two men inside to indicate that Sheriff Boldwig should not have shared with the barricaded fugitives the names of any of the other co-conspirators and was an arrant fool for having done so.

Once again from the Lord Mayor through the thick wooden church door: "This church is no fortress, Reverend Upwitch. If we cannot ram this door, we will fracture a stained-glass window or two and enter easily in that manner. Do you wish your lovely stained-glass windows destroyed?"

"And do *you*," returned the vicar, "wish me to climb to the top of the campanile and ring the bell to convoke a crowd, which I shall be more than willing to address with my voice-trumpet? And what will I say, Lord Mayor, that may be of interest to them? I think I shall tell them, sir, of the true purpose of your July 15 gathering, and how all of the rest of us are to be abandoned to Heaven-only-knows what sort of fate."

"I have no idea what you're talking about."

"Come, come, Lord Mayor. You would actually allow me to climb to the top of that campanile and tell everyone who will listen the truth about Dingley Dell? Knowing the threat that this would pose to the success of your Bon Voyage party? Consider the question carefully, sir. How should you like to be kept here with all the rest of us because you have failed to keep the hordes from finding out about the Tiadaghton Project?"

"Where do you come up with such nonsense? Who has told you these things?"

"I shan't betray my sources, Lord Mayor. Let me simply say that we are not the innocents and simpletons you have long taken us for."

"Good God."

"Yes, God is good, your honour, and takes, methinks, a rather dim view of your complicity in bringing about an end to our Dingley Dell."

Upwitch and Graham could not see the face of the man who had just been told that everything which he thought had been kept quiet and covert and multiply veiled was now known to a select few who had absolutely no right to the purchase of it. But the face must assuredly have been drained of all colour—for there was a sickly pallor to the very voice of the Lord Mayor as he, no doubt, thought through the repercussions attendant upon this significant revelation. Finally he said, "You will stay there, Upwitch, and you will not be disturbed under your absurd declaration of asylum, but if you so much as take one step outside this edifice, you will be promptly placed under arrest. We will have constables watching each and every door round the clock. Your lies stop here, sir, just as they have been put under commensurate lock and key at the gaol. This infestation of opposition and deliberate prevarication will not spread. I hope that there is food enough in your rectory larder to feed the two of you until—"

Lord Mayor Feenix stopt himself, but Uriah Graham, taking sudden and uncharacteristic courage, finished the thought for him: "Until all Bashaws should be gone from this valley—swept away, Lord Mayor, by their fear and by their cupidity and by their contempt for those who would in similar circumstances have never sold their own souls to the Devil the way that you have. We await that day, Lord Mayor—we await it most eagerly— the day that you and your ilk shall be gone from Dingley Dell forever."

Lord Mayor Feenix muttered something in response that was received only by the ears of the Boy Sheriff. Yet the two men who stood behind the door, having won a small victory largely through intellectual ingenuity, could easily guess its apostrophising gist: "Enjoy your short-lived freedom such as it is, gentlemen. Enjoy it well."

And this imagining sent a chill down the spines of both of the part- nered stalwarts—a most frigid chill indeed.

CHAPTER THE FORTY-THIRD

Wednesday, July 9, 2003

With a number of those Dinglians most familiar to the reader either incarcerated in the gaol, committed to the Bedlam Asylum, or self-immured behind the solid stone walls of the All Souls Church, I now turn your attention to that other set of Dinglians who remained at liberty during what would become the final hours in the life of this cursed dale, each of whom would play a contributory role in bringing this story to its close.

Let us begin with Harry Scadger, still at large and still fretful about the declining health of his consumptive daughter Florence. She had received some of the doses of the Outland medicine that was put to work to heal her, but was now coughing without respite and with a frighteningly sanguinary product. Abbey Hexam who, in the absence of her now imprisoned employeress, was working alone in the stationer's shop below the rooms offered to the Scadgers by Antonia, could not help hearing the rasping, unrelenting cough. When the last customer of the day had departed, she quickly shut and latched the door to the street and climbed the stairs to ask if there be anything that she could do for the afflicted girl.

"You are most kind to ask," said Matilda Scadger from the bedside of her daughter. "But Mr. Scadger left only a little while ago down the back stairs to fetch Dr. Timberry. The doctor was to come yesterday but did not."

Miss Hexam gave Mrs. Scadger a curious look. "But do you not know that Dr. Timberry has been arrested with Miss Bocker and the others? He now sits in the Dingley Gaol."

"Bless and save the man, I did not know it!" exclaimed Mrs. Scadger. "Are they to arrest every last one of us before we have done with this terrible season?"

"'Tis my fear, Mrs. Scadger. Only this morning Mr. Meagles told me that Judge Fitz-Marshall has already signed so many warrants that his hand was seised by a cramp and his clerk was sent to procure a bag of ice from the ice house."

"Would that the magistrate's hand fell completely from his wrist," said Matilda Scadger with composed contempt. "For it was Judge Fitz-Marshall who had me whipped in the workhouse when I was a girl for failing to sweep up the ashes from his clumsy pipe when he paid his governor's visit. And now he has put our rescuing angels Frederick Trimmers and Antonia Bocker into the gaol, and I should wish further that the judge's other hand and both of his feet drop off as well and that he should bleed to death from all his limbs!"

"*Mama!*" cried Florence in roopy-voiced awe.

At nearly that same moment, Harry Scadger stood rapping upon the door to Dr. Timberry's cottage. "Dr. Timberry!" he called. "It is Harry Scadger. Are you within?"

"You won't find him in there," said Timberry's next-door neighbour. The man was quite old and wore a broad-brimmed slouched hat and sat upon a low campstool in his cutting garden. He pointed his clipping shears in the direction of Milltown (for Timberry's home was in the working-class village of Tavistock not far removed from Fingerpost).

"What do you mean, sir?" asked Harry.

"That they come for him yesterdee. That they find him at his Pa and Ma's place down the road 'chere. That they take all three of them on to the clinker, the Ma, she a 'hollerin' and a squealin' like a whipped pig all the live-long way."

Harry Scadger thanked the neighbour for the informative, yet disheartening, intelligence and seated himself upon the front step of the doctor's house, tears of hopelessness welling in his eyes.

"You have a sick young one at home do you now?" asked the old man, tipping back his brim for a better view of the weeping young man.

Harry nodded.

"Might be of interest to you to know that he didn't take his medical bag with him."

Harry raised his head to look at the old man who had now risen from his stool and was approaching the low paling that separated the two properties. "You're sure that the medical bag didn't go with him?" asked my half-brother.

"The lawmen don't let a prisoner take nothin', generly speaking. No, the medical bag warn't with him."

Harry stood. "If I go into the house and look for it, will you report me to the sheriff as a housebreaker?"

"Are you a friend of the doctor's?"

"I believe that over the last few days we have become friends of a sort, yes."

"Then it ain't no business of mine if you want to enter your friend's house. I'm turnin' my back on you, sir, and it's no more a concern to me. Good luck and good health to your sick child." The old man did, indeed, turn his back on Harry and then disappeared altogether into his little stone cottage.

Harry tried the front door and found it unlocked. Inside was a most unexpected picture: the front parlour had been thoroughly ransacked. Furniture lay overturned, drawers had been yanked entirely from their cabinets, their contents spilt about. Piles of books and papers lay strewn round in remarkable dishevelment.

As Harry stood in the doorway, surveying the room's troubling state of disarrangement, he heard a woman's voice calling from the lane.

"You there! What are you doing there?"

The one who had called to him was Rose Fagin. She was accompanied by her daughter Susan. The two were going to each of their properties in an effort to raise enough money from their renters, in exchange for future concessions, so that they should have sufficient funds to bargain for the release of Mr. Fagin from the gaol. Whether such bargaining constituted a bribe or no, Rose Fagin did not care. She only wanted her husband home. "Answer me, young man. Are you breaking into my house?"

Harry Scadger knew not how to answer the question except to say that he wasn't aware that this was her house.

"It most certainly is. I am the owner along with my husband, and Dr. Timberry is our tenant. Are you with the Apricot Clan? You have no business here, young man. Get along now before I summon the sheriff."

"Do not summon the sheriff, Mama," said Susan, her face screwed up into a look of strong repugnance. "He is an ogre—a pustular eruption in the shape of a man for what he has done to Papa. Simply let this man go upon his way. He is, no doubt, hungry, having only apricots to eat."

"Begging your pardon," said Harry, who had overheard Susan's entreaty to her mother, "but in spite of the fact that I do hail from that tribe, I no longer reside with them. I live in Milltown and I am not here for the purpose of obtaining victuals, but to fetch Dr. Timberry. Having just been informed of his arrestment, I am now interested in discovering if the doctor's medical bag is kept within, for my consumptive daughter must have her medicine."

Rose Fagin considered for a moment everything that Harry had said as she and her daughter approached the house.

"As I live and breathe!" ejaculated Rose, seeing now the condition of the parlour. "Are you responsible for this whirlwind's visit to my house?"

"Most assuredly not, madam. This is how I found it only a moment ago myself."

"It is not necessary for you to call me madam. 'Mrs. Fagin' is my name, and this is my daughter Susan."

With a bow: "Nice to make your acquaintance."

"He has good manners, daughter. For an apricot-eater. Young man, have you any thought as to what has been sought here?"

"The medical bag, no doubt," said Harry.

"What is so valuable about this medical bag, that one should look for it in such a frantic manner?" asked Rose.

"I believe that *I* know," said Susan softly. "If it is the same bag that was used by Nurse Wolf in her rounds, there are special drugs in there—the most efficacious drugs from the Outland."

"Aye," said Harry, nodding eagerly to Susan to continue.

"I have accompanied the late Miss Wolf upon her rounds and have seen her apply the drugs surreptitiously—for I believe that she was never permitted to use them. And I have marveled at their efficiency. There is great value to the medical bag, for it contains largely those medicines that cannot otherwise be found here in the Dell."

"And is that all, my child?" asked Susan's mother. "Could this be the only reason that such a great worth has been placed upon the bag?"

"No. There is something else therein. I saw her use it once. It was at

Bedlam and I was assisting her in sedating a crowded ward of patients there. The inmates had grown querulous and wild and there were no orderlies available to assist us in subduing them. It is an Outlander device. She took it from the bag and used it upon one of the riotous men and brought him quickly to the point of docility. It so frightened the other men that they became quite yielding."

"And is there a name for this device?" asked Harry.

Susan nodded. "It is called a Taser. She asked me never to speak of what I saw or ever to tell that she had the device, for no one knew that such a weapon had been brought into the Dell. Of course, now someone *must* know, or they would not desire so much to have the bag."

"How does it work?"

"It delivers an electrical charge to the subject, thus interrupting temporarily all voluntary controul of his muscles. It bears similarity to a handgun but doesn't fire bullets or shot. It fires, instead, a wire resembling a stinging sea creature's tentacle. Please don't tell anyone what I'm telling you."

"Or what, my dear?" asked Susan's mother Rose in a sarcastic tone. "It should place the late Miss Wolf into jeopardy?"

Susan coloured. Then Susan said in a sad and regretful voice, "Perhaps if she had had it with her, she would not be dead. It is a most effective weapon."

"Mayhap she thought it better that Timberry should have it. And now, alas, it is in the hands of the sheriff, no doubt," said Harry, scouring the ruined room for any place that the ransackers had not delved.

Rose considered this statement with a light drumming of her fingers upon her temples. "Not necessarily. For I know of a place that perhaps wasn't searched by those who came hither to destroy my house—and mark me, they will pay for this damage, after they have made restitution to my poor husband for arresting him under a spurious charge."

"Where is the hiding place?" asked Harry with great interest.

"Pull back that chair there," replied Rose, pointing. "Remove the four floor boards beneath it. You may have to tug a bit, for they are wedged tightly amongst the others to produce the illusion of close adherence to the other boards. Timberry knew of this hiding place, for I shewed it to him myself."

Harry did as he was instructed and quickly discerned which of the boards could be removed with a bit of applied prying.

Having removed all four, he reached down into the dark space below the floor and drew up the medical bag with a smile.

"Take the bag, Mr. Scadger," said Rose. "It is no longer safe to leave it here. Perhaps you should give me the Taser gun so that I can go to the Inn-of-Justice and electrify all of those constabulary miscreants who are holding my husband without due process of law. That should do the trick to win his release!"

"You will do nothing of the kind, Mama!" proclaimed Susan. To Harry: "Let us keep the bag between us, since there are other patients of whom I am aware who could benefit from the medicine within. Mama, Mr. Scadger and I are going to tend to his sick daughter. You should stay behind and put this cyclone house to rights, and think no more of storming the Bastille with an electric gun."

"It was said in dark jest, my daughter. But now is not the time for levity, is it? Your father mouldering away in gaol. Half this valley under commensurate lock and key or chained to beds at Bedlam. It depresses me to no end."

But by now Rose Fagin was addressing only herself, for her daughter and Harry Scadger had fled.

Susan Fagin and Harry Scadger could smell the smoke, but could not glean its source. As they continued on their way to Milltown, they began to notice a growing darkness in the eastern sky—a darkness that quickly materialised into thick rising puffs of black cloud coming from the direction of the Scadger apricot grove.

"My brothers and their families are in peril," said Harry. "I must help them."

Yet there was nothing that could be done. When Susan and Harry reached the orchard, it was fully aflame, and Harry's half-brothers and their wives and children were huddled together and watching with moist and horrified eyes as their arbour hamlet turned itself into charcoal and ash. Harry pinched at his nose; the smell of baking and burning fruit assaulted it with sweet acridity, as would a fruit pie left too long in the oven.

"Who did it?" asked Harry of his oldest half-brother Sol.

"Uniformed men what came from the wood. Zeph was sentry for the day and saw them first. We had expected an evening assault but nothin' in the broad daylight, brother. The men, they gathered us together in a group and we were afeared that we should be executed upon that spot. Mel had hardly time to draw his bow and arrow to give fight when it was shot from his hand. We were defeated before the battle could even begin, brother— outnumbered and outweaponed."

"And left with no more home," said Harry in sad commiseration with his brothers' plight. "And where are the men now—the Beyonders who did this?"

"Scuttled back into the wood like the Outland rats they are. Ephraim, now, he wants to go after them."

"A fool's mission," said Harry, shaking his head vigorously. "We cannot fight the Outlanders. Not this way. Come with me to Milltown."

"We'll not live beneath a bridge!" proclaimed Sol on behalf of his clan. "Nor will we go to the workhouse. Mel wants to leave the valley altogether—to try to make a home for ourselves in the Terra Incotta."

"And that should be the deadliest course of all, brother. Are not the woods and ridges growing thick with Outlander agents—the same who came to burn down this orchard? Perhaps you have not heard it, but Sir Dabber and his son and a nurse were slashed and stabbed to death only two nights ago to prevent their own passage. You need not go to the bridge or the workhouse. My other two half-brothers now sit in the Dingley Gaol along with Mrs. Lumbey and her apprentice. Their lodgings are presently empty. I will take all of you there and I will take full responsibility should anyone return with objections. But I think that they should not, given present circumstances. Come. Gather your things together and let us vacate this place, lest the Outlanders return to finish the task for which this fire was only prologue. Miss Fagin, please assist the women in gathering up their things, and I will assist the men. Look sharp, my brothers. We should tarry no longer in this dangerous cinder-grove."

And so Harry's half-brothers and their families began to ready themselves to leave their orchard home forever. And there was a great flow of tears and angry murmurs and shakings of fists in the direction of the eastern wood. And Melchisedech Scadger looked upon his ruined bow and his quiver and his stilled arrows, which he had fashioned and carved with his own hands, and he repined his inability to do battle on behalf of his clan as Harry placed a consoling hand upon his shoulder and left it there for a brief tearful interval.

CHAPTER THE FORTY-FOURTH

Wednesday, July 9, 2003

Near the end of the Scadgers' journey to Mrs. Lumbey's lodgings in Milltown, the light of day began to wane, to be replaced by crepuscular half-light and shadow. The band of brothers and their wives and their large litters of barefoot children tread slower than was their wont, their heads bowed in disconsolation, for though little had they ever had, now even less did they possess—not much more, in fact, than the clothes upon their backs and a few rescued tools and personal baubles. Susan Fagin walked along with the women, holding a young infant in her caring nurse's arms, and Harry walked ahead with his older brother Solomon, his four younger brothers marching only a few steps behind.

It was the two brothers in the lead who first saw what sort of reception Milltown would give them, for no sooner had they crossed into the West End by the northern road did they begin to receive suspicious glares from many of those out and about this early evening. There were also whispers interchanged between frowning and contemptuous mouths—clear signs that the clan was to move along and stop nowhere along the way.

One man went even farther in his own show of distaste for the Scadger clan. The man was the apothecary William Skettles, brother-in-law of Montague Pupker. He stood upon the front step of his shop, having just locked up his establishment for the night. "The Westminster Bridge to the

East End is *that* way," he called to Solomon Scadger and his brother Harry, who remembered the ignominious occasion of his ejection from that same apothecary's shop only a few days before. "You are all going in the wrong direction."

"We are not headed for the East End, Mr. Skettles," replied Harry. "And furthermore, it is no business of yours just *what* direction we are going."

"What insolence!" declared Skettles. "To come into this neighbourhood in your dirty, diseased rags and display such extraordinary contempt for your betters. Turn your steps in the direction of the East End, Apricoteater, or I will summon a deputy sheriff to turn them for you."

"Yes, and do be so good as to tell me where we shall go in that neighborhood, since you and your brother-in-law Pupker turned my family out of the mews."

"That was *you*? My, but don't all of you fruit-gipsies look alike!"

"Ignore the man," said Harry to his older brother, sensing that Sol wanted to say something as well, on behalf of his family. Sol, heeding his brother's bidding, checked himself as the two men continued to lead their blood troop in the direction of their own choosing.

It so happened, that to Skettles' delight, there *was* a deputy sheriff in the vicinity of his chemist's shop coming just that moment down the lane. Skettles signalled him with a wave of the hand, though he need not have done it. The deputy, a man nearly as young as his new employer Boldwig, had already made up his mind to learn the reason for the Scadgers' pack-like presence in the West End, since it was common knowledge that gatherings of the destitute in any number generally represented a blot upon the face of any upstanding neighbourhood.

"Deputy Gradgrind," said Skettles, "perhaps you may wish to inform this filthy tribe of the location of that bridge which takes one out of the West End. As you can clearly see, they haven't a clew as to how to gain it."

Before the deputy could oblige the apothecary, Harry stopt. All those behind him stopt as well. Harry spoke up: "We have no intention of going to the East End. There are lodgings for us here in the West End and so here in the West End we shall stay."

Skettles shook his head in sheer and utter astonishment over what he had just heard. At the same time his eye fell upon Susan Fagin, standing amongst the Scadger wives. "Miss Fagin, do you become a charity worker when not about your healing rounds within our local hospitals?"

"I am whatever you may wish to think of me," said Susan, "for I care little for your opinion."

"Upon my word, girl, does your mother know what has become of you?"

Susan hadn't time to answer (even should she have wished to) for at just that moment Deputy Gradgrind drew out his billy club, which had been fixed upon his belt, and held it aloft in a threatening stance. To Harry he said, "Leave this vicinity, sir—you and all your clan. March yourselves to the bridge, or I will have every one of you put under arrest."

Harry Scadger squared his shoulders and bridled his chin. "We are free men. We have done nothing wrong. Our orchard home has been burnt to the ground. We are going to our new lodgings."

"There is no place in the West End that would take you, or do you intend to commandeer a bivouac for yourself? You will go to workhouses in the East End or you will go to the gaol. What be your choice?"

"We have made known our intention, Deputy, and we will not waver from it. Now, you have tried our patience long enough, so we will be on our way."

"Take another step and I will strike you with this truncheon," said the young deputy in a bluff, defiant voice.

"And my brothers and I will strike you down with our twelve fists," struck in Solomon, who as leader of the clan could remain silent no longer.

"That is a bargain that does not favour me," said the young deputy sheriff, restoring his billy club to its slot on his belt. Then, reaching inside his coat, he continued, "but let us try *this* arrangement and see if it doesn't work better to my benefit." The deputy drew out a pistol—similar to that used by Sheriff Boldwig three days earlier. "Go to the East End without delay, or I will shoot, and I will not stop shooting until every member of your stinking clan be dead."

"Capital!" cheered Skettles with a couple of applauding claps of the hands.

"What has come over you, Gradgrind?" asked Harry, taking a step toward the deputy, even though there should be a gun aimed directly at his chest. "That you should turn your back on one of your own to do the bidding of the Bashaws? What are they paying you to debase yourself in this manner?"

"*They*? I'm upholding the law, you jolterhead. And I have no idea what you mean by 'one of my own.'"

"Your own cousin Violetta who married my brother Zephaniah. Is she now dead to you?"

The dark-eyed and olive-skinned Violetta stepped forward from the cluster of Scadger wives so that the deputy could better see her face.

"I did not recognise you," said he. "You are now so thin, your cheeks so gaunt. As children we once played together and now I would not know you for anything but a tatterdemalion indigent."

"Yet that is what I am, cousin," said Violetta, pulling tight the draggled shawl draping her bony shoulders. "But let us pass. Pray let us pass, dear cousin."

The young deputy shook his head. "I cannot. I uphold the law. And I will not hesitate to shoot you as well, should the lot of you not go as I have ordered."

"Then shoot me first," said Sol, his look hardened and his brow set. With that, the oldest member of the Scadger clan augmented his provocation by advancing forthwith upon the deputy. Deputy Gradgrind took a step back and then another as if he had suddenly lost his nerve along with his authority.

"You can't do it," said Sol in sober assessment. "I knew that you couldn't."

Then Gradgrind did something *quite* authoritative; he accepted Sol Scadger's dare and fired his gun directly into that man's chest. As the loud cracking report of the shot echoed throughout the lane, the air was pierced as well by the screams of some of the wives. Solomon's own wife Nell did not scream. Instead she fell insentient into the arms of her sister-in-law Barbara, who watched in horror as the oldest of the Scadger clan clutched at his fast-crimsoning breast and then fell to the ground. Susan Fagin rushed to his side. Solomon Scadger's eyes remained open, but all life had fled from them.

"Right through his very heart," said Susan somberly and clinically, though her own eyes were filling with silent tears. Deputy Gradgrind did not lower his gun. He kept it trained on the other five men, each of whom wore seething expressions of murderous revenge.

No one moved with one exception: Susan Fagin, who went to the medical bag, which Harry had a moment before set down next to his feet. She unbuckled the straps and opened the bag, even as Harry said to her in a low, crippled voice, "There's nothing that can be done for him. Can you not see that he is already dead?"

"There is at least one *small* thing that I can do in his memory," said Susan. And then she did her small thing; she pulled the Taser from the bag, engaged it as she had seen Nurse Wolf do, and shot the deputy with it, the electrified wire striking the young man in his chest at very nearly the same spot where his bullet had entered the body of Solomon Scadger. Gradgrind fell forward, just as Solomon had fallen, crying out in anguish from the pain of the voltaic attack.

The pistol having dropt from the deputy's hand, Melchisedech Scadger swept it up from the ground. "See if there are other bullets on his person," Harry instructed his brother. Gradgrind, stunned by the electric shock and unable to move, put up no struggle. Mel retrieved a box of bullets from one of the deputy's coat pockets.

"Hurry on," said Susan to Harry. "Allow me to stay behind and pay the price for my actions."

"We will not leave you here. Nor will we leave my brother Solomon behind. Brothers, lift up your slain oldest brother and let us be on our way. Susan Fagin, you will come with us."

Susan Fagin thought over her choices for a brief moment, then nodded and cast her lot with whatever fate awaited the Scadger clan. A man was dead, another man brought to his knees by a diabolical but efficient Outland weapon. A third man—Williams Skettles—had disappeared into his apothecary shop and was, no doubt, crouching and quivering behind his counter, having fully soiled his under-trowsers.

"Where are we to go?" asked Zephaniah, as he bore the motionless right shoulder of his lifeless older brother.

"To Fort Lumbey," replied Harry.

Deputy Gradgrind's pistol was not the only one to be fired that night. In several separate incidents, arrests were made amongst citizens in the East End, but not without engagement of the Outland guns that had been distributed by Sheriff Boldwig to each of his deputies. Judge Fitz-Marshall had taken it upon himself with nodding approval of several members of the Petit-Parliament to declare a curfew for this and every one of the succeeding nights until the time of the Summit evacuation so as to better keep the peace in the remaining days of valley occupancy.

There had been concerns by certain members of the Petit-Parliament that such a reining in of personal liberty amongst Dinglians would have the opposite effect—would incite anger and panic and chaos—and it was this faction that had accurately foreseen the quickly-ensuing results of the judge's actions, for there was now just such a reactive backlash afoot and growing more conflagrative with every moment, with each newly retailed rumour circulating through the streets like bellowed flame. The reason was this: that every fear which had dwelt within the breast of the vaguely and perpetually-fearful Dinglian, passed along from generation to generation for 121 years via an ethos of indeterminate unease and doubt and unanswered enquiry, now gave way to the sudden realisation that *anything* could be true—that *everything* could be true—that the sky was indeed falling— that the Dell was now in its dying throes.

Rose saw it for herself as she returned to her jewellry shop. There in the street was a gathering of merchants and tavern-keepers and hostlers and blacksmiths and barbers, and other men and women of middle-class burgherdom, assembled to know what was to be done with so many arrests and so much foment in the streets. At least a dozen shops had been forcibly entered and vandalised in just the last hour. And arrests had not been limited only to the criminal element. Had not the jeweller Herbert Fagin himself been hauled off to gaol; and the writer Frederick Trimmers; and the young doctor, Mulberry Timberry; and the successful businesswoman, Antonia Bocker; and even the former sheriff, Vincent Muntle? What was the charge? Conspiracy? Conspiracy to do what? To stop whatever force now overshadowed the land? Those gathered together avowed to make an enquiry of the Petit-Parliament at the earliest opportunity, but they must first get themselves through this perilous night in which angry East Enders had begun to cross the bridge to roam the streets of the prosperous West End and to break windows and to steal from the shops that had long been closed to their patronage, their having heard rumours that Dingley Dell was now become a lawless province and every man must fend for himself. Sharing those streets were armed patrolling deputies wielding Outland weaponry and arresting whatever man had his name put upon a warrant, and some men and women whose names were *not* put upon warrants, but who (as in the case of Rose Fagin's husband) dared to protest too loudly a constabulary action. These too were placed under swift arrest.

Rose Fagin listened to the ringing, echoing voices of concern and apprehension in the street, and then she repaired to her shop to take to her lodgings above. But once within her showroom she learnt a most terrible thing: she had been robbed, the culprit (or culprits) having taken nearly every ring and broach and choker in her shop. "It's the end of the world," she said to herself, sitting down upon a stool, but she did not weep, for hunger quickly called her to her kitchen, wherein she put some cold boiled mutton with caper sauce upon a plate and devoured it with sad little moans.

CHAPTER THE FORTY-FIFTH

Wednesday, July 9, and early Thursday, July 10, 2003

Maggy stood at her window in her small sleeping quarters off the kitchen. She had put on her dressing gown and had even spent an unproductive interval in bed, tossing and turning and wondering why the man to whom she had given her heart must first lose his position as sheriff and then find himself sitting within a dark and damp gaol cell. Maggy's former state of bliss had been brought to an abrupt end only a few hours earlier when her employer, Mr. Chowser, took her aside after supper and conveyed the most recently disturbing news about Muntle.

Maggy vowed that she would go and see her fiancé as soon as her employer gave her leave. Vincent could not be kept incarcerated forever, and perhaps it was time to ask Mr. Chowser if he had need of another labouring man to help round the school. Then the two could marry and be happy together ever after.

That part of Maggy which did not embrace sound logic wondered if, against all odds, she might catch a glimpse of him in the shadows, his having daringly escaped from his confinement in Milltown, drawn, of course, to her side by the magnetism of her deep affection. It was a silly thought, but one that nonetheless captivated her and kept her eyes fixed upon the road for any sign of him. The hour was late and there should be no one coming down this isolate byway at such a time. But then at just the next moment, there was: two dark figures, in fact, each silhouetted against the moonlit landscape, each furtively creeping out from behind the stand of trees round which the road turned and made its appearance before the school. Since the dirt road terminated at the open and welcoming front gate of the Chowser school grounds there was no other place to which they could be headed. The two figures entered the gates and came very near to Maggy's own window, startling her to such a degree that she shrunk back and slapped a hand directly upon her mouth lest they hear her audible gasp through the open casements.

It was good that the frightened cook should cover her mouth in such a manner, for what the phantoms did next would surely have invoked an even more vocal reaction. A spark was struck in one of their hands and then two large torches were lighted, both bursting suddenly upon their flambeau ends as if there was greatly combustible material packed there. It was now clear to Maggy that the torches had some purpose other than simply the lighting of the strangers' way as they traversed the dark grounds. They were come for a reason far more sinister than mere prowling about; they were set, it now appeared to Maggy, to put the main school building to quick flame—to burn the building to the ground with all of its occupants fast asleep within their beds.

Maggy watched as the men went round the side of the building and disappeared from her view. But not another moment passed before she could smell the smoke of the arsons' incendiary mission. Wasting no time, Maggy raced into the kitchen and threw open the door that gave on the garden. Above this door hung the noisy iron bell that summoned all of the hungry Chowser School residents to their meals. On occasion it was used for other convocational purposes. Now Maggy sought to employ it for a brand new purpose: to wake the sleepers in their beds and call for an immediate evacuation of the burning school.

The tocsin did its business, and shortly thereafter came a scramble and bustle of activity inside the school, which was already burning on its western end where the classrooms were situated. Yet even in the dormitories on the eastern side, one could smell the pungent smoke and all knew instantly what was happening.

All, that is…save young Jack Snicks, who continued to sleep through all the shouting and the hubbub—slept soundly and peacefully upon his cot until Alphonse Chowser retrieved him from the smoke-clouded dormitory.

Alphonse pulled the nine-year-old boy up from his bed, along with a tangle of sheets and blankets, and patted him gently upon the cheeks. Jack awoke with a start; he had been in the midst of a most engaging dream in which he had been sitting before his late aunt's cozy hearth when the flue suddenly shut and the room became filled with smoke.

"Do you not know what is happening, lad?" asked Chowser, setting the boy down upon the floor and taking him by the hand. Then answering his own enquiry as the two hurried in their bare feet toward the door that offered egress from the smoky room: "But of course you could not have known until I woke you. I often forget, my little sleepy man, that you're a deaf mute, for you read lips so very well."

Jack made an unintelligible noise with his tongue and throat that served to forgive Chowser the oversight.

There was a brief and valiant attempt at forming a bucket brigade amongst the pupils and the staff, but the fire raged too great, and the hand windlass turned too slowly above the well to retrieve the buckets fast enough to make any difference.

Before the large stone manse that served as boarding school to some thirty-some-odd boys (the current crop), Alphonse Chowser, Esq., stood robed but still shoeless, along with all of those equally barefooted boys and wide-eyed adult employees. There was Porter (who went by nothing but his occupational name alone); and Mary Katharine, the maid-of-all-work; and Diggory, the gardener; and Mr. Smangle, who handled the accounts and sometimes taught arithmetic and eulogic, which was a discipline developed by this rumple-haired, pock-marked man himself: a philosophy rooted in a Panglossian sort of view that most people are by their inherent nature good and kind, though this evening of arson would prove the exception that makes the rule.

And there was Maggy, the saviour of the night, who, through a sleepless longing for the man she loved, had made possible a full and successful evacuation of the school. Chowser took Maggy's hand in a silent show of gratitude whilst shaking his head despondently as the flames spat and danced within his tired, worried eyes.

"Oh, Smangle," suspired Chowser in a lamenting tone, "all of my years of work, vanishing before my eyes. It is most difficult to bear."

"Who would do such a thing?" asked Mary Katharine, her fingers running desultorily through her sleep-mussed hair.

"Arsonists, as I have said. I saw them with my own eyes." answered Maggy in a logical but not altogether enlightening way.

"We will rebuild, Chowser," said Smangle. "We *must* rebuild. At all events, these flames do not put to ashes all of the work you have already done, for there are hundreds of upstanding men throughout the Dell who are walking testament to your years of self-sacrificing labour. They are testament to all that your father has done and to the efforts of your grandfather before him. The Chowser School does not die *there*," indicating the blazing fire with a gesturing hand, "but that it continues to live *here*." Smangle pressed both of his hands tightly against his breast to show where his heart was.

"Mary Katharine asked the right question," said Diggory. "Why would anyone want to burn down our school? For what possible reason?" The gardener was still wearing his sleeping smock. With one hand he clutched the handle of a spade, hastily drawn from his tool shed. With it, Diggory had hoped to strike blows upon the perpetrators of this dastardly act, though by that point the evildoers had already long vanished into the surrounding darkness. Diggory gave a nervous glance over his shoulder at his prized vegetable patch, which was too close to the darting flames for his comfort.

He turned back to Maggy. "And you're very sure, Cook, that you saw them—the men with the torches? You are sure that they weren't some fancy of your half-drowsy mind?" Diggory patted his callused hand soothingly upon the head of one of the youngest boys, who clung tremblingly to the gardener's knee and would be in tears were such a thing ever to be permitted by his stoic older schoolmates.

"Alas, Gardener, I believe that Maggy's eyes did not deceive her," said Chowser through a sigh that carried a great weight of sorrow with it. "I have always wondered if it was not a bad decision on my grandfather's part to build our school so far removed from Milltown or even from any of the other villages. Here we sit upon the veritable frontier of the Dell. I've sent Anthony on the fleet bay mare to fetch the firemen, but it will all be for naught. The blazes could not be contained even should the engine arrive at this very moment. In no time at all the whole building will be reduced to smoking wooden rubble."

Chowser turned his back to the flames, able no longer to endure the sight of them. Yet still he could not successfully remove the scene from his view, for the fire shone in all the reflections round him: it shone in the blazing eyes of the boys who huddled close together and looked on in amazement at this destructive feat of nature (initiated in this case not by nature but by the villainous hand of man); its bright flames reflected in the coal scuttle held by Porter (thinking that it could be used to carry water to douse the flames, though it was found to be woefully inadequate for that purpose); it was mirrored in the Britannia metal tea pot rescued by Mary Katharine, the maid-of-all-work (because it was lovely and why should it not be saved?); and it gleamed bright yellow and orange from the side of the tin cash box, tucked beneath the arm of the ever practical Mr. Smangle.

It was that last gentleman who broke a silence that was in truth not so silent at all, given the crackling, popping, and crashing down of an old wooden and stone building succumbing to its fiery dismantling: "Do not repine the decision of your grandfather, fearless leader, for this has been a most excellent location for our happy little school, with ample room for the boys to run and play. If your father had bought a building in town, there should be no more romps in the meadow, and I for one could not have inculcated my young charges—under the canopy of that great, beautiful oak tree that puts us all at one with the squirrels—with all my acorns of eulogical wisdom. This has been a joyous, most splendid place of learning. Oh, hither comes the new sheriff. What's that boy's name?"

"Billy Boldwig," offered Diggory with a sneer. "His father never en-roled him here. He was privately tutored. And he has a stench. Have you noticed? There's always a stench."

The new sheriff dismounted his horse and marched up to the knot of frowning, moist-eyed fire-gazers comprised of both the pupils and the instructors and staff of the now *former* Chowser School for Boys (ante-formerly known as the Chowser School for Wayward Boys, the "wayward" being subsequently struck when the school began to invite in other boys not so wayward to ingurgitate "the finest affordable education afforded anywhere to a Dingley lad").

"Thank you for coming so quickly, Sheriff," said Chowser, reaching to take Boldwig's hand.

Not seeing the hand, Billy didn't take it. His eyes were fixed on the fire. "I came quickly, but I cannot tarry here. There is a crime spree in Milltown. What happened here? Who did this?"

"A crime spree? What do you mean?"

"Unrest. We will quell it. Who put this old building to flame?"

"We don't know the identity of the arsonists," said Chowser. "Will you make it your duty to find them and bring them to justice?"

"And how are you so certain that it was arson? There could be any number of possible causes for a fire such as this. Perhaps it grew from a kitchen fire insufficiently snuffed out."

"I am always meticulous in how I put out my fires," said Maggy, taking offence at the Sheriff's suggestion. "Moreover, I—"

"I will say it, Maggy," interrupted Chowser. Then to the sheriff: "We know that it was arson because my cook saw two men approach the school on foot carrying torches."

"And this could not possibly be a deception on her part, to cover the fact that she went to bed having left something burning in the kitchen that should have been doused?"

Maggy's cheeks mantled in sudden choler and rising perturbation.

"Let us say that two men *did* come past your school to-night carrying torches," continued Boldwig. "Perhaps they were merely lighting their way in the dark night. Ask your cook, sir, if she saw them actually put fire to the building."

"I am standing right here. You may ask me yourself, you malapert puppy," said Maggy, her arms placed akimbo upon her wide hips.

"There is no cause for incivility, dear lady," rejoined Billy Boldwig, as Chowser put a hand upon his cook's arm to stay her wroth (knowing, of course, that it was being fed both by the sheriff's charge of negligence on her part *and* by the man's complicity in placing the former sheriff—and Maggy's heart's delight—under arrest). "And let us say that everything you surmise is true—that two men did come all this way for the purpose of setting fire to this firetrap of a school; now, just how would you suppose I go about catching such persons?"

"We cannot say, but at all events you must certainly try!" beseeched Mr. Smangle. "There must be retribution for a crime of this magnitude."

"I will do what I can when I can. There is too much else that demands my attention to make any sort of promise." ·

Now Diggory stepped forward to be heard. "Explain again, sir. Whatever did you mean about there being unrest in Milltown?"

"That very thing, sir. The East Enders are become crazed Jacobins, dashing about stirring up their own Reign of Terror. The Scadgers have come in from their orchard to barricade themselves within Mrs. Lumbey's shop on Dombey Lane. They have weapons and have already attacked one of my own deputies."

"Then by all means go and see to your duties there," said Chowser. "There is not much more that can be done here." The headmaster turned to look again upon that which he could hardly abide: his life's work disintegrating in flames, with scant hope of phlogistic phoenix rising from its ashes.

Maggy fixed her own eyes glaringly upon the sheriff. "And you have no knowledge whatsoever of who these men could be—the men who came here, and *why* they should come and do what they did?"

"For all I know, madam, they are part of that horde that is presently creating pandemonium in town. I cannot begin to think of who these men could be or what they should be about. And now I must go."

"Thank you for coming, you useless lump," hurled Maggy with sarcastic bite.

"She is upset," apologised Chowser, quickly interposing himself between Maggy and the sheriff. "Quite upset. As are we all."

But Maggy was not quite finished. She delivered her valedictory comment from behind Chowser's intervening back: "Perhaps there would not be revolt in the streets if you and your men hadn't gone merrily about arresting every man and woman in Dingley Dell who disagreed with the leadership of this valley for whatever reason served your purpose."

"Or perhaps things might have been even worse had we failed to act," said the freckle-faced Boy Sheriff, quickly grown into his job and standing a bit taller through pride in his office. "And Mr. Chowser, were I you, I should speak to your cook about the wages of disrespect for public officials."

The sheriff went to his horse and undid the reins from the fence post to which they had been tethered. Then as if seised by a sudden parting thought, he turned and said to the group that included both child and adult alike, "How do you know that it wasn't one of your delinquent boys who did it? I ask you that. Check your snot-nostriled ruffians for lucifers—that's what I suggest. That should more than likely comprise the whole investigation, Mr. Chowser, and once you find the culprits, I should be glad to hand them over to Judge Fitz-Marshall for the speediest of trials."

"Our boys are all good boys," said Chowser with an ebbing desire to continue this fruitless exchange. "All fine and decent little men."

But then to make a liar of the earnest headmaster, a rock was thrown in the direction of the sheriff. It came from a knot of especially scowling boys, each quite displeased to be called delinquents and ruffians and perhaps even arsonists. It fell slightly short of its target and struck the sheriff without injury upon the tip of his boot. Billy reached down, picked up the projectile, and displayed it upon the flat of his palm. "Who did this? Who threw the bloody rock at me?"

The boys shook their heads as one. The true assailant, young Jack Snicks, took a few steps backwards. It was hard for him to read the lips of the sheriff from such a distance, but he knew by the law officer's dyspeptic look that he had been saying cruel things about the school, cruel things about Cook who was always especially nice to him because he was an orphan, and cruel things in general because he appeared to be contemptible by nature. Such behaviour provoked young Jack Snicks to strike a blow for his school and for all those who had been kind to him. Jack Snicks did not understand why the Sheriff should not come and shed tears of worry over what was to become of all the boys and all the men and women who took care to educate the boys and to tuck them into bed each night with tender custodianship. Jack Snicks was confused and Jack Snicks was angry and there was only one thing to do about it: smite the uncompassionating sheriff with a rock.

"You will not give the boy up?" barked Billy. "None of you? You'll not give up the boy who scuffed my boot—give him up in the name of the law? Then I say to every one of you low gutter vermin, that you had this coming to you. It was right that this place should burn down and I'm happy that you were positioned in such a spot as to require it."

The headmaster gave the sheriff a quizzical look. "Whatever do you mean, sir? 'Positioned to require it.' I don't understand."

"I'll not tell you. You're not amongst those who should know. Let me say only this: that I find it quite a laugh—and quite telling, really—that all who occupy the periphery of this valley, which must be cleared of all occupancy and habitation, are those which rank the lowest upon that scale of human worth: the vagabond Scadgers, the filthy coal extractors of Blackheath, and this school of delinquents. Quite telling. I'll not weep for the loss of this school or for any of the rest of you. I'll not drop a single tear."

And with that, the sheriff bent low to dust off his boot with his riding glove, then mounted his horse and galloped away without looking back.

"What does he mean?" asked Diggory of Chowser. "About those places that must be cleared of all occupancy and habitation."

Alphonse Chowser clapped his hand upon the shoulder of his gardener and said in a soft but fearful tone, "That those of us on the outskirts are being moved in one fashion or another into the centre of the Dell."

"But why?"

"I plan to ask Muntle that very thing when I visit him in the gaol on the morrow."

In the distance Boldwig could now be seen meeting up with the fire engine, which had been summoned from Milltown. Chowser and the others watched as the Boy Sheriff exchanged a few words with the fire chief and then as the fire chief addressed the driver, who quickly turned his team of horses round and steered them back into town.

"Having come this far, why would the chief not complete his call?" queried Diggory of his colleague Smangle, the former scratching his head in befuddlement.

"Because Boldwig's told him everything he needs to know," answered Mr. Smangle. "No doubt, to-morrow that most helpful fledgling of the law will be sitting down with the insurance claims man and we'll not see a penny. A life-long investment, no recompense, every cinder and ash to be hauled away and dropt into the iron pit. Not that we should ever have seen any insurance money anyway. Because I don't think we're long for this place."

"Is that what you believe, Smangle? Because I am inclined to agree," said Chowser to his school's bookkeeper.

Alphonse Chowser, Esq., had spoken in a voice made so low that it should reach Smangle and Diggory and Maggy's ears only. He presumed that none of the boys was near enough to hear such a bleak interpretation of recent events. However, one of the boys who did not hear had no need to. It was young Jack Snicks who had, of late, taken to chucking rocks at Tiadaghton Bashaws (not because they were Bashaws but because they were soulless blackguards). He had caught every word, each delivered from the lips of the two men, and the words would trouble him from that moment forward.

After the fire had burnt itself down and there was a glimmer of morning light over the dark Eastern Ridge, Alphonse Chowser wandered amongst his pupils and amongst those men and women in his employ, rousing those who had fallen into uneasy slumbers upon the ground and pulling the others from their pensive reveries. "Come," he said. "Wake. Rise. There's much work for us to do this morning. We must gather what little things we have left, which were saved from the fire, and return you boys to your families and guardians."

This injunction was received with a great wail of disappointment, peppered with recalcitrant grumblings and oaths from each of the boys, who most decidedly did not wish to be returned to their families and their guardians. They wanted to be here—here now being, unfortunately, a place of incinerated hopes and dreams—a place that had the misfortune of standing too close to the edge of the valley, and which, as now was slowly coming to the ken of Chowser and Smangle and the others, had been specifically marked for expeditious obliteration.

Alphonse Chowser, Esq., placed a trembling hand into the pocket of his sleeping gown and found nothing there but flue and lint. He had sought to rescue his grandfather's watch from the gathering flames, had dug his hand into the drawer beside his bed in search of it, but then remembered that it had been missing from that drawer (and from every other place he'd looked) for several days. It had disappeared, in fact, on the very day of Newman Trimmers's departure. Chowser could not believe that the boy had taken it, but coincidence often gives an answer where none other can be found. It was a gold Geneva hunting watch, engine-turned, capped, and jewelled in four holes. It had the uncommon ability to tinkle a fairy's chime every quarter of an hour, and it was the one thing that Alphonse Chowser, Esq., had said he would take from his room should he ever find it engulfed in flames and the opportunity given him to rescue only one item of value or sentiment.

Chowser only hoped that Newman had gotten a good price for it.

The Chowser School wasn't the only building in Dingley Dell set aflame on that flagrant night. Blackheath, that small colony of humble huts occupied by the men who worked the coal mine and by their families—set at the farthest point south within the Dell—was burning as well, even though every man, woman, and child in the little miners' outpost was out with buckets and pails and everything that would hold water to quench the flames.

But all efforts came to naught. In less than an hour all of the huts had burnt themselves to the ground, and what was once a slightly dingy but pleasant labouring village had been reduced to nothing more than a collection of jagged and smoking heaps of black ruin.

"Did anyones get a look at dose what did it?" asked a grey-bearded man named Joper, who was assistant to the foreman and the closest thing this group had to a leader.

"Dem wore hoods and capes, best as I could tell," said another man—a veritable eyewitness to the crime—who could scarcely be heard over the blubbering of his wife and six cubs.

"Where be da sherf?" enquired a different man over the keening of his own family. "Ain't he comin'?"

"Sherf ain't Muntle no more," answered the man standing next to this man who held a little Tiny Tim-like boy upon his ash-dusted shoulders. "'Tis dat Deputy Boldwig wit da Pa what sits in da Parlmength—da one what ain't got nothink between his ears but fart-wind."

"I bet it's his own men what burnt our village down," said another man named Stryver, the barrel-chested father of the late Mrs. Pyegrave's lady's maid, Tattycoram. "Or mebe it was dem M.P.P.P.'s demselves what did it."

"And why would you say dat?" asked Joper.

"To move us oot and put all us in da Workhoose. Dint you know dis day would coom? Da way we always complainin' aboot da low wages and da long hours. Dey plan to move us oot and move some others in who'll be doing less of da complaining. Watch and see if what I say don't coom true."

Tattycoram, who stood next to her father, spoke now, the avatar of authority on Milltown, "'Tis death to live in dat Milltown. I seen it. 'Tis death dat awaits us all."

Then she said no more.

CHAPTER THE FORTY-SIXTH

Thursday, July 10, 2003

The Parliamentary Palace of Dingley Dell had only a fraction of the majesty and the august appointments of its stately and far more legitimate British inspiration. Nor would the palace (that word being largely a misnomer, given the fact that the building was less a palace and more of a capacious townhouse) hold its own when set against any of the other more venerable (and legitimate) legislative and governing bodies of the world. There were times that the place was thought little better than a parish meeting hall.

But it was never an M.P.P. who thought it. To each of the members of the Dingley Dell Petit-Parliament, the palace was quite sufficient to its purpose of maintaining preeminent authority in the Dell. It had served quite well the legislative and executive needs of the valley for over a century, and some of its judicial needs as well, for Dinglian judges and magistrates by historical tradition also had a voice and a vote in the Parliamentary chamber—in clear conflict with the generally-held doctrine of separation of powers. The palace was also sparingly furnished for another reason. Whatever money might go into the exquisite furbishing of the hall was thought better allocated for the exquisite furbishing of the individual homes of its constituent members.

There had never been so many men and women squeezed into the sessions chamber as had put themselves into that room by the necessity

of circumstances this pre-dawn hour. All of the M.P.P.'s were present with
one exception, and most of their families as well, along with those other
Dinglians who worked in league with the Petit-Parliament and so had also
been blest with invitations to the July 15 festivities—men such as Montague Pupker and William Skettles and Dr. Arthur Towlinson and Dr. Egbert Fibbetson.

But no one was in a festive spirit at this early morning hour. There was
fear to be discerned upon nearly every face, for the turmoil, though it had
partially subsided—the angry East Enders having retreated back to their
sleeping hovels across the river—was still manifest to some degree within
the breasts of members of the working class and the merchant class, who
milled about in the lanes and met behind closed doors of their own and
shook their heads and gnashed their teeth over the impotency of the Parliament and its subordinate constabulary. Members of the working class and
the merchant class wondered why the general state of unrest had been permitted to escalate to such point that their shops should be vandalised and
their livelihoods placed into serious jeopardy. And was anything to be done
about it? Would the Parliament assemble a militia to restore order? There
was no doubt that the Petit-Parliament had gathered itself into some sort
of emergency session, but why were members' families shuttered in as well?
Who would step up and return things to the way they were a mere twelve
hours earlier? How could the time-revered institutions of the Dell—the
pillars of Dinglian government and society—become so fragile as to bend
and break so dramatically and with such frightening expedition?

Montague Pupker stood at the window and peered through the Venetian
blinds. He could hardly count the number of belligerent West Enders who,
not yet wishing to retire, now shuffled and loitered just outside the Palace,
demanding with their shouts and their intermittent chants that the M.P.P.'s
start to earn at last their long exorbitant salaries and prove at last their long-
boasted mettle, by putting an end to this crisis without further delay.

"Is he out there? Has he returned?" asked Pawker, the Minister of
Trade, a gawky, asthenic man who even in his middle years had not filled
out his skeletal frame no matter how many dollops of clotted cream his
wife spooned upon his scones.

"I don't see him."

"Should we proceed without him?"

Pupker shook his head. "Feenix hasn't been gone that long. Give him a little more time." To Dr. Towlinson: "You should not have left him there to make the call by himself. Now he must go the gauntlet to get himself back here. What a foolish place for the Project to have put that cellular telephone tower at all events. I have always advocated that it go atop this very building."

"Montague," said Towlinson in his wonted imperious manner, "I've had much greater cause to be in telephone communication with the Project overseers than you, especially when one considers my superintendance of all of those Returnees and Limbo Returnees and legitimate lunatics who must be warehoused in my hospital like so many sardines in a tin. Where is *your* need? Where is Pyegrave's and Feenix's? You are businessmen. You concern yourselves only with commerce—improving it and improving your own lot by acquisition of your Outland trinkets. And as to the matter of where the cellular tower should have been placed, it has worked quite well on the Bethlehem grounds up to now, and I cannot help it that there are rioters and revolutionaries who may block Feenix's path back to this building. If there is blame to be assigned for what you currently see out that window, *you*, Pupker, should be its recipient. All of this started with your inability to keep your sub-cellar secure, and I knew that your daughter would talk, and obviously she did, and if I were not a Christian I should have placed her into a permanent coma when she was first admitted to my hospital."

Towlinson glanced over at Dora Pupker, seated upon a banquette between her daughter Cecilia and her newly adopted daughter Alice (formerly of the Trimmers family). Mrs. Pupker raised not even an eyebrow at the suggestion that her older daughter Hannah should be deserving of such extreme treatment by Towlinson.

"There is a great deal of blame to go round, Towlinson," retorted Pupker, giving Richard Pyegrave a passing but penetrating look. "We are all become careless and lax as the day of our delivery grows near. Fibbetson confided to me just to-day that Trimmers and Dabber and the Pilkins mother and daughters could not possibly have missed seeing the Outland calculator that you stupidly left exposed upon your desk."

"Fibbetson, you low scoundrel!" bellowed Dr. Towlinson. "I told you that in absolute confidence."

"And in absolute confidence did I tell it to Pupker. It isn't my fault that he has decided to share it with everybody else."

"We are being ridiculous, every one of us," struck in William Boldwig, who was pacing at nearly the same rate as Judge Fitz-Marshall, the two men walking up and down a narrow cleared path in the crowded room, all four of their hands clasped behind them like robed, cogitating professors. "As we sit here casting blame all about for not keeping a better lid on things before our impending departure, my son is out there doing everything he can to extinguish the violence and restore some degree of calm that will allow us to make our way to the Summit without assault or molestation."

"And has he hired the extra deputies as we have asked?" enquired Judge Fitz-Marshall, stopping in his own turn to face the worried General Agent.

"As many as he has been able. It is not so easy a thing to do as you would think, and I should know, for it is my business to put people into professional situations."

Pupker drew his watch from his fob, opened the clasp and gave it a look. "I will give Feenix five minutes more to come back with word from the Project as to what we are to do. Then we will have to make a decision for ourselves."

"If any of you were any manner of real man," offered William Skettles, "you would form a party of escort to conduct our Lord Mayor and Minister of Health and Justice safely to this chamber."

"Would you care to form such a party with yourself as its leader, Skettles?" queried Pupker dryly of his carping brother-in-law.

"I would if I could, Pupker, but I can barely walk after what was done to me by that attacking Scadger mob. The deputy sheriff was blest to receive only one shock from that electric gun. For my part I was shocked five times."

Skettles rubbed his leg a little to burnish his point as his brother-in-law murmured skeptically, "Five times. That's one more than in your last embellished recounting of this encounter."

Addressing William Boldwig, Pupker asked if his son, the sheriff, intended to arrest "those animals for their attacks" (Skettles having failed to mention the provocation responsible for employment of the Taser: the shooting death of Solomon Scadger).

"There just happen to be matters of even more pressing urgency in contention, Pupker," replied Mr. Boldwig on behalf of his son. "Besides, the Scadgers are armed now with a deputy's pistol and the electrical device, and it would not be wise for Billy—with so few men—to concentrate himself on the Scadgers purely as a matter of revenge. Once things settle down, he can simply set the building on fire and shoot everyone who stumbles out."

Dr. Towlinson groaned. "This talk of shooting people I simply will not tolerate. Have we not always said—and I thought that we were in perfect agreement on this point—that as savage and bestial as our Overlords become, we will not stoop to be like them, that we will endeavour always to keep our own hands clean, to never seek to depreciate our intrinsic humanity?"

"You refer, of course, to the over-lording barbarians whose plan it is to kill everyone in the Dell who is not sitting in this room?" asked Fitz-Marshall with sardonic scorn. "Don't be a hypocrite, Towlinson. Your hands may be as clean as polished brookstones when we leave this valley, but every day thereafter your heart will remain immutably imbrued with the blood of all of those thousands of your countrymen who were not so lucky as to escape along with us. If you believe in Hell, doctor, then I should think that there will be a special place reserved for all of us—yourself included—quite near the devil's own furnace, for that is where the most *inveterate* hypocrites must lodge."

"And what is the alternative, Fitz-Marshall?" rejoined Towlinson in a faultering voice. "That we should now at this late hour renounce the Project only to suffer the same fate as everyone else out there? How will that save a single soul amongst us? What will happen will happen, and we can choose to commit suicide or we can escape with our lives. For fifty-nine years I have looked forward to the opportunity to study all of the advances in medicine that have passed me by in this time-frozen vale, and I do not intend to give up that chance, no matter how much of a hypocrite it makes me."

Dr. Towlinson had scarcely completed his defence when Pupker signalled "quiet" with his hand. "I see him. He's coming down the lane."

"Are they detaining him? Do they accost him?" asked the Lord Mayor's frantic wife, pushing her way to the window.

"No," said Pupker, stepping aside to share space at the window with Mrs. Feenix. "He is speaking to them calmly, as you see, and they are responding in kind. Now a few are retreating. I don't know what he is saying to them, but he does seem to be doing some good."

It took several minutes for the Bulldog to finally conclude his conference with those assembled in the lane and to make his way to the door.

Once inside, he sat himself down and fanned his face with a book that lay within reach. "It is a warm night. Is there lemonade? I should like a glass of cold lemonade."

"What news have you?" asked Pupker, who stood nearest the overheated Lord Mayor.

"I believe, gentlemen, that the crisis is past. I have told those who held me outside—and do you not see that they're now returning to their homes?—I have told them that the Parliament has convened a special session this evening to address this terrible civil unrest. I have told them that our families accompany us only for reason of protection, as threats have been made against our lives and our persons, and it was thought best that we should have our loved ones close to us on this aberrant night. And I put it that way because it *is* an aberration, and things will calm down once people come to understand that it isn't the end of the world, that rumours can make for nasty anomalous situations, but those situations need not endure once sanity and reason are restored." To the bearer of his glass of lemonade: "Thank you, my dear. You are a gem." After a long slurping drink: "So this is what I told them. I believe that the crisis is passing—that it *will* pass, that peace will return."

"And the Project—what did *they* say?" prodded Pupker.

"Oh, yes. Well. Not at all what I'd expected. They disagreed with my assessment of the situation. They fear that things will only continue to deteriorate. For this reason they have moved up the date of our departure."

"What is to be the new day?"

"To-day. Later to-day. This afternoon, in fact. Two o'clock."

There were scattered gasps made about the room, followed by whispers and low chatter.

"But do you think it wise, Feenix?" asked Dr. Towlinson. "So soon and with so much left for us to do?"

"We will do what we have to do to be done with this place," said Pyegrave, now stepping forward and finally making his opinion known. "I for one will be quite happy to leave here in nine hours. I'd be happier still if it were nine minutes. The sheriff will do his duty, I trust, and assign every deputy to guaranteeing our safe passage to the Summit?"

Boldwig nodded.

Pyegrave continued, "I do not care what happens to this valley otherwise. I do not care about the peripheral fires that are burning people out of their homes, nor do I care about those who sit in our gaol or those sardines of Towlinson's in the Bedlam tin. The only thing that matters to me now, and which should matter to all the rest of you, is getting your arses out of this Goddamned place and getting out as soon as possible. So I take this as good news and I am now going to my lodgings to pack my bags and be ready to make my climb to the Summit. When and where do we assemble, Feenix? I assume that we will make our march together in some sort of assembly for safety's sake."

"Let us meet here at 12:15, post meridiem," replied the Lord Mayor.

The widower Pyegrave (widowed by his own offices) nodded, solicited the accompaniment of his two brothers with a second nod, and was well nigh ready to step out of the palace and commence his peregrination home, when he was halted by a beckoning Montague Pupker.

"Mr. Pyegrave, is there not something you're forgetting?"

The redoubtable Pyegrave coloured, returned to where he had been seated, and retrieved his leathern satchel.

"All that Dinglian jewellry you stole this afternoon from the Fagins' shop will do you no good at all with the Outlanders if you accidentally leave it behind," said Pupker archly.

"I have no idea what you're talking about," retorted Pyegrave with a snort as he snatched up the satchel, a jet necklace jangling untidily from beneath the open clasp.

Once outside the Parliamentary Palace, Pyegrave was approached by a worrisome, still-aproned Mr. Chuffey, the baker. "Has something been decided?"

"What do you mean?" asked Pyegrave in an impatient tone.

"By the Petit-Parliament. Is order and calm to be restored?"

"Yes, most certainly," replied the murderous and larcenous upholsterer, sweeping past. Then over his shoulder: "There is a plan to return things to normalcy. It will be announced by Lord Mayor Feenix upon the Milltown commons to-morrow evening." Pyegrave stopped and paused, for it became necessary for him to compose himself to prevent the escape of a cruel smile. Then he added, "I trust that you know how to swim."

"How to *swim*, Mr. Pyegrave?"

"You misheard me, Chuffey. I said: 'This violence—it will be *stemmed*.'"

"Oh, yes. Very well, very well indeed, Mr. Pyegrave."

CHAPTER THE FORTY-SEVENTH

Thursday, July 10, 2003

The Senator had agreed to speak with the Jersey Shore jeweller, though the two members of the Senator's staff who had accompanied him to the Williamsport fundraising dinner had raised objections, the older of the two assistants registering the whispered opinion that Phillips was most certainly "some kind of nut." The Senator had earned a reputation for doing that which was often unexpected, having spent his nearly four terms as senior senator from the state of Pennsylvania following more often the dictates of his own gut and his own head than the ideological prescriptions and partisan directives of his affiliated party. Now he was removing himself from the hotel banquet hall, having wrung more than enough hands for one evening, in the company of a man of coincident age who sold jewellry in a small shop in a very small town and who reminded him in no small way of his own father, a peddler and junkyard owner (in the American parlance, and dustman in the Dinglian).

The Senator was familiar with people who held wild ideas and embraced conspiratorial theories, for had he not many years earlier served as assistant counsel for the Warren Commission, which was charged with investigating the assassination of a United States President named Kennedy? And did he not harbour doubts about its findings based upon a tip or two that was slipped to him about a secret organisation called "The Tiadaghton Project"?

And now he was hearing that same name spoken by the old jeweller all these many years later, in conjunction with the valley in his state about which he had never been told nearly enough, this fact having always been a needling frustration to him.

Phillips told the Senator everything that he knew, as fantastical and implausible as it should sound to the legislator's ears. He told the Senator about Ruth Wolf as well, about how he now believed her to be dead when communications from her had stopt, and what agency he thought had been responsible.

The Senator sipped his tea in the hotel bar and listened to everything imparted by Phillips, without judgement (for he was, at his core, a lawyer, and not one to form a final opinion until every fact had been presented), and even as his staff stood impatiently outside the door and signalled their desire to leave, expressing wonderment over how the Senator should give the old man even a second glance, let alone a long and respectful audience.

At the close of Phillips' lengthy presentation, the Senator agreed to go with him that next morning to the Tiadaghton compound and ask some questions. He may or may not be admitted to the facility, which, though the Project was ostensibly a government-authorised operation, sat upon private land, as did the valley adjacent to it, and there would be proper legal justification should they wish to deny him access.

However, the two never made it to the compound, for on the road that took them there next morning, Phillips, with the Senator sitting next to him, descried a very old man lying crumpled upon the shoulder.

"Is he dead?" asked Phillips, peering past the Senator to get a better view out of the passenger's window.

The Senator shook his head. "No. There seems to be a little movement in his legs."

Phillips stopped the vehicle and the two men went to the aid of the supine man, who was none other than Roger Rugg, the expatriate Dinglian snake-handler. "Do I know you men?" wheezed Rugg (for he was having difficulty taking in breath).

"You no doubt know *this* man," said Phillips, pointing to the Senator.

"I do? And who are *you*?" asked Rugg of Phillips.

"Do you not remember me, Rugg? It was only a few days ago that you and I assisted Ruth Wolf in getting the young Trimmers boy back to Dingley Dell."

"Ah, yes," said Rugg, squinting. "I do recall something of that esca-pade. Forgive me, gentlemen. I have lost my glasses. I've lost nearly every-thing else upon this journey. Everything is a haze to me and I haven't much strength left. I fear that I am destined to fail in that which I set out to do two days ago: return myself to Dingley Dell." To the Senator: "I'm going home, you see—home to die. Do I know you? I've seen you on the news, have I?"

The Senator introduced himself as he and Phillips helped Rugg into a seated position. "It's a pleasure to know you, Senator," said Rugg. "Do you fancy snakes? Some senators do not, though some senators are the very worst sorts of snakes themselves in my humble opinion. Now look at me, gentlemen. I'm still alive. Perhaps I'll make it still, though I am weak."

"What's the matter with him?" The question came from a few yards away. All three men looked up to see a woman in her sixties walking up to them. It was Mrs. DeLove, and her house sat not too far in the distance.

"Exhaustion, I think," said Phillips. "Do you live here?"

"For the last forty years. Let's get the poor man inside and lay him down. He looks dehydrated."

"I'm thirsty, yes," said Rugg with a little smile of gratitude.

Rugg was taken into the DeLove house and put down upon the bed in the spare bedroom where Augustus Trimmers had feverishly lain, and given a drink that Mrs. DeLove said would "restore his electrolytes." There was another woman in the house—a young woman—who introduced her-self to Phillips and the Senator as Mrs. DeLove's daughter Annette. Both Mother and Daughter DeLove spent the succeeding minutes in vocal aston-ishment over the fact that one of the guests to their home that morning was the senior United States senator from the Commonwealth of Pennsylvania, and there was happy relief expressed that the high-ranking governmental visitor wasn't the state's junior senator who only three months earlier had created a public firestorm through remarks that crudely referred to men making love to their dogs.

"There was a time," said Mrs. DeLove, as her daughter served Pirouette Rolled Wafers to her coffee-imbibing guests, "when I would have left a man like Mr. Rugg exactly where he was, assuming that he was already dead."

"And just why would you assume a thing like that?" asked the Senator in the flat accent that matched the flatlands of his Kansan youth.

"Because it was easier that way—to keep myself from getting involved.

My daughter Annette and I have done quite well in holding onto our farm—while all of our neighbours have been run off—by minding our own business, by looking the other way when things happen—terrible things. We've had to. Annette has agoraphobia. She tells me she'll drop dead the minute she's ever made to step off that porch. Don't ask me to explain how a person's mind can work that way. I couldn't even begin to explain it."

"What sorts of things—terrible things—are you referring to?" asked the probing Senator who used to be a district attorney in the early season of his career.

"People killed before our very own eyes!" exclaimed Annette.

"People have been killed on your property and you didn't call the police?" The Senator set his coffee cup down, thoroughly amazed and really quite appalled.

"It goes to what I've been telling you," interposed Phillips. "I'm curious about one thing, Mizz DeLove: you indicated that you didn't used to want to get involved. Yet to-day you didn't hesitate to leave your house and come out to help us. What's changed?"

"Mr. Trimmers' visit, for one. He is a Digglian like Mr. Rugg. He came here and gave a face to all those poor people who live beyond that ridge. And it turns out they're not extra-terrestrials after all. They're human beings just like you and me, who live in some sort of time warp. Like they're all Dickens characters or something—you know the way that Christmas carolers dress up every year and do the Victorian Christmas thing? Well, as Gus describes it, that valley's full of people who do this kind of thing all year long because they don't know any different."

Phillips exchanged a confirmatory glance with the Senator. Is this not exactly the thing that Phillips had told him at the hotel the night before?

"Gus Trimmers," said Phillips, nodding. "The father of the boy my rescue group helped to return to the valley. What happened to him?"

Annette's face brightened. "Did you hear that, Mama? Gus's little boy got home safe." To Phillips: "We're hoping that Gus made it back okay, too. He wasn't completely well yet, but he was pretty determined to get home."

"Just like our friend Mr. Rugg in there," said Phillips.

"Are you going to make the trip yourself, Senator?" asked Annette.

"By trip, do you mean, am I going into that valley?"

Annette nodded.

"Well, it would be difficult, don't you think? First, I'd have to be permitted to enter the compound. Then somebody, I'm sure, would have to be assigned to me. An escort of some kind. More than likely this person would shew me what they wanted me to see, tell me exactly what they wanted me to hear. That is, if they shew me or tell me anything at all. Chances are, though, I'd be barred from entering that gate. Or there could be a far more troubling scenario that might play out. Do you remember what happened to Congressman Leo Ryan in Jonestown back in '78? The only member of Congress to die in the line of duty. Maybe I'm not ready to be number two."

"But there will be *some* sort of investigation, right?" asked Phillips, looking hopeful. "When you get back to Washington?"

The Senator shook his head. "Based only on what the three of you and Mr. Rugg back there have told me? Mr. Phillips, I must tell you: I'd be laughed out of the Senate. Let alone the fact that the timing would be terrible. Maybe you haven't noticed: major combat operations in Iraq may have ended, but we're still in the middle of a strong guerrilla insurgency. How would I get anyone to pay attention to Dingley Dell when all of our time and resources are being channeled into the war effort right now? No, I think what I'd like to do first is to undertake a little enquiry of my own."

"But you said—" No sooner had Phillips launched his rebuttal, did he come to realise exactly what the Senator now intended to do.

"There's a different place to enter Dingley Dell—outside the compound gates?"

Phillips nodded. "Up the Eastern Ridge. You go over the ridge through the eastern woods or you take the path that leads up to the Summit of Exchange. But I have to say, Senator, that either way, it's not an easy climb for men our ages to make."

"Then we'll take it slow," said the Senator with a smile. "I'm not an invalid. For crying out loud, I get a daily workout just serving on the Senate Judiciary Committee. And yes, I want to go to the Summit. I want to see the entire panorama of Dingley Dell—I want the full picture for starters."

"You're going to climb that ridge together—just the two of you?" asked Mrs. DeLove.

"Unless anyone else cares to join us," answered Phillips.

"*I* do." This from Mr. Rugg. The old man stood unsteadily in the doorway, and though he looked as if he might collapse at any second, his countenance was fixed with a look of hard resolve.

"Mr. Rugg, you get yourself back to bed. You're not well!" bid Mrs. DeLove.

"I know I'm not well. I'm one foot in the grave, my dear. But I don't want that grave to be here in the Outland. I want my life to end in Dingley Dell—the place where I was born."

"We can't carry you up that mountain, Rugg," said Phillips. "We'll be lucky if we can make it all the way up ourselves."

"You don't have to do a thing, young man," said Rugg, propping himself against the door frame. "If I die, at least I should die that much closer to my home. Now let me rest for a bit longer and then we can be on our way." With that, Rugg turned and repaired again to the bedroom.

"Quite the determined old codger," said Phillips.

"Reminds me a little of myself," returned the Senator.

CHAPTER THE FORTY-EIGHTH

Thursday, July 10, 2003

Mrs. Gargery sat at her window, holding Mr. Toddles in her lap. The little dog nibbled bits of dried bacon from her palm, tiny crumbles of the little snack clinging to his flattened pug nose. "Prisoners, Sarah! Prisoners in our own home—that's what we are. Mr. Toddles and I should be sitting upon my porch and taking the air as we usually do, that's where we should be. It's a profoundly disappointing development, my dear girl. No, no, my little beauty, it is an outright tragedy!"

Mrs. Gargery's maidservant Sarah, who was standing behind her mistress combing the elderly woman's thinning hair with long, gentle strokes, peered out of the window and said, "But look, my mistress. There are no more ruffians in the street. All is quiet. I dare say that it should be quite safe to open your door now and put yourself back upon that porch."

"I don't know," dithered Mrs. Gargery. "It was such a frightening day yesterday. Someone tread upon my geraniums and a brickbat tumbled my mignonette box from the window. I didn't sleep all the night wondering what sort of mischief might happen under cloak of darkness." Mrs. Gargery promptly turned in her seat to address the other occupant of the room: "Did *you* sleep, Georgianna? Did the ruffians disturb *your* dreams, my dear?"

Mrs. Gargery's overnight houseguest, lounging upon the chaise, did not respond. She was, in fact, fast asleep at that very moment.

"I don't see a single soul in the lane," observed Sarah. "One-hundred ninety-nine, two-hundred. May I stop brushing now, my mistress? My hand has lost some feeling."

"Yes, you may stop brushing. Oho! Who is *that* then?"

"Who?"

"Coming toward us from the opposite direction. It is a veritable mob! Watch them, child. They will throw more brickbats at our windows, and plunder and pillage us, for this is what mobs do."

"I see no mob, my mistress. I see only some manner of slow-moving foot parade. Can you not tell by this, that confidence has been restored in the streets? For there are a host of men, women and children coming toward us in a calm and collected manner. And look at how finely drest they are! There can be no possibility of mischief on the minds of those who dress themselves as well as these, my mistress."

Mrs. Gargery nodded and smiled. Then suddenly it came to her: the identity of the afternoon paraders: "Why, I know exactly what is happening here, Sarah. It is a parade of those who are going off to the celebratory festival upon the Summit. They have apparently decided to gather a few days earlier than the date put upon the invitation. What a splendid means by which to reinstate civility to our deranged streets. We must go and commend them!"

Mrs. Gargery and her maid Sarah crossed to the front door of that respectable woman's ancient abode, the procession of other Dinglian respectables now gaining her house. It was quite a number of them, in fact—seventy, perhaps eighty or more. And interspersed amongst the promenaders were sheriff's deputies, some habited in the formal uniform of their office and others, apparently newly-hired, drest in improvisational equipages of nankeen and leather jerkin. "The chair, Sarah! The chair! I must take my seat and attend the parade as it passes."

Thus installed, Mrs. Gargery began to wave in the royal manner, keeping the forearm fixed and the wrist and hand in constant lateral motion. "Oh look, Sarah—Mrs. Feenix is waving back, and there is Mrs. Kitt and Lillie Pawkins. I should like to go with them, but alas, Sarah, I have no invitation. I *had* an invitation but I gave it to Miss Bocker. Now where is Miss Bocker? For she could go if she wanted; she has Mrs. Pyegrave's own invitation now."

Said a groggy voice behind Mrs. Gargery, "Antonia cannot go, Cornelia, because she is presently locked away in a gaol cell."

"Goodness, Georgianna, why has our friend Antonia been put into the gaol house?"

"For the crime of mannish rudeness, I have no doubt," said Georgianna Milvey in a bored voice, whilst filliping her flask and repining with a frown its present inconvenient hollowness.

The faces of those who marched in the cavalcade of the Eighty-three Elect gave a variety of expressions. Some shewed happiness to be leaving this Paradise-turned-Golgotha. Others could not hold back the tears that flowed from being separated from that place which had been the only home they had ever known and a good and decent home at that. Still others betrayed no emotion at all, but were set in their dutiful look and in their steady, stoical eye. Such a stare of impassiveness characterised the faces of Lord Mayor Feenix, and Montague Pupker, and Judge Fitz-Marshall—who did not avert his gaze from the path ahead, even when bid goodbye by his forsaken little clerk, Mr. Meagles, who held the judge's gavel limply at his side as if it were become some token of painful remembrance.

Sheriff Billy Boldwig, his own eyes in constant vigilant motion, walked alongside his father and mother, and shewed little expression either save that of ever-attentive keeper of the law and of the peace and of the overall decorum of the stately procession. The excessively freckled Boy Sheriff had been charged with taking the Eighty-three Elect to the Summit, whilst his deputies were to remain below at the foot of the mountain, having still not been told the true reason for the fête champêtre. There was, no doubt, another emotion that would have registered upon the face of the young sheriff had he permitted it: worry. Over whether or no he would achieve success in this afternoon's all-important commission. Would the procession proceed smoothly? Would the East Enders misbehave and grow unruly, perhaps even violent, as they had only the day before? Up to now they had staid safely on their side of the bridge. Would they remain there?

Mrs. Gargery waved and Sarah waved and Mr. Toddles was, with some assistance, made to wave his little paw, too, as Miss Milvey crept away to rummage through her friend's dining-room cellaret, which was the cabinet in which Mrs. Gargery had once told her she liked to keep her brandy.

Jemima Pilkins and her daughters Charity and Mercy raised their heads from their current chore: the full soapy laving of their Saint Bernard

Caddy. (And an onerous task it was, the dog being quite large and quite fluffy and really quite in need of a good bath.) The parade was passing along a cross street in such profound, sepulchral silence that the Pilkins would most certainly have missed it had Caddy not barked to inform them. Jemima rose to her feet and wiped her sudsy hands upon her apron. Seeing Dr. Towlinson near the head of the marchers, she called out, "Dr. Towlinson. Whither are you going? Who is looking after my brother Walter?"

"We are merely going to an assemblage upon the Summit," Towlinson called back. "A celebration. Your brother is in good hands."

"That is rather odd," said Jemima to her daughters. "A party upon the Summit. Whilst there has been such trouble in the streets. And look at all these constables that come along. But let us seise this opportunity, darling daughters. Let us go to the asylum and see just who is left in charge of that place. Perhaps the surrogate will give us leave to see Walter!"

Headmaster Chowser and his cook Maggy Finching were delivering the last of the now school-less boys to his parent, the responsibility of this particular placement having fallen to the two by earlier mutual arrangement. Each pair of staff members of the Chowser School had been given a certain lot of boys to escort home, and Chowser and his cook had had eight Milltowner youths to drop off, not including young Jack Snicks who came along as somewhat of a little helper, since his aunt was dead and there was no one else to whom he could presently be assigned. "Now, Mrs. Sliderskew," said Chowser to the woman standing in the doorway, "you will note that master Abraham here has acquired an aversion to split peas and calves' foot jelly, so we would advise against serving either to him in the short term. And feather pillows will make him sneeze. He prefers to lie with a horsehair pillow if you can find one." To young Abraham: "Goodbye, little man. It was a joy to teach you." Chowser touzled the boy's head as the little man blotted away a tear with his sleeve.

"And a joy it was, as well, to *feed* you, Master Abraham," joined in Maggy. "Jack—Jack, look up at me. I'm speaking to you now. Will you not say goodbye to your friend Abe?"

But Jack would not. He was too busy at that moment watching the approaching cortege.

"Good God," said Chowser under his breath, as he also took keen notice. "What's this?"

Mrs. Sliderskew, who stood clutching her boy Abraham to her waist, shook her head.

"They look to be going on a picnic," said Maggy. "See, some of the women hold wicker baskets. Oh fie for shame! The Dell burning itself down and crime and general discontentment breaking out all over, and our Dinglian gentry are off to sit upon blankets and eat sirloins of beef upon sticks. It is all quite remarkable."

"Let the Bashaws have their frolics," returned Chowser in a low voice. "We haven't time to repine it. Did you not wish to see your Mr. Muntle as soon as the boys were deposited with their families?"

"Most certainly," said Maggy, not turning to Chowser, but keeping a hard look upon the parade, which now passed close by. "But if I had a potato, I would throw it."

"Don't give Jack any ideas," said Chowser. "And don't give *them* any reason to put all the rest of us into confinement at the Inn-of-Justice!"

"There you are still," said Harry Scadger to his brother Mel who knelt before the upstairs window, which overlooked the lane. Melchisedech Scadger had not surrendered the pistol since he first took possession of it, even when his curious brothers asked to hold it. Nor did he surrender it when it came time to bury their brother Solomon in a plot of dirt in Mrs. Lumbey's fenced-in rear area. There had been a little service for the dead brother held only a few hours earlier, but Mel had not participated. He had stood amongst his weeping brothers and all the weeping wives and children and had caressed the gun in his hand and had imagined himself firing upon the deputy who had murdered his brother in cold blood.

Mel confessed as much to Harry upon returning to his sentry post at the upstairs bedchamber window—sentry post and waiting spot, for Harry's younger brother vowed that if he should have to wait ten years for Deputy Gradgrind to appear, it would be worth it, the privilege of revenge being all the sweeter with the passage of time and the dulling of memory on the part of the one who deserved retribution. "There are more productive things that you should be doing, brother," said Harry. "And let us say that you see the killer in the next hour for that matter. By firing upon him you will only invite an assault upon this house."

"The assault is coming withal, brother. It only be a matter of time. We meet it early, we meet it late. It makes no never mind to me."

"Well, it matters to *me*. We are not yet prepared to withstand such an assault. There are things that we still must do to ready ourselves for it. You are making no positive contribution to our efforts, sitting here, willing your quarry to come beneath this window like a spider biding time in her web."

"So if I see him I should not shoot him?"

"Aye. Don't be a fool, Mel. And don't be a menace to the clan through vengeful madness."

"You be ordering me not to fire as head of this family?"

Harry nodded. "If that is what is required. Papa is dead. Now Solomon is dead. I am oldest now. I am now the new head."

"You are a *half*-head. Half-brother and *half*-head."

"I still carry some of your blood in me, Puppy, and you still carry some of my blood in you, and even should I discover that I bear no relation to you at all, I was raised amongst you and will always consider myself a part of this clan. Now I can no longer afford to engage you. I must look in on Florence. The move from the Bocker apartments has weakened her further and I fear for her."

"Solomon be dead, Harry. I cannot even think it."

"Nor can I. Persevere, dear brother. Be strong but be wise."

Harry turned to go, but his brother caught his arm to detain him. "Look."

There, moving fully down the street, soon to pass beneath the improvised sentry window, was the procession. "I could fell them all," Mel mumbled, "one by one, to pay them back for what they done to our family over yea these many year. Look at them, brother, every one of them what done hurt to us, every one of them what done laughed at our dirty faces and our simple ways."

"You would fell them all? With your mere twenty-two bullets? By use of the first pistol you have ever held in your hand, let alone fired? Don't be a bigger fool by giving action to the fool's statement you just made. Withdraw from this window. Don't give them further evidence that we reside here. They're nervous. I see it in their looks. They are liable to shoot at this house with very little provocation as it is. I beg you."

Mel considered for a moment his brother's strong words. Then Mel receded. Harry watched from behind the curtain as the parade passed with its cautious, wary gait.

"Where be they going?" asked Harry's younger brother in a raised whisper.

"To the Summit. This is what Trimmers tells me. The festival was scheduled for Tuesday. But they've apparently decided to have it earlier. They're leaving, brother. That is what this is all about. They're leaving Dingley Dell."

"Then let us have our own party for to celebrate it!"

"No, brother. Things will not play the way you think. With these men and women, as much as we hate and despise them, go our best hope for any future at all."

CHAPTER THE FORTY-NINTH

Thursday, July 10, 2003

What are you looking at, you goose?" sought Cecilia of her informally adopted sister Alice.

"Nothing."

"You were looking up at your uncle's apartments above the Lumbey shop, weren't you? Don't deny it. Who were you looking for? Your uncle is in gaol, and so is your worthless mother. Your father is probably hooting like a loon at Bedlam. There is no one in this house that you know."

Alice averted her gaze. "Still I have spent many hours in that place. My mother has bought me dresses in that shop."

"I'm sure that you'll find much prettier clothes to wear in the Outland. Don't be an ingrate, Alice. My father has given you the chance to live a life so wonderful you cannot even begin to imagine it. Don't bumble it."

"I won't. No, I won't," said Alice evenly. She walked on, hand-in-hand with her new sister, neither speaking now—only listening to the whispered conversations of those who walked close by. It felt to Alice as if she were part of a sombre funeral train. In fact, Cecilia was the only one who was bouncing up and down and frisking a little.

Alice patted her breast and sighed. The pendant was still in place, still hanging from her neck. It was a beautiful little chain pendant with a small emerald for the drop. Her mother and father had given it to her when she turned twelve-years-of-age. It had been an expensive gift, made only marginally less expensive by the discount that Rose Fagin had offered her parents. Alice had treasured it, thinking it the loveliest little silver pendant as ever had been made. On some of the nights that succeeded its bestowal, she would sit up late with her candle and observe the play of light penetrating the translucent green stone. Even though the emerald was small, it shimmered most magnificently before her young, appreciative eyes. She loved her mother and father with all of her heart upon those sparkling nights.

But things had changed. Alice had begun to find fault with her parents, and with her insufferable urchin of a brother. She had become ashamed of her family and no longer wished to be seen with them, and had spent more and more time gadding about with her best friend Cecilia. Leaving her mother and father in the end was the best thing that could happen for her. It was good that she was now a part of the Pupker family. Mr. Pupker had bestowed upon her something of much greater worth than a dull emerald pendant; he had invited her to leave the valley with his family—to be brought embracingly into the arms of the Outlanders. What an ineffable honour!

Alice's eyes began to brim with tears. She did not wish Cecilia to see, but Cecilia most certainly *would* see if any attempt were made on Alice's part to wipe them away. Why was she crying? Because she knew in her heart that she would miss her mama and her papa? Miss them terribly? Because she was now ashamed of the way she had behaved towards them? Ashamed most of all over the fact that *she* had been the one responsible for their arrest? How this realisation tortured her conscience! For Alice Trimmers *did* have a conscience. It had lain dormant for quite some time, but now it roused itself from its imposed slumber to remind Alice of how very much she would now miss her mother and father once she left the valley; it gave her to think of her lost brother Newman and to feel great sadness for him; it moved her to imagine what horrible thing awaited her family—her true family—once she and the Pupkers were gone.

Alice Trimmers touched the pendant once again. It had a habit of becoming unclasped and slipping from her neck. Sometimes she would feel it come undone and would re-clasp it. On at least one occasion, she did not know that it was gone from her neck until much later, but she had by good fortune never left her bedchamber and was able to find it upon the rug there.

Cecilia studied Alice as if the girl were become someone she hardly knew. "Take off the dratted pendant if you think it will come undone. Carry it in your dratted hand, goose!" she uttered sharply. "Egad, I've never known one to go on so about such a silly little bauble."

"It is not so silly really," returned Alice in a soft voice, "when you think that it is all that I possess, which was given me by my parents."

"Who are now dead, dead, and nearly buried, goose. If you want to know what I should do—I should take the pendant and toss it right away and be done with any memory of those parental failures."

"But I would never wish to do that."

"Because you are a dolt." Cecilia, who had been looking all about her as she spoke, taking in all the sights of Milltown for the very last time, now turned to behold the visage of her best friend and somewhat sister. "You're crying! Egad! I can't believe it. You're crying."

"I am not the only one, Cecilia. There are others around me with tears in their eyes as well."

"But you are the only one crying over things that need not be worth a tear. As for the silly trinket that still binds you to your family, if you are so needful of keeping it from being lost, then unclasp it and hold it in your hand until we can secure a jeweller in the Outland to replace the damaged clasp."

This was the first thing said by Cecilia with which Alice actually agreed. She undid the pendant and put it into her hand. She closed her fist tightly round it, the tiny coiling chain feeling so small in her palm—as small and slight as the invisible chain that linked her to her blood family.

Soon Milltown was behind them and there were a few sighs of relief that the cavalcade had moved through the town without the smallest incident. The valley opened up now into a broad plain of field and small coppice, with a long, clear prospect comprehending the space that surrounded the muddy Riparian Road—the road that led by spur to the foot of the Northern Ridge. In one direction: the Wang-Wang rice farm—a boggy place with a little pagoda teahouse in the style of the Orientals. In another direction: the black, ruined apricot orchard, burnt to the ground, no doubt, by those vandalising gipsy Scadgers: such an ugly thing for the Eighty-three Elect to see amongst their final departing views of Dingley Dell. A cornfield there, next to an old, weathered barn. And over there another corn field, this one planted in New World corn, or maize, as it was sometimes called. And there straight ahead, the Northern Ridge, standing tall and majestic and carpeted in dark green as the early summer rains had brought its cover of shrub and dwarf trees to even deeper verdancy.

On did the procession move along, some of its constituents in march step, others slackening into a more plodding tread—for many of the Eighty-three Elect had not walked so long a distance in a very long while and were growing quite tired. Finally the group drew up to the spot at the foot of the ridge in which one commenced by wide foot- and barrow-path the climb to the top.

Pupker took the voice-trumpet and commanded attention from his pilgrims for what needed now to be said. "My friends, I have been given the report on conditions at the top and all is fair weather for our descent into the Outland. There are escorts who await us upon the Summit, of more than sufficient number to ease us in the early hours of our first foray into what will very shortly be shorn of its current appellation 'the Terra *Incognita*.' For it is now to be our home, soon to become as warm and familiar to each of us as was Dingley Dell. All of our luggage has been taken up ahead of us, all of your belongings put safely within the waggons which went out this morning. Now I must ask before we ascend: is there anyone amongst us who has changed his mind about making this journey? For this is the last time that you will be given leave to quit this party."

Pupker waited to hear if anyone would speak. Cecilia looked at Alice, who seemed at first upon the verge of saying something, but then did not. Cecilia nodded and smiled and patted an approving hand upon Alice's back. Alice, for her part, attempted to return the smile, but she could not. Cecilia did not know how close Alice had come to removing herself at that very moment from this group and returning herself with all due haste and a loving heart to the arms of her mother and father. But she could not bring herself to do it. For surely they must hate her now. For surely they had already erased her name from the family book and there would be no reconciliation. She had made her choice. She would hold her tongue; she could do nothing else.

"Our merry band of future Outlanders remaining intact, I shall now ask Sheriff Boldwig to deliver instructions to his deputies." Pupker handed the voice-trumpet to the sheriff.

"Men," said he, "you must now be scratching your heads over what Mr. Pupker has just said, or else you have astutely figured it out. You will stop here, gentlemen, for those whom you have shepherded to this spot will not, in truth, be climbing this mountain for the purpose of a party at all, but for the far more important reason of departing permanently from this Dell, and I regret to inform you that you will not be coming along with us. I have made no provisions for whom shall succeed me in my office. But I will now make that assignment. Mr. Magwitch, will you step forward?"

One of the deputies—in fact, its former tipstaff who had groused so vocally over the firing of his friend Vincent Muntle that he was demoted to deputy of the lowest rank—now stepped out of the knot of astonished sheriff's officers.

"Your past insubordination is forgiven in the spirit of my magnanimity. I christen thee the new sheriff of Dingley Dell." Boldwig handed the man his badge and his pistol. "I wish you well. I wish all of you well and we thank you for your kind assistance in facilitating our migration from this valley."

Magwitch was in a bit of a daze. "I am the new sheriff? And you are all going? The Lord Mayor, all the members of the Petit-Parliament? You are leaving us and never coming back?"

Billy nodded.

"Trusting that you will do with all of your power and pistols only the good work of proper law enforcement," said the Lord Mayor with a yawn. And then to Pupker, his under-voiced words picked up by Alice's sharp ear, "They'll riot and pillage the valley till there be nothing left is what they'll do—the savages—and how appropriate that this is how Dingley's penultimate chapter gets written!"

The procession began to snake its way up the ascending switchback trail as the deputies—there were eighteen of them now serving under the newly elevated Sheriff Magwitch—stepped back and watched them go.

"What do we do now?" asked one of the deputies of the new sheriff.

"I suppose it would be best at this point for us to repair to the Inn-of-Justice and gather men and women round us who will decide what the future of our bereft valley holds for those of us who remain."

"I have a gun," said one of the most recently appointed deputies, a young shaver with bristle-brush hair. "Why should I not use it to my own benefit?"

"Because I will shoot you if you do," said Magwitch. "We were left with these arms to keep order in the Dell, and renegade behaviour of any stripe will not be tolerated."

"You will shoot me?"

"Right between the eyes."

"Then we should both be dead, Sheriff, because I will shoot you at nearly the same time."

"If that is what you want, Snagsby, then let us aim all of our guns at one another and have done with it. But if we are to hope for a peaceful continuity following the loss of our leaders, then I would advise each of you to use your authority sparingly and to good purpose. For my part, I intend to take my office and bestow it once again upon the man to whom it rightfully belongs: Vincent Muntle."

"But he is in gaol," said one of the other deputies.

"On a wholly fabricated charge. Do not be dense, Jaggers. Do you not see why all of these recent arrests were made? To facilitate a smooth passage out of the valley by all of those we now see huffing and puffing up that trail."

There were various nods and a few grumbles from those who had greedily thought for a brief moment of using their newly-acquired weaponry to procure a free plum bun or mahogany umbrella stand or fine copper pocket watch or fishing rod or all the porter in a pewter ale-pot that their gullets could hold.

Which the cynical Lord Mayor should never know, his now being out of earshot of the abandoned deputies.

It was not long before Alice, who had not put on the proper shoes, soon began to slip and slide upon the loose stones and upon the slick exposed roots that made the mountain trail less smooth and friendly than it appeared from afar. As her pace slackened, she found herself quickly overcome by some of those who climbed behind her. It was all that Cecilia could do to keep from pushing ahead and leaving Alice alone with her stumbles.

"Why did you wear *those* shoes?" snapped Cecilia. "They are like the tallest pattens ever made. You look as if you're climbing upon clown stilts!"

"They were the nicest shoes I had," was Alice's weak response. "Go ahead if you must, but I simply cannot go along any faster or I will trip and fall."

"I will not leave you, but you so try my patience, goose!"

Alice had made it to within several hundred yards of the Summit when the very worst thing happened; she slipped and fell to the ground in such a spectacular way that heads were turned and there was even a gasp or two from several of the women who climbed ahead of her, thinking for certain that she would somersault all the way down the mountain. Alice dropt to her knees, catching herself upon the hard, rocky path with the palms of both hands to prevent a dramatic tumble. "Have you hurt yourself, dear?" asked Mrs. Gallanbile.

"No, no, I am fine," grunted Alice.

Cecilia shook her head in jocular judgement. "My friend is a walking mishap," said she, while reaching out her hand to help Alice to her feet.

Alice gratefully accepted the proffered hand, but was suddenly thrown into a state of panic. She released a wordless cry of anguish.

"What is it?" There was no more glee to Cecilia's address.

"The pendant which was in my hand—I have just now dropt it."

"Then let us look about our feet. We'll quickly find it."

"No, no, no. It went down there. Into that little indention, below that rocky ledge." Alice was pointing and peering down into a concave portion of the ridge, darkened by the shadows of the angled afternoon sun.

"Then it is lost forever. Let us resume our climb, Alice."

"But I must have it! I really must have it!"

"Don't be a blockhead. You cannot go down there and look for it. There is no time."

Alice shook her head with such violence that she surprised even herself.

"If you do not leave the pendant where it is, I will call for my father to come and carry you the rest of the way. And he would do it, I'm certain, for there is not that much farther to go to the top."

"Please, I beg of you, Cecilia. Give me but a minute or two to climb down there and give a look. The pendant is all that I have left from my mother and father. I must take it with me to remember them by."

Cecilia gave a heavy sigh of exasperated displeasure. She tapped her toe. She put her hands upon her hips. "Take only the time required for those behind us to pass, and then I will not let you delay us even a second longer." Even as Cecilia was granting Alice permission to slip down a little into the brushy indentation to search for the lost pendant, Alice was doing that very thing, removing herself from the trail and proceeding down into the thick foliage that would make for a most challenging hunt-and-probe even under the best of circumstances. "Oh, look at you!" bellowed Cecilia.

"You have lost your mind. I'm certain of it."

"Is that what the girl has lost—her mind?" chuckled Dr. Fibbetson, who now approached Cecilia, quite winded and no doubt happy to take a brief rest from the arduous climb.

"She has dropt some stupid little thing given her by her mother and father," answered Cecilia with a roll of the eyes. "But you know that the Trimmers are daft. They always have been."

"I have known it for years, my dear. I have known it for years." Fibbetson took a few more breaths whilst excavating dust from his nose with his finger.

Alice was inclined to shout up in response to the arrant rudeness of her friend Cecilia and the disgusting medical practitioner that "no, the Trimmers are not daft. They may be different, but they are not half so daft as all of those climbing this mountain round me." But she bit her tongue and narrowed her gaze upon all the green and brown in search of something green and grey and glistening.

"Will you come up *now*?" pleaded Cecilia, as Fibbetson, representing the very last of the train, moved on. Cecilia reached out her hand to assist Alice in climbing back up.

"A moment longer, I beg you."

"Absolutely not. Take my hand. There is no time to lose. They will leave without us if you tarry."

"One moment more. That's all I ask. There is something reflective in that litter of dead leaves. I must have a look at it."

Cecilia retracted her hand. "You blithering, dunderheaded fool! You don't deserve to come with us. You should die in this place for your stupidity. I am going. I have done with you!"

Cecilia righted herself and proceeded to climb up the trail now unaccompanied by the girl who was once her very best friend and then her near-sister, and now was someone who apparently meant nothing to her. "Over a pendant," she muttered to herself. "A ridiculous pendant, which should mean nothing to any *sane* person."

But the pendant did mean something. I meant *everything* to Alice Trimmers, in fact, for as it turned out, it meant her very life.

For here is what happened next. There was a woman's scream. And then another, easily perceptible to Alice's ears, although she was still a few hundred yards removed from the Summit and situated in a small hollow.

Then came the booming sound of a man's voice. "At will, men." And then a sound that would echo in Alice Trimmer's ears forever thereafter: gunfire, terrible thunderous gunfire, that did not relent for a long time—the guns firing away to be thorough, to be certain, to leave nothing undone. Alice clapped her hands over her ears but the terrific sound could not be fully blocked out. She felt faint. She reeled, losing her footing. She fell backwards into a crevice—fell directly into a break in the ground that nearly swallowed her up, that placed her into rocky, cobwebbed half-darkness, but did not dull the sound of the guns, which continued to fire away, to tear at her delicate ears with the intensity of their blasts. Then Alice heard a different sound; she heard something topple down the path as if it were a body falling, tumbling downward. She saw something in the crease of light above her that looked at first like dripping water, but was too dark for water, too red for water. There was blood spilling off the Summit of Exchange—fresh rubiginous blood—blood mixed with the soil and sand of its freshly made rivulet. She heard a rustle and the thumping of feet as unseen persons now descended the path. Was she missed? Had they come looking for her? Or was it the tumbling, somersaulting body they were after—the body that had fallen off the mountain when all the others were felled neatly upon their spots. Was it the last to have reached the top? Was it Cecilia? But no, it was not Cecilia, for there was a moan—a man's anguished moan that could be faintly heard.

"Holy shit! This one's still alive," said a voice. Alice did not recognise the voice. It belonged to a man, and the accent was strange to her ear.

"It's Fibbetson. Don't you know him? It's the doctor—the screw-up— probably killed more people with his one scalpel than all of those we just took out."

"Help me," Fibbetson moaned.

"Be glad to, Doc." And then came a sound like ripping cloth, like tearing flesh, and an agonising cry—a blood-clabbering cry.

And then fading, grunting voices: "Where did you—uhng—learn to gut like that?"

"I…uhng…*fish*," explained the other man.

Then silence.

And then darkness, as Alice Trimmers sank into merciful unconsciousness.

CHAPTER THE FIFTIETH

Thursday, July 10, 2003

Permit me, kind reader, to turn the clock back to a time preceding the massacre on the Northern Ridge—only a few minutes, if you will indulge me—so that you may know what was being said and done in other places when those tragic shots were fired. Let us begin with Newman Trimmers, who stood within the attic room looking down at a man lying asleep upon a pallet on the floor. The man had kept him up for most of the previous night with shouts and groans and troubled thrashings in his sleep. Yet Newman wasn't angry with him. Didn't Newman have such nights as this one himself? Indeed, all of the eight men and one boy who shared this room had been plagued with nightmares of equally terrifying intensity. The dark dreams came, in part, in remembrance of their time in the Outland (for each of the men, save one, had been there and had seen things there of a haunting nature). The dark dreams also came from the fact of their secret imprisonment at the top of an insane asylum—each of these "Limbo Returnees," long thought dead and gone by most—a veritable gathering of ghosts.

"Does he still nap?" asked George Muntle in regard to the sleeping man, putting a hand upon the shoulder of the boy.

Newman looked up into the eyes of the enquirer and nodded.

Vincent Muntle's brother George bore a similarity to his younger brother only in the eyes, which were dark blue and shaded by thick brows. Where Vincent was bluff and hardy and a bit rounded in those places where musculature had softened, George was rail-thin and possessed of a rather cadaverous aspect that shewed not only in the hollowness of his ocular orbits, but also in the concave cheeks and the narrow, withered neck. Perhaps it was the fact that George had lived all of the last twenty-five years of his life in this sunless attic room, which had drained the life and sinew from him, for his brother had always thought him robust.

Newman was the most recent addition to this special isolated fraternity and its youngest member. The men took an instant liking to him; it had been a very long time since most of them had seen a child, although Newman preferred *not* to be thought a child and tried whensoever possible to acquit himself in the blustering, stouthearted ways of men. Sometimes Professor Chivery, during his most confused moments, would mistake Newman for a youthful Harry Scadger, whom he had tutored when Harry was the same age as Newman. And Newman would never correct him, for there were things that Newman learnt from the professor when playing to the old man's faulty memory that were good to know: games and tricks with numbers and mathematical theorems that could be put to practical application. Chivery was especially fond of explaining why a circle could not be squared, basing his staunch belief that this ancient geometric conundrum was insoluble on the fact that pi was a transcendental number. He was alone in this regard, most mathematical scholars of the Dell, and the great arithmeticians who taught them through the *Ensyke*, believing it only a matter of time before quadrature of the circle could be taken to proof.

Chivery was alone in another respect; he had been placed with the Limbo Returnees, though he was not one. The reason could hardly be discerned, though some of Newman's attic-mates wondered if his obsessitor diagnosis made him perfect company for the Outland-obsessed Returnees.

"Newman, why do you stare at him so?" asked one of the men. He was a lean, spindle-limbed man with a long, scraggly beard and his name was Quilp. Christopher Quilp had lived for many years in this cock-loft, though not so long as George, and had spent a goodly number of those years of occupancy whittling little soldiers from blocks of wood. The soldier he presently held in his hand—very nearly finished but for the buttons and pockets of its uniform—was soon to be added to the company of a veritable miniature battalion of other such whittled soldiers. It was not a hard look that he gave Newman, for Mr. Quilp was quite fond of the boy, and enjoyed playing "Waterloo" with him upon the floor during those times in which Newman would allow the young child within him to come out for a bit of a juvenile frolic.

"I have noticed a pattern about the professor," said Newman, happy to explain his sudden interest in Chivery's repose. "I've noticed first that when he has had a hard night and is crying and calling out in his slumber, his restless state continues when he rises in the morning."

"Yes, that is where we get the term 'restless,' boy—from getting no rest." This from a man named Bolo who was quick with a quip. He yawned and then closed his eyes again upon his pillow in a corner of the room. Although the men were pale-skinned from having been separated for so long from the browning rays of the sun—the windows of the attic room having been boarded up and then plastered over many years ago—Bolo's epidermis was without any colour whatsoever, so that one need not look too close to see the trails of all the veins in his face and neck and arms.

"Newman was making a point, Bolo," chastised George Muntle. "Finish your point, Newman."

"I was going to say what else I have found in the pattern. After the turbulent sleep, the professor seems very different the next day—and sometimes he even begins to make sense."

George thought for a moment. "Newman is right. There *are* such moments, as we all well know, and they *do* tend to follow a night of troubled sleep. It is as if the man's brain in repose is attempting to repair itself. I have played chess with him on such days, for he is quite sharp and coherent then. By the bye, Quilp, whittle me a new rook, for there is one that has lost nearly all of its crenellation. Formerly I had thought Chivery wholly healed during such amazing periods. But they do not last. He inevitably lapses back into his wonted state of lunacy."

"Alas and alack," said Bolo, cracking the joints in his thumbs.

George smiled. "But perhaps this will be one of those days in which I shall be in for a good game of chess."

"Unfortunately, Mr. Muntle, I'm not quite up for chess," said the professor, raising his head to rest it upon the shelf of his palm. "For there is far more important business that we must attend to to-day."

The professor rose to put himself into the Hindoo sitting position and to address not only George, but Newman and his other attic companions, at least two of whom greeted this temporary state of sanity and coherence on the part of the professor with commendatory applause.

"My sleep was troubled last night by dreams of what is soon to come and by the fact that I am helpless to do anything about it."

"Yes, we know the dreams well, Professor," said George. "It is the Noah story, is it not? That there is to be a great flood and all will perish save a ridiculous number of animal pairs that could not possibly fit themselves into the ark unless it be the size of France."

The Professor nodded. "That story, Muntle, or at least the way I told it, was wholly symbolistic."

"So what, then, does the flood represent?" asked Bolo in a loud voice from the other end of the long room.

"Why, it represents what it actually is. In true fact, I am fearful that a flood is soon to wash all over this entire valley."

"And kill us all," said Quilp without animation. "Yes, we're quite familiar with how it all plays out, old boy. Have you anything new to add that doesn't include placing your notebooks before us and asking us to glean meaning from all the numbers and mathematical formulæ scribbled in them?"

"Yet there *is* meaning. A great deal of meaning," expostulated the professor. "Newman, do you not believe me? Have even you become so inured to my—my—?"

"Ravings?" offered Bolo, still reclined upon the floor in a lounging aspect.

"That is what I do?"

"Most certainly," said Quilp. "We stopt listening long ago. Because we know that you're mad—generally speaking—except for the stray moment of pure and clear perspicuity, which we now know generally comes after a very restless night, such as the one you just had."

"Is it forenoon? It feels like afternoon."

"Does it matter *what* time it is, Professor Chivery?" asked Bolo. "When every hour feels like every other hour in this perpetually candle-lighted warren?"

"What *do* all the numbers mean, Professor?" asked Newman. "Tell us now whilst it could possibly make a little sense to our dull minds."

"Do you really wish to know?" asked the professor with an excited lift to his voice. "For I have been most eager to tell you since I completed my calculations roughly two days ago."

George laughed. "Is that why you've stopt writing in your notebooks, Chivery?"

"I had thought it was because he had finally run out of room," injected the comical Mr. Bolo.

"No, no, no! I would have celebrated it at that moment, had my communicative faculties been sharper."

"Then what is Stage One?" asked George. "You have mentioned a 'stage one' and then a 'stage two' quite often in your ravings. Tell us now whilst you are lucid. We'll listen."

"Of course we'll listen," added Bolo. "For what else is there to do in this rat-nest but talk and listen?"

"And lose all of your toothpicks to *me* in every game of backgammon we play," jeered Newman in warm jest.

"Of course. For every man here wishes to see at least one amongst us keep all of his choppers, and why should it not be *you*, my boy?" Bolo grinned with a large mouth to shew himself bereft of several of his own teeth (and the ones that remained being quite brown and rotted through.)

Chivery leafed to the back of one of his many notebooks. Free to adorn the walls of his cellar cell, the professor was not permitted here to cover the walls of this room with his chalk, for a vote was taken early on and it was determined that it should not be desirable to have to look at mathematical equations all the livelong day.

"Stage one, gentlemen: we send men down to dynamite the Belgrave Dam. We probably won't have time to take out the whole dam, but if we are able to make an opening of *these* dimensions…" pointing to figures in his notebook, "…it will nonetheless produce an additional outlet for the floodwaters to escape, sufficient to reduce the waters valley-wide by this volume here…" pointing again. "The smaller structures will be unavoidably washed downstream by the force of the cataract entering the Dell at the Tewkesbury Cut, regardless of what is done in the way of expanding egress for the waters in the south, because by my earliest calculations I've concluded that the gorge will be opened by the force of the influx to such extent as to create an initial assault upon the valley of *this* magnitude." Chivery pointed a third time to calculations within his notebook.

"What is he talking about?" cried Bolo, rolling his eyes. "He's gone back to blithering again."

"No, he hasn't," said Newman. "He's telling us how strong the flood will be and he's telling us how to—how to—"

Newman could not find the right words to finish his sentence. George

Muntle finished it for him. "How to reduce its impact upon the valley."

Chivery nodded.

"But then, what buildings do you think *will* withstand the onslaught of that vanguard wave?" asked Muntle, as he sat himself down on the other side of the professor, intrigued by the academician's findings.

"My calculations on hydraulic surface forces tell me that only two structures within Dingley Dell are of such size and have been constructed with sufficient integrity to withstand the swell with some degree of certainty. If we are successful in lowering the water level prior to natural recession, the campanile tower and roof of the All Souls Church, as well as the roof of this very building, should remain above-water and keep us high and dry, as the phrase goes. And *that*, sirs, is Stage Two. Holding ourselves to the top floors of the campanile and to the roofs of the church and the asylum to keep out of reach of those treacherous rushing waters."

"Nothing else in the valley will hold?" asked Quilp, becoming more interested himself and drawing nearer to the professor and his book.

"Perhaps a lucky house here, a lucky factory there, but nothing in the Dell is better constructed that the two buildings of earlier mention, and so I would put all of my money on these two structures alone. And of course, I must reiterate that all is for naught if we cannot breach the Belgrave Dam. If that isn't done, *everything* in the valley will be drowned."

"Stage Three then being the final receding of the waters," said George.

"And all of us climbing down from that tower and those roofs and going for a bathe!" chuckled Newman.

Chivery nodded. "The boy is right. But standing floodwater isn't the best place to have a—"

"Quiet! Silence!" interrupted Quilp, signing with his hand that conversation in the room should come to a stop. "Do you hear that? Off in the distance?"

George nodded. "I hear *something*. Is it thunder?"

Quilp shook his head. "That isn't thunder. That is the sound of guns. Someone is firing guns—a great number of them there in the northern part of the valley."

"'Tisn't in the valley," said the professor, cupping his hands round his ears. "The gunfire emanates from high upon the Northern Ridge."

"How can you be sure?" asked Bolo, rising from his lounging place upon the floor.

"Because sound travels differently *above* the valley than it does across the crowded valley floor. Its texture is clearer with less reverberation. Can you not hear a sharp clarity in the blasts of those guns? Listen."

Newman and the men listened carefully. After a few seconds more, the sound died down to a pop here and a crackling there, and then was succeeded by silence.

"It most assuredly came from the Summit," concluded Professor Chivery.

"That is where Miss Wolf gave me an injection to put me to sleep," said Newman.

"It is as the woman said—the one who wrote the letter I gave to your Miss Wolf. She mentioned something that carried the name 'Phase Seven.' Phase Seven—whatever it is—has apparently commenced."

"Stages. Phases. What does it all mean?" asked one of the other men, all of them now crowding close to the professor to listen even more attentively to what he had to say.

"That a terrible slaughter has just taken place on the Northern Ridge. As we do not possess guns, I suspect that Dinglians were its recipients. And as it is not one of the Mondays when our brokers go there to trade with the Outland tradesmen, I would say that there is another party that has been made the target of such a deadly attack. I cannot calculate how much time should pass before the floodwaters be released, but I would not think that it should be very long to do that which would finish us off. Gentlemen, we should get ourselves up to the roof of this building with all expedition. But we must also warn the others. Men must be found who are skilled and willing to go down to the Southern Coal Ridge to put a hole in the Belgrave Dam or every hope is lost. Someone go and pound upon that door. Appeal to anyone who will listen. Our very lives depend on getting ourselves out of this deathtrap of a room and having our voices heard."

I looked at Muntle and Muntle looked at me. We both shared a look with the other occupants of our crowded gaol cell, as well: Mulberry Timberry, his father Charles, and Herbert Fagin.

"What is happening?" I finally asked.

"The Moles are being killed," said Muntle.

"How do you know?"

"Consider that they comprised the crowd that passed the Inn-of-Justice ninety or so minutes ago. Did we not surmise that they had scheduled their departure for to-day instead of the 15th?" Muntle bounded up from his cot. "Gaoler! Bullamy! Get yourself back here! Where are you?"

Muntle began to strike his pannikin hard against the iron bars of our cell to make a noisy clatter. "Bullamy! Bullamy!"

A plump, paunch-bellied man with a gloomy, sallow face shambled into the anteroom. "D'you hear it? They's some shooting going on out there. Do you think it be the deputies what are taking those to the picnic, Sheriff—I mean, Mr. Muntle-who-ain't-the-sheriff-no-more? Be they a'shootin' at some Scadgers or some wild East Enders d'you think?"

"That wasn't the sound of a dozen pistols we just heard, Bullamy," replied Muntle. "The reports were much louder, much stronger. Those were Outland guns: rifles, carbines, whatever else is used by Beyonders these days."

"Who d'you be thinking they was shooting at—them gun-carrying Outlanders?"

"The Dinglians that went to the Summit would be my guess. Now why don't you unlock this cell so that we can find out what's going on?"

Bullamy shook his head. "The sheriff who be the new sheriff, not you who be the *old* sheriff, left word that I was not to let a single soul out of this place on no condition. So I'll be getting back to my desk now, Mr. Muntle, and wait for my next orders."

"And what if the new sheriff just happens to be dead, Bullamy?"

"Why would he be dead, Sheriff—I mean Mr. Muntle?"

"That's what I'd like to find out."

"We'll all find out together when he comes back here. He'll tell us if he's dead or not, then." With that, the fat, ridiculous turnkey returned himself to the room from which he'd just emerged (and returned himself, as well, to the nap that the gunshots had rudely interrupted.)

"The man's a two-florin idiot," said Muntle. "Well, of course, it makes perfect sense that Billy would leave him in charge. There is such brilliant logic to everything that elephant-eared half-wit does."

"Why would they kill them—all those who went up to the Summit?" asked Mulberry. "I thought they were being given free passage out of Dingley Dell."

"Maybe it was never the Project's intent to allow any of them to leave,"

I offered. "Maybe the plan had been all along to execute them with all of the rest of us—only, maybe a couple of hours sooner in their case."

"It juggles the brains," said Mulberry's father, shaking his head slowly, incredulously.

"The Moles knew too much," I expounded. "They knew that the valley's days were numbered. Let's say that there was *never* a plan in place to permit them to emigrate—to remove them from harm's way. Wouldn't the Project administrators have been fools to tell them? They had to set up this ruse, or else the Pupkers and the Towlinsons and all the M.P.P.'s would have found no further profit in doing their bidding. My guess is that they had to be lulled into thinking that they were being allowed to leave, or else they would have been inclined to band together with the rest of us, to use their far greater resources to help us stand our ground."

"As theories go, Trimmers, I can think of none better."

"Or none more ghastly," put in Herbert Fagin. "What of your niece, Trimmers? Was she with them?"

"I fear that she was." I felt slightly light-headed and sat down. "We have to get out of here, Muntle. Right now. We have to get all of these people to safety before they blow up the Tiadaghton Dam upriver. Can you not make another appeal to this idiot Bullamy?"

But Muntle didn't have to. At just that moment Harry Scadger and his brother Mel stepped into the anteroom, Harry in possession of the key to our holding cell. Harry had something else in his hand—something that I could not identify. Mel was in possession of his precious recently acquired revolving pistol. The men were well armed, it appeared, and I could not have been happier.

As we passed out of the anteroom to a different room, which communicated with the women's cells, I looked in on the ridiculous Mr. Bullamy. He writhed upon the floor as if in the midst of some fit.

"What has happened to the man?" I called to Melchisedech Scadger.

"He's been electri*fried*," said Mel. "By your brother Harry and his magical Taser. Fried him up pretty good, don't you think?"

CHAPTER THE FIFTY-FIRST

Thursday, July 10, 2003

The shots were heard throughout the Dell by every ear save those of Jack Snicks and that small group of other Dinglians who were equally deaf. The deputies, who had heard them best of all, had scattered in a panic, but then, regaining their wits (along with a little of their lost mettle), regrouped, and headed back to Milltown with no desire to confirm any more for themselves than that which their imaginations had gruesomely constructed.

There were even those outside the valley who had heard the gunfire. Three men who were climbing through the woods to reach the mountaintop had gained a point halfway to their destination when the shots rang out. They heard not only the shots themselves, but also the anguished screams and cries of those upon whom the guns were trained. The jeweller knew what it all meant and explained it to the Senator and to the nonagenarian snake handler in stark terms. The snake handler nodded and accepted the intelligence without questioning it, for he had seen what Outlanders were capable of doing. He knew the hearts of those who administered the Project and he had watched those hearts grow blacker and blacker with the years.

The men did not know whether or no they should proceed, for they did not wish to risk injury or even death at the hands of those who would bring an end to all things Dinglian and to all those who knew what Dingley

Dell was. For his part, Rugg could not move on even if he most desired it, for what little stamina he possessed had been drained away by the hard climb. "I will stop here," he said. "Here is the end for me."

"We'll go to the mountaintop and find out what has happened," replied the Senator. "And then we'll return and take you back down."

"Go if you wish, Senator. But all that you shall find upon your return will be a body to collect."

Phillips studied the grim face of the Senator. The legislator's gaze was now fixed upon the forest path to the Summit. "Do you still want to go, Senator? After what we've just heard?"

The Senator nodded. "Of course, this may be the end of me as well."

"You would do this?"

"I can't defend what may be the most impractical decision of my fairly long life, Mr. Phillips, except to say simply this: that millions of my own people perished in Europe because the world paid little attention to what was happening there. Now people are dying on this mountaintop here in my own state, and I cannot simply turn away. If you don't want to come with me, I'll go alone."

"Senator, I've spent the last two years of *my* fairly long life trying to undo the evil that those people do—to the Dinglians, now to my friend Megan, and I don't intend to suspend my efforts with that evil having reached its culmination. I think that what we'll find up there will sicken us. But I'm in this thing for the duration, come what may."

Upwitch and Graham crept out of the church and looked about. There were no deputies waiting to arrest them amongst those who had assembled on the steps and front lawn—a ruffled and rattled congregation of Milltowners trying to cobble some meaning from what they had just heard. Their number included the school headmaster Alphonse Chowser and his cook Maggy Finching, and the orphaned boy Jack.

"What is happening, Vicar?" asked Chowser, speaking for the group.

"Nothing good, Mr. Chowser. For now, though, we must keep the people calm. Take those who will go with you into the church. The church has always been our refuge and it will prove to be so in its most literal sense to-day."

"My school was burnt down last night, Reverend Upwitch. Do you think that those who did this now intend to do even greater harm to this town?"

"I do, Mr. Chowser. I think that what we've just heard is only a prelude to that which is to come. For now, I would advise that you spread the word to all that you can to come together here. There is strength in numbers, sir, and power to be gained from the Lord's offices."

Chowser nodded. Maggy had stepped away from him. She looked about, a distressful shadow crossing her face. "Maggy, help me do as the vicar advises. Help me direct these people into the church."

"I must find Vincent."

"In time, dear woman. I need your help here and now."

"Yes, I understand," said Maggy, taking the hand of a frightened old woman. "Into the church, madam. There is safety there."

❦

Mr. Howler's voice could be heard outside the door of the attic room. "I cannot let you out, Muntle. Dr. Towlinson has forbidden it. It's a preposterous request."

"And what if there *is* no more Dr. Towlinson?" asked George Muntle.

"What are you talking about—'no Dr. Towlinson'? Don't be daft. Keep yourselves quiet. I know that you have missed your dinner. I'll try to find you something to eat and put it through the slot at the bottom of the door. I assume that this is how Towlinson delivers your meals."

"No, Mr. Yowler," said Mr. Bolo with twitting bite, "he generally glides in wearing a waiter's habiliments, and we all sit politely as he tucks a bib beneath each of our chins."

"Silence, man!" chid George Muntle, casting daggers at his darkly droll attic companion.

"Mr. Howler, 'tis Professor Chivery here. Attend me, sir. There is no likelihood whatsoever that your employer Dr. Towlinson will be returning to this hospital. Nor is Dr. Fibbetson. Indeed, no one who climbed up to the Summit this afternoon is in any shape to come back down. Which puts *you* in charge, young man. You and only you. Now you may choose to awaken that long dormant conscience that lives within you and do the right thing and unlock this cursed door that has unfairly entombed us, or you may continue like a booby to follow the orders of dead men until you too should be dead—drowned under the thousands of tons of water that will soon be visiting this valley."

"Tons of water? Foh! I should heed the entreaty of a lunatic? Double foh! You waste my time, gentlemen. There are people pounding at the front door and I must see what it is that they want. There are only three orderlies and myself attending the Bedlam circus to-day, and I haven't another second to engage you."

The Limbo Returnees, now clustered close round the heavy steel door, listened to the retreating footsteps of Dr. Towlinson's beleaguered assistant and sighed and groaned. George Muntle pounded a fist angrily into his opposing palm.

"What a shit!" said Mr. Bolo.

"We must break out the windows," suggested Newman. "No one will come to stop us, for didn't you hear that Howler and the orderlies have more important things to do?"

"Ah, yes," said Quilp. "But first we must *find* the windows. Where are they, Muntle? You were here when they boarded them over."

"Somewhere along *that* wall," said George Muntle pointing. "But mind how you bring sunlight in the room, for some of us could go blind!"

"A warm purblindness I would relish!" declared Bolo, looking about for something with which to begin to tear away at the false wall. "Each of you: find something to break through that wall. Professor, there is a chair beside you that you may use."

Professor Chivery's countenance had now changed. It was a most queer look, which seemed to indicate that the window of lucidity had unfortunately closed. "Stage one, and then stage two, and after that, stage three," he mumbled. "But there is no stage four." Taking Newman by the arm with a wild-eyed look: "You will tell it that way, boy? You will tell it that way to the letter?"

Newman nodded. "I will, Professor. Go and sit, sir. We have work to do."

❧

Before Howler opened the front door to Bethlehem Hospital upon Highbury Fields, he made certain that all three of his orderies were standing with him. Amongst the surviving quartet of asylum employees was Oscar, the cellar attendant. The young man was especially interested in finding out who was so bent upon disturbing the quietude of the building he helped to superintend that they should pound upon a door with such rudeness. Oscar clutched an India rubber hose in one hand behind his back to be ready should the reason prove to be a hostile one. The hose had always served him well to keep those under his care from objecting too strenuously to his rough treatment of them, and it would most certainly do the trick here as well, he thought.

Waiting upon the portico before the front door of Bedlam was a larger crowd than Howler and his associates had anticipated, for those present included not only myself and all of those who had been gaoled along with me—both the men and the women—but Mrs. Pilkins and her husband and their two daughters, and several others who had family members locked inside.

"Good afternoon, Mr. Howler," greeted Muntle brusquely. "Please step aside. We are taking over this institution."

"By whose order?"

"Our newly-formed Council of Concerned Citizenry," said Antonia Bocker.

"I don't recognise it," said Howler.

"Matters not, sir," I returned. "Give us your keys. We have very little time and intend to release everyone from their cells."

"Are you mad?" returned Howler.

"No. And neither are most of the men and women you have locked up in here."

Howler shook his head. "I cannot allow it. I have my orders."

Muntle put a heavy hand on Howler's shoulder. "As sheriff of Dingley Dell, Howler, I am countermanding all of your orders in the name of the law. Kindly surrender your keys to Miss Bocker and Mr. Trimmers and Dr. Timberry. Then move aside and suffer us to remove these people to safety."

"They are safe where they are. And besides, Mr. Muntle, you are no longer the sheriff of this Dell and consequently have no authority here."

"On the contrary," said a man standing to the rear of the gathering. "I was made sheriff when Boldwig left with the others to climb to the top of the Summit." It was Magwitch, and he stepped forward to clap a hand of support upon Muntle's back. "In turn, I have restored Mr. Muntle to his former office. He is the soul arbiter and enforcer of the law in Dingley Dell now, for there is no longer a Petit-Parliament. All of its members have been slain."

"How do you know this?" asked Oscar, dropping his India rubber hose from a hand that had suddenly gone limp.

"We were there at the foot of the ridge when it happened," answered Magwitch. "The M.P.P.'s and the others had climbed the ridge, and when they reached the top, they were slaughtered—every man, woman and child who went up there, we have little doubt. They were to leave the valley. They left it, of course, but only through forfeiture of their lives."

Oscar, suddenly seised by a terrible fear for his own safety now that there be Outland marauders with guns poised to do harm to him, made a vaulting leap past Howler and scudded away.

Howler looked over the faces of those who were come to make his job difficult and then capitulated to the inevitable, unfastened the ring of keys that depended from his belt, and turned it over to Muntle. "Is it true that we are all to be drowned?" he asked fearfully of the reinstated sheriff.

Muntle nodded. "There is to be a cataclysmic flood of this valley, yes."

"Then we must leave Dingley Dell without delay," said Mr. Fagin, who was flanked on either side by his wife and daughter with whom he had just been reunited.

I shook my head and explained to the growing crowd why such action would not be prudent. Already we had begun to hear a stray gunshot now and then, which I suspected came from an Outland sniper meeting up with some Dinglian acting upon those very same thoughts of escape. "By the bye, Howler, from whom did you hear that we were to be drowned?"

"From one of those we keep in the attic. I believe that Professor Chivery was the one who said it."

"Take us to him," said I. "Take Muntle and me up to those who reside beneath the roof, for my nephew is there and Muntle's own brother."

"How do you know this?" asked Howler with a look of surprise.

"We know more than you can possibly imagine," said Antonia, examining the ring of keys in her hand. "Mrs. Pilkins, Miss Casby, Mrs. Lumbey. You will come with me. The rest of you, take these other keys. Be quick about it. All must be removed from this place immediately. Muntle, Trimmers: whither shall we take them?"

"To the Respectable Hospital for now," offered Dr. Timberry. "Those who still require care beyond what a family's restorative embrace can give them."

"Which of these keys opens to the door to the attic room, Howler?" I asked.

Howler shook his head. "I don't have that one."

"What do you mean?"

"I mean that Fibbetson still has it. Dr. Towlinson gave me all of the keys prior to his departure but one. That one I was to get from Fibbetson, but he refused to give it up to me."

"You fool!" thundered Muntle. "How could you have let him keep it, when Towlinson directed that you should have it?"

"It never pays to tussle with that man. And how was I to know that they would not be returning? No one tells me anything." Howler had become flustered. His agitation manifest itself in a head that would not stop shaking and hands that had suddenly taken up a circumstantial tremor. Spenlow Howler was clearly a man at his breaking point.

"Think, Howler: is there any other way into that room?"

"There is only the door, and it cannot be breached without a battering ram."

"Then we must find a battering ram and break it down," suggested my literally minded sister-in-law Charlotte. "My boy is there. We simply must find a way to release him!"

Indeed, Charlotte and Gus both knew now that their son was alive and where he was being kept, for I had a made a point of finally divulging the facts of his whereabouts as the three of us were being transported to our respective addresses of incarceration. Knowledge that their son was no longer abroad had, no doubt, been of great comfort to them during these last two days, and I was happy finally to be able to unburden myself of the weight of it once and all.

"You cannot break down that door, as hard as you try," explained Howler in a pet of exasperation. "For it was made of solid steel for the express purpose of putting all thought of escape out of the minds of those who would dwell behind it."

"Lest all the secrets of the Outland and the Tiadaghton Project be revealed," said I in an undertone of disgust. "Still, Howler, take Muntle and me to the door and we will find out what can be done from inside by the inmates themselves to assist in their rescue."

What had already been done was this: the plaster had been carved and chipped and chopped away, and the under-boards of strong wood cut and pried back enough to emit a sliver of light into the room. The sliver was being broadened inches by inches through the application of clawing, splinter-lacerated hands and rude makeshift tools: Quilp's dull whittling knife, the leg of a chair, the iron cross bar from one of the room's now disassembled cots. "What do you see below?" asked George, as my nephew put his eye to the open slit in the wood.

"There is glass here, but it is so dirty, I cannot see anything through it."

"Can you crack it, boy?" asked Quilp. "Can you crack it with this knife if you jab it through the cleft in the wood?"

"I'll try," said Newman, taking the knife from the whittler. Newman began to thrust the blade through the narrow space that had been carved away in the wood—to jab and stab until finally the glass was penetrated, the whole pane shattering and falling away.

Nearby, walking along the cobbled lane that ran behind the asylum grounds, was Uriah Graham and his friend, the Vicar Upwitch. In the course of stopping all whom they would meet to send them to the All Souls Church for an emergency assembly, the librarian Graham, hearing the sound of the breaking glass, looked up in time to see sparkling shards and splinters raining down from the top of the large building. "Look, Slingo. Do you see it? A pane of glass has broken from that high window. Someone is up there, Slingo. Do you see?"

The men leapt over the paling and raced across the back lawn. "Halloa up there!" Upwitch cried. "Can anyone hear me?"

Newman turned to his companions in the attic room. "Someone is calling from below, but the opening is too narrow for me to see them. And they will not hear me."

George Muntle nodded, pulled the boy aside and began to yank and pull and pry at the wood with his frenzied hands. George's fingers began to bleed profusely from his efforts, but he did not stop until he, in turn, was pulled away by one of the other men in the room—a larger man with an even more powerful grip. Together the two men took turns by dint of the energetic, elemental force in their own strong hands to free themselves and their mates from the room that had entombed them for such a long and terrible season in their lives. The crease of light that angled across the room's wood and plaster-strewn floorboards began to widen as the portal expanded. The room grew brighter too as the carapace of the men's long imprisonment became violently ripped away. Into the dank, musty, stifling space irrupted the fragrance of trees and flowers and freshly mowed glass.

Into the attic tomb wafted the call of two men below who represented that which was so strange to those locked inside: a desire from someone *not* within that room that they should be free, that they should be allowed to leave forever that place which had for so long entrapped both their bodies and their beleaguered spirits.

Newman returned to the spot where George Muntle and the other man had broken through, a large opening having now been created there. "I see them!" cried Newman. "Do you see *me*?" he called down. "Do you hear me?"

"We do, Newman! By God, we most certainly do!" Upwitch waved both hands in the air as my joyous nephew put his head entirely outside the freshly created portal.

"There are others up here with me, Reverend Upwitch!" called Newman. "We want to leave this place but cannot go through the door. Have you an idea as to how we may get down?"

"We will think on it, young man," said Upwitch. The vicar then turned to his companion. "Think on it, Uriah. How in bloody hell are we to get these men out of there?"

Inside the room, George Muntle put his hand upon Newman's arm. "If we are to heed the words of the professor, Newman, it isn't *down* that we should go, but *up*. And we should tell the vicar to broadcast all that Chivery has told us. For was not the All Souls Church one of the places that he said that people should go?"

As George Muntle was about to speak to Upwitch and Graham, there came a loud pounding upon the heavy steel door from without.

"Howler has had a change of heart. Bless him!" said Bolo. "Is that *you*, most worthy and honourable Mr. Howler?"

"It is I. I have brought others with me. Alas, I cannot open this door, gentlemen, for I haven't the key."

Now there came another voice from outside the door: my own. "Newman, are you in there? It's your Uncle Frederick."

"I'm here!" said Newman. "You have found me!"

From Charlotte: "Newman, my baby! My baby!"

"I am well, Mama. I am safe. But I am quite tired of this dull room."

Now another voice still, a voice choked with tears: "George?"

"Yes? Who is it?"

"It is Vincent. It is your brother."

"I can scarcely believe that we are speaking to one another," said George, wiping back a trickling tear from his own joyful eye.

"Your voice has grown old," said Vincent.

"As has yours. We're no longer boys, my brother." George touched his hand to the door at just the place in coincidence that Vincent touched it on the other side. And only an inch or so separated their two hands, the hands of two brothers parted by twenty-five long years.

CHAPTER THE FIFTY-SECOND

Thursday, July 10, 2003

In the ensuing moments a great deal was discussed, both with those who stood outside the steel door and those two men who stood below upon the grassy back lawn of the asylum. All that had been said by Chivery during his brief window of lucid self-possession was relayed to me and to the others who were most receptive to it, and there was confirmation in the telling of it, for now I knew what had driven the professor in his obsessitor way to put so much upon those cellar walls and upon his classroom board and into his thick notebooks. The professor was attempting through the brilliant intellect that had been gifted to him by the Almighty to save us from the impending deluge, and so we listened closely and spread the word that there was soon to be convened at the church an important meeting to which all would be summoned who could help to put into place the things that Chivery had advised.

We would send a contingent of colliers skilled in explosives down to Belgrave Dam to dynamite out a part of that barrier which otherwise would doom us to total submersion beneath the impending floodwaters. They would be accompanied by an armed escort of deputy sheriffs. We would send men and women to every house and farm throughout the valley to spread the word and draw the residents to the asylum and All Souls' roofs and to the upper floors of the campanile for protection from the deluge. We knew that not every man and woman would believe us, would choose to heed the warning, would be so willing to leave his or her own place of seeming safety. We knew, as well, that there would be those who would not be content to sit upon a roof and wait—that they would wish instead to leave the valley entirely and would not listen to what we had to tell them about the dire consequences pursuant upon such a precipitant course of action. But we would do our best—our army of forewarners—to reduce the number of casualties with solid logic, the freight of emotional urgency giving ballast to our entreaties.

Betweenwhiles, the locked doors to the rooms and wards of Bedlam were being unbolted and flung open. Walter Skewton was being restored to his sister Jemima Pilkins and a very drugged and drowsy Hannah Pupker was being handed out of her cell to Amy Casby and Mrs. Lumbey, who did not have the heart in that liberating moment to tell the young woman what horrible tragedy had befallen her father and mother and sister. Though Charlotte had the pleasure of telling Gus that his son was residing only a mere two storeys above where they stood, she was loathe to let him know what was presumed to have happened to their estranged daughter Alice, and perhaps she could not have spoken the sorrowful words even should it have been her immediate desire. Yet Gus knew the truth from the way that she hung round his neck and wept heavy tears, the source of her grief assaulting both of their souls.

As Antonia and Mrs. Lumbey and Dr. Timberry made their rounds with their keys throughout the bleak asylum, Timberry taking special care to make certain that the Rokesmith "Ruins" were handled as gently as possible, Antonia Bocker whispered to her friend Estella that she had something to say and that it could not wait, for the time to say it may never come again.

"What is it, Antonia?" asked Mrs. Lumbey with a quizzical look. "That you are sincerely sorry for all those years of gall and wormwood between us? Because I am, too. Most sorry. We could have been good friends, had we only gotten past our early enmity."

"That is all water under the bridge, Estella. Orderly! Be careful with that patient; he has a bad foot."

"Then say it, Antonia. Say whatever you wish. We are all probably destined to die anyway, so nothing you say will matter much in the long term anyway."

"My, but are you not the inveterate pessimist! Orderly! Who is in this room? Is there anyone within? We will find out. Estella Lumbey, I have loved you since we were young girls and you first stole my heart with that gift of a child's mud pie."

"You have *loved* me?"

"Yes. I gave my heart to no one else, because it was only yours I wished to have. Orderly! Get me a cloth, for this man is drooling like a Great Dane!"

"Well, I'm happy that you let me know, Antonia. I have always valued your good opinion and now I have reason to value it even more."

Antonia embraced Estella, and though she held her only briefly, it seemed to Antonia Bocker a veritable eternity of warm bliss.

As she pulled away, the accompanying orderly finally found the key to unlock the door before her.

"That took you long enough!" Antonia admonished the young man, who had a cleft palate and was perhaps all too often and cruelly admonished simply for the way he looked. The orderly opened the door to a small ward of a dozen or so beds, each empty, for their occupants stood clustered together in one corner of the room, cowering fearfully. There was quite a range to their ages: the youngest perhaps in his thirties, the oldest a man perhaps in his eighth or ninth decade. And they were a rather odd-looking lot: men *and* women, some drest in hospital-issued gowns and pyjamas, others wearing ragged and tattered Outland clothing. A man who sported a front-brimmed Outland cap bearing a large letter "P" on it spoke for the others: "Are we being liberated?"

Antonia nodded.

"Can we all go home?"

"Where is home, young man?"

"Pittsburgh," answered the capped man.

"Jonesboro, Arkansas," said another.

"Brooklyn Heights," said a woman wearing a long nightshirt bearing the caricature likeness of a yellow-hued boy with a serrated head requesting in caption that someone should eat his shorts.

"How on earth did you get here?" asked Mrs. Lumbey.

"We all hiked in at one time or another," said the first man.

"To see the aliens," said the woman. And then brightening: "Are *you* one?"

Upon reaching the Summit of Exchange, Phillips and the Senator saw that which at first glimpse could only be thought to be some sort of magician's mirage—a diabolical illusion of death and carnage such as one would produce to shew a battlefield in its quiet, elegiac aftermath. But this was no proscenium concoction, no grand sculptural tribute to human depravity. What lay spread out before the blinking, disbelieving eyes of the two men was real—as real as the flies that buzzed and flitted among the fresh corpses. Here lay not soldiers, fallen upon their guns and swords, but men and women and children, riddled with bullets and pierced and bludgeoned, crumpled one upon another in odd configurations of twisted, twining limbs, some with frozen, horror-stricken gazes, each bathed and streaked and mottled with deep red blood—their own blood shed together in the suddenness of their fall.

Phillips felt himself choking at the sight, and even the Senator, being no stranger to death from his life spent as soldier and criminal lawyer, had never witnessed anything to match the wholesale butchery evinced in this place. And so he stepped back, and so he held his hand to his mouth in involuntary, incredulous revulsion. What was even more incredible about the scene was the fact that amongst all the dead bodies was one man who was very much alive. He was a young man, and he wore uniform drabs that mimicked in their grey and green blotched pattern the look of forest foliage—a solitary man performing the solitary task of putting leaden bodies into barrows. The man, who was quite young—not much older than his late teens—turned to see his two visitors standing at the other end of the killing place.

He dropt the body that he had been tugging, which had earlier been enlivened by the soul of Mr. Skettles, the apothecary, and quickly drew his gun.

"Who are you? How'd you get here?"

"We came up through the compound," lied Phillips. He took a deep breath through his nose in an attempt to calm himself so that he could better put forth the counterfeit necessary to preserve his life and the life of his companion. "Flatiron sent us."

"Well, I knew you couldn't have come up from the valley because we've got men guarding the barrow trail."

"No, we didn't come from the valley. We came up from the compound," repeated Phillips.

"Flatiron."

"That's right."

"Are you here to do a count? It's eighty-two. It was supposed to be eighty-three but somebody must have changed their mind at the last minute."

"I see," said Phillips, nodding his head slowly and thoughtfully to look appropriately administrative. "And how is the mop-up going? Why are you undertaking this task by yourself? You were supposed to have help."

"Do ya *think*?" said the young man with undisguised rancor. "The story *I'm* getting is that all my fucking help got reassigned to the South Sector."

"What happened to the contingent of shooters that were already detailed to that sector?"

The young man relaxed and lowered his gun. "A couple of them bailed, I think. Cold feet. Something. Only two hours before Diluvian."

"But when was this exactly?"

"I don't know. Forty-five minutes ago, maybe."

Phillips consulted his watch. By his calculation, there was now roughly one hour and fifteen minutes until release of the floodwaters.

"Anyway, I'll get some help later. I mean, I *have* to. Some of these fuckers must weigh three-hundred pounds. What kind of lard-ass meals do these fatso Dinglian dudes eat, anyway?"

"Some of them have been known to eat quite well," said Phillips. "What's your name?"

"McIntyre. But look, I just want you to know: I'm not complaining. I got the best seat in the house for the main attraction. I mean, check it out. It's gonna be awesome. And yeah, I guess I'd like to be down there, you know, picking off the survivors, but I'm on probation. I mean, they didn't *say* I was on probation, but I know I am."

"What did you do?"

"I guess you don't know."

"Don't know what?"

"They say I'm the one who got Andrews killed—the guy we lost when we took out the nurse and those other two dudes. They say I shouldn't have left Andrews to deal with the wack job by himself—the one who went all postal. I mean, what the fuck was *that*? Thinking he could take us on with—I mean what *was* that—a Swiss Army knife or something? I was, like, just shoot the three of them in the heads and get it over with, but no, it had to be a fucking stealth job. And now Andrews is dead and I'm hauling bodies in wheelbarrows like some kind of a, like, custodial worker, or something."

"The desire to survive can be strong," said Phillips. "Especially among these people."

"Whatever."

So this was one of the men who killed Ruth, thought Phillips. The role he had decided to play was becoming an even greater challenge. He tasted bile. He swallowed.

"Who's *this* dude?" asked McIntyre, indicating the Senator with a jerk of the head. "He looks familiar."

"He *should* be familiar," replied Phillips. "He signs your paychecks."

"Yeah, okay. I guess that means helping me with these bodies is probably gonna be a little above your pay grade."

Phillips looked away, as if pretending that such a statement didn't deserve a response.

At just that moment there came a sound that commanded the attention of all three men: a pronounced rustle behind a hedge of shrubbery just beyond the gazebo. McIntyre put a finger to his lips to signal silence. He stepped over the bodies to place himself next to Phillips and the Senator. "Looks like we got us a little company," he said in a low voice. "Are you packing?"

"*I* am," said Phillips, drawing out a small Outland revolver. The Senator, having no knowledge that Phillips had been carrying a firearm all along, gave the jeweller a look of contained surprise.

"Good," said the young cadaver-remover, raising his pistol to his chest. "You go left and I'll go right. Probably just a fawn—there are a lot of deer up here—but you can't take any chances."

Phillips nodded and did as he had been instructed, moving off in the opposite direction. The Senator, unarmed and feeling slightly vulnerable, decided to stay where he was.

It was McIntyre who noticed her first: Alice Trimmers, crouched behind the shrubbery. "Stand up!" he barked. "Step away from the bushes!"

Alice pulled herself tremblingly to her feet.

"Step out. Shew yourself. Hurry up."

Alice stepped out from behind the greenery that had not done such a very good job of concealing her. With great difficulty she produced the beseeching words, "Please don't hurt me."

"Who are you?" asked the young man.

"A-A-Alice Tr-Trimmers," stuttered Alice.

"Are you the eighty-third?" Over his shoulder to Phillips: "*Here's* your eighty-third, Suit."

"I don't know what you mean," said Alice.

"The man is asking," interposed Phillips, "if you are the last of those who were supposed to come to the Summit to-day."

"I don't know."

"How can you not know, young lady? Either you're supposed to be up here or you aren't."

"What are you going to do to me?"

With a leering smile and a nod, McIntyre indicated that he would like to answer this question for himself. "I don't know what *he's* going to do with you, A-A-A-Alice, but I know what *I'm* going to do. I mean, *before* we lay your dead body on that pile over there."

Alice shuddered. The Senator closed his eyes and swallowed. What was Phillips doing? What in God's name was he permitting to happen here?

"Please. I beg of you."

"Beg. Yeah, that's good," said the barrow-boy through a toothy grin. "How old are you?"

"Th-thirteen."

"You look older. Which is why I'll still do you. Unless these Suits want to do you first." Turning to the Senator: "Age before beauty. I can wait my turn."

The Senator shook his head, his look fixed, intentionally unrevealing of the terror now striking his heart.

"We don't have time, kid," said Phillips calmly. "Let me go ahead and take her out."

The Senator felt faint.

"You want to, really? Because I was actually starting to look forward to doing it myself. See, I came too late for the party and by the time I'd gotten here, it was already clean-up time. Okay, okay, okay. Here's an idea. Let me have a little fun with her first, and then you get to put her out of her misery. Is that a deal?"

"I have an even better idea," said Phillips. "I'll kill *you*…" The first shot went cleanly into the young man's jabbering mouth, the second squarely into his neck. "And *nobody* has fun with her. Does that sound like a good plan?"

The young man dropt to his knees, blood spraying from his neck like a geyser. Then he fell flat upon his face.

The elderly jeweller, as it turned out, was an excellent shot.

The Senator remained frozen where he stood. Alice was equally immobilized by what she had just seen.

"Well, what would *you* have done, Senator?" asked Phillips.

"Exactly what you did. Although I probably wouldn't have waited so long."

Phillips turned to Alice: "Miss Trimmers. You're safe. You're coming with us." The jeweller took Alice's hand and together the three turned their steps away from the Summit and toward the forest path that had delivered the two men to this spot only a few minutes earlier.

For the Senator, the time that had just passed seemed like an eternity. He fumbled with his cellular telephone, his hands shaking.

"Phillips, can I—can I get a signal up here?"

"There's a tower not too far from here. I should caution you, though."

"About what?"

"About whom you call. The president, the Pentagon—you'd be amazed at who's in bed with these people."

"I could never in a million years think that—"

"Think what you want to. I'm telling you what I *know*."

The Senator stared hard at the jeweller. "Look, Phillips: I've been in government service for decades. And I've known corrupt administrations and I've known trigger-happy Joint Chiefs. But I'd wager all the money I have that this particular president and this particular Pentagon would not countenance this 'final solution' being played out to-day. I wager, as well, that they've been intentionally left in the dark about all of the other more nefarious aspects to this operation."

"Say I give you that, Senator. You're still not going to get swift action from a bunch of suits and uniforms who'll more than likely spend the first several hours of this crisis comparing notes—wasting precious time thinking of every way possible to spin their personal versions of plausible deniability as they watch the shit on its way to the fan. By the time they finally get their heads out of their asses and their index fingers out of each other's faces, it'll all be too late. Eleven thousand people will be dead. Right in the heart of your state. And with you standing impotent on a mountainside while it plays itself out."

The Senator thought for a moment. "That doesn't leave us a lot of options. There are men in the Senate whom I would trust with my own life, but they can't be of any use to me unless they've got the ability to beam themselves over to the Tiadaghton Dam like *right now*, Phillips, and defuse whatever bomb is set to go off there. But if what you tell me is true, and some of these Dinglians know about the flood, then they're probably spreading the word right now and taking the necessary steps to brace themselves for it, and I pray that the body count will be kept low. What I'm most worried about is the snipers who will go after all those survivors. We need to stop them. And if we can't depend on the federal government to do it, we've got to figure out some other way."

Suddenly, the Senator's eyes brightened. "There is one man I trust who could do us some good. We've been close friends for years—worked under me in the Philadelphia D.A.'s office."

"You're referring to the new governor."

With a nod: "He may be a member of the other party, but we've both been crabbing for years about the great political divide in this country. Now we get to put our money where our bipartisan mouths are. How are you doing, Alice? You holding up okay?"

Alice nodded. The Senator put his arm around her to guide her down a short rocky incline.

"The governor's already been complaining to me about how hard it's been getting any information from the administration about what has been going on in this damned valley. And I've been of no help to him. But now he can be of great help to *me*."

"How?"

"Something called the Pennsylvania Air National Guard. Maybe you've heard of it."

Chapter the Antepenultimate

Mizz Kreis had called us an ant farm, and for this afternoon at least we did quite resemble a hustling, bustling little insectival operation. With no designated leader (save my friend Muntle in whom some of the offices of maintaining order and lawful civility were invested), we were a fairly headless army, and like workers in the formicary of Mizz Kreis' analogy, each of us took upon his own shoulders the weight of a particular important responsibility for which he (or she) felt most suited.

When he realised, for example, that the Respectable Hospital—nay, *any* of the hospitals in the Dell excepting Bethlehem would not be a safe place to deliver the invalid and infirm, Dr. Timberry began to direct Susan Fagin and those other nurses and orderlies and the two doctors still remaining in Dingley Dell to convey patients to the All Souls Church and put them high within the campanile where they could lie flat and not roll away, as the slanting roof of that church could not make the same promise.

A good many Dinglians had already fanned out to evacuate the homes and shops of the Dell long before the Reverend Upwitch had made his public plea from his pulpit and explained in stark, realistic terms what was soon to happen to our valley home.

Mrs. Lumbey and Jemmy the stableboy had taken it upon themselves to go and release all of the horses from the Regents Park stables, so that they could gallop off to the woods before the floodwaters came. Other animal-lovers, shewing equal concern, rode off to pay expeditious visits to farmers in the Dell, and with a "Hi-ho, the derry-o," purposefully leave the cheese standing alone.

A few matters took some coordination of intention: the resourceful minds bursting forth from the attic of Bedlam through a shattered window and those other resourceful minds that dropt a sturdy rope from the roof to pull the men and the one boy to safety had to work together in mechanical concert and by use of an improvised pulley system to accomplish their goal. When it was done and all were atop, George and Vincent Muntle held each other in a fraternal embrace for the first time in a quarter century (though only one of the two had eyes to see his brother, the older having been blindfolded along with some of his companions, since the harsh light of the afternoon sun would surely have seared their sun-sensitive retinas), and a father and mother gave copious kisses to the cheeks and neck of their prodigal son Newman.

Mr. Chowser, who had made it up to the asylum roof as well (but more conveniently through the internal stairwell) in the company of little Jack and Maggy the cook, waited his turn to shake the hand of the brave Trimmers boy who was once a student at his school, and then found passed to him by that hand the pocket watch that Newman had stolen to sell for himself in the Outland.

"So did no one wish to buy it—a watch so fine as this?" asked Chowser, shaking his head, bemused.

"On the contrary, Mr. Chowser. A jeweller did buy it. But he returned it to me before he and Miss Wolf brought me home. He said that it belongs here in Dingley Dell, and I agreed. It belongs with *you*."

There was one other important matter that required some planning, and Vincent begged leave to go to the All Souls Church to help with its organisation (and with some reluctance, Maggy Finching gave him that leave in exchange for a kiss upon the lips that blest the departure). A company of men was required to go down to Belgrave Dam and dynamite a part of it as Chivery had directed. The sheriff's tipstaff Magwitch had learnt the names of two Blackheath men, Joper and Stryver, who were well versed in the placement of charges through their explosives work in the coal mine. They knew the amount and ratio of nitroglycerin (three parts), infusorial earth (one part) and sodium carbonate (a small admixture) necessary to do the job, and could easily be found encamped at Regents Park, their village having been destroyed only the night before.

The men were at first unimpressed by concerted efforts to impress them into service to save the Dell. "And what be da reason me mate and me should t'help a valley dat gave no thought ever elseways of ourselves and our families?"

"Because the ones what disregarded you ain't around no more," answered Ephraim Scadger. "And the ones who be left are your friends now."

Harry Scadger, standing with his brothers Ephraim and Melchisedech, nodded in agreement, though he couldn't help being distracted by the jarring collision of the two distinctly different Dinglian dialects.

"What is more," added Mel to what his brother had just said, "I have a gun and my brother Ephraim has the electrifier and we'll give you the protection you need all right."

Magwitch shook his head. "That's a job best done by a sheriff's patrol, gentlemen."

Mel shook his own head to counter the statement. "We never *done* nothin' for the Dell and we never *take* nothin', but all that be changing now. We give and take like the citizens we always shoulda been. And right now, sir, we *give*."

"I cannot stop you if you wish to go," said the assistant sheriff. "But it's best if you're properly deputized. Come over here, gentlemen. Give me your hands. Consider yourselves duly deputed."

"Thankee sir, and you'll not regret it. Me brother and I know well the ways of the Outlanders who have always gone a'lurkin' hither and thither in our wood. As low and snaky a bunch they be as some of your own men, Mr. Tipstaff." This last pronouncement from Melchisedech Scadger came just as the speaker caught sight of a particularly low and snaky deputy who had just stepped into the narthex of the church: Nick Gradgrind.

The two men exchanged dark, mutually suspicious looks, each laying a palm upon his pistol as if there were to be a duel in short order.

"What is this?" asked Muntle, who had just arrived himself, and had inadvertently put himself into the middle of the freshly brewing confrontation. "We haven't time for this."

Harry attempted to explain: "Sheriff Muntle. This man—one of your most recently-hired deputies—shot and killed my older brother Solomon."

"In self-defence," returned Gradgrind.

"Despicable lie," retorted Harry. "My brother wasn't armed. Moreover, there was no reason for the deputy to impede our journey. He sought first to intimidate us and then to do worse—much worse."

"Yes, I see." Muntle sniffed and scratched his forehead. "Gradgrind: although I didn't appoint you, I do have the power withal to remove you. Surrender your badge and your pistol. You no longer serve the sheriff of Dingley Dell."

Nick Gradgrind shook his head. "But I will not."

"What do you mean, 'I will not'? I'm sacking you, Puppy."

Nick Gradgrind would not go without making further asseveration in his own defence. He pointed to Harry. "This man has no standing to make charges against me. He is a Scadger. A *Scadger.*"

"To-day, Gradgrind, we are all of us Scadgers. Those who once divided us are gone. And if we cannot learn to work together, then we are all destined to die—together, apart, it makes no difference, man. We shall all be dead. Is this your choice, Gradgrind? To be as dead as those you have always so vaunted and esteemed?"

Gradgrind shook his head.

"Then give me your gun and go off and do some good. Go to the East End and see how the workhouse evacuations are progressing."

"The *East End?*"

"Yes, Nick," said Muntle, taking the pistol and handing it to Magwitch. "Have you never been there?"

"He has been there," said Violetta Scadger with a knowing look. Zephaniah's wife continued: "He was born there and he grew up there."

Resigning himself to the inevitable, Nick Gradgrind drifted out. Muntle turned to Harry and Mel. "I am gravely sorry to learn what Gradgrind has done. I should put him into a gaol cell at the Inn-of-Justice, but he would only drown there before his trial." Then, addressing the men standing in the narthex as a whole: "To Belgrave Dam, men. You have your instructions. You will be forever in our debt, should you succeed."

"And what if we shall fail?" asked Magwitch archly.

"Then we shall all be dead together and nothing will matter then, now will it?"

Rugg was dead.

The Senator, kneeling next to the still body of the aged Dinglian, felt for a pulse that he knew would not be there. "We'll have someone come back for the body. There's nothing we can do right now."

"Make sure that he's buried in Dingley Dell," said Phillips. "That's what he wanted."

"If it's possible to do it. Does someone wish to say a prayer?"

Phillips said a prayer. There was a curious but altogether appropriate reference to snakes. There was also mention of the fact that Rugg had been instrumental in saving the life of Newman Trimmers. To this Alice sub-joined, "God bless his soul."

"A good man, dear Lord. The Outland was lucky to have him for so long. Amen."

The trio continued down the forest path.

After a lengthy ruminative silence, Phillips picked up a thread that had earlier been left dangling: "And the governor actually believed you?"

"He did."

"You told him the most incredible story he'd ever heard in his life and he took it for gospel truth right then and there?"

The Senator nodded. "He first asked if I was drunk. Having established that I was neither drunk nor stoned nor suffering from a sudden cerebral hemorrhage, he said that he had no choice but to believe me. He knows that I have never lied to him. The governor also knows that we are neither of us 'Show me' Missourians. We're 'I trust thee' Pennsylvanians."

"What about the dam?"

The Senator shook his head solemnly. "He agrees with me that the charges are probably concealed far below the waterline and set to go off by remote activation. It would be impossible to find them in the hour that remains, even if there were men willing to risk their lives looking for them." The Senator sighed. "I suppose we'll know when it happens."

"Hell, they'll hear it all the way to Harrisburg."

"These people actually think they can get away with this?"

"They've had a perfect track record up to now."

"Let's pray their luck has finally run out."

The Euphemia Trimmers Memorial Society had one last member to collect. Antonia had already gathered up Mrs. Potterson and her daughter

Betty, and Mrs. Venus and Mrs. Blight. Rose Fagin had no need of being collected for she was off helping her daughter and Dr. Timberry remove patients from the Milltown Respectable Hospital and from the Indigents' Hospital and the Lung Hospital. The only member left either uncollected or unaccounted for was Miss Georgianna Milvey, who was missing from her tiny garden cottage.

"She stops with Mrs. Gargery fairly often," Antonia informed her fellow society members. "I'm confident that she'll be there, and this will be a convenience since I had intended on collecting Mrs. Gargery as well."

The Society watched with eager and expectant looks as Antonia knocked on Mrs. Gargery's front door. When no one answered, Antonia knocked louder and more pressingly, employing both the knocker and her fist, and even the old bell cord that she knew had stopt working some time in the early 1980s. Then she began to shout, "Someone come and open the Goddamned door! Good Christ, Georgianna, if you've pulled up the draw-bridge again I shall cane you until you be dead."

Mrs. Potterson swooned to hear such coarse language, whilst her daughter tittered behind her hand.

From just above Antonia's head came a voice from out a window. It belonged to the lady of the house herself. She held Mr. Toddles in her arms. "Bless my life, Antonia! What are you doing here? You should be sitting in your upper rooms. There is to be flood, or have you not heard?"

"Upper rooms? Cornelia, dear, this area isn't safe at all. All of these buildings are going to be washed away!"

"Washed away? But Georgianna said that we should all be fine."

"And just how would Georgianna know such at thing?"

The eminently sagacious Georgianna Milvey's head now popped up next to her friend Mrs. Gargery for the purpose of making her own case. "*Because*, Antonia, I remember that when the Thames flooded back when we were girls, these streets became like canals, but all were safe and dry who could climb above their soggy ground floors."

"Yes, we all remember that flood, Georgianna. But this one is different. Quite different and really quite deadly. Come with us now. Quickly."

"On the contrary. I intend to stay precisely where I am," replied Georgianna Milvey through pursed, determined lips. "I have done with your ordering me about as if you are the fount of knowledge spraying all of us with your wet plashes of wisdom. It is infuriating on ordinary days, but on extraordinary days when we are already to be put in the way of significant inconvenience it is beyond maddening."

Antonia was set to respond, but her friend Malvina Potterson pre-empted her. "Hear me, Georgianna. I hardly ever listen to Antonia because she is generally obnoxious and imperious and I can't abide her."

"I hope to God there is a contrasting predicate to your sentence," muttered Antonia.

"*But* she is telling the truth. The Outlanders are going to destroy a dam upriver and flood the valley in a terribly large way, and you and Mrs. Gargery are not at all safe where you are. Come with us to the All Souls Church. We're going up into the campanile."

"What do *you* think, Sarah?" asked Mrs. Gargery of her maidservant. "Should we heed them?"

"I believe that we should, mistress. If only for Mr. Toddles' sake."

"There is a good girl. Thinking of Mr. Toddles' welfare. You are a priceless treasure. Georgianna: we must go. You will come with us."

Georgianna Milvey shook her head.

"But girl, you simply *cannot* sit here and be washed away. I'll not allow it."

"I have a point to prove, Cornelia. Antonia Bocker isn't always right. This time I will prove her wrong. I will sit here and watch the canal waters rise and then recede, just as they did when I was a girl."

"And you'll do that whilst drinking yourself into a comatose state!" shouted Antonia in a pitched and angry voice. "I am with Mrs. Gargery: I too will not allow it. Georgianna Milvey, you are everything that I oppose, but it is not my wish that you should die. Now get your besotted body down here this instant or we will drag you by force and you will be blue and black with bruises as a consequence."

Betty Potterson had taken a great interest in Miss Bocker's brash handling of the recalcitrant Miss Milvey. If only she could find courage herself to speak to her mother in that way when the two found themselves in opposition over some such matter, the most recent being Mrs. Potterson's continual playing upon her harmonica glasses long into the night. Betty smiled to herself. For she remembered what she had done before joining her mother and the others upon the Potterson lawn not twenty minutes before: she had taken a heavy hearth shovel to every one of those noisy goblets, and squealed with glee as they sang themselves into a thousand little pieces.

In the end, Georgianna Milvey was effectively vanquished, though her displeasure was somewhat mitigated by Mrs. Gargery's offer of her very best bottle of brandy, which the inebriated woman accepted with a lip-licking tongue and nestled in the crook of her arm as if it were some live thing to be cuddled.

❧

With grateful thanks to Mr. Graham for his updated map of the southern region of the valley, the dynamite crew found its way quickly to the foot of Belgrave Dam. As Joper and Stryver discussed betwixt themselves the best places within the earthen structure to emplant the charges and thereby restore to the Thames its historical outlet, Ephraim and Mel Scadger and several deputy sheriffs under the command of Tipstaff Magwitch created a half-circle round them, reconnoitering the surrounding trees and brush for any sign of the Project men, whose job it was to prevent escape from the valley. Had these men also been ordered to prevent a dam from being dynamited? Perhaps not. Because for at least the first few minutes of occupation, the area remained quiet, and there were no signs of a threatening Outlander presence.

Joper and Stryver worked briskly and assiduously to plant eight separate sticks of dynamite into the northern side of the dam, all of which had been carefully transported from an underground storage pit near the entrance to the coal mine. One by one the blasting caps were attached and carefully crimped into place. One by one the cylinders went into cavities trowelled into the dam wall. Those cylinders installed highest in the dam were given the longest fuses to allow time for the igniter to light them in succession as he descended the dam, and finally time enough to quit the area altogether before the dynamite began to do its business.

Several additional minutes passed and there continued to be no sign of the Project men. Magwitch consulted his pocket watch and released an impatient sigh. Things were still moving along too slowly for his comfort. He whispered to one of his deputies, a young man named Elwes: "We'll take the Blackheath bridle road back to Milltown. The ground is higher there in case we get caught in the flood." Again, he pulled out his watch—a nervous habit. As he was clasping it shut for the seventh or eighth time, he felt a stabbing pain in his hand, accompanied by a loud crack. A bullet had pierced the lower half of his palm, shattering his watch along with most of his carpal bones.

Magwitch dove for the ground as his deputies scattered and dropt to their stomachs. Melchisedech Scadger pivoted and fired his pistol into a thick stand of trees, fired in the direction from which the bullet had come. In turning his body, he gave a shooter from the opposite blind the chance to put a bullet directly into his shoulder. The powerful projectile ripped through flesh and bone and knocked him backward into the grass.

More shots rang out. It was difficult to tell how many men comprised the ambuscade. Shots were pinging off the earthen dam now, as Joper slid down the side to remove himself from the hail of bullets.

Stryver did not. The blasting caps had now been attached, the fuses fixed. There was nothing left to do now but to light them—all eight of them.

Faulty aim from the Tiadaghton shooters.

Strong returning fire from his own men.

And luck.

Matthew Stryver counted on each of these three things to help him finish the job that he had been sent to do, even if there be insufficient time to remove himself wholly from the critical area of detonation. In that brief moment, one important fact had become clear to the father of Tattycoram: that he would be sacrificing his own life in the cause of saving Dingley Dell.

One. The first fuse hissed and sputtered as all around Stryver pebbles ricocheted right and left, little puffs of dust rising up where a bullet meant for the obstinate collier missed its mark. On the ground below, the deputies and their tipstaff fired from their improvised entrenchments in the stony field, shielding themselves as best as they could behind small piles of rocky detritus that had tumbled down from the dam over the years. They exchanged fire with the Project men from within gutters and hollows in the broken, uneven earth, giving shot-for-shot, though the more sophisticated Project guns dominated the exchange. Twenty seconds into the firefight, Magwitch's own pistol found purchase; there came an anguished cry from behind a large tree and then an Outland agent revealed himself by falling stricken to the ground. Was it a lucky hit or were Magwitch and his men quickly learning how to use the Beyonders' weapon with success? The tipstaff thought the latter. Proudly so.

Two. A second fuse lighted and popping and sparkling as the flame worked its slow, carefully calibrated way down to its blasting cap.

Three. Fewer bullets now searching out the hunkered Dinglians below, most of the guns now trained on the most important target of all: Stryver. For it had not taken long for the Outlanders to glean the reason for all of the activity upon the dam. And so the objective narrowed. Stryver would have to be stopped. For only in killing the collier, in halting the destruction of *this* dam, could the greater, more important objective of the Tiadaghton Project be achieved.

Four. This stick was very nearly lost, for Stryver's foot kicked it and it rolled halfway down the incline. As Stryver slid down to retrieve it, a bullet grazed his knee. As he was climbing back up, cylinder in hand, a bullet ricocheted off his boot. As he was planting the stick, a bullet ripped a gaping hole in his right arm. It was difficult for him to steady his hand to light the fuse, to steady his nerve to keep going. Joper saw it. Joper knew what must be done and Joper sallied forth from his covert and scrambled up the side of the dam to relieve his partner.

Five. This one was Joper's doing. And it took three lucifers to successfully engage the fuse as Stryver began to move himself toward safety. Seconds later, as Joper slid down to number six, Stryver's chest was torn open by an Outland bullet, his life coming to sudden end.

Six. Joper taking a bullet in the stomach. Joper coughing blood upon the sixth fuse, lighting it with a weak and quivering hand. Joper cursing the unseen gunmen, cursing the Tiadaghton Project, cursing the Bashaws, cursing the God that never smiled upon himself or his family. Joper praying to that very same God for deliverance.

Seven. Lighted as Joper's world fell away. As Joper descended into unconsciousness, his body sliding down the dam, his arms outstretched like our crucified Christ.

There was one final fuse to be lighted, one final cylinder of nitroglycerin that was to take out the bottom section of the dam. Would the first seven be sufficient to the purpose of reducing the level of the floodwaters? Ephraim wondered. But only for a moment. In that next instant the youngest of the six Scadger brothers was up and moving in a zigzag foot pattern toward the dam, dodging a swarm of bullets to take the box of lucifers from the most recently slain of the two colliers, and to light the last fuse that would give his valley home every chance for survival.

Just then an explosion. Not here. Not this dam. But the one farther upriver: the Tiadaghton Dam. A great blast was followed by a second and then a third, each explosion shaking the valley and ushering in the deluge—the great "Diluvian" that was to take Dingley Dell out of the present and put it forever into the past.

The flood had come.

CHAPTER THE PENULTIMATE

Magwitch signalled his men—those still alive—to follow him to what was left of Blackheath. The entrance to the mine was several hundred feet above the valley floor, overlooking the town. There was a good chance of survival at that height. Two men rose and quickly followed their leader as bullets continued to fly toward them—toward them and the Scadger brother who put flame to the final fuse.

And then he was dead. Ephraim Scadger was shot cleanly through the head. Mel was witness to it. Mel watched as his brother crumpled and then fell, as he rolled and tumbled to the bottom of the sloping dam. Mel wanted to go to him; he wanted to cradle his brother in his arms, to say goodbye to his youngest brother, just as he had said goodbye to Solomon, the oldest of the Scadgers. But he knew that it could not be. He knew, as well, that there was a man who lay near him who was alive and who very much needed his help. It was the deputy named Elwes. He had been shot in the leg, and though thankfully no place else, was unable to walk without assistance.

Mel crawled over to Elwes and helped him to his feet. They would try to make it out before the blasts began, and before the waters of the swollen Thames made their way to the southern portion of the valley. Mel put his arm round the grateful young man's shoulders, as his own shoulder protested with jarring pain, and as he bid goodbye to his fallen brother with a tearful final glance, and as he nodded his respect to the fallen colliers.

In the distance, the rumble of the raging, rushing, roiling floodwaters could be heard. Yet here for just a moment more was silence, all the guns now stilled, the Outland gunmen having fled for their own lives, knowing what was coming. Together the two Dinglian men, one a fruit picker and fashioner of bows and fletcher of arrows, the other a novice deputy sheriff and former poulterer, began to hobble away. They had got no farther than a few hundred yards from the dam before great gashes were suddenly ripped out of its side, explosively torn from that manmade wall that had redirected a river to the far side of a valley, where its clean, powerful current was needed in the extraction and processing of iron and coal, where industry transformed Arcadia. Now the dam was nearly gone and now it was urging the wild waters of the Thames in its death throes to return. *"Come this way, this way again, I pray! Out through this opening. Out and away."*

I watched, transfixed, standing upon the flat roof of the asylum as the great wave rolled in—a massive, surging comb of water, turned brown from alluvial shearing of the Tewkesbury Cut, turn browner still from all the earth it had scoured up from below. Within the wave there churned and tumbled everything that had stood or lain within its path to the north, both the inanimate and the animate: uprooted trees, a horse trough, an old harrow, the side of a barn, a pony-chaise without its pony, paddock palings still linked together, an abandoned, insentient cow, and that most tragic sight of all: a Dinglian man riding the waters in arm-flailing terror—riding the waters to his imminent death.

The waters swept over the entire valley, immersing the downs and the agricultural fields and the charred apricot orchard; toppling and dismantling Mrs. Wang-Wang's proud pagoda; sweeping away the black sticks that had once been Alphonse Chowser's lifelong pride. I could see it all from my perch upon the roof of the asylum, in the company of my brother and his family, along with Maggy and Vincent, and Vincent's brother George; near Chivery and all of Newman's other attic companions; each of the four Pilkins and Jemima's embittered brother Walter Skewton who had not let off celebrating with hoots and whoops the death of his medical tormenters upon the Summit, even as the approaching waters put thoughts of everything but the flood from the minds of all of the rest of us. Hannah Pupker stood next to me. Although her look was vacant, her brain still muddled from the drugs she had been given, she took my hand, and squeezing it tight, refused to let go.

There were several hundred of us wedged tightly together upon the Bedlam rooftop, several hundred Dinglians and their silverware and their shaggy dogs and their squirming, indignant cats. Just as hundreds more of their kinsmen and kinswomen clung to their spots upon the pitched All Souls roof two blocks away, and hundreds others stood and lay upon all the floors and stairs of the church's sheltering campanile. And there were still others: still more Dinglians that had crowded themselves into the church's sanctuary, for several of the town's carpenters at Graham's behest had taken immediately to the task of boarding over the stained glass windows and closing off every other place that the waters could invade.

I regretted that more of my countrymen could not be saved—so many there were who had not attended the warning. So many there were who had climbed to the tops of their own houses, thinking that they should be safe there. And miraculously, a good many *were*. For though Professor Chivery had been accurate with most of his calculations, there were a couple of things he had got quite wrong, in our favour. The stone cottages of Tavistock had largely withstood the initial wave and did not wash themselves away. They had been built by Dinglians—by men who took pride in their work and would never build a house that wasn't solid and sturdy. A number of Milltown structures also held together—more so than Chivery had predicted: the Library and the Burghers' Hall and the flower and vegetable pavilion (though the Petit-Parliament building a block away fell quite quickly, it having been most shoddily constructed by one of the corner-cutting Pyegrave brother contractors). This select group of buildings had defied the professor's projections to provide additional harbourage to those less fortunate Dinglians who found themselves apart from the asylum and the church, and floundering in the muddy sluice, clambering for a dry berth.

The wave washed through Milltown with slightly less force than it had exhibited farther north, slackening as it spread out width-wise across the valley. By the time the brown waters reached the opening that had been blasted in the Belgrave Dam, there was little of a discernible wave left, the swollen turbid river passing out of the valley in an almost orderly fashion, though it be choked and knotted with debris and scourings of every possible description.

Magwitch and Melchisedech and Elwes and two other fortunate

deputies watched from the opening of the mine as the waters rose to slosh their feet and then rose no more, and as an Outlander rifleman, hiding himself in that same spot to fire upon Dinglians when the time came, was discovered and "electrifried" into a bug-eyed ball of human convulsions.

From the roof of the All Souls Church, Alphonse Chowser and his ward Jack Snicks studied the waters as they rose and then settled, the church holding itself firmly in place. Tattycoram sat thinking of her father and praying in vain for his safe return. Next to her, Mr. Meagles took the gavel that he had devotedly carried with him since his employer's brusque departure and tossed it contemptuously into the snuff-coloured water below. To himself, he said, "Good riddance to a judicial bastard. May you rot, sir. May you rot!"

The remaining members of the Scadger clan, including Harry and Matilda and their five children, sat not off to themselves, but intermingled with all their fellow Dinglians. "Look, Papa," said David to his father, "the water came nowhere near us."

"Aye," answered Harry, distracted by thoughts of his younger brothers Mel and Ephraim, the heroism that marked their character making him proud to call himself a Scadger apricot-eater.

Florence remarked that she would write of this some day, when she was well, and when the consumption had been cured. And Matilda, for the first time since her oldest daughter had taken sick, believed that such a thing could now come true.

High within the campanile Susan Fagin, her father Herbert, the doctor Mulberry Timberry and his other medical colleagues ministered to the sick of Dingley Dell, carried from their beds, sometimes on litters but often on the backs of their caring family members or neighbours to this high tower of refuge, to this place that like ancient Babel climbed into the sky, but, unlike its Biblical predecessor, was filled with those who spoke the *same* language and shared a part of the same great heart that was Dingley Dell.

Here in the campanile were Mrs. Lumbey and her friend Antonia Bocker, and Mrs. Gargery and her maidservant Sarah. Here were Charles and Julia Timberry who had lost their Punch and Judy puppets in the flood and would now have to make new ones to entertain those children who in the coming days would so desperately need to laugh. Here were Upwitch and Graham, founding members of the Fortnightly Poetry League, who knew that were it not for their delving, enquiring league no one should be sitting dry within this great edifice and Dingley Dell should be washed away.

And here sat the full contingent of distaff members of the Euphemia Trimmers Memorial Society.

"I won't say that I told you so," said Antonia Bocker to her friend Georgianna Milvey.

"Good," returned Georgianna. "And I won't say how you continue to be insufferable even when we are faced with the likelihood of a swift, wet demise."

"Fine. Because I don't wish to hear it," said Antonia.

It was Mrs. Potterson who spoke next. She tapped Graham on the shoulder. "Mr. Graham? My dear Mr. Graham, when do you think that the waters will drop to a point in which we should be able to vacate this tower?"

"What is it, madam?" Graham's head was out of the open arching window. He was using his field monocular to determine if the stained glass windows had held, if indeed the sanctuary of the church had withstood the flood. It appeared at first sight that all of those who had taken shelter within the structure had been saved. Putting Dinglians *into* the church instead of on *top* of it, directing carpenters early on to board over the windows, had been *his* idea, for he had made his own calculations to discover if Chivery had fallen short here. If he was right, he should be a proud man to know that his own scientific brain had served as well as the most brilliant mind in the Dell. And unlike Chivery, he still retained his wits in the bargain!

"I *asked*," said Mrs. Potterson, "when you think that we will be able to climb down from this place."

"I think not for some time, madam. There is perhaps ten or twelve feet of water below, and I do not anticipate a rapid recession."

Graham now turned his telescopic glass on the pitched roof of the church to continue his intermittent monitoring of the hundreds of people situated there. It was at that moment that a shot rang out. A man seated near the edge of the roof, fully within the librarian's view, clutched at his crimsoning chest and then fell sideways like a toppled skittle, rolling himself right down the pitch and then completely off the roof.

Then came a second shot seemingly from out of the empty blue, and a woman near the peak of the roof was struck. More shots rang out in rapid succession, and more of those who had put themselves atop the All Souls church began to fall. Panic now broke out and there was a mad scramble toward the outside fire stairs that connected the roof with the choir loft inside. Matilda caught the hand of one of her two little girls as the other child slipped away, falling back into the arms of Mr. Chuffey, the baker. "I've got you, girlie!" he cried. "Onward! Hurry!"

A moment later other guns were turned on the occupants of the Bedlam roof. There was now a similar panicked scrabbling surge toward the door that communicated with the internal stairwell.

Vincent tried to shield his beloved Maggy from the gunfire, but a bullet found her, penetrating her neck. Too heavy to be held, she fell from my friend's arms. Vincent dropt to his knees before her and raised up her limp and dying body, clutching her warm full bosom to his own breast, beholding her face as the light fled from her eyes. She gave him a glimmer of a smile before passing on. He held her there, not moving, as all around him others pushed past, stepped aside, entreated him to save himself.

I was too far away to add my voice to theirs. I took Hannah's hand and moved us along in the throbbing, jostling, jolting throng. Preceding me were Gus and Charlotte and my nephew Newman. I watched as Newman was shoved to the ground by a wild-eyed man, as he tried to rise and was knocked down again by the knee of a different man thrust stumblingly forward by the hysterical crowd. I reached down and strained to pull Newman to his feet.

The crowd crushed closer now and tighter still, as those having reached the door to the stairs bunched and bottlenecked themselves within the straitened stairwell. There were even more guns firing away at us now and more Dinglians dropping all round me: people I knew, people I did business with, people I wrote about, people I'd had a pint with, thrown a quoit with, people I esteemed, people I loved: Gummidge the lamplighter; Mrs. Flintwitch, the doll's dressmaker; Mrs. Chillip, my brother's neighbour; the schoolmistress Miss Clickett; the distiller Cratchit; the dentist Copperfield; the pieshop owner Mrs. Nickleby, the veterinarian Micawber, and the unfortunate Mr. Howler who in the end had done the right thing and perhaps would be rewarded for it in the quiet, far less flustering afterlife.

From the campanile, Antonia and Estella watched in terror as their friends, their neighbours, their surviving countrymen and women were stricken down one, two, three at a time by the diabolically-exacting aim of the Project marksmen—expert Outland sharpshooters hired to finish the task that the floodwaters had started.

The sound of guns was joined by the cries of those who had been hit and by the horrific screams of those who watched as others were shot, by the grunts and moans, gasps and sobs and hasty injunctions and brisk exchanges and nearly monosyllabic good-byes swirling from within that brutal, bloody, cold-hearted assault upon the "ant colony," upon that cage of subhuman guinea pigs, upon the "Victorian freak show" darkening behind its descending curtain.

We had tried valiantly to save ourselves. We had engaged our intellect and our muscle and our intrepidity, we had come together as the Dell had never before united itself to deliver our valley from a powerful mysterious force that had played us like chess pieces until we should lose all of our crenellation, until we should be wholly discarded, disposed, ultimately destroyed. The fear in me gave way to deep, burning anger. How could such a thing be? How could the universe be so indifferent? Where was God? Where was fairness and justice in this cosmological equation?

I returned my ranging thoughts to Newman who stood before me. "Are you all right, nephew?"

He nodded. "I've lost Mama and Papa."

I pointed. "They're there. Just ahead. Keep moving along."

But Newman didn't keep moving. He stopped, risking again being swept under the mob. He cocked his head. Listening. Listening to something quite different from the tumult of panic and peril and death. He was the first to hear the curious drone of the manmade birds as they approached—the sound of their spinning horizontal wings, turning in rapid oscillations like the wings of the oddest sort of hummingbirds. The drone quickly became a steady mechanical groan, as the flying machines began to descend over Dingley Dell, moving both vertically *and* horizontally. There were twenty of them, then thirty, then perhaps forty of these manmade mechanical birds, less like a flock now than like a gathering swarm of giant mechanical bees, hovering above, spinning their blades in the manner of Leonardo da Vinci's famed aerial screw.

Some drew so close that I could feel a strong wind from the air they displaced, so close that we could see the faces of the men and women who rode inside. They were drest as soldiers. They were pointing guns—not at us, but out and away—aiming their arms at those who were aiming *their* guns at *us*. The spinning, flying machines buzzed over Milltown as if to announce their arrival, and then they pulled themselves apart and spread themselves out along the periphery of the valley, fluttering over the place where the shooters had been about their killing business.

Here and there could be heard an exchange of rapid gunfire between the flying soldiers and the Tiadaghton marksmen. But quite quickly did the shots die away. The Project shooters were outnumbered. The Project shooters were fleeing back into the woods, fleeing Dingley Dell. The Pennsylvania Air National Guard under orders of the governor of the Commonwealth of Pennsylvania had come to Dingley Dell to save the aliens.

CHAPTER THE ULTIMATE

Newman Trimmers touched the sky.

The mechanical bird called the helicopter lifted him, along with his mother and his father, up into the air, flying him high above the flooded valley and on to a place called the "FiG." Fort Indiantown Gap, as it was also known, was headquarters for the Pennsylvania National Guard. All of the surviving Dinglians were airlifted there. The rescue operation continued throughout the long night and then through all of the next day and even through several days thereafter. By late afternoon of the second day, most of those who had made it safely through the flood had been taken away and put into an encampment that was being set up for them on the grounds of the FiG. There were a few Dinglians who had made their way into the Eastern and Western Woods and who, not trusting the Pennsylvania guardsmen, hid there for a while. These men and women would later be found and placed into the camp as well.

The Senator and the Governor appealed to the United States Congress for special emergency funding to provide for all of the displaced and homeless Dinglians. There were many months of investigations to be held, many charges of criminality to be prosecuted. These are ongoing even as I write this eighteen months later. Hundreds of Tiadaghton employees were rounded up and taken to prison. There were suicides. An arsonist took a match to New York's landmark Flatiron Building and destroyed two of the upper floors. The newspapers called the growing revelations about the

Tiadaghton Project the "The Scandal of the Millenium." "Extraterrestri-alsinPA.com" lost most of its readers and all of its advertisers.

Hundreds of questions remained: What would be done with those who had lived in Dingley Dell and knew nothing of the ways of the Out-land? How would they be integrated into modern society? How would these relatively primitive people be protected from illness, from cultural prejudice, belittlement, and exploitation? How would their livelihoods, many no longer applicable in a modern world, serve them? Who would re-train these people? Who would re-educate them? Where would they live? For even as of this writing there has been no decision made as to what will happen to the ghost valley of Dingley Dell (Langheart Steel's plans for the Dell having been declared null and void). Would the Dinglians be allowed to return to the valley and to live some semblance of their former lives? Things would, no doubt, remain unsettled for many more months, per-haps even a good many years to come.

But more immediately, there were funerals to be held and a search for places to inter the Dinglian dead. And there were, at final count, nearly three thousand of them. A Pennsylvania Congressman noted that the number almost equaled the final toll of death exacted by the terrorist at-tacks on the United States on September 11, 2001. In both cases, the deaths need not have happened. Religious obsessitors killed Americans in the fall of 2001. Corporate playfellows, crapulous with an overdose of power and privilege, killed the denizens of Dingley Dell on July 10, 2003. Greed, said one American newspaper columnist, will motivate a man or a group of men to descend to the depths of human depravity, but there are other rea-sons for degeneracy upon such a staggering scale. The corporate overlords of Dingley Dell were avaricious men and women who had become deadlier still in the manifestation of their boredom. The Dinglians were to be tossed out like a child's toy that no longer enchants or enthralls. Wealth corrupts, said the columnist, but it also habituates one to lackadaisical acceptance of the inhumanity that may be engendered by it.

Maggy Finching was dead, and my friend Vincent Muntle mourned her with all of his heart. But there was some compensation in the return of his long-lost brother to his side. Hannah Pupker found no consolation in the loss of her father and mother and younger sister, for she had always hoped in that small place within her heart where the most improbable things are wished for, that their own hearts should some day be softened, that they should become more Dinglian in their feelings for her and in their feelings for others. I would hold Hannah in my arms for many of the ensuing days and I would comfort her, and over time we would come to love each other and to mend our souls in romantic affection. My family became *her* family as our union was officiated by the Vicar Upwitch (Uriah Graham and Antonia Bocker tossing the petals).

Though his medical credentials were no longer valid in the Outland, my friend Timberry and his fiancée (and subsequent wife) Susan Fagin assisted in the care and treatment of all of the Dinglian consumptives, and nearly all were healed, including each of the Scadger children so afflicted. The Scadgers and the Trimmers grew close over those tented months and learnt from one another, and indeed there was so much that was to be learned about the Outland that a special school was set up, The Chowser Institute for Outland Studies, wherein Dinglians were versed in the culture and practicalities of Outland living. Dr. Chivery joined the school's faculty and made substantial contributions when he was lucid. He was delighted to learn that his hypothesis with regard to the impossibility of squaring the circle was proven correct, and that pi was a transcendental number just as he had always believed (and that a supercomputer had truncated it at over one trillion digits!)

Alice came to be restored to her mother and father (and brother and uncle) on that second day. She came by special escort, accompanied by a jeweller by the name of Phillips and by the senior senator from the Commonwealth of Pennsylvania—by the two men who had not only saved *her* life, but also the lives of eight-thousand denizens of Dingley Dell through their swift, courageous actions. For though it had been Outlanders who had marked us all for extinction, it was also Outlanders who had pulled us back from the brink.

Charlotte wept with joy to have her family intact once more, and Gus, who scarcely ever cried himself, could not turn off his own spigot for worlds.

Phillips told us much that we did not know about his friend Ruth Wolf, and her brave spirit communed with us ever thereafter.

I cannot say much more about us on this day, a year and a half after the destruction of Dingley Dell, for so much has yet to be decided. We continue to reside at the FiG and are grateful to be so well cared for there, but it is not a life that we would permanently wish for ourselves, and we are eager to return to some form of normalcy. We know that to achieve normalcy here in what was once known as the Terra Incognita will require a long period of adjustment—a period about which I may well write some day.

Suffice it to say that there is nothing to be learnt here of any great inculcatory benefit. We are no object lesson for future study. We are simply a little people from an orographically anomalous valley where the words of Charles Dickens sprang from the page and directed our steps and our hearts. We are of no particular importance otherwise, except that we have been uprooted and now as refugees must make our way in a strange and foreign land, and such a journey may fascinate some. There are African pygmies who are being similarly watched in the state of Utah.

There is bad in what was done to us and good in how we came to be rescued, and pride in how much of our deliverance was effected through our own industry. This is a familiar story at its core—a story of human survival, a story that gives evidence of the potential for both good and evil in the species. We are not so very different from *you*, kind reader. Embrace your child. Bake a loaf of bread and lather it with butter. Go and wash your dog.

I'm certain that he needs it.

—THE END—

Acknowledgements

The author wishes to thank his publisher, David Poindexter, and his editor, Pat Walsh, for their long and undiminished support for his work and for this book in particular. A grateful nod should also go to Dave Adams and Joe Di Prisco for their editorial input, and to the staff of the Center for Southwest Research and Special Collections at the University of New Mexico's Zimmerman Library who gave the author unrestricted access to their delicate 120-year-old set of the Ninth Edition of the *Encyclopedia Britannica.* The author also wishes to thank his friend Susan Guinter, who made herself available for even the most oddball sorts of questions about Lycoming County, Pennsylvania.

A few somewhat quixotic thank-yous are also in order: to Mr. Dickens, whose voice and literary spirit were greedily channeled for this book; to the Community Theatre League of Williamsport, Pennyslvania, whose support for the author's work for the stage kept him returning over and over again to the beautiful valley of the West Branch of the Susquehanna River, which would play so prominent a role in his novel; to Teddy Roosevelt, subject of the author's yet unpublished fictional biography, whose bully literary voice animated the account of the firefight at the foot of Belgrave Dam; and to Pennsylvania Senator Arlen Specter and Pennyslvania Governor Ed Rendell, who were unbeknownst inspirations for the characters of the "Senator" and the "Governor."

The author wishes most of all to thank his wife Mary—soulmate and most trusted critic—who touches his heart every day with her love and kindness, sound judgment and herculean indulgence of this most emotionally needy and demanding author. Without her, he should never have found the inspiration or stamina to take that long journey to Dingley Dell.